THE PRIDE

THE GLORY

arrow books

This edition published by Arrow Books in 2004

Arrow Books
The Random House Group Limited
20 Vauxhall Bridge Road, London SW1V 2SA

Random House Australia (Pty) Limited
20 Alfred Street, Milsons Point, Sydney
New South Wales 2061, Australia

Random House New Zealand Limited
18 Poland Road, Glenfield
Auckland 10, New Zealand

Random House (Pty) Limited
Endulini, 5a Jubilee Road, Parktown 2193, South Africa

The Random House Group Limited Reg. No. 954009

www.randomhouse.co.uk

A CIP catalogue record for this book
is available from the British Library

Papers used by Random House are natural, recyclable products made from wood grown in sustainable forests. The manufacturing processes conform to the environmental regulations of the country of origin

ISBN 0 09 190295 9

Printed and bound in Great Britain by
Cox & Wyman Ltd, Reading, Berkshire

Judith Saxton

THE PRIDE

arrow books

AUTHOR'S ACKNOWLEDGEMENTS

Writing this book has been rather like writing a real-life detective story, with the facts given in old letters, stories and newspaper cuttings forming the framework around which my tale is woven. In building up a picture of the places and people amongst which and to whom these events occurred, a great many people have given generously of their time and knowledge. I cannot mention them all by name, but here are some of them:

In my efforts to find out about Texas in the nineteenth and early twentieth centuries I first got in touch with Stephen L. Roberts, Librarian at the U.S. Embassy in London, who gave me the names of various people who might prove helpful. On his advice I wrote to Martha Lilly of the Palestine Carnegie Library and she provided me with material which helped to build up a picture of that area. Next, I wrote to Robert Cunningham, Principal of the Elementary School in Humble, Texas, and he passed my letter to Dr J. Alford Moore, President of the Humble Bi-Centennial Museum Society, who found a great deal of information including photographs, mostly collated by the local D.A.R. Chapter, and Amelia Shrader copied the documents and forwarded them to me.

For the New Zealand background I wrote first to Marjorie Shepherd of the New Zealand High Commission, who allowed me to use a variety of her library's excellent source books, and who also gave me names and addresses of citizens of Dunedin. The Principal of the Otago Girls' High School passed my enquiry straight to Helen Spooner, the Research Librarian of the Otago Early Settlers' Association, who must surely be the epitome of speed and efficiency. At the time she received my queries time was running short and my deadline was near, but Helen Spooner found, photostatted and sent me documents and photographs which proved invaluable. She seemed to know by instinct exactly what would be most helpful and answered every letter by return of post and with great clarity and preciseness.

In Britain my uncle, Geoffrey Saxton, showed me his collection of old documents, letters and newspaper cuttings and told me about his father's early struggles in New Zealand, America and England, and made his own childhood, in the early twentieth century, come alive with his vivid reminiscences.

Elizabeth Ziman, of the American Library at London University, helped me to find out what life was like in the Deep South in the '80s, helped me to trace the course of American railways, and generally guided me through her department.

From the staff of the Branch Library, Inverness, the staff of the Liverpool Local Records Office, and the staff of the Wrexham Branch Library, I received a great deal of help. I would particularly like to thank Lynne Butler and Marina Thomas of Wrexham, who worked terribly hard to get me the information I needed.

And last but not least, since the idea for this book sprang from my grandmother's charmingly written memoirs, I would like to thank my father, Ivor Saxton, for letting me read them and for encouraging me to continue whenever I flagged.

PROLOGUE: Waihola, 1870

As Edna Kittle reached the ridge, the sun came up. She had visited the Neyler place several times since Anna Neyler became pregnant, but never at this time in the morning, and the view before her brought an involuntary gasp to her lips.

It was so beautiful that despite the need for haste she paused, seeing as if for the first time the great mass of the forest, the clear colours of the pastures and hayfields painted by the early sunshine, the misty blueness of the distant hills.

The Neyler place nestled – there was no other word for it – in a fold of the hill, with forest on one side and cultivated fields on the other. It was a log cabin, but the front wall was a mass of flowering creeper and even the farm buildings had a look of permanence. Smoke was issuing from the chimney and a flock of hens and ducks were cackling and quacking round something on the ground; they had obviously been fed.

Down there, Edna reminded herself, a woman is in labour. She began to cross the meadow, the grass almost waist-high. She hoped that the child would be a boy, because that was what Karl Neyler wanted and he was a man no one liked to cross. It would not be a pleasant task, she thought uneasily, to tell him that his wife had only produced a daughter!

On the other side of the meadow there was pasture, with a boggy patch poached by the cows, and then she was in the farm yard. She barely had time to reflect that teutonic efficiency did have its merits if it could produce the only tidy yard she had ever seen when she heard, faintly, a baby's cry.

She ran the last few steps, and burst into the cabin.

It was a moment she would never forget. Karl had the child in his arms as he knelt by the bed; the baby was pink from its birthstruggles, the small face suffused with red, the mouth open on a wail. Hair, yellow and wet as a new-hatched chick, stood up on the small head.

Karl looked lit from within, as if joy, an emotion he scarcely knew, had suddenly flowered in him, irrepressible, forcing the watchful look from his eyes, the dour line from his mouth.

'It's a boy!' he said simply. Then, reality beginning to asert itself, 'And you're late!'

'I came as soon as I got your message.'

She went swiftly to the bed, took the baby and laid him flat on the sheet, and tied off the cord. She cut it, handed the boy to Anna, whose placid face was wreathed in smiles, and began to knead the woman's flattening stomach.

'Why do you do that? Is it twins?'

She had never heard Karl's voice so animated, she thought, but said briefly, 'No, it's the after-birth.' To Anna, watching with round eyes, she added comfortably, 'Nothing to worry about, you'll hardly know . . . ah!'

She noted with approval that boiling water, bowls and clean cloths were laid out in readiness. She also knew that untidy, dreamy Anna would not have shown such methodical forethought. It had been Karl who had seen to such details, and she was grateful as she disposed of the afterbirth and cleaned up mother and child.

When Anna was comfortable and the child sleeping, she made a cup of tea for the three of them and looked round the cabin. It was a simple, one-room place with an open fire at one end, a camp oven, a big double bed, a few chairs and a scrubbed wooden table. Shelves were stacked with food and clothing; hooks hanging from the beams held a tin tub for taking baths, a huge woven fly swat and a meat safe within which a flitch of bacon was secured. It was a primitive place, earth-floored, the windows small and too high for convenience, but Anna had made it a home.

Idly, Edna said: 'You'll be building on now, I daresay, Karl? You'll need another room or two.'

'Yes. We'll add a room when she's on her feet again.'

'Don't you have a hired man?' the midwife said, rather startled. 'Those logs are heavy for a woman to handle.'

'Pay out good money when I've a strong woman?' Karl raised his blond brows mockingly. 'Anna knew when I wed her how it would be.'

'I see.' Edna finished her tea and put down the cup. 'What are you naming the boy?'

'Edward.'

It was the first time that Anna had spoken, but she smiled as she pronounced the name, looking tenderly at the child in the curve of her arm.

'Edward? That's a nice name, Anna.'

'Aye, it's a nice name.' You could hear the soft Scottish burr in the girl's voice. 'You like the name too, don't you, Karl?'

There could be no mistaking the nervous pleading in the girl's tone.

'It'll do.' His voice was still heavily accented, the way he turned his sentences Germanic, even after the years he had spent in New Zealand.

'I'll tell the minister.' The midwife got to her feet, crossed to the bed, and gently touched the child's fluff of hair. 'He's a fine boy, blond as yourself, Karl. I'll come in each day for a while, to see Anna's managing him.'

'She'll manage. She won't need help.' Karl's tone was defensive and the midwife knew he grudged the expense.

'I always home visit for a first,' she said mildly. 'Is there anything I can bring you from the village when I come tomorrow?'

'I fancy a cup of coffee,' Anna said, her voice yearning. 'Could you bring me some coffee beans?'

'Too expensive,' Karl snapped at once. 'Drink tea, girl. Or milk. The cows are yielding well. I won't have you starting fancies.'

Anna sighed, then nodded weakly. 'Very well, Karl.'

Edna Kittle, fuming, let herself out of the door. 'I'll see you tomorrow, Anna.'

She was crossing the yard when she heard Karl behind her.

'Wait! Edna!'

She turned back, brows raised.

'Buy some coffee.' His voice was gruff, as if he were ashamed of his words. 'It's a boy, and . . . well, I don't often make a fool of myself over money, but I don't have a son every day. She can have coffee.

Edna held her mirth until she was back on the ridge, then she stopped for a moment to have a laugh out. A fool over money! Karl was twice as mean as any Scot, and they were supposed to be tight. He was paying his wife with a few coffee beans for producing a fine, healthy son!

She moved off again, humming to herself as the sun climbed. At least it was a start, a softening. After a few more sons had been born to him, Karl Neyler might be almost human!

1: Spring, 1887

It was a grey day. Above the spires and rooftops of Liverpool the sky lowered, threatening rain. Tina, hurried along with her small hand in Grandma's, found excitement and anticipation lost in breathlessness, felt a stitch stab her side like a knife. But she knew better than to complain or hang back, for Momma was ahead with baby Cecilia in her arms, following the man who was wheeling their boxes on his cart, and they must not lose sight of those boxes! One contained Tina's best clothes, her wax doll, her much-thumbed story books. So she gritted her teeth and struggled uncomplainingly on.

Grandma slowed, caught in the press of people, and bent towards the child. 'See the ship, Tina? The *Aurania,* that is. A big ship, eh, for a girl so small to ride on?'

Tina, who was not quite five and small for her age, could see nothing but the enormous woman in front of her, her bustle draped in many folds of dusty black crepe. She smiled at Grandma, however, glad to stand still for a moment, tilting her head upwards towards the grey sky. Grandma, not understanding, said again, 'A big ship, eh, *bubeleh*? So safe it will carry you across the ocean, all the way to America!'

She had scarcely finished speaking before the crowd began to move once more and they were pushed forward, mounting the gangplank at a snail's pace to arrive, bewildered, upon a busy deck, then to descend into the darkness of the steerage space, which smelt of people, food and mildewed linen.

Deborah was already ensconsed in a narrow cabin containing a bed for herself, a cot for her little daughters, and their boxes and bundles, for freight was expensive unless it was carried in your own quarters. Tina's eyes flew to the box holding her things and saw, with relief, that it was securely stowed. Her doll, Pigeon, was safe.

'Momma! Can I unpack Pigeon now?'

'Not yet, sweetheart.' Deborah smiled and stroked her daughter's cheek softly. 'Do you like the ship, Tina? It will take us to Poppa! Shall we go back on deck now? It's very stuffy down here.'

'All right. Shall I take Cecy's hand?'

'No, I'll carry her. Her fat little legs are tired.'

Tina could see no reason why Cecy should be tired, since Momma had carried her all the way from the boarding house where they had spent the night, but she followed the adults obediently back on to the deck. A fine rain had begun to fall and the freshening wind blew it against their faces. Deborah said awkwardly, 'Better go ashore, Mutti, or you'll get carried off to New York with us.'

'All ashore!'

The warning, shouted stentorially from near the gangplank, scattered the old woman's careful composure. She snatched Tina up and hugged her fiercely, her seamed peasant face working with the intensity of her emotion. In times of stress she reverted to her native tongue. 'I pray to God I shall see you again,' she muttered in German. She gave the child one more hug, then stood her down, kissed Cecy, and patted her daughter's shoulder. 'You maybe done right,' she said in English. 'Take care of my *bubelehs*, and of yourself.'

'I'm sure I'm doing right,' Deborah answered, striving for briskness though the tears were running down her cheeks. 'You'll see us again soon enough, Mutti, and just you take care too. Hear me?'

The voice called out again, warningly, and Deborah watched the old woman making her way across the deck, her shoulders stooped. She did not look back until she reached the quayside, and then she paused only a moment before hurrying off into the thinning crowd.

Tina was puzzled. Where was Grandma going? Had she left the ship to fetch something they had forgotten? Then, suddenly, light dawned. Grandma was not going to New York with them! She was going back to Norwich! She would catch the railway train and tomorrow she would be back in Grapes Hill, unlocking the front door of the small house squeezed between the Chandler's and Porrit's, the game dealer. It was Grandma's home and Tina's too, for she could scarcely remember the home they had shared with Poppa before he went away. Nothing of that time remained in her memory, not even the shape and smell of the rooms.

The house in Grapes Hill smelled of chicken soup and wax polish, and, indefinably, of Grandma. For she was always there. Momma worked as a seamstress, and when she came home was much occupied with baby Cecy, but Grandma was different. Sometimes cross of course, sometimes impatient, but reliable as a rock, endlessly loving. She said she had no favourites, but she understood Tina's desperate desire for the kisses and cuddles Momma showered freely on baby Cecy, expecting Tina, the elder by eighteen months, to be content with a more temperate show of affection.

And now Grandma was leaving them. Tina's cold despair thawed into action. 'Grandma, Grandma!' she screamed, 'Wait for Tina! I'm coming with you!' In her anxiety she attacked the people nearest her, kicking and pushing, squeezing between the waving passengers towards the gangplank.

It was useless. A woman caught at her skirt, a man, laughing, barred her way, and then her mother clutched her arm, turning her away from the rail, imploring her to be sensible. 'Tina, little one, don't you want to be with Poppa? Grandma will still be here when we come back!'

'I want to go with Grandma,' Tina wailed. But the gangplank was there no longer, and the ship was separated from the shore by a rapidly widening line of choppy grey water.

Thinking that Tina would realise the uselessness of further displays, Deborah turned to lift Cecy into her arms once more.

Immediately Tina hurled herself at the rails, bawling loudly. Then, seeing that nothing could turn the ship from its steady passage out to sea, she tore off her new bonnet in a fury of disappointment, hurled it on to the deck and trampled it flat with small, booted feet.

'Grandma! Grandma!' she shrieked. 'I *hate* Poppa! I want Grandma!'

Cecy, infected by her sister's grief, began to wail. Deborah bent her efforts to soothing the younger child while Tina continued to rail and weep.

A ship's officer, passing the small group, bent down and smiled at the small girl with the shining black curls rippling down her back, her face wet with tears and red with fury. Not understanding but anxious to help, he bent and lifted her up. 'Can't you see properly from down there? Would you like to wave goodbye to Liverpool?'

It was the last straw. Eyes blue as drowned periwinkles stared into the face close to her own for a moment, then she leaned forward, took a grip on his short brown beard, and sank her teeth into his cheek.

The officer, taken by surprise, yelped. He held her at arm's length, the teethmarks showing white on his tanned skin. 'What was that for?' he asked reproachfully. He was young, and fond of children. 'Come on now, let's see if you can smile!'

But Tina was past smiling. How *dared* Momma deceive her! How *dared* she try to part her from Grandma! And this man came along and treated her like a baby and then expected her to smile at him! She lunged forward, fists flailing, and found herself snatched from the officer and held tightly in her mother's arms, close to Cecy's bewildered and flower-like countenance.

Ever since Cecy's birth she had constantly been told to take care of the baby; never frighten her, always succour her. The sight of the younger child's tear-filled eyes and trembling lips quieted her as nothing else could have done. With one last, hiccupping sob she raised her hands and knuckled her eyes dry.

'That's my good Tina. My little daugher, so good, so patient, who wants to help her momma! Don't you love Momma and baby Cecy? How could we go such a long way without our big Tina to take care of us?'

Deborah stood her elder daughter down, her voice soft. With new understanding, she did not mention Arthur. She realised Tina must scarcely remember the father who had gone to the States when she was not quite two years old. She was being taken from her home and from her beloved grandma for the sake of a man who was no more than a name.

Tina, mistress of her emotions once more, picked up her bonnet. Flattened and jumped on, it was still recognisable as the white silk affair trimmed with rosebuds and satin ribbons which she had been so proud of when Grandma had first given it to her. Now she patted it into shape, her small face serious. 'When we've found Poppa, can we go home? To Grandma's house?'

Deborah tried to smile, to instil a teasing note into her voice. 'Would I take you from your grandma for ever? Am I a monster? Of course we'll go home to Grandma's house when we've found Poppa.' The ship was well out of harbour now, moving uneasily on the increasing swell, and Deborah was suddenly aware that her stomach was churning and her head felt hot and dizzy. 'I think I shall go to our cabin for a little,' she said. 'Will you look after Cecy?'

'Yes, Momma.' Tina took Cecy's dimpled fingers in her own and the two small girls followed their mother down to the cabin. Deborah collapsed thankfully on the bare, lumpy mattress.

'I shall feel better lying down,' she said as Tina brought her a thin flock pillow and a frayed grey blanket. 'You'd best take . . . take Baby out and play with her. Is . . . is there a basin?'

Tina glanced round, then resourcefully produced the chamberpot from beneath the cot she and Cecy would presently occupy and stood it close to her mother's head. She looked at Deborah's ashen face and pale lips, then, with care, spread the patched blanket over her shoulders.

She wondered what else Grandma would have done, but there really seemed nothing, so she took Cecy's hand and led her out of the cabin.

Deborah was alone.

Throughout the first part of the voyage Deborah was racked with seasickness, and during that time the children looked after themselves as best they could, bringing their mother drinks and waiting obediently by the bed until she had finished with the cup, emptying the chamberpot when it was full, comforting her with promises that when the weather cleared she would be well again.

Then one morning she awoke feeling empty, light-headed, but no longer nauseated. She realised that the motion of the ship had changed, no longer seeming designed only to curdle her brains and twist her stomach, but to rock her almost pleasantly as she lay in bed.

She glanced around her. The children lay curled up like puppies in their cot, their blankets long since kicked off, their nightgowns rucked up round their waists, their naked lower limbs sprawled in contented slumber. She knew she should be shocked, but they were only babies, after all. The muddle was indescribable, however. Someone, probably Tina, had opened one of the boxes, and toys, clothing and books lay abandoned all over the floor, together with two empty tin mugs and two plates, still crumb-laden. She thought guiltily that she really should get up, cover the children warmly, clean up the mess and then find herself something to eat. But though she was hungry, her hunger had no urgency. She would eat later, when the children woke. Now she would lie quiet, luxuriating in simply feeling better.

Her mind roamed uneasily over the past days. Weeks? She had no idea how much time had passed since she had staggered down here at the start of the voyage. With a pang of guilt, she wondered what the children had been eating with no one to stop them. Had she not promised her mother that to the best of her ability she would see that they ate as befitted a Jewish emigrant family? She comforted herself with the thought that in the circumstances inadvertent dietary sins would be forgiven them. She had brought food – biscuits, oranges, bars of bitter chocolate – but since it had not occurred to her to mention it, Tina would scarcely have searched for it amongst their luggage.

Sunshine fell palely through the tiny, smeared section of window which let daylight into the cabin, and Deborah remembered that other voyage, the one her mother had so often told her about: the long sea-journey from the little baltic port where after terrible vicissitudes, the Cohenz family had at last been split up. They had fled from their restricted and persecuted lives in Lithuania with almost nothing but each other and their three tall sons. At the seaport they had sold their last remaining possessions and the boys had worked to earn money for the passage to a land where they would be welcomed, allowed to live their own lives without religious persecution.

They wanted to go to America, where others had fled before them. The land of opportunity where, already, Jewish communities were growing up. But there was not enough money for them all. So Deborah's parents bought themselves steerage space down in the hold of a sailing ship bound for America, and their sons waited to sign on as deck-hands. They would all meet, they told each other, in the *Goldeneh Medina*!

For Deborah's parents the voyage had been indescribably hard. Penned below in foul weather, with the cargo breaking loose and threatening to crush the Jewish immigrants who huddled in the hold, they had almost died; had certainly lost count of the weeks and months which passed. And then, one day when their food had run so short that they had been driven to chew the hides which made up part of the cargo, the captain came amongst them and told them they had reached America at last; a small port. He advised them to disembark at once rather than wait until they reached New York or Boston, for the food situation was worsening and he could not let them share the sailors' rations.

Accordingly, the immigrants went up on deck and

watched as the ship entered the harbour. It was a quiet little place, dozing in the grey light of a winter's afternoon. Not one of them spoke English, but this had not worried them, for they had relied on being landed at one of the major cities where they knew there would be Jews who spoke Yiddish, the common tongue, even if they could not converse in any other language.

But now they regretted their lack of knowledge. A few men were mending nets on the quay, but when the immigrants tried to question them they only shrugged uncomprehendingly. Even in the small town they could not make themselves understood, though they bought a hot and sustaining meal for themselves with a little gold necklet owned by one of the women.

When they had eaten and recruited their strength a little, for they were worn out and cold and many of the women still weak from seasickness, they set off up the road. The widest road.

'Where it led we knew not,' Deborah's Mutti used to tell her small daughter as they sat snugly by their parlour fire. 'We just wanted a big city where we might find other Jews. But we tramped on, and the road divided, and the names on the signpost were not those we longed to see. So your Poppa, he took the walking stick belonging to one of the old men, and spun it round in the road. And where the stick pointed, we followed. And so we came, at last, to Norwich.'

Although she knew the answer, Deborah always said the same thing. 'Norwich? But the captain had taken you to America!'

'The captain wanted to be rid of us,' her mother told her. 'He had only wanted our little supply of gold. I daresay his cargo was destined for some port such as Yarmouth, along the East coast. He had landed us at Wells.'

'And my brothers?'

Mutti's face softened, as it always did when her boys were mentioned. 'Ach, my fine sons! Herman, David and Solomon. They had more sense than their old parents! They took ship and arrived in New York where they are to this day, making a good living.'

'My brothers.' Deborah had been born in Norwich within a year of her parents' making their home there. She had been brought up as the only child of elderly parents, and with her father's death shortly after her twelfth birthday had never fully understood her mother's obstinate refusal to pack up and leave England, to join her sons in America.

There was the shop, of course. Selling working clogs and boots just that little bit more cheaply than his competitors had enabled her father to build up a small business, but it had never made them rich. Until Deborah married, Mutti continued to run the shop, but then Arthur took over. He was a tall, dark young man with a big Semitic nose and sparkling dark eyes. He worked hard, but he had big ideas. He knew himself to be intelligent, forceful, resourceful. What he did not realise was that he was not cut out for marriage and responsibilities.

However, when they received a good offer for the shop from a rival firm, he persuaded his mother-in-law to accept it. 'I shall go to America and make our fortunes, and you must stay here and live on the money from the shop. When I'm rich, I'll send for you,' he told the two women.

To do him credit, he meant every word at the time. And, at first, he sent money regularly. Only it was never enough, so that Deborah had left her children and returned to her old job as a seamstress, saving as much as she could from her wages so that when Arthur sent for them she would be ready.

But he did not send. He wrote, of course. But the gaps between letters got longer and longer, the letters themselves shorter and shorter, and the months slipped by and turned into years and it occurred to Deborah that Arthur was forgetting her.

'He's left you, girl,' her mother said. 'Some day he'll maybe come back. In the meantime, forget him, eh? We must for the children work!'

'He hasn't left me,' Deborah protested. 'He's going to send for us all!'

The older woman, darning a stocking that was more hole than wool, rolled her eyes towards the ceiling and pulled down her mouth into an expressive grimace. 'He is? *Mazel tov!*'

Deborah's mind had darted back to the sweet, secret days of their courtship, to their honeymoon in Great Yarmouth, one as virgin as the other, though Arthur had been nearer thirty than twenty. It had been summer and they had not had much money, nor needed it. Exploring the town with its rows and its harbour, watching the fishing boats returning from the banks laden to the bows with their catch, laughing at the antics of the bathers descending into the cold North Sea from the brightly painted bathing machines; this had occupied their days. In the evenings they strolled along the beach in the sunset glow, their arms round each other, Arthur splendid in Norfolk jacket and soft felt hat, herself elegant in a walking dress of cream satin, tight in the bodice, trimmed with coffee coloured lace, the skirt draped over a huge bustle.

The nights had been the best, though, so full had they been of love! Both gentle, both shy at first, yet Arthur had proved an imaginative and demanding lover whose caresses had roused an ardent response from his quiet little wife.

When they returned to Norwich they had taken up residence in the rooms over the shop, and it was here that their two daughters had been born. It had been an idyllic time, with Arthur so much in love, so proud of his children and his pretty wife. How they had dreamed and planned, Arthur always sure that he would make their fortunes, Deborah content with life as it was, or content to share his dreams.

All that, to end like this! Arthur in the States and herself in England, struggling to bring up his children with no companion to give her support, no lover to warm her heart and bring that pleasure which comes from experiences shared. It was then that she had resolved to follow him, sitting in her mother's parlour, seeing on her mother's face the conviction that Arthur would never return to her. Perhaps, she told herself, he was too proud to come back as penniless as he had left. But she had no pride! She wanted him – he must want her! She would go after him and then at least they could share their poverty, if that was all he had found in the New World.

It had not been easy, for Mutti had fought against the idea from the first.

'A man you have to chase, he's no good,' she affirmed. 'Wait for him, yes. But follow?' She raised her hands, pulling her face into an expression of amazed disbelief, wagging her head from side to side. 'Ay-yi-yi, only a madwoman – a *meshuggeneh* – would do that!'

'So now you know I'm a madwoman,' Deborah said coldly, months later, when she had saved enough to pay for the journey and a little over for lodgings in New York. 'But I have to go; he's my man.'

The older woman appreciated the stubborn peasant possessiveness in the statement and nodded reluctantly. 'To bring children up alone, this is hard. But to go all that way alone ... .'

'Arthur went, and he didn't have the children for company.'

Mutti shrugged. 'Worse than alone, with little ones tugging at your skirt. And Arthur said to wait!' She sighed, then capitulated suddenly. 'If you must go, you must. But leave the children you should! I could take good care of them.'

This, however, Deborah refused to consider. She knew that her mother would look after her grandchildren but she knew, too, that money was growing short. She had saved what she could from her earnings, but each week she had been forced to pay more for groceries as the children grew up and their demands became greater. No, she would take the children with her. They were her responsibility.

'Momma?'

Abruptly, Deborah came back to the present, to the frowsty cabin and the movements of the ship. She had closed her eyes, the better to see into the past, but now she opened them to find Tina's small face only inches from her own, a smile on her lips.

'Momma, you're better! I'll get you some porridge, and coffee.'

Deborah swung her legs over the side of the bed, tried to stand up, and fell back, half laughing, half alarmed. 'I'm weak! I should get up and get breakfast for you and Cecy!'

Tina was already dressing, tucking her shift into her frilled pantaloons, dragging her petticoat over her head. Her voice, faintly muffled, said matter-of-factly, 'Johnny gets our food.'

'Johnny?'

Tina put on her smock dress, her head emerging ruffled out of the neck opening. 'He's nice. The one I bit.'

Deborah chuckled. 'Perhaps he gets food for you so you won't bite him again!'

Tina sat down on the edge of the cot to pull on her woollen stockings and boots. 'I don't think that's why. He likes us.'

She jumped to her feet and was about to leave the room when Deborah said sharply, 'Tina, your *hair*!'

The child came over and stood beside the bed. 'I brush it myself,' she said with some pride. 'But I can't tie the ribbon.'

'Oh! Well, I'll brush it for you and tie it back after breakfast,' Deborah said weakly. Tina's hair was matted and unkempt, though she had no doubt done her best. And Tina was dirty! Shocked, Deborah peered down at Cecy's rosy face. Yes, her neck and cheeks were smeared with dirt and her hands little better than grubby paws.

'Can I go now?' Tina said hopefully. 'I won't be long.'

Deborah lay back, nodding assent, but as soon as her daughter had disappeared she got shakily to her feet and bent over Cecy, running a finger cautiously through the child's springy, light brown curls. Then she snatched back her hand as if Cecy's head had been red-hot. Something had *moved*, something small and dark had scurried across the white scalp between the silky strands.

Bugs! She jumped back, her heart pounding beneath the

stained nightgown which she supposed she must have worn ever since she arrived on board. What must she do? Who would help her? She put unsteady fingers to her head, already feeling as if her own scalp crawled with life. She took two steps towards the door, remembered her dishevelled state and hesitated, even as the door opened inwards to admit Tina, prancing cheerfully ahead of a young man with a laden tray.

'Good morning, Mrs Rosen! I'm glad to see you looking better.'

Too upset to guard her tongue, Deborah said faintly, 'The children have bugs in their hair!'

The man grinned, teeth white against his tan. 'Indeed? Well, ma'am, some of the steerage passengers have much worse things! But never fear, I'll commandeer some paraffin. I believe that kills the creatures. And now sit down for a moment, and see if you can't clear your tray! It's only porridge and hot coffee, because it is not at all the thing to overload the stomach after a prolonged bout of *mal de mer*, you know.'

He gestured to the bed and Deborah sank down upon it, holding out her hand for the coffee cup, her mouth watering, suddenly voraciously hungry and thirsty. 'I am most grateful,' she said, sipping the bitter, burning liquid. 'But surely it is not your job to take care of the steerage passengers?'

He watched her sipping eagerly, burning her mouth, sipping again, and thought her beautiful, despite the stained nightgown and untidy hair, seeing the pure oval of her face, the downward tilt of the long blue eyes, the sweet, drooping mouth. 'No, it isn't my job,' he said gently. 'But you get a rough crowd in steerage and your little girls are young to fend for themselves.' He reached out and rumpled Tina's head; she was spooning porridge into her mouth with enthusiasm and did not so much as glance at her benefactor. 'Not that they're grateful. This one is sure she could manage quite well without me! A strong character, Miss Tina! Knows what she wants and goes for it regardless.'

Deborah, draining the last drop of coffee, began to eat porridge with exquisite slowness. How delicious it was, quite the nicest food she had ever tasted! She smiled up at the young officer, scarcely taking in his words, only seeing that he was kind and had befriended her children, was willing to befriend her. 'I hope the children have been good,' she said.

'They'll do.' In her cot Cecy sat up, hair on end, face still dazed with sleep. 'I've got porridge for the littl'un, too. I've been helping her to eat it, but perhaps you would care to do so now you're better?'

Deborah stared. 'But she feeds herself! She's over three years old!'

'I think you'll find she needs help on board ship. Now I'll leave you to dress and I'll come down later with paraffin and some hot water.'

He took the tray with her empty plate and mug and had turned to go before Deborah abruptly remembered her manners. 'I thank you, sir, you've been truly good. What is your name?'

'I'm the second mate: Feversham. Good day, ma'am.'

Tina was squatting down beside Cecy, holding the bowl steady while the younger child ate. 'He's Johnny. I *told* you,' she remarked over her shoulder as the door closed behind the young man. Then, to Cecy, 'Try not to spill your porridge on the cot, you bad girl!'

Deborah stood up and selected the clothes she wanted to wear, blushing to think that she had sat in her nightgown and chatted with a man. What would the children think? One could place no reliance on Tina not taking due note of her lapse.

Dressing under cover of her voluminous nightwear, Deborah thought guiltily that she must not blame Tina for being intelligent. The child was dressing Cecy now, dragging her clothes on with scant regard for the little one's comfort or dignity. Deborah, watching, made up her mind to teach both children to dress themselves as she was doing, for Tina had simply stripped Cecy's gown off without a qualm at revealing her sister's nakedness. She was very self-possessed. In fact bossy! And she was not yet five! Mr Feversham's words came back to her: 'Knows what she wants and goes for it regardless', and this time she knew what he meant. Her quiet, obedient little daughter had changed; she had been forced to change, learning to take care of her little sister and herself because her mother could not do so.

Deborah began to brush her own hair. It would be different now. She was well, and able to cope; Tina could go back to being a little girl again. She finished brushing her hair and coiled it into a soft bun at the nape of her neck with a practised hand, sticking four long hairpins into its thickness before turning to the children. 'Have you finished dressing? Good. I'm going to wash you both presently, and do your hair as well.' She lowered her voice as if the walls had ears. 'Cecy's got . . . got *lice* in her hair!'

'Has she? I expect they came from Marigold. She's got things, I heard Mrs Scantling say.' Tina scratched her head reflectively. 'My head itches. But I 'spect Johnny's stuff will make it better. Was that why he said he'd bring paraffin?'

'Er . . . yes, that's right.'

When the paraffin came, and the hot water and the strong lye soap, Mr Feversham also brought a pair of shears. Despite her resolve to care for her children from now on, Deborah found herself quite willing to let the second mate clip Tina's long black curls and then shear Cecy as well until two small strangers stood before her. Two tough little boys in skirts!

With tears running down her face Deborah combed the wriggling little horrors out of the tufts of paraffined hair and watched, appalled, as Tina and Cecy, with every sign of enjoyment, stamped on the lice as they fell to the floor. Then she washed their heads with soap and hot water, rubbed them with a rough towel, and collapsed on to the bed.

When Mr Feversham had gone she fell a prey to despair. She thought shrinkingly of her mother; what would Mutti say if she knew that her darlings had been scrubbed and de-loused, and now looked like miniature convicts? I am a bad mother, she thought. I should have left them in Norwich, where they would have been well cared for.

The children, oblivious of this heart-searching, were playing with their dolls on the floor. What good little souls they were, despite everything! Deborah lay back on her pillow, thinking that presently she would take a walk on deck, when an ear-splitting howl rent the air.

'Momma! Momma! Look at Saya!'

Sara was Cecy's doll, a stout, linen-bodied creature with abundant brown locks and jutting china cheeks. Deborah sat up, then echoed Cecy's shriek.

Sara lay on the floor between the two children, her round, painted eyes fixed reproachfully on the ceiling. Her abundant locks were in Tina's left hand, Mr Feversham's shears in her right.

'Tina, you wicked child! How could you ruin poor Sara! And you've upset your baby sister! You're a bad, naughty . . .'

'I am *not*,' Tina said, aggrieved. 'The child had *lice* in her hair. I had to do it!'

Deborah's mouth fell open. She tried to speak, then felt a giggle rising in her chest. She turned her head away from the two little girls, saying in a tight, unnatural voice, 'And what about Pigeon, pray? I trust you are going to crop her curls!'

'Oh, Pigeon had lice last year; you can't get them twice. When I had the measles and then Mrs Crowther's grandchild got them you said you couldn't get them twice.'

An answer for everything, thought Deborah grimly. She said firmly: 'It was wrong of you, Tina. Now take your sister, and make a neat bonnet for poor Sara out of the material scraps in the small box. It will be . . .'

A strong smell of lye soap reached her nostrils and she turned hastily, in time to see the longsuffering Sara plunged into the tepid, grey-scummed water, linen body and all. 'Just bathing her,' Tina said airily. 'Then we'll take her up on deck. She'll soon dry up there.'

Deborah got off the bed and stood up, clasping her head. 'No; no, you can't go on deck! What will everyone think?

Your hair . . . even poor Sara . . . You'll have to stay down here until . . .'

'We can't stay down here till we get to America! Come on, Cecy.'

And despite Deborah's protesting wail they went, Tina holding Cecy's little paw and Cecy trailing the soaked and hairless Sara behind her. As soon as the cabin door closed behind them, Tina began to sing. Deborah felt the hair stand up on the nape of her neck. That *terrible* child! Growing gradually fainter as they neared the deck, the dreadful refrain reached her.

'You can't get lice *twice*, you can't get lice *twice* . . .

2

The room was full of people. People who gesticulated as they talked, and they talked constantly, laughed loudly. Mostly men. Her uncles.

Tina had made herself as inconspicuous as she could, sitting beside her mother's chair, Pigeon's flock-stuffed body held close, comfortingly familiar amongst so much that was strange. Cecy slept on their mother's lap; open-mouthed, sprawling.

Deborah was talking to a pretty, plumpish woman whose ankles, Tina was fascinated to observe, bulged over her tiny high-heeled shoes. From her lowly position, in fact, she could see almost nothing but skirts and trousers unless she looked upwards, to catch glimpses of the undersides of chins, beards, bobbing bodices, eloquent, finger-flickering hands.

Above her head, the comfortable talk continued. Domestic talk of kitchens, recipes, sewing patterns. It was interrupted by Uncle Herman who walked over and patted Deborah's shoulder, booming, 'Foolish little one, not to send word sooner that you were coming to New York! Less than a month ago Art was in this very room, eh, Mirah? And the sly dog never mentioned that he'd sent for you! Didn't think you'd leave at once, eh? Never mind, never mind, you can telegraph him in the morning and he'll be back here before you can say knife!'

Uncle Herman was the eldest of Tina's Cohenz uncles. It had been he who had met them on the quayside where she and Momma and Cecy had stood beside their luggage, cold and alone amidst the alien crowd, whilst Momma said, her voice thin with despair, 'I telegraphed; I asked them to meet us.'

Then, suddenly, they had been claimed. Tall Uncle Herman had swept Momma into a bear-hug, then he had swooped on Tina and Cecy like a warm wind, lifting them up, one in each arm, as though they weighed no more than feathers, kissing their shorn heads, saying, 'Aha, my little nephews, my little *boychiks*!' There followed a gust of laughter and another kiss, this time on their cold cheeks. 'Your Uncle Herman is joking you, eh? Two pretty little *faygelers*, that's what you are!'

He had taken charge, calling a negro to bring their boxes, dispensing money with a lordly hand. He had bundled them, gaping, into a cab, taken them through a maze of straight streets lined by buildings so tall they seemed to graze the clouds, and finally helped them down outside a tall building where they were welcomed in and introduced to a bewildering number of aunts, uncles and cousins, including Aunt Bessa Lubutz, who owned the house.

Tina remembered sitting down at a long dining table covered with a starched white cloth. Uncle Herman said grace in the rich, guttural language of the *Shul*, and then they began to eat. A wonderful meal, starting with chicken soup, clear and gold-bubbled with *matzoh* balls bobbing in it, and ending with a *strudel* sweeter and flakier than any she had ever tasted. She was hungry and ate eagerly whilst the talk rolled around her; sometimes in English, sometimes in German, sometimes in a third tongue which she dimly recognised as Yiddish. And then, to her shame, she had fallen asleep. Sprawled amidst the empty plates and glasses she had finally woken, deeply embarrassed, only to find with profound relief that the talk and laughter continued unabated. No one had noticed her lapse.

After the meal they had gone back to the parlour, and it was here that Momma and Aunt Mirah were chatting when Uncle Herman began to talk of Poppa. Tina noticed a slight flush warm her mother's cheekbones, but Deborah replied composedly, 'Yes, Herman, I'm sure Arthur will return as soon as he knows I'm here.'

'Good, good. And how is Mutti? Oh, I know she has a good business, which needs her, that she's busy and happy. This she tells in every letter! But what of her health, her friends? You left her in good hands, eh?'

Tina's startled upward glance was not lost on Deborah. 'Goodness, I must get the children to bed,' she said, getting to her feet with Cecy, sleeping still, in her arms. 'Mutti's just fine, Herman. Say goodnight to your uncles and aunts, Tina love!'

Tina began to follow her mother from the room but found herself picked up in Uncle Herman's strong arms and held close to his wise, lined face. 'You are tired too, eh, *liebling*? Then Uncle Herman shall be you horsie!'

Tina snuggled against the side of his neck, completely at ease with this big, good-humoured man who obviously adored children and was at his best in their company. 'Trot then!' she demanded. 'Trot faster than Momma!'

He speeded up, overtaking Deborah and saying over his shoulder as he did so, 'I'll take these two off your hands tomorrow, little sister. They can come to the store with me. 'We're only a stone's throw from the park and you can lie in a while.'

He left them in the bedroom they were to occupy during their stay. It was small, with dark, elaborate wallpaper and a mantelpiece crowded with knick-knacks, but the bed they were to share was huge and looked inviting, the velvety chairs on the rug looked comfortable, and a fire burned in the small grate.

'Can you undress yourself, chick?' Deborah whispered after the door had closed quietly behind Herman, laying the sleeping Cecy on the bed. 'I'm going to try to undress Baby without waking her.'

'Yes, of course,' Tina said, swaying with tiredness, wanting more than anything to be cuddled and helped, then popped into the bed to sleep and sleep. But she undressed slowly, her tired fingers fumbling with buttons and hooks, laying her clothes neatly on one of the velvety chairs, folding her petticoats, standing her boots beside the fender. At last the nightdress slid sweetly over her head and she was able to climb into bed, to feel blessed warmth enfold her. Her toes felt the heat of a stone hot-water bottle and she snuggled down, sighing with pleasure.

Cecy, nightgowned and still sound asleep, was slipped into bed beside her and then Deborah began to undress.

'Momma? Who is Aunt Bessa Lubutz and why are we all in her house?'

'Uncle Herman is a widower and lives here as a parlour-boarder. So do David and Elsa and their big sons. Mrs Lubutz is a Russian Jew, so this is a *kosher* household; I suppose it is convenient for them, though for my part . . . But there, try to sleep now, there's a good girl. Tomorrow will be a busy day.'

Tina, watching in the light from the gas mantle, saw Deborah shed her jacket trimmed with persian lamb, her draped and bustled silk skirt, her tight, figure-clasping blouse and bodice and then her boots. Still demurely petticoated, she reached up and turned off the gas, then, with only the light of the dying fire upon her, slipped out of the last garment, pulled on her nightgown, and unpinned her bun. The light brown hair bushed out under the brush, flying into a halo in the dimness.

How pretty, thought Tina, her lids drooping. She felt the bed sag as her mother climbed in beside Cecy, felt moth-soft lips caress her cheek, felt the springs settle as her mother turned on one side and began to breathe slowly and steadily.

I'm awake after Momma, was her last, astonished thought before sleep claimed her.

The days that followed were happy ones for the children. Herman owned a thriving delicatessen store east of Broadway, quite near the Union Square Theatre, with a lunch counter, a soda fountain, and various other attractions. Each morning, he and the two children set off on the streetcar for 'Herman's', unlocked to let in the hired help, old Mr Samuels and Janie Kepzel, and then went into Union Square Park. Tina and Cecy grew familiar with every inch of its attractively set out walks and flower beds. They ran races, played ball and invented games of tick, 'home' being the Washington statue, where they congregated to chatter with other little girls, usually accompanied by grand nannies from the magnificent hotels and private houses surrounding the square.

When they had raced off their early-morning energy, the three of them returned to the delicatessen and the children perched on tall stools behind the counter and played at chequers or jackstraws. They drew on slates, did sums, practised writing and spelling, and experimented with simple word games. Sometimes Tina was allowed to serve customers with help from an adult.

When the lunchtime rush was over they were allowed to choose their own food from the lavish display which the customers scarcely seemed to reduce at all. Mouth watering, Tina would fish for pickles with the long ivory-handled fork, or dole out a helping of *sauerkraut* on the side of her plate. She loved pickled herring too, and salt beef sandwiches with dill cucumber, or a slice of delicious, pinky red salami on rye bread. Sometimes, for a treat, Uncle Herman would slip a sliver of *lox* on to the edge of her plate, for smoked salmon was expensive. Cecy had different tastes, adoring *pletsl* rolls with jelly and peanut butter – Uncle Herman always shuddered dramatically when he served this – and slices of *halvah*, an oblong block of flaky sweetstuff made of honey and chocolate and garnished with sesame seeds.

Within a few days, Tina was a real help when the place was busy. She was quick witted and quick fingered, and she soon understood the money, handling cents, nickels, dimes and quarters, adding up in her head, giving change for the big, shiny dollars. Uncle Herman taught them to play *Pisha Paysha*, largely for Cecy's benefit, since the simple card game taught them to use numbers in the right order. Then he let them copy out price tickets and menu cards and dispensed nickels for good efforts.

'Tina's sharp as a needle, and ought to be in school,' Herman told his sister a trifle ruefully. 'So good she is, such a help! And then, not long in New York you will be; not long enough for her to start at a kindergarten, eh?'

Deborah agreed, a trifle nervously, that they might indeed leave New York any day. She could not bring herself to tell either her brothers or their wives that she did not have the faintest idea where Arthur was. Nor that he fondly believed her to be still in Norwich with Mutti. She had gone out with instructions on how to reach the telegraph office, and when she returned, prepared to admit she had sent no message, was further confounded to find it was simply taken for granted that she had telegraphed. And as the days passed, it became more and more difficult to admit the truth. Not for her own sake, she told herself, but for Arthur's. Her brothers were such fine men; generous, capable, full of laughter. They would think Arthur a poor creature and herself a fool, for who but a fool would follow a man who did not want her halfway across the world?

Every morning she woke full of good intentions. She would tell Herman; or David, who was a younger edition of Herman; hair darker, body leaner, but otherwise a carbon copy of the eldest brother; or Solomon, nearest to her in age, who laughed with her and teased her and said she would make a terrible store-keeper, being far too young and lively for such a fate.

But in the end, it was Mirah who heard the true story.

Mirah was Solomon's wife, a plump, untidy woman in her fifties, with a wide, toadlike mouth and greying hair.

But her eyes were kind and she was closer to Herman than most, since she and Solomon, after Herman had lost his wife, had helped to bring up Herman's only son, Paul.

'Not that we interfered in any way,' Mirah told Deborah as the two of them worked in her kitchen one Friday. 'But he could not manage the boy alone, so we all moved into Mrs Lubutz's place and shared Paul. Good for Solly and me, good for Paul, good also for Herman, his worries to share. Solly and I have not been blessed with children.'

'I see. And how long have you lived in your own apartment?' Deborah said, gesturing at the small, clean kitchen.

'We moved when Paul grew up and went to college.' She was washing up at the sink while Deborah made *challa*; braiding the rich dough, painting it with egg white, sprinkling the poppy seeds on top. 'Oh, that Paul! Such a *bren* he is, so clever at school and now such a good businessman!' She turned from the sink, hands flicking soapy water on to the floor as she gestured enthusiastically, 'Everyone admires him, for he's done so well! A bachelor yet, though God knows why, for women adore him. Ah, but why am I telling you, who must know it as well as I? Paul and Art are such good friends, such *chavarim*. At first, Paul advised Art on what to buy, where to go. But now, he says, Art knows best. A natural salesman your man is, Deborah.'

Deborah, putting a *challa* loaf on to a greased baking tray, smiled but said nothing.

'Soon it will be Passover; will you join Art for the feast, or will he come back for our *Seder*? You've not heard yet, eh? Then why not telegraph again, telling him to come to New York for *Pesach*? It is a time for families to be together.'

'I don't know where he is.'

The words fell baldly into the warmth of the kitchen, like little drops of ice sizzling on to smoking logs. Deborah kept her head down over her baking, not daring to look up for fear of seeing the friendship in Mirah's mild brown eyes turn to contempt. Instead, she found herself being impetuously hugged, felt Mirah's lips warm on her cheek.

'You don't know, *faygeler?* You should have said! We're

your family, your friends too. Then he didn't send for you, the *kalikeh*! Paul did say . . . but there, don't cry, little one. It is only thoughtlessness; but not easy to forgive. He is a fool, to hurt a wife so beautiful and loving.'

'He stopped writing, sending money . . .' Deborah gulped, glad to pretend no longer. She allowed Mirah to guide her to a chair and collapsed on to it, feeling the hard knot of secrecy and hurt melt in the warmth of the other's concern. She let the tears run freely, snuffling into her handkerchief, feeling relief at the end of deceit almost stronger than her grief over Arthur's mistreatment.

'Yet he loves you,' Mirah soothed, going unerringly to Deborah's worst fear. 'He wants only the best for you. Forgetting to write is nothing – probably he did write, but the letters were lost. Never think he doesn't love you, for you were made to be loved, you pretty thing! Such a good mother you are, such a good cook, a clever manager! See how I trust you to make the *challa* for a family party? Not many would I so trust, I promise you!'

'Men d-don't love women because they're g-good cooks,' Deborah said through her tears. 'Nor j-just because they're pretty. Perhaps he's met someone else!'

Mirah put a comforting arm round Deborah's shoulders. 'We must be practical, yes? Firstly, he has gone West; everyone knows women are scarce in the West so where will he find this . . . this *tsatske*? This woman who would take up with a married man? And then he moves on, always selling. What father would let his daughter marry such a one, even if he were free?'

'I don't really think he's got another woman,' Deborah admitted, giving a watery smile. 'I think he doesn't want to be burdened with a wife and two babies! But however he feels, I'm going to find him, and hear from his own lips why there have been no letters.'

'That's right! He'll be grateful to you, mark my words. And now, may I tell Paul? He knows Art so well he may easily be able to contact him. And perhaps we could tell Herman also? He is a good man and will not condemn.'

'I was a fool to lie,' Deborah said, colouring. 'Please tell them all.'

But Mirah, pursing her lips, shook her head. 'Not everyone, for some would be sharp. But I'll speak to Paul and arrange for you to go see him. Just for a start, eh?'

'I'd be most grateful,' Deborah said. She dried her eyes carefully and squeezed Mirah's hand. 'You make me sure I'll soon be with Arthur.'

'I, too, am sure,' Mirah said, getting to her feet. 'And now let's finish our baking.'

Paul Cohenz sat in his office, waiting for Deborah. Though he was her nephew he was, in fact, her senior, having been born whilst his parents still waited for a passage to the States. But he was older than his aunt in more than years. His education and upbringing, and now the experience of running a highly successful wholesale business, which needed both tact and toughness, had given him the maturity and sophistication which Deborah patently lacked. A tall, thickset man with broad, muscled shoulders and a deep chest, his hair prematurely greying at the temples, he had an ugly, craggy face, stern-seeming in repose because of deep lines running from nose to mouth. But his eyes were bright and dark, and his full, sensuous mouth could smile with great charm.

He had not seen his aunt, having been unable to attend the Sabbath dinner party, and awaited her arrival with a certain amount of curiosity. Arthur he knew well. A handsome young man with little interest in women, he would have said. Not so young, really, yet he gave an impression of youthfulness. Pondering Arthur, Paul came to the conclusion that it was his complete lack of responsibility which made him think of Arthur as a youngster. His wife would probably be a giggly, simpering little thing with fluffy hair and no clothes sense. The sort of woman he himself would have run away from within a month of the consummation of the marriage. He concluded that Arthur, living in a close-knit, insular Jewish community in England, had believed marriage to be the only chance of losing his virginity. Well, he would help the silly little thing find her man because his father wished it, and his Aunt Mirah, the only woman he had ever loved. But he felt sorry for Arthur.

Outside, in his typist's little room, he heard a murmur of voices and knew Deborah had arrived. There was a tap on the door and he stood up, smiling, waving her into a chair, closing the door behind Miss Frosdyke.

'So, Aunt! Mirah has explained your problem, and I've been taking a look at Art's last order.' He smiled at the sudden colour which flooded her cheeks. 'You prefer that I call you Aunt? I don't want to be disrespectful, ma'am.'

She glanced up at him, her cheeks burning, her eyes full of reproach. 'Don't! I know you think me ridiculous, but at least I cannot help being your aunt!'

His ready sympathy was roused, and besides, she was no fluffy little creature such as he had imagined. She had character, this woman; she held herself well and her clothes were simple but suited her. He got himself a chair and pulled it close to hers, then picked up a ledger and sat down, holding it between the two of them. 'No, no, you aren't ridiculous. I was teasing you, and in very bad taste too. You have a worrying problem and you must let me help you with it.'

Close to her, like this, he could see that she was beautiful. The long, downcast eyelids were faintly shadowed with violet; by nature, not artifice. Her skin was milk-smooth, and she smelt, faintly, of flowers and freshness. He found himself wanting to touch her, to run his fingers up into the clean, pale brown silk of her hair. He caught his breath, feeling a surge of desire as she bit her soft lower lip in small white teeth, glancing up at him shyly out of her long, dark blue eyes.

'I wish you would, Paul.'

He blinked. For a second the words seemed an invitation, then he remembered he had offered his help to find her husband. He cleared his throat, opening the ledger, running his finger down the columns, horrified to think that he had, for a moment, lusted after this young relative of his as if she had been one of the merry little prostitutes who promenaded hopefully along the sidewalks of Broadway, looking for custom.

'Yes. Well, I've been glancing at Art's last orders, and I think I can make a guess where he's headed. Normally I could tell you more, but last time he was in town he was talking of setting up a permanent store someplace. I'd say, from the goods he took with him, that he'd a mind to visit around a little and not just follow his usual route.'

'A *permanent* store? Is he doing well, then?'

'From these figures,' Paul said carefully, 'I would assume that your husband was a rich man, my dear. But I don't think for one moment that he knows it! He's told me at various times to bank sums for him and I doubt if he's ever kept proper accounts. Just draws out to buy goods and pays in on his return. This time I reckon he'll go out West, perhaps as far as the Rockies. He follows the railroad, visiting the whistle-stops, outlying ranches and so on. I think he'll go out much as usual, but will turn back or change direction anywhere he might think to set up for himself.'

'I see. Then what had we best do, Paul?'

'I'll telegraph folk I know, try to trace him. In the meantime, you sit tight. Take a look at New York, relax.'

'But . . . that won't be easy. I mean . . . could I get a job? Just as a shopgirl, or something. Or a dressmaker! I'm a good dressmaker!'

He patted her shoulder, then got to his feet and returned the ledger to its place on the shelf. 'My dear girl, do you think your brothers would allow such a thing? Out of the question! We will take care of you and your children while you remain in New York.' He had turned to face her as he said this, and now he turned back, keeping his voice deliberately casual. 'You've seen nothing of the city; I'll take you around myself. I'll make some enquiries about what's showing at various theatres and then I'll come round and pick you up at seven this evening. We'll do the town! How about it?'

'You're very kind. I should enjoy a visit to a theatre.'

He smiled and walked over to the door. She got quickly to her feet and he took her hand, patting it. 'No more worries, eh? You can find your way back to the Lubutz house?'

He saw her out, then returned to his desk and began to formulate suitable messages to telegraph. When he had done that he despatched Miss Frosdyke to the telegraph office and turned back to the order-list he had been checking before Deborah arrived. Only when this was dealt with did he allow his thoughts to return to the evening ahead.

He enjoyed the theatre, and mulled over the various choices, though he thought shrewdly that most things would please her. She was no sophisticate, yawning behind her hand at an operatic aria or fidgeting through a fine piece of acting. Opera! That was the very thing! An Italian company was doing *The Bohemian Girl* at the Academy of Music; he would send Miss Frosdyke to get two tickets. And afterwards they would eat at a quiet *kosher* restaurant on Twenty-third Street. Usually, he took his woman friends to Del Monico's, where the food was excellent and the atmosphere impressive, even though the prices were frighteningly high. But he usually confined his attention to well-born Gentile women who had spent most of their lives in New York. One did not entertain young Jewish girls unless one had marriage in mind, and he enjoyed his bachelor state far too well to risk changing it.

But this was different. This was his friend's wife, who must be entertained and even pampered a little. God knows, Art hadn't gone out of his way to pamper her, he told himself righteously. He did feel a pang of guilt when his conscience told him that had she been plain and stupid, or a vapid little empty-head, he would never have dreamed of entertaining her, but such thoughts did not outweigh his pleasure that he was to see her again so soon. He settled down to his ledgers and was soon absorbed, but not even his work could take away a feeling of exuberant anticipation.

They went to the Academy of Music, Deborah in a borrowed evening dress, for Mirah assured her that not even the prettiest of her gowns would do justice to the occasion, and Paul would be wearing tails. Handing her out of the cab and escorting her through the huge auditorium to their seats, he felt proud to be seen with her. She wore a low-cut gown in palest pink, with her hair piled up in a pyramid of gleaming curls and a necklace of brilliants sparkling at her throat. Her cheeks were flushed with excitement, her eyes brightened by it. As they passed down the narrow way between the rows of seats, with the brilliant chandeliers making the scarlet and gold of the decor look barbaric and splendid, Paul could not but notice the glances they received. The women admired his good figure in the severe black and white of his evening clothes, but every man present envied him Deborah. Her freshness and beauty could not have been shown to better advantage, and when the opera began he, who loved music, got almost more pleasure from her breathless enjoyment than from the excellence of the large orchestra, or the first-rate performances of the cast.

Afterwards, they sat opposite one another in a booth at his 'quiet little restaurant', which Deborah thought a wonderful place, and she found herself talking easily and with authority about England, the upbringing of children, her view of New York. They laughed together, making gentle fun of the absurd story of the piece they had just seen. Time flew, and when he left her in Mrs Lubutz's front hall they had already arranged to meet next day, to lunch together at Nash's in Park Row.

'And you can tell me how far you've traced Arthur's movements,' Deborah said, as they shook hands in the narrow hallway. 'Goodnight, Paul, and thank you for a lovely evening.'

'Where are you going tonight, Momma? Somewhere shabby?'

Deborah laughed at Tina's acumen, for she was wearing an old black cloth pelisse and a pair of faded grey gloves, besides the plainest hat she possessed. 'Clever girl! Uncle Paul and I are going to be very unfashionable tonight, and

I must not look too tidy. I might even exchange my hat for a scarf tied round my head later on!'

Tina sat up in bed, her eyes like saucers. 'Uncle Herman says there are bad men on the streets at night. Be careful, won't you?'

Deborah laughed and promised, but she was touched by the child's concern and told Paul about it as they made their way by street car to the Bowery.

'Tina's an old-fashioned little thing,' she said. 'She sounded really concerned, just as Mutti would have been.'

Soon enough, however, Tina was forgotten in the enjoyment of the admittedly vulgar attractions of the Bowery by night. The street was lined with shooting booths and enlivened by the proprietors bawling out their 'Five cents a shot', and 'Hit his heart and hear de trumpet sound!', or 'Win de best knife in de Bowery wit' a shot at de King of de Beasts!' Brilliantly lit, lined with open stores, gambling dens, strip clubs and even more dubious forms of entertainment, the street was at this hour the haunt of every nationality. In ten short minutes Deborah heard as many languages spoken on either side of her. Alone she would have been terrified but clinging to Paul's arm, buffeted by the good-natured crowd, she knew herself to be safe. Together they laughed at the antics of a clown, threw nickels into a street musician's hat, and Deborah fed a red-coated monkey with peanuts and applauded when Paul took a quarter's worth of shots, winning a Mexican sombrero which he slung round his neck on its long cord and promptly forgot about.

After this, they went into one of the theatres and saw a melodrama. As soon as the curtain rose Deborah forgot everything but the play, and her wholehearted enjoyment did much to make Paul forget an uneasy feeling of guilt, because he should never have brought her here.

They emerged, blinking, into the brightly lit street, Deborah stifling a yawn. 'It's been lovely, Paul,' she said sincerely. 'The nicest evening I've ever had.'

'Good, good. Now we must get a cab.'

In the dark, musty cab Deborah sat dreamily reliving the

melodrama, so that when Paul helped her down on to the sidewalk she was jolted out of her reverie, amazed to find herself on a strange street and not at the Lubutz house. 'Oh, I thought we were going home! Are we going to dine out again? What a treat!'

Paul took her arm. 'As if I would take you home without a meal! And I thought, for a change, we would eat in my apartment. I've done all the hard work, but you can make yourself useful by warming up the soup. Come.'

He tucked her hand into the crook of his arm and led her towards the large brownstone building which stood on the street corner. Deborah did hesitate, but to say one was visiting a man's apartment at night when the man was one's own nephew sounded absurd. Accordingly, she walked meekly beside him into the foyer of the building and into an elevator which whisked them smoothly up to the third floor.

As he fitted a key into his front door he glanced down at her, saying bracingly, 'You're not worried about visiting my apartment? I promise you, no one would think badly of an aunt visiting her nephew! And I've prepared a good little supper so you can see how handy I am. You may serve it, for you'll do it so much better than I, but I reserve the right to pour the wine, pull your chair out for you, and wash up afterwards!'

After that, it would have seemed absurd to have voiced any objection, even had she felt that the situation was not, perhaps, as acceptable as he seemed to think. They entered the apartment, Deborah gave up her shabby coat and hat and tucked her gloves into a pocket. Her shabbiness did not extend to her dress, which was a neat blue merino with cream lace at the throat, and as he led her into the kitchen he reached for a capacious apron, saying as he did so: 'What a pretty gown that is. You must not get soup on it! Can you deal with this and boil a kettle, while I put the finishing touches to the table?'

He tied the apron round her small waist and then disappeared, leaving Deborah to pull the heavy pan of soup on to the stove and fill the kettle. As she worked, she looked about her. So modern, this kitchen, all shining surfaces and gleaming tiled walls, the taps, or fauçets as she was learning to call them, shining like silver! Yet for all that it was a cosy room, well lit, the bright curtains drawn to shut out the night. A kitchen, Deborah reflected happily, was homely! No one could ever think anything out of place about someone who had been helping in a man's kitchen!

But when she poured the soup into a heavy tureen and carried it into the dining-room, doubts returned. A table for two, lit by tall wax candles. Shadows flickering, Paul putting out two crystal wine glasses and a bottle of some pale golden wine, misted in the warm room, standing by a vase of flowers.

He looked up at her, and there was a look in his eyes which dismissed the fiction of entertaining his aunt, so that she gave a little shiver. Suddenly she could see Mirah's face, the eyes hurt, watching her. She set down the tureen, her hand shaking a little, and licked her lips, wanting to ask him to take her home. But he was absorbed in pouring the wine, his eyes steady on the glass, and she hesitated.

He finished his task and crossed the room in a couple of strides, and went behind her, untying her apron, saying, 'Sit down and eat your soup while it's hot. There's salad, and cold chicken, and a baked potato wrapped in the napkin. See?'

He dropped the apron to the floor and she froze, conscious of his nearness, his breath fanning warm on the side of her face. She felt his hands gently imprison her waist, felt his body hard against her own, felt his mouth against her neck. Her heart gave a frightened bound and she pulled away, hearing her voice saying 'No, no, no' in a husky whisper. She struggled, putting her hands over his, tugging at his iron-hard fingers. Yet even as she made the conventional motions of escape, a part of her wanted to lean back against that broad chest, to let him do what he would, if only he would continue to cherish her.

He said, 'Oh, my dear! My darling Deb!' and then, on a breath, 'Deborah?' For she was no longer struggling, the fingers which held his own were still, and though he could feel the leap of her heart and hear the soft panting of her breath, he was man enough to know that this was a different panic. Quietly, without fuss, he turned her in his hands, so that they faced each other, she looking up at him with candid eyes in which shame fought with another emotion.

'Deborah? Dear God, you're the same! You feel as I do! Ah, but I love you, Deb!'

His mouth took hers, he crushed her close, felt her lips soften and part beneath his. On the table candles flickered, the wreaths of steam fading as the soup cooled.

Two days later Deborah and her daughters boarded the train which, they hoped, would carry them to Arthur. If Herman and Mirah were surprised by the suddenness of the decision they made no comment, either to each other or to Deborah. Paul, helpful as ever, had bought the tickets, checked out their luggage, arranged for them to travel by Pullman sleeper for the first part of their journey, quietly funded them for meals and lodgings.

At the station, he accompanied his father and Mirah to see the small party off, kissing the children, giving Deborah a chaste salute on the brow, calling her 'Auntie' to make the children laugh.

When they had gone he returned to his office and sat at his desk for a long time, thinking. He knew that they had done the right thing by parting. Knew, too, that he would miss her sorely. And, at last, told himself that he must thank Heaven it had stopped with that one long, starved embrace. That they had both come to their senses in time. There could be no happiness for either of them in an illicit relationship which would bring such deep sorrow to their family.

He found it cold comfort.

3

'But Momma, how do you know Poppa will be at the town we're getting off at?'

Tina and Cecy were sitting demurely beside Deborah on the long, mohair-covered sofa of their sleeper. It was homely, Tina thought, with the table and a lace-edged cloth, a table lamp to light when it got dark, a niche in the wall with a vase of paper geraniums in it, and curtains which could be drawn when the sofa was made into a bed. Opposite them an elderly couple, the McCabes, had already shown a friendliness entirely devoid of curiosity which Deborah found comforting. She and Mirah had decided that her best policy would be to explain that she had saved from the money Arthur had sent her, and had set off to America earlier than he had dreamed possible, to 'surprise' him. It was not, Mirah reassured the younger woman, so very far from the truth.

So now Deborah said frankly, 'I don't know whether Poppa will be there, dear, but I *do* know it's a town he often visits. When Poppa arrives in a town he stays several days, but we shall only stay long enough to find out where he went on to next, so we should catch him up quite soon.'

'Oh. Cecy, when the night comes we go to *bed* in this train! Isn't it going to be lovely? Like being in a tiny, tiny house.'

'A tiny, tiny house,' Cecy crooned. 'Shall Cecy avva nightgown on?'

'Certainly not!' and 'Yes, of course you shall!' came simultaneously from mother and sister. Tina promptly reinforced her view by saying in an injured tone, 'Why not, Momma? We always put our nightgowns on at home!'

'Because everyone else is going to bed too, and it wouldn't be ladylike,' Deborah said, blushing. 'We shall sleep fully clothed.'

Mrs McCabe leaned across and patted her knee. 'You'll be a might uncomfortable if you don't tek somethin' off, dear. It gits turruble hot in the sleepers, come night-time.'

'We shall wear our nightgowns then,' Tina said, in a tone which brooked no argument. 'Cecy and I hate to be hot.'

'Yes, 'ate to be 'ot,' Cecy echoed, and Deborah was forced to conclude that the bossy side of her elder daughter's nature, mercifully hidden in New York, had come to light again.

And, it transpired, not a moment too soon. The extreme heat in the car, which the Americans seemed not only to take for granted but to enjoy, soon had Deborah feeling queasy, and the fights for meals at the twenty-minute whistle-stops were worse.

'Is the food always so bad?' she said timidly to Mrs McCabe. 'That tough beef, those potatoes boiled to a pulp, that *beastly* slice of pie . . .'

''Tweren't bad,' Mrs McCabe said, looking faintly surprised. 'If you think that's bad cookin', child, wait till we gits further West!'

So for three days Deborah had to endure the heat, the rush for food which she considered almost inedible, the poor toilet facilities and long, sleepless nights. The children took it in their stride, eating vast quantities of stewed tomatoes and stewed corn, chewing their way through beef tough as leather and apparently feeling none the worse for it. Between stations they played in the aisle, rushing up and down, chattering to total strangers, hanging about near card-playing cowboys, begging for a game.

Deborah, watching them enviously, thought that at least they slept at nights. But she could not. Oh, the bed was wide and comfortable, the blankets and sheets clean and ample. It was the closeness of the other passengers which stole Deborah's tranquillity. Across the aisle from them were two of the best-looking cow-hands imaginable; tall, tanned, fair-haired. During the day they were courteous and friendly, eager to help a young woman travelling alone with two small children. But at night, when the curtains were drawn and lights extinguished, in Deborah's mind both men all but developed horns and tails. All her commonsense told her that she was scarcely likely to be raped in a sleeper containing over a score of fellow travellers. But who could tell what might happen when one slept – if one slept? Someone might run amok with a knife! Her children might be slaughtered in her arms or she might be killed, leaving them motherless and unprotected.

She was even afraid of the Indians who joined the train from time to time. Poor, filthy, blanket-wrapped, they climbed aboard, whined for food, begged for nickels or charged passengers a quarter to hold one of the well-wrapped papooses which the women carried on their backs. They knew almost no English and were plainly a cowed and dispirited people, a far cry from the redskins of fiction. But at night, in her mind, they became once more the 'noble savages' of whom Fennimore Cooper had written so movingly. Every sound became an Indian, stealing on smooth, moccasined feet along the aisle, searching for a victim. A dozen times a night she almost woke everyone with a scream of terror, a dozen times the sounds proved innocent. And so she lay wide-eyed, sick and afraid, praying for morning.

Increasingly wan, she stepped gladly down on to the platform at the end of the third day's travel. The cow-hands accompanied them, carrying Deborah's overnight bag, collecting her baggage and announcing in their soft Western drawl that they would 'see you-all to the hotel, ma'am'.

Tina, trotting at her mother's side with Cecy's hand grasped firmly in her own, was the only one of the three to notice the small town. The shack-like appearance of many of the buildings, the boarded sidewalks, the saloon with its weird swing doors, a larger building which she took – rightly – to be the hotel. She saw a hitching post with horses standing by it, idly switching their tails, a range of stabling, a man sauntering along on foot, a gun at his hip.

Then they were inside the hotel, in a dark, ugly hallway. Tina looked round her appreciatively. There was a long wooden counter with rows of little pigeon holes behind it, a clerk with a solemn white face who leaned back in his chair studying a newspaper, a skinny mongrel dog who scratched his fleas contentedly on the half-landing. The place had an air of dusty neglect which would have dismayed many – it certainly dismayed Deborah – but Tina was intrigued. It was so different! Different from New York, from Uncle Herman's shop, from the train. I like things to be different, she told herself, as the man handed her mother a key and began telling her in a nasal whine about the price of the rooms and the times of the meals. They headed for the stairs, the clerk carrying their baggage, for the cow-hands had smiled their farewells as soon as they had seen their charges into the foyer; they could not risk missing the train.

Deborah and the clerk climbed the stairs wearily, but Tina jumped from step to step, jerking the unfortunate Cecy with her. A new phase in her short life was about to begin and Tina was looking forward to it.

They had no news of Arthur at the first stop, save that he had been and gone. As they got further West, the folk in the small towns remembered Arthur better, but it seemed that he had always passed through weeks before and had not been seen heading back to New York again.

Everyone grew weary of the long journey, even Tina. Western towns ceased to be different, became merely another stuffy hotel room or crowded eating house. Even brawls, which happened from time to time, could not be enjoyed to the full by Cecy and Tina because they made Deborah cry, and that made her nervous and irritable, clutching them to her bosom in a way they found infuriating.

In one of these fights they had watched open-mouthed as a big Irishman, redhaired and full of whisky, had fought with the conductor, who threw him through a plate-glass window. Amidst all the excitement, Tina could be heard remarking wisely that it was as well the man had red hair; his wife would no doubt take the blood for a mere darkening of his glowing locks.

Occasionally they struck lucky, choosing a town where the hotel was well looked after and the food excellent. And wherever they went, they were met with unfailing courtesy and kindness.

At Kansas City, where the people at the hotel remembered Arthur well, Deborah decided to take a day off to visit an outlying ranch where 'Art' usually called. They hired a waggon with an ancient nag and a driver called Bob, and set off early in the morning, arriving at the ranch by noon. The rancher's wife was friendliness itself, entirely understanding Deborah's anxiety to be reunited with her husband, but could be of little practical help save to assure them that 'Art' had promised to bring her a dress length in blue velvet before the fall. Tina promptly asked, 'Before the fall of what?' and was unfairly laughed at – unfairly, because one glance at her mother's pink cheeks told her that she had barely got the question out before Momma!

However, it had been a day to remember. They had driven through a veritable forest of sunflowers, each bloom well above the heads of the passengers in the waggon so that they could see nothing of the surrounding prairie. Then, later, they had seen huge roses hanging heavy heads in the rancher's wife's little garden, and what seemed like a wall of woolly sheep, packed as close as peas in a pod, being driven into the corrals.

'We had a whole melon,' Cecy remarked, wide-eyed at the recollection, as they climbed stiffly down from the waggon at the end of the day. 'And then nice milk.'

'Wasn't it strange to be given canned milk on a ranch?' Deborah said idly, as they pushed open the hotel door. 'I should have thought they of all people, would have enjoyed fresh milk.'

'Momma, it was a sheep ranch!' Tina said, giving her mother a glare. 'You are silly!'

'Oh! Well, of course I noticed that, but I still don't see why they shouldn't keep a cow or two. And don't call me silly, please, Tina. You're only a little girl, and . . .'

Tina retorted at once, with more spirit than good manners, and Deborah gave up, thinking, horrid child, how managing and abrupt she is becoming! She bit the thought back, dismayed. How could she think such a thing about her beloved daughter, who was such a help, such a comfort! But in a way she would almost have preferred a child who hated this life as much as she did, who needed comforting. To see Tina, so much younger than she, taking charge made her own lack of authority worse. She knew that in some strange way leaving Paul so suddenly had taken the zest out of her search before it had begun. *Did* she love him? He had seemed so sure, but she was not. She loved Arthur, so how could she love Paul too? It just was not possible for a woman to love more than one man at a time, she knew that well enough.

They had begun to climb the stairs when a voice hailed them from the hallway below. 'Miz Rosen? Ah guess you must be Miz Rosen! Ah've a message for you, ma'am, telegraphed through from Noo York this mornin'. Feller by the name of Paul says "Try Shreveport". Mean anythin' to you?'

He was a droopy-eyed man with a walrus moustache and a star in his shirt. Deborah descended the stairs far faster than she had climbed them and clutched his arm, her eyes shining.

'Shreveport? Can you reach it by railroad from here?'

'Guess so, ma'am, though it's a powerful way. It's in Louisiana, ma'am, hundreds of miles off. Tain't on the ole U.P. line either, so you'll hev to change some.'

'I see. It will . . . cost a good deal, I daresay?'

The man reached into his pocket, grinning shyly at her. 'This Paul feller, he's sending money, and I 'tend to loan you a sum myself, so's you kin ride out tomorrow, if you keer to.' Deborah began to thank him, but he waved his generosity aside. 'Nothin' to it at all, ma'am. Only a loan, after all, an' glad to do it.'

'But how can I repay you?' Deborah said, her voice full of anguish. 'It may be a while before I find my husband.'

'This Paul's sendin' money out from Noo York; he's already despatched it. Barrin' accidents it's halfway here already. You only have to repay him, ma'am.'

The man's voice was patient, soothing. Deborah smiled uncertainly. 'I see. Then I will take the money. I should like to leave first thing in the morning.'

'I'm 'greeable, ma'am.' He took a thick envelope out of his pocket and handed it to her. 'Best check it,' he advised. 'Should be fifty dollars.'

'Fifty? That's a lot of money.'

He chuckled. 'It's a lot of miles. He touched his hat, which had remained on his head throughout the interview. 'Good day, ma'am.'

He leaned down and rumpled Cecy's curls, winked at Tina and was gone, leaving Deborah staring speechlessly after him. It seemed that he had been an angel in disguise, bringing them the good news of Arthur's whereabouts and the wherewithal to reach him.

'Momma, I'm hungry!'

Cecy's shrill little pipe cut across her thoughts. With a sigh, she began to shepherd both children towards the stairs once more.

It was easily the worst and longest journey she had ever imagined, Deborah thought, climbing wearily down off the train. She helped Cecy down, watched Tina jump scornfully on to the platform, and began to rummage in her capacious sealskin handbag for her brass check. A young negro came running, his delighted grin bringing answering smiles from the children. He picked up the overnight bag as if it weighed nothing.

'Hotel, ma'am? De bes' is de Mortimer. Shall us go dere?'

'If you please. And my baggage has been checked to the station. Had I better to see to that first?'

With his free hand he took the brass check and trotted over to a wooden shack grandly labelled 'Baggage Repository'. He handed over the check and returned. 'Yo' baggage will be at de 'otel afore yo' is, ma'am.'

And so it proved. Deborah and the children entered the hotel to find their luggage already standing at the foot of the stairs. They crossed the foyer to the usual long counter, with the usual bored clerk in attendance. He shoved a key at them, and the hotel guest book. Tina beamed up at him, trying to make him grin back so that she could see if all black men had huge white teeth like the boy who had carried their luggage. But he would not smile, gazing gloomily into space, tapping his long, pinkish fingertips on the counter, bored with them already.

'I see you've got a M-Mr R-Rosen staying h-here,' Deborah said, stammering, now that the end of their search seemed in sight at last. 'M-may I ask where he is now?'

The clerk yawned and rubbed his finger round the inside of his ear, inspected the result without much interest, then turned the book round to face himself. 'Yaas'm. Checked out, day befo' yistiday.'

'Oh, God!' Deborah let her shoulders sag. She tried to straighten herself up, then began to move listlessly towards the stairs.

'Where did he go?' Tina said impatiently. 'Do you know where he went?'

'Ah sho' do, missie. He's gone down de coas', to Galeport. Seems he had business dere.'

'Is it far?' Tina demanded. 'Will the railroad take us there?'

The man seemed to throw off his inertia. He grinned suddenly, showing teeth every bit as white and huge as the boy's. 'Railroad don' go no furder dan Shreveport, missie. But dere's a stagecoach leaves each mo'ning, fust light.'

Deborah had turned back to listen to this exchange but now she said suddenly, 'I'm not budging from here!' She glared down at Tina, who glared straight back. 'We'll wait here, and catch Poppa when he comes back to the railroad. I *won't* go off on another wild goose chase. I'm tired to death!'

'Momma, we *must*,' Tina said urgently. 'Suppose Poppa moves on from Galeport, in some other direction? We must follow. You said so yourself when we left New York.'

Deborah bit her lip, smiled weakly, giggled, then began to laugh outright. 'Heaven defend me from a child who's always right! Tina, you're going to grow up to be a most objectionable young woman! But you're right. We'll go.' She turned to the clerk, who had been following the exchange with deep interest. 'Please book us seats on the first stage to Galeport tomorrow, and see we're woken in good time to catch it,' she said briskly.

The stage was ancient and the horses elderly, but it went at a steady pace and they reached their destination by mid-afternoon. This was not Galeport, because the coach did not travel that far. As Arthur must have done, they took the stage to Binnacky, where the clerk at Shreveport, once his interest had been roused, had been sure they would find the small hotel satisfactory.

'Yo' kin git to Galeport in a hired buggy,' he told them. 'Dere ain't much at Galeport, acos it ain't a place so much as a kinda pier stretching out into de sea, for de ships to stop by. Folk come from de big houses an' sich fur to git goods offa de ships. Yes, sah, dat's all dere is to Galeport.'

As she stepped down from the stage the heat hit Deborah like a blow in the face. She winced involuntarily, then glanced round her. A few frame houses, shade trees, patches of garden. A store, a smithy, a saloon. Right at the end of the street was an old colonial house, stone built, with a strip of lawn round it, more shade trees, a glimpse of an orchard. It looked pleasant, and Deborah guessed it must be the hotel, an old private house before the Civil War, perhaps, which had been made to earn its keep when the family fell upon hard times.

But apart from themselves the place seemed deserted. Helplessly, Deborah looked down at their luggage. She could certainly not carry it, nor did she intend to try. 'Oh, dear! Why is no one here to meet the stage? What shall we do with our baggage?'

'Leave it here. We'll get the boy in the hotel to fetch it,' Tina said firmly.

'How do you know there's a boy in the hotel, Miss

Know-it-all?' Deborah said disagreeably. But she picked up her overnight bag, took Cecy's hand, and led the way into the hotel.

In the cool, marble-floored hallway a clerk sat yawning behind the counter, his feet up, his shirt unbuttoned down to the waist. He jumped to attention when he saw them, however, and opened the register with a pleasant smile. 'A room, ma'am? Suttinly, ma'am.'

Deborah bent over the book, then stiffened. The last name in it was Arthur Rosen. She checked the opposite column this time; it did not seem that he had checked out.

Casually, she said, 'Is Mr Rosen still here?'

'He'm still here, ma'am. Leastways, he's gone down the street a piece, to Jacobs' Store. You musta passed it as . . .'

'C-could you send someone for my luggage . . . baggage, I mean? It's down by the coach stop, I'll just go along to the store and see . . . '

Before the clerk had recovered from his surprise, his new guest had left, leaving behind her overnight bag, a sealskin handbag and the copy of Harper's Monthly Magazine with which she had been fanning herself as she entered the hotel.

He ran to the door, stopping to pick up her belongings, and was in time to see her vanish into the store. Shrugging, he returned to his place. She would be back!

Inside the store Deborah was halfway across the swept wooden floor before she stopped, one hand going to her heart. By the counter a stout woman was dictating a grocery order to a lanky black youth. They heard her saying, 'Grits, Cy; and some of that maple syrup Ah had las' month. It sure pleased Mr Evan Frost, so we'd best have more.'

She turned her head at that point to stare openly at the newcomers. Cy, on the other hand, gave them a glance of professional indifference but called laconically over his shoulder to where a door stood slightly ajar, 'Mistah Jacobs, sah, 'nudder customer!'

The door, Deborah imagined, must lead to the storekeeper's private quarters. Now two men emerged from it.

The first man was small and fat, his face shining with sweat. He glanced across at them with an automatic smile, however, wiping his hands on his large white apron as he said, 'Yes'm? Kin I help you?'

But Deborah scarcely heard him. She had eyes for no one but his companion. Tall, leaner than she remembered, dark hair flopping across a tanned brow, dark eyes screwed up against the prairie glare even though it was dim in the store.

'Arthur?'

There was a moment's complete stillness, then the tall man gave a whoop and vaulted over the counter, taking Deborah into his arms in one quick, hungry movement, hugging her tightly, looking incredulously down at her. 'Deborah! Oh, Deb! But how . . .'

He turned to Mr Jacobs. 'It's Deborah, Fred. Can we go into the back for a moment? There is so much I don't . . .' He did not wait for the other to reply, but pulled Deborah round the counter and through the door behind it, which he then closed firmly.

Left behind, the people in the store looked at one another. Mrs Frost raised her brows at Mr Jacobs, who shrugged helplessly and cast an equally questioning glance at the two small girls who stood, hand in hand, gazing blankly at the closed door.

Cecy broke the silence. 'Is this our poppa's store?'

Mr Jacobs bent over the counter, giving her his most winning smile. 'No, li'l girl, it ain't your poppa's store. Is that young fellah your poppa, then?'

Cecy smiled up at him trustfully. 'I dunno. *Is* it our poppa?'

Mrs Frost drew in a scandalised breath, but before she could speak Cecy said plaintively, 'Have we any pennies, Tina? I want some sweeties.'

'Momma maybe has some pennies,' Tina said. For once, she felt at a loss. Her recollections of her poppa were vague, yet surely Momma would not have hugged and kissed a stranger? But why did the fat man not *know* his friend had two little girls? If they were the tall man's little girls!

'Ah'll buy you some candy, honey!'

Tina turned with a certain relief to the stout white woman who addressed her. 'Thank you, ma'am. When my mother comes back she'll repay you. Or my father, of course.'

'Then he *is* yo' daddy! Guess they wuz so tickled to see each othuh, after this long time, they done forgit their li'l chillun. Yes, sah, Ah'll buy yo' some candy an' then, iffen you've a mind, Ah'll tek you down the road fer a soda! How 'bout that?'

Tina smiled and bobbed a curtsey. She was intrigued by this white woman who spoke like a negro, and nothing in her previous experience had given her cause to doubt a grown-up's good intentions. If the lady wanted to buy them sweets and a soda, why should she be denied? 'Yes please, ma'am, we'd like that.'

'Hev you done orderin', Miz Frawst, ma'am?' the black boy said. He alone seemed impervious to the drama which had just been enacted and Tina warmed to him. He was a boy after her own heart, singleminded enough to ignore the sloppy huggings and kissings of two old people.

'Add some candy to ma bill, Cy,' Mrs Frost said imperiously. 'Which sort do yo' prefer, honeys?'

Cy, turning to the shelf behind him, began to reel off the names of the sweets in an almost inaudible mumble but Tina cared nothing for names. 'The pink ones, please,' she said grandly. 'We'll have two bags; one each.' She saw no reason why she should not make the most of this unrivalled opportunity.

Cy, who would have thoroughly appreciated this point of view had he understood it, dipped a scoop into the big bottle of pink sweets, shot them on to the scale and then into a cornet-shaped bag. Tina watched sternly as he dipped out the second bag, then graciously accepted both with her most beguiling smile (which was wasted on Cy). Turning to Mrs Frost she thanked her in her most 'society' manner for the gift. Cecy, prompted by a savage elbow, hastily echoed her elder sister's thanks and bobbed a wobbly curtsey, enchanting Mrs Frost, a childless woman.

'Ain't she the cutest thing, Mistah Jacobs? Ah sho' shall enjoy buyin' a soda for such a purty thing!'

'Yes, ma'am,' Mr Jacobs agreed politely. He cocked a worried eye at the closed door to his private quarters. 'D'you think I oughter maybe . . .' He paused delicately, raising his brows in tactful enquiry.

'Ah really think yo' might go in, presently,' Mrs Frost agreed. 'Tell their maw and paw Ah's tekked the chillun down to Maude's drugstore. They'll be fine with me.'

As she spoke, she put out two hands and was flattered at the way two small hands were instantly thrust into her own. Flanked by Tina and Cecy she sailed out of the store and down the street towards a small, unpretentious frame house with the legend 'Drug Store' in gilt lettering above the front window.

Mrs Frost smiled proudly down at her charges. 'There ain't many drug stores this far South, an' the soda fountain's all the rage,' she declared. 'Your maw an' paw sho' chose good when they chose Binnacky to rear their chillun.'

Tina recognised the hint of a question in the last remark, but ignored it. 'Yes, ma'am,' she said.

They entered the house and Tina saw that some enterprising person had turned the parlour into a soda fountain by adding a long marble counter on which was perched the soda dispenser. Behind it the wall had been lined with mirror and a long shelf held glasses, biscuits and cakes, confectionery, and tall bottles of fruit syrup.

Behind the counter a thin woman in a plain dark dress and frilly white apron looked up enquiringly as they entered.

'Yes? Oh, it's you, Dorrie. Didn't reckernise you fer a moment with them young 'uns in tow.'

'Ah've brought ma li'l friends in fer a soda, Maude. What'd you fancy, honey? Bless me, I never axed your names!'

'I'm Tina and she's Cecilia, and we'd like . . .' The two heads drew close for a moment, faces hidden behind bonnet brims. 'We'd like a yellow one and a red one.'

Maude reached for the bottles of syrup and measured

some of each colour carefully into two glasses. 'One pineapple soda, one raspberry soda. What about yo'self, Dorrie?'

'Not a soda, Maude,' Mrs Frost said. 'But Ah sho' wouldn't say no to a slice of yo' vanilla layer cake.'

Once the sodas and the cake had been dispensed, Mrs Frost led the small girls to the window table and hoisted them up on to the tall stools. Seating herself, she commenced an artless form of questioning which she hoped might yield all the information she required without labelling herself a prying female. After all, strangers were not the norm in Binnacky, and it would be nice to have all the facts at her fingertips.

'How old're yo', Tina? And babby sister here?'

'I'm five and she's going on for four.'

'Mm hmm. That sho' is big! An' hev yo' come to live at Binnacky with yo' maw an' paw?'

Tina, aware as are all children that treats must be paid for, sighed, took a satisfying drink from her glass of pineapple soda, and said cautiously, 'I think so, for a little while. Then we must go home to Grandma.'

'Yo've got a granmaw at home, then? Now Ah wondah why yo' grandmaw didn't come with yo'? Would she be yo' maw's maw, or yo' paw's maw?'

Tina looked as puzzled as she felt. 'She's just Grandma, ma'am.'

Mrs Frost looked across at Maude, who was listening avidly whilst pretending to polish the counter top, and raised her brows slightly, then tried another tack. 'And yo' paw? Guess yo've not seen him fer a while, Miss Cecilia not reckernisin' him the way she did. Why would that be?'

Tina might be only small, but she knew the value of a frank 'don't know'. Not many people could get round that one. 'I don't know, ma'am.'

'Where've you bin afore Binnacky, then? Noo York?'

That was easy; she could give good value for the sodas here! 'Yes, we were in New York for a long time. We stayed with Uncle Herman and Mrs Lubutz in the Bronx, and we helped in Uncle Herman's delicatessen. At least, I helped, Cecy just played. Then we went West, on the train, for weeks and weeks, to all sorts of places. We went on a sheep ranch, and into hotels . . . oh, all sorts of places! But I'm glad I helped in Uncle Herman's store, because Momma was pleased and said I would be a help in Poppa's store, when we found him.'

Found him! This was manna indeed! Mrs Frost pounced. 'So yo' come all this way to find your paw! And weren't he glad to see yo'! Ah declare, he nearly hugged yo' maw in two! So why'd he go off without yo'-all, Ah wondah!'

'Mebbe there waren't no cash fer all of 'em,' suggested Maude from her vantage point behind the counter. 'Happened before, Dorrie.'

Her friend snorted. 'He's doin' mighty well for hisself, that young man. Bought property, Ah understand.' She turned back to Tina. 'Did you know, back in Noo York, that you wuz comin' to Binnacky?'

'No, ma'am.' Then, just as Mrs Frost was pulling her 'very odd' face she added innocently, 'Momma may have known, but me and Cecy didn't.' She finished her soda, tipping the long glass up and licking her lips regretfully as the last sweet, flavoursome drop trickled down her throat. 'All done, Cecy? Good girl, say thank you nicely to Mrs Frost.' And before Mrs Frost could think of any further delaying tactics the two little girls had curtseyed, chorused their thanks, and left, trotting back up the street towards the store.

'That thar's a purty sight,' Maude said, with a hint of malice in her tone. She and her friend stood in the window watching the children nearing the store. 'Two real nice . . . well!'

The exclamation was uttered as Cecy suddenly lunged at her elder sister and a short but fierce fight ensued, ending, had the watchers but known it, with Tina handing over one of the bags of sweets as Cecy's 'I'll tell!' squeaked out into the empty street.

'What in tarnation was that about?' Dorrie Frost turned a scandalised face towards her friend, who chuckled gently. Running the only drug store in town had made her more au fait with children than her friend.

'Nothin', most like. How come you had them chillun in tow, Dorrie?'

Nothing loth, Mrs Frost told her friend about the drama in Jacobs' store. 'Ah reckin them chillun know more'n they'd say,' she ended darkly. 'Why, Maude, that Art fellah 'most et the woman up! A-carryin' on before the chillun, to say nothin' of Cy! And not a bit of notice did he tek of the chillun, come to think. Never threw 'em a word or a look, I swear it. Jus' grabbed aholt of the woman an' lit off into the back.'

'Perhaps they ain't hissen,' Maude suggested charitably. 'Mebbe they'm love-begot.'

That was going a little too far and too fast for Mrs Frost. Nevertheless, she pretended to consider, head cocked to one side, eyes screwed up in thought. 'No-oo, Ah don't reckon,' she decided. 'Fer one thing, that Tina's got a look of the young fellah about her, an' fer another, why would she bring 'em here, if they waren't hissen? She mighta bin unfaithful and repented, or p'raps *he* wuz unfaithful an' left her, an' she's run him to earth at last.'

There was a short silence whilst the two women digested this, never knowing how near the truth they had come. At last Maude said regretfully, 'It don't seem likely, Dorrie. If it war true, why'd they kiss like you said, and go off into the back? There would've bin a scene, Ah reckon.'

She contemplated this idea with relish, but shook her head slowly at Mrs Frost's expressed opinion that the scene might even now be taking place in the back of the store. ''Tain't likely,' she rejoined. 'But we'll know; if they settle here there won't be much we don't know in a few weeks.'

Sadly, Mrs Frost had to acknowledge that she had lost her initiative. Soon enough, everyone would know all the strangers' business; small town living was like that. But, making her way back to the livery stable where she had parked her buggy, she knew that what she had actually seen would provide food, not only for thought but for gossip also, for many days to come.

The thought cheered her on her drive home.

4

Deborah sat in the stuffy little hallway which was Dr Kingsley's waiting room, dreading the interview to come. It seemed hard that she should have to take the blame for being pregnant again, as though she had deliberately sought the condition out of stupidity or stubbornness; she had not in the least desired another child but since it had happened she supposed, drearily, that she must make the best of it.

In the two years since her reunion with Arthur, Deborah had born him two more daughters. Rebecca was fifteen months, Rachel a mere twenty-five weeks. And she was pregnant again. She took a deep breath, trying to steady her nerves. But she remembered too well Dr Kingsley's frank words after Rachel's birth.

'This climate don't suit you; too humid. Reckon you've gotta be born here to stand it. And bearin' a child every ten months don't suit you either, Miz Deborah Rose. Tell your man to choose; either he stays home and minds the store, or you stop gettin' in the fam'ly way. Understand?'

She understood, for of late she had often been too tired to sleep and the exhausting bouts of morning sickness which had attacked her during her last pregnancy left her weak and lethargic. She had spoken shyly to Arthur and knew Dr Kingsley had also had words on the subject, but Arthur was unimpressed. 'Babies you love, Deb,' he said, turning over in bed and kissing the side of her neck. 'Making love is good, when I come home. Surely this pleasure you would not wish to deny me?'

She had been tempted to say she was too tired to enjoy

his lovemaking and that much though she loved babies, she did not want another one too soon. But the thought of losing him kept her silent, for it was a constant fear. If she protested that she could not stand the climate, that she feared being alone with only blacks for company, the reply was always the same. 'Did I ask you to come over to the States? If you aren't content, it might be better if you went home.'

So she submitted to his desires, hoping that this time she might be lucky, and not quicken. He was home for such short periods, yet each time she conceived. And she had soon realised that her hopes were in vain. Another baby was on the way, and her back ached, her head ached, even her mind seemed to ache at the prospect of managing with a fifth child.

Sitting in the waiting room while Dr Kingsley lanced a boil on Sam Braid's neck, bandaged Sue Ellen's sprained wrist and gave Mrs Mansell a bottle of medicine to cure the hookworm contracted by all of her fourteen children, Deborah felt the first stirrings of real resentment against Arthur. He knew she was pregnant yet he had gone off less than a week ago, having been home no longer than was necessary to load up his waggons. All his promises of remaining by her side once the early months in the store were over had been conveniently forgotten.

When the store had first been built, with the house adjoining, Arthur had told her that with Galeport being no more than a stopping-off place for ships bound for the Delta and other customers restricted to a few poor whites from the forest and the owners of the big holiday houses which lined part of the coast, he would have to continue to take his waggons out 'from time to time' in order to make ends meet.

'But Galeport, it will grow,' he said confidently. 'Then enough trade there will be to keep us both busy.'

He had been right, Galeport had grown. In addition to their own store there was a smithy, an eating house, a drug store, two saloons, a boarding house and a livery stable. At first, ships coming to the pier to offload had scarcely stopped, but soon it was borne in upon the captains that Galeport was a thriving little place where shore leave might safely be granted. The men bought oddments at the store, drank in the saloon, ate the famous crab gumbo of the Gulf Coast. Some of them even left their ships here instead of continuing up the Delta, because the stage no longer terminated at Binnacky; it came right on to Galeport. Tina and Cecy, indeed, travelled on it to school each day. Dr Kingsley, seeing how the houses were springing up around the tiny settlement, predicted that in a few years Galeport would have its own school too.

The town was growing, but Arthur's promise had long since crumbled into dust. Far from remaining at home, his periods of absence were longer, rarely less than four months and often more. And he left Deborah with so much work and so many responsibilities! Four little girls, the hired negro help, the store. And with its expansion, Galeport began to have its dangers. With the crews now allowed ashore there could be trouble. Once, a knife-fight had taken place between two buck negroes right in front of the store. A man had died as a result of that fight. And a girl, one of the poor whites from the forest settlements, had been raped. After that, Deborah had asked Arthur half-humorously if he was not afraid to leave her alone in such a place.

'Afraid? For a sensible woman, surrounded by servants? Certainly not! Mabel and the boys would not let harm come to you. And in the store there is Mel. No, with them I can leave you safe.'

So Deborah struggled on alone, living behind screens because of the mosquitoes which swarmed to the coast at certain times of the year, buying, bargaining, pricing, selling. Serving in the store, trying to bring the children up properly. Ranged against her were the humid heat which sapped energy and brought illness, the awesome weight of responsibility, and her inability to deal with the blacks without showing her fear of them.

Mabel, her housekeeper, was wonderful. Fat, motherly, sensible, she ran the house like clockwork. But the men –

Rufus who did all the heavy work around the store and looked after their large garden, Jimmy who looked after the horses and drove the buggy when she was unable to do so, and Truman, the loutish lad who helped Rufus – all filled her with sick uncertainty and fear. They were so different; they even smelled different! She watched Tina and Cecy run to Jimmy after school, chattering, fearless, and envied but did not understand their ease.

Mel, of course, was different. The eldest son of a desperately poor family of whites who scraped a living from the forest, he had come to the store asking for a job. He could neither read nor write and his knowledge of money was confined to a great need of it. Yet both Arthur and Deborah saw that behind the skinny, tow-headed youth with the pasty skin and the frightened eyes there was a person of intelligence. Tina saw it too, and proceeded to give Mel lessons. As fast as she learned at her little school she passed it on to Mel so that now, with two years of education behind him – albeit secondhand – Mel could read, write and figure as well as Tina herself. In fact, he was reading English classics and wading his way through a dog-eared copy of *A Midsummer Night's Dream* whenever time permitted.

Yet despite this he was still skinny and underfed, a boy who thought he was sixteen or seventeen but could not be sure! And Arthur, who had once loved her so dearly, was content to leave her for months at a time with no more protection than that which Mel and Mabel could offer!

Dr Kingsley's voice calling 'Next!' brought her out of her reverie. Her heart thumping, sweat breaking out on her brow, she walked with what self-confidence she could muster into his consulting room.

Arthur, driving a hired buggy, contemplated the pleasant fields and mountains, the woods and streams of Pennsylvania and remembered, a little resentfully, a conversation he had had with Dr Kingsley just before he left Galeport. Knowing Deb was pregnant again and would have to face the doctor, he had gone over to the surgery in Binnacky to tell the doc, man to man, that what had happened was as much his fault as his wife's. To his surprise, Dr Kingsley had not been at all impressed with this man-of-the-world frankness.

'She's your wife. 'Bout the only legal way a man kin kill a woman's the way you've chosen, boy. But don' come runnin' to me for a share o' sympathy when she's gone. You kin bring up the li'l gals without her, I suppose?'

'*Kill* her? But why? She's had four already!'

'Because she's past thirty, and the climate at Galeport ain't natural for any white woman. Most of 'em either gits waited on hand an' foot by black servants, like Mrs Elliot at Plains House, or dies young.'

'No. No! She's strong, she's . . .'

'Not thought of it like that?' Dr Kingsley said. 'Well, mebbe you're not bad, Art, so much as plumb thoughtless and careless of your li'l wife. Just remember when she's gone that you won't be free no more. Tied by the apron-strings to them young 'uns, you'll be. Guess you can't afford a mansion and two-three dozen black servants yet?' And as Arthur dumbly shook his head, 'Then I sure hope you enjoy bein' a mother to five young 'uns, Art.'

It had frightened Arthur badly; so badly that he had humbly asked Dr Kingsley for his advice.

'You got no call to leave her here the way you do. Either stay, so's she doesn't git all the work of the store and kin share her troubles, or take her someplace else. Why not sell up and go East? In a more equable climate she'd thrive, I guess, even on a baby a year.'

Strangely enough, that very same day he had seen an advertisement in a paper Paul had sent. Paul had ringed it round, because for some time he had been trying to persuade Arthur to invest some of the money lying idle in the bank, and like Dr Kingsley he was sure that living in the sub-tropical South could not be good for Deborah or the children. The advertisement was for a store in Johnstown, Pennsylvania. Against the advert Paul had written, in pencil, 'Widow woman who has made her pile and wants out. Conemaugh Valley growing fast.'

On impulse, Arthur had gone into Binnacky and telegraphed Paul to buy, adding the rider, 'Shall go to Johnstown self, 30 May. Hope to move family. Join me?'

Paul's answer came quickly. 'Deal made. Will join you 31 May. Delighted.'

It had been arranged like that, quickly and with ease, but Arthur had not told Deborah; innate caution held him back. Suppose he saw Johnstown or the store and disliked one or the other, or both? He loved the West as other men loved women, but had no desire to settle his wife and family there. He was sure they would not enjoy the great spaces of the prairie, the strange, freakish violence of the weather, the idea of being in a world which was made for men without women. So he neither expected nor wanted to like Johnstown, any more than he expected or wanted to live there himself. But he would visit regularly, as he visited Galeport, so he wanted the place to be pleasant.

Now, driving back to the hotel where he had spent the previous night, he decided that Johnstown would do very well for Deborah and the children. It was a typical small-town neighbourhood with all the drawbacks of a small, insular community. No doubt gossip was rife, and back-biting, and narrowmindedness; but this would not displease Deborah, who had been virtually alone for two years in Galeport.

He took the hired horse and buggy round the back to the stables, then strolled into the hotel. He dined well, and then retired to his room for that good night's sleep which would enable him to meet Paul tomorrow at his best. He knew it was early, but felt he could do with the rest after rushing around the way he had been lately. With a feeling of virtuousness, he climbed into the comfortable bed and sank quickly into a deep, untroubled sleep.

He did not know what had woken him. Almost in his sleep, he stumbled to the window and looked out across the quiet town. It was still dark but there was a moon and he could see quite well; he noticed the river, glinting silver, the mountains, black against the stars. And then he knew what had woken him. Something was moving, rushing down the mountain, something which hissed and muttered and roared as it came. He felt his skin rise in bumps, the short hairs on the back of his neck prickle erect. It was a great wall of water twice as high as the hotel, rushing down on the town like a huge Atlantic roller.

Horror and incredulity rooted him to the spot for perhaps two seconds, while his mind strove to deny the reality of the scene. Then the water was in amongst the houses and its roar was augmented by other sounds. The creaking groans as wooden houses took the onslaught, the screams as the houses buckled and bent and were torn apart. Then the hotel screamed too, like a woman, and he saw the walls caving in on him.

There was no more noise then, and no more light. There was blackness, and a weight on him, forcing him into water which gurgled into his mouth, tried to invade his nostrils. He could neither call out nor fight the weight, which seemed to be increasing. His hands moved with small, helpless gestures, trying to discover where he was, what was happening, for his eyes could tell him nothing. Then the weight shifted, though it did not leave him, and he felt objects passing him and knew he was being carried along. Sometimes obstacles thrust him deeper into the water, at other times his face was almost free of it. He could hear, above the rushing water, cries for help, small and faint and far, and sounds of splintering wood, breaking furniture, and dull thumpings which he could not identify. Then something struck him on the back of the head and he knew no more.

He regained consciousness, how much later he could not tell. He was no longer in total darkness; he could see light. He strained his eyes, saw that the light flickered, orange, red, a pale, wicked yellow. Flames! His body from the waist down was in numbing, ice-cold water yet his face was scorched by fire. He felt the heat increasing and tried to move away from it but he was held fast. His hands told him he was trapped in a great mass of heavy wooden planks, and he knew he was floating on the water in the remains of the hotel and that above him the wooden building must be on fire. A sudden hot blast fanned red-hot air into his face and he felt his eyebrows catch, then his hair. The pain was intolerable! He screamed, a thin, reedy sound which sounded nothing against the roar of fire and water. He beat at the encroaching fire with futile, weakened hands. A log above him fell, flaming, throwing hissing embers into his face and on to his wet clothing; then another, knocking him silly but not bringing loss of consciousness, so that when the great pile suddenly began to move he was aware that somehow they had entered running water and he was being borne at a tremendous pace towards the inferno.

The railroad workers were the first rescuers to arrive at what had once been Johnstown. They saw charred bodies, the ashes of buildings, and everywhere the flood. They knew the dam above the town had burst and that a fire had started in the great pile of bone-dry timbers which had once been snug dwellinghouses, but they had not been prepared for the numbers of the dead, nor for the stench, sweet and sickening, which hung thick in the air.

'This one's almost whole,' a railroad man observed, lifting a bolt of timber away to reveal a blackened, hairless, bloodied figure which, nevertheless, had all its limbs and features.

'Let's have him outer that, Paddy, and on to the pile.' He heaved at the body's legs, then nearly dropped it as he heard it groan. 'Begod, Paddy, I t'ink it's alive!'

'Never,' Paddy said sceptically. 'There's none alive, man! It musta bin air rushin' outa the lungs.'

But a second, whimpering groan convinced both men that here they had no corpse, even if the man was dying. So they carried the shattered wreck that had been Arthur very carefully across to firm ground and put him on a waggon already loaded with the pitifully few wounded, bound for the nearest hospital.

It was there, later that same day, that Paul found him.

'Can I see him?' he asked the young Irish nurse who told him that the man certainly seemed to be his uncle-in-law.

Papers found in his pockets proved his identity beyond all reasonable doubt.

'Well, you *can*; but he's not a good sight, I'm tellin' ye! Awful beat about, he's been.'

'Will he live?' Paul asked in an awestruck voice after he had been allowed to peep at his uncle-in-law. He supposed it was Arthur; in his present state, deeply unconscious as the man was, it was impossible for him to be sure.

The little nurse patted his arm. 'Only God could tell ye that, but I'm thinkin' he's gone through too much to give up at this stage. I think he'll live, though he'll never walk again.'

Paul drew in his breath sharply. 'Not . . . not walk?' He tried to think of Arthur confined to a chair, or a bed, never striding out to his wagon, never returning to the Western prairies. 'Dear God! He's a wife and four children down in Louisiana. How am I going to tell them?'

'Why, it's been all over the papers for days. She'll surely think him dead,' the little nurse said, her small face brightening. 'You'll be bringing good tidings!'

'I think she won't know he's here,' Paul said quietly. 'He would not tell her. A secretive man, Arthur. I must go to her.'

'Of course ye must. I'll tell him where you've gone when he comes round.' She patted his arm again, smiling up into his grim face. 'Remember, you're bringing her *good* news; 'tis life that matters, when all's said and done.'

Back home, Deborah struggled on. The visit to Dr Kingsley had not been anywhere near as bad as she had feared, the doctor merely saying that she must be sensible and leave the store to Mel in the afternoons. He did ask her, casually, whether she and Art had ever thought of birth control, but did not pursue the subject in the face of her obvious embarrassment.

As she jogged home in her buggy, Deborah's mind played with the idea of birth control. She knew it existed, had seen discreet little advertisements in the drug stores when she had visited New Orleans, but had never considered it for herself. It seemed . . . sinful, as though limiting the number of little Roses was against God's law.

For they were known as Art and Deborah Rose here, due to a simple accident. Soon after they moved into the store, Arthur had gone off with his waggon to arrange for some more stock to be delivered. She had watched him go happily enough, believing in her innocence that this would be an isolated occasion.

A day later, a young fellow had come into the store and offered to paint their name on the fascia board outside, since he had noticed the board was empty. For a very moderate sum plus his meals for two days and a bed at the back of the store or in the stable he promised to do her a really good sign.

Pleased at the thought of Arthur's pleasure when he returned, Deborah had agreed. The young man asked for some money in advance which he promptly spent on a bottle of whisky and as promptly consumed. He could not have been used to strong drink, for all next day he lay moaning on his shakedown in the loft while Deborah, very concerned, made him drink beef tea.

Unrepentant but extremely grateful, he had appeared next morning, consumed a hearty breakfast, and disappeared outside with his pots of paint, to 'do the durndest job you ever did see, ma'am, so's you'll know Ah sho' am grateful fer your kindness'.

He had done a good job. The name, Arthur Rose, was executed in bold yellow and black lettering and the fascia board was smothered in painted roses. Scarlet, pink, yellow, their green leaves so real, as an admiring customer pointed out, 'you could've touched 'em'. And Deborah, summoned out to admire, had not felt able to complain that he had omitted the final 'n' of their name. Particularly as the fascia board was now so rose-bedecked that there was not room for another pin on it.

When Arthur came home, he admired the board and dismissed the missing letter airily. 'You're pretty as a rose, so we'll use the name,' he said. 'My father started life as Rosenbaum and knocked off the last four letters; if I change to Rose I'm following the family tradition.'

Preoccupied with her thoughts, Deborah was halfway home before she remembered she should have waited for the girls to leave school. It would have saved her a second journey. But she must do as the doctor said, and rest in the afternoons, so she continued on her way. She thought of the babies, snoozing in their room, and of how she would ask Mabel to make her a pot of real English tea when she got in. She was so relieved by Dr Kingsley's unexpected understanding and kindness that nothing seemed as bad as it had earlier. Though not precisely happy, she felt better than she had for some while. Lazy, contented; waiting.

Arriving back at the store, she called to Jimmy to unharness the horse and went quickly into the kitchen. Mabel, busily making bread, said with easy friendship, 'How yo' done go on, Miz Deb?'

'Oh, fine. Dr Kingsley was so kind,' Deborah said. 'He wants me to rest in the afternoons, though, Mabel, and I really think I shall this time. Would you make me some tea and then keep an eye on the babies until about four o'clock? They've been good?'

'Slep' like two li'l angels,' Mabel reported. 'Is yo' set on fetchin' Tina an' Cecy, Miz Deb, or shall Ah tell Jimmy to go gettem?'

Deborah wavered. It would be so nice not to have to go out into the hot sunshine again. Abruptly, she decided that just for once she would spoil herself. 'Yes, Mabel, tell Jimmy to fetch them.'

She was halfway across the hall when Mabel called after her, 'Miz Deb! Did you done tell Rufus 'bout the vegerbles?'

'No, I forgot. Tell him for me, will you?' Deborah heard Mabel's placid assent as she closed the bedroom door. Methodically, she removed her bonnet, her cashmere jacket, her skirt and the loose smock top. She undid her button boots and kicked them under the bed. Lying down on the covers she thought with amusement that at least she had got out of one task she thoroughly disliked. Rufus was an immense negro with a small, bullet-shaped head and hands like cow-catchers. She was afraid of him, though she came into daily contact with him and had done so for two years, and her reason told her he was a huge, good-natured, slow-witted creature who would not harm a fly. But reason, of course, had nothing to do with it. Her fear was something which she could no more escape than she could avoid growing older day by day. So now she lay in the quiet bedroom, feeling a little breeze wafting across her sweat-damp skin, and hoped that the baby would be a boy and that Arthur would stay with her for the birth.

Presently, she slept.

When school finished, Tina and Cecy stood in the school-yard for five minutes, then began plodding along the shady road in the direction of home. It was not the first time Momma had been late, and although the walk was a long one they felt sure they would soon see Cloud, the pony, with the buggy rattling and swaying behind, hurrying towards them.

'I'll go straight to the store when we get home and get my chores done,' Tina said casually. 'I just hope we aren't too late because Mel likes me to make up the orders.'

'I will too,' Cecy said. Since she rarely disagreed with her elder sister, Tina had rather taken this for granted, but she said at once, 'Good. I'll do the livery stable one.'

'Oh! You did it last time! It isn't fair, Tina!'

'Let's play spellings,' Tina suggested diplomatically, and immediately suggested a word which she knew Cecy would be able to cope with. Allowing herself to be sidetracked, Cecy rose to the bait and for some time they proceeded quite happily to play the game invented by Tina, master-minded by Tina and usually won by Tina. In fact, both were in a fair way to forgetting the heat and dust of the afternoon when a buggy drew up beside them, coming from the direction of Binnacky.

'Hey, gals, where's yo' maw? Ah've got a message for her.'

Tina looked up and smiled at Mr Ellis, from the railroad depot. He sometimes brought them messages from Poppa or from New York, and they packed him a box of goods every now and then. 'Hello, Mr Ellis, sir! Momma didn't call for us so she'll be at the store, I guess. Why? Is it a message from Poppa?'

'It's a message,' he agreed briefly. 'Hop in.'

Nothing loth, both girls climbed into the buggy and were driven the rest of the way home. Arriving outside the store, Mr Ellis jumped down and fairly hollered out for Rufus, then made for the house, leaving the girls to climb down themselves. As she did so, Tina reflected that this was not usual. Mr Ellis was a southern gentleman and prided himself on treating ladies, even young ones, as if they were made of finest china.

Rufus had come running and was leading the buggy round into the stableyard. The girls ran to the front door, where Mabel was screwing up her face anxiously, appealing for silence. 'Hush, sah, Miz Rose, she's asleepin',' she began, and then, 'Suffin' wrong, sah?'

'Ah think you'd better wake Miz Rose,' Mr Ellis said carefully, stepping into the dim hallway and glancing down meaningly at the children by his side. 'Wake her gently, Mabel.'

Mabel waddled up the stairs and presently returned with Deborah, sleep-flushed, in a pink woolly wrapper with her hair fluffed into untidiness and her eyes still heavy-lidded from her recent nap. 'Yes, Mr Ellis? I'm ashamed to say I wasn't feeling too well, so I had a little sleep, and . . .'

'Miz Rose, there's been a turble thing happen at a li'l place called Johnstown, in Pennsylvania. It's down in a valley, see, with a dam above it. Seems like the dam burst, an' flooded the valley.'

'That is terrible,' Deborah said, her face faintly puzzled though still serene. 'But I don't think I've heard of the place. Mr Rose goes out West with his waggons.'

'I know it, ma'am, and Johnstown was only a tiddy place. Seems your husband had his eye on some property there, though, and . . .'

'Art?' Suddenly she was fully awake, the colour drained from her face, her eyes black with terror. 'Is he dead?'

'Hurt, ma'am, and mebbe not bad, at that. The message was from a relative of yourn, a Paul Cohenz. Says he's on his way here, and will take you to your husband. Readin' between the lines, Ah guess Art's in hospital – and lucky to be so. There's precious few come out of Johnstown alive, ma'am.'

'I must go to him,' Deborah said, her breath coming short in her chest, one hand laid to her palpitating heart. 'I must go to . . .'

Tina gasped and Cecy began to cry as, slowly and gracefully, Deborah collapsed in a heap at their feet. Mabel, ever practical, bent over her mistress, saying, 'Kin yo' help me git her on to the sofy, sah?'

Despite being three months pregnant, Deborah was light enough to make it an easy task to carry her across the hall and into the parlour, where she was laid gently down on the sofa. Once there, she came round quite quickly but her face was so white and pitiful that Mr Ellis drove off at once to fetch the doctor, leaving Mabel with Deborah and the four children.

'What's for our supper?' Tina enquired practically, as Mabel bathed her mistress's temples with lavender water and soothed her with such heartening remarks as 'Better in 'ospital dan six feet undah, Miz Deb!'

'Supper? Dear Lor', don' say yo' is hungry! It'll be chipped beef an' them fresh vegerbles, only I ain't biled 'em yit,' Mabel said, chafing Deborah's ice-cold hands between her own warm, rosy palms. 'Kin yo' gittem on de stove, Tina-gal?'

'Of course I can.' Tina turned to her mother. 'Momma, when will Uncle Paul arrive?'

Deborah had been lying with her eyes closed but at that her lids lifted slowly, revealing eyes still dark with fright. 'Uncle Paul? Coming here?'

'Dere, de poor crittur di'n tek in a word,' Mabel said compassionately. 'Ne'er yo' mind, Miz Deb, yo' cousin is comin' to tek care of yo'.'

'I do remember something about a telegraph message,' Deborah said, frowning. 'I wonder how long it will be before the doctor arrives? And Paul! He'll hurry, but . . .'

For a while Tina and Cecy busied themselves about the kitchen, preparing the meal and getting out the dishes. Then Tina remembered the babies, and went back to remind Mabel that her small sisters had yet to be fed.

'Dear Lor',' Mabel said. 'Ah wish Ah had three pairs of hands!' She glanced at Deborah. 'Miz Deb, she's asleepin' for a while. Tina-gal, do yo' reckon yo' could nip out and fetch Rufus? He kin fuel up de stove an' git a room ready fo' yo' Uncle Paul whiles Ah get Rachel's feed an' mek some porridge for Becky.'

Things went smoothly for a while after this. Mabel served them a meal and made her mistress drink a cup of hot, sweet tea. Then she sat down and spooned porridge into Rebecca and fed the baby from a bottle. Rufus, apprised of the present state of affairs, did everything that was required of him and then departed down the road to watch for the doctor.

Tina went quietly through to the parlour, to find Momma pale, complaining of a terrible backache and asking how long it was since Mr Ellis had left and why they thought the doctor had not yet arrived.

Afterwards, Tina acknowledged that she should have remembered Momma's feelings about Rufus. Not that Momma had ever said she was afraid, but Tina had always sensed how Momma felt about black men. For herself, black faces were a part of her life, as good and as bad as the few white faces she met. Now, when she knew that Momma was not well, that she had fainted and was suffering from a bad pain, she ought to have remembered that Rufus was watching for the doctor, and might suddenly appear.

But they were all busy. Tina, with great care, was filling the enamel baby-bath with alternate jugs of hot and cold water. Mabel was undressing Rachel, Cecy was rather unhandily trying to change Becky from her scuffed pink crawlers to a nightgown.

Tina was the first to hear the buggy turn from the dusty road on to their gravelled frontage. 'The doc's arrived!' she shouted, jumping up from where she had knelt, pouring the last of her water half on to the floor. She ran out of the kitchen and across the hall, eager to be first with the good news, heading towards the parlour with its half-open door.

Then, from the parlour, came the most terrifying scream she had ever heard. It was ripped from her mother's throat, sounding more animal than human, and it rooted her to the spot for a moment. In that moment the screen door burst open and a man pushed into the hall, passing Tina without so much as a glance, all his attention fixed on the parlour, where the appalling scream was dying away in whimpers.

Simultaneously Rufus, his eyes starting out of his head with fright, came out of the doorway backwards, shaking like a leaf, and collided with the stranger.

There was a shout and a scuffle. The man swung out wildly at Rufus even as Tina shrieked, 'Don't, sir! Don't hit Rufus!' But there was no need for fear on that score. Rufus fled with amazing speed for one so huge and they could hear his wails disappearing into the distance.

The man charged into the parlour and knelt beside the sofa, putting his arms round Deborah. Much to Tina's disgust he began behaving in a very soft and stupid manner, kissing Momma's face and hands and groaning, asking over and over, 'What's he done to you, my poor little one? What has he done?'

From the direction of the kitchen she could hear Mabel's startled voice, then the sound of a chair being pushed back. Tina sighed and rolled her eyes towards the ceiling. Grown-ups! If it was not one thing it was another, and if she did not say her say soon all sorts of complications would develop. Accordingly, she marched into the parlour, shook the man's shoulder and announced, 'I'm Tina Rose. Are you my Uncle Paul?'

'Yes, I'm your uncle.'

The man turned towards her, and she saw he was suffering from a strain every bit as great as that which had caused Momma to faint. Impatience at the foolishness of the entire race of adults made her say sharply, 'She's all right, you know. Rufus didn't hurt her, I expect he went in to tell her you'd arrived. She's afraid of blacks.'

'Oh!' He stared at her rather blankly for a moment, then turned back to gaze searchingly into Deborah's pale face. 'I thought . . . Why is she lying on the sofa? Has she been ill?'

'She fainted when Mr Ellis told us Poppa was in hospital, and again when Rufus frightened her. Look, her eyes are opening.'

He turned, in time to see Deborah's eyes widen in panic as they saw him, then soften as recognition dawned. Then, suddenly, she was sitting bolt upright on the sofa, both her arms rightly entwined round Paul's neck, weeping and clutching him, and saying, 'A dream! Was it a dream? I thought you were a black man, come to . . . Oh Paul, I've been so frightened!'

He put her away from him for a minute, very much aware of the child standing so still at his elbow. 'Frightened? For two *years*?'

She nodded convulsively, her eyes fixed on his face. 'Yes. Afraid of the blacks, afraid of the responsibility of the store and the children. Afraid of having babies. Afraid Art might go one day and not come back. Always afraid. Until now.'

'What's different about now?' He spoke in a low voice and still held back from her, but she smiled up into his face, her eyes shining with a tenderness which made her small daughter feel most uncomfortable.

'Now, you've come. You won't let me be alone, will you? You'll tell Art that he must stay with me?'

Tina watched as his hand reached out, almost of its own volition, and began stroking the soft, shining hair off her mother's brow. He said, his tone caressing, 'I won't leave you. Poor little *bubeleh*, poor Deb! I'll take care of you.'

For some reason which she did not care to analyse, Tina felt she could remain in the room no longer, watching such a private moment. She withdrew as soundlessly as she could, closing the door gently behind her, to find Mabel standing in the hall with the strangest expression on her shining black face and the baby Rachel cradled in her arms.

'Did we oughter leave 'em?' she began, and then became

suddenly practical. 'Dey should eat, den dey'll feel better! C'mon, Tina, le's git a nice supper on a tray for de uncle and yo' mudder!' She bustled back into the kitchen and began to tuck Rachel into the cot which she had brought through from the bedroom, supervising the laying of the tray at the same time, whilst Cecy and Tina flew round doing her bidding.

The doctor arrived, examined Deborah and left again, saying that the pains were probably nothing more than shock, and would pass. The children went to bed early without demur, but later Tina was woken by a commotion; voices, cries, scufflings. She climbed out of bed and went out into the upper hall where she met a distraught Mabel, clad in a garish purple wrapper, her tired face anxious.

'I'se goin' fer de doctor,' she said tersely. 'Yo' Momma's losin' de baby.'

'Losing *Rachel*? But how . . .'

Mabel was halfway down the stairs. 'Go back to bed,' she called over her shoulder. 'Be a good gal, huh?'

Tina turned and made for the door to her mother's room, to be met by Uncle Paul, coming out. She registered that he wore a dressing-gown which belonged to Poppa and that his face was sheet-white, his mouth grimly set, and then heard her own voice, high and shaking, saying wildly, 'What's wrong, Uncle Paul? Where's Rachel?'

He put his arm round her and hugged her to him for a minute, and in that minute Tina knew why Momma had been so glad to see Uncle Paul. He was warmth, safety. He reminded her with sudden clarity of Uncle Herman, far away in New York. She understood now why her mother had felt safe with Uncle Paul. She felt safe herself.

'My poor chick! I heard Mabel, who is so good, so kind, but muddled! She doesn't mean Rachel, *faygeler*; you didn't know Momma was making another baby, eh? Well, she is, but the baby, he wants to come now, which is too soon. There's nothing you can do, so best go back to bed, eh? Then when you wake in the morning, everything will be all right.'

He turned her neatly, propelling her gently back into the

room she shared with Cecy. She was going willingly, comforted, when through the half-open door to her mother's room came a whimpering cry. 'Paul? Paul? Oh, Paul, don't go, don't leave me! It hurts me so!'

'Does it . . .does it hurt very much, when a baby comes too soon?'

She heard him sigh, and felt his breath on her hair as he squatted down beside her, then turned her to face him. 'Tina, you know it hurts when the babies come? And you know poor Momma has had a nasty day, eh? Your poor poppa is in hospital and this gave her a bad fright, so the baby is disturbed, and thinks now is right to be born. Understand so far, eh?'

She nodded, eyes fixed trustingly on his strong, ugly face.

'Then a baby being born is just a baby being born, only a little like a fruit being picked, perhaps. When the fruit is ripe, it comes off easy in the hand, but earlier, not so easy. See? You want to help?'

She nodded again, though she did not feel too sure she would be of much assistance. The urgency of her mother's cry, the fact that she had appealed to Uncle Paul and not to her eldest daughter, bred fear and uncertainty. However, she looked up questioningly into Uncle Paul's face.

'Good girl. You're not too tired?' When she shook her head, the doubt plain on her small face, he gripped her shoulders encouragingly and then stood up. 'Right. Go downstairs into the kitchen and put a pan of water to boil on the stove. Wrap yourself up warmly first, mind. When the water's on, sit down in Mabel's comfiest chair, and wait until the water boils. Then you may turn it down to simmer, and when it is needed you shall be told. Can you do that?'

'Oh yes,' Tina said eagerly, unutterably thankful that she would not be expected to go into her mother's room and be a helpless witness to whatever pain she was suffering, yet glad that she would be helping nevertheless.

'Good girl,' he said again. He accompanied her to her room and made her put on her warm woolly wrapper and slippers, then saw her to the top of the stairs before returning to her mother's room.

Tina trotted down the stairs and into the familiar warmth of the kitchen. It could not be as late as she had supposed, for the fire still burned in the grate. She filled a pan with water, lugged it into the middle of the stove and then cuddled down in the big chair. The kitchen door was closed and it was solid, so no sounds penetrated from the rest of the house. The clock ticked, the fire settled, and presently the water began to bubble softly.

It seemed a long time since she had stood at the top of the stairs and heard her mother's cry for help. Tina felt her lids growing heavy. She thought she really should climb down off the chair and see if the water was boiling yet. She would, in a minute, but now she was so cosy and comfortable, the chair so soft and the firelight so gentle and warm.

Tina slept. She did not stir when Mabel returned with the doctor, nor when the water she had heated was taken from the stove, nor when Mabel came through the kitchen with a dreadful burden, for Deborah lost the child.

She woke when dawn was lightening the sky, and streaks of rose, heralding sunrise, showed in the east. She stirred, opening her eyes slowly, seeing the flames flickering still round the edge of the stove door, wondering what on earth she was doing in the kitchen instead of her own warm little bed.

She sat up, and with the movement memories returned and anxiety rushed in. She jumped down from the chair and made her way through the quiet house. Outside her mother's room she paused, then, driven by some impulse she could not explain, she opened the door slightly and poked her head around it.

Her heart jumped, then steadied as she saw her mother lying in bed, her face tired but peaceful, colour in her cheeks, the fan of her dark lashes lying on her cheek.

She could see her mother breathing softly, could see, too, that the bedlinen was clean and white, fresh and good to look at. She feared to find it bloodstained and terrible, for she remembered too well the mess and misery which had attended baby Rachel's arrival, with Momma vomiting right up to the birth, and a dreadful, stale smell hanging over everything, and Mabel afraid to leave her mother's side to send someone for the doctor.

Then she saw Uncle Paul. He was asleep too, in a chair beside the bed, and his face looked worn and weary. One strong hand hung loose at his side, but the other clasped Momma's slim fingers.

Tina withdrew, closing the door very softly behind her. It was all right! Momma was alive, and would be well. Rachel slumbered in her cot by Mabel's bed, no doubt, and Becky in the truckle bed by the cot. In her own room her little bed waited, with Cecy, unaware of the drama of the night, sleeping too.

She crept into her room and into her bed, then curled beneath the covers and pushed her thumb into her mouth. Her last thought was that everything would be all right now, because Uncle Paul would see that it was.

She had never given a thought to her father, or his injuries. Indeed, he had made so little impression upon his children in his rare visits home that not one of them felt deeply for him. Even Deborah, caught up in the agonies of giving birth to a premature baby, had not thought about Arthur.

And as the sunrise stole across the sky and painted it rose, Arthur lay in his hospital bed and turned his eyes to the distant mountains. He did not think of his wife or children either. He just wished he were dead.

5: Waihola

Edward Neyler was building a bank around the new pasture. He cut sods with his spade, then piled them up, one on another, firming them into place. Eventually a hedge would be planted on top, fencing off the new stretch of land and adding another good acre to the Neyler holding.

Standing up for a moment to rest his aching back, Edward looked down towards Waihola Lake, blue beneath the October sun. About halfway between himself and the water's edge a small figure saw him straighten and stopped for a moment in its own toilings to wave vigorously. He waved back, then bent to his task again. That would be Pearl MacPherson. It looked as though she was picking berries, but he would know soon enough. No doubt she would make her way uphill, in his direction. She made no secret of her admiration for him, though goodness knows he gave her little enough encouragement.

Grunting with effort, he spaded a particularly fine sod and fitted it into place on the bank. He must get this job done tonight, for although his father no longer wielded his stock whip on his sons he had a sharp and spiteful tongue, and a way of making life uncomfortable for them all if someone transgressed. Mainly it was Anna who suffered, and Edward nursed the ugly suspicion that Karl would beat her if he could do so without his sons finding out.

Sometimes, Edward wondered if his father were a little mad. Karl had come to New Zealand in '65, drawn by the finding of gold in Otago. He had been a twenty-eight-year-old cabinet maker who knew nothing of mining, but even then he had been a hard and persistent worker. He had slaved at his diggings and when he struck gold had not frittered it away, nor returned, rich, to his homeland. Instead, he had remained in Otago and bought land. A great deal of land.

For three years he had tried to create a farm from his acres of wilderness, living in a one-roomed sod hut, cutting down the forest and clearing the land, making and mending for himself. Then, one night, he sat down and thought. To run a farm such as he envisaged a man needed sons, and to get sons one must first get a wife. It had been, for Karl, that simple. He had cast his mind back to his days at the mining encampment, and to a Scottish girl who had watched him, smiled on him. He knew himself to be tall and handsome with his blond hair and even features. He never doubted his ability to get the woman he wanted. That very night he had arranged with one of the Maoris who sometimes laboured for him to move into the hut and keep an eye on the stock, and had begun the trek back to the goldfields.

When the boys had been small they had heard him taunting their mother over his choosing of her. 'I cut you out from the herd as I would cut out a good cow for the bull,' he said scornfully. 'I saw you came of a family of brothers, saw your broad hips and strong arms. I thought you would bear me good sons so I took you.'

Anna never protested when he spoke like that, though sometimes the colour surged up under her fair skin and she would take herself off to some other part of the cabin to complete other tasks.

The sod hut was replaced as soon as the couple could do so with a two-roomed edifice of wattle and daub, the windows covered in calico, which let in some light but no air or insects, and which gave no view. Later, Karl began the homeric task of cutting down the great fern trees, fashioning the lengths into planks which, with the rough, chocolate-coloured bark outside, formed the outer walls of the cabin in which they still lived. It had a very large living-kitchen with a wide fireplace for burning the massive logs the boys were for ever cutting, and small windows which were glazed now that money was not so tight. There were two bedrooms, one for Karl and Anna and one for Edward and his younger brother Mark. A parlour, seldom used but regarded reverently by Anna, was the latest addition; she was furnishing it, slowly, to be sure, but with great pride. She kept poultry, and Karl allowed her to spend any money she made from the eggs on her beloved parlour.

Thinking of his mother's poultry made Edward remember a scene he had witnessed when he had been no more than five or six. He had been collecting nuts in the forest and had run a splinter into his finger. Returning to the house in the mid-afternoon, he had found it deserted and had gone out to the barn, his finger dripping blood, to search for Anna.

He heard her before he saw her; a high, tuneless humming, coming from the direction of the barn. The door was open, and he stole up to it, the pain of his finger forgotten, thinking to surprise her. He peeped round the barn door, then stood where he was, for though his mother was in there, her apron half-full of eggs, singing to herself as she searched for more, so was his father. Karl must have been in the loft and was just descending the steps, walking with a cat-like quietness, so that Edward guessed at once that his father, also, wanted to surprise Anna.

Straightening up from rummaging in the manger, Anna caught sight of Karl. 'Oh!' She turned towards him, smiling a little uncertainly, the colour rising up from the low neck of her brown wool dress. 'I didn't know you were in the loft, Karl.'

'So I see.' He crossed the haystrewn floor between them, and took a lock of her thick, honeybrown hair between finger and thumb. 'How untidy you are, Anna! Your hair is coming down.'

She began to apologise, to explain, then stopped as Karl said roughly, 'Don't whine, woman!' He pushed his hands up into the net which held her hair in a bun and loosened the strings of it so that her hair tumbled about her shoulders, framing her flushed, wide-eyed face. Then he caught hold of her, crushing her against him, manoeuvring her so that her back was against the manger. She seemed to pull away, to twist in his grasp, and Edward saw his father's fingers tighten as he pulled her away from the manger, only to push her backwards on to a pile of hay.

Anna gasped, an incoherent protest, then there was a muffled cracking sound, Karl cursed, and Anna said, half-laughing, half-tearful, 'The eggs! You've broken the eggs!'

She was looking up at her husband as he knelt above her, her mouth curved into a tender smile, her eyes frankly loving, but Karl drew back, gazing down at the mess of broken eggs smeared over her apron and his breeches. Then, without warning, he grabbed her shoulders, jerking her upright as though she had been a rag doll.

'*You* broke the eggs, you stupid bitch!'

Before surprise had more than opened Anna's eyes wide, he had slapped her, hard, across the face. She gasped, shock whitening her cheeks, and he hit her again, so hard that blood leapt to her lip and ran down her chin. He was literally growling with rage by now, and Edward was far too afraid to move.

Karl jumped to his feet and Anna came up too, unresisting, held between those strong, cruel hands. He shook her until her sobs ceased and her hair entirely covered her face, then he threw her down on the hay again and began thrashing her with his fists, pounding her hips and thighs, hearing her sobs and pleas begin but heeding her not at all.

Then, as suddenly as the beating had begun, it stopped. Karl pulled Anna into his arms and his mouth crushed down on hers. Anna's arms crept round her husband's neck and her sobs died down into gasps and whimpers which, Edward could tell, were quite different from the sounds which had gone before. Completely bewildered, the child continued to watch. The savagery had gone, and though he felt a pang of fear when his father began to undo his mother's bodice, he could tell by Anna's reaction that she was no longer afraid. She was almost purring now, beneath his father's hands.

As though his young mind had been sharpened by what he had seen, Edward noticed after this that his mother was often marked. He would notice how, even in company, his father would grasp his mother's arm or waist in seeming amity, but that the hand which seemed so casual would often sink cruel fingers into the flinching flesh. He realised, with dismay, that his father enjoyed inflicting pain on Anna, and that she accepted it almost with equanimity.

Now that he was almost a man himself, Edward sometimes wondered if there was, in fact, an element of enjoyment in his mother's attitude to his father's behaviour. He could not forget how she had submitted to the beating in the barn, showing no resentment or surprise when Karl's blows had turned to caresses. *Did* women like being thrashed? He shrugged. He and Mark had loathed their father's uncontrollable rages which always ended in one or both of them being whipped. As soon as they were able to resist, they had put a stop to *that*. Karl had not hit either boy for several years now. But the uncontrollable tempers, the bouts of savagery, had not cooled with the years. It was this which kept the boys from leaving home; what would Karl do to Anna without two sons to intervene? Anna had her faults, no doubt, but her children adored her. Neither would dream of leaving her alone on the farm with Karl.

A movement in the far corner of the new pasture caught Edward's eye; it was Pearl, coming up the slope towards him. Passionate Pearl, Mark called her, laughing at him because he showed no interest in the tall, comely Scots lass whose grandparents had come to Dunedin when it was little more than a handful of mud huts built around the curve of the bay. But despite the fact that women were still outnumbered almost two to one by men, he could not feel complimented by her preference. Instead, it embarrassed him. Damn it, he had no desire to be encumbered with a wife! The fact that his father was in favour of the marriage made him even less keen. Karl had actually offered to speak to old MacPherson, and to let the young couple build a small cabin near the home farm.

What might have been an enticement to some men sounded like the knell of doom to Edward. If he married and moved into a cabin on the property he would never be free! His greatest desire was to leave the farm one day, try his hand at something entirely different. Already he had plans. There was a fortune to be made, for instance, by treating milk in such a way that it might be kept when it was plentiful and used when the cows were dry and grass short. And butter! Fresh butter did not remain so for long in the summer time, yet there must be a way to preserve it! They had a great many dairy cows and it annoyed Edward that in times of plenty they could well lose money if others had herds that were yielding well. No, marriage was not escape, it was the final, echoing slam of the prison door!

However, striding down the sunset-gilded meadow towards Pearl, it seemed churlish to think of her as a prison warder. Despite the fact that he would not encourage her, she was a very pretty girl! This evening her dusky curls flowed on to her shoulders for she carried her bonnet by its strings, and when she smiled she showed her strong white teeth and a deep little dimple sprang to life beside her mouth.

'Edward! I thought it must be you, working at such a rate! How well you've got on! I was toiling to fill my basket with berries, while you built the whole of that bank!'

She stood close to him, her strong, shapely body clad in a blue stuff working gown, made short so that he could see her calves in their striped woollen stockings. She was tall, about five feet nine or ten inches, but she had to throw back her head to look up into his eyes.

'Walk me home, Edward? Through the forest?'

Edward hesitated. Then, suddenly, he felt recklessness rise like a tide in him. The girl was throwing herself at his head; what was the harm in walking her home? It was his evening off, too, so he would not have to hurry. Each boy had a number of tasks to perform, but now that he and Mark were grown they took it in turns to get away from the place sometimes. When he was not working he would take one of the horses and ride into Dunedin to the theatre, if a play was being performed. Or just go for a ride, sometimes, into the bush, where the only sound would be the shrill clatter of paroquets as they fluttered from tree to tree, or the sweet notes of the green and black *tui* bird.

He stood, smiling down at Pearl, checking over in his mind what he had done, and what Mark would do. The logs were cut and he had fetched plenty of water before coming to this meadow. Mark would milk, and see to the dairy herd with the aid of Penny, the cross-eyed, cross-grained old Collie bitch who was, nevertheless, invaluable with the cows.

'What are you thinking of, Edward? Will ye walk with me?'

He heard the little Scots burr come into her voice

because she was confused by his silence, and caught her lightly by the shoulders, laughing at her, inviting her to laugh too. Her lips parted in an uncertain smile and, as he watched, her tongue darted out and licked her full lower lip. Edward swallowed.

'I . . . I'll walk you home.'

Inside him, a little voice moaned an anxious warning, but he ignored it. Throwing caution to the winds, he slid his arm round her waist, feeling the firm young flesh beneath his fingers.

'Yes, I'll walk you home, if you want me to.'

She had round, sherry-coloured eyes fringed with lashes dark as her hair. Now she glanced at him through the lashes, replying demurely, 'Oh yes, I want you to,' but the twinkle in her eyes gave her words a much bolder meaning.

For one moment more Edward hesitated. Ahead of them, the sun shone still, slanting red-gold through the trees, making the forest look different. Stagey. Exciting. Then, overhead, he heard the honking of wild geese as they made their way to their roosts beside the lake.

Edward took a deep breath, tightened his hold on Pearl's waist, and led her into the trees.

It was dark before Edward returned to the Neyler farmhouse, and the fine day had given way to a blustery night, with the wind scudding clouds across the sky at a great rate so that the dappling moonlight fell only intermittently to light his path. But it worried him not at all; indeed, he scarcely noticed the wind which tore at the treetops and blew his hair up into a plume. He was thinking of Pearl. Making love to her had been sweet, her kisses, eagerly given, fresh yet stirring. For the first time marriage no longer seemed so unattractive. He pursed his lips into a soundless whistle, then grinned. So soft, so cuddlesome, so willing! Would marriage be so bad? They could live in a neat little cabin and keep themselves to themselves. Pearl could help his mother with her many backbreaking tasks; it would be pleasant for Anna to have another female about the place. And then he and Pearl would be together with everyone's blessing, to be man and wife. If kissing and cuddling could make him feel so good, what would he feel like when Pearl did not gently stop his increasingly eager lovemaking?

He entered the farmhouse garden which Anna had made, painstakingly, over the years. He could smell the sweet, nutty scent from a positive forest of phlox plants growing in one of the borders and he saw a pair of glowing lamps in a dark shape turn towards him, then streak away, across the garden and round to the barn. Mother's cat, Selly.

He circled the flower beds and followed the cat round to the back yard. No one ever used the front door, except the minister, and perhaps an odd passerby, wanting directions to the village. It occurred to him, as he passed the shuttered kitchen window, that it sounded as if they had company, but then he was at the door, opening it, stepping into the warmth and light from the noisy world of the wind and the flickering moonlight.

The kitchen was crowded, or seemed so at first glance. There was the minister, the Reverend Proudfoot, and Mrs Kittle, the fat old 'howdy' who had delivered himself and Mark, and the five babies which Anna had borne – and lost – since Mark's arrival. Mrs MacPherson was presiding at the stove, and Mr MacPherson, Pearl's father, was standing by the fire talking to Karl.

For a moment, guilt swamped every other feeling in Edward's mind. How had they found out that he had been with Pearl? Would they be disgusted, furious? Hot colour flooded his face and he sought for some innocent, innocuous opening remark which would tell him what was going on. Then, sharply, realisation struck him.

'Where's Mother? And Mark?'

He knew at once that they had waited for the question. Mrs MacPherson said soothingly, 'You'll be wantin' a cup of tea, lad. Karl, where's Mark?'

Even that simple remark shouted a warning; the neighbours had never called his father anything but Mr Neyler. He looked around, recognising now that the faces turned to his were not accusatory but sympathetic. He began to speak, then stopped as Mark slipped into the room from the direction of the bedrooms and parlour. He saw that Mark's face was unusually pale, his freckles standing out in sickly relief against his waxy skin, his light, reddish hair rumpled. Mark crossed the room and grasped his brother's arm. He said, without preamble: 'Mother's had a heart attack, Ted. The doctor's with her now, but she seems to be unconscious. Up to ten minutes ago she was awake; she smiled, she even spoke a few words, but . . .' He pulled on his brother's sleeve. 'Come through.'

Together the brothers went into the bedroom where their mother had slept every night for the last twenty-one years. It was a sombre room, because Karl, for some reason, had forbidden the use of whitewash or wallpaper on the wooden walls but had merely polished the wood, not caring as it darkened with the years. Now it was lit by half-a-dozen candles. They illuminated the doctor, and the figure on the bed.

She was very still. Maynard, who had known the boys all their lives, beckoned them over. 'I think she'll not wake again,' he whispered gruffly. 'She's in a coma.'

Edward bent over the strangely white, grim-faced woman on the bed. 'Mother? It's me, Edward.'

He could see no movement in her, not even the slightest sign that she breathed or lived.

The doctor leaned forward and picked up Anna's wrist. He held it for a moment, then sighed and pulled the sheet up over that quiet face. 'She's gone, boys. Go and tell your father.'

But Edward, without ceremony, suddenly pulled the sheet down again. Right down, to reveal his mother's rounded, creamy shoulders and the plumpness of her smooth skin above the opened cotton nightgown.

Weals, purple, bitter against the white skin, showed in the candlelight. Her neck was bruised as if someone had gripped her by it whilst administering the beating.

Breath hissed out of Mark's mouth as Edward, gentle now, pulled the sheet up once again. He bent then, kissing his mother's cold cheek before turning towards the kitchen, his face alight with his furious intent.

'Edward! Where are you goin', son?'

'I'm going to kill that bastard,' Edward said almost conversationally. 'Coming, Mark?'

But the doctor had hold of his arm, shaking it. 'No! Do you think that's what she would have wanted? Dear God, is it for *you* to punish him and end up being hung for it? Mark, tell your brother!'

But Edward needed no telling. In his heart he knew that beating his father to a pulp would give him no satisfaction, and would show him to be no stronger than Karl, no more capable of bridling his fury.

'It's all right. I won't kill him. Won't hit him, even.' He passed a shaking hand across his burning forehead. 'But I'll not spend another night under his roof! I'm going, and Mark'll come with me. Eh, lad?'

'I will.'

The doctor looked from one to the other. 'It'll look bad,' he said slowly. 'Two lads, leaving their father with their mother's body not cold.'

'Not as bad as two lads beating their father to death,' Edward said. 'It's one or the other, doc. I either leave here now, or I'll kill him.'

The doctor shrugged. 'Very well. I'll go and clear everyone out; there's nothing they can do now, anyway. I'll tell them . . . what do you want me to tell them?'

It occurred to him that never had he seen eyes colder than those Edward Neyler turned on him, yet they burned with a scarcely suppressed passion. A cold fire. He shivered.

'Tell them? Please yourself.'

He and Mark made their way to the small room they shared. Without speaking, they packed their few belongings. They heard the neighbours leave but continued with their task, stripping the beds to make two bed-rolls, using a flax mat each to roll round their belongings. At last the room was stripped of everything but the bedsteads. Edward walked to the door and held it for his brother.

Neither looked back.

In the living-kitchen, Karl was cooking pancakes at the stove. As they entered he said expansively, 'Aha, I've cooked you some supper! We must stick together now, eh, my sons?'

'We're leaving,' Edward said shortly. 'We'll take the grey and the dun.'

Karl abandoned the stove and picked up his stock whip – then put it down again, though his face was darkening with rage. He must have realised that both boys were longing for him to turn on them so that they could retaliate. 'Take my horses? That's stealing! I'll have the law on you!'

'Put it down to the money you never paid us,' Mark said, his adolescent voice cracking. 'Blood money, Father.'

They heard Karl begin to scream and swear as they slipped out into the night, softly closing the back door behind them. Edward looked back, but the door remained closed.

Once they were riding down towards Waihola, Edward said tentatively, 'Mark, was there . . . was there a heart attack? Or did Doc Maynard just say that?'

'It was true. I didn't know about . . . the other business until you . . .' He swallowed. 'I came in to find them both in the kitchen. Mother had a pan of batter, Father was whittling at a wedge for the stable door. I could see Mother had been crying, but . . .' He stopped and Edward saw the pale triangle of his face swing towards the house.

'But she often cried,' he concluded quietly for Mark. 'Go on.'

'Father was grumbling at her, the way he did. Something about burning his shirt. She'd been ironing and I daresay she'd let the flat get overheated. She went to the stove – there was a pan smoking on it – and tipped some of the batter into the hot fat. Then she sort of grabbed her side, and then her arm and shoulder. She swayed, and cried out, and then crashed to the floor.'

'I see. But nevertheless, he killed her.'

'Yes. I'm glad we've left, but . . . Edward?'

'What?'

'Where shall we go?'

Edward had given no thought to the matter but now he said decisively, 'Why, to Rimmer's Accommodation house in Dunedin, of course! They'll give us a bed for the night and tomorrow we can decide what to do.'

They were silent then until the horses were clattering down York Place, when Mark said suddenly, 'Have you any money?'

'Oh God!'

With one accord, both boys started to laugh, Edward almost falling off his mount. Without exchanging another word, they turned their horses and rode out of town again.

'Good thing it isn't raining,' Mark said, as they tied the horses up to a convenient post-and-rail fence and spread their bed-rolls out in the dubious shelter of a small copse of trees. 'We ought to have brought the dog, though.'

Edward, straightening out his blankets, grunted.

'Should we go back for her tomorrow?'

'You can if you want, Mark. I'm never going back. Not while he lives.'

They had slept out in the open before, but this was different. Neither had any money nor the slightest idea what they would do on the morrow. Edward, raw from his mother's death, still could not but enjoy the sense of freedom. If he wanted to marry he would do so! If he wanted to leave New Zealand he would do so! And he owed this freedom to his mother's death, which should make it bitter. He groaned, turning over on the hard ground. He knew he ought to be sad because Anna had died and yet a bubble of excitement and pleasure kept rising up in him, so that he could have sung and cheered, despite the hard ground and the cold wind tugging at his covers. The recollection of Doc Maynard's words came back to him. 'Is that what she would have wanted?' All her life his plump, pretty, frightened mother had only wanted one thing. Happiness for her sons. If she could see them now, know that they had escaped from Karl's humourless, grudging presence, she would be smiling.

Comforted, he allowed himself to sink into sleep.

Tomorrow would be time enough to worry about what they must do.

They awoke next morning a little stiff from lying on the ground all night, but with their sense of freedom won still stronger than their feeling of loss. The gale of the previous night had given way to a soft and sunny spring morning, and the dawn chorus of the bellbirds and *tui* which they had heard through their sleep was still a shout of birdsong that made them glad to be alive.

Without exchanging more than smiles, the boys tidied up their bed-rolls, harnessed their mounts, and slung their things up on to the animals' backs. Then Mark said, a touch of apprehension in his tone, 'What next, Ted? Don't you have *any* money?'

'Not a penny! But we've got friends; let's go and cadge some breakfast.'

They had camped almost at the summit of a great, scrub-covered hill and now, mounting their horses, they had an excellent view of miles and miles of the surrounding countryside. Almost at their feet was Waihola lake, its blue speckled by waterfowl, and just above it their own home. To the left, deep, fruitful valleys and darkly forested hills hid Dunedin, and to their right the spectacular beauty of the Blue Mountains showed against the horizon. Directly in front of them was the coast with its picturesque fishing villages and the white-sanded bays and inlets where they had longed to play as children.

'You don't mean . . .'

Edward followed Mark's glance and grimaced. They could see the farm clearly and from its chimney now a thin thread of smoke was rising; Karl was up, and getting breakfast.

'No, I don't mean Father! Actually, I meant the MacPhersons. Shall we ride to their place?'

'They'll feed us,' Mark agreed. 'But won't they want to know why we aren't eating at home?'

Edward slapped the reins against his horse's neck and they began to move downhill, the horses picking their way carefully down the steep, mossy slope.

'Everyone will know soon enough. Though the MacPhersons live in the opposite direction from Dunedin, and we . . .' He stopped abruptly and hit himself on the knee. 'What a fool I am!'

Mark turned, brows raised in enquiry.

'Why should we go to Dunedin, Mark? Why not to the Clutha?'

Mark jerked on his reins, his eyes widening. 'The Clutha? What on *earth* . . . ?'

'Gold, little brother! There are plenty of people panning for gold still, you know, and they make a living – a fortune, sometimes! Or we might work on the dredgers, though that seems tame compared with prospecting. Are you game?'

'I suppose so. But it seems kind of idle! The sort of thing . . .'

'The sort of thing our father would rail against us for doing! Right, that's good enough for me. I'm sick and tired of being sensible and hardworking and deadly dull! From the time we were toddlers everything had been done the hard way. We threshed with a flail, we chopped turnips with a knife nearly as heavy as we were ourselves, we scrimped on every penny so that Father would not have to spend. I daresay we'll find panning for gold hard, or driving a dredger , but at least we'll be doing it because we want to, for our own benefit!'

'All right, I'm game.' They had reached level ground and Mark touched his heels to his mount's sides. 'Let's *ride*, big brother!'

They were over a year on the Clutha, seeking – and finding – gold. They grew tanned and hard from living in the open twelve months of the year and sleeping in the shelter of the two-roomed stone cabin they built for themselves. They grew to know and to love the mud-caked banks of the river where the dredgers worked, the wild scrub of the plains where the tussocky snow-grass grew thigh-high, the mountains with their thick, secret coverings of native beech and larch. They grew to admire and respect their fellow workers, particularly the Chinese, who worked incredibly hard and with such neatness and thoroughness that they found more gold than anyone. Indeed, when they built their cabin it was within a stone's throw of the Chinese. There was little Sun Yu, with his tea-brown face and huge white teeth; there was fat, perspiring Chi Ming, who was always laughing at himself, always slipping in the mud, losing a slipper, cursing the heat and the cold alike. And there was Ho John and his wife Li, and their daughter, Wan Leng. Ho was a giant of a man but extremely good-natured and placid, and his daughter, a plump, merry little creature with a round, creamy face and a plait of thick, shiny black hair which fell to her knees, spoke English as good as that of Edward and Mark.

They trusted the Chinese and enjoyed their company, so that it soon became a matter of course to boast over one's finds and rejoice with their neighbours when they, too, had good fortune.

It was a hard life, but exciting and varied, and both boys found it satisfying. They found gold and took it to Dunedin in the fine summer months and sold some for supplies. The rest was safely banked. In winter, when even the paths and roads down to the coast were blocked, they simply stowed the gold away in a box in the corner of their cabin and scarcely thought about it.

And then, almost two years after they had first arrived on the Clutha, when spring was showing in the sweet greeny-yellow of new grass and the fresh scent of mint and wild thyme, Ho John made his big find. A large nugget of soft, dark yellow gold from one of the fastest, rockiest stretches of the river, where no one else had bothered – or dared – to search.

'I go in, slow-slow, the water push, pull, glab, spin; and then foot he slip down clack in lock, feel something smooth, like pebble, or egg. Put he hand in water, bling up him!'

He held up the large chunk of precious metal, smoothed to a perfect oval by the constant batterings of the rapids.

'What'll you do with that, Ho John?'

A wide smile creased the shiny, yellow face.

'I no stay here, boys! Li, Wan Leng and John go buy eating house in Dunedin. Do good tlade!'

After the Chinese had left, the boys turned to each other, the same thought in each head. As though they had discussed it many times – though in fact it had never been mentioned between them before – Edward remarked, 'All good things come to an end, Mark! What shall it be? An eating house in Dunedin, to do "good tlade"? Or a shop? A fishing boat? Or a farm?'

'A dairy farm, on the Peninsula. We could start a real dairy, to make butter and cheese, and perhaps even to condense milk. You'd like that, wouldn't you, Edward?'

Edward got to his feet and lounged across to their box. 'I would. There's enough money in the bank in Dunedin to finance a farm, I'm pretty sure, but we've done well this winter. Let's try to weigh our loot!'

6

It was three months before the Rose family and Paul Cohenz left Galeport, and when they finally set out on the long journey to the East it was for the last time.

Paul had told Deborah that, in his opinion, it might be many months before Arthur could walk again, if he ever could, and that it was her duty to be nearer him.

'You must sell up here,' he said. 'And then move back to New York. I've telegraphed to the hospital explaining what's happening, and they have agreed that as soon as Arthur can be moved they will send him to Mirah. She has a spare room and she's a good nurse. She'll look after him until you arrive and take the job from her.'

'I can't accept any more help or money, Deborah said wildly. 'I can't let Mirah . . .'

'You can and you must let Mirah help,' Paul interrupted her. 'As for accepting money, there's no need! Financially, Art is sound. More than sound; he's a very rich man. Now, no more grumbles, eh? We'll put the store and the house on the market and it's my belief that both will sell easily.'

He had been proved right. But though the new owner, a man who had made a pile goldmining and wanted to settle down, paid over his money with gratifying promptness, he was unable to take over immediately. So Tina and Cecy were taken away from school and everyone helped to pack up furniture and goods, to stock the store to the very brim, to sell the waggons and horses which were costing a great deal in the livery stable where Arthur had left them, and, finally, to show Mr Rhet Fincher, the new owner, how to run the store.

Tina had been incredulous at first when Deborah had told her they would be moving back to New York and selling the store. Then she had been rebellious, seeing herself once again as a helpless puppet in the hands of grown-ups. First they had taken her from Grandma, then she had been snatched from her happy life with Uncle Herman and trailed over America for months and months. Then they had allowed her to settle down in Galeport and to make friends at the Binnacky school. Now, for no good reason (for her father had scarcely ever been in Galeport, and they had managed perfectly well without him), she was to be uprooted once more.

And it would mean leaving Mel. That was what hurt! For Tina loved Mel, and had quite decided to marry him, when she was sixteen or so. To others, Mel might appear a silent and uninteresting youth, but not to Tina. She knew everything about him, knew that he was courting a plump, foolish looking servant girl who worked at one of the big holiday houses on the Delta. Her name was Maybelle and Tina felt she could afford to be indulgent over his fancy, for though Maybelle was no beauty, she did have scarcity value. Since taking the job with the Andersons, she had been to and fro between their holiday home and their real residence at New Orleans, and Maybelle was openly boasting of her 'beaux'. Long before Mel could support a wife, Tina was sure, the fat and self-satisfied Maybelle would be wed.

Tina had not told Mel of his ultimate fate. For one thing, he might have objected to her airy dismissal of Maybelle. Or, worse, he might have laughed at her. In this case, Tina was convinced that ignorance was bliss. She would break the news which would make him a happy man when she was about sixteen, and until then he could indulge in his hopeless passion for stodgy, drawling Maybelle.

As soon as she realised that there was nothing she could do to change her mother's mind, however, Tina became philosophical about the move. After all, New York was not the end of the earth! She would just have to do her growing up there, and then hurry back to Mel. She told him severely that she would write each week and would expect him to reply promptly; she gave him her Aunt Mirah's address and told him she would let him know as soon as they had an apartment of their own. Then she busied herself with the move, for what could not be cured must be endured. But as she packed away her belongings and tidied up her room for the last time, she reminded herself that one day it would be her turn to say when to stay and when to go. And she would make them sorry, then, that they had pushed her about!

She kept a brave front up until they were leaving the store for the last time, then she flew round the counter and cast herself upon Mel's skinny chest. 'I wish I could stay with you,' she muttered against his shirt.

Mel patted her shoulder awkwardly, and promised to write, and Tina detached herself from him with what dignity she could muster and followed the rest of the family to the coach stop. She glared at her mother's straight, slim back and at Uncle Paul's broad shoulders. This time, scorning to be a baby, she had packed Pigeon away and she and Cecy held Becky's hands and had promised to look after their little sister and keep her amused, but, trudging along in the wake of the grown-ups, she thought wistfully that it would have been nice to have Pigeon to hug.

Uncle Paul was very nice, of course, but he was busy looking after Momma; he had no time for playing games with his young cousins. She sighed, shifting her hold on Becky's damp little paw. It was going to be a long journey!

'Are you better, Art?'

Deborah made the enquiry timidly, gripping Paul's hand as she spoke, for she scarcely recognised her once handsome husband. In three months his hair had grown back in, and the worst of the burns were just visible as pale, shiny pink marks. He had grown a big, droopy moustache which gave him a lugubrious look, and his skin had a waxy pallor. The large, dark eyes which he lifted to hers were almost indifferent; certainly the energy and vivacity which had characterised him before were absent now.

'Yes, I'm better,' he said in a drained, colourless voice. 'Why are you here?'

Despite Mirah's generosity, Arthur was still in hospital, though he had been moved to one on the corner of Seventeenth Street where great care and skill had been lavished upon his hurts.

'I've sold the store,' she said, trying not to sound surprised. 'Don't you remember? I wrote you, and Mirah visited, and you said to do what we thought best.'

He glanced up at Paul and for the first time, a little animation showed in his face. 'Paul! You're back, then? I've missed you. You thought it best to sell at Galeport?'

'I did. You wouldn't have wanted to go back there, and New York has life, good schools, plenty work, plenty play.'

A faint grin crossed Arthur's countenance, but he said peevishly: 'Play! They say I'll never walk again! And I couldn't live in New York. Couldn't!'

'You could,' Paul said firmly. 'For a while, at any rate. When you're getting around again, we'll discuss what next to do. For now, you need treatment here still, and your wife and children will be near at hand.'

Arthur closed his eyes. 'Oh, very well. Now I'm tired.'

Deborah hesitated, then bent over and kissed the pale brow. 'We'll leave you then, Arthur. I'll come in again tomorrow.'

He opened his eyes to give her a strange glance; almost as if he disliked me, she thought. 'You can come if you like,' he said rudely. 'I shall still be here, that's certain.'

As they left the building, Paul said tentatively, 'You were hurt by him, eh, Deb? You must not mind. For an active man to be told he'll never walk – that is very bad.'

They were standing on the street, the autumn sun warm on their heads. 'Hurt? I suppose I was, in a way.' Suddenly she turned to him, clutching his sleeves. 'Paul, it was as if he was a stranger! *Can* love die?'

'Did it ever live?'

She stared at him, shocked. 'Why . . . why yes, of course! Why do you think I followed him all the way from England? Why did I search and search . . .'

Her voice trailed away.

'Only you can answer that, Deb. We'd best return to Mirah's place. You are comfortable there?'

'Yes, indeed,' Deborah said uneasily. 'Paul! I should not have said what I did. Please forget I . . . I . . .'

He took her arm, then let his hand slide down until their fingers touched. He felt the little shiver that passed through her, but merely said comfortingly, 'Of course, my dear, anything you say. Do you mean to come to see Arthur alone tomorrow?'

'Yes. No! Oh, I'm not *sure*! Paul, forgive me, but I must think! You go back to your office.'

'I will do so, when I've seen you back to Mirah's apartment. Don't say you can find it yourself, for even if that were true Mirah would think me a poor nephew not to take you to her.' He grinned down at her. 'Come along, we'll catch a street-car.'

All that night, Deborah lay awake and struggled with her conscience. It was plain to her now that what had seemed friendship between herself and Paul had turned to love almost without her noticing. Or was it love? Dependence, certainly, and a warm affection. She thought about returning, as she must, to be Arthur's wife, content to take the initiative, do the work, run the family. What was worse, she must be content to be a small and unimportant part of his life, the gilt on the gingerbread, instead of the centre of her man's existence. She acknowledged, now, that she had been the centre of Paul's existence during the three months they had been together, although they had never even kissed as lovers might. Arthur, she knew now, wanted to enjoy her only when he had the time and the inclination. Companionship, sharing, were no part of his plan for a marriage.

She thought wistfully that she might insist they remain in New York. If she did so, Paul would continue to visit her, to give her his wordless support in everything she undertook. And sooner or later, regardless of the fact that they were related, they would become lovers. She acknowledged, at last, what Paul had known two years ago. His love for her was total; he would willingly give up his business and take her away from the family, to live with him alone.

The weaker side of her nature almost swooned with longing at the picture this presented. To be alone with Paul! She thought his craggy face far more beautiful than Arthur's romantic profile; the touch of his powerful, blunt-fingered hands brought not only comfort but desire. If only he had come to me before the accident, she thought bitterly, as dawn stained the sky outside her window. Then, it would have been almost justice if I had left Arthur as he so continually left me.

But now? To leave a man of action, crippled? To take from him at one stroke his mobility, his family, his pride? She could not do it.

By the time morning came, Deborah had made up her mind. She felt ill and knew she looked wan and heavy-eyed, but with the decision made a kind of peace eased her. She breakfasted with the children, fed the babies, and then made her way, alone, to the hospital. She came to the point as soon as they allowed her to see her husband. 'Arthur, we must go home. To England.'

She had braced herself for protests, arguments, reminders that they were in a fair way to making their fortunes and could not abandon the country for her whim. But, wrapped in his cocoon of self-pity, Arthur scarcely took in the import of her words. 'As you wish,' he said indifferently.

'Good. I'll book our passage and make all the arrangements as soon as the matron says you're fit to travel.'

Once again, she noticed a gleam of what appeared to be dislike in the dark eyes. She said anxiously, 'Will you be very unhappy in England, Arthur? I can't explain why I feel we should go home, but I do feel it, most strongly.'

He shrugged. 'No more unhappy than I shall be here,' he said. 'I don't expect happiness.'

His voice was so bitter that for a moment Deborah hesitated, then she said quickly, 'Well, I'll go and speak to matron, then,' and escaped from his uncomfortable presence.

Matron, when consulted, assured Mrs Rose that her husband could travel, provided a nurse accompanied them to dress the burns on his chest, which were still painful.

'He'll ride in a wheelchair,' she said. 'We'll loan it to you, and then the nurse can bring it back to New York with her. You'll pay her passage both ways, of course.'

This Deborah was happy to do, and so she made her plans. She told no one, not even Paul. Why should I not have his loving attention whilst I can? she thought. Once I'm in England I shall be just a fading memory.

A week before the voyage, she told Mirah they were leaving.

'You've done right,' Mirah told her. She had watched her adored nephew fall in love with this girl, and had been filled with apprehension for them both. She knew Paul's strength, the way he could take one's burdens and make them seem light, and Deborah had more burdens than most. She had doubted, at one time, whether Deborah had the strength to deny Paul's love. Now she saw that Deborah had taken the hard path, and her heart smote her. Poor child, to go back to England, so far from Paul, with her four little girls and her crippled husband!

'Yes, I think so. I telegraphed my mother and she will hire us accommodation. Something quite simple, at first.'

'You are a good, sensible girl,' Mirah said. 'Some day, Arthur will know what a good wife he's got.'

For the first time, Deborah smiled. 'I wonder! At the moment, I think he almost hates me.' Then, as Mirah's eyebrows shot up, 'Why? Why, because I can walk and he cannot.'

It was less easy telling Paul.

'I *can't* stay,' Deborah said piteously, when she broke her news and saw how white his face became. 'How can I stay, Paul, feeling as I do?'

It was her first admission that there could be anything between them but friendship, and for a moment his face brightened. Then the pain returned. 'I guess you're doing right,' he said heavily. They were alone in his office and he got up from behind his desk and moved over to her, standing with his hands on her shoulders, looking down into her upturned face. 'If there was some way . . . but I guess this *is* the way. The only way.'

She nodded, feeling tears form in her eyes.

'You've made all the arrangements for this journey? A nurse you have got?'

She nodded again, not trusting her voice.

'Is there any way I can help?' he said humbly. 'Art has investments here, I know. Could I take care of them for you?'

She started to speak then stopped, her mouth pulling itself into odd shapes. Then, with a cry, she threw her arms round him and their lips met in a kiss so charged with hunger and love that she knew she would remember it all her life.

It barely lasted a moment. Then she tore herself out of his embrace and left, walking quickly out of the office, her head high, her back poker-straight.

It was the bravest thing she had ever done.

*

Tina, heading for home in all the luxury of a first-class cabin, with a real nurse to take care of the little ones and watch out for Poppa, found the voyage oddly lacking in excitement. She knew she was going back to Grandma, but even this held little allure and several times she found herself wishing that she was travelling outwards once more, with a crowd of unwashed, ill-educated immigrants, and with a friendly officer like Johnny to play with her.

Momma was strange, too, on this pleasant, idle journey. She sat on a deckchair and read a book, she jumped up and ran to fetch and carry for Poppa. But when Tina wanted to talk about America, or the store, or Mel, she would just smile the small, tight little smile which was all she seemed capable of these days, and change the subject. Poppa, it soon transpired, could not bear the nurse. She was a tall, stringy, bespectacled woman of a nervous disposition and after he had yelled at her two or three times and clouted her accidentally – or so he said – as he swung his arms around to exercise the muscles, she was only too willing to take over the charge of the children and leave the care of Arthur to his wife. After that, Deborah hardly left her husband's side, and the other passengers remarked upon her devotion. But Tina, studying her parents, had her doubts. It was a cold devotion, she thought dubiously, as different from Momma's old, clinging attitude to Poppa as chalk from cheese.

When they were halfway across the Atlantic, as if he had been in a waking dream until then, Arthur suddenly began to take notice. He decided that he must exercise his legs, in the hope that by so doing, he would one day be able to walk again.

'All right, then I shall crawl!' he shouted irascibly when Deborah remonstrated over what she saw as foolish recklessness. 'But one day I intend to walk, woman, with or without your help! And when I can, I'll walk away from you! Yes, hold me for ever you shall not!'

In the privacy of his cabin he made his first clumsy, frightening attempts to stand whilst Deborah and Tina watched, Deborah exclaiming and rushing forward when the attempt ended, as the early ones always did, with his legs refusing to take his weight so that he sprawled on to the floor.

Once, he balanced for a second or two and then took a swaying, unsteady step forward, though it was less of a step than a broken, crab-like crawl. But he was triumphant over it, looking slyly at Deborah as though she had deliberately tried to hold him back. 'See that?' he panted. 'You think you've got me, don't you? But you haven't. Just wait till I can *really* walk! I'll be off, back to the West. You can't hold me, not even half-crippled!'

There was a cruel taunt in his tone and Tina, hearing this one-sided exchange, knew vaguely that Poppa was baiting Momma in an unpleasant way. But strangely enough she found herself much more in sympathy with the crabby, spiteful invalid than she had been with the self-assured man who had swept in and out of their lives in Galeport, making Momma weep with joy at his arrivals and with grief at his departures. Indeed, by the time they docked, she found herself watching her father with real interest. He had such courage! She had watched him when he believed himself to be unobserved, flexing and straightening the cruelly crippled legs over and over, though the pain made beads of sweat stand out all over his face. And though he snarled and growled at Momma he was cheerful and easy with the other passengers, so that they spoke admiringly of his good temper in adversity.

When they went to get on to the train which would take them to Norwich, he shouted at Momma to wheel him into the guard's van and 'for God's sake, leave me alone there, woman!' Momma, her little smile faltering for a moment, murmured that surely it would be better . . . and then, when he shouted again and the baby began to cry, pushed his chair into the van with a sigh and left him there. But Tina quietly squatted down beside the wheel chair and smiled up at her cantankerous father.

'I'm staying here too,' she announced firmly. 'I don't want to be in a carriage with the babies, and that stupid nurse.' She waited for his protest, but when it came, merely smiled sweetly at him and produced a book from the pocket of her dress. 'I *know* you don't need me; I don't need you, either,' she remarked cheerfully. 'I'm staying here because I want to!'

Once back in Norwich, they moved into a small furnished house in Duck Lane, a stone's throw from Grandma's house in Grapes Hill. Grandma was ecstatic over their return, and began to plan how Momma would be able to manage with a bedridden husband. But Tina sat with Poppa in his downstairs bedroom, and watched as he began his first serious attempts at walking.

It was a dark, quiet room, with too much heavy furniture, thick, dusty drapes, ruched and tasselled, whatnotted, over-elaborate. Poppa's bed stood amidst all this, cabined, cribbed and confined by furniture.

'But an advantage it is, Tina,' Arthur would say, grinning sourly. 'An advantage to half a man!' And with that he would grunt and sweat and swing his legs over the edge of the bed. Such an effort, for a movement which, once, he would have performed without a second thought! He would sit there for a few moments, getting his breath, and then he would begin the slow work of heaving himself to his feet. Then he was glad of the furniture, to grab, to fall against, to use to pull himself back to bed.

He never got out of bed now, if Deborah or Cecy was in the room, not even if baby Becky toddled in. 'It's our secret,' he would say to Tina, and she knew that once he was on his feet the door must remain locked until he was back in bed, no matter who knocked. Once, it was the doctor, and then Poppa did not actually get back into bed but merely sat on the edge whilst Tina let the man in. He examined his patient, making no comment until Poppa was safely tucked under the covers once more. Then he said shrewdly, 'Want to surprise us all, eh, Arthur? Well, you're a tryer, I'll say that for you!'

Tina could tell by his tone, the reluctant admiration in his eyes, that he did not believe her poppa would ever walk. But he was wrong. She watched as gradually one side of the room was conquered, and Poppa, grabbing, crabbing, got to the window and back. A month later, he had painfully circled the room and turned to his small daughter, a flush mantling his cheeks, his eyes bright with elation. 'How about *that*, eh? I knew I could do it! Tomorrow, Tina, on your way back from school, I want you to buy me two walking sticks.'

'Where shall I get the money?' Tina said practically.

He chuckled, a jovial conspirator. 'Don't you think Momma would hand out two shillings for a little treat for Poppa? She would, but no need for that; I want to surprise her.' He delved into the bedside drawer and produced a handful of small change. 'Take some of this. You know what sort of shop sells sticks?'

'Of course. Mr Lamb, the tobacconist in St Giles, sells lovely ones. You could have plain, or ones with carved handles, or the sort that has a proper knob on top of the stick part.'

Poppa grinned, his face boyish with glee. 'We'll have the plain sort, Tina, with a curved handle.' He made the shape in the air with his hand. 'Know what I mean? It will be better for me to grasp. And then, when I've practised, to school I'll come, and meet my girl! How about that, eh?'

'Better not. It's a long walk to school,' Tina said, taking the money. 'Besides, I want to go with you the first time you go out. We could walk down to the gardens.'

'A date, *faygeler*! Aha, we'll surprise 'em all!'

Within a week he had exhausted the possibilities of his room, because the furniture which had been so useful when he had no sticks was now nothing but an additional hazard. Deborah, when he first swung out of his room fully clothed, a big grin almost splitting his face in two, was genuinely delighted.

'Arthur! You're *wonderful*!' she gasped, and spontaneously he flung his sticks aside and grabbed her, kissing her with an exuberance she had forgotten he possessed, until she was flushed and laughing like a girl, her hair coming down, delighted that he seemed to have forgotten, for a moment, the grudge he had borne against her because she had got him tethered at last.

From that moment, his recovery was certain. He could manage amazingly well with the sticks and soon became dextrous, swinging himself along the pavements at an astonishing rate, stopping to talk to friends, gesturing with one of his sticks to make a point, manoeuvring up and down kerbs, across uneven roadways, up and down steps, as though he had been on two sticks all his life.

'I'll never walk alone, as I once thought I might,' he confessed to Deborah one evening as they sat beside the fire after the children had gone to bed. 'The muscles which used to work my legs aren't there. But there's almost no pain, and to walk well is a challenge. To work, also. Soon, I shall work.'

'But at what, Arthur?' Deborah asked diffidently. She could not forget as easily as he apparently could the long weeks of resentment, the sarcasm, the bitterness.

'I'm going to buy a shoe manufactory. What do you think of that? I shall make good stuff, the sort of boots and shoes I used to dream of making, stuck in Mutti's cobbler's shop.'

'That sounds wonderful,' Deborah said cautiously. 'Where is the manufactory situated?'

'The other side of the city. That's why we're going to move house.'

'Move *house*? But, Arthur, this is so convenient! Near to Mutti and the school . . .'

He swept this aside with an impatient movement of his hands. 'Ay-yi-yi, you women, how you *argue*, and before you know what you're arguing against! Two days ago I went a walk with Cecil Hibbert, yes? We took a cab to see a house, but this I did not tell you. I waited.' He paused dramatically, but she said nothing, so he continued. 'The house is large, and we need a large house. It has a walled garden, an orchard, and a long lawn which runs down to the river.' He looked at her again, a slanting glance with a laugh in it, out of the corners of his eyes. 'We've four children now; who can say that in two years we shan't have six? In six years, nine?'

Deborah coloured, glancing at him shyly. 'Arthur? The Rabbi asked . . . I was so embarrassed, I didn't know what to say! Do you mean . . .'

'First, I had to know that I could walk, and earn my own living,' he said, reaching out and taking her hand. 'My poor Deb, I have been unbearable, no? So cruel, and angry! But I am a man who likes to be doing! I could not bear to see a woman on her feet, doing my walking for me. And I like to make love, eh?' He laughed when she blushed and turned her head away. 'So? What is to be ashamed of, eh? I like it, and feared it was for me no longer possible. But now, I accept. I shall walk on sticks always, but that is not so bad! And more babies we will make, my pretty Deb! This house is too cramped, you upstairs with the *bubelehs*, me stuck downstairs. In the new house, a nurse we will have for the little ones, and you and me both will be downstairs.' He chuckled, squeezing her fingers, pulling her close. 'And then! Aha, *then* you'll see!'

They moved to the new house just before Chanukah, with a snow storm outside and the children in their usual confused state of excitement over the Christmas season at school and the Feast of Lights which occurred just before it. The new house seemed huge, and was only partly furnished, for Arthur had decreed that he would have only the best, and would prefer to buy and pay gradually rather than in a rush, but it was a paradise for the children.

In the hall, on a pretty, pie-crust table, stood a small fir tree. 'Our Chanukah tree,' Arthur called it.

'It's our Christmas tree,' Tina corrected him, but he only laughed, telling her that Jews had put lights on Chanukah trees long before the custom had spread to Christians.

There was a long, parquet-floored room at the back of the house, and standing with her nose pressed against the french windows Tina could see the frozen garden and beyond it the frozen orchard and beyond that, dimly, the stretch of white lawn. She could not see the river, but knew it was there because when boats came past their shapes could be seen moving slowly up and down.

'This shall be the children's room,' Arthur said, clumping in behind her and waving with his stick at the silent garden outside. 'This year, not much furniture, eh? This year, no carpet, only a table and a chair or two. But next year, and the year after, you shall choose what to have in here, until it is a nice room for you.'

Tina was speechless with delight. The best room in the house and one from which, in summer, the garden would be all theirs to run in! She hugged Arthur, then broke away from him to run into the parlour, where Cecy was helping their mother to straighten the rugs.

'A room! A room all our own!' she gabbled, clutching her sister. 'Come and see!'

It became a favourite place, that holiday. At Chanukah, the beautiful silver *menorah* was brought out, and the *shammes* candle, which would light all the others, was lit one evening when it was dark outside and the meal had been laid in the children's room, on request. There were no curtains or blinds at the window, and the night pressed in as Arthur performed the simple ceremony of lighting the first candle and then said grace and they fell to on the food. Lovely food, cooked by Grandma, for she had moved into this big house with them, to help Momma, and to be near them all.

Later, illogically perhaps, they ate a Christmas dinner in there, with a pudding to which Arthur set fire far too expertly so that there were shrieks, and Deborah threw a glass of wine on to the flames, and the children laughed and shouted.

It became a room which meant happiness and togetherness for the children. Their own place, but one where the adults they loved were welcome. And when the Passover came, the table in the children's room was set with the traditional food – the *matzo*, or unleavened bread, the shank of lamb, the fat bunches of parsley.

Deborah sat at the foot of the table, watching Arthur as he intoned the prayer which began the *Seder*. She had prepared many *Seders*, or helped Mutti to prepare them, but none, she thought, so full of meaning as this one. They were in a home of their very own, in their own country, with their family and friends around them. This ritual in which they were taking part was ancient, well-loved. Presently Rachel, as the youngest child present, would pose four questions to her father. She had learned them by heart and looked seriously from face to face, eager to show her knowledge and earn her parents' praise.

The prayer ended, and Arthur raised his wine glass. 'Not only once have they risen to destroy us, but in every generation . . . But the Holy One, blessed be He, always delivers us from their hands.'

He smiled at Deborah and she smiled back. Tonight, just for a little while longer, they shared a secret. But soon they would tell the family; when the meal was over, when the wine had been spilled, and drunk, when the door had been opened for the Prophet and a hymn had been sung to welcome him. Then it would be Deborah's turn to speak. To tell them that by next Chanukah they would be lighting a candle for another little Rose. For Deborah was pregnant once more.

Tina was pleased that there was to be a baby. She had wondered, sometimes, why her mother did not repeat her attempt to have a son after the miscarriage in Galeport, but now she wondered no more. It had never occurred to her that both a mother and a father were necessary for the production of babies. Why should it, indeed, when her mother had produced, without apparent effort, two babies in two years when they were in Galeport, when her father had so seldom been there? When her mother had broken the news that she was to have another baby, Tina simply concluded that Momma had been too busy with the new house to think about adding to her family.

But now it was winter again and the baby would be coming soon. Tina, wrapped in a cosy blue coat and scarlet muffler with matching mittens and a pom-pom hat, hurried home from school, a small parcel tucked under her arm. It was a present for the new baby, laboriously made. A fluffy shawl, with lace on the hem, which had taken Tina months of effort. Indeed, one glance at the hem, with tiny bloodstains here and there where she had dug the needle into her finger by mistake, and larger, grimy areas where she had unpicked her work, showed that it had taken much time and effort in its manufacture.

As she always did, Tina ran from her friend Lizbeth's gate, because there was no point in loitering when she was alone. She turned once, to wave to Lizbeth's small figure, tramping up her own garden path, then began to run again, her breath puffing out steamily before her, so that the house looked as though it were wreathed in mist.

A brief delay as she opened the gate, then a struggle to shut it properly because of holding the parcel. Then a quick dash up the path, with its rosy bricks and neat edgings, and she was at the front door. She hurled herself at the door, was through it in a moment and standing, panting, in the hall.

'Grandma!' she called softly. She could not wait to see Grandma's face when she spread the shawl out in all its glory! 'Grandma?'

The kitchen door stood open, but the room was deserted. Usually, at this hour, Grandma was there, baking or cooking. She would bustle out, ask how the day had gone, suggest a good hot cup of tea and something nice which she had just made – potato *latkes* were a favourite – and then she and Tina would sit and gossip round the kitchen table until everyone else arrived home.

Tina hesitated. 'Grandma?'

Then, from overhead, she heard a door fly open, and the clatter of her father's sticks. She heard a faint mew, like a kitten, and then her father was clattering down the stairs, his hair on end, his face red with excitement.

'It's a boy, it's a boy!' he was shouting. 'My son, at last! Louis Rose!'

'But that's a girl's name,' Tina objected, running up the stairs. 'Can I go in and see the baby?'

'Not yet. And I said *Louis*, not Louise, you *schlemiel*! It's a great name! You can see him when you've done an errand for me. Run round to Mr Zelner's house and tell him it's a boy. Tell him I want my boy circumcised, there's a good girl. Louis Rose! My son!'

7

On September 28 Tina awoke very early, and was immediately conscious that this was a special day. Today she would begin the term, but not at the small junior school Cecy, Becky and even baby Rachel attended. Today she would be a senior at the High School. Her uniform lay on the bedside chair by the window, her new books were piled neatly on the dressing table, and new boots stood between her bed and that of the still slumbering Cecy.

She could bear to lie in bed no longer, with so much awaiting her! She got up, padded across the cold linoleum and pulled back the thin cotton curtains. Pale early sunlight flooded in, casting its glow over the pile of bedclothes and the rumpled brown curls that were all one could see of Cecy. Tina glanced up towards the eaves. The sky was a clear blue, without a cloud. She smiled to herself. A perfect day for her first day at senior school!

Returning silently to the washstand, Tina poured water from the tall, poppy-decorated jug into the bowl and washed, then cleaned her teeth, trying to do everything quietly so that she did not disturb her sister. But nothing woke Cecy until her usual rising time. She slumbered on, unaware of her sister's wakefulness, her cheeks rosy with sleep, her mouth open, a tiny, curling snore escaping from her now and then, for she suffered from catarrh in winter and hayfever in summer.

Tina brushed out her hair and then plaited it with a certain amount of difficulty. Usually she and Cecy plaited each other's hair, for Momma had her hands full with the younger children before school besides being pregnant again, and painfully sick some mornings. However, she managed to obtain a neat hair style, and then she dressed herself in the starched, high-necked blouse with its leg o'mutton sleeves and tight cuffs, the dark green tie, and the full, dark green skirt which reached almost to her ankles instead of being halfway down her calves like a junior's skirt. She put on black stockings and her stiff new boots. A final touch was the leather belt with its heavy silver clasp. She tightened it and glanced approvingly into the mirror. The belt accentuated one's tiny waist, if one had a tiny waist. Looking at her own, Tina was glad she did not bulge, like Eudora Simkins, or go down straight as a lathe, like Betsy Pilling.

Her school hat, navy straw with a green and silver ribbon, lay on top of her books. She picked it up and tried it on at several different angles, then laid it down again and consulted her small gold watch. She noted that several hours would elapse before she need arrive at school – it was barely six o'clock and on the first day school did not commence until ten – and pinned the watch proudly into place. Not even Paulina, who lived further up Bishopsgate in a much grander house and was hopelessly spoilt, had a finer watch! Poppa had given it to her when she knew she would be going to the senior school, his hands behind his back, keeping the small jewellers' box hidden.

'So you done well in the examination and the interview, eh?' he said gruffly. 'But is it right that you should go to this *goy* school, where go only *shiksehs?*'

'I am only the first; other Jewish girls will go, you said so yourself,' Tina protested. 'And why say *shiksehs?* They're girls, just like me. English girls, Poppa!'

He pretended to scowl at her, but she could see the pride in his eyes. 'English, eh? And you want we should all be so English? You want I shouldn't speak Yiddish? Other Jewish girls work in the home, speak like Momma. But you and your sisters! Ay-yi-yi, how English you will be!'

He often teased her by accentuating his accent, rolling his eyes, peppering his sentences with Yiddish expressions, so now she only sighed in an exaggerated manner, saying,

'Is that wrong, Poppa? We *are* English! We were all born here, except Rachel and Becky, and they were born in the States.'

'Ach, born is nothing.' He drew his hands out from behind his back, his smile broadening. 'You done well, Tina. I, your poppa, say so. Here, for you.'

He thrust the box into her hands and she opened it, then could only gaze. The watch had a tiny, blue-enamelled face with the numerals picked out in gold, and it hung from a short length of gold chain. Carefully, her father took it from its box and pinned it to her blouse.

'Oh, Poppa!' Tina cried, her eyes shining. 'Poppa, I love you! And I won't be too English!'

He scowled, heavy eyebrows descending in mock wrath. 'You better not! I wish you well to wear it, and it's I who am a fool, to tease you because you are English. Be off with you now, and show Momma, and Mutti, and the young ones.'

Cecy, turning over in bed with a muffled groan, brought Tina back to the present. She took one more penetrating look in the glass, pushed a tendril of hair behind her ear, and made her way downstairs.

Passing across the hall she glanced at Momma's bedroom door, but it was firmly shut. Her parents would be asleep still, no doubt, but Grandma would be up, and Alice, the servant girl who did all the rough work of the house and looked after little Louis, who was now three and a terrible handful.

Pausing a moment, she listened. Yes, Alice was in the living room, laying the fire. No doubt she would then make her way to the breakfast parlour and light the fire in there, so that when the household woke up they would be able to eat their breakfast in a warmed room.

As she had expected, she found her grandmother in the kitchen, the fire roaring up and the stove hot, a bowl of dough proving near its warmth. Mutti, turning as the door opened, said in her heavily accented voice which had never grown used to the English language her grandchildren spoke as of right, 'For this vonderful new school you are ready, eh? And so early! That I should live to see the day!'

'It is a bit early,' Tina admitted. She glanced at the dough. 'What are you cooking, Gran? Not honey-cakes! I'm not a child, you know.'

Mutti's eyes filled with tears of pride but she said scoffingly, 'A woman you are, at twelve? *Mazel tov*! And do you think I would give such a great girl honey-letters?'

The words rolled back the years. Tina remembered her first day at the school in Binnacky, and of how she had come running into the kitchen behind the store, afire with the excitement of being with other children and having a little desk and some books all her own, to find an alphabet of honey-cake letters set out round her place at the table, to remind her that 'learning is sweet'.

'No, I suppose not. What's the dough for, then?'

Her grandmother's voice was smug. 'Oh, only a few plain old bagels. To go with the blackcurrant preserve you hate so much.'

Tina crossed the kitchen and kissed her grandmother's lined cheek. 'Gran, you're a queen! My favourites! Don't think I'll be late for tea today, no matter how my friends beg me to stay and talk! I'll be home so fast you'll think I took a hansom!'

Mutti, smiling, reached for the dough, turned it on to a floured board, and began swiftly shaping it into wheels. 'Pull the water over the fire, will you? I thought school ended at one o'clock?'

'It does, except for extras. This afternoon there's a hockey practice for my year. Lizbeth and I thought we'd attend.' As she spoke, Tina pulled the heavy saucepan over the flames and watched as bubbles began to form on the sides. 'It's a long walk, but I should be home by tea-time.'

You'll walk, then? All the way to Theatre Street?'

Tina laughed. 'Gran, it's not so far! If it was raining, I might catch a bus, but otherwise I'll walk. Shall I make the coffee?'

Mutti picked up half a dozen dough-wheels, took them over to the now boiling water, and dropped them in.

'Certainly you may. You wan' some breakfast?'

'Yes, please, though not too much.' She took down the coffee pot, measured ground beans into it, filled it with water and stood it on one side of the stove. 'Could I have some bread and butter?'

Her grandmother clucked disapprovingly. 'You want you should faint, your first day? Bread and butter! Have some hot parritch, or a couple boiled eggs.'

'It's *porridge,* not parritch, and I don't want anything cooked. I mustn't forget to put my knitting into my school bag. All the seniors knit during recreation.'

'Knit schmit,' Mutti grumbled softly. 'Why should they knit?'

'They knit for the heathen,' Tina explained. She and Lizbeth had noted the young ladies' habit of strolling side by side, their tongues going faster than their needles, as they knitted sagging woolly vests and strangely shaped socks for the unfortunate heathen.

Mutti scooped out the bobbing bagels as they rose to the top of the water, spread them out on a greased baking sheet and popped them into the oven to brown. 'Bread and butter she will have, to start the day! And a cup coffee! Too fat, does she think she is? Oy-oy, what a *schlemiel*!'

Nevertheless she sliced bread, buttered it, then stood it on the table and brought out a jar of orange marmalade. 'There! You'll take a packed luncheon? Liverwurst sandwiches? Some fruit?'

'That'll be lovely. Could I have a piece of your chocolate *torte* as well?'

Over her grandmother's face spread a gratified smile, but she only said as she bustled over to the pantry, 'Not so bad, eh, your old gran's cooking? Why not? Two pieces I'll give you, one for you and one for Lizbeth.'

Tina, aware that she had redeemed herself for a bread and butter breakfast, winced slightly as Mutti jammed two enormous slices of the *torte* into her small sandwich box, then got up from the table, still munching bread and marmalade.

'The coffee smells good. Will the girls be all right, Gran?

I can't walk them to school now that I'm at the Assembly House.'

Mutti snorted. 'You want they should depend on you? Because you aren't there, will they lose their sense? Cecy is good, Becky also, and Rachel . . .' An ecstatic sigh, accompanied by upcast eyes. 'I tell you that child is an angel! And clever! Why . . .'

Tina drained her cup, set it down on the table, and said briskly, 'Yes, she's very clever. And I must go up and finish getting ready. Shan't be long.' She left the kitchen with Mutti's paeon of praise for her favourite grandchild fading into a mutter of anxiety about the bagels as she swung the oven door wide. Tina ran up the stairs and burst in upon Cecy, standing dreamily at the window in her bodice and a pair of darned drawers. Cecy jumped and turned pink, then relaxed.

'Tina! You startled me! And you're dressed already! You must have got up at the crack of dawn!'

Tina grabbed her toothbrush and began scrubbing her teeth. Muttering through the brush, she said, 'I did. I wanted to be in good time, and this is the second time I've brushed my teeth this morning!' She rinsed her mouth, spat vigorously into the basin, and turned to her sister. 'Take care of the little ones, Cecy. Don't go dreaming along with your head in the air, leaving them to their own devices. I know what you are!'

Cecy was the same height as her sister but quite a lot plumper. Her pretty, rosy face went rosier at the implied criticism and she tossed back her bush of curly hair and pouted at her sister. 'I'm not so much younger than you, and of *course* I'll look after Becky and Rachel! As for dreaming, I'm not the only one in this family who does *that*!'

'Good,' Tina said. She reached into her top drawer and grabbed a ball of grey wool and a pair of needles. 'I'm off now. Bye, Cecy!'

'Off? You must be ma-ad!' Cecy's wail followed her swift flight down the stairs. 'You'll be hours too early. You'll be the first . . .'

Tina knocked perfunctorily on her parents' door and opened it. Momma was dressed in her petticoats and bodice and turned a surprised face towards the door. Of Poppa there was no sign.

'Tina? How early you are! I'm about to get Louis up, and then I'll go down for breakfast. Your father is down already.'

'I'm leaving, Momma,' Tina said. 'I'll be home at tea-time because there's games practice after luncheon.'

'Of course, the new school. Have a good day, darling child.'

Tina dashed across the room, kissed her mother, and went rapidly across the hall to the breakfast parlour. Poppa, reading the paper while eating a huge pile of scrambled eggs on toast, beamed at her over his reading glasses. 'Off already? You'll be the first to arrive, unless you intend Lizbeth to visit? No? I don't blame you, for, good girl though she is, late for everything that child has been all her life!' He got to his feet, wiped his mouth on his napkin, and kissed his daughter heartily. 'Work hard, my child, and may good luck and good fortune go with you.'

Tina left the breakfast parlour and returned to the kitchen, grabbing her school bag and pushing her knitting down beside the books it already contained. 'Goodbye, Gran. I'm off now,' she said, taking her luncheon box off the table and pushing that into her bag as well.

Mutti crossed the kitchen and hugged her, a smear of flour decorating her forehead and a wooden spoon in one hand. 'Goodbye, *bubeleh*, and may you do well,' she said.

Tina went to the front door, opened it, screamed 'Goodbyeee!' over her shoulder and heard answering shouts from all over the house. Then she was off down the short drive and through the wrought-iron gates into Bishopsgate. To her left was Bishop's Bridge, spanning the river, but she turned right and began walking briskly along the pavement, passing the Old Men's Hospital and a number of ancient dwellings with creepers turning bronze and red in the autumn sunshine, and gardens brilliant with dahlias and chrysanthemums. She did consider calling for

Lizbeth as she passed her friend's house, but decided that Poppa was right; it was pointless getting up early and setting off betimes, only to be held up by Lizbeth, for the sweet, scatty creature would scarcely have got out of bed yet, let alone breakfasted! So she continued her walk, enjoying the warm sun striking through her blouse and the sweetness of the early morning air.

She turned into Palace Street, and was walking along beside the tall flint wall which hid the Cathedral Close, glancing up at the reds and yellows of the turning leaves which overhung the wall and sniffing the sweet, nutty scent of them, when she saw a group of schoolboys ahead, bound no doubt for the Grammar School in the Cathedral Close. She walked even more sedately, sternly repressing an urge to straighten her hat and peep down to see that her belt was not twisted nor her boots dusty. She recognised Malcolm Butterworth and Roy Sutton but they did not pause in their hasty strides, and as she emerged on to Tombland she saw them disappearing through the Erpingham Gate into the Close.

For a moment she felt a clutch of dismay at her heart. Was she late, after all? Then she remembered that Malcolm and Roy were both in the choir; doubtless they were hurrying to early service. Relieved, she paused on the pavement, waiting until it was safe to cross. The city was busy although it was still early, with carriages taking workers to their shops and offices, bicycles wheeling sedately between the vehicles, carts up from the country with produce for sale, and maidservants hurrying off to the market to buy vegetables while the dew was still fresh upon them.

She crossed the wide road, then hesitated for a moment over her choice of route. There were several different ways she could walk to school but since she was so early she would go the long way round. Up Elm Hill. It would take longer, especially if she stopped at the corner shop, but she had plenty of time. It was wonderful to be alone in the city, without her sisters or other persons who might impose their will upon her.

She turned right along the pavement, passing the shop

which always made Rachel shudder. Harvey's sold game, and although it was early a long string of hares, their bulging eyes fixed and staring, hung from one side of the doorway. On the other side woodpigeons, eyes meekly closed, and ducks with immaculate green and black plumage, were suspended like beads on a necklace. Tina took a breath and held it until she was past, so that she would not smell the blood. Then she crossed the square where, later, the flower-sellers would congregate in the shade of the tall lime trees, and dived up Elm Hill.

It was an attractive street, cobbled, with ancient houses and cottages leaning perilously over the pavement, some of them supported by stout wooden pillars. But for the Rose children the main attraction of Elm Hill was the corner shop.

Tina, feeling that she had a treat in store, hurried to where the street widened into a small square, made smaller by a huge, leafy elm tree, and headed for the window of the corner shop.

Today it was full of puppies. Pale brown, rich chocolate, mottled, their fur asking to be stroked, their liquid baby eyes beaming at her, their small mouths opening in soundless yaps as they grinned at her through the glass. Sometimes she was lucky, and a grimy hand would reach into the window even as she watched and put down a dish of scraps. Then what a commotion there would be! Tiny tails wagging, eager paws bouncing in and out of the dish, puppies pushing, squealing, rolling over each other. The Rose children thought it good as a play – better – whether it was puppies, kittens, or any other young animals, and Tina felt a positive surge of satisfaction as she reflected that now she could have a private view of the pet shop window every morning, if she left home early enough.

Today, however, the puppies must have been fed. She moved to the second, smaller window, which was crawling with tortoises. With slow, idiotic determination they climbed over each other, chewing limp lettuce indifferently. Tina noticed that one or two of the smaller ones were sprightlier and might prove to have characters, but it was no good wishing. Momma thought pets unhygienic and wasteful and Grandma agreed. Moving away from the reptiles, Tina risked a quick peep into the shop itself. The man who kept it did not care for children, thinking them mischievous and idle, suspecting them of a desire to tease or steal his animals. This morning, however, he was rooting round in a big sack, then weighing up pellets on a scale which he kept behind the counter. She stared, her gaze wandering over the soft, nose-twitching rabbits, the tanks of tropical fish, the seedy, hunched parrots.

A second glance showed her bantams, ferrets, and a half-grown dog, already too big for the cage into which he had been thrust. He saw her looking and whined a little, but she moved back from the doorway before the man could glance round, and turned back to the puppies.

A young man was standing by the window now, watching the playful occupants. As she moved to stand within a foot or so of him she saw his eyes slide furtively over her. She ignored him. The young ladies at the senior school knew better than to notice young men, however much they stared!

One puppy, bolder than the rest, came over and stood up against the glass, revealing its soft pink underside, cocking its head, bright eyes begging her to play. She cooed to it, 'Lovely boy, lovely fellow,' not caring that it could not hear her, knowing her loving glance spoke through the glass as did the puppy's silent yaps.

A hand, heavy and hot, fell on her shoulder and she was swung round away from the puppies to face the young man who had been standing beside her. Now he loomed above her, tall and thick set with a red, shiny face and very small, wet eyes, like blue beads. He said softly, 'Jew girl! Dirty little Jew girl!' and gripped both her shoulders, hurting her so that she instinctively tried to wince away, though his fingers forbade movement. Her mind was still half with the puppies and the fanatical hatred which shone from the little eyes seemed unreal. She said stupidly, 'What?' and he repeated, 'Dirty Jew girl,' his face alight with malice, his fingers seeming to bite into her flesh. Then he took a deep breath and the grip on her shoulders relaxed. He spat, full in her face, and stepped back from her.

She staggered back against the window, her hands going up to try to wipe the spittle out of her eyes, to stop it from trickling down towards her mouth. For a moment shock stunned her, held her rigid. Then terror and disgust flooded her so that she turned and ran, feeling her plait bobbing on her back, her school bag banging against her knees.

Behind her she heard him call, 'I'll find yer! Every day, somewhere, I'll find yer! Don' you fret!'

She spoke of it to no one, yet it marked her deeply. At first, all she could think of was that which made her different. What was it? How had he known she was Jewish? She wore the same school uniform as a hundred other girls, behaved in the same way, enjoyed the same games and pastimes. What was the mark of Cain which had made her immediately identifiable to an unknown young man? Her father, with rare understanding, had always told her that one did not flaunt one's faith. Certainly she would be the only Jewish girl in the High School, for the Jewish community was a small one and the education of girls still a matter for consideration and argument. Poppa had refused to insist that she miss assembly or religious instruction, maintaining that hearing and learning about other religions would broaden her mind without lessening her faith.

'Behave nicely to other children, yes, and to the teachers, show politeness and thought,' he advised. 'Then they will love you for yourself, Tina. And when you are loved for yourself, it matters not that, in one little way, you are different.'

She had taken this advice at her junior school, yet still the young man had known. Lizbeth knew she was Jewish, and they were still best friends, but now she waited for the girls in her class at the new school to shrink from her, for the teachers to be sharp. She remembered her momma once saying in a vague sort of way that if ever she heard children begin to ask who killed Christ, she was to come home at once – at *once*, and not to stay to argue. Then, she had not understood; now she did. At her new school, everyone behaved unexceptionally towards her, yet she could take no comfort from it. Did they realise she was Jewish? If they suddenly found out, as the young man had done, would they shun her, turn against her? A dozen times that first week she almost told Lizbeth, or Poppa, or Grandma, the whole story, a dozen times her lips closed despite herself. This was her problem, she knew, and one which only she could resolve.

By tea-time on that first day, she had decided it was an isolated incident, an act of temporary insanity on the part of an unknown young man. On the second morning she went a different way to school, though some instinct kept her from seeking Lizbeth's company.

Every day, for a week, he found her. He would appear somewhere on her way to or from school, bend over her as if solicitously, befoul her face, and vanish.

She became nervous, flinching at sudden movements, crying secretly in bed at night, absent-minded and stupid in class. Her work began to suffer. At school, teachers thought she had problems at home; at home, her parents discussed anxiously whether they had been wise to allow her to go on to the High School. Tina noticed nothing. She was obsessed by her tormentor.

It might have gone on indefinitely had not Rachel come home from a music lesson howling loudly, telling the world at the top of her shrill young voice that a horrid man had come up to her in the Close, had shouted 'You girl! You girl!' and had spat down at her, soiling her pinafore and her school bag.

Fortunately Deborah was out, but Mutti gathered her darling in her arms, her little, withered face flushed with perplexity and fury, her mouth a button of annoyance. 'A man grown, to behave so?' she said grimly. 'To my innocent child? This I will not stand! Tomorrow I shall come to the Close with you, and you shall show me this man!'

Tina, scrubbing the dirtied school bag, opened her mouth – and shut it again. For the first time, pure anger killed fear and the sick trembling that the thought of him had brought. How *dare* he attack her little sister? And suppose Grandma did meet him? Or Momma, who sometimes strolled up to meet the little ones from school? She knew, suddenly, that he would spit into Grandma's face or into Momma's, and that they would be hurt by it in a way more terrible, and longer-lasting, than the way she herself had been hurt.

On the instant, her main purpose in life became to stop the man before he attacked Momma or Grandma, and before they realised what, in fact, he had shouted at Rachel. She felt real astonishment that she had borne with her tormentor for so long, had allowed him to crush her vivacity and undermine her self-confidence. She said nothing, but that evening she ate a good meal, and sat down afterwards to do her homework with a will.

Next day she set off for school early. Today, she told herself, I am searching for *him*! She walked with her old briskness, her thoughts no longer confused, no self-doubt clouding her mind. She knew what she must do and felt neither fear nor shrinking.

Halfway up Elm Hill she saw him, strolling casually towards her, looking into windows, stopping to adjust his tie in the glass. She kept her head lowered for fear he might read her intention in her face and avoid her, but he suspected nothing. He came on, crossing the road towards her so that presently they would meet face to face.

Tina felt the coldness of her resolve begin to blur into a lust of rage and fury so strong that she felt armoured by it, invincible. He had made her feel guilt because she was a Jew, instead of feeling honoured to be one of God's chosen people! He reached her, bent over her, a hand on her shoulder. Quick as thought she brought her umbrella up, pushing the steel ferrule as hard as she could into that gloating, hated face.

He gave a choking, terrible shriek. He fell, half on the pavement, half on the cobbles, blood spurting, the great mouthful of saliva he had been holding to spit into her face pouring down his chin in a glistening flood.

He was screaming, clawing at his face. A door opened

nearby and a woman, aproned and with a brush in one hand, called out to a neighbour, who was scrubbing her front doorstep. Together the two women approached the writhing figure. Tina bent over him.

'Next time, I'll kill you,' she said.

Then she walked on, stopping by the two women to say the young man seemed to be having some kind of fit, that he had clawed at his own face and was foaming at the mouth. Then she continued to climb the hill, leaving the women to be joined by others, clustering uncertainly on the pavement, exclaiming, trying to get the young man to speak to them. Giving no thought to the fresh-faced schoolgirl with her long plait of hair bobbing on her back as she left the scene.

8

Once she knew that she had no more to fear from the young man who had tormented her, Tina settled down very happily at the High School. She was intelligent and soon rose to the top of her class; she was naturally athletic and revelled in games, becoming a keen member of the hockey club and playing against other schools for the junior team. And then, at Christmas, she found out why the young man had behaved so cruelly towards her.

'Remember that young fellow I sacked, Deborah, back in August?' Arthur said one evening, as they sat round the fire roasting chestnuts and reading, the younger ones having been banished to bed. 'Alf Biggins, his name was. I told you he was bad, a bit *meshugge*; he had trouble made, in the factory.'

Deborah, manoeuvring nuts into position beneath the glowing coals, nodded. 'I remember.'

'Well, he got a job, with Colmans. And here in the paper is a frightening story! He went into the offices of the new boss with some trifle which had annoyed him, and pulled a knife! Ay-yi-yi, how easy it could have been *me*! He hated me enough!'

Tina glanced up. 'Did he hurt the man, Poppa?'

Her father shook his head. 'No. It says here . . .' he gestured to a paragraph on an inner page, then read out loud: 'Biggins insulted Mr Parslow, calling him a Jew, and tried to stab him in the stomach with a knife which he produced from his pocket.' He snorted. 'To call him a Jew is an insult? Well, it would seem so perhaps, for Mr Parslow is a strong Methodist.' He shook his head, then returned to reading from the paper. 'Mr Fowler, a clerk in the office, seized the man and held him whilst Mr Parslow fetched help.'

Tina split a hot chestnut and began, gingerly, to peel it. 'I see. What did Biggins look like, Poppa?'

'Nothing out of the ordinary. He had funny little eyes, though: like blue beads, they were. Small, glistening.'

'Oh,' Tina said. She took a bite of the smoking nut. 'This is delicious! Shall I peel you one, Poppa?'

Spring came, and Tina went off to school one morning with a headache and a sniffle, sitting through an arithmetic lesson, a French conversation class with Mamzelle and half a music lesson with Miss Barret before quietly excusing herself and making her way to the headmistress's room.

Tapping on the door she entered, to find Miss Gadesden sitting at a desk opposite the door, writing in a large ledger. She was wearing her gold-rimmed reading spectacles and looked up enquiringly at the opening of the door. 'Yes, Tina?'

'Miss Gadesden, I've got an awful cold; I wonder if I might go home,' Tina said thickly. 'I would have waited until luncheon but I've got drill with Sergeant-Major Collins next, and this afternoon I've a painting class with

Miss John. I don't really feel well enough to get through the whole day.'

Miss Gadesden got up from her chair and walked over to Tina, placing cool, impersonal fingers on her pupil's forehead. 'You're very hot,' she observed in her precise voice. 'I do trust it isn't the onset of influenza, child! Are you able to reach home alone, or shall I send a senior pupil with you?'

'I would rather go alone,' Tina said quickly. 'It isn't a long walk. I'll be quite all right.'

'You wouldn't prefer to wait quietly in the small store room until the luncheon break? Then you could be accompanied by those members of your own class who do not have painting with Miss John this afternoon.'

Tina, however, remained steady in her resolve to go straight home, and as soon as she had received Miss Gadesden's permission to do so, made her way across the school playground. Already the rest of her class, in gym skirts and blouses, were forming up on the asphalt while Sergeant-Major Collins strode up and down, exhorting them to 'Git hinto *fowers*, young leddies, in horder of your 'ight!'

Tina waved to Lizbeth, then unlatched one of the tall wrought-iron gates and sallied forth into Theatre Street. She hesitated for a moment, wondering whether she should catch a tram. But she knew from bitter experience that she might have a considerable wait before one came along, and despite the sunshine, which had tempted Miss John to announce that they would go into Chapel Field that afternoon to immortalise the drifts of daffodils in their sketches, there was a chilly breeze.

Accordingly, she began to walk briskly in the direction of her home and was aware that she felt much better in the air than she had in the stuffy classroom. By the time she passed the Old Men's Hospital, in fact, she was beginning to be sorry she had given in to her cold. It would have been fun, sketching in the park with her friends, and Miss John was an unexacting teacher. At home, with Grandma and Alice busy, she would very soon grow bored.

It was not until she had opened the gate and was walking

up the short drive that the realisation hit her. Thursday! It was Alice's day off, and Grandma was going shopping and then having luncheon with old Mrs Glantz, who lived on Grapes Hill near Grandma's old home. After luncheon, she would go on to the Jewish Ladies' Circle meeting, which was being held in Unthank Road this week.

Tina groaned. Her cold was beginning to make itself felt again and she had just been thinking how pleasant it would be to be spoiled, for once; to totter in through the front door and explain to a sympathetic and clucking grandma that she was ill. She had imagined Grandma's concern, a hot stone bottle being taken up to warm her bed, the kettle being put on to boil, lemons being squeezed. And then, the snugness of being tucked up warm in bed during the daytime, a light luncheon being carried in on a tray, her favourite books to read!

But it was not to be, though her mother would be in. She seldom went out nowadays, saying that pregnancy made her feel awkward in company. Besides, she had not been well; she had suffered from attacks of giddiness and nausea, and was so lethargic that she was apt to fall asleep whenever she sat down. So Momma would be in, but it was unlikely that she would exert herself for her daughter, cold or no. Bending down and finding the key under the stone where Grandma always left it when she went out, Tina thought wistfully how nice it would be if Momma took this opportunity of spoiling her eldest! How lovely to feel Momma's soft, cool hand caressing one's hot brow, to see a gentle, anxious look in her eyes!

She unlocked the door, opened it, and stepped quietly into the hall. How silent and empty the house seemed! She wondered if Momma might be in the kitchen, and quietly tried there first, but the room was empty though a bright fire burned and the air was redolent of good food. Tina, sniffing, decided that Grandma had left a stew in the oven; her mouth watered, but she closed the door gently and was about to make for her parents' bedroom, which was up a short passage just off the main hall, when she thought she heard a small sound from the study.

Her heart lifted. Was Poppa home? How she would surprise him!

She stole to the door and opened it softly. There was no sign of her father, but her mother was sitting at his desk, her head down on the pink blotter. For a moment, Tina thought she was asleep, and then, unmistakably, she heard the little catch in the throat, the ragged, uneven breathing, which every child knows so well. Momma was crying! She hesitated, then, closing the door as softly as she had opened it, stole back across the hall and made as much noise as possible in opening and closing the front door.

'Grandma? I'm home!' she called a little hoarsely, then went deliberately to the kitchen, opened the door, slammed it again and went over to the study. She entered, to find Deborah sitting upright at the desk, apparently writing a letter. Her face was very pale, her eyes red-rimmed, but she smiled at her daughter, though it was obviously an effort to do so.

'Tina! Is it luncheon time already?'

'No. I've been sent home from school with a cold. Momma, you don't look at all well. Are you all right?'

Deborah laid down her pen. 'Perfectly all right, just a little tired. To tell you the truth I fell asleep in the middle of writing a letter, and I still feel somewhat heavy-eyed.'

'Poor Momma! Who are you writing letters to?'

'To Auntie Mirah; do you remember her, when we stayed in New York after Poppa's accident? I had a letter from her this morning. She writes a lovely letter; it's almost as good as hearing her talk. She tells me . . .' There was a pause, and Tina heard, with dismay, a tiny tremor come into her mother's voice. 'She tells me that Paul is to marry! Yes, and she's a lovely girl, though years younger than he! Do you . . . remember Uncle Paul? He came to Galeport and fetched us back to New York. I'm writing at once, of course, telling Mirah to wish them happy.'

'I see,' Tina said in a small voice. She felt, suddenly, as if her heart would burst. She took out her handkerchief and blew her nose, saying in a muffled voice, 'Give them my best wishes too. Uncle Paul was so kind to Cecy and me.'

'He was, wasn't he? Now you go off to bed, dear, and leave me to finish my letter. Presently I'll bring you up a hot drink and some luncheon. I daresay Mutti's left something which we can share. How will that be?'

'It would be lovely,' Tina said gratefully. 'But I'll make myself a drink – and a hot bottle at the same time.'

She left the study and went into the kitchen, her thoughts in a turmoil. She had never acknowledged, even in the innermost depths of her mind, that her mother had cared for Uncle Paul, had felt for him a warmer affection than that which was customary between relatives. But now she knew that this was so. In her junior school there had been a teacher called Miss Matty Bloom. She was young and very pretty, with black, curly hair, dark brown eyes, and dimples. She had taught Tina when she was ten, and Tina could still remember Miss Bloom's warmth and gaiety, the way she had hugged her little pupil and rejoiced with her when Louis had been born. And then she had come to school with a sparkly ring on her finger, and the head mistress had made a little speech about how they would hate to say goodbye to Miss Bloom, but that her fiancé taught in a school in the south of England and after their marriage Miss Bloom, too, would seek a position there.

The following term, however, had seen Miss Bloom back in school, still teaching. And the sparkly ring had gone from her finger, the bright happiness from her face. The older children whispered that she had been jilted but Tina, not understanding the word, had only known that something, or someone, had made Miss Bloom so deeply unhappy that she would never be quite the same person again.

Tina began to lay two trays, one for her own luncheon and one for her mother's. That look had been in her mother's eyes, oh, for ages! She had noticed it but had never bothered to analyse it, never asked herself what had happened to take the lightness from her mother's step, the warmth from her glance.

Working automatically but efficiently, she laid a clean traycloth on her mother's tray, heated Grandma's chicken broth and poured it into an earthenware bowl, sliced and thinly buttered bread and cut off the crusts, prepared chicken salad and cut a slice of Grandma's light and fluffy sponge cake. On her own tray she simply put a selection of food she liked most – a slice of peppery German sausage, some pickled onions and dill cucumber, a raw carrot, an iced bun and a mug of hot lemon tea. She had already filled her bottle and carried it up to her bed, and now she took her mother's tray through to the study.

'Oh, Tina, that was kind,' Deborah said, patting her daughter's cheek. 'Now off to bed with you. I'll come up presently, when I've eaten this delicious luncheon.'

Tina, climbing gratefully into her warm bed and beginning to tackle her own meal, began to speculate on the changes in her mother which, she now realised, had been becoming more marked ever since they had reached Norwich. Also, her own relationship with her parents had altered. Now that she thought about it, she realised that in America Momma had meant everything to her and Poppa less than nothing. She had not even liked him very much! Yet now Poppa had first place in her affections. She supposed, rather confusedly, that it had come about because Momma was no longer happy; she never laughed or sang around the house or lit up in Poppa's presence, the way she once had. Nor did she run the house and manage the family; Grandma and Poppa did. Oh, Momma smiled, and listened to their talk of school affairs and friendships and quarrels, she presided over meals and mended their clothing. But the warmth had gone out of her interest. She no longer cared as passionately as she once had.

Tina forced herself to look back, to Momma as she had been when they were in America. Busy, frightened, worried; but always *involved*. Crying with grief when Poppa went off with his waggons and with joy when he returned. Shouting at Mabel, picking her way down on to the boats when they came in, her forehead creasing with the effort of remembering what she need to order. Back they came after the years between, the little, bright pictures. Mel lived again, his lanky form bent over a book, his face screwed up with the effort of understanding. Tall, stupid Rufus, loping around the garden, scaring Momma and never knowing it. And Uncle Paul. She could see him so clearly, his craggy profile, his broad-shouldered figure, his dependable strength. And Momma, standing close, slender and straight beside him. A pair.

Quickly, guiltily almost, she dismissed Uncle Paul from her mind and thought about Poppa. He was a wonderful father, always interested and concerned, always noisy, exuberant and popular. Everyone liked Poppa, his own children most of all. He made life easier for them, and more interesting, too. He had insisted that Tina should attend Hebrew classes with the Rabbi, though she was the only girl in the class. Momma thought it strange, but did nothing to prevent it. He saw to it that Tina had more freedom, too, than other Jewish girls. She went to and from school alone, went by train to Brundall to visit Alice's parents, accompanied her friends to the Theatre Royal sometimes, to see a suitable play.

He was unorthodox in other ways, too; a good Jew, bringing his children up to be good Jews, but having no patience with the little things. If he wanted pancakes on the Sabbath, he would swing into the kitchen on his sticks and make himself pancakes, propping himself up beside the stove and turning the delicious yellowy rounds with a dextrous flip of the wrist, although he knew as well as the rest of the family that one should never cook on the Sabbath. And if he wanted cream in his coffee he would have it, no matter what meat had preceded the sweet course. He would raise his brows at Deborah and she would go into the kitchen and return with the cream jug. Oh, he might shake his head and pretend to slap his hand, but he tipped the cream into his coffee just the same!

Remembering Galeport, Tina saw more than ever how different Momma had become. There, against tremendous odds and with no one to care how she behaved, she had koshered all the meat they ate and never served pork, or shellfish, though the coast was famous for its crustaceans. And she had taught the children the rudiments of their faith and their religious observances so that on their return their religion came naturally to them.

Yet now she made no effort to reform Poppa, had never even remonstrated with him when he told the children that they might play on the Sabbath. 'First comes Shul, natural,' he had said genially when they had settled into the Bishopsgate house. 'But after, your time is your own. Play with your friends, bring them home. But tell them not to expect a hot dinner. No roast beef for us, on the Sabbath!'

In Galeport and later, in New York, Mother had made friends, enjoyed a social life. Here in Norwich she attended Shul, went to the Ladies' Circle meetings, came to parents' evenings at the school. But the warmth had gone out of her interest. When Poppa took her to see a play at the theatre, or down to the coast for a meal, she accepted it without question, always saying placidly that she had enjoyed herself but never instigating an outing. Could it be that she really did not want to go out any more? That a calm, emotionless existence was what Momma had always wanted?

Then Tina remembered something else. Momma had shown emotion this very day! She had cried because Uncle Paul was getting married!

With a shiver, Tina crept right down the bed and pulled the clothes over her head. It was her imagination, that's what it was! Miss Bayley, at school, was always either congratulating her on her imagination or telling her to keep it in check. She would think about something else, because the way she felt, her thoughts were not much comfort to her. Resolutely, she tried to think of the painting class, to wonder what they were doing. And presently, worn out, she fell asleep.

Three weeks after her cold had cleared up, Tina and Cecy went into the city with Grandma to choose silk for light dresses. Alice was in charge of the younger ones and a nurse, Mrs Elgood, was already installed since Momma's time was near.

The children had set out with enthusiasm, but by the time

Grandma had trailed them round every silk merchant's warehouse in the city, arguing, bargaining and complaining, they were tired and eager for their tea. Grandma, however, was in fine fettle, trotting briskly across Tombland and down Palace Street, chattering about the scandalous prices she had been asked to pay, the way she had beaten them down, and their father's pleasure when he learned how economically she had behaved with his money. Tina was vaguely aware that her friends' mothers did not bargain, but five years of Grandma's shopping methods had inured her to embarrassment and her only thought was that she wanted her tea. As they passed the Old Men's Hospital she waved surreptitiously to old Mr Ramsden, who came twice a week to help their gardener out, and remarked to Cecy, 'I wonder if Alice will let us make flapjacks?'

'Oh, I hope so! Covered with syrup, Tina! I adore flapjacks.'

They were at the front door before the subject of their tea was exhausted and Grandma fished out the key which she carried round her neck on a gold chain and let them in. They walked into the hall and were horrified to hear a long, throbbing moan which turned, frighteningly, into a series of short, exhausted wails, then died away in whimpers. Grandma pushed past them, snapping, 'Go to the kitchen, girls!' and went rapidly up the short passage and into their parents' room.

Tina began to follow, then checked as Cecy grabbed her sleeve. 'It's the baby, isn't it? Oh, Tina, don't go in there! We should not, I know. Where's Poppa? And the little ones?'

'You go into the kitchen. Alice will be there,' Tina told her sister. 'I must go and see if they need any help.'

'Are you sure? Oh, Tina, why is Momma crying out like that?'

'Because it hurts, of course!'

Tina left her sister and hurried off down the passage, to find Grandma still standing in the doorway, conversing with someone in the room. She turned as Tina approached, saying, 'Off, off with you, *faygeler*. Momma is . . . busy. Go to Poppa; he's in the study.'

'I want to see Momma,' Tina said obstinately. 'Just for a minute, Gran!'

There was a murmur from within the room and Grandma, reluctantly, stood aside for a moment. Tina, peering round the old woman's spare frame, caught a glimpse of her mother lying on the bed, her face shiny with sweat. Mrs Elgood, starchily dressed in an apron and cap instead of in the more comfortable grey gown she usually wore, stood on one side of the bed and Dr Goldstein on the other. He had his back to Tina, but she knew him at once, for he had attended her ever since her birth, with the exception of the years in America.

'Tina? Tell Poppa . . . I'm . . . all right.'

Deborah's voice was faint, but her smile determinedly bright. She added, in a stronger voice, 'And you may come in properly, as soon as the baby is born, which should not be long now.'

Dr Goldstein turned round, saying briefly, 'Yes, yes, go tell the good poppa! Now off with you, Tina mine. This is no place for a child, eh?'

Tina, retreating, heard her mother say in a ghost of a voice, 'You must tell my son that, doctor, when he puts in an appearance,' and heard the doctor chuckle. Then the door closed and there was nothing she could do but make her way to the study. Arthur was there, sitting beside the fire with Cecy at his side. They were both studying the flames intently but as the door opened they both looked up, and Arthur's face showed his relief.

'Tina, my love! You've seen Momma? It has a long time been! Is she . . . is she suffering?'

'Of course she is, Poppa. Why don't you go and talk to her?'

He shrugged, glancing uneasily from her face to Cecy's. 'It wouldn't be right, *bube*. It's woman's work, and she wouldn't want a *kalikeh* like me in the room.'

'She would. But perhaps the doctor and the nurse wouldn't,' Tina conceded. 'Would you like some tea,

Poppa? Shall I ask Alice to get us a tray?'

Alice took Becky and Rachel and Louis round to the Feltons,' Arthur said. 'But tea I would like! Let us go to the kitchen and make tea – all of us!'

'I think that's a good idea,' Tina agreed, looking at Cecy's pale, set little face. 'It will help us to pass the time.'

They repaired to the kitchen and the girls bustled about, making a pot of tea, finding a tin of *kichelach* and putting the small, sugar-dusted biscuits on to a clean plate, cutting slices of Grandma's soggy fruit cake which Arthur adored but would eat only rarely, because it was so indigestible.

'I've made cheese and pickle sandwiches,' Cecy said, putting the plate down on the kitchen table. 'There is some of Gran's egg and onion pie left, too, if you'd like a piece.' She patted the chair drawn up beside the table. 'Sit here and have some tea, Poppa.'

'I will indeed! You two girls will make some lucky fellows first-rate wives!' He picked up a sandwich and bit into it. 'Delicious!'

Tina, pouring tea into shallow blue cups, smiled at her father. 'Why don't you say we're good daughters? It will be a while yet before we think about being wives!'

'You're the best daughters a man ever had! No milk for me, *faygeler*, nor lemon either, I'll just have it sweetened.'

He was raising the cup to his lips when they all heard a door open, followed by a brief, faint wail. Tina dropped the sandwich she was holding and ran to open the kitchen door. Clearly now, it could be heard; a baby, crying thinly.

'My son! He's born! Thank God!'

The three of them hurried across the hall to where the door of the bedroom stood open with Grandma, wreathed in smiles, waiting for them. 'A boy it is, natural! A boy my daughter brings you, Arthur!'

Cecy, her face pink with excitement, peeped round the door, smiled at her mother, and said, 'I'll go and tell the others.' She vanished, but Tina and her father entered the room, both a little shy now that the moment had come.

Deborah was lying back on her pillows, sheet-white, her eyes dark-circled, but there was a smile on her lips and her long blue eyes seemed to be smiling too. 'A boy, Arthur! A brother for Louis!'

Her smile encompassed them both, then she closed her eyes wearily. Arthur started forward to take the baby from the nurse. 'Deborah, my dearest, what a fine boy he is! Small, always a baby seems small when you compare him to the other children, but a grand fellow!'

Deborah made no comment and Tina said anxiously, 'Momma? Are you all right?'

Mrs Elgood rustled across, smiling. 'Yes, just exhausted, dear. Would you like to hold your new brother for a moment? I'm sure Papa will allow you to do so, just for half a second!'

'Not sure I am if I should trust a mere girl,' Arthur said, grinning at her. 'What shall we call him, eh? Think of a fine name. A good, British name, like Arthur!'

Tina held out her arms and received the small, blanket-wrapped scrap of humanity into them. He was a tiny, dark-skinned baby, with long, thick black hair and a bud of a mouth.

'He's like the Indian babies, the papooses the Indians used to bring on to the railroad trains,' Tina announced. 'We'd better call him Cherokee, Poppa, or Blackfoot!'

The nurse began to exclaim but Arthur laughed, and took the baby from her. 'What a suggestion! Envy it is, because she is a mere girl and cannot change herself. No, no, my new son shall have a good, British name. I like David, myself.'

The doctor was scrubbing up, the nurse running water from a jug into the baby bath which stood ready. As her father joked over his new son's head, Tina became aware of an odd sound. A small, steady *tick, tick*, which reminded her of a clock, or a dripping tap. She glanced at the bed, whence the sound seemed to come, and thought she saw a slight stir of movement beneath the valance. She tugged at Arthur's sleeve. 'Poppa. What's that?'

Arthur glanced cursorily towards the bed, then bent his gaze upon his son once more. 'What? There is nothing! Shall we call him Herman, for your momma's brother? Or

Paul, perhaps? Now Paul was a good friend to us.'

But now Tina was quite certain that something was moving beneath the bed valance, creeping, gleaming. She knelt on the floor, ignoring her father's admonishment to behave herself. 'Poppa, there *is* something under here . . . Oh!'

For a moment she was covered with confusion, thinking that the moving pool that was creeping towards her like a dark tide was merely the result of an overturned water jug. Then she saw that it was dark red, and was soaking, scarlet, into her petticoat hem. She gasped. Above her, Arthur cried out and the doctor, who was still lathered up to the elbows, reached the bed in one bound and dragged back the covers. Beneath them, Deborah lay in a pool of blood which had already drained right through the mattress, the drip and patter of it on the linoleum beneath the bed Tina's mysterious sound.

Everyone moved quickly after that. Tina was scarcely on her feet before the baby was thrust into her arms and Arthur had cast himself down beside the bed, calling, 'Deborah, Deborah! Don't leave me, my darling!'

Tina stood, blood-bedraggled, her heart pounding and her mouth dry with fear. Her arms were shaking so much that the baby began to mutter, his tiny hands clenching beneath the blanket as her insecurity transmitted itself to him. She dared not move, she dared not speak, she could only stand and shake, trying to pray for her mother with words that refused to make sense.

Dr Goldstein turned, remembering her. 'Tina! Take the child to Grandma, there's a good girl. And don't *worry*. Go on!'

She longed to go, but could not. It was as if fear had rooted her to the spot. Working furiously, trying to save a life that had already almost escaped them, doctor and nurse had not a moment to spare for the petrified child by the door and Arthur could think of nothing but Deborah.

She was so still that they forgot her. She was still until the doctor said gently, 'Arthur, it's no good. I'm afraid she's gone,' and until Arthur began to sob. Then, very quietly and without any fuss, as neatly and unobtrusively as Deborah had slipped from life, Tina's knees crumpled and she fell to the floor.

'She's fainted! God, she should not have been . . . I *told* her to go . . .' Dr Goldstein went to lift Tina up off the floor and saw that she had fallen on the baby. He lifted them both up, and carried Tina out of the room and up to her own little bedroom. The baby he handed to the nurse, and after she had laid it in its cot whilst she cleaned up its dead mother, she put the baby in the crook of Deborah's arm.

It was probably for the best, Mrs Elgood thought philosophically, as she put on her bonnet and prepared to leave. Arthur Rose had enough on his hands with four daughters and a son. He might mourn the death of the new baby, but in his heart he could not regret it. And this way the little girl would never know whether she was in any way responsible for the baby's death.

Come to that, Mrs Elwood thought as she went towards the room where the family was congregated, come to that, no one will ever be sure.

9: Dunedin

Edward strolled down Rattray Street towards the building which, for the past three years, had housed the Edma Dairy Processing Company. The winter had been a hard one, with days of snow and blizzards so that now he lifted his face thankfully to the blue sky, enjoying the warmth of the sun and the pleasant breeze which touched his skin.

His enjoyment, however, was not sufficient to dispel the feeling with which he had been struggling ever since he had woken that morning; a feeling of discontent, of impatience with life in general. Thinking of his desk and the pile of work on it he felt rebellion rising up in him. No! Why should he go in to work on a day so beautiful? When he reached the familiar frontage, therefore, he continued blandly past, reached the corner of Princes Street and turned left along it, heading for the Octagon. Arriving there, he headed across to where a wooden seat stood facing the town hall. He sank down, feeling pleasantly idle. He could keep an eye on the town hall clock and just do nothing for a whole thirty minutes. It would probably do him good!

He liked the Octagon, the very centre of life in Dunedin. When Anna had been alive he and Mark had been driven into the city once a month to attend a service at First Church, and afterwards they had come here, to the Octagon, to meet their father with the waggon. They occasionally attended services still, driving in from their home on the Peninsula, though they also went to St Paul's. He turned his eyes from the baroque splendours of the town hall with its palm trees and flowering bushes towards St Paul's, and winced. Once he had thought it a beautiful building, but just lately he had ceased to regard St Paul's with anything but resentment. He knew why, too, though it had taken him time to admit it. St Paul's was Sylvia's place of worship, and Sylvia wanted to marry him.

Edward took a deep breath and expelled it in a gusty sigh. That was why he felt so restless and discontented, so . . . so trapped! Sylvia wanted to marry him; she had made her wishes all too plain. She had looked around her at all the eligible young men in Dunedin and chosen him, and instead of being flattered or delighted he was horrified.

Yet surely, at his age, he should think of marrying and settling down as both pleasant and inevitable? He was twenty-seven years old, a prosperous farmer and a successful businessman. To underline his need, he and Mark were at present suffering from the many inefficiencies and ineptitudes of an elderly housekeeper, because even in 1897 men outnumbered women by almost two to one on the South Island, and women tended to marry young. So why could he not count his blessings and settle down with Sylvia? She was an intelligent young woman, having recently emerged from Otago University with an honours degree in modern languages. She said she intended to teach, but Edward knew better. She intended to become Mrs Edward Neyler! She was also extremely pretty, with curling gold-blonde hair and blue eyes.

Then why did he not want to marry her? There were, he knew, two good reasons. The first and most important was that he did not want to marry anyone and, though he liked Sylvia very well, he had no desire to be tied to her for life. The second reason was that he had known for some time that Mark imagined himself deep in love with Sylvia. Whether he was really in love scarcely came into it; he thought he was, so Sylvia's blatant attempts to wring an admission of affection – and a proposal of marriage – out of his brother could only be painful to Mark.

The worst of it was that with every day that passed he knew how easy it would be to imagine himself in love. Suppose he was fooled by a romantic moonlit drive into popping the question? He had no doubt that, should he do so, mad or sane, drunk or sober, Sylvia would hold him to it. For there was a streak of ruthlessness about her which accorded ill with her milky skin, the cerulean blue of her eyes.

So what was to be done? Whilst there was the faintest chance of marrying himself, Sylvia would never so much as glance at Mark. Nor, on the other hand, at any of the beaux who surrounded her. He played with the idea of going away, leaving Mark a clear field. It would be good to get away from civilisation for a bit. He could return to the goldfields, or go overseas. He could visit Australia; he had business associates there who would make him welcome!

The clock chiming the hour brought him to his feet. That was his time up. He would go into the dairy, check his letters, see that all was well and then persuade Mark to get a horse from the livery stable and ride with him. They could go fishing, or go back to the farm; there was always work there. Anything except thinking of marriage, in fact, would pass the day pleasantly.

Then, striding straight-backed up the street ahead of him, he saw his father. He hesitated. Was Karl going to the dairy? Strangely enough, his sons' success in business had given Karl the affection for them, which had been previously notable only by its absence. He was proud of them, and took their advice in most things, from the way he dressed and behaved to the way he ran his farm. In fact, he was one of the many local farmers who supplied them with the raw material they needed – milk – to run the dairy on a sound commercial basis.

Seeing Karl about to turn into the dairy foyer, Edward hurried his pace a little, and caught the older man up before he had actually entered the building.

'Father! You look very smart! Are you here on business, or just calling? I had planned to get Mark to throw down his work and come fishing with me.'

The older man turned and greeted his elder son with a smile. Karl's hair was snow-white and he was thinner than of old, but he was sprucely dressed in a dark coat and riding breeches, with highly polished boots on his feet and a soft felt Wide-awake hat on his head. All the bitterness which had lain between them because of Anna's death had dissipated in the years of separation. Edward could see his father's strengths now as well as his weaknesses, even believing that he had truly loved Anna and had bullied and beaten her only because she seemed to expect it.

'Good morning, Edward. You look smart yourself, son! But you won't wear those good clothes to go fishing? What's wrong with overalls and rubber boots?'

Edward, taking his father's arm and steering him into his office, laughed. 'Nothing! Except that I dressed for the office and the sunshine tempted me to take a holiday! Now, what can I do for you?'

He waited until Karl had seated himself in the comfortable visitor's chair opposite his own, then sank into his leather upholstery.

'Nothing; I want nothing. But would you and Mark come on a rabbit shoot, and bring some friends? The MacPhersons, the Murrays, the Seymours, all are over-run with rabbits. So we thought we'd organise a big shoot and get rid of the pests. Or as many as possible, anyway.'

'Yes, we'd enjoy that,' Edward said at once. His business instincts taking over, he added, 'What will happen to the meat, Father? Have you a market for it?'

'Not yet. Have you any ideas?'

'Why not freeze it, and ship it to Australia? No, perhaps not. They've rabbits in plenty of their own. How much sale would there be locally for the meat?'

His father sniffed. 'For vermin? They won't pay for what ruins their own pastures! Do they have rabbits in England?'

Edward began to make a joking reply, then stopped in mid-sentence. 'Hold on! I've had a thought!'

For a moment he struggled with it, then recollection came flooding. He said triumphantly, 'Yes, there might be a market for it in England, if you can persuade your guns to clean and skin their rabbits, and then bring them straight in for freezing. Lately, the top men in the New Zealand Refrigerating Company have been bewailing the fact that Dunedin sheep no longer fill their holds. After this bad winter, with farmers losing large numbers of stock, I'm sure rabbits would sell well if we could guarantee a sufficient quantity.'

Karl nodded. 'I'm sure that can be arranged.' He turned as the door opened to admit his younger son. 'Good morning, Mark.'

'Morning, Father. I didn't know you were in town. What are you plotting, you two?'

A rabbit shoot. And, subsequently, the sale of the meat,' Edward said, rubbing his hands. 'A *big* shoot, Mark, so that there are sufficient rabbits to ship to England.'

Mark grinned. 'I see my brother's business instinct at work here! And the skins, Ted? I suppose you've arranged for them to be sent to London too, so that Queen Victoria may have a Jubilee robe made of New Zealand bunny fur?'

'Now that's a point. I wonder if there would be any sale . . .' Edward stopped short, staring at his brother. 'Mark! You may well be right! The fur is soft and pretty, and, above all, cheap! It could sell very well for trimmings and such, with the Diamond Jubilee next year! I'll mention it to the shipping company when I talk to them about the meat.'

The conversation then turned to other matters, but four days later, on a fine morning with the sun coming up red over the shoulder of the hills, the brothers rode out of the Waihola farmhouse, guns beside their stirrups and friends and neighbours in attendance.

'It's beautiful countryside round here, but not a patch on the Peninsula,' Mark said as they rode down the hill and into the scarves of mist still rising from the silvered surface of the lake. 'Why do you suppose Sylvia wanted to come, Ted?'

For Sylvia had no sooner heard about the shoot than she was hot to accompany them, even when it transpired that she could not shoot and would have to be one of the women who remained at the Waihola homestead to prepare food for the hunting party's return.

'I don't know,' Edward lied. He looked at his brother with affection and compassion. Mark was one of the best, but there was no denying that he was plain – downright homely, in fact. He had reddish hair, freckles, and a thin, anxious face. Edward knew, however, that Mark was worth two of him. He was loyal, loving, and a tremendously hard worker. Sylvia was a fool – but then what woman wasn't, when it came to men?

'She still wants to marry you, Ted. You've only got to say the word, you know that.'

They were riding ahead of the rest of the party, leading the way to the best pastures, and their low-voiced conversation could not be overheard above the soft thumping of horses' hooves on mossy pasture, and the jingle of bits and harness.

'Well, I'm not going to say the word.' There was a pause, and then Edward said quietly, 'Mark, I'm thinking of going away for a bit. Right away, you know, leaving you to manage the dairy and the farm alone. Do you like the idea?'

'Not much. Why?'

Edward shrugged. 'Why not? Look, you know I don't want to marry Sylvia! If I wasn't here, she might turn to someone else.'

Mark tightened his lips. 'She wouldn't turn to me, if that's what you mean.'

'You've got no self-confidence whatsoever, Mark, so how can you expect other people to treat you the way you deserve to be treated? For God's sake, man, Sylvia doesn't *love* me! She just thinks she does.' Not for worlds would he have told Mark that Sylvia loved the Neyler money, the Neyler property, and the thought of being married to an up-and-coming young businessman! 'If I go away, Mark, will you promise me you'll make a push to get Sylvia's interest?'

Mark glanced sideways at his brother. 'If it means so much to you,' he said gruffly. And then, on a lighter note, 'Best dismount now, Ted, and start working our way nearer to the hedges. Don't want the bunnies taking fright.'

The shoot was successful, and the Neyler brothers wended their way home that night, Sylvia riding between them on a neat little blood mare, knowing that rabbits in plenty had been shot.

But it was not until a few days later that Edward's dimly conceived plan to go away and leave Mark a clear field finally crystallised into reality. He was talking to the shipping clerk who was negotiating the sale of the rabbit meat for him.

'Skins? That's not a bad idea, to take a cargo of skins to England,' the man conceded. 'But we couldn't handle it. Why not? Because we've no agents the other end who would know how to sell the furs. What you want to do, Ted, is take them yourself. They'll be decently cleaned and so on? Well then, it won't matter if you can't charter a fast ship, for they'll be none the worse for being at sea a while. I've a brother-in-law who charters sailing ships; he'd undertake the voyage for you, if you went along yourself to sell 'em the other end. Want me to put you in touch with him?'

In the end, it was as simple as that. Edward chartered the

Candida, owned by her captain, Elias Peake, got his affairs in order, and arranged for Mark to have extra help in the office and on the farm for six months.

'Not that I'll be gone that long,' he told his brother with easy optimism. 'It may take a while to reach England, but once there my business will be over in no time and I can get a passage straight home on a fast steamer. A mere thirty-five days, I believe.'

Then he broke the news to Sylvia. He chose his moment well, a fine, summery night when Christmas was passed, and he and Mark had gone with a group of other young people for a moonlight picnic to St Kilda's beach. It was a perfect night, with the full moon shining from a sky as clear and dark blue as ink, and the softest of breezes from the land blowing the good scents of grass and pines over the firm, white sands. The young men built a big bonfire and roasted joints of lamb over it, they pushed potatoes into the red embers, and then they feasted, greasy fingered but happy, boys eyeing girls, girls cuddling closer to the boys of their choice.

Then some bright spark suggested a moonlight swim. Anxious reminders that sharks could – and did – take bathers surrounded by their friends and in full daylight could not deter the would-be swimmers. The men stripped off their clothing, throwing down the straw hats, the gaily striped blazers, the elegant, highly polished shoes. Some went in mother-naked, others clung to their shirts. Edward, laughing and shouting at Mark to make haste, dropped his trousers on the tide line and ran into the gentle, creaming surf. He kicked it up, into his own face, then dived through an incoming wave, feeling the water sparkling like fizzy champagne over his shoulders, knowing he could swim like a fish and had a magnificent physique, that at least half the girls on the beach had been watching him as he entered the water.

He swam well out, then let the water cradle him on his back and looked up at the infinity of stars. I am not leaving New Zealand for Mark, but because I don't want to be tied to Sylvia, he told himself severely. Come to that, I'm not leaving New Zealand, because it is the land of my birth and I love it with all my heart. I am just going away, for a little while, and when I come back I most sincerely hope that Sylvia will be married to someone else. Then Mark and I can go back to our pleasant, carefree, bachelor existence.

He liked women and enjoyed their company, so he had no intention of becoming a hermit. If, when he returned, Sylvia was still keen on him, she would have to be firmly discouraged. Indeed, had it not been for Mark he would have discouraged her pretty firmly a while back! As it was . . . he turned on his front and began swimming for the shore again at a fast crawl, his arms curving out of the water with the speed and rhythm of a war canoe's paddles. As it was, he would grasp at this chance to see England and perhaps do some good business, and enjoy every minute of it. And when the shore was reached and he was respectably dressed once more, he would hand Sylvia up into his waggonette and break the news to her.

The fact that this did not go entirely according to plan was his fault for not allowing for the human factor, he thought afterwards. Sylvia, it seemed, was very angry with him for bathing. Mark, she pointed out, had been about to join him when he had realised that this would leave Sylvia alone on the beach without an escort! Edward nobly refrained from pointing out that she would have been in good company, with a large proportion of the other young men disporting themselves in the sea also. Instead, he humbly begged pardon, and assured her that Mark was much more the gentleman than he.

'But I'm off to England, you know, in a few days,' he told her, as though it was the most natural thing in the world, and no more than a walk down the street. 'Perhaps my manners will improve then, amongst all the lords and ladies!'

She was silent for a moment, then said stiffly, 'I see. And when, pray, may we expect to see you home once more?'

He shrugged, glancing sideways at her face, white with anger and moonlight. 'Six months, nine months? Something of that nature, I suppose.'

'You've planned this to make me look ridiculous,' she said bitterly, her voice tense with anger. 'You must know that people say what a lovely couple we make, how we're made for each other! They're waiting for us to tell them *when* we mean to marry, not if! But you are going away, without any sort of warning, just to spite me.'

This was too uncomfortably near the truth for Edward to deny it with much conviction, but he said, 'Sylvia, my dear, what nonsense,' as bracingly as he could, following it up with, 'Everyone knows you could have any man you choose! Why should they assume you would choose me?'

She gave an angry sob, but made no attempt to answer him, and the rest of the drive was accomplished in icy silence on her part, while Edward only felt capable of the most trivial remarks.

He saw her to the door of her parents' house, and then drove back out to the Peninsula farmhouse, half pleased with the evening, half sorry.

'We quarrelled,' he told Mark, who was waiting up for him in the large kitchen with a hot drink and a plate of sandwiches. 'If you ask me, little brother, she's a shrew, for all she's got a pretty face and a degree in languages.'

But Mark, grinning, would not allow her to be less than perfect, so the brothers went to their beds, both quite satisfied with the evening's work.

The evening before his ship was to sail, the Otago Hussars gave an all-male party for Edward. He and Mark had joined the Hussars when they first moved into Dunedin, and very much enjoyed the meetings and manoeuvres, since both were bruising riders, proud of their skill with a rifle.

In the way of such events, it turned, fairly rapidly, into a drinking party and Edward, knowing his ability to hold his liquor, downed countless pints of the strong dark local brew, and grew at first merry and loquacious, then taciturn, then downright dejected.

Mark, also drinking heavily, admitted in a slurred voice that he was dreading being in charge of the farm and dairy.

'N-not got your shtrength of p-purposh, ole Ed,' he mumbled. 'Nor your way wi' the shtaff, either.'

'Can't think why I ever 'greed to go,' Edward admitted. 'Don' wanna see England, don' care about th'old Queen, don' like the Brits above half. Wi-wish I'd not booked a pashage.'

It was remarks like this which led to the entire party abandoning the hall and taking to their horses. Edward, feeling the night air on his face as he rode down the street with his fellow Hussars, felt remarkably fit and not at all the worse for drink. In fact, on the road which led to the beach he distinctly remembered thinking that he had never felt better.

That was the last thing he did remember, apart from a confused picture of the road and the trees which lined it suddenly changing places, a feeling of flying through warm air, and then a bump which slid him painlessly into oblivion.

He came to himself once, to hear drunken giggles and hoarse cries as he was half carried, half dragged, up a flight of stairs and tumbled inexpertly into a bed. Then he slept.

He was woken by long fingers of sunshine reaching his face and exploring his closed eyelids. He opened one eye and sweat broke out on his forehead as the top of his head became roughly detached for an instant, then crashed back into place with an appalling judder.

He lay still, afraid to move, the inside of his eyelids glowing a brilliant, head-splitting scarlet. Presently he moved his head, very, very carefully, out of reach of the sunbeams and into cool blue shade. With infinite caution he opened one eye again, then the other. Where was he? And what, in the name of heaven, had he done last night to wake up with a hangover like this?

He squinted round the room; it was strange to him, and yet . . . suddenly it leapt back into his mind. This was the Maxwell place on Princes Street South! Otto, a fellow Hussar, had given them beds before in his uncle's Accommodation House and Restaurant; no doubt, realising that

Edward would want an early start . . .

An early start! Suddenly it all came crashing back to him and he sat up too quickly, cringing, statue-still, until his head returned to its perch on his shoulders.

Today I was to have sailed at dawn for England. Captain Peake had made it plain that a sailing ship could not just up anchor and leave when it chose; it had to do so when the tide and wind were right. They had been right at dawn. And the skins had been loaded yesterday. Therefore, judging by what he'd seen of the sunshine pouring in through a crack in the curtains – a quick, shrinking glance confirmed his fears – then he had missed the *Candida!*

Quickly but carefully he reached for his clothes. He had been put to bed in the raw, for which he was grateful, since the thought of taking off a borrowed nightshirt, probably several sizes too small, was not pleasant. He dressed, clumsy-fingered in his careful haste, then stepped across the floor as if it were made of ice and went into the corridor.

It was dim out here; kind to bloodshot eyes, he thought with wry humour. There were four doors, any one of which might hide Mark – unless his brother had been well enough to get home, which he doubted. He tried the door next to his own and knew he was right, seeing Mark lying on his back, his mouth open, a snore issuing from his lips. He woke at once to the sound of his name, hoarsely hissed.

'Ted? What's the matter?'

'I think I've missed the ship,' Edward said. 'I'm going down to the harbour. Coming?'

'Oh my God! I'll come.'

'Thanks, Mark. My luggage went down yesterday; I wonder if they took it to England with them? Or perhaps something happened to delay the sailing. You follow me. I've got to know.'

Soon enough, he knew. There, on the sunny quayside, was his luggage. Alone it stood, with a skinny cat curled up in the patch of shadow it cast, watching with hungry curiosity the antics of some birds pecking and scratching at the cobbles nearby.

Edward's eyes went to the patch of water where, yesterday, the *Candida* had swung at anchor. Nothing. Only lazy ripples slapping against the harbour wall and sunshine glinting on a patch of multi-coloured oil. A solitary gull, eyes half-closed against the sun, bobbed with the sea-swell.

'What's to be done, Ted?'

Mark's anxious voice jerked him out of his trance.

'That steamer – right at the far end of the harbour, near the warehouses – it's a refrigeration ship, isn't it? Where's it bound? When does it sail? Today?'

'That? It's the mutton ship, for London, I think. It should sail fairly soon, but . . .'

'Mark, I must buy a passage, and at once! The skins will arrive at Ipswich in three months or so, and no one will know what to do with them. On the mutton ship, I can be in Ipswich before them. I must go!'

'Have you enough money?'

Edward patted his pockets. 'Curses, no! Rush back to the dairy, Mark, and fetch me . . . well, say fifty pounds; bring it straight down here. With a little bit of luck, and some fast thinking . . .'

He watched as Mark set off, at a run, back towards the dairy, then turned towards the shipping offices.

Two hours later Edward stood at the rail of the fast steamer, watching Dunedin fade into the distance. They had done it! He had a cabin berth, quite a good one, with plenty of room for his trunks, and he would arrive in England in thirty-five days – considerably sooner than his own ship!

There was a stiff breeze blowing but Edward, who was never seasick, was untroubled by the motion. Fortunately, his hangover had dissipated under the influence of working to get his berth booked and, it must be confessed, after four cups of strong black coffee, administered by a disapproving waitress in a nearby coffee shop.

Leaning on the rail, seeing the waves grow larger as they drew further off from land, feeling the wind tugging at his hair, Edward thought wonderingly, all this so that I can get rid of Sylvia and Mark can take up with her! All this because one strong-willed, spoilt girl makes up her mind to marry . . .

A voice at his elbow said: 'Isn't it a beautiful day to start a voyage, sir?'

He turned sharply, and for a moment his heart sank; he saw golden hair and blue eyes, a shapely figure clad in navy and white, and thought for a ghastly moment that Sylvia had somehow contrived to follow him aboard. But then he saw that this girl had hair which was more honey-coloured than gold, that her eyes shone more grey than blue.

'Yes, a very good day,' he said politely. 'May I introduce myself? I'm Edward Neyler, of Dunedin. And you are . . . ?'

'Susan Reid, of Invercargill. Are you travelling all the way to England, sir?'

'I am indeed, Miss Reid. I'm going over on business, in connection with my firm. And yourself?'

She smiled, revealing small white teeth and a dimple beside her mouth. 'I'm going to visit my grandparents. Imagine, I'm nineteen years old and they've never seen me! So Grandpapa, who lives in Ayr, sent my parents my passage money, and he will meet me when the ship docks and take me to Scotland.'

She smiled again, dimpling at him, and Edward swallowed. He had a weakness for dimples.

'And you are travelling alone, Miss Reid?'

'Well, yes. But in the captain's care, of course.'

'Then since I, too, am travelling alone, we must be friends,' Edward said. Upon her blushingly declaring she would like that, he took her hand, tucked it into his arm, and proposed that they should explore the ship together. As they strolled along, peering into hatchways, investigating the dining saloon, the lounges and the shelter deck, he thought of the old proverb, 'When one door closes another opens.' It was true, evidently, of love affairs as well as of doors!

Happily casting Sylvia's wiles into oblivion, Edward prepared for his first shipboard romance.

10

'I assure you, Poppa, a domesticated Tina is not nice to live with! You don't know, you're out of the house so much, but for us, especially during the school holidays . . .' Cecy shuddered expressively. 'Well, it's become almost more than I can bear! She's so bossy one cannot have a discussion, much less an argument, with her. She lays down the law and will listen to no one!'

Arthur, sitting comfortably in his red leather armchair drawn up before his study fire, turned slightly reproachful eyes up to his daughter, standing before him, her face pink at her own temerity but her eyes pleading for understanding.

'She does well, your sister. This family she runs like clockwork, a mother she is to the younger ones. And yet you, who should support her, complain? Cecy, your poppa thought better of you! More generous I thought you!'

Cecy's face went a deeper pink, but her gaze did not waver. 'I'm sorry, Poppa, but I had to tell someone, though I knew you'd be angry. You don't understand . . ..'

'Why angry? Should I be angry because my little girls disagree?'

'Not angry, perhaps, but hurt, because you think I'm criticising Tina.'

Arthur picked up his pipe from the table near his elbow and began to fill it from his tobacco pouch.

'Yes, hurt is right. I am a little hurt. But my hurt is for Tina, not for myself. So hard that child works! Marketing, planning, cooking . . . and still she finds time for the little things Momma did! The evening story before bed she reads, the homework she helps with, the special gifts she buys. You are jealous, perhaps, of her abilities?'

'No, Poppa! She's so good in many ways; I could not be jealous of her. But Poppa, I want to help too! She lets me do nothing. Suppose she were to marry and leave us. When Momma was alive we used to learn cooking, dressmaking, how to trim the lamps, the best way to dress a cheap joint. But now, Tina either does things herself, or sets the maids to do them.'

'Now, that is not right, Cecy! I have heard complaining, when you say Tina makes you too hard to work! Groans from you, miss, when Alice was away and you had to do the ironing! And Becky, who is nearly eight, complaining because to a party she had to take Louis, her own brother!'

'I don't deny she lets me help with the dull jobs,' Cecy said rather bitterly. 'I'm sure I'd make a very good washerwoman, or indeed housemaid, for she's very happy for us to wash, and iron, or dust and sweep carpets, especially when Alice or Tess is away. But I don't *want* to be a housemaid, Poppa! I want to be someone's wife, and cooking, shopping, using the sewing machine, these are things for Tina alone. Anyone would think koshering meat was some sort of secret rite, the way she carries on! Not letting me into the kitchen, screaming at me if I so much as look at her beef, koshering away. As if I would defile it by looking too closely! Poppa, such things are important for girls to know. Momma taught Tina, and had begun to teach me. But now . . .'

'I see, I see. Yet you must try to understand, Cecy. You go to school, but Tina left when Mutti died, and never has a complaint passed her lips, never a reproach to Poppa who forced her to give up so much! School she loved, for she was so clever, so good at her lessons, yet she uses her good brain now just to do your homeworks, when you are puzzled. Hockey, too, she loved. She must miss it, yes? To rush across the field, waving her hockey stick, smiting the ball, screaming for her team!'

'No, well, at least she doesn't come home with her ankles black and blue,' muttered Cecy, no lover of hockey. 'But

Poppa, I *do* understand how she feels. And I *still* think I should be allowed in the kitchen. I'm fourteen, and I can't make a bagel, or cook pancakes, or sew a straight seam. At school, they say such things will be taught us by our mothers. And I say again, if Tina *did* leave home, we should be in a pretty pickle!'

'Tina won't leave home! Foolish little Cecy, she is not yet sixteen! Where would she go, what would she do? But I believe you are right. Is it just that you aren't allowed to cook that worries you? Or is there something more?'

Cecy blushed and sat, without being asked, in the chair opposite Poppa's. She rested her chin in her hand, then sat upright, giving herself a brisk shake. 'It is mostly that I think I ought to be able to cook and sew. But there is something else, something which has brought this to a head and forced me to tell you how I feel. The truth is, if we're forced to eat another of Tina's suppers I think we shall *all* leave home, even Louis!'

Completely bewildered, Arthur took his pipe out of his mouth and stared at his second daughter. 'Leave home? Suppers? What means this?'

'You have dinner at night, right? But we children have high tea, then we do school work, play games, read books. And then, just before bedtime, we have supper.'

Arthur nodded impatiently. 'Right, right, right! So what is this about leaving home?'

'I'll tell you, Poppa, but in my own way. This supper is served by Tina in our room, usually about eight-thirty, because by that time Louis and Rachel have had their baths and have come downstairs in their dressing-gowns, to say goodnight and have their bedtime story. And Becky hasn't gone up for her bath.'

'Yes, yes. So?'

'So every night for a year we've had rye bread, salami and pickled onions for supper. Once or twice, when even Louis has complained, she's changed the salami for liverwurst, or for that peppery German sausage she loves, and sometimes she serves a granary loaf instead of rye bread, and gherkins instead of the onions. Every night, Poppa!'

Arthur's lips twitched, and he hastily began to puff on his pipe. 'Every night? No change for a whole year? Ever since Grandma died, in fact?'

Cecy nodded. 'Every night the same,' she confirmed. 'And luncheon on the Sabbath, in Momma's time, used to be a *cholent* in winter, or some other food which could be kept hot from Friday. But now it is nearly always cold meat and pickles. You aren't often home, you see. It is only when you're home that we get a good hot meal. And those suppers!' She borrowed from his vocabulary. 'Ay-yi-yi, how sick of them we are!'

'But why so monotonous a diet does she choose?' Arthur asked, in genuine astonishment. 'Good, varied dinners we have! A fine breakfast she puts before me each day. I don't understand!'

'It's her favourite food,' Cecy explained. 'She can't see that other people don't want to live on salami and pickles! And also, of course, it's easy to prepare. Alice is usually busy at suppertime, bathing the younger children and seeing that everything is ready for breakfast next morning. That means Tina gets the supper.'

Visited by a horrid suspicion, Arthur said abruptly: 'Cecy, *can* Tina cook? Momma taught her a little perhaps, and Grandma may have let Tina make a cake occasionally, but now I think about it, Tina never cooked a meal while Grandma was alive! Do you think Alice does *all* the cooking?'

'I don't know,' confessed Cecy. 'She won't let us into the kitchen to find out! But if I could learn to cook – well, Poppa, you may say that Tina won't leave us, but what about Alice? She has a great many admirers, and will certainly marry one day. What about *that?*'

Arthur, thinking of the magnificent roasts, the fluffy Yorkshire puddings, the stews and casseroles and jugged hares, swallowed nervously. He had always assumed that Tina was responsible for these delicacies, not the maid, who might indeed leave tomorrow!

'You done right to tell me,' he said. 'I misjudged you, *bubeleh*. Certainly you must learn to cook and so, if she cannot already do so, must Tina. Send her to me!'

'If I do, she'll guess I've been complaining,' Cecy said, showing the whites of her eyes. 'She'll be mad as fire, Poppa!'

Arthur gave this his consideration. 'I'll go and see her, bring the cooking up casual,' he decided. 'Where is she now?'

Cecy glanced at the clock. 'Making our supper, in the kitchen.'

Despite himself, Arthur chuckled. 'Opening a jar of pickled onions, eh? Now is the time! You return to your room and I'll take a little stroll towards the kitchen.'

He heaved himself out of the chair, adjusted his grip on his sticks, and swung himself out of the study. Following, Cecy watched as he thumped across the hall and disappeared into the kitchen. He had put on a little weight and his hair was greying at the temples, but he was still a fine figure of a man. He was a wonderful man, her poppa!

In the kitchen, Tina's reaction was somewhat different. 'Give Cecy cooking lessons?' she said incredulously. 'Oh, no, Poppa, I'm far too busy.'

'Then Alice may do so,' Arthur said imperturbably. 'It will be to your advantage in the long run, my child. Now, an idea! How would it be if Cecy, just for a start, made supper every night? Not a big meal it is, not difficult, but it would give her some idea, no?' He met her suspicious gaze limpidly. 'You have the little ones to bath and put to bed, so many things to do. It would of the greatest assistance be!'

'Yes, but . . . well, there isn't much work in making supper, and I don't want Cecy muddling and messing in my kitchen! Just at supper-time too, when Alice and I are far too busy to guide and assist her. I really don't think . . .'

'But what is this I see? My poor child you are in such a hurry that you have only cut bread and salami for supper? Fie upon you for not begging Cecy's help, for so bad for the digestion is sausage, late at night. And pickles . . . ! But I don't need to tell you. To try to sleep on a bellyful of pickles! Ach, horrible. If this is Alice's work, a good thing to have Cecy to help you.'

'It doesn't stop *me* from sleeping,' Tina snapped, stung. 'What's wrong with a nice slice of salami on good fresh rye bread? They've had it every night for ages, and no one's said they couldn't sleep!'

'Every night for . . . but Tina mine, how dull, and how their little stomachs must rebel,' Arthur said sternly. 'Is it that I don't pay you sufficient money for good food? Is there nothing else in the house for supper tonight?'

Tina hesitated. If she confessed there was other food, he would insist that she use it and perhaps she might no longer be able to serve salami and pickles every night. It was so quick and easy, she thought wistfully. And so delicious! On the other hand, if she pretended there was only sausage and pickles, he might send Cecy poking round the pantry to see what she could find. She said reluctantly, 'Well, there's a madeira cake which Alice made yesterday, and I've always got eggs, fruit, vegetables, that sort of thing. And bread of course, and milk.'

He beamed at her. 'Good, good! Then tonight the children shall have lightly boiled eggs with bread and butter, followed by Madeira cake and hot milk. You can manage that?'

'Of course. I suppose I had better put the eggs on soon, since Louis must be in the bath now.'

Arthur crossed the room and gave his eldest child a hug. 'Tina mine, tell me the truth! Good meals you serve, and a beautiful, welcoming home you keep. But how much of the cooking is done by you and how much by Alice?'

'I do a great deal of cooking,' Tina said, but she avoided her father's eye. 'I bake all the bread, and I can make chicken soup and potato *blintzes*. And then the special things, like preparing food in a kosher way, making *farfel, matzo* balls, the Jewish things, I do them. And I *could* do all the cooking! All the roasting and baking. But . . .'

Arthur hugged her again, then lifted her chin with his free hand so that she was forced to meet his eyes. 'Tina, Tina, Tina! Would it not be a good idea if you and Cecy had some lessons from Alice?'

'You mean that knowing is not like doing?' Tina sighed.

'I suppose you're right, Poppa. But . . . but I won't have lessons with Cecy. I don't want her to know I don't do all the cooking!'

'I think perhaps already she suspects, Tina mine. But does she think badly of you for it? Of course not! Why should you cook, when Alice is here to do it? So many other things to do you have! Only you would like to learn, eh?'

'Yes, I would. And Poppa, I can teach Cecy to bake bread, and make a good strudel, truly I can!'

He patted her cheek, then crossed the kitchen and opened the door into the hall. 'That's my girl. Tina, mine, you will find out as you older grow that the hardest thing is to let go a little. Today you have done a hard thing.'

He closed the door gently behind him and Tina went across to the pantry and found the tin with the Madeira cake in it. Presently the door opened again and Cecy came in, looking self-conscious and pink cheeked.

'Tina? Poppa said to come and help you get supper.'

Tina looked up with well simulated surprise. 'Oh, thanks, Cecy. Could you get out five eggs, and put them on the stove, in a pan of water? We're having boiled eggs with bread and butter, followed by Madeira cake and hot milk, so if you could put the eggs on to boil that would be a help.'

'Of course. I do want to help! How long should the eggs boil for, Tina?'

Tina considered, frowning. 'Well, we want them lightly boiled, so I should think twenty, twenty-five minutes would be long enough.'

It says a lot for Cecy's good nature that she ate her bullet-like egg that evening without one word of complaint, and sternly suppressed attempts by the younger children to complain while Tina was present.

And later, in the quiet of their own bedroom, Cecy said humbly, 'Poppa said you and Alice are to give me cookery lessons, Tina. When will I have the first one, and what shall I learn to cook?'

'Well, not tomorrow night, because Poppa's bringing a business acquaintance home for dinner, and everything will have to be just so. But you might have a lesson on Sunday.

You'll start with something simple, of course; perhaps you could make the porridge.'

'Or boil the eggs, perhaps?' Cecy said innocently into the darkness.

In the silence which followed she wondered apprehensively whether Tina was going to be offended and then, with relief, heard a smothered chuckle. 'Yes indeed, boil some eggs! For I don't mind telling you, Cecilia, that those eggs we had for supper tonight had been cooked far too long!'

Arthur, sitting beside the dying fire in his study, drinking hot milk generously laced with rum, thought smugly that he had managed a difficult situation rather skilfully – no, damn it, *very* skilfully! But he could not help reflecting that it had forcefully brought home to him the fact that Tina was living an unnatural life, and had been doing so ever since Mutti's death. After Deborah had died, things had changed remarkably little. They had employed a nursemaid, Jessie, to keep an eye on the children still not at school, and a kitchenmaid, Tess, to help out with the rough work. Alice had been promoted to Mutti's right-hand woman, and in the main things had gone on much as before. Tina and Cecy had continued to attend their classes at the High School, had gone off to dancing lessons and hockey practices with their friends, had filled the house with giggling young girls.

Then, barely a year later, Mutti had died in her sleep. It had been a quiet, almost contented passing, for Mutti was over ninety. But it had turned the house upside down in a way which Deborah's death had not. Tina had left school, had given up her dancing classes, her piano lessons, and, without perhaps even realising it, her friends. Oh, Lizbeth, Barbara, Sarah and Paulina had been faithful at first, but gradually their visits had ceased until only Lizbeth remained. And even she, with school and classes and a budding interest in young men, was not as often at the Roses' as Arthur would have liked.

And what of Tina herself? She certainly managed the house beautifully, but Arthur knew she was stricter with the children than either Deborah or Mutti had been. Games which might untidy their room were no longer allowed, even when school preparation was completed. No friends might be brought back to play unless Tina had been consulted and had given her permission. Often it was easier to play at a friend's house than to run the gauntlet of obtaining Tina's permission for the same friend to spend an hour with them.

Louis, to be sure, suffered little, because Arthur insisted that his son should play freely with his peers and not be subject to unending petticoat government, but Tina kept her younger sisters on a very tight rein.

Tina's social life, Arthur acknowledged now, is simply non-existent. She is a young girl, a pretty young girl, rising sixteen, yet she goes nowhere, meets no one. Oh, she goes to Shul and meets the half-dozen members of the congregation who are of a similar age, but she's known them all her life, and has never shown any interest in or friendship for any of them!

She ought to be at school still, he told himself. Mixing with girls her own age, playing games, learning to dance and sing. He had noticed that at Shul it was tall, handsome Sybil Goldstein who had two or three boys talking to her after the services, and never his Tina, though they were of an age and Tina, he was sure, far the prettier. Sybil had a large nose which would become a commanding beak in five years, whereas Tina's small, straight nose, inherited from Deborah, seemed unlikely to change.

Tina had no self-confidence with young men, he realised. She was mistress of his house, a substitute mother to her younger sisters and brother, but she was losing the trick of easy intercourse with her peers.

He comforted himself with the reflection that it was highly unlikely her future husband would be one of the boys who attended the Shul in Norwich. In a year or two, when she was more mature, he would see that she met other young people; would take her up to London and introduce her to business acquaintances of the faith. It would make up to her for these lost years.

He realised, of course, that he would have to overcome some opposition from Tina herself, who was wholly absorbed by her housewifely tasks. He did not understand her well enough to realise that she was merely filling the aching void left when first her mother, then her grandmother, and finally her school life and friends, had been taken from her, but he did see clearly that she was an extremely intelligent girl who suddenly found herself with nothing to occupy her brain. At the High School her brain had been stretched to its full intellectual capacity and she had revelled in the challenge of competition. So when all this had gone she had determined to make herself into the best housekeeper and substitute mother anyone had ever known.

Once she had confided in him that hard work in the house was good for keeping depression at bay, and that being sharp and practical with the children stopped her from missing Momma. His heart had bled for her; though he missed Deborah more than his children could possibly have imagined, for he was a man who had always enjoyed the physical side of marriage. He had wondered, at first, whether he might marry again, but the thought of a young woman trying to take over the house, arguing with Tina, possibly giving birth each year to another child, discouraged him. If he had been questioned on the subject, he would have said piously that he owed it to Deborah's children not to marry again. The truth was that he was too lazy to begin trying to meet someone suitable, and dreaded the thought of being forced to please a young wife by taking her to social events, entertaining her family, and sacrificing the even tenor of his days, which gave him, on the whole, a good deal of satisfaction.

Abruptly he remembered his dinner guest. He was glad he had asked him back for a meal, because he was a much-travelled young man, cheerful, independent, with plenty to say for himself and an intelligent way of saying it. It will be good for Tina to meet a young man from the Antipodes, he told himself. The fact that the young man in question was over six feet tall, had thick golden hair and blue eyes, and must be considered strikingly handsome, never occurred to him. Tina was a child, after all!

The clock struck midnight and Arthur heaved himself out of his chair and made for the door. He was late to bed, and that meant he would probably find difficulty in waking when Alice brought his early-morning cup of tea. And tomorrow he wanted to be at the factory in good time, to show his prospective guest the very shoes he wanted trimming.

In the hall he turned off the gas and made his way through the darkened house to his lonely bed.

11

Swinging his cane, dressed in his striped flannel suit and his stiff-collared white shirt with the red silk tie, Edward made his way, unhurriedly, across the city of Norwich. He was still unfamiliar with the place, but had taken the precaution, when Arthur Rose had issued his invitation, of getting a copy of a street map from a local newsagent. Now, with the help of the map, he could make his way quickly and accurately to Bishopsgate.

He wondered as he walked what his host's home would be like. He was lodging in a small house in King Street run by a friendly little soul, a widow-woman called Mrs Ellen Capper. Her rooms smelt of cooking cabbage, of coppers boiling load after load of sheets and towels, of stale food and of dust. The small parlour where Mrs Capper's 'gentlemen' might sit of an evening was crowded with furniture, all hard and prickly, with ornaments on every surface, and fringes, cushions, antimacassars, runners, lace drapes, bobbles and many other strange objects which Edward could not name.

Was this how the average Englishman furnished the average home? Edward did not think so, but he could not be sure. This evening he would find out! He hoped that Mr Rose's wife would be a good cook, for poor Mrs Capper was not. He had only been lodging with her a week, but already he had suffered her shepherd's pie, her boiled cod in white sauce, and a solid white object which she assured them was rice pudding. A fellow guest, correctly interpreting Edward's half-hearted attempt to stab an undercooked, greenish potato, whispered, 'Wait till you taste 'er cabinet pudding, mate! It's made out of a real cabinet, I swear!'

As he neared Bishopsgate, Edward could smell the river. It was a good smell on a mild February evening with the stars pricking the night sky above his head. It smelled of clean, country river banks, and, faintly, of salt.

He turned into Bishopsgate and began to glance at the numbers as he passed them. He reached the Roses' establishment and lifted the latch on the tall wrought-iron gates. In through them, up a short gravelled driveway and the house was before him. He thought there was a creeper over the walls, but could not be sure in the dusk. The front door was gained by a short flight of steps, scrubbed to a glistening white and clearly seen because a gas light illumined them. The door had a brass knocker shaped like a lion's head. He lifted it, let it fall. It rapped briskly, the sound echoing in the evening hush.

The door shot open immediately, so quickly that he suspected someone had been watching for him. It was Arthur Rose, standing tall on his two sticks, his face beaming with pleasure at his guest's arrival.

'Mr Neyler! Welcome to my home, sir!'

He stepped into the hall, a little dazzled by the sudden light after so much darkness. Shaking Arthur's proffered hand, he heard him asking how he had found the house, heard himself answer. But his attention was not with his host.

Standing behind Arthur and a little to the left, plainly waiting to be introduced, was a girl. She was small and slender, with black hair parted in the middle and drawn into a thick, soft bun on the top of her head, giving her additional height. He gazed and gazed, seeing that she had the most beautiful dark blue eyes, the straightest little nose. He smiled at her and she smiled back and two deep dimples sprang to life beside her kissable mouth.

'And this, Mr Neyler, is my eldest daughter, Miss Tina Rose.'

He held out his hand and took hers, feeling the slender, strong little bones, the smoothness of her skin, filled with a deep delight in her.

'Would you let Alice take your coat, Mr Neyler?'

He wrenched his eyes from her small face, suddenly horribly aware that he had scarcely heard a word that had been said, wondering if he had been guilty of other social solecisms while his attention had been so totally caught.

'My coat. Yes, of course, of course,' he stammered, letting Arthur help him off with it and handing it to the maid almost without registering the fact that she was a very pretty girl too; blonde, pert-featured.

'And now, before we dine I must ask you to accompany me to my study, to try a glass of a new sherry wine which has only recently been delivered. I think it good, but your opinion I would value, eh, Tina? Mr Neyler, you know, comes all the way from New Zealand, where no doubt they have a good local wine.'

They had crossed the hall and entered a pleasant, masculine room, the walls lined with books and sporting prints, the furniture consisting of a huge desk with a chair behind it, and some comfortable red leather armchairs. Arthur poured him a drink and waved him to a chair.

'Sit down, Mr Neyler, drink your wine, and enjoy! Tina mine, sit for a little also, and I will pour you some sherry, for you are a big girl, eh?' He laughed, indicating his daughter's small stature, then pressed her into the chair. 'My Tina is my housekeeper, ever since her momma died,' he informed his guest. 'Such a good girl she is! Such a cook! But you shall see presently.'

Edward sat down and sipped at his brimming glass. The

sherry was good, he realised, through the bemusing mist in which he moved. 'Your health, Miss Rose,' he said.

She smiled at him, taking a sip out of her own glass and trying to prevent the look of startled distaste which sprang to her eyes. He guessed she was not much in the habit of drinking sherry.

'Thank you. Dinner will be served very soon, but before then you must meet the rest of the family. We shall all dine together tonight, for we're very informal, are we not, Poppa?'

Arthur murmured assent and Edward replied, 'We New Zealanders aren't given to overmuch ceremony, Miss Rose. You have younger sisters and brothers, then? Your mama . . .?'

Arthur surged forward, dragging another chair before the fire. 'My dear wife died two years since.' He shook his head, his expression lugubrious. 'Tina has to be mother to three younger sisters and my son, Louis. Hers is not an easy life.'

'It's a very pleasant life,' Tina said primly. She turned to Edward again. 'What do you do in the shoe trade, Mr Neyler?'

Edward laughed. 'Well, nothing, Miss Rose!'

'Mr Neyler is a farmer and dairy owner from Dunedin, Tina mine. He is also in shipping!'

Both men laughed, and Edward said easily, 'Your papa is teasing me, Miss Rose. The truth is that my brother and I farm and run a milk processing business, and I have come to England to try to sell rabbit skins. You see, rabbits are a pest to farmers, and we organised a big shoot to rid our land of them. It occurred to me that, with the Queen's Diamond Jubilee in June, I might very easily sell the furs in England. They are pretty, and will do very well for trimming boots, shoes, mittens and the like. They don't cost as much as ermine, but are every bit as soft and warm! So I chartered a ship and set out for England.'

'And Poppa is buying some of the skins for his boots and slippers!' Tina put in. 'Is the fur pretty? May I see some?'

'My ship hasn't arrived yet, Miss Rose. I . . . er, I didn't travel aboard her. Business matters kept me, and I caught a later vessel. But when she does arrive, I will escort you to Ipswich myself and you may see the skins brought ashore – that is, if your papa will allow me to do so.'

'But if you caught a later sailing, Mr Neyler, why are you here before your chartered vessel?' That was Arthur, finishing his sherry and getting up to pour more into the tall, crystal glasses.

'The *Candida* is an elderly sailing ship,' Edward admitted. 'I couldn't have afforded to charter a fast steamer, because then I should have been forced to charge more for the rabbit skins than I wished. My own sailing time was thirty-five days, but the poor old *Candida* will take more like sixty or seventy days. In a couple of weeks I shall go down to Ipswich and ask at the port for news of her. If I've not been telegraphed by then to say that she's docked, of course.'

At that point there was a knock on the door and what seemed, to Edward's bemused eye, to be a positive tribe of small children entered the room. They lined up on the hearthrug by Arthur's chair while he introduced them.

'Cecilia, next in age to Tina.'

The eldest of the small group, a plump girl with curly brown hair and a heart-shaped face, curtseyed and smiled shyly.

'Becky and Rachel, who are inseparable.'

Two little girls of eight or nine, with dark hair, blue eyes and sweet, shy little smiles.

'And my son. My Louis.'

A handsome little boy of about five, with curly black hair, bold black eyes and a nose which already showed a tendency to be masterfully hooked, grinned at Edward and stepped forward to hold his hand out, but said in a voice of deep disappointment, 'I thought he'd be *black!* You said from the Antip . . . well, I did, anyhow!'

The other children were laughing; Arthur was trying to look shocked and not succeeding very well. Louis, plainly, was the apple of his father's eye.

'I'm sorry to disappoint you, Louis, but it's the Maoris, the native New Zealanders, who are . . . well, not black, precisely, more brown,' Edward said gravely. 'I'm a first-generation New Zealander, you see.'

The boy stared. 'What were you before?'

'My father was German, my mother Scottish,' Edward explained. 'I guess that makes me sound like a mongrel dog, but a great many New Zealanders who live in the Otago Province have Scottish ancestors.'

Another tap on the door heralded Alice, the words 'Dinner is served' on her lips.

Louis, his questions promptly forgotten, gave a cheer and Tina said reprovingly, 'Louis! Tell our guest that we ourselves are first-generation English! If one can call Jews first-generation anything, that is.'

Edward had not realised they were Jewish, but he said at once, 'Why not? Why, I cannot even call myself of one religion, for my mother was Presbyterian and my father Lutheran.'

He held out his arm, and tucked Tina's small hand into the crook of his elbow. 'There we are. We shall go into dinner in style. Only you'll have to tell me where to go, or we'll end up in the kitchen!'

Arthur, following them, thought what a nice fellow Edward Neyler was. Treating his little Tina like a fully-grown woman, taking her arm and smiling down at her in such a kindly fashion, and answering Louis in a calm, sensible way; not talking down to him as some people did.

Once seated, grace was said and Alice served the soup. Arthur beamed as Edward exclaimed at the delicious flavour.

'It is chicken soup with *farfel,*' he explained. 'My Tina had the recipe from her grandma. She was a wonderful Jewish cook, and Tina will be as good, when she is full-grown.'

Edward raised his brows and smiled at his young hostess. Her dress was a smoky blue, cut low across her white breasts, the puffed sleeves making her arms look slim and childish in contrast. 'Is it difficult, Miss Rose? Cooking according to the Jewish law?'

Tina smiled back and took a spoonful of soup before replying. 'Cooking in some Jewish homes must be very complicated. But though we would not eat pork or shellfish, and I always kosher any meat and poultry we buy, we are not as strict as many. I think it may be because we spent a number of years in America, in a very tiny town, and though my mother did her best, it was impossible always to eat as we ought. And Poppa lived rough in the American West, where he ate what food was available and cooked it himself. So you see, we are not very orthodox.'

'What rules do you observe then, Miss Rose?'

He had asked the question to hear her voice again; it was a clear, decided little voice, but with a musical quality which made it fascinating to him.

'Rules? Well, we don't eat flour in any form during the Passover, we don't eat meat and milk at the same meal – not often, anyway – and I never use animal fat for cooking,' Tina said, ticking the items off on her fingers. 'But Poppa says that many of the laws were made for hygienic and not religious reasons, so he doesn't think it necessary to adhere too strictly to such laws.'

'This is for your ears only, Neyler,' Arthur broke in, placing a finger on the side of his nose. 'We have many Jewish friends and business associates who would be horrified to hear Tina speak as she has done. And when we are entertaining them we respect their feelings. Tina will then prepare, cook and serve just as an old-fashioned Jewish housewife should. Eh, Tina mine?'

The soup finished and cleared, Alice appeared again, her trolley laden with a very large sirloin of beef flanked by roast potatoes and a well-risen Yorkshire pudding. Other vegetables were placed on the table in tureens, and a gravy boat full of rich, meaty gravy was set before them.

'This is a typically English meal, and one we very much enjoy,' Arthur said, as he carved the joint. 'We should not be serving Yorkshire pudding to a strictly Jewish party, because Tina tells me that it's made with milk, but for tonight we bend the rules a little.'

They ate the food to the accompaniment of chatter from the children about their school day. Edward was pleased, but a little surprised, to find that in this household at any rate children were not expected to be seen but not heard at mealtimes.

Seeing his curious glance going from face to face, Arthur said; 'The children rarely dine with me, and when they do it is like a holiday for us all. Besides, an intelligent child adds to the pleasure of a conversation and becomes more intelligent as a result. We Jews have great faith in education, and encourage our children to learn all they can.'

Edward remembered his own childhood, the lessons grudged by Karl because they kept the boys from the farmwork. 'My own mother felt the same,' he said. 'Unfortunately, it is not a view shared by many parents.'

Alice, clearing the main course from the table and putting out a large dish of fresh fruit, leaned over Edward and a firm young breast, garbed in crisp grey and white checked cotton, brushed against his arm for a moment. Edward, intent upon Tina, never even noticed.

'No, I fear not,' Arthur agreed. 'Do you like apple strudel with syrup sauce? They are Louis's favourites. Or would you rather share *my* favourites? Crêpes suzettes!'

'Or chocolate mousse?' Cecy suggested shyly. 'Tina and I made that this afternoon!'

Edward made himself popular by choosing the apple strudel. It left Arthur to dispose of the entire dish of crêpes suzettes and the girls to polish off the chocolate mousse, and it made Louis think that his choice of pudding had been just what their guest most liked.

The meal ended with cheese and a variety of home baked biscuits and coffee.

'Often we have it black,' Arthur explained. 'But tonight it is late for black coffee, so we will all have it with cream.' He turned to Edward and gave a conspiratorial wink. 'Already we have sinned with Yorkshire pudding; why not be hung for a sheep, eh?'

When the meal was finished the elder girls excused themselves and disappeared in the direction of the kitchen to wash up and clear away, Edward guessed. He was sorely tempted to offer his assistance but, from the sprightly and eager way in which his host headed for the study, guessed this would be most unacceptable to Arthur. Indeed, the evening passed pleasantly, for Arthur was widely read and very interested in New Zealand, in gold mining, in milk processing – in fact in discussing anything with a young man who had lived rough and made money as he himself had once done. It was left to Edward, longing to ask if he might call on Tina, to lead the conversation round to his host's children.

'They are nice, yes?' Arthur said, beaming expansively and lighting up a fresh cigar. 'Tina is just sixteen, but she runs this house better than most fully grown women could do. All goes right with my Tina in charge.' He conveniently forgot the squabble over the salami suppers, the children's resentment at Tina's strictness. 'Cecy is a help, of course, but she's at school all day and there are only two maids beside Tina. Becky and Rachel are clever, as their eldest sister was, and . . .'

'Does Miss Tina not go to school?'

Arthur sighed and shook his head, exhaling cigar smoke towards the ceiling. 'Not any more, my friend. Not since Mutti died. Too much work there is in the house, too much organising. It is sad, because she has a good brain, but then who wants brains in a woman? Better it is that she helps me to rear her sisters and her brother, and learns how to cook and keep house.'

To himself, Edward thought that he preferred a woman with a good brain to a little empty-head, and that a clever woman would probably pass on her intelligence to her sons. Aloud, he said, 'So she is alone here all day, except for the servants?'

The unsuspecting Arthur agreed that this was so, and went on to explain that Louis was at school now and was little bother to his sister in any case, for he was bright, popular with other lads, and good at games.

'So you must not think her a slave to the house, for she goes out when she does the marketing. She meets her old school-friends sometimes during the holidays, and she's a keen cyclist. Every day, she spends some time on her bicycle. Right up on to Mousehold Heath she goes, and cycles along the flat for miles. She says it keeps her healthy, and stops her moping.'

'Even in the winter?' Edward asked craftily.

'Yes, yes, at all times. Now I shall tell you about Louis. He will, of course, follow me into the business . . .'

Listening with a degree of sympathy, Edward forced his face into an expression of spurious interest. For I must make him like me so that I can visit again, he kept telling himself. And besides, he's just told me without being asked that I may meet my little darling any time I choose if I walk on the Heath all day!

And then, by a piece of good fortune, Alice popped her head round the door and announced that Mr Keller was in the hall and would like a word with Mr Rose.

'Excuse me, my dear fellow,' Arthur said, getting to his feet. 'This will take only a moment.'

Within a few seconds of his host leaving him, Tina came slipping round the door, stopping in seeming confusion when she found him alone. Edward, wise in the ways of women, said tactfully, 'Are you looking for your papa, Miss Rose? He's been called out for a moment, on business. Do stay and talk to me until he returns!'

'Well . . . but what shall we talk about?'

'Why, you, Miss Rose!' She glanced up at him coquettishly, her eyes frankly admiring, and gaining courage he went on, 'Will you be going shopping in the city tomorrow? I should very much like to meet you! I could carry your shopping bags, and take you to Rayna's Refreshment Rooms for coffee and cream cakes. Would you like that?'

'Oh!' The treat was plainly something which did not often come her way. 'But you know the city so well, sir! I thought you had only just arrived!'

'I noticed Rayna's when I was out strolling the other day, and lunched there. Will you meet me?' She nodded, her eyes flicking towards the door. 'Where? Do you know the Royal Hotel on Agricultural Hall Plain?'

'Of course I do! Though I've never been inside.'

'Then meet me in the foyer of the hotel tomorrow at ten o'clock.'

She hesitated, then heard a sound outside the door. Her hands flew to her hot cheeks, and she whispered distractedly, 'Yes, I'll be there. A ten o'clock.'

He resisted a sudden impulse to lift her off her feet and kiss her pointed chin, her soft, inviting mouth. Instead, he said quickly, 'That will be pleasant. And now, Miss Rose, tell me how you amuse yourself when your brother and sisters are at school.'

She was as quick witted as she was pretty, he noted with approval, for she immediately began to speak in her clear little voice of the way she ran the house and of their rare outings. By the time her father returned – for it had been the thump of his sticks which had made Edward change the conversation – nothing could have been more innocent than their demeanour. Tina was standing demurely by her father's chair, apparently lecturing the young man, who leaned against the mantelpiece and watched her face with avuncular interest.

The evening took its appointed course and Arthur, increasingly pleased with Edward, told him that they hoped to see more of him during his stay in the city. Edward said with truth that he, also, had enjoyed their talk and hoped it would not be the last evening they spent together. He was careful to leave quite early, too, so that his fund of anecdotes – and his host's – would not begin to seem repetitive.

By the time he reached his lodgings in King Street, he felt that he had known Miss Tina Rose all his life – and had loved her all the time he had known her.

The strangeness of it amazed him. He was, after all, no innocent youngster, experiencing the pangs of first love. He was twenty-seven, experienced, even a little cynical. And one glance from those big dark blue eyes had had him reeling like a seventeen-year-old!

Did she feel the same, that was the question. He could scarcely bear the thought that she might have forgotten him already, but it had to be faced. He wished he could look into her mind now, this very moment, and read her thoughts!

Tina, undressing quietly so as not to wake Cecy, was struggling with her conscience. Had she been deceitful, to agree to meet the young man tomorrow? She thought not, for her father liked Mr Neyler and would encourage her, surely, to show friendship to one so far from home and friends! On the other hand, she had not attempted to tell her father of the meeting, nor did she intend to do so now.

If we meet often, she told herself as she climbed into bed, I shall obviously tell Poppa all about it. Then it occurred to her that she was, after all, only a young and inexperienced child when compared with this much-travelled young man. At twenty-seven he must have had lady friends, probably very beautiful lady friends. And I am small, and dark, and ordinary, she reminded herself disconsolately. Probably it is just his kindness, wanting to meet me for coffee and cream cakes. A treat for a child from an indulgent adult. Turning restlessly in the warming covers, she reminded herself crisply that she had been happy yesterday, when she had not so much as heard his name, and would doubtless be happy tomorrow, if she were never to see him again.

But sensible though this attitude might be, she found it unaccountably depressing, and it took her longer than usual to fall asleep.

12

The next day there was a strong wind blowing, though the sky was blue and the sun shone brightly. Tina was glad of the gale, for it gave her the chance to change her usual practice, which was to cycle into the city when there was not too much shopping.

'I think I'll catch the tram. It's quite dangerous to bicycle with shopping when the wind is so strong,' she said off-handedly to Alice, entering the kitchen already dressed in her coat and hat. She went across and picked up her basket, then went into the hall, to examine her reflection in the long mirror there. She smiled at herself. Yes, she looked nice in the three-quarter length figure-hugging peach coloured coat, with its brown velvet collar and cuffs. With it she wore a brown velvet hat, the brim upturned to support a very large bow of peach coloured silk, brown kid gloves, and brown doeskin shoes.

'Mind you don't mess up that decent coat,' Alice said from behind her. 'Why so fine to do the shopping?'

'It's a lovely day, and I felt like dressing up,' Tina said airily. 'Don't forget to clean out the conservatory, Alice. Be sure you tell the gardener to set those new plants, too.'

'And don't you forget the master fancies beef curry for tonight,' Alice retaliated. 'Best add shin beef to your list.'

'I certainly shan't forget,' Tina said. She grinned suddenly at Alice. The other girl was five years older than she, but they managed to get along extremely well despite 'mistress', in this case, being considerably younger and less experienced than 'maid'. 'I'm off now. Get luncheon for one o'clock.'

She tripped out of the house, down the garden, and then turned to her left, to cross the narrow, ancient Bishop's Bridge, to pick her way across Riverside Road, and to stand with rather more patience than was her wont at the tram stop.

She felt pleasantly adventurous and slightly wicked as she took her seat beside a fat matron also bearing a large basket. It certainly added spice to her trip to say to herself, I am going to meet a Man! It is a Secret Assignation! She imagined herself boasting about this illicit meeting to Lizbeth when next they met, and dreamed blissfully of how she would tell the story until the driver drew his horses to a halt outside the Agricultural Hall. Then, of course, she was in a flurry to jump down and in so doing caught the hem of her peach wool skirt with her heel, and nearly fell into the gutter.

Recovering, she crossed the road, wending her way cautiously between the traffic – for despite the earliness of the hour the Plain was crowded – to where the wrought-iron and glass portico of the Royal Hotel stood out over the pavement. There she hesitated, suddenly unsure of herself. She had never been in a hotel in her life, apart from in America, and there the hotels she had visited with Momma had not been imposing, like this one! She approached the doors, then turned and surveyed the street. She was early; he could scarcely be inside yet. She would wait out here, watching the people bustling along the pavements. The road was wide here, and, because of the multiple crossroads, busy. People dodged across the road, hurrying out of the way of the traps, carriages and waggons, several of which would be bound for the market since it was market day.

She stood close to the doors of the hotel, therefore, and watched the comings and goings, feeling that she was unlikely to be accosted at ten o'clock on a windy February morning, with what seemed to be half the citizens of Norwich passing along in front of her!

A file of schoolgirls, crossing the road two by two, with a teacher at each end of the procession, made her think wistfully of her own schooldays. They would be heading for the Castle museum and she noticed that most of them carried luncheon boxes. No doubt, as the day was so fine, they would be allowed to eat their luncheons in the Castle moat gardens, and to play hide and seek amidst the evergreens, the pavilions, and the bandstand, all deserted so early in the year.

Remembering similar school trips of her own made her wonder what Lizbeth was doing; would it be art, or conversational French, or drawing? But one must put childish things behind one, she reminded herself severely. Here was she, waiting to meet a Young Man for a Secret Assignation!

A much more exciting pastime than school!

Her eyes flickered over the crowded pavement. Women in fur-trimmed coats and elegant hats strolled along in pairs, no doubt going to buy beautiful dresses in Bunting's before meeting for coffee somewhere incredibly smart and fashionable; men, out from their offices, loud-voiced, black-suited, heading, no doubt, for some horrid place where they might drink strong liquor. Tina tightened her lips. Men! Women were not given to conducting their business over whisky or sherry!

'Miss Tina! Here!'

She looked round wildly, but could see no one she knew on the pavement and, with heightened colour, glanced down at her neat doeskin shoes again, pretending she had heard nothing.

'Miss Tina, here! Right under your nose!'

This time the voice had a laugh in it and she shot a furious look at the roadway, to meet a teasing glance from Mr Neyler's bright blue eyes. Mr Neyler was sitting at the driving wheel of a motor car!

Surprise and curiosity got her across the pavement almost before she had had time to draw breath. 'Mr Neyler! I didn't know you had a motor!'

He leaned across, looking down at her and patting the passenger seat invitingly. 'Do hop in! I dare not get out for fear the engine dies on me. I was in great apprehension driving along Prince of Wales Road in case you were already in the hotel and I had to climb down.'

Nothing loth, Tina jumped in, her eyes shining. 'None of my family have been in a motor,' she announced gleefully. 'Not even Poppa!'

'Have they not? I've brought you a dust-coat, if you care to slip it on, and a hat cover, though I daresay you won't need that. Indeed, I hope you don't, for I want everyone to see what a pretty girl I'm escorting!'

Compliments were lost on Tina at this moment, however. Draping herself in the dust-coat, she said regally, 'Drive on, Mr Neyler!' and then, as he laughed and obeyed, she added, 'Is it yours? I say, how fast we are going! Is that because it's on a downhill slope? Oh, all those things to pull and push! I'm sure it is difficult to learn to drive such a creature! Do women drive motors? I would dearly love to do so!'

Forgotten was her shopping, the promised coffee and cream cake! Forgotten, also, the fact that Mr Neyler had made her look foolish outside the hotel – and since Tina hated, above everything, to appear foolish, this was a triumph for the motor car indeed! She did not even notice the eyes which followed their progress as they drove off. She was far too intrigued by this modern and wonderful mode of transport.

'I've hired it,' Edward said. 'As to driving it, anyone with a practical turn of mind could do so – even a woman, I imagine! Stopping it is not difficult, but starting it is, however, which is why I shouted to you to jump aboard! As for speed, one cannot go fast in the city; quite the opposite.'

He was indeed driving with extreme caution, keeping well clear of nervous horses and even more nervous pedestrians. He had not, however, forgotten the object of their meeting.

'There is an old inn backing on to River Green, Miss Tina, where I may park the motor whilst we have our coffee and cakes. I thought we would go there first and then I'll take you back into the city to do your shopping. I can park easily enough, I suppose?'

'Oh, yes. I've seen a motor parked on the cobbles on Orford Hill,' Tina said quickly. 'Do you know it? It's right outside the Bell Hotel.'

'I'll find it, with your assistance. Tell me, are you expected home for luncheon, or might I escort you to a restaurant in the city to share my meal?'

Tina consulted her conscience, which told her very decidedly that nice girls did not have luncheon with young men unless they had first obtained parental consent.

'I'm sorry, I have to be home for luncheon,' she said regretfully. 'Poppa comes home, you see, and today the children will be home as well since it's a half day at school.' Then, on impulse, she added, 'Though it would be perfectly acceptable if you were to come home and share our meal, since I happened to meet you in the city.'

He grinned at her, showing very white teeth. 'Capital! I shall be delighted to accept your invitation!'

It was not far to the River Green. Edward parked the motor carefully and then took Tina's arm and led her into the low-beamed coffee room. They chose a table near the blazing log fire yet in the window embrasure, so that they could overlook the river scene as they drank their coffee and ate their cakes while, as Edward put it, 'simultaneously toasting our toes'.

'Oh, the swans!' Tina cried at one point. 'I wish we had something to give them!'

'Next time we'll bring some stale bread, if your kitchen will furnish such an item,' Edward said. 'Doesn't your garden back down to the river?'

'No, there's a high fence and a path beyond,' Tina admitted. 'Poppa would worry about Louis otherwise, because he's far too adventurous. He's rather spoilt, you see, being the only son; Poppa has so many daughters!'

'And such pretty ones!'

Tina glanced up at him through her lashes, uncertain how to deal with the compliment. Natural curiosity won. 'Do you say such things to all the young ladies you meet?' she asked without coquetry.

He answered her as seriously. 'If it's true, Miss Tina. I think pretty girls deserve to be told they're pretty.'

'Suppose they already know?'

'Do you object, then, to being told something you already know? When friends meet, they say "How cold it is!" or "What an oppressive day!" For my part, I say "How pretty you look!" '

'What would you say to Poppa, then?'

He laughed, throwing up a hand. 'You win! I daresay I should make some mundane remark about the weather.' He got up from the table and offered her his arm. 'Shall we drive into the city now?'

She slipped her hand into his arm as naturally as though she performed such an action every day, smiling up at him.

'Yes, do let's! How lovely it will be to have my basket carried for me, and to drive up Bishopsgate like a queen!' As they approached the car she added, 'It is Queen Victoria's Jubilee in June; do you suppose you will still be here then?'

'June! I ought to be back in Dunedin by then, I fear. Unless, of course, something keeps me in Norwich.'

'Must you go home? What a pity, for the city will be *en fête,* you know. There will be fireworks, parties, a parade. I think it will be wonderful!'

He cranked up the car and was delighted when the engine sprang almost at once into noisy and vibrating life. Climbing into the driving seat, he said: 'I daresay Dunedin will be *en fête* too, for the Queen is our ruler as well as yours. Only fancy, Miss Tina, if you were to find yourself in Dunedin for the Jubilee!'

She gave a delightful gurgle of laughter. 'As if such a thing could happen! And I'm sure Dunedin won't have such things as Norwich has planned! Captive Air Balloons on Cattle Market Hill for those who can afford such diversions. Fireworks which all can watch, of course. And a great many other things!'

She had not taken his remark in any way seriously, he realised, as they drove into the city. And why should she, indeed? She was only a child, when all was said and done. She was enjoying his company but she had no thought of him as anything but a companion in adventure. He guessed that his sex added spice to her thoughts of him, but was very certain that she was not woman enough to wonder what his intentions were.

He soon discovered that Tina was not the only member of the Rose family to be blind to his interest. When all the shopping had been done they piled it on to the back seat of the car and he drove her home. She jumped down to open the gates for him, then insisted on remounting for the short journey up the drive. At her command he beeped on the horn and brought the household running, Louis wide-eyed and envious, Alice tutting her disapproval but plainly intrigued by the horseless carriage, the girls nervous, giggling and pointing.

Last but not least Arthur came out on to the driveway, swinging along on his two sticks, still chewing – for they were a little late and luncheon had started – but enthusiastic about the new toy. He accepted without question the fiction that they had met by chance and that she had invited Mr Neyler in to luncheon in return for his kindness in bringing her and her shopping home.

'After we've eaten, I would like much to see how your motor works,' he said enthusiastically to Edward. An invitation to 'go for a spin' was promptly offered and as promptly accepted. 'Louis may come too? Also the girls? Well, well, what a treat! Alice may run round to the office and tell them I shan't work this afternoon. And Tina mine, a real good tea you shall make us, *faygeler*, for our return. We must see that our guest does not go away hungry.'

'We'll see more of that young man,' Alice said as she and Tina prepared a substantial high tea for the motoring party. 'You can fool Mr Rose, young lady, but you can't fool me! Met by chance in the city, indeed!'

Tina, cutting bread at a great speed, glanced up and smiled self-consciously. 'Don't tell, whatever you do!'

'As if I would! He's going to get his legs under the table, you know that.'

'What on earth do you mean by that, Alice?'

Alice snorted. 'Make himself at home, miss! He's uncommon handsome, so he wouldn't waste time on charming Mr Rose unless he was serious. Mark my words, we'll see plenty of Mr Neyler.'

'Have I done enough bread? If so, I'll start buttering it. Don't you like Mr Neyler?'

'Like him? I don't *know* him,' Alice said scornfully. 'I reckon I'll get to know him, though, in the next few months.'

'Wrong again! He goes back to New Zealand once he's sold all his rabbit skins,' Tina said derisively. 'He's lonely, that's all.'

Alice pounced on the buttered bread and began cutting off the crusts with quick, decisive movements. 'Perhaps.

Getting up a flirtation, I suppose. Well, you be careful, miss.'

'I don't care if he is; so am I! After all, if I was still at school I'd probably be swooning over the art mistress, or having a crush on that young man who goes in twice a week to help with the science lessons,' Tina said defiantly. 'I'm sure you had flirtations when you were my age, Alice.'

Alice stopped buttering bread for a moment and thought, head on one side. 'Lumme, yes! Young George Carter, him what brought round the bread at the big house. And then there was the footman, Charles. He *did* fancy me, and I led him a dance, I did!'

'Well then, don't disapprove of me if I begin to enjoy myself a little. I intend to see Mr Neyler as often as I can. If he wants to see me again, that is.'

'He will.'

This proved to be the case. During that first car drive, Edward had explained to Arthur that he was both bored and lonely, waiting for his ship to dock, and would be most grateful if he might be allowed to visit the Roses and to take the young ladies and Louis out sometimes.

Arthur was only too delighted to have another man about the house, to see him quite at home there, helping Cecy with her schoolwork, teaching Louis how to hurl a ball overarm so that when summer came he might excel himself at cricket. He certainly never thought that Edward had any deeper interest in Tina than in the other children, except that, since she was not at school, he naturally saw more of her.

And with every day that passed Edward fell more deeply in love. He most earnestly wished to kiss Tina, but hesitated to do so even when they were quite alone. He had no wish to frighten her off and realised that this might be easily done. Fortunately, he thought, his ship had been delayed, and though the month was mid-April there was no word from her. For he knew that to go home without taking his little love would be torment. He was amazed at the suddenness and the completeness of his captivation. As the weeks passed, he began to know her well, and to love everything about her. Her protectiveness towards the younger children, her briskness, her bouts of domineering bossiness, her quick temper which could flare and then die away with equal speed. He knew her now not just as a pretty girl, small and dainty as a porcelain figurine, but as a person. One fine Sunday he took her on the river in a boat and laughed when she attempted to row and only succeeded in splashing them both. Because he had laughed and she felt foolish, she flew into a rage and boxed his ears so hard that his eyes watered. His straw hat fell into the river and she growled and spat like a kitten attacking a wolfhound. He laughed again when he fished the hat out of the water and brought it inboard on an oar, and drips of water fell from the oar on to Tina's straw bonnet. This time, he had to imprison her hands and speak firmly to her or she would have hit him again and jumped out of the boat, despite the fact that they were several yards from the bank.

'You've got a shocking temper, my girl,' he said, still holding her hands imprisoned, laughing down into her pink and furious countenance.

'I hate being laughed at,' she growled, glowering.

'Why should I not laugh at you? I laugh at myself! And can you swim? What would you have done if I'd not prevented you flinging yourself off the boat in a rage?'

She giggled, glancing up at him through her thick, curly lashes, her temper forgotten.

'I don't know. I didn't think! I just wanted to punish you for laughing. But it isn't deep here. I'd have reached the bank.'

He still held her hands, but more gently now. 'Wouldn't you have looked a lovely sight, dripping off along the pavement with duckweed in your hair and mud thick on your new skirt! I suppose no one would have been allowed to laugh at you then?'

He saw an arrested expression in her eyes. 'You mean that losing my temper can make me a laughing stock? Oh, but I can't *help* it! I mean to be calm and sensible and then something happens and I just hit out blindly.'

He lifted her small fingers to his lips and lightly kissed them. 'Remember, next time, that when you hit out blindly you may do a worse hurt than you ever dream. Now I shall row us back to the bank – without splashing!'

He no longer thought her an angel; he thought her the only girl for him. But how did Tina herself feel? He knew she liked him very much but shrewdly suspected that the thought of marriage had never crossed her mind. And, by now, he knew that his main objective in life was to marry Tina.

But how to discover her feelings without frightening her away? He wondered whether to speak to Arthur, then decided against it. It never occurred to him to wonder whether he would be welcomed as a son-in-law; why should it, when Arthur showed him nothing but the friendliest face? The man was not religiously bigoted, as was shown by his whole attitude. No, he had no fears on that score. It was Tina's own feelings which worried him. He believed that even if she did not love him now, she would come to love him. Before he asked her to marry him, he wanted her to realise that she loved him. How, he wondered, did one persuade a very young girl, fresh and innocent as a spring lamb, to fall in love? It was all very difficult.

Then he had a telegram from the port authorities in Ipswich. It stated that the mate of the New Zealand ship *Candida* had arrived in port and wanted to see him. It was forty miles from Norwich to Ipswich and no car was supposed to exceed a ten mile speed limit, but Edward thought that if he set off early in the morning he might contrive to do the journey in both directions before darkness fell. Accordingly he approached Arthur with the idea that Tina and Louis might enjoy an excursion with him, to see his ship and the piles of skins.

Arthur agreed without any qualms, bade Tina pack a good picnic in a hamper, and told Alice to prepare a hot dinner for their return. But when Edward called for the two Roses, he found general consternation. Louis had fallen from an apple tree in the garden and broken his leg. He was in some pain still, but grinned, pale but perky, at his father's dismay.

'I'll be all right, but I shan't be able to go to Ipswich,' he remarked. 'Could you take me over to Solly Keller's house, Poppa? I can play with him while Tina's away.'

Arthur had truly meant to tell Tina that she and Edward had better take Alice with them. Unfortunately, he forgot; so Alice remained in the kitchen and Tina and Edward set off in the sunny early hours, bound for Ipswich. Later, realising what he had done, Arthur comforted himself with the thought that Edward was more like an uncle than a beau to his daughter, and that in any event Tina was a well brought up child; she knew that no decent Jewish girl would ever get emotionally attached to a *goy!*

Tina, blissfully unconscious of her father's faith in her, climbed into the front seat beside Edward and settled down to enjoy her day. They drove to the outskirts of Ipswich without mishap, other than about three or four stops to cool the engine, and had their luncheon in a pleasant meadow, the grass dotted with wild flowers which Tina longed to pick.

'I'd better not though, because they'll fade and die before I can get them into water,' she said regretfully.

When their meal was over they packed everything away in the luggage boot and drove into town. It was not difficult to find the docks and Edward assumed that he would have no difficulty, either, in finding the *Candida,* but though they roamed up and down the quayside examining the shipping there was no sign of her. Baffled, Edward tucked Tina's hand into his arm and went in search of the harbour master.

'The *Candida?* Sorry, sir, no ship of that name in harbour at present,' the harbour master said briskly. His eyes slid admiringly over Tina's trim little figure, clad in naval fashion – a navy and white walking costume with a white straw hat. 'What made you think she was here, may I ask, sir?'

'She *must* be here,' Edward said, a frown creasing his brow. 'I had a telegram from Brett saying they'd arrived.'

'She most certainly is *not* here . . .' the harbour master

began, then broke off. 'Can I see that telegram, sir?'

Edward drew it out of his pocket and handed it over, seeing light dawn on the harbour master's face as he read the contents.

'Ah, *that* Mr Brett.' He darted a quick, curiously diffident look at Tina, then at Edward. 'He came in two, three days ago, on the *Ocean Queen*. You'll want to speak to him, I daresay. He's putting up at the Crown.'

'The *Ocean Queen?* But he sailed on the *Candida!*' Edward felt a terrible suspicion rise up in his mind, like dark fog. 'For God's sake man, tell me the whole! What has happened to the *Candida?*'

The harbour master, looking acutely unhappy, wiped his hand across his brow, then took off his spectacles and polished them vigorously on his sleeve.

'I don't rightly know, sir. You'll have to speak to Brett to get the full tale. All I know is Brett came in on the old *Queen* because his ship had foundered. But the name of the vessel . . .'

'*Foundered?* She's sunk? I can't believe it!'

'No, sir, and I've not said it's your ship, for I don't know it. I would be much obliged, sir, if you'd go to the Crown and see Brett yourself!'

Edward swung round, almost lifting Tina off her feet. 'I shall do so at once,' he flung over his shoulder. Then, at a murmur from Tina, he turned round, saying remorsefully, 'I'm sorry, but I had no idea . . . I did not mean to be rude!'

'No offence taken, sir, I'm sure,' the harbour master assured him. 'Was your ship insured? If so, you may gain from the mishap.'

'It wasn't my ship. I only chartered her. The cargo wasn't insured,' Edward muttered. 'Good day, and thank you.'

He and Tina hurried to the Crown and were fortunate enough to find Mr Brett still in his room. He came down to the coffee room and told them that the *Candida* had indeed foundered, and that three lives had been lost, including the captain's.

'She was an old ship,' he told them sadly. 'Cap'n Peake,

he di'n't take the care he oughter, consid'rin' her age an' all. But he sure di'n't deserve to drown.'

After many explanations and a description of the storm in which the ship had gone down, the couple finally managed to get away from Mr Brett, who intended working his passage back to New Zealand as soon as might be. They returned to the car and drove off in silence, but after a short distance Edward drew up in the shade of some trees, with a distant prospect of the river, and turned to his companion.

'Tina?'

It was the first time he had used her name without the prefix but she never even noticed, looking up into his face with frightened eyes. 'Yes?'

'If I'd not got roaring drunk and missed that ship, I'd probably be dead by now. Drowned.'

She nodded, her face quite white. 'I know. Oh, Edward, I'm so glad you got drunk!'

'And me. But this changes things. There's nothing to keep me in this country now, nor any money to get me back to Dunedin. The skins were to make my fortune, you see! Most of the money I brought with me has gone.'

For the first time since they had heard of the fate of the *Candida*, a smile dawned in her eyes. 'Then you'll stay here? You won't go back to Dunedin?'

'Tina, I must go home. There's nothing for me here! I've a good business back in Dunedin, besides the farm. Oh, my brother Mark is running everything at present, but I couldn't let him continue to do so. There's too much work there for one man. I shall take a job as a clerk or something of that sort, and earn enough money to get me home.' He leaned across and took her hand, feeling it tremble in his own with a clutch of the heart. 'Tina, will you come with me?'

She said cautiously, 'To New Zealand? How could I? Don't be absurd!'

'It isn't absurd. I'm asking you to come to Dunedin as my wife!'

'*Me?* She giggled, her voice rising to a squeak. 'How *could* I do such a thing? I'm much too young, and who would look after the children? Besides, I'm Jewish!'

'I know that, but what does it matter, if two people love one another?'

She looked at him doubtfully, as though fearing for his sanity. 'Doesn't matter? But Poppa would never agree to my marrying outside the faith! And someone must look after the children. I couldn't possibly just leave them. Who could take my place?'

Ever practical, Edward said: 'Cecy would. She's longing to do more for the family, and you know it. I believe she'd be almost as good at it as you, what's more.'

It was the wrong thing to say. Tina's pointed chin jutted and her lips closed in a tight line, giving a look of mulish obstinacy to her small face. She turned her head away pointedly, looking blindly out over the meadows beside which they sat.

'Tina?'

She half-turned towards him, and found herself seized and held firmly against his broad chest. She struggled, startled and still offended, and turned her face up to his, ready to wither him with invective.

And was kissed. His lips took her own so gently at first that she relaxed almost without meaning to and then, as his hold tightened and the warmth of his lips drew a response from her own mouth, her arms went round his neck as naturally as she might have hugged her father. She pushed her fingers into the thick hair at the base of his scalp, giving a tiny moan of pleasure, but when he tried to deepen the kiss she pulled away, alarmed as much by her own reaction – the slow parting of her lips, the strange, tugging sensation in her stomach – as by his boldness.

He made no attempt to draw her back into his embrace, but held her at arm's length, smiling down into her eyes. 'That was your first kiss, Tina Rose! And it won't be your last. You liked it, I could tell, and if you marry me you'll get kisses every morning, every evening, and ten million in between. Does that tempt you?'

She sighed and then, incongruously, yawned. He laughed at that and she laughed too, then grasped his wrists, gently but inexorably pulling herself free from his hold.

'Don't let's spoil it,' she pleaded. 'We've been such good friends, Edward. I've never had such a good friend, nor enjoyed myself so much. We think alike, and laugh at the same things – please don't spoil it! Tell me, Mr Neyler, will you still be in England for the Jubilee celebrations?'

Edward sensed that this was the time to capitulate, or to pretend to capitulate. He climbed out of the car and swung the starting handle, shouting above the din, 'Guess I'll be here. It will take me a couple of months to earn a berth home.'

All the way home, Tina discussed the Jubilee celebrations, commiserated with him on the loss of his rabbit skins, suggested various jobs which he might undertake. But beneath her surface chatter lurked a sense of disappointment that he had not tried to woo her further. Had it not been a little faint-hearted of him to give up so easily? Not that she had the slightest intention of marrying him! Nor of going to New Zealand, a world away, leaving her beloved family to Cecy's tender mercies. But nevertheless, if he loved her the way he said he did, he should have tried harder!

She sighed, aware of her inconsistency, then brightened, remembering that he would be in England now for at least two months. No doubt, during that time, he would continue to pester her! The thought gave her considerable satisfaction.

13

He had not given up, and Tina soon realised that Edward Neyler was not the man to meekly take no for an answer. His job as an office clerk at the chocolate factory did not give him as much free time as he had hitherto enjoyed but when he was free he spent the time with her.

And after a while Tina, kissed once and not again, found herself dreaming of his arms, the feel of his mouth on hers. It had been, she remembered, the strangest sensation, giddying yet sweet. She did not put into words in her own mind that she wanted to feel that sensation again, but she did. Curiosity over her own reactions, pique at his apparent lack of desire for her kisses, put her in a receptive mood and she was annoyed when he resumed his almost brotherly attitude towards her.

As the weather improved their outings grew more venturesome. He called for her, not in a motor now because he was saving all his spare money, but in a pony cart. They jogged out of the city and into the softness of country lanes, stopping to eat the picnics she had prepared. Sometimes they took Louis and the two little girls, sometimes they went alone. Soon enough, the inevitable happened. Their hands touched as they packed dishes away and he smiled at her and kissed the tip of her nose, then continued to tidy up as though nothing had happened. She glanced at him speculatively, but he neither looked up nor moved towards her so that she wondered for a moment if she had imagined that butterfly touch.

Next time they picknicked alone and their hands touched he was almost sure she had engineered it, and caught her fingers, sliding his hands up her arms to the elbows, the shoulders, giving her ample opportunity to stop him. But though she looked a little apprehensive, she allowed him to draw her close until their faces were only inches apart. Then she closed her eyes.

The kiss lasted longer this time, and when he drew away from her he was aware of a reluctance in her. I am a swine, he thought remorsefully, wooing her with kisses so gentle and harmless when my whole soul longs to crush her in my arms, cover her face with fierce kisses, make her mine! But damn it, I love her, and if I go gently I'm sure she'll discover that she loves me too!

Yet knowing he must go slowly, he was still aware how quickly time passed. Mark had been informed of the fiasco of the rabbit skins and had written back telling his brother that, though the affair with Sylvia was progressing to his satisfaction, business was not.

'I am no substitute for you,' he wrote ruefully. 'I cannot sell the *idea* of milk processing the way you do, which means we've no new suppliers. And because it's been a bad season, some of our regulars have stopped sending in milk; they can sell it nearer home, they say. You would put a stop to this. I find I cannot. However, the farm is doing well and Sylvia seems to have decided that an inferior Neyler is better than no Neyler at all. When will you be back? Shall I send you some money?'

But Edward was stalking game which needed no more money than he could earn. He had saved enough for his passage by the end of May but had decided in any case to stay on for the Jubilee celebrations. He could see that Tina was growing more and more dependent on him for companionship and understanding, beginning, perhaps, to believe that he would stay in England indefinitely. He was almost sure that, this being the case, she would be both shocked and miserable when he announced his departure.

When she's still raw from the thought of losing me, I'll propose again and this time she'll accept, ran his cunning thoughts. Arthur likes me, and will scarcely refuse his consent when he realises we love one another. Despite Tina's horror at the idea, Cecy will manage the family very well. I shall have to delay my departure, of course, to allow for the wedding, but I'll telegraph Mark. He'll understand.

Accordingly he booked a passage for June 24, but wrote to Mark telling him it was unlikely he would be aboard, since he anticipated being required to remain for personal reasons. Then he went and saw Arthur, to beg his permission to squire Tina throughout the gala day.

The schools had arranged various parties and functions for their pupils and Louis would be spending the day with his friend Solly, so Arthur knew that unless he agreed to send Tina with Edward she would probably spend the day alone, both maids having begged a day off. He was a generous father, and, besides, had no desire to escort his daughter through the raff and scaff of the city, so he graciously gave permission and waved the young couple off in the motor car which Edward had recklessly hired with money left over from his passage.

'Well, what's to be first?' Edward asked as they turned into Prince of Wales Road. 'Would you like to see the procession of decorated carts and carriages, or a cricket match at Lakenham with the players in fancy dress? Or would you rather go down to the market place and watch the school children getting their commemorative medals? Becky and Rachel will be there, I guess. And will Louis and Solly go along?'

'Anything but that,' Tina said, bouncing on her seat and adjusting her rose-pink parasol at a becoming angle. 'Both Becky and Rachel were away from school at the beginning of the week with sore throats, and yesterday Louis went berserk and cut the heads off all the roses by the front gate. I don't want to see one schoolchild, let alone twenty-two thousand.'

Edward laughed. 'Is that how many there are? I rather agree with you! Then I vote we go and watch the procession first. After that we ought to go to the Cattle Market and start getting in line for our balloon ride, if you're still set on it.'

'Yes, please! That's to say . . . Can you afford it,

Edward? You're saving, remember!'

'I've saved,' he said, not looking at her. 'I've actually bought my passage. And I've got money left over.'

'You've . . . you've bought your passage home? she said faintly, 'That's . . . that's wonderful. When do you sail?'

'On June 24, but I leave the city by train tomorrow evening. Look, I think we'd best park the motor and walk to Castle Meadow to watch the procession. Will that suit you? Are those very pretty shoes comfortable?'

'Perfectly, thank you,' she said dully. Then, with forced cheerfulness, 'What a wonderful day for the Queen's Jubilee! I'm sure it's what we've all been praying for.'

Walking beside her along the crowded pavement, he knew he had spoilt her pleasure in this special day. But it was all in a good cause, he told himself. He must hurt her in order that she might realise how much he meant to her!

As they stopped at a good vantage point to watch the procession pass, he had to admire her courage. She might not know she loved him but she depended on him, and now he had cut the ground from under her feet by telling her that he would soon be gone. Yet she continued to smile and chatter, her expression determinedly cheerful, and he knew she was slowly assimilating his news and trying to come to terms with his departure and what it would mean to her. He felt sincerely sorry that his leaving stood between her and the pleasure of this bright, never-to-be-forgotten day, but the deed had been done. Now he could only stand back and watch her take it on the chin.

And presently he knew she had won. His news had been banished to the back of her mind, a spectre which would break out and pounce as soon as she was alone. But now she was giving him her full and excited attention again, trotting along beside him chattering brightly, her hand resting, feather-light, on his sleeve.

'The procession was wonderful, wasn't it?' she said, hopping a little to keep up with his longer stride. 'Shall we go to the Cattle Market now? Are you *sure* it isn't too much money?'

Lovers were everywhere, the people in holiday clothes

and a holiday mood. He bent down and kissed the side of her face, tasting her skin, a little salty, very sweet. 'Today is special. Nothing's too much money today. Come on, there's a crowd waiting already.'

They stood in a line until they reached the man selling tickets, then Edward parted with a vast sum and they were led over to one of the captive balloons. They climbed in, gas and heat hissed and smelled strange, silk swelled, revealing rainbow stripes, and they were rising through the air, they were high as the birds, higher than the castle battlements, slowly turning on the spot while Tina leaned over the side and exclaimed at the ground so far below, at people like ants and carriages no bigger than beetles. Then, because it was so exciting, and such a beautiful day, she flung her arms round Edward and kissed him, laughing and wriggling when he made the balloon rock with his fervent response.

They had a luncheon of breast of chicken, salad and bread and butter, followed by strawberries thickly sprinkled with sugar, and then drove to Lakenham and watched the cricket match. They returned to the city and had tea in Chapelfield Gardens and listened to the band of the 3rd Battalion Norfolk Regiment and ate sponge cakes covered with lurid pink icing.

Dusk fell, and they strolled in the moat gardens, admiring the electric lights, the first either had seen, gleaming in bright colours, cunningly interwoven amongst the branches of trees and shrubs. They thought them brilliant and astonishing, but when darkness fell at last they returned to Castle Meadow, arms entwined, and saw a display of fireworks which had Tina gasping.

'Weren't the set pieces beautiful?' Tina murmured as they made their way back to the motor car. 'That Star of India! And the portrait of the Queen! It looked so like, yet it was only fireworks, after all. I wonder how they do it? And the silver rain and golden rain, the catherine wheels!'

'It isn't over yet. Climb into the car and we'll watch the end from here.'

The end was rockets, hundreds of them despatched

simultaneously, setting the night afire with a brilliant, many-coloured bouquet. In the silence which followed Edward realised that Tina was crying.

He put his arm round her and kissed her tear-wet face. 'My poor darling, you're tired out,' he murmured. 'It's been a long day.'

She moved her head until their lips met and, when he drew back, gave a tremulous sigh. 'I'm not tired. I don't want you to go away,' she wailed, her voice breaking on a sob.

'But I must, my darling girl! Now if you were to say you'd marry me . . .'

'I cannot! If I could . . . but you know I cannot!'

'I don't know that you can't, I just know you won't! Tina, you know I can't stay! I can't continue to live here, as a clerk, earning a pittance, when I've a good business at home which needs me. Mark needs me, too! And you, my darling, do not! You can't have your cake and eat it.'

'I kn-ow,' Tina sobbed. 'And I d-do need you. I want to be w-with you. I can't bear the th-thought of being l-left alone again!'

His heart lifted at her words. 'You truly can't? You truly need me? Then come with me, my darling! Marry me! I've enough money for a double passage to Dunedin.'

She trembled in his arms, then said slowly, her voice still quavering, yet firmness coming back with every word, 'No. I won't even think of it. Take me home, Edward.'

He was taken aback, for he had felt sure of her. 'Look, Tina, it isn't just your life you're ruining, it's mine, too. What about that? I don't want to go home without you. I don't know how I'll bear to leave you. Don't hurt us both so!'

'It's been a lovely day, Edward, but it's over. I'll never forget it – or you. But please, I want to go home now!'

Baffled, he drove along the still humming streets and into the quiet backwater of Bishopsgate, drawing up close to the front door, seeing that the house was in darkness. It was very late, but Alice would still be up; she would not go to bed while one of the family was out. He turned to Tina, who had stirred in her seat. 'No, don't get out yet, there's a good girl. We really must talk.'

She turned towards him. In the dim starlight her face was tear-streaked but serene. 'Edward, there's nothing to talk about. Not any more. I understand that you must go home and you must try to understand that I'm a Jewish girl, the daughter of Jewish parents. I can't marry you without my father's consent because I'm too young, and he would never give it. If you think otherwise I'm sorry, but you're mistaken. I've *always* known that Poppa meant me to marry a Jew, even though I've not talked about it. And another thing. You've had plenty of girls, but you are my very first young man. I can't exactly pretend I'm making a choice, can I? Poppa would say I was just flinging myself at the first man who asked me!'

It was a far more mature and reasoned response than he had expected, and he felt his heart sink. He had hoped to make her see that she needed him as badly as he needed her. Instead, she was making him see. He had scarcely given a thought to the religion which she had known all her life, or to her cloistered existence. She must know Arthur better than he; must know her sisters better, too. He heard himself saying humbly, 'I know you're young, and I know the family needs you. Perhaps I'm wrong to say you love me, when you've not known other men. But I'll wait for you.' Even as he said the words, he regretted them. How could he say such a thing? He certainly did not intend to hang around in England for years, nor could he visualise himself leading the life of a monk back in Dunedin.

'You'd wait? Do you mean . . .' Her voice lifted. 'Oh, Edward, do you mean you'd come back?'

He leaned across the car and took her by her shoulders, gripping her so hard that she winced. 'If I come back in a year, would you marry me? I think you'll know, you see, once I've gone.'

She gazed back at him, her eyes brimming with hope. 'Would you come back? Would you really?'

'I really would. If you loved me and meant to marry me.'

She thought about that, a frown creasing her childish

brow. 'Once you've gone, you think I'll know whether it would be right to marry you. I'll miss you, of course, but there'll be another feeling, won't there? A worse hurt than just missing a person. And if I have that feeling I'll know?'

'You'll know,' he said, suddenly confident. 'You're very young and you've not met many men, but love is something special. I know I love you more than I could ever love another person, and I think you'll find you feel the same. Yes, I'll come back for you.'

'What about Poppa? Do you suppose he'll consent when he sees we still want to marry after a year apart?'

'I'm sure of it.'

'That would be wonderful. But why didn't you tell me earlier that you'd saved enough for your passage home? We've no time left together, not even a day!'

He grinned wryly in the darkness. 'I thought I'd be taking you back to Dunedin with me.'

She laughed, saying 'Coxcomb!', and then threw her arms round his neck, hugging him convulsively. They kissed more passionately than they had ever done before, then he handed her down and jumped down himself to start the engine. It stuttered and coughed into noisy life and jumping back behind the steering wheel again he said above the racket, 'Goodnight, my darling. I'll come round tomorrow to say an official goodbye. I love you! Goodnight, little one.'

'Goodnight, dear Edward!'

She watched the motor car disappear from view, walked down to the gates and closed them, then made her way back to the front door. How happy I am, she thought incredulously. Yet he is going away! She was beginning to realise already how much she would miss him but it had not, as yet, touched her heart. Later she would begin to feel the pain of parting, but now everything was bathed in brilliance because he loved her.

How have I done it, she asked herself as she fitted her key into the lock. Tina Rose who had never had a beau, who found it difficult to be natural with boys, who never flirted or even thought about marriage, had somehow won the love of a handsome and charming young man.

She opened the front door and slipped into the darkened hall. She must be later than she had thought, for Alice had obviously gone to bed. Even as this occurred to her, she saw a light come on in the study. She smiled; Poppa must have told Alice that he would wait up for her, and he must have fallen asleep and been woken, perhaps, by the noise of the car engine as Edward left. How she would tease him!

Before she could reach it, the study door opened and Poppa appeared in the doorway, dark against the light. She went towards him, saying cheerfully, 'Am I late, Poppa? I did not mean . . .'

Her words were cut short as he grabbed her by the shoulder and dragged her forcibly across the threshold, slamming the study door shut behind her.

'*Schlump!* Ach, slut, to behave so!' Before she could protest his hand hit her across the face so hard that her head jerked back and she yelped. 'Shut up, you dirty little bitch!' He hit her again, viciously, sending her white straw hat flying. Then he grabbed her piled-up curls and dragged her across the floor, flinging her into an armchair. He towered over her, muttering words she had never heard on his lips before, his face working with passion, his eyes slitted with a fury which was beyond her comprehension.

'What *is* it, Poppa? What have I done?'

'What have you done? So innocent you sound! Why, you . . .' As the abuse began again he hit at her legs with his stick, using all his strength so that the blow cracked on the bone and she whimpered, drawing her legs up and curling into a protective ball, sobbing and pleading for an explanation.

'Shut up!' he barked. Abandoning the stick he seized her hair again, pulling until she was jerked to her knees, tears streaming down her face, her mouth twisted with pain, sobbing, not heeding his hissed instructions to be quiet. He jerked at her hair again, saying through gritted teeth, 'What did he do, eh? What did you give him, you *chozzer?* You serpent!'

To be called a pig and a serpent in one breath brought her

eyes wide, despite the pain. She tugged feebly at his hands, trying to break his grip, while her sight was clouded by tears and the skin of her forehead tightened excruciatingly as he lifted her almost off her feet.

'Poppa, are you mad? Why do you call your Tina such names?'

'Because you deserve them, slut! Why should I not tear the hair from the head of a *yentzer* who goes with a *shaygets*?' His tone had been one of unalloyed fury, now it changed to a subtler insult. 'Did he pay you well, you whore? Was it worth being beaten? Did you enjoy, to feel him on you?'

He heaved and Tina's feet left the ground so that, for an instant, she hung by her hair. She screamed then, a high, animal scream, and he flung her down with such force that she felt something give in her ankle as she struck the floor.

She lay where she had fallen, dazed, bruised and sick, but he could not leave her even so. He began to hit her with his stick, exclaiming, 'You shall be shut up in this house! Never again shall you go out of it!' Then, abruptly, he sank into one of the chairs, letting his sticks slide out of his grasp and clatter to the floor whilst he passed a shaking hand across his forehead. 'To think that I, a man full-grown, with the natural urges of such a one, have denied myself since my poor Deborah died. Yet this . . . this Jezebel, who is a child almost, runs whining for it, even from a *goy!*'

At last Tina understood what he was talking about. She moved cautiously, and when he did not hit out at her, forced herself to sit up. Her father was leaning back in his chair, his face that of an old, defeated man.

She said, her voice coming out higher than she intended: 'Poppa? You think Edward and I have done wrong?'

He did not open his eyes, but passed his hand over them as if to shut out the light. 'Think? I saw you!'

'But I only kissed him! I was saying thank you for a lovely day out!'

His eyes opened and he grabbed for his sticks and lurched to his feet, pointing a stick at her, foam glinting at the corners of his mouth. 'You *only* kissed him? I saw that kiss! I heard him shout that he loved you! Get out of my sight, slut, before I beat you to the floor and crush you with my feet. GET OUT!'

She dragged herself to her feet, whimpering with pain as one foot touched the floor and would not take her weight. Like a wounded animal she skirted him, gasping, holding her side, trying to keep out of reach of his stick. At the door she turned, and he was following her. Blind panic seized her. She choked on her sobs, forcing herself to hurry, dragging her injured limb across the hall and up half the flight of stairs before she dared to look back.

He stood, swaying, in the centre of the dimly lit hall. He was looking up at her, his skin grey, his mouth trembling, and to her horror she saw tears were coursing down his cheeks.

For a moment she hesitated. Part of her longed to run down and fling her arms round his neck, assure him of her love and untarnished innocence, beg for his love in return. But fear was too strong. He had torn her hair out by the roots, beaten her with his stick, flung her to the floor with enough force to do her ankle some grave injury. She dared not go back! She opened her mouth to speak to him, plead with him, and saw that the whole hall was swaying, advancing and retreating before her eyes. At once, uncertainty crystallised into terror that she might faint and fall at his feet, to be crushed as he had threatened. She turned and began to plod upstairs, dragging herself up by the banister. Behind her, she heard him begin to make strange, frightening noises. A part of her was torn by his weeping; another part refused to believe that she was hearing the sounds of grief. They must be a threat, a mutter of bad words which would presently break out into shouts and screams. And blows. Her tender, bruised flesh cringed at the thought of further punishment. She was no longer brave, she was just a little girl who had been treated cruelly and must escape her tormentor.

She reached the head of the stairs and began to limp along the corridor. The door to the room she shared with Cecy stood open. She got inside somehow, closed the door and slid the bolt across. It went easily, considering it had never been bolted before, yet though she was safe she could not reach the bed. She took one wavering, uncertain step and then her knees gave way and she crumpled on to the cold linoleum, feeling it against her face like a friend; cool, impersonal, a hand on the hot brow.

'Tina?'

Cecy sat up in bed, her face ghost-white in the starlight. 'Tina, what's the matter? Are you ill?'

For a moment Tina did not answer. She could not. Her heart was beating so loudly that it almost deafened her and she lay listening to it until it quieted so that she could also hear the coursing of blood through her veins, the ticking of her pulses, all the frightening sounds from her frightened body. She heard her breath rasp in her throat, sucking air slowly into overworked lungs, and moved her head, but could not lift its weight.

'Tina? What's out there? Why did you bolt the door? Shall I go fetch Poppa?'

She opened her eyes and saw Cecy bending over her, eyes black with fright, shivering in the cool darkness.

She tried to move, but only jerked her head against Cecy's bare foot. She muttered, 'Help me up, Cecy. Help me to reach my bed!'

Cecy bent over her sister, then drew back a little. 'Tina, you're hurt! You're all bruised and torn! I'm afraid!'

'Help me up, dear Cecy.'

The soft whisper brought tears to Cecy's eyes but she bent over her sister again, and caught her arm. Her hands did not grip firmly enough; softly, ineffectually, she only dared to touch, afraid to hold and do hurt.

'Help me!'

The command came out almost strongly, and as she spoke Tina began to try to sit up. With Cecy's aid, she got to her feet and managed to collapse on to her bed.

'Who's done this to you, Tina? I really must fetch Poppa! Was it . . . ?'

Poppa beat me. You must not go downstairs tonight, indeed you must not! He's very angry with me, and it would not do for you to question him.'

'*Poppa* did this? But he's never raised a hand to any of us!'

Tina loosened her skirt waist and began, painfully, to unfasten the stiffly buttoned bodice. 'He hit me with his stick. He thinks Edward and I . . .But it isn't true, Cecy! Oh, never mind, just help me off with my shoes, would you?'

Kneeling, Cecy unbuttoned the shoes, tenderly removed them and the stockings from her sister's feet, then saw the ankle, swollen, blue, the flesh stiff and shiny. 'He thinks Edward and you did bad things?'

'I suppose so.' Tina shook her head, wanting to forget the attack and her fear, wanting to sleep, to drown in sleep, never to wake again. She felt muzzy and strange. The moonlight, in squares on the floor, kept jigging around in an unpleasant and unnatural manner.

'Tina mine, you should see a doctor about this ankle,' Cecy said with unexpected firmness. 'It's sprained, if not worse. I'm sure Poppa could not have meant to do you harm! Do you think he's gone to bed? I could sneak downstairs and bring up cold water and a cloth, to bind round your foot. I could even dress and fetch a doctor!'

'Don't be silly, dearest. I'm all right, just bruised and shaken.' Tina rolled into bed and sighed with deep thankfulness. 'Oh, thank God, to be lying down! Only let me sleep!'

Cecy snuggled the covers round her sister's body. 'Yes, sleep. In the morning you can see a doctor. Everything will be explained when morning comes.'

Presently Tina heard Cecy cuddle down, and soon after that knew from her sister's even breathing that Cecy slept. But Tina could not follow suit. She ached from her beating, but it was not that. Worse, she ached with the knowledge that Poppa had been saying, with every blow he struck, that to love Edward was wrong and to show such love an offence which not even the most lenient father could forgive.

At first she lay shivering, her nerves stripped raw by Poppa's fury, but later she was quiet, thinking. Arthur was a good father, who had never hit one of his children in anger until tonight. He had wanted, she knew, to burn into her flesh a sense of the great wrong she had done. And lying in her bed, watching the stars fade and dawn slowly grow in the sky, she could see that he was right. The Jews were a race apart and for centuries they had been persecuted by people who called themselves Christians. To turn to Edward, to allow him to love her, was to betray.

It was bitter to acknowledge her guilt and to know that her father had justly punished her, for if she believed he was right she should never see Edward again. At the thought of such self-sacrifice pain went through her like a knife; she groaned as from a physical blow. She could not! She loved Edward and could not agree to spend the rest of her life away from him. If she had doubted her feelings before, she doubted no longer. She would have to choose between her faith, her family, and her love.

When the alarm went off and Cecy woke, Tina was pale and heavy-eyed from lack of sleep, but she had come to a decision.

To betray one's faith and one's family was bad, but to betray one's love and oneself would be worse. She might not marry Edward, but she would not deny her affection for him. And if he wanted her badly enough to return to England, she would marry him with or without Arthur's consent!

However, there was no sense in asking for disgrace and humiliation! One must acknowledge that Edward was going a long way away, and might change his mind about a little scrap of a Jewish girl back in Norwich. So she would tell Poppa, truthfully, that Edward was returning to New Zealand because she had told him she was too young to talk of love, and that all he had seen had been a goodbye kiss. She would tell him, too, that she understood why he had beaten her, and bore him no grudge. He was a generous man and would surely accept both her story and her promise to behave more circumspectly in future? Especially when he knew that Edward would soon be twelve thousand miles away!

Nevertheless, it took courage to go downstairs and face the new day. And Poppa.

14

Edward climbed down from the train and looked around him. The platform was not crowded and the people waiting for trains, glancing up at the clock, buying papers for their journey, looked very little different from those who had been here when he left Norwich nine months ago. He walked under the dome of the station roof and out through the booking office to where a line of hansoms stood waiting, the horses drooping between the shafts.

'Hey, cabby! Give me a hand with these trunks!'

'Yessir, sartinly! Do that big black 'un be yours?'

Edward nodded, grinning to himself as he climbed into the cab. That accent! It had amused him before but now it had a homely and familiar ring. He heard the last trunk heaved into place and leaned forward. 'The Bell, if you please.'

'Verra good!'

Edward sank back into his seat. He was actually here at last, after all the aggravations and delays, and he hoped that never again would he live through such worrying and hectic months. For a start, he had been forced to leave the city without again setting eyes on Tina. He had tried, of course, walking through one of the worst storms in living memory to her house, while the wind tore the roofs off houses, flattened crops, howled down the deserted streets. Above him the thunder growled and cracked incessantly and next day he saw that lightning had set fire to a farmhouse and several barns.

But despite the elements he had enjoyed the walk. It made it almost romantic as he slogged along, battling against the wind, now pelted with hail, now drenched by a cloudburst, now deafened and awed by the thunder and lightning. He was glad of his Scarborough waterproof, a garment with an arm-length cape to protect one from heavy rain, but even that could not save him from weather such as this; he was soaked to the skin by the time he arrived at the house in Bishopsgate.

Alice answered the door and ushered him in, full of concern at his being out in that terrible storm. She fussed about him, and as she helped him off with his waterproof she hissed, 'Don't ask to see miss; nor don't write to her 'ere,' and had then gone on to tell him, in her normal voice, that she was about to put crumpets on to toast for their tea.

Arthur, appearing as if by accident in his study doorway at that point, had been his usual charming self, thanking Edward with apparent sincerity for the pipe and the expensive tobacco which were his parting gift to his host. Handing over large boxes of chocolates for the young ladies and a toy steamship for Louis, Edward shook hands, thanked again and again, then thought it would be natural to enquire why Tina had not come in to bid him goodbye.

'A mishap,' Arthur said jovially. 'Downstairs she fell, my poor Tina, carrying a tray of china, no less! No, no, not badly hurt, but stay in bed she must for a day or so.'

There had been little he could do or say after that. He drank a cup of tea from one of the delicate china cups, and ate a buttered crumpet. Then he reiterated his goodbyes, and left, with all the family except for Tina, waving him off.

He did not go far. Despite the fact that it was not yet five o'clock it was dark, the sky overhead clouded black, the thunder rumbling still. Edward crouched against the gate-post out of sight of the front windows of the house, and waited. Soaked, shivering, but sure that Alice would get out for a moment if it was humanly possible.

Presently his vigil was rewarded by the sound of foot-steps crunching on the gravel. Light footsteps. He peered round the corner of the gatepost, ready to walk quickly away if he saw Arthur, but it was Alice, wrapped in a hooded cloak.

He went to open the gate but she shook her head, then pressed her face to the lattice-work. 'It squeaks, sir, don't you go opening it! I dussen't be long, either, he thinks I've gone to the privy.' She grinned quickly, then sobered. 'You mustn't write 'ere, sir. The master beat miss something cruel last night.' She saw his face darken and grabbed the gate latch, saying quickly, 'There i'n't nothing you can do 'cept go, sir! The master won't touch 'er once he knows you've gone for good.'

'I must go, but I'll be back,' Edward promised grimly. 'Tell her that, Alice! Where may I write?'

'Draper's Cottage, The Street, Brundall; my mother's,' Alice gabbled. 'Sir, I must go. I dussen't let him suspect I'm helping miss.'

He put a cold, soaked hand through the bars and squeezed hers. 'Thank you. You're a wonderful girl! I've got that address committed to memory now. Goodbye, Alice.'

He watched until she had slipped round the corner of the house and then made his way back to his lodgings through the storm-tossed and deserted streets.

The voyage home had been a nightmare. Eight days out they had been caught in a storm and had taken considerable punishment. Some time after that, it was discovered that there was a fault in the engine. They limped into St Helena's harbour and there the disgruntled passengers and crew had been stranded for two months, until a replacement part could be brought by sea from England. Upon arriving in Dunedin, he had found a scrap of a note from Tina explaining that the atmosphere was still stormy and that she might find it difficult to write. He also found Mark in a state of considerable perturbation.

'Come down to the dairy and see for yourself,' was all his brother would say, however. And indeed, one glance at the formerly busy place had been enough to explain his hang-dog look. A rich farmer, it seemed, had set up in competition to them and had enticed most of their best workers away. Edward looked quickly round, at the vats which should have been seas of milk in various stages of preparation, at the two or three untrained youngsters fumbling their way through the processes, and said one word.

'Sell!'

It had been easy to say, more difficult to accomplish. But Edward knew his business and within a month of arriving back in Dunedin had made it plain to the rich farmer that, if he so chose, he could bankrupt his competitor's flourishing new business in a few months simply by undercutting his prices, paying more for the milk, and getting the Edma Dairy rolling once more.

'Needless to say I didn't add that, since my own business venture in England had been a resounding failure, we had no means of building up the dairy again,' he told Mark with a rueful grin. 'Here in Dunedin they've never known us fail, so they take it for granted we could make good our threat. And the fellow says he'll buy us out! He'll pay a reasonable price, too.'

'Well, since you say you must return to England in a few weeks, it's better that we sell,' Mark said. 'I never was a businessman; I'm a farmer. That was why old Ashburton decided to try his hand at milk processing, of course. He realised that the farmers wouldn't bring their milk to me for processing, because I've no head for business or dealing. He also knew that once you were back they would prefer to deal with you, knowing you would do right by them, than with him, who's just another farmer like themselves.'

With the problem of the dairy on the way to being solved, he confided in Mark about Tina; that he must return, marry her, and perhaps remain in England for a time.

'I shan't want to bring her straight back here when she won't have had a chance to mend matters with her family,' he explained. 'Nor do I think she would come! Besides, when I come back I want to do so with money in my pocket! So we shall stay in England for a while.'

'I can manage the farm, of course,' Mark admitted. 'But I'll miss you! Don't be gone too long!'

'Of course not! This is home to me as well as you, Mark.'

And then another letter arrived from Tina, and it showed her unhappiness more clearly even than the first.

'I'll wait for you,' she wrote rather pathetically, 'and if you decide not to come back I'll understand. But I would like to know, please, Edward. I am in disgrace and not allowed to leave the house alone, nor to ride my bicycle. If you will be coming back I should like to know. Your letter despatched from Southampton arrived safely at Draper's Cottage, but nothing since. Please, Edward, how long will it be before you come back? I should like to know.'

Edward showed the sad little note to Mark and wrote back by return saying that he was in the process of selling the dairy business to fund himself. When the sale was complete the money would pay for him to return to England and take her away. He explained that Mark's share of the money would go into buying more cattle for breeding purposes, so that she realised they would share the profit, but said he had decided to retain his half-interest in the farm so that, one day, he might return to New Zealand with her and bring her to the home he and Mark had built.

Then, as if on cue, Mark contracted a virulent infection which laid him low. Edward remained on the farm and the sale of the Edma Dairy waited on Mark's health. Sylvia, who had kept away from the farm once Edward returned, came calling. She assured Edward that there were no hard feelings, that she was too fond of Mark to risk losing *his* friendship. She was teaching at the Otago Girls' High School and brought Mark small presents, books to read, fruit, puzzles. Best of all, she stayed with him while Edward went into the city and conducted negotiations for the sale of the dairy. And at last things began to happen. They sold the dairy and the money came through and was divided. Mark, pale and weak on his legs but rapidly mending, began to take on his fair share of the farmwork. And at last Edward was away, by ship, by train and now in a cab. He would soon be ensconsed in the Bell, able to make plans to see Tina!

He had arrived in Norwich on a Wednesday and they met on the Friday. He had despatched a mixed posy of early daffodils, catkins and primroses to Alice by messenger boy, this being agreed as a suitable sign of his arrival. He got a verbal message back, simply saying, 'Friday morning 11 o'clock on the market, by the fish stalls.' The fish stalls! He chuckled to himself, feeling brighter than he had done for many a day. How unromantic was his love, but how practical! This, he knew, would be Tina's work. Few people, seeing a young man eyeing the fish and a young woman buying them, would think of secret assignations.

He dressed carefully, clipping his thick hair, cleaning under his nails with an orange-stick. It was a grey, miserable day, with the far end of the street hidden in a veil of light rain, but he dressed with care in his new tweed lounge suit, blue and gold Ascot tie and an uncomfortably high Shakespeare collar, then hid it all with a sigh beneath a waterproof, and sallied forth under a large black umbrella. No point in dressing up and arriving at the rendezvous drenched!

He was early, so he took a look around, then bought a posy of snowdrops from a flower-seller. The daffodils and catkins he had sent Tina through Alice had been imported, of course, but these frail, snow-scented little blossoms were blooming in country gardens all around. Presently it occurred to him that a young man carrying flowers might be supposed to be meeting a young woman, so he gave them to a small girl who was crying because she had dropped her new muff into the mud. It was still raining and he was loth to get out his watch, so he walked up through the stalls to the Oxford Hotel and glanced at the clock in the foyer. Five to eleven! He had best be getting to the fish stalls!

He strolled up to the nearest stall right on the hour and purchased a pint of shrimps, which he stowed in the pocket of his waterproof. As he was turning away a small girl in a mud-coloured cloak and bonnet came up to the stall, her face turned away from him towards her companion. The companion, a tall, golden-haired girl, was undoubtedly Alice, clad a trifle startlingly in an electric blue Chesterfield and matching hat trimmed with scarlet cherries.

'Alice! Where is she? Couldn't she get away?'

As he spoke, he felt a small hand on his arm. He glanced down, into dark blue eyes beneath the rim of a dowdy brown bonnet.

'Tina! Darling!'

He dared do no more than grasp her hand fervently, while his eyes devoured her. She had not changed! The dark blue eyes were brimming with love, the dimples appeared beside her soft little mouth as she smiled up at him. But a second glance showed that there were differences. She was pale, and the eyes which flickered over his face brimmed with more than love; presently, a tear trembled on the ends of her long lashes.

'Edward, I'm so *glad* you're here!'

'We must talk,' he said urgently. 'When must you be back? Is there anywhere we can go? A coffee house, perhaps, where you aren't known? I dare not take you back to the Bell; businessmen meet there, especially on rainy days.'

Tina wrenched her eyes from his face to glance uncertainly at Alice. 'We're all right until luncheon time,' she said. 'But where could we go? If only the weather were not so horrid!'

'No problem, miss,' Alice said briskly. 'We'll go to the Castle museum. There won't be a soul there unless it's a school party, which I doubt on a day like this. You two go in and 'ave your talk, and I'll take a cup of tea at the Central Café. You can join me there about noon. I'll stand outside if there's anyone we know within.'

'You're a marvel, Alice,' Edward said warmly. He released Tina's hand, which he had been holding as if he dared not let it go, and turned towards Davy Place. 'Shall we walk together, or must I go ahead?'

'You go ahead, we'll follow,' Tina said. 'Wait for me in the British bird gallery. I shan't be far behind you, I promise.'

Edward, collar turned up, umbrella held low, charged across Gentleman's Walk and down Davy Place, then across Castle Meadow and up the steps of Castle Mound and so into the museum. There, in the deserted bird gallery, he and Tina kissed for the first time for nine months, and he held her close enough to feel the thud of her heartbeat and the trembling of her limbs.

'I don't know how I've kept sane,' he groaned against her hair, when they began to walk, arms entwined, along the gallery and into the foreign bird room. 'I've worried and worried about you, left alone here. It was dreadful, not knowing.'

'If you'd have known more you'd have worried more,' Tina said. She pulled herself out of his arm, casting a nervous glance behind her as she did so, though she allowed him to retain her hand. They were passing cases full of exotic birds now, and Tina glanced sideways at the brilliant colours. 'When Alice comes in here, all she keeps saying is how nice the feathers would look on her Sunday hat. She has no soul, I tell her!'

'Don't change the subject! I'm here now, and I must know what's been happening! Has your father forgiven you? How much does he actually know?'

'He knows nothing, apart from the fact that I kissed you when you brought me back from the Jubilee celebrations. As for forgiving me, how can you ask that?' She saw by his surprised look that he did not understand her and tweaked the edge of her mud-coloured bonnet distastefully. 'Look at my clothes!'

He obeyed, and what he saw dismayed him. Her brown cloak was too long for her and had trailed upon the ground so that the hem was muddy and frayed, and with the cloak she wore cracked, elderly button boots, darned woollen gloves and the despised bonnet.

'You don't look as elegant as you used,' he admitted. 'Is this part of the punishment? Just for kissing me? How cruel and unworthy!'

'That's not all.' She glanced round her again, then untied the strings of her bonnet and pulled it off, turning to face him, her eyes ashamed and angry. 'See?'

Her thick, curly hair had been cropped level with her

ears; badly cropped too. It was uneven and chunked off, an abuse of the beautiful shape of her small head.

He could not prevent his gasp, and took her in his arms, gently dabbing at the tears which shone again on her lashes. 'Poor baby, poor little love! When we're married you shall have it properly trimmed and shaped and I'll buy you one of those wig things.'

'A transformation,' she cut in, briskly drying her own eyes and beginning to smile.

'That's right. A transformation, to wear until your hair grows long again. As for those horrid clothes, that's a blessing in disguise. When we leave, your poppa will circulate your description in those brown things, but I shall buy you clothes fine and bright as a peacock's feathers, and no one will recognise you from your father's description!'

She laughed, snuggling against him, her eyes bright with anticipation. 'Then we really will run away? It isn't just a dream?'

'We really will. I've made enquiries and we shall take a train to London and another to Scotland. We may marry there without parental consent, despite your being under age. I had hoped to take you to New Zealand fairly soon, but . . .'

She interrupted him without ceremony. 'New Zealand? No, Edward! Not so far away before I've had a chance to win Poppa round! Cecy has been wonderful, and the younger ones are very fond of me. But above all, Poppa will forgive me, I'm sure, and take me back into his love! When I'm reconciled with Poppa, then I'll go anywhere you say.'

He had expected something of the sort and said pacifically: 'Well, I wouldn't think of marrying and sailing immediately, because I daresay your father will have the ports watched – with especial closeness in the case of vessels sailing for the South Island.'

'That's very true,' she conceded. 'He would guess I must have fled to you, for there's no one else. Shall I leave a note to tell him, though? I should hate him to question my friends, though goodness knows I've not seen any of them to speak to since . . . since you left.'

'Why didn't you meet them in secret?' he asked, horrified that she should have been treated so.

She sniffed. 'And let them see my hair? And these horrid, ugly clothes? Do you know, my hair begins to look quite pretty after a little while, but as soon as it begins to curl he hacks it all off again. He says in olden times he would have shut me up in a nunnery sooner than see me given to nothing but vanity and Christians.' She giggled, despite herself. 'I can't hate him as I ought! His eyes on me are cold and ruthless, he tries to give me pain, yet underneath his soul weeps for the hurt he does me!'

'That sounds very fine, but he's not forced to treat you the way he does,' Edward pointed out. 'I didn't know there were Jewish nunneries, actually.'

'I don't think there are; it was just a figure of speech. Now, shall we make our plans? When shall we run away?'

'On Monday morning, early. Can you come out as if to do some shopping but go straight to Thorpe Station?'

'How could I?' Tina shook her head regretfully. 'Alice has to accompany me and she'd get into awful trouble. Poppa would know I couldn't have given her the slip.'

'I forgot that. Then it'll have to be the ladder and the window at dead of night! And the milk train to London.'

He was half joking but she nodded eagerly. 'Yes, please, Edward! Only wouldn't the midnight train be best? I go to bed at ten and I can sneak out of the house any time after that. Sunday night is a quiet night, too. We could be in London by dawn on Monday!'

He laughed at her eagerness. 'And married, perhaps, by Tuesday or Wednesday!'

'What part of Scotland are we going to visit, then?'

'Inverness, in the highlands. It may seem a long way to run, but my mother was born there and when we were small she told us many a tale about the town, the river, the shipyards. I really feel I know it quite well, and would like to visit it. There are several hotels and guesthouses – and churches for marrying, of course!'

She hugged his arm. 'Of course. Then will you come to the gates at . . . well, at eleven o'clock on Sunday? What about a bag with all your clothes and toothbrushes and combs and things?'

She giggled. 'I'll pack a bag tonight and Alice can bring it to the Bell on Saturday morning when she goes to Brundall to see her mother. Will that do?'

'That will do very well. And when you get on the train, you will have to seize an opportunity to change your clothing. Then we'll put your horrid brown clothes into our luggage and you will arrive at Liverpool Street Station looking smart and pretty – and less like a little orphan school child.'

'It'll be nice to wear pretty clothes again,' she said seriously, 'But don't forget the transformation, will you? And some black hairpins. And a hat with a veil, perhaps.'

'I won't forget. And now we've laid our plans, I think we ought to join Alice at the Central Café!'

She left just before eleven on Sunday night, slipping down the stairs and across to the front door, shooting back bolts she had previously oiled, avoiding the crunchy gravel and stealing across the grass instead. She had oiled the hinges on the gates as well and they opened beneath her hand without a whisper, so that she slipped through them and was beside him before he knew it. He turned towards her, and she saw his teeth gleam in the dark. Neither spoke but he squeezed her hand and patted her shoulder. Then they set off in the direction of the railway station.

They scarcely exchanged a word until they were on the train and it had pulled out of the station. Then Edward said: 'Did your escape go according to plan?'

'Yes. Cecy was asleep. I left a little note just saying I'd gone to Edward, and that I'd write properly later on. I shall, shan't I?'

'Of course.' He had piled the luggage rack with their bags but now he thrust one on to her lap. 'Good thing we've a compartment to ourselves. Corridor trains seem to be the exception rather than the rule in England! But I want you to change, so I'll take a nap while you do so.' He tipped his hat over his eyes and said, from behind it, 'Will that do?'

She rummaged in the bag. 'A blue tailored coat and skirt, a beautiful pale yellow hat and gloves, and even some little smart shoes,' she said, with satisfaction. 'How very pretty, Edward! What's that black thing? Oh, my transformation! You've thought of everything!'

'I know I have. The hairpins are wrapped in that scarf thing. Put them on, there's a good girl.'

She looked doubtfully at his face, almost hidden from view by the hat. It seemed very strange to change one's garments in front of a gentleman, even if his face was obscured beneath a hat! However, the shabby brown cloak was nothing if not voluminous. She disappeared inside it and after what seemed like hours to Edward, stifling beneath tan velour, she emerged, flushed and breathless but clad in the cheviot wool suit.

'I knew it would suit you,' he said smugly. 'Now let's get that transformation in place.' He took a comb from his pocket and dragged it through her ragged curls and then, with her help, pinned the transformation to the top of her head. 'There! Now for the hat!'

He perched it in place, aware that her face was suffused with blushes and that his hands were trembling. It was simply being close to her, he realised with wonder, and having his hands entangled in that soft, baby bird hair. He longed to kiss her, but knew that from now on, until they were married, he must treat her as he would a younger sister. She was in his charge and at his mercy. He must not abuse her trust.

The next few hours passed quickly for them both. They arrived in London and had a hasty breakfast in a small workingmen's café just outside the station. Tina sat demurely opposite him, sipping coffee from a chipped earthenware cup and eating great doorsteps of buttered toast, her eyes never still, following every vehicle, every passerby, every dog and cat, interested in each one. They hailed a hansom as soon as their hunger was satisfied and arrived at the other station just in time to see their train draw in. Before Tina had time to do more than widen her eyes at the press of people on the platform they were on the train, sitting this time in a crowded carriage, and were off, bound for Inverness.

As they sat side by side it occurred to Edward to wonder what the other people in the carriage thought about them. Did they realise that this was an elopement? That the child he could see reflected in the picture of some highland glen, tender and wide-eyed, and the tall, broad-shouldered man sitting beside her, were about to be married? It was then that the truth burst upon him like a bombshell. Tina was not just innocent and trusting *looking*, she *was* innocent. And trusting. How could she be anything else? Her mother and grandmother had died when she was no more than eleven or twelve. Tina, bringing up her sisters and brother, missing out on school, on girls' chatter, on biology lessons, knew nothing. Unable to keep an animal, not even a singing bird, because her father disapproved of pets, she was totally ignorant of the facts of life!

He had not told her, but it had entered his mind that he would prefer her father not to run them to earth until Tina was pregnant with his child. He felt heat steal into his cheeks. Good God, what sort of a swine was he? He had stolen this beautiful child from her home and family, to take her far away to a strange place. And there, in a grimy hotel bedroom, he had meant to perform a rite which, he suddenly realised, would disgust and terrify her.

At that precise moment she turned from her fascinated contemplation of the countryside through which they passed and gave her sweet, dimpling smile.

'You look rather hot,' she murmured. 'Shall I open a window a little?'

'No, it's all right.' He smiled down at her, trying to seem avuncular or elder brotherly. Anything but the goatish seducer of innocence he had suddenly felt himself to be! He patted her hand. 'Are you thirsty? Next time the train stops I may be able to procure you some lemonade, or a cup of tea, perhaps.'

She tilted her head and beamed at him, then put her mouth so close to his ear that her breath tickled him. 'I'm hungry.' she whispered. 'I'd rather have a great big currant bun!'

She was so close that the faint perfume she wore was all around him, and suddenly the madness which had brought him into this scrape engulfed him once more. So he had stolen her away – she had been very willing to be stolen! So she was innocent – well, so should any gently-bred girl be, before her wedding. He took her hand, murmuring that he would try to find her some food when the train next stopped for a few moments, and curled his fingers into her palm. He traced a heart on the soft, cushioned flesh and saw the colour flood her face, knew it had quickened her breathing. He smiled. All right, so he was a scoundrel and a cad, to elope with a baby! But he loved her!

He did what he could to make the journey interesting for her, but there was not much he could do. They were unable to obtain a meal, though he did get her some lemonade and a small dried-up sponge cake. By the time they climbed down from the train at Inverness station, he knew he was in charge of one very weary young lady. Too eager to get her installed to worry about cost, he hailed a porter and told him to take their luggage to the nearest hotel. It proved to be an imposing building with a foyer the size of a young ballroom, and a uniformed staff who sprang to attention every time a customer came through the revolving doors.

As he and Tina made their way towards the clerk at the desk Edward looked once more at Tina through a stranger's eyes. She looked so tired and pale, her face smudged with smuts from the train, her new yellow hat grimy. She also looked very, very young!

On the spur of the moment he said to the clerk, 'Miss . . .Edith Draper and Edward Draper. Brother and sister. We've come to see . . . to see our parents' birthplace.'

He signed the register, still chatting wildly, while the clerk, not at all interested, selected two keys and pushed them across the desk, remarking in a broad Scots accent that they were both on the second floor. A hovering page-boy and an elderly porter picked up their luggage, and they followed them up the curving staircase.

'Have a wash and then we'll go downstairs and get some food,' Edward advised her. In a lower voice, he muttered, 'We'll stay here tonight and move on tomorrow, after we're married.'

Her eyes were still bright but he thought her shoulders drooped a little. She nodded, however, and disappeared into the first room they were shown, shutting the door firmly.

He went into his own room, two doors further along the corridor. It was a decent apartment, carpeted and comfortable, with a large double bed, an ornate washstand and dressing table, and a huge wardrobe covered with sinister looking carving. While the boy lit the gas mantle Edward pulled the velvet curtains, glad to shut out the cold darkness outside.

'Here, lad.' He pressed money into the boy's hand, tipped the old man as well, then closed his door and surveyed the room with some satisfaction. It looked quite cosy in the gaslight and the water in the jug was steaming; probably poured when the train was heard entering the station!

When he had washed and changed into a clean shirt he went along to Tina's room. He knocked gently. No reply. He knocked again and then, after a pause, opened the door.

She was lying on the bed, fully clothed except that she had removed her suit jacket and her hat and shoes. She had evidently washed, for her skin shone daisy pale and fresh, and she was equally evidently fathoms deep in sleep. He tiptoed across the room and stood looking down on her. She seemed so small, so desperately tired! Very gently he pulled up the coverlet and she sighed, then stuck her thumb in her mouth in a purely childish gesture, bunched up her knees and settled down to sleep the night away.

I haven't got the heart to wake her, Edward thought, but since I'm very hungry I'll go down to the restaurant . . . His thoughts jerked to a halt. How could he leave her alone up here? She might want him, come padding along the corridor and find herself alone, neglected, not knowing where he had gone, how she had got here, anything! He walked across and turned down the gas until it went out with a quiet *pop,* and then he went to the door, glancing back as he did so. No movement, no sound save for her steady breathing.

Returning ruefully to his own room, he began to undress. He was down to shirt and trousers before something suddenly occurred to him. He crossed the room and tugged impatiently at the bell. Remarkably quickly, there was a knock at the door. He opened it. A liveried pageboy stood there, hat on the back of his head, round eyes enquiring.

'You rang, sir?'

'Yes, it was me. Could you bring me a beer and some sandwiches up here? A lot of sandwiches?'

'Certainly, sir. Ham? Beef? Potted shrimp?'

'All three,' Edward decided. 'And a meat pie, if you've got one.'

'Yes sir.'

Edward relaxed. So he was not doomed to starve, after all! He felt sorry for poor little Tina but she was asleep. Hunger would not disturb her dreams. And he would see she had a good breakfast in the morning.

15

'What do *you* want?'

Edward, who had knocked politely on his love's door, stood with his mouth half open, considerably astonished by this strange reception. Recovering himself, he said gently, 'It's time for breakfast, my darling.'

He saw that her hair was rumpled, her blouse creased and her eyes still heavy with sleep. Patiently, he said, 'Tina,

I'm waiting.'

'I don't *want* breakfast. Go away! I'm going back to bed.' She glared at him malevolently.

'Tina, you must be starving.' Heavens, what a moment to spring a temperament! 'Be a good girl and get dressed, then you can come down to breakfast.'

She knuckled her eyes, then stared at him. 'Breakfast?'

'Yes! It's nine o'clock, you know!'

'Then why . . . how . . .' she looked helplessly down at her tweed skirt, then up into his face.

'You fell asleep on your bed, quite worn out. I hadn't the heart to wake you, so I covered you up and left you to sleep.'

To his dismay the scowl descended once more.

'Oh, did you! Well, it was very thoughtless. I feel all sticky and disgusting, and I've got backache from sleeping in my clothes, and it's all your fault!'

'I like that!' Edward exclaimed, not liking it at all. 'How am I to blame because you fall asleep?'

'You should have woken me! You shouldn't have covered me up! You . . .'

'I'm not standing in the corridor arguing with you,' Edward said with spirit. 'Let me in. Someone's coming!'

He stepped forward, only to have the door slammed almost on his nose. He hurled himself at the handle just as the key turned triumphantly in the lock.

With the pageboy trotting towards him up the corridor, there was only one course possible – retreat. Edward returned to his room, no longer blaming himself for stealing a lovely innocent from her home and family. Little vixen, he thought, it would serve her right if I took her at her word and went down to breakfast without her! Nevertheless, he returned to her door when he felt she had had time to tidy up, and knocked again. No reply.

Suppressing a wild desire to scream and shout and, if necessary, attack the door with a battering ram, Edward said in a low but (he hoped) carrying voice, 'Tina! I'm going down to breakfast. Then I'm going for a stroll around the town. I'll be back here in an hour or so.'

No sound from within. After waiting for a nail-biting moment he strode off down the corridor, so angry that he could have slapped his beloved.

'Hey!'

He turned, reluctantly, to see Tina's rumpled curls sticking round the corner of her doorpost. 'Edward? I can't get the trans . . . transformation to stay on.'

At the pathetic little quaver in her voice all his annoyance vanished. Poor child, what a dilemma! He walked back to her room and she held the door open politely then closed it after him, looking as if butter would not melt in her mouth. She had the transformation in one hand and his lip twitched. She held it distastefully between finger and thumb, like a badly made bird's nest.

'Give it to me. I'll have a go.'

He took the transformation, pinned it in place, then looked seriously down into the blue eyes raised to his. 'In a better mood now?'

She smiled up at him, totally unabashed. 'Oh, yes! I was tired and cross, you know. Let's go down to breakfast. I'm starving. You must be very hungry too!'

He opened his mouth to admit that he had eaten sandwiches and drunk a glass of beer, then closed it again. Perhaps not! He had a shrewd suspicion that if Tina knew he had eaten last night he would be taking a regular termagant down to breakfast!

After the meal, he suggested they walk into town and find the register office so that they might make arrangements for their wedding. 'Then we'll move our stuff to a smaller hotel somewhere nearby before we go searching for my mother's old home.'

However, plans of any sort were speedily to be overset. Edward went to the register office leaving Tina with sufficient money to buy herself another outfit, for it transpired that she had brought nothing save the brown cloak and skirt in which she had escaped, plus a change of underclothing and a nightdress.

They arranged to meet at a café on Bank Street, overlooking the wide river, but twenty minutes later, as Edward entered the place, his self-confident pleasure in a fine but blowy morning had evaporated.

'Fifteen days!' he exclaimed as the waitress set coffee and scones down before them. 'We have to prove to the clerk or whatever he calls himself that we've resided in the district for fifteen whole days before he'll marry us!'

'That's sad,' Tina said, but her tone lacked conviction. 'This is a lovely place, Edward. I've been looking round, and fifteen days will seem just like a holiday! Might we take a trip to Culloden? If we go on the four-in-hand coach tour which leaves the town tomorrow we can visit Culloden, Kilravock Castle, and then Cawdor Castle. They even provide you with luncheon, at an inn near Cawdor! And that's only one trip! Did you know that Queen Mary – the Mary Queen of Scots one, of course – stayed in Inverness? The house is on Bridge Street. And there are pleasure cruises on the loch, steamer trips on the firth . . .'

She reeled off a list of enticements and, as he agreed to take her anywhere she wanted to go, Edward grew more than ever convinced that his love had no more idea of what marriage was about than a kitten. She wanted to wear a new dress and call herself Mrs Neyler, and be with him for always, but she saw little point in grieving because they must spend fifteen more days – and nights – in separate rooms! He realised, with a sinking heart, that if he told her a honeymoon was more usually taken after the wedding than before, she might very easily say 'Why?', and he did not fancy trying to answer such a comprehensive question!

He had been pleasantly surprised, however, to find that prices up here were very reasonable. He booked two more rooms at a hotel called the Glenalbyn, on Huntly Street. It was a homely place, overlooking the river though on what he imagined to be the 'unfashionable' side of it, and their rooms were clean, the fare at table plain but good. But what particularly tickled his fancy was their advertisement which he had spotted on a billboard: 'The only Second-Class Hotel in Inverness,' it ran. 'Not Patronised by the Nobility of Europe or any other Country,' and then it went on to list its prices, which were quite as reasonable as he could wish.

After they had hired a cab and moved their luggage to their new quarters, they walked to the premises of Messrs Macrae & Dick and booked seats for the coach trip to Culloden next day.

As the tickets were not expensive and the shops not yet shut, Edward agreed to some shopping. Finally, in Mathieson's, a large store on Union Street, he saw the very thing for his Tina to wear on her wedding day.

'Dark yellow silk, with an overdress of primrose gauze,' Tina breathed rapturously. 'An Empire tea-gown, which I never thought I'd own! Oh, Edward, I *love* you!'

She flung her arms round him and he hugged her back, still carefully brotherly, and told her his reward would be in having the prettiest bride Inverness had ever seen. They would order more clothing to be made before they left, he promised her; she must have her trousseau and he would greatly enjoy buying it for her.

They returned to their hotel and had a good dinner of roast mutton, vegetables and gravy, followed by pears in wine sauce, excellent cheese and biscuits and coffee. Afterwards they played billiards for a little, or rather Edward showed her how to hold a cue and laughed at her efforts.

As they climbed the stairs at last, tired but happy, Edward resolved that since he had been forced to accept fifteen days' grace, he would make good use of them. Somehow, before their wedding, he must educate his bride a little.

'Thank you, Mr Neyler, Mrs Neyler. Good day to ye!'

The official had a deep and sonorous voice, making the most trivial remark sound important. Tina glanced uncertainly at him, then clutched her brand-new husband's hand.

'Is it done? Can we go now?' she whispered.

'Yes, we're married now.' Edward went up to the official and there was a clink of money changing hands, then he was back at her side, his face wreathed in smiles. 'Come on, darling! We'll have an expensive luncheon to celebrate, and then afterwards what would you like to do? Go for a cruise on the loch? Or how about visiting Fort Augustus on the canal steamer? We could have tea there, and . . .'

'Edward, you're gabbling,' Tina said accusingly as they emerged into High Street. 'What's the matter? Don't you like being married? I do!'

'I do! Yes, of course I do! But where would you like to go, my sweet? I'm afraid you found the visit to my mother's little cottage rather dull, and I know you found Culloden a bit depressing, but anything else you'd like to do . . .'

Beneath all his talk and gaiety he was remembering how little he had managed to convey to his rather puzzled bride about the facts of life, how often he had allowed himself to be led off the subject. Come to think of it, he had never actually got round to talking about warm-blooded mammals at all, let alone the human race!

I should have tried harder, made her listen, he told himself miserably. Could he not say a few words now? But she was so happy! Mentally shrugging, he decided he would have to let things take their course.

They had a delightful day, for the sun shone without once going behind the clouds, and, though there was a breeze, it scarcely lifted Tina's curls from her forehead. They found time to take their canal trip, but they had missed the steamer so instead Edward hired a boat and they took turns with the oars, and then they had luncheon at the Peacock, with wine and a tiny glass of liqueur for Edward.

'And now we must go and book a room at the Imperial Hotel, which seems a decent place,' Edward said, conscious of some embarrassment.

'Why? We aren't leaving tomorrow, are we?' Tina asked, instantly suspicious, for the Imperial was on the corner of Union Street and directly opposite the station.

'No, darling of course not. But we're married! It would look odd if we went out as Mr and Miss Draper and returned as Mr and Mrs Neyler.'

Tina giggled. 'So it would! Shall we do that next, then? I love my new dress and coat but I don't want to get them soiled, and I like to wear my tweed suit in the evenings, when it gets chilly. Shall we dine at the Imperial?'

'Very well. I told the porter at the Glenalbyn to take our traps round to the Imperial; I daresay he thought we would be leaving soon. I think we might dine there, if the menu suits us.'

They went back to the Imperial and Edward got the room key from the desk clerk. He went before her up the stairs and along the corridor and opened the door for her, standing aside for his wife to precede him into the room. Tina smiled her thanks very sweetly, and almost shut the door in his face.

'Tina, this is *our* room,' Edward said gently. 'Take off your coat, my love, and you can wash and change. Or would you prefer a bath? For my part, I'd rather bathe.'

Tina was staring at him, a flush creeping up her cheeks.

'*Our* room! Oh, but I thought . . . That is, this is a *hotel!* I thought we'd have our own rooms until . . .'

'No. We share a room once we're married. I'll go and run you a bath and I'll take the second one.'

He was quite glad to escape from those wide, uneasy eyes.

Tina, feeling very foolish and uncomfortable over her silliness in not realising that they would be sharing a room, soon forgot her troubles in the pleasures of a hot bath. She climbed nimbly into the tub, lathered herself lavishly with the scented soap which Edward had given her, rubbed vigorously at her curls, then lay back and indulged in a little day-dreaming.

She was married at last! Mrs Edward Neyler. Tina Neyler. She wondered what Cecy would think if she knew that her sister was a married lady. And what Alice would say. And . . . no, she would not think about Poppa, not when she was so happy! The nicest part of being married, she reflected, was now no one could separate her from Edward. No one, not even one's father, could part husband and wife! She held out her hand and twisted it this way and that, admiring the deep gold of her wedding ring.

She was married! Truly married!

As the water began to cool she climbed reluctantly out of

the tub and rubbed herself dry on the hotel's largest bath towel. Then she slipped on her poplin blouse and blue tweed skirt. Her hair looked wild, all damp, tumbled curls, but it would dry while Edward took his bath.

She left the bathroom, padded along the corridor and entered their bedroom, then stopped short, her hand flying to her mouth.

Edward was standing there, clad only in his trousers. He turned and she felt a hot tide of blood rush up from her neck to the top of her tingling forehead. She said, on a gasp, 'I . . . I'm sorry . . .' even as he turned back towards the mirror, saying lightly, 'Come in, love. I've taken my jacket and shirt off and hung them up, so that I don't get them all steamed up in the bathroom.'

There was no way she could control her blushes, but she had too much pride to allow him to see how he had startled and dismayed her. She said casually: 'How sensible. Let me pass you your dressing gown.'

She did so, and to her relief he slipped it on without demur and went for his bath.

If he thought her unusually silent at dinner he did not remark on it, but went out of his way to make her laugh, teased her, and once leaned over the table when no one was looking and kissed her with a lightness which she found reassuring. But throughout the meal she was conscious of his physical nearness and the fact, daunting, strange, that they were to share a bedroom. She was not *afraid*, she told herself; just taking her time to grow accustomed to this new idea.

After their meal they lingered in the dining room for a little, and then returned to their own room. Tina, with real courage, did not suggest a walk by the river nor a last game of billiards. No use putting off the evil hour, ran her thoughts. If this is marriage, then I must be married.

Nevertheless, when they were in their own room and Edward had locked the door, turned down the gas and suggested that she might like to get ready for bed, she was so embarrassed that she could not look at him.

'Shall I ch-change in the bathroom?' she suggested, her

eyes on the floor.

'No. Why?'

'It seems immodest to take off my clothes with you in the room,' she muttered. 'It seems . . . fast.'

He knew her too well to laugh, but mirth bubbled within him and was sternly suppressed.

'Tina, darling, we're man and wife. Nothing about you can shock me. What we do with each other . . .' His voice shook, but only a little, 'can *never* be . . . fast.'

He crossed the room and took her in his arms. 'I love you!'

For the first time since they had come to Scotland he tilted her chin and kissed her firmly on the mouth, prolonging the kiss luxuriously, feeling once again her stirring, the quickening of her breathing, then the instinctive withdrawal. As before, he released her, smiling down into her flushed face. 'If you want, I'll change in the bathroom.'

Her dimples peeped. 'Oh, if you please, Edward! I will grow accustomed, I promise, but . . .'

He grinned, his teeth gleaming and reflecting the soft gaslight. 'You'd better be in your nightgown and in that bed before I get back, or I might kiss you again,' he teased. She smiled uncertainly, then he was gone.

She lay waiting for him, demurely nightgowned in white cotton from chin to ankle. Her heart beat fast, a little unevenly, but she told herself she was certainly not afraid! It was only that she could not help wondering, a little apprehensively, what young men wore to go to bed. Poppa wore a striped nightshirt, very respectable and not in the least frightening. But would a *young* man wear such a garment?

Edward returned, handsome in his green silk dressing gown, his golden hair brushed till it shone, smelling deliciously of soap and toothpaste. He grinned at her, turned off the gas, and climbed into bed, first taking off his dressing gown. She saw the last glimmer of light reflect on bare skin, and gasped. So *that* was what young men wore in bed!

He slid under the covers, then put out his hand and felt for her face. When he found it he leaned over and kissed her. Such a kiss! They had kissed before but always fully clothed. Between them had been shifts, boned bodices, cloaks, gowns, jackets; waistcoats, stiff collared shirts, vests. Now she was held against his bare chest, his skin warming her through the thin cotton nightdress, his hands fondling her fragile shoulderblades as their mouths met. She gasped a protest even as her stomach gave a sickening lurch of pleasure, and as her lips parted his mouth invaded hers. She whimpered, trying to pull away, pushing feebly against his bare shoulders. And then he had released her, though his arms still gently imprisoned her.

'What's the matter, my darling? Are you afraid?'

'Afraid? No! Why should I be . . .well, a little, perhaps.'

'Why? You know I wouldn't harm you.'

'It isn't that! You're different, you do funny things, and you . . .'

She broke off with a squeak and next moment a fury had attacked him, hitting and slapping, sobbing and exclaiming.

'You beast, stop it! How *dare* you? I think you're very rude! Keep away! Stay on your own side of the bed! If you do rude things I'll hit you again!'

He lay still without speaking and gradually she calmed down. After a few minutes' silence she said defensively, 'Do let's go to sleep, Edward! I'm tired, I truly am!'

'Tina, take your nightdress off, or I'll take it off for you.'

She stiffened, clenching her hands into fists. 'How *dare* you! So that was what you were trying to do! Just you leave me alone, Edward Neyler!'

She was sitting up, shaking in every limb, prepared to leave the bed in one leap if she felt his hands on her bare flesh again. She felt besieged, surrounded by strangers, her breathing was fast and shallow, the heart-beats pulsing through her body were suffocatingly loud.

He did not move but his voice came out of the darkness and it was her own dear love's voice; gentle, understanding.

'My poor darling, don't be afraid! You know women bear babies and men father them; you've read it in the Bible. Well, that's as much a part of being married as exchanging rings and being called a wife. I swear to you that nothing I shall do or have done is wicked or . . . or rude.'

'And . . . and must I take my nightdress off?'

'Yes.'

With a sigh, she began to obey him. Trembling fingers fumbled with the small buttons at her neck, the smaller ones at her wrists. She began to cry silently, not sniffing or gasping, just letting the tears form in her eyes and spill down her face. After a moment, buttons undone at last, she pulled the gown over her head in one desperate, brave movement.

'Edward?'

'Yes, love?'

'I've done it.'

She felt his hand, trembling a little, touch her shoulder, then travel firmly down her upper arm to her elbow. 'Brave girl. Give me a kiss.'

She had thought that the removal of her nightdress would lead to some sort of terrifying attack and was immeasurably relieved when it did not. She moved a little closer to him, feeling her own interest in him stirring. She found his shoulders, stroked up his neck to his chin, and gave a nervous gasp when his lips kissed the palm of her hand.

'That . . . that did something to my stomach,' she said breathlessly.

'Kiss me Tina. I dare you!'

With her hands resting on those broad, muscled shoulders, she leaned closer, until their lips met. This time the kiss was long and sweet, with no frightening strangeness, no probing, pushing intimacies. She gave a small, contented mutter and cuddled closer. His arms rested lightly round her and it was she whose fingers suddenly tightened as, unexpectedly, a wave of desire rose in her. She had been holding back a little, almost unconsciously, but now she allowed the whole length of her newly aroused body to touch him, feeling her small, apple-shaped breasts press against the curly hairs on his chest, her hips touch his.

He broke the kiss, but still made no attempt to grab or ravish. Instead, his lips began a slow, intimate journey which banished fear and brought her newly awakened feelings to a peak. She moved under his mouth, like a cat responding to a caressing hand, almost purring at this sudden, new pleasure. He lifted his mouth for a moment.

'Tina?'

'Mm hmm?'

'Do you still feel frightened?'

'Oh, no!'

'Is it all right for me to go on?'

She felt so lovely! Her body felt like warm silk, beautiful to touch, soft and supple, as though his touch was a kind of magic which aroused fresh wonders and beauties in her body that she had never known about. She felt good. satisfied. But not yet sated; something which knew more than she did herself told her there was something else yet, something better.

'Please do,' she said courteously, and heard him chuckle against her silky skin without resentment.

He went on.

Tina was awoken next morning by the soft click of the door shutting. She sat up, then groaned and lay down again. She was so stiff! Her legs felt as if she had run a thousand miles the day before, and her back ached. Whatever . . .

Recollection came flooding in and she swallowed, feeling the blush burning up her body. Cautiously, she pulled back the sheet. Did one blush all over? She had never taken the slightest interest in her body before but now she knew she would find it fascinating. Edward liked it very much, therefore it behoved her to know all about it.

She was intrigued to find that the blush which poured so hotly over her did indeed show up over most of her skin, though only her face and neck were dyed scarlet, leaving the rest of her the palest rose. She rather liked herself in pink! Then she remembered what had woken her and stretched out her hand to where he had lain all night. The sheets were still warm. He had crept out of bed to go to the bathroom, leaving her, as he thought, still sleeping.

She got out of bed rather stiffly and padded across to where her own dressing gown hung on the back of the door. She glanced at her nakedness in the dressing table mirror, and thought she looked rather comical. Never again, she realised with surprise, would she think nakedness wrong or sinful. It could not be wrong to be naked, because Edward said so.

Reaching up she unhooked the gown, slipped into it, and belted it round her small waist. She opened the door and peeped cautiously up and down the corridor. Not a soul about; it must be early still. She padded, barefoot, along to the bathroom door and scratched on the panel.

'Edward? Let me in!'

There was a pause, then water sloshed violently about in the tub and the door opened, letting wreaths of steam escape into the corridor.

'Nip in quickly, darling. I was in the bath.'

She slipped round the door and he locked it behind her, then turned and kissed her, their lips meeting briefly. His strong, tanned body was rosy from the hot water and his shoulders steamed. She looked at him deliberately, trying not to blush; but she knew the colour was suffusing her face and smiled up at him, acknowledging her blushes by putting her hands to her hot cheeks.

'Have you come for your bath? Share mine!'

She slipped out of her dressing gown and threw it down carelessly on the floor. 'Yes, I want to bath. But there isn't room in the tub for both of us!'

'Of course there's room. If we keep close to one another, that is.'

He picked her up like a baby, pretended to rock her, then lowered her splashily into the water. She smiled up at him as he climbed in as well, and then saw his lids droop over his eyes, his nostrils flare, something happen to his mouth. He lowered himself into the water, then caught hold of her, dragging her into his arms. Water sloshed up the sides of the bath and she began to laugh, then his mouth covered hers and there was no sky, no moon, no stars; only Edward, and the loud song of their love, their wet, tangled limbs, their burning, heart-stopping kisses, and the water crashing out of the tub and puddling the floor.

Much later, she pushed his wet hair off his forehead, and kissed the side of his mouth. Languorously, he returned the kiss.

'I am yours,' she said softly. 'What you want, I want. Where you go, I follow. You've made me *real*, Edward. There is only you.'

He tilted her face up to his, a finger beneath her pointed chin, and kissed her soft, eager mouth.

'I know, my darling. I know.'

16

They had been in Inverness a week, enjoying being married, sharing things, before Edward decided the time had come for a serious talk.

'My money's running out,' he explained, sitting Tina down on a bench and watching the river slip past. 'We must have some capital in order to get established, and I must keep some aside for our passage back to New Zealand, so I dare not just go on spending. I've been keeping my eyes open as we walked around the town, but there are no openings for someone like me. No wonder my grandparents emigrated! There's a lot of poverty and hardship here when they aren't engaged in ship building.'

'Then where shall we go? Back to Norwich?'

'Not Norwich, no. I think Liverpool would be our best bet. I met a fellow – Hecky White, his name is – who's started up in the building trade in Liverpool. Apparently the city fathers have decided to go in for slum clearance in a big way, so that's why openings in the trade are better in Liverpool than elsewhere. Hecky would welcome us, because I've got the knowledge of building which he needs – Mark and I built our farmhouse, you know, and our dairy – and because I've some capital. Shall we try it for a while?'

'It sounds all right,' Tina said. To be honest, anywhere seemed better than Dunedin, twelve thousand miles away! She had not missed her father or her family in the same way since that blinding moment of love when she had given herself unreservedly to Edward but she was still conscious, occasionally, of feelings of guilt because she had run off, leaving them to manage as best they could without her. 'I'll write to Poppa once we've got our own home in Liverpool, shall I?'

He put his arm round her shoulders, drawing her close until her head rested on his breast. 'Not immediately, my love. It hasn't occurred to you, but your poppa might prefer to drag us through the courts and get the marriage annulled rather than see you married to an uncircumcised man. Or he might decide to come after us and circumcise me personally!'

She pinched his chin. 'You are *rude*! As if Poppa would! But I may write, mayn't I, provided I don't give them our address too soon? We don't have to wait until I'm pregnant, do we? You said yourself that I'm young and it might be a while.'

He kissed the top of her curly head. 'So you are – young, I mean. As for waiting until you're pregnant, we might have to wait months! Years! No, but we won't get in touch until we're settled in and I've seen how being a builder suits me. Which reminds me, Tina Neyler, you know I married you without knowing the dreadful truth about you? I wonder if the marriage is legal, in the circumstances?'

'Not legal? What are you talking about? You know *all* about me!'

'I do now, Valentina! What a mouthful for such a small girl!'

She laughed, twisting out of his grasp to stand up and hold out her hands, pulling him to his feet. 'Didn't you know until our wedding day? What a horrid shock! I never tell anyone because I can't stand the name. Well then, we've decided. Liverpool it is! When do we leave?'

He hugged her, then tucked her hand into the crook of his arm.

'No fuss, no outcry,' he said admiringly. 'You're an admirable little wife, Valentina!'

Mark came into Dunedin most days to deliver the milk to the dairy in Rattray Street, no longer trading as Edma but as the Ashburton, and then he usually drove the pony-cart up Princes Street so that he could collect his mail from the post office.

Today he had already dumped his milk churns and picked up his letters and was walking slowly back towards the cart, scuffing the snow off the pavement with heedless toes, for the letter was from Edward, and therefore of great interest.

'Mark? Can it really be you? How lovely to meet you after all these years! Do you remember me?'

He almost cannoned into the speaker and apologised, blinking, for although it was very cold and in the countryside the snow lay thick the sun was brilliant, reflecting off the snow.

At about shoulder height a small face was beaming at him. He frowned. Recognition swam just out of reach, tantalising him, but the strong sunshine and the years between combined to baffle him.

The girl said: 'Dancing Dan, do you remember him? I have him still!'

'Wan Leng!' He seized her hands, squeezing them. 'No wonder I didn't recognise you! You're a fashionable lady!'

It was true. At the gold diggings she had dressed Chinese-style in thick blue wool trousers beneath a long woollen tunic; in the cold weather, indeed, she had scarcely been visible except as a dumpling of coats, scarves and cardigans. Now she was a Western lady. Her hair was curled and dressed high on her head, her gown was the green of a young beech leaf, her topcoat, a three-quarter length tweed, was tailored to show off her tiny waist.

'I am a fashionable lady to look at, but beneath my pretty clothes I'm still your friend from the Clutha,' she said solemnly.

'And you still have Dancing Dan? I can't believe it!'

He had bought her the small wooden doll on a stick years ago and had shown her how to make it dance and leap. He remembered the little plays she had performed with the doll taking all the parts; the small houses she built for Dan out of river mud and stones, the flax mat she tried to weave for him when she was pretending he was a great Maori chief. Of course she had kept the doll. It had been her one and only toy!

'Yes, I still have Dan. He's a little battered, and his paint is scratched, but I have him still. He reminds me of my good friend Mark. And of Edward, too.'

Mark dropped her hands which he had been gripping while they spoke and took her arm.

'Come into the Old Times Restaurant and we'll have coffee and some cakes and talk in the warm. You must tell me everything.'

'Old Times, eh? That's appropriate. Very well, I can spare a little while.'

They were outside the door of the restaurant when Mark remembered the pony-cart. He clapped a hand to his head.

'My God, I'll forget my own head next! I left the pony-cart tied up outside the post office. Do you think it will be all right there?'

'Same old Mark, always worrying! Of course it will be all right, why should it not? Tethering posts are for tethering, aren't they? Now buy me those cakes!'

Presently, comfortably seated at a window table with hot biscuits and the promised coffee and cakes before them, he re-opened the conversation.

'Now, fire away! What are you doing here? You went back to China, didn't you, years ago? How are your parents?'

She took a hot biscuit, licking melted butter from her fingers and considering his questions. For a moment she looked very like the Wan Leng of Clutha days.

'To begin at the beginning, we didn't return to China, we went to England. My parents are there still, but I was homesick for Otago, for the shore and the hills. I've been to college and have my degree, so when I saw an advertisement for a teacher who could teach mathematics to young ladies between twelve and sixteen I applied. It was at the Girl's High School on Dowling Street, and I got the job.' She glanced up at him archly. 'They were a little surprised when I arrived, but so good and kind! I came for a trial period on both sides, but I think I'll remain.'

'Why should they be surprised?'

'I don't use my old name any more. I am Wendy Lang.'

He laughed.

'Why, for God's sake? Wan Leng's a very pretty name.'

'Very foreign, you mean,' she corrected. 'I assure you it is better if people meet me first and see for themselves that I don't have four inch feet and a needle through my nose; then I stand a chance of being fairly judged.'

'A needle through your nose! But is Wendy Lang your real name now? Must I call you Wendy?'

She nodded seriously, though her eyes sparkled. 'Yes, it is my real name; I changed it by deed poll. But you can call me Wen; most of my friends do.'

'What a relief! It isn't that different, really. And your parents?'

'Still in London, though they would like to return to Dunedin if only to see me settled in! They're better off in England in a way, though, because I've a host of relatives there.'

He was still gazing at her as if he could not believe his eyes, though he ate his cakes and drank his share of the coffee nevertheless. 'Little Wan Leng, a school teacher! Wonders will never cease! But it's marvellous to meet you again!'

She beamed at him, her dark eyes almost disappearing.

'And good to see you, Mark. How is Ed? I always think

of you together, you and your brother.'

'He's in England too, in Liverpool. He's married to a girl called Tina; they eloped together a year ago.' He fished the crumpled and forgotten letter out of his pocket. 'I got this from Ed this morning. He says he's taking his wife home again to make it up with her papa. He's hoping to come home to New Zealand in a year or so for a holiday. He's in business with a friend and they seem to be doing pretty well.'

'Oh, poor Mark! You and Edward were so close, more like twins than brothers. I suppose you have commitments which prevent you following him to England?'

'Commitments? Oh, you mean the farm. No, I couldn't leave, but I wouldn't go anyway. I'd be no good at the building trade; the only thing I'm good at is being a farmer. I need the land and the animals.'

'Well, I quite see that the farm is a commitment, but I meant more personal things. You have a wife, children?'

'*Me?* Good God, no! What about you, Wen?'

'*Me?* Good God, no!' She laughed up at him, but there was a good deal of understanding in her dark eyes. 'But you must have thought about marriage. You're a lot older than I am.'

'I was engaged for a bit,' he admitted. 'I bet you've got a lot of beaux.'

'Why didn't you marry her? Your fiancée, I mean.'

'It's a long and very stupid story. Her name was Sylvia and she was in love with Ed, but when he left the South Island she decided to make do with me. Then fortunately someone with more money and better prospects came along and she went off with him. She's Mrs Albert Booker now and lives in Christchurch.'

'Were you truly glad? You meant fortunately?'

Mark leaned back in his chair and breathed in until his cheeks were puffed out like oranges, then expelled the air in a long whistle.

'Phew! So glad, Wen! She was a predatory blonde, cold as ice and determined as a bull seal. Not my type at all.'

'She doesn't sound any man's type! Why did you become

engaged to her?'

'She was very pretty,' Mark admitted grudgingly, then grinned as her laugh rang out. 'On the surface, she was just a pretty young girl. Ed warned me, or tried to, but I only began to see for myself when the ring was on her finger and she began trying to push me towards her idea of success. But let's not talk about her. Tell me about you! Where do you lodge? How long have you been back in Dunedin? When . . .'

'Mark, I've enjoyed talking to you more than I can say, but I must go!' She consulted the small fob-watch dangling at her lapel. 'I have a class in twenty minutes. Would it be very forward of me to suggest you walk me back to the High School?'

He was on his feet at once, offering his arm.

'Of course I'll walk you back! But I don't intend to lose touch with you again. Do you have weekends off? Then would you do me the honour of lunching with me on Sunday? I'll drive into Dunedin and call for you and we can spend the day on the farm. I can show you round the house and outbuildings and we'll find plenty to talk about. Say you'll come!'

'I'd love to,' Wendy said at once. 'It will be like old times.' She hesitated, glancing up at him a trifle shyly. 'Mark, I must ask you, because I value my job. Is there . . .'

'I've a housekeeper, an elderly and respectable female. I don't mind you asking, honestly.' He patted her hand, lying on his sleeve. 'Here's the school. Where shall I meet you on Sunday, and when?'

'I've lodgings in York Place, so if you could pick me up at the MacPhersons' place at about ten . . . ?'

He agreed eagerly and stood watching her as she swung into the building, elegant and neat, then turned and waved. 'Till Sunday, Mark!'

Returning to the tethering post outside the post office, Mark suddenly remembered he had not finished Edward's letter; an unprecedented occurrence, for usually the letters were read and re-read until the next one arrived.

With pleasurable anticipation, he got the thin, crumpled sheets out of his pocket and drove off down Princess Street, one eye on the page as he found his place. He turned left into Anderson's Bay Road and once under the railway bridge gave his full attention to the letter. The pony could have found his way home quite unaided along this familiar stretch of coast road.

Beneath the wheels the snow squeaked a protest as it was compressed. The sun had melted the ice on branches which stretched, in places, across the carriageway, and there were small noises of running water, tinkling droplets meeting lower branches, and the ever-present sound of bird-song. To his left, the murmur of the waves never ceased, a constant background which one never heard on the Peninsula because it was there all the time.

He frowned down at the letter. Liverpool sounded grim no matter how good business might be. He wondered how Edward, reared in the deep forests of Waihola and then living on the Peninsula coast, could bear it. It must be Tina, wanting money, tying him to her wretched country. He pictured her small and thin, blonde like Sylvia because Edward liked blondes. A small, weaselly creature, ruling Edward with a rod of iron. It *must* be her! Edward spoke of the reconciliation between his wife and her family as though that were the only bar to his homecoming, but despite Mark's words to Wendy the letter did not actually mention their return to the South Island.

Mark was not like Edward. He was painfully shy, a real introvert, but he had never felt this to be a disadvantage until Edward had left. The two of them were so happy in each other's company. Edward was popular and outgoing, yet he had never needed or wanted close friends because he had Mark. And Mark, shy, hard-working, loving the work he did perhaps better than any other farmer on the Peninsula, was content because he had Edward. No woman had ever come between them because women answered a need which had nothing to do with their fondness of each other.

With Ed gone, Mark had known real loneliness. He had

two farmhands and Toddy and his wife Freda so that, indoors and out, he was seldom actually alone. He scarcely counted Mrs Stitch the housekeeper as company, she was so cross-grained and deaf.

No, it was not other people he was lonely for, but Edward. No one to congratulate when things went right, no one to commiserate when things went wrong. And then Edward had married and Mark had known that nothing could ever be quite the same again. So there was a gap, a soreness in his life, where once there had been understanding and comfort.

There's so much for him here, Mark thought, jogging home in the snow and sun. So many opportunities. But he's willing to set them all aside and stay in England, a stranger in a strange land, because of a selfish little bitch of a girl. God, how I hate that Tina!

I hate that Mark! Tina thought angrily. But she did not say the words out loud. Edward was reading a letter at the breakfast table, his face wearing the wistful look she had come to associate with letters from Mark. During the year they had been married she had come to recognise that her only real rival in Edward's affection was his younger brother. She knew about Sylvia, who had once been Edward's girl and had gravitated to Mark, but she never wasted a thought on her. Sylvia had meant nothing to Edward. Her husband only loved two people, herself and his younger brother.

At the moment she knew his love for herself was in the ascendant. Why else would he remain in England when it was plain that his wretched Dunedin and Mark called to him? There was the business, of course; but he and Hecky were doing well, and she knew he could be spared for a few months. But he had promised that until she was reconciled with her family he would not expect her to go to New Zealand, even for a holiday. So here they were, and she knew he loved her best, and was determined that he should continue to do so.

She was trying so hard to be a good wife! She had made

mistakes, of course; she acknowledged that now though at the time she had not been prepared to do so. There had been the bacon and egg pie, for instance, but she preferred not to think about that. And the pair of trousers, Edward's best, washed well but not wisely. And their next door neighbour's youngest who, invited in to see Mrs Neyler's pretty new hearthrug, had calmly squatted down and defecated upon it.

But she was learning all the time, and, because Edward loved her and helped her whenever he could, her falls from grace were less painful now and less frequent too.

There was the loneliness, of course. She had not reckoned with the awful, mind-crippling loneliness which had assailed her the first time Edward had left her alone in their little house to go off with Hecky on business. At home she had thought herself lonely, but now she realised she had not known the meaning of the word. The eldest of a large family, with two servants living in the house, pleasant neighbours who had known her for many years, Poppa home every day at lunch-time and the children home by four o'clock, yet she had thought herself deprived! Now she could look back on the Tina of a year or so ago and wonder at her foolishness. Surrounded by people and friends she had been. She had scarcely known a moment's loneliness!

They had bought the end house in a row of terraced dwellings, theirs being a trifle bigger and a good deal better than the neighbours' homes. It had been built for a milkman and he had insisted on a square yard at the back with stables and a hayloft, and a small washhouse and lavatory built on to the back kitchen. He had planted trees, too. A pear which he had trained against the wall of the house, a fig which grew beside the stable, a Victoria plum tree which children stripped bare before the fruit had even begun to turn colour.

Edward bought the house because it was cheap, convenient for his work, and had outbuildings which the business could use to advantage. He gave little thought to the neighbours or even to the district. It simply did not occur to him that it was not kind to set his Tina down in a slum, to live amongst people so far removed from her own kind. Edward thought Mrs Snelling, whose house abutted theirs, a friendly, outgoing woman, and advised Tina to visit her and become friendly.

Tina did make timid overtures, but soon realised that she and the older woman were poles apart. Mrs Snelling was an Irish Catholic with a dozen children, ill-clothed and ill-fed, two mongrel dogs which peed on Tina's clean doorstep and stole her bread if the baker left it on the threshold, and a fund of gossip and dirty stories. Her house was fast deteriorating, as were the dwellings in the rest of the row, into an enormous rubbish heap which smelt bad in hot weather.

For her part, Mrs Snelling had no desire whatsoever for Tina's friendship. She did not grudge her the piped water which Edward had caused to be brought right into her kitchen, nor the bedroom which Edward had converted into a real bathroom, nor the modern stove which he installed. She certainly did not envy Tina her constant battle against the dirt and grime, the line of washing put out daily, the meticulous ironing of all Edward's stiff-collared shirts, her own petticoats, blouses and drawers. She did not even envy the fact that Tina was plainly not short of money for she knew herself to be better off than most. Her man was in regular work and three of her sons had good paying jobs down at the docks. She saw Tina on her hands and knees, scrubbing up the dirt as soon as it was laid down, up to her elbows in suds for hours at a time, rushing out every day to buy fresh food and vegetables for her husband, and felt nothing but resentment. She had no desire to do such things herself, but she resented the fact that, by keeping the place clean and tidy, by turning her husband out impeccably and by always looking spruce as a pin herself, Tina was proving that it could be done.

Gone were the days when she could sigh to her husband, ''Tain't no use, Frederick, the dirt's gorrus all beat! You can't fight it, chuck! Pass us a sup of ale!' Now, her man and her sons only had to glance next door to see what war could still be waged on the filth; waged and won. So it was no wonder that she disliked Tina and could not wait to pass round rumours about that skinny, black-haired little witch!

Relations did not improve when Tina, desperate for company, walked home with Bill Snelling as he was coming back from a day's work at the docks and mentioned to him that she had bought a book which she thought quite the funniest thing she had ever read.

'You read, then, Mrs Neyler?' Bill said eagerly. 'I do, an' all! Anything I can lay me 'ands on! What sorta books 'ave you got?'

Encouraged by his interest, Tina promptly asked him in and the two of them spent an hour with their heads together in front of her small bookcase, already crammed to overflowing though she had come into the house without a book to her name.

'I've got a few,' he admitted to her. 'I'll lend you some, if you like. Say, how about you coming to the 'aymarket with me? There's a power of bookstalls there. It's like a dream, honest! I spend all me spare cash there!'

She accepted his invitation without a second thought and next day the two of them, both voracious readers, came staggering home up the Row with armfuls of reading matter.

'I lent 'er four, and she's lent me four,' Bill muttered, stowing his books away in a corner of the general living room. 'I say, Mam, you 'aven't been next door, 'ave you? Like a little palace, she's gorrit! But books! Blimey, they're everywhere. Not a bit toffee-nosed over 'em, either. Borrow any as you've a mind to, she says, very pleasant-like.'

Mrs Snelling, answering with a grunt, was in a dilemma. She had waited hopefully for Mrs Neyler to put a foot wrong, to invite a man into the house and prove herself a loose woman and at last she had done it. But it was Billy, her favourite son! If it had been anyone else, she told herself furiously, the story would have gone round, with suitable embellishments, before morning, and Tina's reputation would have been effectively smutted. But Billy? How could she accuse her neighbour, only a slip of a girl when all was said and done, of seducing her Billy, who was twenty-five, big and tall with it, and a one for the girls into the bargain? People just would not *believe* that she had lured him into her house to have her wicked way with him! They would nod and wink and put tales about concerning her son!

So Billy and Tina continued to enjoy each other's company in the most innocent way possible, unsmeared by gossip. In fact, the other neighbours were extremely surprised that Mrs Snelling's oft-repeated criticisms of 'that stuck-up bitch' suddenly seemed to tail away to nothing other than a few vague remarks about her neighbour polishing out in the street next.

'What are you dreaming about?'

Tina looked up, startled. They were still at the breakfast table and Edward had just laid down Mark's letter, yet her thoughts had spanned almost twelve months of living in Spanner's Row, had re-lived her friendship with Billy, had even taken in the neighbours!

'Dreaming about? Who else but Billy Snelling?'

He glowered at her. 'Dream about me!' he commanded. 'Do you know we've been married a year tomorrow?'

'It had crossed my mind. Do you want more coffee?'

'No thanks.' He leaned across the table and stole the last piece of toast from her plate and popped it into his mouth. Speaking rather thickly, he said: 'A year's long enough. I'm going to get in touch with your father.'

It was so totally unexpected. She felt a flutter of fear begin in her stomach. 'But what about Cecy? She says in all her letters that he won't have my name mentioned. She keeps trying to get him to forgive me, but he says he never will. He threw my letters on the fire, Ted! He says I'm dead to him.'

Edward pushed back his chair and got up, folding his newspaper into a small square to fit into his overcoat pocket.

'I've wondered, lately, why Cecy is so vehement; haven't you? But a year's a long time, Tina. I'm going to telephone him today at his office. If he really won't speak to us then at least I'll know the truth and can begin to plan accordingly.'

'Ted, I wish you wouldn't . . .' she began, and then stopped. To see them again! To walk through Norwich in the springtime, bound for the Bishopsgate house! To walk up the familiar path, lined with crocuses, narcissi, daffodils, and to knock on that much-loved front door! She could see it all; the hall tiles shining in the sunlight which would pour in when the front door opened, the children, lining the doorway of their room, and the room itself, with its comfortable, faded rugs and chairs, the games and toys, the french windows leading out into their glorious garden!

He took her in his arms and kissed her eyelids. 'Well? Changed your mind? Would you like to see them all again?'

'I *would!* If I could be sure Poppa wouldn't disown me, or . . . or . . .'

'I'll telephone.' He kissed her mouth with the slow tenderness which she adored. 'Goodbye, darling. See you this evening!'

'So Edward telephoned me, at the office, and they are to come home for a long weekend. Well, Cecy mine, what do you think?'

Cecy's complexion darkened until she looked the picture of guilt but she said: 'Lovely!' as brightly as she could.

'Edward said Tina had been corresponding with someone, Lizbeth perhaps, all this past year. Someone, it seems, said to Tina that no longer would I speak her name, nor receive her in my house.'

Cecy glanced at Arthur's face, and read sad knowledge there. 'It was me! I . . . I said it because I didn't want you upset, nor . . . nor the children, and I . . . I . . .' Her voice became suspended by tears.

Arthur went to her, putting his arm round her plump shoulders. 'Cecy, Tina's place here is no more, you know that! You have a place in your own right, earned by you! You are my right hand, my dear little helper. I gave you nothing that was Tina's and I could not, therefore, take from you to give back to Tina. What did you fear? It was wrong to lie, to make your sister unhappy, your father unhappy. Written to me I thought she never had, yet Edward tells me many letters she sent. Begging for forgiveness, beseeching me only to answer! How could you do this thing?'

'Oh, Poppa, it was so lovely to be your favourite,' Cecy sobbed, burying her head in his velvet jacket. 'To hear you say to the others "Do as Cecy says", and "That's a good girl, Cecy mine". I knew I was running the family as well as Tina had and better. And then she wrote to me, enclosing a letter to you and saying she wanted to be reconciled . . . I just couldn't *bear* it! The thought of her coming home, bossing us, being your darling girl again . . . I couldn't bear it! So . . . so I burned that first letter and wrote back to her, saying you'd thrown her letter on the fire without even looking at it. She wrote again, direct to you, and again, and then again. I burned all the letters! I didn't *read* them, or anything like that, I just destroyed them.'

Arthur got out his handkerchief and wiped Cecy's eyes tenderly, tilting her chin up so that she met his gaze. 'Cecy mine, it is a bad, a wrong thing that you did, but it is over, eh? Forgotten by me it shall be. Tina must know, because I cannot have her think it was I who burned her letters, but she need not know who . . . and she will forgive, for she has done us a wrong, and knows it, I think. But it is not right to forget that for many years Tina worked very hard for us.'

'But Poppa, she left us! Ran off with Edward, not even saying where she was going! I'll never forget your hurt, Poppa! Nor the little ones, crying, begging me to bring her back, when I could not! Then the letters came, so . . . so complacent, so smug. "Edward and I", "Edward thinks", "our dear little house"! She has everything, but she still wants what I've got! She wants you, and the family. When she first went you said she'd forfeited her right to a place as your daughter, so I . . . I . . .'

'That was said in anger, Cecy mine. Tell me, do you not wish to marry one day? Ach, hope I must that you will meet and love a good Jewish boy, but then you will leave us, no? I was a fool with Tina, I guarded her too well, tried to keep her a child when a woman she was! I was content with my home and my children and thought she should be content also. I forgot that a young woman has desires which . . .' he broke off, looking self-conscious. 'Such talk, it is not for you. Not yet, eh? But you will welcome Tina when she comes? Make her at home to feel?'

'Oh, Poppa, I will! And do you forgive me truly?'

He bent and kissed her, rumpling her hair. 'With all my heart I forgive, Cecy mine. I much worse things have done, and have been forgiven. Love your sister, my child, don't envy her. It has been hard for her, alone and believing herself cast off. Make up to her for the grief you caused.'

She smiled up at him, tears forgotten, though her cheeks were still wet. 'I will, Poppa. You see!'

17

'Edward what made you suddenly decide to ring Poppa? Was it just that we'd been married a year, or was there something else?'

They were walking up Bank Plain, hurrying home, with Edward carrying their small weekend bag as if it weighed nothing. He glanced down at Tina, grinning teasingly into her small, fresh face. She still looked like a schoolgirl despite the year of marriage she had lived through since last she walked this pavement.

'There were other reasons. I wanted your hair to be a proper length, of course. And I wanted my business to be sufficiently established so that when Arth . . . Poppa asks questions I can answer them properly. Questions like "Are you giving my daughter the life to which she had become accustomed?"'

'As if Poppa would dare to ask you such a thing! Why, he must know that you give me everything I want!'

'Naturally! Like a piano, for instance!'

She pinched his hand, digging her fingernails into his skin so that he yelped.

'Don't be so mean, to mention that wretched piano! I was much younger then, and so foolish! You won't tell Poppa?'

He grinned. 'What, tell him that you got into a furious rage with me because I said we couldn't have a piano, and stormed out of the house shouting like a fishwife and ordered one? And when it came, and the men saw the front room and told you it would never fit . . .'

'Edward, if you don't stop this moment I'll turn right round and walk back to the station and go home to Liverpool,' Tina said, her eyes very bright, her mouth pinched into a straight line.

He caught her shoulders and hugged her to him for a moment. 'My darling! Do you realise you said "home to Liverpool"? Don't worry. I'll bury that wretched piano along with the first custard tart you made, and the shirt with the turned collar, and all the other natural disasters. And before you hit me, there is another reason why I thought we should come to Norwich and make our peace with Poppa.'

'What? Do tell me before we reach Bishopsgate.'

'Well, you know about a month ago you had several nasty attacks of sickness? You vomited at about breakfast time, on and off, for a while?'

She nodded, eyes clear and innocent of any knowledge. 'I remember.'

'Well, darling, I think you may be pregnant.'

The hand tucked confidingly into his elbow tightened on his coat sleeve until the knuckles showed white. 'Pregnant? How could I be? It's nonsense.' Then, when he made no reply, 'Isn't it?'

'I think you may find I'm right,' Edward said carefully. 'I hadn't intended to say anything to you until I'd spoken to Alice, or . . .'

'How would Alice know anything? She isn't even

married!' She had stopped in her tracks at his statement but now she gave a little skip and commenced trotting along again, glancing up into his face now and then for all the world like a puppy hoping for commendation. 'Can it be true? Can I really be going to have a dear little baby? When, Edward?'

He was amused and touched by her instant acceptance of his suspicions, and laughed a little unsteadily. 'Darling, I don't know! I did have a word with Hecky's mother, but she said I should take you to a doctor and we've both been fit since we arrived in Liverpool so of course I didn't know anyone suitable. Then I remembered Dr Goldstein had been your family physician for years. So I thought, if you wished, we could consult him.'

'Shall we tell Poppa? And Cecy? Alice, of course, and Becky and . . .'

'Hold hard, girl! I only think you might be! Suppose I'm wrong? I'm no doctor!'

'I expect you're right; you usually are,' Tina said with sublime faith in his abilities in all directions. 'When may we tell them, then?'

'When the doctor confirms it. Not a word till then. Now hush yo' mouth, gal, we'm awmost on de do' step!'

Nothing could have exceeded their welcome. Arthur crossed the hall, flung down his sticks, and enveloped Tina in a huge hug. With tears running down his cheeks he held out a hand to Edward, saying simply, 'Too long it has been; too long.'

The little ones rushed at Tina, then giggled and hung back until she produced the presents she had brought for them a year ago, in Inverness. Tartan pencil cases stuffed with fat coloured pencils for Becky and Rachel, a clockwork train set for Louis, a fringed and crocheted evening wrap for Cecy. For Poppa there were thick sheepskin slippers, and even the maids had not been forgotten. Alice had two pairs of gloves, one made of pearl-grey kid embroidered with white swans, the other tan suede, and Tess, the little maid of all work, had two pairs of red silk stockings embroidered with thistles.

The presents were received with rapture, and then Cecy drew Tina aside on the pretext of seeing improvements made in the kitchen.

'I'm sorry I told you Poppa could not forgive you,' she mumbled. And then, eyes brightening, 'See how well I'm managing, Tina! Do you remember how you wouldn't let us have friends in, or play games, because you said the house would become a bear garden? Well, I allow games, and friends to visit, but see how nice and clean and tidy everything is! We hardly ever argue, either.'

'Everything looks lovely,' Tina said truthfully. 'What a beautiful house this is! But my own little home is nice too, though there is only me to keep it so. We don't have a maid or a cleaning woman or anything like that.' She laughed. 'When Edward first took me round it, I looked at the two little bedrooms, one of which Edward said he intended to convert into a bathroom, and I said, "Where will the maid sleep?" Edward said you could have knocked him down with a feather! I mean, Cecy, two tiny bedrooms, a parlour and a kitchen and I ask a question like that!'

'Oh. I didn't leave school, you know, Tina, like you did; I'm there still, although only in the mornings. I don't mind that, though I miss sketching, and music, and hockey. Poppa decided that his big mistake with you was in taking you away from school and from your young friends. Yet despite still having to study I run things very smoothly. You must ask Alice how we go on!'

'I will,' Tina said absently. Her eyes flickered over Cecy, in her pretty pink and white gingham gown with a spotless white pinafore over it. She glanced at the huge kitchen with its shiny surfaces, the large, walk-in pantry, the larder for meat and other things which needed to be kept cool, the amount of space all around. And outside, the clear air, the garden, the flowing river. She faced Cecy squarely. 'My dear little house is very small, Cecy. And I have to work all the time just to keep it clean and nice. The railway is so near, so there are smuts everywhere, and mud gets trekked in from the street . . .' She sighed at the blank look on her sister's face. 'Look at my hands!'

Cecy looked at her sister's small, work-roughened hands, the nails cut short, unpolished. 'So?'

'Spanner's Row is a *slum*! The woman next door has twelve children and she's rearing them in a two-bedroomed house like mine. Next door to that they keep chickens in the *house*! Not in the yard, but in the house! When I come back with shopping they jump up at me, fluttering around my basket.' She shuddered briefly. 'Smelly, disgusting things, pecking at each other, getting underfoot! You've no idea what it's like.

'Edward took you to a *slum?* But why? I thought you were so happy!'

'I am terribly happy,' Tina admitted. 'But the work is very hard. The road outside is full of filth and I seem to spend half my life – more – washing and ironing and scrubbing and cleaning windows. If you leave it for a day or so the dirt gets so bad that it won't ever come perfectly clean again, so you have to keep on at it. I have to market every day because there is nowhere to keep fresh food, and I make most of my own underclothing and all the curtains, and bake all my own cakes, though I buy bread.'

'I have to clean nearly every day too,' Cecy said earnestly. 'I am very busy, supervising the maids, and . . .' She broke off, looking at Tina for the first time. 'I thought it was such a paradise, your little home! That was why I destroyed your letters, Oh, what have I done! I thought you were so happy!'

'I was, you silly girl. And I am still. I told you about my home because I want you to understand! Look, when I ran away with Edward I just thought about being with him, being married. I never thought about the hard work, being alone for hours and hours, living in a neighbourhood where the people next door would resent me just because I kept myself clean! Nor that we should be short of money because of having to plough every penny back into the business! But it didn't matter. I work terribly hard, and I'm terribly happy. See?'

Cecy did not quite see, but she did manage to understand that Tina did not grudge her her place as head of Poppa's house despite the fact that her own life was not quite as Cecy had envisaged it. She longed to ask her sister about being married, but when she did so Tina went red as a beetroot and gruffly advised her to mind her own business.

The weekend flew. On Monday they saw Dr Goldstein, who confirmed that Tina was indeed pregnant, and on Monday night, as they changed for dinner, Edward asked Tina if she would like to stay a bit longer.

'Well, but Ted, you told Hecky we'd be back by Wednesday! It would be wonderful to stay, of course, and look up our old friends, but . . .'

'Not *us*, sweetheart. You! I can manage at home without you. I'm quite good about the house. Have yourself a little holiday. Arthur will put you on the train in a week or two – a month, if you'd like it – and I'll meet you the other end. How does that appeal to you?'

'To stay without you? It would be a penance!'

He tried to look doubtful, but only succeeded in looking absurdly pleased. 'You foolish child! I don't deny I'd miss you, but . . .'

She put her hand over his mouth, silencing him. 'Not another word! I refuse to be treated in such a way. We leave tomorrow morning, as planned!'

It was hot in the kitchen. August was gone, but the heat showed no sign of lessening. Day after day dawned hot and still, and there had been a number of cases of enteric fever in Spanner's Row. Worse, typhoid had been brought into the city by one of the immigrant ships from Europe and now there were rumours of cholera, though Tina gave little credence to that. She knew that during the past ten years cholera had been almost wiped out in England.

She was ironing Edward's shirts, having put off the hated task until the pile waiting to be dealt with was so formidable that she was forced to light the fire and stand the flats by it before Edward noticed he had not a shirt to his name. She bent over the table, hefting the iron in both hands, and saw her sweat sizzle down on to the heated metal. Ironing, she reflected, was her most difficult task now that her pregnancy was so advanced. She could no longer stand close to the table and to iron from a distance, so to speak, meant that she needed both hands just to lift and maneouvre the flat.

Today the wretched iron seemed to weigh a ton. She glanced at the pile of shirts and sighed. There were petticoats too, but they had got very dry in the extreme heat and would have to be damped before she could press them. She finished the first shirt, folded it, and reached for the next. Just for once, she would wear her petticoats rough-dried. She could not face the thought of having to iron her own things as well as Edward's.

She had nearly finished the second shirt when she heard a knock at the door. Carefully she stood the cooling iron down near the fire but did not reach for the next one. Instead she left the kitchen and went into the short hall. She opened the front door, not caring if it was just one of the guttersnipes playing a trick on her. Anything to get away from the ironing for a moment!

But it was not a trick. Bill Snelling stood there, his face sweat-streaked, his mouth at half-cock.

'Mrs Neyler? Mam's out and she's left me to see to our Claud, the littl'un. He felt sickly this morning, it seems, but he's awful bad now. Would you . . . could you tek a look at 'im?'

'Well, I could,' Tina said doubtfully. 'But I don't know that I could do much, Billy. What's the matter, do you think?'

'Me mam says just a fever, but I was wondering about typhoid,' Billy stammered. 'You know 'ow Mam can be, Mrs Neyler – a bit muddled and fuddled, like. Well, it do seem to me our Claud's awful 'ot, and . . .' He paused, his face reddening even more. 'Well, kinda smelly!'

'I'll take a look at him,' Tina said. She walked past him, out of the front door, a short way along the pavement, and into the open front door of the Snelling house.

Inside, the stench hit her like a blow in the face. A most terrible, foetid smell! She stopped short, then a whimper from a pile of assorted rags in the corner drew her on. The youngest Snelling lay there, scarlet-faced, gasping for breath, and smelling, as his elder brother had indicated, quite appalling.

Cautiously, Tina laid her hand on the child's forehead, then with more confidence examined his chest and stomach.

'It's all right; it isn't typhoid, I don't think,' she said over her shoulder to Billy. 'I *think* it's measles.' She turned to Claud and began to stroke his brow soothingly. 'Poor little man! Does the light hurt your eyes then?'

'Oh it does, it does,' moaned the small sufferer. 'It 'urts me heyes something cruel!'

'I'm sure it must be measles,' Tina said decidedly. 'I've had them, and I know the light hurt my eyes dreadfully for several days, and I was terribly hot and feverish.' She had been speaking to Billy, but turned back to address Claud. 'Are you thirsty, my lad? Would you like me to bathe your forehead?'

'Thirsty, thirsty,' Claud muttered. 'Can I 'ave some stout?'

Tina's horrified 'No you cannot!' and Billy's indulgent 'I'll fetch some!' were spoken simultaneously. There was a short silence, then Tina said decidedly, 'This child needs caring for, Billy. Have the rest of you had measles?'

'Not a one!'

'Then help me to carry him next door. 'I'll give an eye to him until the worst of the fever's over. I can make him up a bed in the parlour.'

'It's good of you,' Billy said gratefully. 'But . . . but he's awful niggly and whiny, and . . .'

'I've a little brother not much older than your Claud,' Tina said briskly. 'What he wants now is a nice cool wash, and then a good long drink, and then plenty of sleep. If you could send for the doctor, perhaps he'd recommend laudanum. It does help ill persons to sleep, I know.'

By the time Edward returned from work his house had been rearranged. His shirts, neatly ironed, had been put away, and the fire was out. In the middle of the parlour, hot, red in the face and extremely fractious, but sweet-smelling and clad in an old shirt of his host's, was Claud Snelling, lying on a bed of cushions which he pronounced to be 'prime', and noisily sipping a glass of lemonade.

'He's over the worst, and now the rash has come out he'll be better in no time,' Tina told Edward smugly. 'He's quite a nice little boy really. And Billy was so worried, Ted.' She drew him into the kitchen, lowering her voice. 'Ted, the smell in that house next door! And the filth! He was lying in rags, with nothing to drink, his clothes still on and soaked with sweat. He wouldn't stand much chance of recovery in those conditions, but under my care I think he'll be all right.'

'I hope to God he is,' Edward said, feeling extremely worried. 'It's a big responsibility, Tina.'

'I know it. The doctor said how good I was, though,' Tina said. 'Don't fret, Edward. Claud will get well quickly with me to mind him.'

She had reckoned without Mrs Snelling. The older woman returned home late that night, and very drunk. She had been, she informed the street, on a day trip to Chester, and had enjoyed an excellent time, an excellent meal, and a great deal of booze.

Tina woke and lay listening to these rumbustious remarks without so much as a qualm. When she heard the shriek which echoed up and down the street, indeed, she merely thought maliciously that her neighbour had probably tripped over her own sizeable feet. But then there was such a rattling and a banging on her own front door, accompanied by raucous yells and a great deal of swearing, that she felt bound to wake Edward.

'What is it?' he said sleepily. 'I can hear old Snelling blinding away. Did you wake me up to tell me that?'

'She's banging our door down,' Tina said apprehensively. 'Do get up and see what she wants, Ted.'

'Oh, God! No doubt she wants her ewe lamb. I told you it was a mistake to interfere, my child.'

'Interfere? Me? I never did; I helped out,' Tina said indignantly, climbing heavily out of bed and beginning to pull on her dressing gown. 'That poor little boy! Surely she isn't going to try to take him from me in the middle of the night?'

But Mrs Snelling was past reasoning. As soon as the door opened a crack she hurled herself at it and burst into the hall, took a brief, tipsy look round and smashed the only thing in sight: the umbrella stand.

Tina stepped back as the older woman swayed towards the parlour where Claud lay innocently sleeping.

'My baby! The snooty bitch took my ba-aby!'

Mrs Snelling collapsed on her knees beside her son and gathered him up with what seemed like superhuman strength.

Tina said feebly, 'Must you take him now, Mrs Snelling? Couldn't he stay till morning?' but it was doubtful if Mrs Snelling heard her.

Lumbering along with the now wakened and weeping Claud clasped to her massive breast, she began to scream abuse at Tina until Tina's patience snapped and she shouted back.

'All right, take the poor little boy away,' she cried. 'Take him back into that stinking room, to lie in rags. And don't blame *me* if he's dead in a week!'

Twice before she reached her own home Mrs Snelling dropped her burden. Tina watched, shivering and crying, while Edward's arm went warmly round her and he murmured reassurance and love in her ear.

Back in their own bed, Tina said sadly, 'Why, Ted? She can't love him! She went off on her trip to Chester knowing full well he was ill! Why did she take him back?'

'Because she does love him in her own way and because she's jealous of you,' Edward assured her. 'One day you'll understand.'

'I shall not,' Tina said defiantly. 'I don't want to understand her, the wicked woman. I only hope she doesn't kill the kid.'

Edward chuckled in the dark. 'She won't. He's used to that filth, remember. He'll survive. They're tough, the Snellings.'

And indeed, for several days Tina heard nothing more

about Claud from next door. Billy, either from shame or because his mother would not allow him, came neither near nor by and the other children seemed subdued, playing in their own tiny, filthy backyard or further up the Row.

Then, about ten days later, there was another knock at the door. Tina went with some trepidation, to find Billy outside.

'Mrs Neyler, I'm sorry to bother you, but I know you go down to the shops most days. Could you get us some lemmings? Claud keeps arsting for that drink you made 'im.'

'Oh, *lemons!* Yes, of course. How *is* Claud?'

Billy smiled diffidently. 'A good deal better, thanks. And there's a message from me mam.'

'Oh? What have I done now?'

Billy looked hurt. 'Only good, Mrs Neyler, Mam's mortal sorry for the way she grabbed our Claud off of you, an' says to say she was a trifle merry at the time. She says to say you'll know 'ow she feels, when you've gorra littl'un of your own.'

The lemons were duly bought, and a bag of oranges too. Quick to recognise an olive branch, Tina went out of her way to send small gifts in to the sick child and presently she knew the breach was healed. Better, Mrs Snelling became very partisan over her once-despised neighbour.

'The doctor says you acted very prompt with our Claud, missus,' she told Tina. 'Reckon I were a bit 'asty with you, that night?'

I wonder how much she remembers, Tina thought, but aloud she only said, 'Perfectly understandable, Mrs Snelling; you're very fond of Claud, I know.'

And, amazingly, she did know. It had been love which had brought that terrible, drunken old woman swaying and roaring round to the house in the middle of the night to save her child. Love, Tina reflected sagely, is a very strange thing!

'Yes, the baby's coming quite soon, dearie. But not for a while yet.' The midwife turned away from Tina and addressed herself, in an undervoice, to Edward. 'Mrs Neyler is only a small woman but she's young and healthy, and small women are often very good breeders. No need for you to worry yourself. Why don't you go downstairs and make us all a nice cup of tea? I'll look after your wife.'

Edward was turning away when a voice, small but determined, said, 'Stay here. I want you here!'

He turned back at once, looking with love and pity at the small face with the big eyes looking twice their usual size from fear of the unknown.

'Of course, sweetheart. See, I'm here. I'll stay and talk to you.' He turned his head and addressed the midwife. 'Perhaps you would like to go down and make some tea?'

The nurse, with a disapproving sniff, left the room and could be heard clumping heavily down the narrow stairs. Tina smiled up at Edward, then the smile trembled and a frown took its place. He saw pain etch into her features and bent to kiss her cheek.

'Poor darling! Can I help you in any way?'

'You can rub my back.' She turned on her side and curled her hand round the arm that was not massaging her lower spine. 'I suppose I should be saying thank goodness the baby has decided to come at last. Especially now that the worst of the heat seems to be over. Only . . . only . . .'

'Only what?'

'Only I very much wish it was all over, and the baby born,' Tina confessed. She gripped his arm tightly as the pain began once more, pulling and tugging at her insides as though the baby intended to bring them with him into the world. She knew she should not hold her breath or tense up but she did both, pain closing her eyes and curling her fingers into claws until it began to ebb.

At first she was grateful for Edward's nearness and was able to converse with him between pains. But the pains grew longer and longer, the respite between them shorter and shorter, until she scarcely knew who else was in the room, and was barely conscious that the doctor had taken Edward's place until he said bracingly, 'Not long now, Mrs Neyler! I'll be bound you're going to have a big son, because he's giving us so much trouble!'

Tina, exhausted by the pain which had clawed at her unremittingly for nightmare hours, still had enough spirit left to remark sharply, 'Us? Did you say us?'

From far away she heard the doctor chuckle, then he was saying urgently, 'Hey, that's better! Push now, Mrs Neyler, your baby's head is showing!'

'Push?' Tina said vaguely. 'Push what?'

'Push down, woman! Push the baby out.'

'Is that right, to push?' She struggled up on one elbow, dazed, so weary she could hardly open her eyes, but game still. 'Can I sit up?'

She could feel the pain changing, becoming less pain than a demand to her to push down with all her force. Yet she was so tired! She dragged herself into a sitting position and began to heave on the midwife's arms, straining, pushing with all her power, because something in the back of her mind told her that only by pushing out that wretched obstruction would she be able to get the sleep she craved. She had quite forgotten the baby, she had no idea that Edward lurked in the shadows near the door, watching her agony, his own mind afire and guilt consuming him.

She was unaware that she cried out, unaware of everything except the almost exultant need to expel the child from her body. She drew up her knees, laid her head on her arms, and pushed.

Edward, standing rooted to the spot, saw something dark and terrible appear in front of Tina, saw blood puddle the sheet and spread, heard Tina give a little shout . . . and he swayed forward and fell heavily on to the floor in a dead faint.

'It was our baby being born, my poor darling,' Tina said later, when he came to her bedside to explain that he had thought . . . had thought . . . 'I think I may have screamed, and then you fainted, only the doctor said not to move, so I didn't, and very soon you were sitting up.'

'It was awful,' Edward said. He felt he had acquitted himself very badly, fainting in that stupid fashion. But he had thought she had ruptured herself in some awful way; he had not realised . . .

With a gulp, he relegated the scene to the back of his mind. 'The midwife says he's a big baby, but he looks a tiny scrap to me,' he said. 'He's very red and wrinkled, too.'

'He felt large,' Tina said with a shudder. 'However! He's in the cot, asleep. He is asleep?'

'I think so,' Edward said, peering into the befrilled and canopied cot. 'Oh, confound it, my voice must have roused the little blighter. He's screwing up his mouth and his face is going red . . .'

'Give him here,' Tina demanded at once. She held out her arms, feeling the soft folds of her clean nightdress against her skin with some satisfaction. It was so nice to be clean and fresh and flat again! 'Come to Momma, little Desmond.'

'Desmond? Why Desmond? Edward picked up the small blanket-wrapped bundle and handed it cautiously to his wife. 'That's an odd name!'

'It is not! It's the name of the hero in my serial in that lovely magazine you've been buying me.' She turned back the blanket and very gently touched the baby's cheek. 'Edward, his skin is so *soft*! I wish I might unwrap him and take off my nightgown and hold his skin close to mine!' She raised wide eyes to her husband's face. 'Do you know, I never told you before but I didn't want a baby! I didn't think I liked babies very much, and I thought it would just get in the way and be a nuisance to us. But I have the most beautiful feeling with this little baby, not at all how I felt when Louis was small. I feel that he's still a part of me, and his little face is very like yours, only he's ugly and you're handsome. I do think I like him!'

'Good. We'll keep him then, shall we?'

She chuckled, gazing contentedly at the baby's puckering face. 'Oh yes, let's! He hasn't opened his eyes properly since he was born. I wonder what colour they'll be?'

'Blue. They must be.'

'I don't see why. Look at Poppa. He's got dark brown eyes. But mine are very blue, aren't they?'

'Yes, but I expect your mother had blue eyes. Though two brown-eyed people can have a blue-eyed child. It's just two blue-eyed people who . . .'

'Never mind, he's awake.' Beneath the swollen, almost hairless lids, a pair of milky blue eyes appeared, then the small face wrinkled up furiously and a surprisingly loud wail rent the air. 'Gracious, how he yells! Shall I feed him?'

She unbuttoned her nightgown as she spoke and turned the baby a little clumsily but with increasing confidence towards the fullness of her breast. The child, tiny hands groping, head weaving like a blind kitten, found the nipple and fastened on to it. Edward laughed at the loud and vulgar sucking sounds which followed, but Tina, shining eyes fixed on her son's mossy head, only smiled contentedly.

'You look so beautiful,' Edward said softly. 'The two of you look beautiful. Madonna and child; a perfect picture.'

Without lifting her eyes from the child's burrowing head, Tina held out her hand to him. 'Madonna, child and father,' she corrected. *That's* a perfect picture.'

18

Mark was taking the waggon into Dunedin, because he was calling, not only for Wen, but for some boxes of her things as well. That first chance meeting in Dunedin had been the beginning of a friendship which had ripened rapidly into something much more. Indeed, from the outset he had realised his old playmate meant more to him than Sylvia ever had. She came to the farm and loved it as he did. Not just the house but the land, the shore, the creatures which lived so close to him.

Mark had always been shy but right from the start he was completely at ease with Wen, quickly knew that he loved her. But did she love him? Could she bear to live in a place so far from civilisation, with no neighbours within easy reach?

On her third visit, he decided to put it to the test.

It had been a bright winter day, and as he drove her up to the farm he tried to see it through her eyes. The low, stone built house, creeper covered, its tiled roof cushioned with patches of mustard lichen; the garden which looked dull and neglected now, though for almost nine months of the year it was a riot of flowers.

It had, Mark decided, a settled look, as though it had always been there. He and Edward had built it with their own hands barely eight years previously, yet it had so sunk into the landscape that it looked a part of it.

He remembered nostalgically the making of the garden. Unlike most farmers, he had no contempt for flowers. Right from the start he had spent all his leisure time making it beautiful, planting, cosseting, transplanting, glancing occasionally at the great seascape which he could see from this height, hearing the sound of the waves as a muted purr.

He looked at Wen; she was sitting straight up in the dog cart, gazing affectionately at the farmhouse. Yes, but visiting was one thing, living here another! He cleared his throat.

'It's such a grand day, Wen, I'd like to take you to see some friends before we go in.'

She glanced around quickly, looking a little surprised. The farm was built on a promontory, flanked and protected by forest, before it the sloping turf which ended at the steep cliffs. Neighbours could certainly not be seen. But she smiled her agreement and, after he had stabled the horse, came with him on the path which led towards the cliffs. Smiling at her inquisitive glances, he scrambled down the cliff path to the half-moon cove below.

They reached the weed-strewn rocks and he caught her arm, stopping her from going further.

'See? Our neighbours!'

The korora, little penguins which nested in the tussock grass above high water, were fishing; diving, hopping out of the water on to the rocks with their catch, then returning to the crashing surf as though impervious to the pounding of the waves on the wicked looking rocks.

'Oh!' It was a gasp of pure delight. 'Mark, what charming neighbours you have!'

He caught her hand and led her further round the coast, to where the seals lay on the rocks, sunning themselves, big, inquisitive eyes rolling round to stare at the intruders. Further yet, and he showed her the albatrosses, taking off in alarm at their sudden appearance, their ten-foot wing span impressive against the wintry blue sky.

'I think it's a paradise, Mark. How lucky you are!'

They had turned to make their way back to the farm but now he stopped her, turning her to face him.

'Lucky? But it's lonely, Wen. Could you bear to live with blue penguins and seals and albatrosses for neighbours instead of people? Wouldn't you be lonely. Feel you needed folk?'

'I wouldn't be lonely. As for people, I'd have the only person that mattered.'

He felt his cheeks go hot. Now for it! 'W-would you m-marry me, Wen?'

'Oh Mark, I'd love to!'

They kissed then, for the first time. With the sun on them and the wind, unheeded, ruffling the black hair and the red. Lips cool from the sea air, tasting faintly of salt. It was a tentative kiss; a sealing of friendship perhaps, before the beginnings of passion had entered their relationship. He knew then, with quiet certainty, that this was the best thing which had ever happened to him.

When they drew apart he went on holding her gently, and smiling up at him she said: 'That must be a record for these modern times, Mark! You asked me to marry you before you had even kissed me!'

'So I did! Let's do it again.'

And now, a bare six months later, the wedding was all arranged. Wen's parents had come to New Zealand for this great occasion, and Karl insisted that the reception be held at the Waihola farm. But best of all, Edward was coming home for a holiday, to be his best man! It filled Mark's cup. Ed had known Wen long ago, but she had only been a child. This new Wen would be as much a stranger to his brother as she had been to him when they met in Dunedin.

Karl thought Wen the perfect daughter-in-law, singing her praises all over the South Island, and Mark was sure that Edward would be delighted with his choice. Also, whatever he might think of Tina, he wanted to meet her. The girl who had taken Ed from him must, he grudgingly admitted, have some good points!

Tina had won Karl's approval by providing him with a grandson. So delighted had Karl been when he heard the news that he had written to Edward offering him the farm if he would bring his wife and son Desmond back to Waihola to live.

It was generous, and Edward's refusal had been equally so.

'I could not, in all conscience, take over the farm you've given your life to perfecting,' he had written. 'But when I do come home I'll be in a position to buy land and build property, and I promise you that I'll settle as near you as is possible.'

So although Edward's return was to be a holiday and not a true homecoming, Mark still longed for it. He had done so much on the farm since Edward left! He had built up the dairy herd and they had more merino sheep than ever before. There would be so much to talk about, so much to show!

The rough little pony pulling the cart knew this journey as well as Mark did. Its pace began to slow as they reached the busiest part of Princes Street and Mark hopped down, slung the reins over the téthering post, and ran into the post office. He came out with a long blue envelope postmarked Liverpool. Impatiently, he tore the envelope open. Why were they writing, when they would be here themselves so soon? They must have posted it as they sailed, unless . . .

Leaning against the waggon, Mark pulled out the single

sheet and read it rapidly, then went back and read it a second time, his mind numb with disappointment. They were not coming! Tina was pregnant again and the doctor did not think she should undertake the journey. Edward said, simply, that they were both bitterly disappointed but hoped that some time in the future . . . A present followed . . .

Mark jerked himself upright and swore, surprising himself by the fluency of his curses. That *bloody* woman! Why did she have to get pregnant now? She must have done it on purpose to stop Ted from coming home!

Presently he climbed back into the waggon and drove off down the street, but the sunshine seemed paler, the day less promising. Not to see Edward again, after two years apart! It was unfair, unfair!

Wen was waiting outside her lodgings, two boxes on the paving at her feet. Mark climbed down, hoisted her belongings into the back, then helped her into the seat beside his own. As soon as they were both comfortably seated and the pony had moved forward once more he handed her the letter.

'They're not coming!' she exclaimed at once, without even unfolding the page. 'Poor darling, what a disappointment!'

'She's pregnant again. I'll swear she's done it so that they couldn't come. Ted will be so disappointed!'

Wen read the letter, then put it back in its envelope and patted his arm. 'Tina must be heartbroken, love! She's had to give up a trip halfway round the world to see her husband's home and people! And for what? To stay at home feeling ill until the time comes for her to suffer childbirth again. She cannot have wanted such a thing!'

'Perhaps not,' he said grudgingly. 'I'd not thought of it like that.'

'I don't suppose you had! Just think of what Tina's missed, Mark. She's never seen Ted's home or relatives, and she must want to, if she loves him. She didn't even have a proper wedding, did she? Look at me with my white lace dress and my parents come all the way from England to see me married; all my friends sending gifts and messages. And your father being so good! What did Tina have?'

'Not much. Only two cleaning women as witnesses. No presents, I suppose, since it was an elopement. I suppose she would have liked a white wedding. But she's got Edward!'

'And I've got you! But I've got so much as well, Mark! I'd like to write to the poor girl.'

Mark put his arm round her and drew her close, kissing the smooth ivory of her cheek.

'You are the kindest soul alive! I'll write too, and say I'm glad she's having another baby, but sorry she won't be at our wedding. And I'll mean it!'

They were married in St Paul's church and their reception was held in a big marquee outside the Waihola farmhouse. There was dancing, music, laughter and friends everywhere. The Otago Hussars made an archway with their swords outside the church and then drank themselves hilarious on Karl's champagne. It was a lovely wedding.

Afterwards, they set off home, with the dogcart hung all over with bunches of silver and gold ribbon, and tin cans, bouncing on strings, trailing behind them. They reached the coast road as dusk was falling on that perfect summer day.

A mist hung over the shore and came creeping up the cliffs as they travelled so that they could no longer see the waves below, though they could hear them. The dull, muffled pounding came to them as they climbed down from the cart in the stableyard and Mark called Toddy to see to the horse and cart, then picked Wen up in his arms and carried her over the threshold into the lamplit kitchen.

As he stepped inside she turned in his arms, her skin gleaming honey-coloured in the light. 'Dearest Mark, we're home!'

He stood her down, pretending to pant and clutching his heart. 'You weigh a ton, Mrs Neyler! Kiss me!'

They kissed. Then, hand in hand, they crossed the room and went through the small square hall. They stepped carefully over the glossy tiles which had been polished to a fine brilliance by Freda, Toddy's wife, before she departed for her own cottage. They entered the main bedroom. It was a large room with a wide window overlooking the splendid sweep of the sea. Even tonight, Mark was struck by the drama of the view; the belt of pines stark against the moonsilvered water.

'I'll light the lamp and draw the curtains,' he said prosaically, however, going over to the window. But Wen stopped him, a hand on his sleeve.

'Don't Mark. I want to go to bed with the curtains drawn back and that wonderful view in front of me. Do you mind? Does it seem wrong?'

He shook his head. 'Not wrong. But I do trust you don't think I've brought you in here to admire the view?'

She laughed and sat down beside him on the bed. Then she unpinned her hair and the night-black locks tumbled down, straight as rain, framing her round, sweet face. She changed, in that instant, from a fashionable young lady to the little Chinese girl he had known so long ago.

He watched her without moving as she unfastened her dress with rapid, neat-fingered movements. When it was undone she stood up, shedding the garment as a snake sheds its skin, with one long, sensuous wriggle. Beneath it she was naked and Mark's breathing quickened at the sight of her body, bleached by the moonlight, perfect and white and lovely.

'Wen, you're so beautiful!'

His voice broke the spell. She smiled and sat down on the bed.

'I'm glad you think so.'

He undressed quickly, hung his clothes over a chair and moved back towards the bed; as he approached she stood up to wind her arms round his neck. He kissed her and they fell on to the bed and it occurred to him that there was no fear in either of them, no embarrassment or shrinking. They were two people very much in love, in perfect harmony with each other. Now they were gentle, slow moving, intoxicated by each other's nearness; later they might wake to a fiercer, more demanding love. But always the harmony would be there, the quiet accompaniment to whatever tune they played.

The new baby was a son, Francis, another lusty, fair-haired boy with Edward's features who clutched and squalled and lay in the cradle close to Tina's bed. But this baby was not given the same attention and affection which Desmond had inspired. He had made himself known at the wrong moment so that Tina had missed the trip to New Zealand. She had had a sick pregnancy too, and now he was a fractious child, needing more time than she wanted to give.

Frank was born in June and by the time he was twelve weeks old Tina felt drained by him. Desmond was walking and into everything. The new baby cried to be fed, or to be changed, or just cried. Tina, cleaning, cooking, washing, ironing, taking two children instead of one out with her, felt her brow was permanently furrowed and her back permanently stooped. When Frank had been a month old she and Edward had taken the children back to the house in Bishopsgate for a week's stay, but Tina had not enjoyed the break as much as she had expected to. For the first time she had felt the stirring of a degree of envy of Cecy. Cecy was seventeen and respectably engaged to Abraham Solstein a Jew of impeccable lineage and faultless orthodoxy. They were to marry in a year and Cecy would take her trousseau and a large dowry to Abe's luxurious London flat. She would have a maid and a cook, and a woman to do the rough work.

I'm only a year older than Cecy, yet I've got two sons and responsibilities I don't know how to bear and work which never seems to get done, Tina thought dolefully, when she was back in her own house. Where is justice? What had Cecy done to deserve so easy a life?

Of course when she remembered the contrast between Edward and Abraham she felt ashamed. Edward was tall and handsome, a kindly, golden-haired god of a man. Poor Abe was scarcely an inch taller than plump little Cecy and he had a dark little monkey's face and beady monkey's eyes. There could be no greater difference between two men than between Edward and Abraham.

Nevertheless, her little house was such hard work! Nappies were everywhere, and it always smelled of babies' food, washing boiling on the stove, and cooking. They all slept in the same bedroom, of course, and often Frank's cries woke Desmond so that some nights Tina barely got two hours' sleep.

Things were not good between her and Edward, either. When he fell asleep as soon as his head touched the pillow, tired after a long day at work, Tina felt bitterly deprived. Yet when he tried to make love to her the sickening fear of another pregnancy caused her to try to resist, to cry, to stiffen. She knew she must not deny him the right to make love to her, but fear over-rode all other emotions and she was, in addition, nervous of the tiniest sound. Just the tell-tale creaking of a bedspring and Frank would wake and begin to mutter.

With the joy and spontaneity gone from their love-making, and his young wife impatient with him and always busy, Edward began to work harder, stay out later. He began to be away for the odd night, when business took him far afield, and then it stretched to two nights; three.

He had been away for three nights, on legitimate business up north, when Tina's patience finally snapped. During his absence baby Frank had been ill with a growling chest cough and Desmond had fallen on the hearthrug and blacked his eye on the fender. She had expected Edward to be away two nights, so when he breezed into the house at tea-time on the fourth day she was furious with him, her sense of grievance stronger than the desire to greet him with her usual overflowing affection.

Edward, unaware of this, stopped on the threshold of the living room with a bright: 'Here I am, darling!'

Tina was kneeling in front of the fire, which had burned low, lifting the sluggishly burning coals with a poker to try and induce a blaze. She had not expected him, so she was wearing a limp wool dress and a stained pinafore; her hair was untidy and there was a smut on her cheek.

'So you've decided to come back! How kind! And just in time for tea, if I ever get a chance to make it.'

Edward was tired too, but basking in the knowledge that he had done well for the firm, buying a vast quantity of bricks for far less than they had previously paid. Now Tina's attitude smashed his pleasure like an empty egg-shell. He looked around the room. Because the fire had been allowed to burn so low it was chilly, and the line of nappies dripping across the hearth, Desmond's whines for his tea, and the faint cry from upstairs as Frank awoke, depressed Edward's previously volatile spirits.

'If you feel like that I can go out again. Hecky wanted me to go for a drink and then a meal.'

Tina knelt back on her heels and glanced up at Edward, standing in the doorway, rosy from the winter cold, warmly wrapped in his new overcoat. He had lived a life quite separate from hers for days! He was a person in his own right! What was she?

'Get the coal in first,' she snapped.

He stood looking down at her for a moment without moving, except that a muscle twitched in his cheek. Then he turned without a word and strode out of the house.

She might have wept, run after him, but at that moment the fire caught and began to blaze. She reached for the guard, rehung the nappies, and began to do all the jobs necessary to keep the home going, too tired to rebel, caught like a mouse on a wheel, endlessly running, never arriving.

When the children were in bed at last she fetched herself some bread and jam – she was far too tired to cook – and sat down by the fire, thinking about their first real quarrel.

It occurred to her that this was how marriages ended. Babies, tiredness, cross words, no more love. Did she want her marriage to end? Did she want to go to Poppa with her two little unbelievers in tow and ask to be taken back? No alternative occurred to her because there was no alternative. A woman burdened with two small children could not support herself and them. But in any case, she knew in her heart that she could never leave Edward. She adored him even when she was cross!

And yet – what sort of life was she leading? Edward enjoyed his work but she could not be said to enjoy hers! It was so narrow, nothing but babies, perpetual housework, and perpetual weariness.

She sat in the chair, so tired that the bread and jam never got eaten because she simply fell asleep and slept until she was woken by Frank, howling for his next feed. She stumbled upstairs, dazed with exhaustion, and began to unbutton her dress. She picked the baby out of the cradle, sat down, and held him to her breast. But after a few desperate sucks the child rejected the nipple, crying, screwing up his face, his body rigid with fury.

Tina forced herself to wake up properly. She washed her face at the washstand, then examined Frank closely. No pin stuck into his dimpled flesh, no wind seemed to be troubling him. She tried him at the other breast. The same thing happened. A frantic sucking followed by screams, red-faced anger; he seemed a miniature fury.

Edward, letting himself into the house after a few drinks and a good meal at a steakhouse, heard the howls as soon as the front door opened. He was tempted to turn tail and return to Hecky's house and the bed his partner had offered. But the baby sounded really desperate. With a sigh, he closed the door softly behind him and climbed the stairs.

He entered the bedroom quietly. Tina sat on the bed, her dress round her waist, tears pouring down her pale cheeks. The child in her arms was screaming and waving dimunitive fists while she vainly tried to get him to take the nipple. As Edward entered she looked up, her eyes red-rimmed and puffy.

'Ed-Edward, he wo-wo-won't s-suck,' she hiccupped. 'He kee-keeps c-crying and he m-must be hun-hungry, but he w-won't suck!'

Any ill-feeling between them forgotten, Edward strode across the room, took the hot and tearstained baby from his equally tearstained wife, and bent to kiss her quivering lips.

'Get into bed. I'll calm him down and then I'll make him

a bottle. I'll bring you up a nice hot drink presently.'

'A b-bottle? Oh, Ted, what's happened?'

'You're worn out and your milk's probably a bit short,' Edward said tactfully. 'Is there some milk downstairs?'

She sat on the bed, rubbing her eyes and sniffing, but he heard her mutter, 'Yes, in the pantry,' before he patted her shoulder and then turned away.

With the still howling baby draped across his shoulder, Edward went downstairs, heated milk on the stove, poured it into one of the bottles they had used for Desmond, and cooled it in the sink. Then he heated more milk and poured it into a glass, added, upon reflection, a generous tot of brandy, and carried baby, bottle and glass up to the bedroom.

Tina was in bed, her hair loose, her face cleaned of all signs of her tears, but she was paper-white and there were shadows beneath her eyes. He handed her the baby and the bottle and watched a smile light her face as Frank seized the nipple and began to suck vigorously.

'Ted?' she said presently in a small voice. 'I'm s-sorry I was cross.'

'You had a right to be cross, my poor darling. This is no place for you. I'll see Hecky in the morning, and tell him I want work started straight away on a new house for us. It will have four bedrooms, and one for a maid, you can have a nurse to help with the boys . . .'

'Oh, Ted! But can we afford it?'

'We can. I've only put off moving because I hoped we might go home, to New Zealand. But the business needs me for a while yet, and a new house will be an investment.'

Her face was radiant and it occurred to him that he had not seen her smile like that for a long while. Poor kid, he thought remorsefully, I've treated her badly! Apart from the week in Norwich he had not taken her out once since Desmond was born.

As the milk in the bottle slowly drained away he talked softly of how their lives would change once they moved into the new house. He fancied Everton Heights; what did she think? A garden would be nice, somewhere for the boys to play. A croquet lawn, too. And stabling, of course, so that she could have a pony cart. In a year or two, he intended to buy a motor; she would enjoy going out for trips, would she not?

When the last drop of milk had been drunk, he took the already sleeping baby from her arms and put him into the cradle. Then he climbed into bed beside Tina, but how different a Tina from the one who had greeted him so sourly earlier! She was her old, loving self, desperately sorry that she had lost her temper with him.

He snuggled down the bed then turned to her, kissing her full on the lips. She neither pulled away nor stiffened but responded warmly and eagerly, anxious to make amends, throwing caution and fear to the winds. They made love then, with a freedom and passion they had not shared for months, and fell asleep in each other's arms, perfect harmony restored.

Six weeks later, Tina knew she was pregnant again. But it was nothing to dread now, with the new house gradually growing, with trips to the theatre and opera almost every week, with a woman who came in to do the rough work and a young girl to take the boys off her hands sometimes.

Once Edward had stopped telling himself that they were only in Liverpool temporarily, he threw himself heart and soul into making the place seem home to them both. They went out, entertained friends from time to time, dined at smart restaurants, even took a hired motor into Wales and exclaimed over the beauties of the scenery.

He and Hecky were working harder than ever, having had the good fortune to obtain the tender for an enormous building scheme which incorporated several streets of new housing, shops and offices, and of course the work on the new house in Everton continued.

Christmas came, and the little house was gay with paper chains and a Christmas tree. Hecky and his wife, Charlotte, came to dinner and the Neylers went to the Whites' for tea. It was all very jolly and Tina, though she cooked and served a turkey and all the trimmings unaided, enjoyed it most of all. She loved to entertain Edward's friends.

This pregnancy was proving different from the last, too. She was well, able to cope, suffering little or not at all from morning sickness.

'It will be wonderful to have my new baby in that lovely house,' Tina told Charlotte. 'The views! And so much space!'

Charlotte, a self-opinionated young woman who had married beneath her and never forgot it, smiled condescendingly. But much Tina cared! The promise of a beautiful new home, the love of her two little boys, made her richer by far than Charlotte, but best of all she had Edward's love and understanding. The breach which had begun to grow between them had healed over and actually strengthened their marriage. She could not have been happier.

And then, out of a clear sky, disaster struck.

Tina was making a shepherd's pie in the kitchen of the house in Spanner's Row while the boys played in the front room when Edward came bursting in through the front door. He crossed the hall and crashed into the kitchen, eyes blazing. Tina, startled, stood with her mouth open, then pulled herself together.

'Ted? What's happened?'

'Hecky's gone!'

'Where? Up to his mother's again? That's too bad, after he had a full week off for the New Year.'

'He's *gone*, Tina! Skedaddled, vamoosed, cleared out!'

Tina sat down on a kitchen chair with a thump. 'Gone? Left Charlotte?'

'Yes. Charlotte knew he'd gone yesterday, the silly bitch, but she didn't think to let me know. He's had a full day's start!'

'Start? I don't understand! Ted, what are you doing?'

He was riffling through a pile of ironed linen, taking his shirts, ties and socks out from amongst the other clothing.

'I'm going after him. Be a good girl and help me pack.'

He headed for the stairs and went up them two at a time. Tina, following, said plaintively, 'You're going to go after him? But where's he gone, Ted? Will you be away long?'

We don't know exactly where he's gone, but we think it'll be Texas. In his office wastepaper basket there was a newspaper with an article about a big oil find somewhere near Beaumont, in Texas. After I'd found that, I searched around a bit more and darned nearly every paper he'd read had all the bits about oil or drillings ringed in pencil.'

'*America*? You're going to follow him to the States? Ted, it's madness! Let him go. You'll do just as well without him.'

Edward had been hurling clothes into a suitcase but now he glanced at her, grinning ruefully. 'My dear girl, if it were just that! But he's taken every penny out of the bank; I've not a feather to fly with! All the money we've been paid for the last job, all the advance money for the new building development . . .' He reached out and gripped her hand tightly. 'Poor darling, what dreadful news to spring on you! Even our lovely new house will be forfeit. But think of Charlotte! He married her for her money, I believe, and he's taken it all. Some he put into the business of course, but the rest he just took. She's penniless.'

'Poor Charlotte! But Ted, you can't just go! What about the business? And me and the children! What shall we live on?'

It stopped him, but only for a moment. 'I'll have to hand over all our property and building materials to the authorities and ask them to get someone else to do the work we've won the tender for. I may still be in debt, but you should be safe in this house. I'll send you money, of course . . .'

'Ted, it won't do,' Tina said. 'Why can't you settle things here and then go? I'm sure I'll be clapped into prison if you go off!'

'If I don't go, I might be clapped into prison,' he admitted. 'But I've got assets: The new house we're building, the stuff Hecky didn't take. I simply must go, darling, to catch Hecky before he spends the money! No use waiting until he's sunk all our chink in some mythical oilwell! I must go now, right away!'

'Then take us with you,' Tina cried, running to her own

clothes chest. 'Take us as well, the boys too!'

'I wish I could! But I can't do that. You've got to stay here to sell the new house and see that we're not cheated, and to take care of the babies. Whilst you're living in this house, I don't think anyone will try to repossess it. I'll either come back or send for you.'

He jammed the last article into the case, snapped it shut and came across to put his arm around her. 'Poor baby! Look, I'll ring the council offices and tell them what's happened and do my best to keep you in the clear. They're good fellows, and if I can find Hecky quickly, before he's spent up, I'll be home in no time. Be good, and take care of yourself.'

He kissed her hard and was gone, clattering down the stairs and out of the house.

Very slowly and carefully, Tina began to tidy the bedroom, putting away the clothes Edward had cast down. As she worked, her mind was busy and soon she thought she knew what best to do. She would ring Poppa and then she would put this wretched little house on the market. Once it was sold, she would join Edward in America. She smiled at Edward's optimistic resolve to find Hecky before he had spent the money. He could have no conception of the vastness of the continent he was setting out to explore! She remembered that journey so long ago, how the train tracks had run on and on across the prairie, how the mountains had loomed up for mile after mile, how vast New York City had seemed. She doubted very much whether he would ever find Hecky, but she quite saw that he must try. And she saw with equal clarity that she must follow him; no other course was bearable.

19

Wen and Mark had been swimming from their private bathing beach, just below the farm. It was not private really, but since other people scarcely ever dared the steep cliff path they thought of it as their own special place. They shared it with the seals, but the animals had all followed the sea as the tide went out and basked on the further rocks, so that Mark and Wen, lying on their backs in the hot sun, were able to enjoy solitude.

Their marriage was idyllically happy. Exploring each other's minds and enjoying every shared moment to the full, they had let a year slip by almost without thinking about the world outside their farm. Wen was a good wife for a farmer; she could rear a baby lamb on a bottle, milk the cows, ride a pony and drive a straight furrow with the old-fashioned plough. These arts had to be learned, of course, but with Mark as her teacher learning had been a pleasure. Their social life bored them both, secretly, a little, but they knew it was a necessary evil. Neither wanted to be thought a recluse or a snob.

When they wanted the world, therefore, they drove into Dunedin or attended a social gathering. But occasionally, despite their lonely position, the world sought them out.

This was one of those occasions. Naked in the sun, salt drying on their skins and a beautiful lethargy possessing them, Wen was the first to realise their solitude was about to end.

'There's someone on the cliff path,' she remarked drowsily. 'A man, I think. Pass me a towel.'

Mark stretched out a lazy hand and dropped a towel on

her middle. 'I shouldn't think whoever it may be will come down here – no one ever does – but it might be as well if you covered yourself. My skin's tingling and I don't want you burnt in such intimate places.'

'It's you that burns, not me! He is coming down, though, Mark. I wonder what he wants?'

Wendy sat up, tying the towel, sarong fashion, round her breasts. 'I think it's Godfrey with the post.'

That brought Mark out of his sun-drugged indifference. He sat up, reaching for his own towel. 'Curses. I'd best go over and see what he wants.'

Wen, lazily watching, saw Mark pick his way over the slippery rocks, splash through a couple of pools, and reach the foot of the cliffs just as the intruder set his foot on firm sand. The two men greeted one another, something changed hands and then Mark returned, to flop down on the seaweed covered rock again.

'Guess what? The old Queen's dead! That's why Godfrey came hunting for us, instead of just leaving the letters at the house. I suppose Toddy told him we'd been bathing; I'll give him one for that!'

'Why? Have you ever told Toddy we don't want to be disturbed down here?'

He punched her gently in the shoulder, grinning. The sun had freckled his face to brown and his eyes looked very blue.

'Of course I haven't, but he knows, the old devil! There's a letter for you, from your parents I think, and one for me, from . . . ' He frowned at it, his attention caught. 'That's odd! It's from England, but it's not from Ted.'

'Open it and then you'll know who it's from,' Wen said patiently. She opened her own letter, briefly scanning the page. 'Yes, it's from my mother. She's very well and would we like Su Yung to come over and work for us? She's my cousin.' She flicked the letter in her husband's hand. 'Go on, open it!'

Slowly, he slit the envelope and drew out the contents. A quick glance, and he was saying, 'It's from Tina!'

Her eyes widened. 'Oh, Mark, is Ted ill?'

He shook his head. 'I don't think so. It seems he's left Tina and the children and gone to America. He's chasing after that White fellow, who's run off with all their money. Tina says she thinks he may not have much opportunity to write to us for a bit, so she's writing instead. She doesn't want us to worry.'

'Poor Tina! What's she going to do?'

Mark frowned. 'She's in a difficult position, it seems. She's pregnant, which is why Ted didn't take her with him, I suppose, but she says she's put the house on the market and hopes to follow Ted to the States. The snag seems to be that the company has just taken on a big construction contract and of course there's no one to do the work now, and no money. Poor kid, she obviously doesn't know which way to turn.'

'I wonder why she turned this way? She's got a father of her own.'

'Who can say? Anyway, she isn't asking us for help. She's terribly worried about Ted, though. Here, read the letter for yourself.'

He passed the pages across and there was silence while Wen read. She finished, and glanced up at Mark.

'That poor little thing! I can't think what Ted's doing, going gaily off and leaving his wife with two little children and another on the way. Let alone all the worry of knowing the business is in trouble. And where will she find money for herself and the boys? It isn't like Ted to be so thoughtless. Is it?'

'Of course it's not. He must have been frantic to catch that swindling fellow. Look, Wen, if I were to leave you in charge of the farm . . .'

'Mark, we've not got that sort of money! I couldn't do more than keep the place ticking over and you can't afford to go chasing off to America and ruin yourself. It wouldn't be right to throw the farm aside and do what Ted did. Why, you don't even know where he's gone.'

'It's so damned far away,' Mark grumbled, bending down and picking up his shirt. 'You're right, of course. It would take me all my time to find Ted, and when I did find him ten to one he'd be doing fine – making his fortune and wondering why I'd bothered! But I must do something, Wen!'

'Certainly you must.' She stood up, slipped her loose gown over her head, and began to gather their things together. Their happy day on the beach was plainly over and real life had to be faced once more. 'But this time do it for Tina, Mark. Send her some money so that she can pay for a few extras. In time she'll want to go to Ted, well or ill, pregnant or not. Perhaps we can help then.'

The pain woke her. Familiar, nagging, it clawed rhythmically at her back, ebbing and flowing like a tide but never quite disappearing. Tina sat up, her hand going automatically out to where Edward should have been. Then she remembered. He had gone to America and she was alone in the house with her two babies.

It was dark, but peering towards the window curtains she could see that there was a light line on the horizon. She sat up, sweat prickling her skin. It was far too early for the baby to be born so this must be a miscarriage. She fought to subdue the panic which rose chokingly in her throat, to forget the stories of women struggling with miscarriages, dying, suffering dreadfully. She made herself lie down and tried to relax, closing her eyes and thinking that morning would soon be here.

An hour later she knew she was in labour and that whatever she did the baby would come now. She knew too, that she needed help. Behind the curtains it was light and soon the first workers would be making their way down Spanner's Row to their factories and cleaning jobs. Between waves of pain she got herself out of bed and stumbled across the room. She knelt on the cold lino and began to try and raise the sash, but it had been a bitterly cold night and it was iced up. As she strained to free it, it shot up suddenly and she toppled forward, cracking her chin on the windowsill. It startled her and brought tears to her eyes, but it also made her smile and when a woman, capped, aproned, and carrying a mop and a bucket full of cleaning materials, glanced up at the window she was able to show her a fairly cheerful countenance.

'Could you give a knock next door?' Tina called down softly. 'I need help.'

The cleaner knocked and Mrs Snelling came to the door. She was draped in a number of dirty shawls and sporting a magenta blanket over all, but she grinned affably, if toothlessly, up at Tina.

'Are you 'aving a miss, chuck? You'll be wanting old Ma Sharp, I reckon.'

'Please. And Dr Rowsell, if you would be so good. And . . . well, I don't like to ask . . . '

'Helen! Mek you da's breakfast gel. Albert, go for Doc Rowsell. Fanny, fetch Ma Sharp!' After these peremptory orders to her offspring Mrs Snelling lumbered out into the Row and approached Tina's front door. 'Hubby there, is 'e? Thought not. Can you let me in, chuck?'

'Yes, in a . . .' Tina, hands clenched, waited for the pain to subside, then got laboriously to her feet and toiled down the stairs. She unlocked the door and Mrs Snelling surged through it.

'Good gel! Come into the living room,' Mrs Snelling said. 'Are your lads still abed? When our Helen's got the porridge on she'll see to your lads.' She glanced round the living room. 'On to the couch with you. Lie down. I see you've laid the fire; I'll put a light to it.' She did so, then waddled back to the still open front door and stuck her head outside. 'Suzie!'

'Yes, our mam?' The voice belonged to the ten-year-old Snelling and came, faintly, from the Snellings' own home.

'Git over 'ere.'

Suzie's small, anxious face appeared round the door. 'Yes, our mam?'

'Go up to the bedroom and git a piller and a blanket.'

The child obeyed and, sooner that she would have believed possible, Tina found herself snugly tucked up on the couch with a hot cup of tea in her hand and the fire roaring up in the grate.

'You are good,' she said as Mrs Snelling lowered her

enormous bulk rather gingerly into the chair opposite her. 'I was afraid! But nothing seems so bad now I'm not alone.'

'Aye, you're right there,' Mrs Snelling agreed, sipping her tea noisily. 'I won't give you no grub, 'cos I know they don't like women in labour to eat heavy.'

'I'm not hungry,' Tina confessed. 'Will . . . will the doctor be long?'

'Not long.'

She closed her eyes. Tina marvelled at her lack of curiosity. Not a word about Edward's whereabouts! Yet her presence was immensely comforting. She had borne twelve children and had gone through the horrid business many times. She had once admitted that she would have had eighteen children by now except for miscarriages.

Presently, Tina opened her eyes and the doctor stood there, talking to Mrs Snelling and another woman. He turned and frowned at her with mock severity, but his eyes behind the gold-rimmed pince-nez were kind.

'Mrs Snelling tells me you're in labour, my dear. Well, that's unfortunate, but it can't be helped. How far on are you?'

'About five months.'

'Hmm. Pain bad?'

'Sometimes.'

'I see. Well, Mrs Sharp has put some water on to boil so, if Mrs Snelling will find me a clean towel, I'll see what I can do to help.'

She lost the baby after a difficult and protracted miscarriage. Unable to look after the boys, she had appealed to her father and he had sent Alice. The older girl remained a month, and at the end of that time departed for Norwich once more, with Tina's assurances that she was quite capable now, and would immediately contact the family if she fell ill again, ringing in her ears.

And before she had really begun negotiations to sell the half-built house in Everton Heights, or the machinations which would enable the firm to pass on their work to another contractor, Charlotte came calling. It was a chilly day and she sat down beside Tina's fire with a fur hat on her head and a fur coat huddled round her shoulders, the tip of her nose pink and shiny but her mouth firm.

'Hecky took all my money when he left me,' she said. It was a statement, neither asking for nor expecting sympathy. 'If Ted catches Hecky, I still won't get my money back; not that I think he'll catch him. America's a big country and Hecky's not a complete fool. But there is a way to save myself – ourselves, if you are willing, Tina.'

'Well, now that I'm not pregnant any longer, I hoped we might join Ted,' Tina said slowly. 'After things are tidied up here, of course. What had you in mind, Charlotte?'

'I want to finish this contract. As though Hecky and Ted were still here.'

'Finish the building? *Us?* But I know nothing about building, nor do you,' Tina exclaimed, staring at the other woman. 'How could we hope to succeed?'

'For a start, we already have the contract. Provided we begin to demolish, clear the ground, and then build, I think no one would object. We've got good men, you know. They want to keep their jobs and would do their best for us. What do you think the corporation will do if we try to hand over the work to someone else?'

'Do? What could they do?'

'Claim we were in breach of contract and sell us up for half what we're worth. The houses, the materials, the yard, the lot. But if we go ahead we'll have all the co-operation Ted and Hecky had relied on. Have you met Mr Roger M'Clusky?'

'Once. Ted thought a lot of him.'

'So did Hecky. And so do I. I've not been idle this past month while you've been ill. I've gone through the books, Ted's calculations, the materials which have already been purchased. If we could raise a loan we could do it, with Mr M'Clusky's help.'

'Yes, but . . . who would lend money to two women?'

Charlotte was sitting by the tea-tray which Tina had put near her on a small table. Before answering she poured herself another cup of tea, then raised her brows at Tina.

'Can I pour for you? Milk? Sugar?'

'Yes, I'll have more tea; I need it,' Tina said rather grimly. 'Tell me who would lend us money!'

'Your father?'

'Poppa? You must be . . .'

'No, listen, Tina. Your father wouldn't want you to go chasing off to America, I'm sure, with his two little grandsons. And more than that, even, he wouldn't want you to stay there.'

'What do you mean? Why should lending us money mean I wouldn't stay in America?'

'Because if we had sufficient money to continue with the contract, you wouldn't go to America until the work was finished. And because if the corporation make Ted and Hecky bankrupt, they won't be able to come back to England to start up in business again.'

This put an entirely different complexion on the proposal. Tina, chin in hand, stared at the fire and thought deeply. It would mean putting off her journey to the States for a while – several months, probably. But already the sheer magnitude of the challenge was making her heartbeat quicken. It would really be something, to take over the contract and make a success of it!

'It's worth a try, anyway,' she decided. 'I'll ring Poppa and then, if he agrees, I'll come down to the yard and we'll go through the books and talk to Mr M'Clusky together.'

Arthur laughed indulgently at first, but he agreed that, if the plan seemed feasible, he would willingly lend the money sooner than see his daughter rush off to America leaving behind her a dishonoured name.

Two or three days later, Tina met Roger M'Clusky properly for the first time since Hecky's flight. He was a handsome man, black-haired, blue-eyed and full of Irish charm. But his very frankness made both young women think he would do his best for them and for the company.

'Sure and I'd not a penny to bless meself with, when forst Mr Neyler hired me as a foreman,' he said cheerfully. 'But I worked hard, and I'm glad to work harder. 'Tis the only chance, I'm thinkin', of becomin' the owner of me own form, in time.'

'Your own firm? How do you make that out?' Tina asked suspiciously. 'You're not planning to leave us before we've even started, are you?'

'No indeed, Mrs Neyler. But when this contract's completed, won't I be gettin' most of the credit for it, indeed? And won't you and Mrs White here be wantin' to sell out to someone else, so's you can go about your business, whatever that may be? And though I've no money to put into the company, sure an' I'll work like a black for you. An' Mrs White has said that you'd be willin' to give me a t'ord share, if all goes merrily.'

'Very well. But Charlotte and I won't be idle, Mr M'Clusky. We shall do the books and as much of the ordering as may be. There are females working for building contractors, in the offices, are there not?'

'You've children, Mrs Neyler,' the man reminded her. 'If you would allow us to do so, the firm could pay for a baby-minder whilst you're here workin'. Would that suit?'

'That's fair, Tina,' Charlotte put in quickly. 'It only means that the three of us share the expense of a baby-minder; it would not do to penalise you because you are the only one with family responsibilities.'

'Very well. I do know someone who would take care of them.'

So things changed in Spanner's Row. To save money, Charlotte moved into the house, sleeping on a truckle bed in the living room and sharing expenses. During the day Helen Snelling from next door came in to take care of Desmond and Frank. She might have become a slut like her mother, but Tina would not employ a slut. With work for women both uncongenial and difficult to obtain, Helen was far too grateful for a well-paid and comfortable job to object to what she first thought of as Mrs Neyler's fussy ways, and soon they became her ways too.

At first, continuing with the demolition of the old houses was nerve-racking. Tina lay awake at night, her mind filled with the hideous vision of having to admit to the corporation that they had bitten off more than they could chew, so that her father's good money would be wasted. But it soon became apparent that the men knew their work and that Mr M'Clusky, charming though he might be with women, could handle most ably all the enquiries of the corporation.

Within six months, both young women were beginning to feel confidence in their own ability to see the thing through.

'It's the most exciting thing I've ever done,' Tina wrote to Edward. 'We do the books, order materials, bargain and scheme to keep costs down. We are busy every moment of the day, yet how we're enjoying it! No wonder men keep such a way of life to themselves!'

She and Edward exchanged letters two or three times a week, both longing to be together once more though both enjoyed their different lives. Edward was working at the Beaumont oilfield, Spindletop, running a supply depot and keeping an eye out for Hecky, though he had seen and heard nothing of his erstwhile partner yet. He was making money, but in almost every letter he stressed that an oilfield was no place for a respectable woman, let alone two small children.

'Hecky's bound to turn up sometime, being so interested in oil,' he wrote. 'In the meantime, I'm making money and saving most of it. If I continue like this I shan't *need* Hecky's thievings; we'll be rich by my endeavours alone!'

Tina, wistfully reading the letters in the lamplit living room once the boys were safely in bed, wished that Edward could see his sons, wished he was here, with his arms round her. But she savoured the responsibility and excitement of her new life. She would make the best of what she had here and now, and look forward to seeing Edward very soon.

Edward was building. First he had worked in a store, then he had set up for himself in a tiny shack made of corrugated iron and cardboard. Now, with money in his pocket, he was building himself a proper store. Kneeling on the rafters, he was nailing a plank roof into place, squinting against the sweat which trickled down his face, for the heat was intense and the sun, baking down on him despite his broad-brimmed hat, made it imperative to keep the nails in the shade of his pocket until he needed them. Left out on the roofing, they quickly became far too hot to handle.

'Ted! Hey, Ted!'

Edward glanced down at the small figure standing in the dust of the roadway, bellowing against the roar of sound from the field.

'Yeah, Stubby?'

'Got yo' mail, fella. Yo' a-comin' down?'

Edward blew a moustache of sawdust away from his mouth and brushed his streaming face. It would be pleasant to stand in the shade for a moment. It must be a hundred degrees or more up here in the full sunshine.

'Yes, I'll come down. Look out!'

He jumped, then swore as dust rose head high.

'God, will I never learn? Give me the letters then, Stubby.'

'Here y'are, fella.'

The letters changed hands and the short, square mailman stumped off, muttering that he'd rather have an ice-cold beer right now than a whole night with Dinah Daintee herself. Since Dinah was the latest attraction in Deep Crockett, and since her favours were the costliest and therefore, presumably, the best, Edward grinned at the mailman's avowed preference. A good thing he felt as he did, since a cold beer was within the reach of his pocket and Dinah certainly was not!

Then his eyes saw Tina's writing on the first envelope, and Dinah, Deep Crockett and Stubby were wiped from his mind. He missed her so terribly! Even the feel of the envelope was good because it came from her, seemed to hold a part of her in the round, childish handwriting and the outspoken ideas which she poured out to him as though she were simply writing down her thoughts. Most people became a little stilted when they wrote a letter. But to him Tina was just her loving self.

He glanced quickly at the second letter. It was from Mark. He wondered which to open first, and decided on

Mark's. He would save Tina's until last, and savour it longest.

He remained in the shade of his building, leaning against the log wall. Mark was well and happiness positively sang in every line he wrote. He obviously adored this Wendy girl he had married. Edward wondered what she was like. A blonde, he thought, like Sylvia; a big girl, with a high, jutting bosom and heavy hips and thighs. Mark had said in one letter that his brother must remember Wendy from the Clutha. Edward had racked his brains, but could remember only one girl clearly from those days and that was the storekeeper's daughter at Alexandra. Had her name been Wendy? He really could not remember, but he did know she was pale haired, with a come-hither eye and a wiggling walk.

Perusing the pages, he mentally shrugged. Whoever she was, his brother thought she was wonderful so she probably was. It seemed that the farm was flourishing; Mark had bought some new dairy cattle, Friesians, and they were doing well. Their milk was so rich that it made almost twice the butter per gallon that other animals yielded. Crops were good, though wheat prices had dropped; Mark was thinking of putting in a root crop next year, and of buying some southdown rams; they had better lambs for meat production.

A little further down the page, Mark informed his brother that they were to have someone to help Wen in the house. 'In her condition it isn't good for her to be doing so much,' he said shyly. Too shyly. Edward simply thought that Wen must have been overdoing it, what with all that milking, sheep shearing and lamb rearing.

The news that Karl was well and had danced five times with widow McRae made him chuckle. Surely Father was not searching for a second wife at his age? Then he folded the letter, put it in his pocket, and opened Tina's.

As always, pleasure and anxiety blended until his eye had skipped down every page and made sure that she was well. Then, pleasure alone reigned. He read the letter slowly, savouring every word, seeing each scene in his mind's eye.

She was blooming and very happy, though she missed him as much as he missed her. The boys were well too; there followed a description of their charms and naughtinesses which he read indulgently, because she had written it, not because he found it absorbing. She was worried about Charlotte. Her friend was allowing Mr M'Clusky to grow too friendly; surely she should have learned her lesson with Hecky? The man was a charmer and a good worker but he would, wrote Tina severely, make very poor husband material.

Edward grinned. He could see her saying it, her mouth tightening in disapproval, a frown bringing the baby-soft brows close for a moment.

He read on, half applauding the business acumen which had made her refuse offers of help from a big competitor, half dismayed by it. She was growing shrewd, his child-wife, and he was not sure he altogether approved!

He would be pleased to learn that they had paid Poppa back every penny, the letter continued, and had seized the opportunity to buy cheap when a building firm in Southport was declared bankrupt. Edward, always soft-hearted with the unsuccessful, hoped she had paid a fair price for the materials but feared she had not. Women, he concluded, could be hard business rivals, even when they were small and slender, with soft skin and softer hair, and were not yet twenty.

He finished the letter, which ended with all her love to her dearest Edward, flanked, followed and surrounded by battalions of kisses, and immediately the noise which he had not noticed while he read his letters came flooding back. He climbed back to his perch on the roof with the shouts of muleskinners, the thunder of the rigs and the whirring and grinding of the donkey engines ringing in his ears. He reached into his pocket and pulled out some nails, then picked up his hammer. As soon as he began to pound the nails into place the sun nailed him to the rafter and the sweat began to pour off him. He felt his eyes begin to sting and licked salt away from his lips. But he felt serene and happy. Tina missed him, but she could not hide the sense of achievement which she felt, nor her pride in her success. He, too, felt proud of himself. He had come here with nothing and soon he would be serving behind the counter in his own store and making more money in a month than many of the boomers made in a year. Being apart was hell, but it was a testing time for them both and he was sure neither would be found wanting. When at last he could send for Tina their love would be deeper, their marriage more loving and secure, for the months of growing strong alone.

20

Wen was in the kitchen, standing before the low, stone sink, washing dishes. Outside, the setting sun gilded her garden and the pine trees which bordered it had their rough, gnarled trunks flamed to orange by the light.

She finished the last dish and turned to dry her hands on a towel, glancing up at the clock on the wall as she did so. Almost six o'clock! Mark should be back soon. He had gone down to the harbour to meet Su Yung, the little cousin who had wanted to come to New Zealand a year or so back. Now she was coming, because Mark had insisted that Wen must have some help in the house. It was sensible, really. Su spoke good English, or so her own mother assured her. She was neat and willing and a good worker, and she hated cities and loved the country. Her education had been somewhat neglected, but Wen intended to remedy that as soon as she herself had some spare time.

The ship should have docked two or three hours ago, but there was Su's luggage, which would have to be brought up from the hold and checked out by the immigration officials.

Then everything had to be piled into the waggon and fastened on, and the drive back from Dunedin was a long one. Nevertheless, it might be as well to get the kettle on. Doubtless both Su Yung and Mark would welcome a cup of tea when they arrived, and a meal soon afterwards.

Wen moved to the stove and pulled the kettle over the heat. She would have liked to meet Su's ship herself, but Mark had forbidden it. Too much hanging about in her condition could not be good, he had said, and Wen, glancing down at her heavy body, feeling the occasional heave and stir as the baby moved, had to admit that he was probably right. She found the extra weight exhausting and often her ankles and back ached until she could have wept, but she remembered her mother's advice and continued to be as active as possible.

'Babies born to women who work in field come quick and easy,' her mother had said once, long ago. 'No tlubble, such babies. But when high-born lady who does no work have baby, then come tlubble.'

Wen, who had no desire to ask for 'tlubble', had passed this sage advice on to Mark when he had tried to stop her from helping with the milking, weeding her beloved garden, and riding her mare, Snowberry.

'You're not just saying that to stop me trying to persuade you to rest?' Mark said suspiciously. But fortunately the doctor had confirmed that Wen's mother was probably right, so he had grown less jealously protective. And once Su had arrived, she was sure he would worry less.

'It will be marvellous for us both,' he said earnestly, 'because it will mean that you have time for the baby and for me. Not only that, but you'll still be able to help me on the farm because Su will be at hand to keep an eye on the child and cook meals. It's so much better than having you tired out all the time.'

'Why should I be tired with one little baby to look after?' Wen protested. 'We've got our dear Freda to do all the heavy housework, and she does a lot of the cooking now that I'm growing so huge, and there's Toddy to help with the milking and work with you, and . . .'

'Look, I know how you like helping me around the farm, and I'm sure you'll like taking care of the baby. I'm not trying to dictate to you, you know; I'm giving you freedom of choice. With this girl actually living in the house you'll be able to pick and choose. Work with me one day, stay with the baby the next. See?'

'Yes, but . . . well, to have someone else living in the house! Won't you hate that, my love?'

'I'm going to build on,' Mark said decisively. 'Two rooms; one for Su Yung and another for the baby. After all, he'll want a room of his own when he's bigger so I might as well build it now.'

She argued no more, because she saw the strength of his viewpoint. To have a girl in the house would make her life easier. Indeed, the very day the letter from her uncle arrived telling them when to expect Su Yung, Mark and Toddy had begun to build the new rooms.

They were finished now, of course, and furnished, too. Mark had simply put a doorway in the short corridor leading to the bedrooms and then extended the corridor by about six feet. Both rooms were small and square, with windows which overlooked the vegetable garden, bright floral curtains, and single beds covered with gay quilts. Freda had polished the floor boards to a high gloss and Mark had boarded the log walls and then painted them white. To make the girl's room look more homelike, Wen bought frail Chinese ricepaper pictures for the walls and on the small, white-painted chest of drawers she had placed a blue Chinese bowl filled with full-blown scarlet tulips and sprays of white lilac. On the marble washstand (for there was only one bathroom) was a jug and ewer with a rim of blue cornflowers, vermilion poppies and flaunting yellow sunflowers. It would have been useless to give the girl books since she could not yet read, but Wen had bought some beautiful leaf-green taffeta material and some white linen, a handful of brilliantly multi-coloured silks, and a clutch of fat pencils, standing on a block of good drawing paper.

She checked over the room in her mind. She could not have

thought of everything, but at least the little unknown cousin would see that she had done her best to please.

The kettle began to sing and Wen bent down, with a certain amount of difficulty, and swung open the oven door. Inside, a mutton and potato pie simmered gently on one shelf and a bowl of rice with shrimps and beansprouts steamed on the other. She knew that Su Yung had been born and reared in London, but since her parents kept a restaurant she might never have grown accustomed to English food. Hence the rice dish, and the pan of sweet and sour sauce simmering on the back of the stove.

The table was laid and the meal done to a turn when the clatter of a carriage driving across the stableyard came to Wen's ears. She moved across to the kitchen window and looked out. Yes, Mark was back, swinging the horse round to a halt in front of the stable. Beside him was a tiny little Chinese girl dressed in blue trousers and a black tunic. She had a long plait of shining black hair and her small, pale face was dwarfed by an enormous pair of slanting, liquid black eyes which were fixed on the house with an anxious expression.

Wen opened the back door and went to greet the newcomer. Su Yung's anxious look faded at Wen's warmth, and she began to chatter about her voyage in excellent English, but with an appallingly broad cockney accent.

'I shall enjoy having you with me all the time,' Wen said presently, when Su had been shown over the house, had freshened up, and they were sitting down to their meal. Su, showing a healthy appetite despite her diminutive size, took a portion of meat pie, two floury potatoes, some early peas and a generous helping of rice and shrimps. Then she poured sweet and sour sauce and gravy indiscriminately over her meal, and began to eat neatly but with great enthusiasm.

'I, also,' she said gravely. 'Anuvver woman abaht the 'ouse will be better.'

'Woman? You're a child,' Mark protested.

'Naw! I've 'ad me fifteenth birfday,' she assured him.

'I beg pardon; you're quite an elderly person, I suppose,' Mark said solemnly, and watched her try to hide her giggles with a small, golden-skinned hand.

Later that night when they were safe in their bed, he turned to Wen and nuzzled a kiss into her neck.

'She's so small! Mind you don't start feeling sorry for her and doing all the work again. Do you think she's capable?'

'I'm sure she is. She's strong and willing, and that's what matters. I love her already, in fact. But darling, that accent!'

He laughed. 'Terrible, isn't it? You'll have to train that out of her or our son will end up sounding like a limey!'

'Suppose it's a girl? Would you be terribly disappointed?'

'Bless you, no! I don't care what we have, so long as he's healthy.'

She pinched him, loving him more because she knew he did care. He wanted a son far more than a daughter, though she was shrewd enough to know that, if left to himself, he would have preferred to remain childless. He enjoyed being just the two of them and saw no merit in producing children.

'That's all right, then. I'd hate to think that if I had a girl you'd want to farm it out, like they used to do in ancient China. Or was it Greece?'

He laughed. 'You should know! How long is it before the baby comes?'

'Babies don't always come when they should, you know. But it's due in a week.'

'Hmm. That should give you a few days to show Su how you like things done. And you can introduce her to people, too. She's awfully pretty; I just hope she doesn't get married before you even have the child.'

'Mark! You said earlier what a babe she was. She'll fit in very well, I'm sure of it. And now, go to sleep! It's your turn to do the milking in the morning!'

Su settled down every bit as quickly as Wen had foretold, and by the time the baby did put in an appearance, ten days late, she was even beginning to model her speech on Wen's, whom she adored.

The baby was a boy.

Mark tiptoed into the room after the birth and saw Wen lying on her pillows, bright-eyed, smiling, perhaps a little paler than usual but quite undeterred by her experience.

In the crook of her arm she held her shawl-wrapped son, and as Mark approached she turned the bundle so that he could see the child.

'Are you all right? Truly?' Mark said, sitting down on the bed and scarcely glancing at his son.

'Truly. And so is Master Neyler. Do look at him, darling!'

Mark looked and grinned. He saw a little round, yellowish face, eyes wedged shut, and a fringe of black hair.

'He looks just like your father! Shall we call him John?'

'I thought you wanted to call him Karl.'

'I thought I did, but he doesn't look in the least like a Karl. However, Father is waiting for this moment with bated breath and I'd hate to disappoint him. I'd sort of hinted that if it was a boy it would be named for him. How about Karl John, and we'll call him John to avoid confusion?'

Wen smiled down at her son, then looked straight into Mark's eyes. 'I know what you mean. He does look very Chinese, doesn't he? To give him a blond, Teutonic name like Karl might cause some eyebrows to rise. But I'm sure he'll change and look more like you when he's older – perhaps three or four weeks. I think babies often look Chinese, even when they aren't. I do want a son who looks like you!'

He kissed her and then, cautiously, the baby.

'Fool! I'm an ugly devil! As for John, I daresay he'll just look like himself. He's an individual already, I can see that.'

'The next street to be rebuilt is entirely demolished,' Tina wrote, her tongue curling out with the effort of keeping her large handwriting small in order to get more words per sheet. 'Your choice of Mr M'Clusky was a good one. Though most people know Charlotte and I are working hard in the office, I don't think they realise that we're actually running things. And this is a good job, because there is a lot of prejudice against women in the business world.'

She turned round in her chair and stared at the stove, where a beef stew bubbled. Things were good with her and Charlotte. Each was beginning to understand the other, and they took turns to prepare the meals, even to keep an eye on the boys, though Helen Snelling was still working for them all day.

It was easier now the boys were older. Desmond was four and attending a small school; Frank was three and eager to start in his turn when Tina felt he was ready.

There had been a bad patch a few months ago, when the first rebuilding project had been almost completed. Charlotte had been growing steadily quieter and quieter, her attitude to Tina and the boys more and more withdrawn. And one morning, when Tina came downstairs to get the breakfast, she could not wake her friend. Fortunately, she had panicked, running into Spanner's Row, knocking wildly on the Snellings' door, begging for help.

Bill Snelling had sprung to the wrong conclusion – he thought that Charlotte had had a drop too much drink and was suffering from an overdose of alcohol instead of an overdose of laudanum. However, his experience in such matters was to prove invaluable. He drenched Charlotte's head in cold water, dragged her roughly to her feet, and began to march her up and down the room. As soon as she was able, he made her swallow a nauseating mixture of salt and water, and presently held her head over a basin while she vomited.

By the time the doctor arrived, Charlotte was conscious, guilt-ridden, and amenable to a lecture.

Tina had delivered it. She had pointed out that even if Charlotte was fed up with them they were fond of her. She told her friend that to escape a contract by deliberately dying was every bit as bad as running out on them as Hecky had. She impressed on the other woman the effect it would have had on the corporation if they had suddenly seen the work slow down and perhaps even stop. 'For whether I could carry on without you, Heaven knows,' Tina said severely. 'I do beg you to consider others, Charlotte, before you do such selfish things!'

In a way, it had done Charlotte good. It had made her see that her life was still worthwhile, still useful to others and to herself. Hecky, to be sure, was lost to her. She believed it and certainly Edward had long ago ceased to search for his partner. But others cared for her. Mr M'Clusky, told of the near tragedy, came visiting with flowers and a beautiful iced cake from the most expensive and exclusive baker in Liverpool. He sat in the living room and made Charlotte laugh, and told her that he could never get on without her and that she really must not do such a thing again. 'Frightened the life out of us, you did,' he said. 'Why, you're the best of the t'ree of us at chasin' slow payers and persuadin' folk that we're on the level. We're a partnership, ma'am, an' don't you forgit it!'

And with their personal lives running smoothly and the contract in a fair way to finishing within the stated time and well up to standard, Tina felt it was safe to think about going to America.

Edward had done well; so well that he intended to move away from Spindletop and settle elsewhere before he sent for Tina and the boys to join him. Already he was talking of different towns within a day's journey of Spindletop, where he might set up in business. Tina had written suggesting that he buy land; she knew he had farmed once and enjoyed it, why not again? And country living would be good for the boys.

So she sat at the writing desk which she and Charlotte had purchased and dreamed of America, of showing off her fine sons to their father, of boasting – just a little – about the firm of White & Neyler and of how they had worked to save the contract.

She knew in her bones that her time in Liverpool was

drawing to an end. A few months, and the last building would rise from the rubble of the slums and she and the boys would be on their way. To the New World, and to Edward!

21

'Have you come back for a cup of tea, love?' Wen said lazily. She smiled up at Mark from the sun-bed in the dappled willow tree shade, and patted the grass beside her. 'Why didn't you come in for lunch? We had cold meat and salad and the loveliest pudding, and now I've come out here for my rest while Su makes a pot of tea. Presently she'll remove young John, which will be even more restful.'

Mark bent and kissed her, then sat on the grass, leaning against the sturdy sun-bed. His eyes followed John, placidly playing with soldiers in the grass. His son still looked more like his mother than his father, but both parents adored the naughty, quick-witted toddler.

'I have to admit our Johnny isn't restful, but I suppose it's largely curiosity which keeps him so active. And he's spoilt rotten, of course. This baby brother or sister will do him the world of good.'

Wen patted her bulging stomach. 'I try to tell myself it will be a companion for Johnny, not that it will put his nose out of joint,' she protested. 'Johnny, don't hit the soldiers, darling! Don't, darling, you'll break . . .' She closed her eyes as the wooden soldier cracked beneath a decisive thump from a toy cannon. 'That gun is meant for . . . for . . .'

'Killing in a more civilised fashion,' Mark concluded for her. 'Johnny, you're a little brute, d'you know that?'

'He isn't,' his indignant and indulgent mother protested. 'He's a broth of a boy, and so . . .' she broke off, leaping to her feet with all the agility she could muster and pouncing on her son. 'What've you got? Give it to Mummy; oh, you bad boy!'

She inserted a cautious finger into his mouth, then yelped as John's teeth closed crunchingly.

'Hey, you mustn't bite!' Wen turned appealing eyes to Mark. 'He's got a worm or something in his mouth, the disgusting little brute!'

'Open your mouth, Johnny,' Mark said, joining in the fray. He picked the child up and shook him slightly. 'Come on, open up!'

John swallowed and then obligingly – if belatedly – opened his mouth.

'It's gone, Wen! God, I hope it wasn't poisonous.'

'It looked just like an ordinary earthworm; you know, sort of pink and wriggly,' Wen shuddered. 'The bad boy! I refuse to worry myself into an early grave every time he eats something he shouldn't.'

Su, carrying a tea-tray carefully across the lawn, put a stop to conjecture. Mark hastily stood Johnny down on the grass and put the wobbly bamboo table near Wen. Then he took the tray from Su and stood it on the table, bowing from the waist.

'Tea is served, honourable lady!'

Wen sat down on the sun-bed and smiled at Su. 'Thank you, love. Whatever did we do before you came? Will you pour out? I don't know whether Johnny wants milk just before he goes in for his nap? What do you think?'

'Tea, tea!' Johnny exclaimed, hurling himself at his father's legs. 'Tea, tea! Bicky for Donny?'

Mark picked him up and swung him over the tea-tray, making him giggle helplessly.

'Can he have a biscuit, girls?'

'Yes to a biscuit, but no to milk, I believe,' Su said. She now spoke clearly and without a trace of a cockney accent. 'He shouldn't have a drink just before a nap. One of the little shortbread fingers would be best, Mark.'

Mark had lowered Johnny over the plate of biscuits and the small, grubby fingers had already selected a chocolate one which he thrust in the general direction of his mouth, scoring a direct hit on his nose the first time and, at the second attempt, smearing chocolate right across one cheek.

'Ah, hum,' Mark said, conscience-stricken. 'I'm afraid it's a bit late to change his mind. Any attempt to wrest a chocolate biscuit from those hot and wormy fingers would lead to a fight!'

'The worm!' Wen shrieked, sitting up. 'He's been playing with worms and I let him have a biscuit! Oh Johnny, Johnny, what a naughty mummy you've got!'

'Too late now,' Mark said philosophically. 'Can I have a cup of tea? We're cutting hay in the top meadow, and . . .' He was standing his son down as he spoke but suddenly broke off, his eyes widening. 'Oh, no!'

'What's the matter, darling?'

'Look!'

Wen and Su followed his pointing finger. There stood Johnny in his white shirt, red knickerbockers, white stockings and little red boots.

'Yes, I see him,' Wen said. 'So what?'

'His bootlaces!'

'What's the matter . . . oh, dear God, he's eaten his bootlace!'

'Pink and wriggly indeed,' Mark said, when they had finished laughing. 'Well, I don't suppose a bootlace will poison him.'

'No, I shouldn't think so,' Wen agreed. She turned to Su. 'Take him to bed, dear, and then perhaps I shall be able to nap for a little while. Though it's so hot! Perhaps I'd be better taking a quiet stroll, or coming up to the meadow. Not to haymake, I suppose, but I could sit in the shade and watch.'

'No, darling, because that isn't resting,' Mark said firmly. 'You stay here and have a nap and then later you can come up to the hayfield. In fact, you and Su and Johnny will probably bring the workers' tea.'

'Oh, well.' Wen watched Su's retreating back affectionately. 'What we did before Su came I can't imagine. She's worth her weight in gold. Why did you come down to the farmhouse so early though, Mark?'

'We shot some bunnies and I brought them down for Freda to skin and prepare.' He licked his lips. 'She's taken them back to her cottage to do, and tomorrow she'll bring 'em in for dinner. She'll roast 'em with whole onions and gravy.'

'Delicious. And now, what shall we talk about? Would you like another cup of tea, if there's one in the pot?'

'No more tea; I'm afraid I'm off, darling. I want to repair the fencing up around the far cliffs. It's been nothing but luck that's stopped us losing stock over there, the fence is so weak. I've left it until now, but I need extra space for the yearlings so I've got to get down to it.'

He leaned over and patted her shoulder, then dropped a kiss on top of her head.

'See you later, darling.'

Wen waited until he was out of sight and then lay back on the sun-bed, not entirely unwillingly. She would not have admitted it to anyone but she was finding this pregnancy rather trying. It was partly Johnny, of course, for good though Su was Wen had to take her turn at looking after her son, and his boundless energy and undoubted naughtiness were very exhausting. Johnny had not been a large baby, but the doctor had confirmed her own feelings that this baby was bigger and she herself heavier and more cumbersome.

Their fears that Su might marry and leave them had proved groundless, for though she had a long string of admirers she showed no particular interest in any of them; although Mark and Wen told each other that she would make someone a marvellous wife, and regarded each new young male visitor with indulgent interest. Su, they had decided, was young for her age, and they were so happy, the four of them! Mark had taught Su to swim and she was an enthusiastic bather now, though when she first arrived at the farm she had been terrified of the water. Now, the three adults would take the little boy down to the beach for a whole breezy, sandy day, and Su and Wen took turns to look after him while the other swam and frolicked in the waves. Johnny would sit, naked, in a little pool, slapping the water with his palms and reaching for shells; staggering, pot-bellied, along the beach after the penguins, kicking the soft sand at the top of the dunes, sliding down in a flurry of giggles and applause. Su was like a child then, sliding down dunes on her tummy, her eyes tightly closed against the flying sand, her plait heavy with salt.

Thinking of the beach made Wen realise that she had not bathed once this summer. She had paddled, watching Su and Mark as they swam; she had gathered shells and fished for shrimps with a flour-bag on a split cane, dug for cockles, used the crab hook to locate the big pinky-brown crabs lurking under the kelp.

The trouble was her size. She and Su had swimming costumes, but she would have been self-conscious in hers, since it was made for a slender and supple Wen and not one with a waist measurement of about fifty inches! What was more, she and Mark usually escaped for a while during the evening and bathed naked from their private bay, but this year she had not liked to suggest it. I look like a great whale, she thought crossly, and I don't want Mark to laugh at me.

Sitting up cautiously, she glanced towards the house even as a rivulet of sweat ran down her spine. It was so hot! Freda was at her own cottage, Mark said, preparing the rabbits, and Su would be lying on her bed keeping an eye on Johnny in his cot, perhaps even snoozing herself in this heat. Presently tea would have to be taken to the haymakers. She glanced at her lapel watch. Presently! Not for nearly two hours would the workers gather in the shade of the trees to enjoy the great jugs of tea, the chunks of meat pie with lettuce and tomato, the thick slices of homemade bread spread with their own yellow, salty butter.

She swung her legs over the side of the sun-bed and stood up, squinting ruefully down at her prow-like stomach. She would just go down to the beach, and if it was really quite deserted she would slip out of her loose dress and underclothing and have a quiet, leisurely swim. She would be very careful and stay well within her depth, but it would be wonderful to feel the cool sea-surge, and to have the weight of her hot, cumbersome body supported by the silky water!

The walk to the clifftop was not long, but under the blazing sun it was tiring, the scramble down the cliff path more so. But at length, sweating, short of breath, heart hammering, she stood on the white sand at the top of the beach. The tide was out and the wet sand beckoned. She kicked off her slippers and walked slowly down to the edge of the surf. It creamed over her toes, cooling her beautifully, and there was a breeze down here which certainly had not stirred the leaves in her garden. She smiled blissfully. Presently she would bathe, wallowing like a seal in the shallows, letting the little waves break over her hot face. She imagined them, hissing on burning skin, caressing her as they caressed the smooth sleekness of the seals.

Thinking of seals made her glance round for them. They were down where the long tongue of rocks reached out into deep water, as they usually were, lolling in the sun with the breakers only inches from their flippers and every opportunity to simply roll over and slide beneath the green and white of the lazy waves.

She walked along the edge of the sea towards the seals, keeping in the surf so that her feet were constantly submerged. When she was level with them she stopped, seeing a fight or a scuffle break out. Two of them, suddenly no longer charming, reared up, mouths agape, roaring angrily. Behind her, like an echo, she heard another roar. She glanced inland. A huge bull seal had been giving himself a sandbath up in the dunes but now he was tearing down to the sea like a runaway steam train. Wen guessed that the bull seal would not allow fighting between his wives and was determined to put a stop to such nonsense once and for all. She smiled, trying to imagine Mark's reaction if she and Su were to roar at each other and try to bite as the female seals were now doing, then turned to face the bull.

He was nearer than she had supposed. It occurred to her that he looked really fierce, his nostrils flaring, his mouth opening to bellow, his eyes glaring anxiously towards his womenfolk. He was humping himself down the sloping beach at an incredible rate and she moved quickly, meaning to get out of his path. At the same moment, the bull saw her. He swerved, equally anxious to avoid her, and the two bodies met with a stunning crash; then the bull continued on his rush down to the sea, flopped, still bellowing, into the surf, and began to swim towards the tongue of rock.

Wen felt the great shingle-smeared shoulder hit her in the knees like a battering ram. A moment's amusement, mingled with annoyance, that she had not realised he would inevitably swerve, and then she was thrown right over his back and crashed down, stunning herself on the ridge of rock as she fell.

There was silence. Then small noises returned as a tern landed on the tide line, ferreting with its sharp beak in the debris, looking for food. Presently others joined it, and then had to move up the beach as the tide turned and the wavelets scrambled inshore.

In the encroaching surf a strand of hair floated, the wavelets hissed against cooling skin.

'Where's Wen?'

Mark walked briskly through the kitchen door, brows raised, and Su, packing the haymakers' tea into baskets, said placidly, 'She's on the lawn, resting. Johnny's still napping.'

'Mark frowned and took a piece of shortbread from a plate. 'This is good, Su. Who made it, you or Wen? She isn't on the lawn, incidentally. I looked as I crossed the yard.'

'Freda made it. Perhaps Wen's already on her way to the hayfield.'

'Without offering to help you with the baskets? That's not like Wen. I suppose you could be right though, particularly if she decided to go for a walk and found herself nearer the field than here. I'll take the baskets for you and go ahead while you wake Johnny. Will you be long?'

'Not long. I think I can hear him moving. I'll put his boots on and give him a piggy-back. We'll be there nearly as soon as you will.'

'What about the jugs of tea? Can you carry them when you've got Johnny?'

She smiled at him, her eyes nearly disappearing with her amusement. 'A pretty girl never needs to carry anything in this country, Wen says. Freddy Boardman is coming in to carry the jugs.'

'Freddy! Is he your latest beau, young woman?'

She was on her way across the kitchen to fetch the child but she looked back over her shoulder, twinkling at Mark.

'I'm too young to think of beaux, you and Wen say so! Freddy is just an obliging young man.'

'He wouldn't oblige me by carrying heavy great jugs,' Mark murmured. 'All right, Su, I'll take the baskets, and see you presently.'

He picked up the heavy baskets, peeped under the white cloths which protected them from insects and the sun-glare, and swung out of the back door and across the stableyard. As he crossed the sheepyard, for some inexplicable reason, he hesitated. He had the weirdest feeling! A pulling, tugging sensation, as if he were absentmindedly walking in the wrong direction. He frowned. He knew full well that the hayfield was this way, because he had been cutting with the men earlier in the day.

He swung the gate open and walked through. Stronger, more urgent, came the desire to retrace his steps.

Mark was not a particularly imaginative man, but he began to feel as if someone was trying to turn him round, pulling on him with invisible strings, a puppet in the hands of an expert manipulator. He continued to walk steadily up the hill towards the hayfield but the hair on the back of his neck was prickling erect; gooseflesh was springing up all over his body and he felt cold, despite the heat of the sun on him.

Halfway across the meadow, he gave in. Not knowing why he did so, he turned and began to go down towards the house. The relief was instantaneous and the feeling of wrongness, of blindly heading for some sort of doom, left him. He walked swiftly, easily, but made no attempt to re-enter the house, merely dumping his baskets unceremoniously on the back doorstep and continuing across the yard, vaulting over the stone wall into the front garden, striding across the still-empty lawn, through the front gate and, led by an insistence which knew better than he what was required of him, to the cliff edge and then down to the shore.

Once there, he stopped, feeling like a sleep-walker awakened. What on *earth* was he doing here? He should have been in the hayfield with Wen and the others – if Wen was already there. He scanned the beach closely. The tide was on the turn and seals were dotted on the rocks and shoreline, but not another soul was in sight.

He turned back to the cliff path, furious with himself, and instantly the tugging recommenced. He made for the cliff, then stopped. He should never have given in to a whim – for what else could it be – but having arrived on the beach, he might as well take a look round. Suppose Wen was down here somewhere? He began to make his way slowly down to the edge of the breakers. If he went right round to the beginning of the tongue of rocks where the seals liked to lie, he could see into the tiny cove where they always went in the rare event of a stranger's presence. If his naughty darling had decided to bathe she might well have chosen the more inaccessible cove because it would be more private for a pregnant woman. She had never said so, but he knew she was self-conscious about her size this time. He grinned to himself as he reached the water margin. He would tease her if he found her swimming naked in her condition! Ahead of him a seal basked in the fringing froth of the waves, moving gently as the sea took it. He frowned. Usually the seals preferred the rocks; could it be injured? He began to hurry, continuing to muse on the strangeness of finding a seal on the tideline long after he knew in his heart that it was no seal.

He reached her. She lay on her side, her blue dress darkened by the water clinging as sleekly as a seal's skin.

Terror filled him. Had she fainted? He fell on his knees in the water, taking her in his arms, trying to raise her. She was all right, of course she was! She looked as though she were asleep, wet lashes lying on wet cheeks, her hair floating as the waves came in. He could not see her face too well; little waves kept breaking over it and it was half buried in the sand, because the turning tide brought sand in the breakers coming inshore.

He tried to lift her but could only manage to drag her on to his lap. He was shaking terribly, that was the trouble, weakened by the shock of finding her. Presently he would carry her up the beach and shout for help. But for now she was safe in his arms, her head cradled against his breast. The water was quite pleasant, cooling his heat, calming his worry.

Presently, sitting there, he laughed. He had not meant to come bathing, but that was just what he was doing! The water was up to his waist. How Wen would laugh at him when she woke up, and they waded ashore together, she teasing him for his impromptu wetting!

Time passed, but he was content, with Wen in his arms, a comfortable weight, and the sea no more than halfway up his chest. A voice, exclaiming, made him realise that there were people on the beach, and that the sun had set. He would have felt cold, perhaps, had he not been so numb.

People splashed into the water and someone was coaxing him to stand up but he could not stand on numb legs with Wen's weight in his arms. He tried, but his knees just gave and he must not drop his heart's darling! Her head lolled as he moved and as he looked fondly into her sleeping face her mouth fell open and inside he saw sand. Sand! He began to cry because he knew she would hate to wake up and find sand in her mouth. She was so fastidious, his Wen. He freed one frozen, numbed hand and began to try, very gently, to clear the gritty stuff from her lips and tongue but he could not feel his fingers and suddenly he knew he was going to let her drop. His arms were frozen too.

'Let me take her, Mark.'

That was Toddy, good old Toddy. Perhaps he had better

let Toddy take her; he was not feeling too good, and he knew he must not let her fall; she was an expectant mother!

The weight left his arms and he was dragged to his feet and up on to the beach. A bottle clattered against his teeth, then fiery liquid gushed down his throat. He swallowed, choked, swallowed again. As it coursed through him he began to shiver, then to shudder, then to shake so violently that the whole beach seemed to tip and tilt. He was ashamed that he had forgotten about the child she carried. Wen would not forget; it would be her first thought when she woke up.

Faintly, he heard his voice. 'Will she be all right? It won't hurt the baby, will it?'

For the first time, he looked into the faces. Familiar faces. Friends, neighbours. Toddy, Freddy Boardman, old Micah. Strange, how pitiful and serious they all looked.

'Come on, Mark, old lad. Up the cliff path and then we'll get you home. You'll feel more yourself after a hot drink and a meal. You must be nearly dead with cold.'

That was Freddy, unusual concern on his ruddy, weatherbeaten face.

He was too weak to make the cliff path, though. They carried him up it, and, since they insisted, he allowed them to carry him right into the farm kitchen. Su was at the stove, red-eyed from weeping, and Freda's homely face was greenish white, her eyes red-rimmed. It was silly to cry, but understandable; a terrible tragedy had been averted. Hadn't it?

The men helped him into a chair and Su ran across to him. He said firmly, 'Is Wen all right? Have you put her to bed? Sent for a doctor?' but Su just put her thin little-girl's arms round him and hugged him hard.

'Mark, my dear. Wen is drowned.'

He heard his own weak laugh, heard his voice scoffing at such a ridiculous remark, but inside him the knowledge was steadily growing. A vast, incomprehensible, aching emptiness grew in his head. They spoke of his own life. Life? Without her?

He let them lead him to his lonely bed.

*

For many days, Mark just lay in his bed. He would eat nothing, drank only water, never spoke. Su brought Johnny to him but he did not seem to know the boy, certainly he never acknowledged his presence. The doctor said it was shock, and that Mark must be given hot drinks and doses of laudanum so that he could rest. Su, confused and deeply unhappy, knew that there were things she should do but she hesitated to do any of them. Neighbours arranged Wen's funeral but neither she nor Mark attended. Words like 'exhaustion', and 'overtaxed nerves', and 'exposure to the elements' were used of Mark's condition, but Su thought that he had gone away to a quiet place, and that when he returned he would understand that Wen was dead but that for Johnny's sake he must begin to live again.

She knew she should tell his brother of Wen's death, but it seemed wrong to go through Mark's desk when he was here, in the same house. People called to give their condolences, for Wen was loved by almost everyone who had come in contact with her, but she could let no one see Mark. He was too ill; only Karl went into the bedroom, and came out weeping, snuffling into a huge purple handkerchief, looking an old man.

Then, ten days after Wen's death, Mark got up, dressed, and went into the kitchen for breakfast. He looked ghastly, thin as a rake, his eyes dark-shadowed, his freckles standing out against the pallor of his skin. He greeted Su quietly, but ate half a round of bread and butter and drank two cups of tea thirstily. When Johnny came in in Su's arms he smiled at the little boy, and when Johnny threw a rusk across the room he rebuked him in an almost normal tone of voice.

Toddy, who had been visiting the house a dozen times a day to find out how Mark was progressing, came into the kitchen, stopped short, then said cheerfully, 'Mornin', boss. You workin'?'

'Not too hard,' Mark said. 'But I'll walk round and see what's been happening. I'm rather weak still.'

'I'll be glad if you'll take a look at Snowberry. She's

standin' on her heels, and I think she may have got a touch of laminitis. She's not been ridden, so she's been spendin' more time than she ought stuffin' grass.'

'All right, I'll follow you.'

Mark got his old jacket from the hook on the back door and put it on, then opened the door, saying over his shoulder, 'Dinner at noon, please, Su.'

Truth to tell, he felt as cold and detached as though he floated a couple of feet above the ground, surrounded by a glass wall which sound could only just penetrate. He had watched Su spreading jam on her bread and butter, pouring the tea, making Johnny's breakfast. He saw Johnny cram a chunk of rusk into his mouth and then spit it back on to his plate, fiddle with his spoon, begin to unpick the stitching on his bib, rub his shoes calculatingly on the legs of his chair to produce a rich, earsplitting squeak which always incensed his elders. But he could not summon up the strength of interest to listen properly for these sounds. Conversation would need careful listening, more careful than he was yet prepared to give.

Walking across the stableyard in Toddy's wake, he found that in this sepia world he inhabited it no longer mattered whether the sun shone or the rain poured down or the wind blew a gale. Caught behind his glass wall, which moved when he moved, imprisoning him constantly, he could not even smell the coffee which Su made, and when he reached the stables the good smell of horse and leather and hay which should have assailed his nostrils was absent.

Colours, too, had gone. Browns, greys, off-whites ruled supreme. And touch was muted by the glass so that his hand on Snowberry's flank might have rested on a brick wall for all the response in his once sensitive fingers.

A quotation which he had never understood came into his head. ' . . . if the salt have lost its savour, wherewith shall it be salted?' He knew what it meant, now. The bread and butter had as well been ashes, the tea water. The salt had indeed lost its savour.

It had been Wen, or the memory of Wen, which had brought him out of his room this morning and set him to trying for some sort of normality. She would want it, he knew, and for her sake and for Johnny's sake he must try to get back to life again.

He worked beside Toddy all morning, and if the other man noticed anything wrong he did not comment on it. At dinner-time he went back to the farm alone, for Toddy would eat with Freda in her cottage, though he would take his evening meal with them today.

Mark walked into the kitchen, taking off his old jacket. His son was playing with a wooden truck on the floor, Su was laying the table. She smiled up at him as he closed the back door, making some remark about the meal.

One moment he saw her small, ivory face, her friendly smile. The next there was a movement in the air, a sort of shimmer, and her hair hung wet, seal-sleek, against wet cheeks, and there was sand in the open mouth.

He drew in his breath sharply and Su was there again, a hint of anxiety in her eyes, telling him that there was mutton stew and dumplings for dinner, saying that she had heated the plates and was all ready to serve, if he would wash quickly. He went to the sink as the back door opened and Toddy came in, rubbing his hands together, saying cheerfully that Freda had gone into Dunedin to do some shopping, and could Su find him a sandwich or something?

After dinner, Mark slipped away from Toddy and made his way down to the shore. Would it hurt unbearably to visit the spot where he had found Wen's body? But it produced no reaction in him whatsoever. He looked at the sepia beach, sepia sea, sepia sky, and thought he would hardly have known it for their special bay, the place where they had laughed and loved a lifetime ago.

At tea-time, it happened twice. Twice he glanced up at Su and twice her face seemed to shiver and dissolve and there was Wen, her eyes closed, her head lolling to one side, her lips a little parted to show her sand-filled mouth.

After tea he tried to play with Johnny. He thanked God that the child did not bring the cruel picture of drowning into his mind. But he found Johnny tiring because the child constantly asked where Mummy was, when Mummy was coming back, and after Su had whisked the boy off he made his way to bed himself, worn out beyond words by the mental and physical strains of the day.

Next morning he got up and breakfasted with Su, and she reminded him, a little diffidently, that he had not yet written to his brother Edward to acquaint him with his loss. For a moment it was as if the sun had come out, banishing the glass wall, the sepia world. Edward! Out of everyone in the whole world, only Ted would understand, would know how he felt, would realise how . . . how *nothing* life had become. Su was right; he must get in touch with Edward at once.

When breakfast was finished he told Su that he would send Ted a letter that very day and enquired, for the first time, whether Wen's parents had been informed. Su was able to reassure him on that point and she began to wash up, immensely cheered by the change in him she had sensed at the first mention of his brother.

Mark took a cloth and began to wipe up the dishes, and Su, chattering, turned to him with some mundane remark about their dinner. And suddenly, there was Wen, her sand-clogged eyelashes fluttering, the terrible, sand-filled mouth trembling as if it longed to speak.

Mark gave a hoarse cry, dropped the plate and the tea towel, and fled from the kitchen. He strode across the stableyard, shaking, tears coursing down his face. Was he going mad? Would this terrible transformation take place every time he looked at Su? He knew, suddenly, that he was on the very edge of madness, that he must get right away for a time. But where? Back to Waihola? To the Clutha, where he first met Wen?

He went into Brownie's stall and the gelding gave a whinny of delight. Mark fondled the smooth chestnut withers. He had not had much exercise lately, poor chap, and a powerful horse like Brownie needed to stretch his legs.

It was the work of a moment to saddle and bridle the gelding and get into the saddle and turn his mount towards Dunedin. As he rode off, Su ran into the yard and called something; he glanced over his shoulder and caught a glimpse of her pale face, then looked hastily ahead. Not again! He could not bear it!

The horse's stride was lengthening; he was impatient for a canter. Mark allowed him to trot, then to canter, scarcely noticing the direction in which he rode. And when, later, he saw the city on the skyline, he felt positively elated. He knew now what he must do! He must go to Edward! There was no one else in the world who could understand and perhaps help him as his brother could. They had been more than friends because for years they had had only each other; they had stood, the two of them, against Karl, the hardships of the farm, the rest of the world. Edward knew him to the heights and depths of his soul, in a way which only Wen had ever bothered to learn.

He had not the haziest idea of where Edward was, though the letters always went to a post office address in somewhere called Beaumont, Texas, but he would find him. Why should he not, when he had no other mission in life?

With complete confidence, he headed towards the harbour.

22

Tina stood by the ferry rail, watching the shore of the Battery draw near, her baggage at her feet, her sons standing close. She had passed safely through Customs and Immigration at Ellis Island, being obviously in blooming health, and having no fears that she might be detained or refused entry.

Mind you, she thought judiciously, remembering the

terrifying inspection hall, a huge place divided into what looked like cattle stalls where she and the children had been physically examined, quizzed and cross-questioned, if I had known what it was going to be like, I might have been as nervous as the rest! But she had remembered her first trip to New York, when Momma had sailed through the old Custom and Immigration post at the Castle Garden without once being stopped or questioned. Momma's English accent and self-confidence had doubtless been in her favour, and Tina soon realised that her own accent and placid demeanour had saved her from the ordeals suffered by so many others.

Standing watching New York getting bigger and closer, she let her mind go back to her departure from England. It had been, in the end, so hurried! The house in Spanner's Row was sold and the furniture put into store, and she and the boys moved into lodgings whilst passages were bought, farewells were said, and the books handed over to Charlotte.

For Charlotte was staying with the firm, and most of Tina's share of the money was remaining too, so that Edward could still be a shareholder.

'I have enjoyed working with the company, and since I wish to continue to do so I shall leave all my own capital in,' Charlotte explained. 'Indeed, how else would I manage? If I draw my money out, it won't last me very long!'

'You'll draw a salary from the firm, then? Tina enquired. 'I'm only leaving my money in because of you, Charlotte.'

'Indeed I shall.' Charlotte licked her lips and the colour rose in her cheeks. 'I think it only fair to tell you that Mr M'Clusky has asked me to be his wife, and, whilst this is impossible at the present moment, I have agreed to move into his new house at Crosby and call myself his wife until such time as we may legally marry.'

'Charlotte!'

'I know what you must be thinking.' Charlotte retained her cool, detached air but her face was a dark and painful red. 'But who will know? We shall tell no one that we are not legally married. And I assure you I have no illusions about Mr M'Clusky. I shall insist that I be treated as an equal partner, and since I shall act for you and Edward I shall have twice the voting power Mr M'Clusky has should it ever come to a disagreement. I have thought very hard about this, and have come to the conclusion that I might do a great deal worse.'

'You're ruining yourself, you know that.'

'Only if people find out, and why should they? I shall say I'm a widow and Hecky is dead if anyone asks.'

She and Tina had parted friends, but Tina was shocked to find someone as precise and pedantic as Charlotte bent upon becoming a Scarlet Woman – and apparently without a qualm.

There had been an emotional farewell over the telephone to Poppa; his favourite daughter going all that way, and with his only grandsons. Cecy and Abraham were now married but had not started their family.

The ship grazed the pier and Tina drew on her grey gloves and tightened her hold on her sons. They had been demons during the voyage. They had pestered the sailors, pinched food from the galley, scribbled over some valuable books belonging to the first officer, and tied a woman's fur coat on a string and towed it around after them, telling everyone it was 'our dog'. However hard she tried, she always seemed one step behind them, apologising for their ingenious naughtiness but never able to forestall them.

Now, four-year-old Desmond scowled and tugged, eager to run ahead, and then lapsed into a sulk when he could not escape. Frank followed suit, his yellow, downy brows drawn together in imitation of his elder brother, though his bright eyes scanned the crowd with considerable interest and speculation.

As they shuffled off the ship, scanning the faces below, Tina told herself that she could not possibly expect to recognise Herman after all these years. But she knew him as soon as she set eyes on him, recognising something in the elderly face, some lion-like strength, unchanged by the passage of time.

'Uncle Herman!'

He came towards her, kissed her cheek, then grabbed Frank and hoisted him on to his shoulder, holding out his free hand to Desmond.

'Aha, Frank! Aha, Desmond! Uncle Herman shall be your horsie as he was once your momma's! Tina, *faygeler,* how good it is to see you, and how beautiful you have grown! The *boychiks,* too, so handsome! Fine fellers, eh?'

It is just as it was, Tina thought nostalgically. She had wondered if her marriage to a Gentile might make Uncle Herman cool, but he was too big a man for such pettiness. Ties of family were strong; she was still Tina, Deborah's girl, and her sons were loved for themselves. Uncle Herman, she remembered, had always been wonderful with children.

When they reached the apartment, though, she saw that life had marched on here as it had in England. Aunt Mirah, kissing her, was white-haired, her fat fallen away, the great dark eyes dominating a thin little face. The hands which clasped her own were shaky, but they were warm and loving.

'A good girl she is, like her momma,' Mirah murmured. 'How I loved your momma; to her family a saint, no less.'

'We loved her,' Tina agreed rather diffidently.

'So young to die.' She shook herself, then brightened, turning to the boys, asking their names, telling them there were sugar biscuits, animal ones, in the kitchen for them. She would fetch the tin and then they could choose whether to eat a tiger, or a leopard, or a little pussycat.

'I'll have a elephant,' Desmond said craftily. 'Elephants are biggest,' and the children left the room eagerly in their great-aunt's wake.

'Tonight a party we have,' Herman told Tina. 'In this good apartment I have lived these six years, since Mrs Lubutz passed on. But Mrs Klein looks after me like I was a delicate plant! The best is not good enough, eh, Kleinie? And her cooking – ay-yi-yi how good! But soon, for yourself you will judge.'

His housekeeper, a plump, dark-haired woman with a considerable moustache, bridled and blushed and presently, the boys fed and popped into bed, Tina joined the family assembled in the dining room. She needed no introductions, save to Paul's wife.

'This is Rhoda,' Paul said. 'Rhoda, my cousin Tina.'

Tina held out her hand and smiled, but her heart gave a doubtful thump. She had expected someone beautiful, but different. Rhoda was tall, slim and dark with creamy skin and beautiful, shining dark hair. She wore a ruby velvet dress cut to show off her deep breasts and tiny waist, but though she smiled there was a hardness about her, a glitter rather than a sparkle, and there was more than a trace of spite in her voice when she spoke.

'So you're Paul's little cousin! You sure *are* little! Hello there, Tina!'

Her accent was pure New York, with no trace of the idiosyncrasies which characterised Tina's other relatives.

'It's nice to meet you,' Tina said conventionally, then turned, with relief, to Paul. 'Do you remember me, cousin? I remember you very well and you've not changed at all.'

Prematurely grey twenty years ago, when they had first met, he was grey still, his face as craggy as ever, his dark eyes as intense. But there was an air of watchfulness about him which she did not remember, as though he observed life more than he lived it. The Paul she remembered had lived every moment, and savoured every moment, too.

Conversation over the dinner table tended to be nostalgic, and after the meal the women withdrew to the drawing room while the men drank port. After a few moments, Rhoda approached Tina.

'The truth now, cousin! Do you see many changes?'

'Not really. Oh, heads are a little greyer and movements a little slower, but in other ways they've not altered. The uncles always boomed and laughed a lot; they still do.'

'And Paul?'

'Just the same. Truly.'

'Hmm. I'll let you into a secret. Did you know Paul had a breakdown just before he met me? It was a woman, of course. I thought it was you, which made me curious to meet you, but it couldn't have been; you were a child then.'

Mirah came over to them with a tray of coffee and Rhoda adroitly changed the subject.

Tina had one moment alone with Paul. He and his wife had left, but Paul came back for his gold cigarette case. He entered the drawing room to find Tina alone, tidying up after the guests.

'I must talk to you,' he said urgently, pocketing his case. 'When do you leave?'

'First thing tomorrow,' Tina said. 'My husband is meeting the train.'

'I see. Then I must ask you now. Tina, was your mother happy with Arthur once they got back to Norwich?'

Tina opened her mouth to tell the conventional lie, to say that her parents had been very happy, then stopped. The expression in those dark eyes! If ever a man had suffered, it was Paul.

'No. Never happy,' she said, her voice pitched so low that he barely caught the words. 'She didn't know a day's real happiness after America.'

He nodded, then held out his hand. 'It's been the same for me. Goodbye, little cousin, and good luck!' He turned and left the room and she heard him calling, 'Just coming, my dear.'

'Tina!'

'Oh, Ted!'

For long moments they clung, oblivious of the crowded sidewalk, curious onlookers, the pile of baggage still on the train. Then they broke apart, Tina's eyes starry with happiness, her lips bruised from his kiss.

'So long . . . you're so *brown* . . .I've . . . I've . . .'

There were too many words. She stammered, stuttered, then began to cry, tears running down her face and making tracks in the smuts, for they had been on the railroad for many hours.

'Don't cry, don't cry. You're here with me, you're safe . . .'

A voice broke in on their self-absorption; a plaintive, testy voice.

'Don't nobody know whose li'l boy dis is? What's youah name, son?'

'Oh, Edward, it's Desmond,' Tina cried, wrenching herself from his arms. 'Dessy? Dessy? Come over to Mummy at once!'

'He wants paddling,' Edward grumbled. He took the smaller boy by the hand and grinned down at him. 'Hi, Frankie? Do you remember Daddy?'

Frank, sucking his thumb, shook his head.

'No? Well, I suppose you wouldn't. Let's find Mummy, shall we?'

Tina, red in the face, her hair and clothing showing signs of the lengthy journey, was reclaiming Desmond from a black and goodnatured muleskinner who had picked the boy up and perched him on the driving seat behind his team. Desmond was resisting his mother's efforts to get him down with kicks and squeals.

'That's enough! When Mummy says do a thing, you jump to it, young man!'

Edward's strong, hard hands whisked Desmond from his perch, shook him, and deposited him on the ground once more. 'Now, let's make for the lodging house. Perhaps, once they get into bed, we'll be able to talk.'

He felt furious and disgruntled; he had dreamed of this reunion, planned it in every detail, and now it had turned into a school trip! He knew the boys must have grown, of course, but had still not reckoned with having to compete with them!

However, they were both very tired and Mrs Calder, the lodging house owner, promised to keep an ear out for them.

'Yo' git yo'selves a meal,' she advised kindly. 'Iffen they wake – *which* they won't, bein' wore out – Ah kin see to 'em.'

'She's a kindly soul,' Edward said, as, washed and changed, they set out down Pearl Street towards Tobe Hahn's Restaurant. 'I've been lodging with her for more than two years now and I know her better than most. Of course she's making money hand over fist, but why not?

She's not one to let a friend down.'

'Good. I shouldn't say it, I know, but it is such a *relief* not to have the boys tagging along, just for once.' Tina gave a little skip, and looked curiously about her. 'How dusty it is! And there are men everywhere! They seem very jolly!'

'Yes. They're heading for Deep Crocket, where . . . where the saloons and dancehalls are.'

'What were you going to say?' Tina asked suspiciously, as Edward held open the door of the restaurant for her. 'I don't think it was either saloons or dancehalls!'

'Nor it was. And you must be content to know that I nearly forgot my company. Let's have that corner table. We can talk better there.' They sat down, and Edward drew the menu towards him. 'Shall we both have the house speciality? It's whole chicken pot pie, and has to be tasted to be believed.'

After their meal they walked through the town, but Tina kept straying towards Deep Crockett, where every second building was a brothel and where whores, touting for business, were liable to accost anything in trousers and insult anything in skirts, so Edward took her out towards Spindletop, almost deserted at this time of evening.

'My store's good enough, but there's no living accommodation and with land the price it is I could no more afford to buy sufficient to build on than fly! But I've got an itch to own land again. So I've bought us a smallholding, a way from here, at a little place called Humble. They're drilling for oil there, and if they find it our place will be worth a small fortune. And I want to start a store there, because there's money in being the first.'

'A smallholding! Oh, Ted, that's a sort of farm, isn't it?'

She stopped, looked furtively round, flung herself into his arms and kissed his chin, then drew back, laughing.

'Ted, you're all bristly! Oh, a *farm*!'

'It's very small, Tina, I warn you. Not enough to make us a decent living unless I did something else.

'Can I keep chickens? And some pigs? Will we have carthorses, and a plough? Oh, how the boys will love it!'

He had his arms round her and he squeezed her to him.

How to explain that it would not be quite as glamorous as he could see she supposed? But his main thought, at the moment, was to get her back to bed. It had been three years and more since he had made love to her and he felt like any eager young groom on his wedding night except that, in his case, he knew that loving her was the most wonderful experience in the world.

He almost ran her back to Pearl Street and to their small bedroom with its coconut matting on the floor, its functional wash-stand and peeling board walls, its creaking, old-fashioned double bed.

She undressed quickly, sponged herself down whilst he stared, trying to see every inch of her, and then hopped into bed, rosily blushing.

'Tomorrow, we'll take the train to Houston and then hire a buggy and go to our place. We'll stay in Houston overnight, and come back here next day, just to make the final arrangements. I've put a fellow in charge of the store, for though I want to sell it wouldn't do to rush things.'

She murmured agreement, snuggled down beneath the sheet, her eyelids drooping with weariness.

At last, however, he climbed into bed and took her in his arms. He was trembling, content for a moment just to hold her, to smell the sweet, familiar perfume of her hair, to touch smooth skin, to feel the slim, strong little bones beneath the silk, wanting to enjoy his possession of her to the full.

He kissed along the side of her face and down her neck, then across her shoulder. He could hear her sleepily purring with satisfaction. How soft and sweet she was! How . . . Purring? He lifted his head and listened. She was fast asleep!

Ten days later they moved into the shack which Edward had euphemistically called the farmhouse on their smallholding. It was, Tina agreed, set in very lovely country, though she found the heat and, above all, the humidity called for the same type of leisurely movements as that of Galeport.

Edward, however, used to the climate, got on with his work at very much the same speed he had used in Beaumont, and within a month their shack, which stood on four short, thick piles, had running water, a small but adequate bathroom, and a bedroom for the boys, beside their own room.

Tina soon realised, though, that loneliness would have to be conquered. They were some way out of the small town of Humble, though that was rapidly growing larger with the promise of oil discoveries fairly soon.

While they waited for their home to be furnished, the Neylers had lived in the town, at the Thomas Payne Hotel, and had talked to the townsfolk. In the cooler weather (is there cooler weather, Tina had said incredulously) there was a school which the boys might attend. There were not many shops yet, though it was only a matter of time, everyone assured her. Already there was Rogers & Grossman's Dry Goods store and Sterling's Feed Store; it was a good beginning, though Tina thought wistfully that a grocery store would have been nice. As it was, Edward drove into Houston, caught the train for Beaumont, transacted his business there, and then returned to her with the pony cart brimming with necessities.

And then, when they had scarcely been in the house a week, Edward walked in and announced that he had hired a man and his wife to help them.

'Ribbons will help you with the housework and the vegetable plot, and Rube will see to the stock and plant out,' he said jubilantly. 'Just you mark my words, Tina, there'll be a gusher soon! I was at Spindletop long enough to know the signs!'

'Ribbons? No one's called Ribbons,' Tina protested incredulously. But she was wrong, and the Blackmans proved to be a hardworking negro couple who adored the boys; more, perhaps, because in ten years of marriage they had not had any children of their own.

The creek which ran through their yard was the delight of the boys' hearts, though Tina blessed it many times, for there would be a shriek, a resounding splash, and she would rush out and fish the unfortunate Frank out of the watery depths while he wailed 'I *di'n't* fall in! Dessy pussed me!'

Then there were the jungly woods, as Tina called them. Because of the humid, semi-tropical climate, the undergrowth was unusually rich and varied, and to be able to pick wild grapes and cherries, if one did not mind getting scratched and impeded by the lush creepers, was wonderful to a city-bred girl like Tina.

She knew better, however, than to wander too far from the house. Ribbons told her that there were cougars and wolves in the woods, and sometimes, if she woke in the night, she would hear bears, rustling around and grunting, or a wolf howling at the moon.

The boys had friends: two identical, chocolate coloured twins called Labby and Boss who came calling one day and stayed to show these small blond boys how to bait a crayfish trap. During the long, sunny day they played by the creek, and Tina got Ribbons to take them lemonade and a tray of cookies. She was glad to see that the twins seemed responsible lads, and since they must have been two years older than Desmond she left her youngsters quite happily to play with the twins. Nor was her confidence misplaced. The twins might be – and were – naughty and mischievous, but they were proud of their small friends and took every care of them, even when leading them into naughtiness which the younger boys might never have thought of, left to their own devices.

And then, the first gusher came.

The very day the news broke, Tina told Edward she was pregnant, and a strange letter came from New Zealand.

It was, though neither of them knew it, the end of their peaceful country life.

'I'm going to get the rest of the stuff transferred to Moonshine Hill just as fast as I can move it,' Edward declared. They were having breakfast and he was shovelling eggs and grits into his mouth as fast as he could. The little boys, with bowls of bread and milk, watched his plate enviously. Tina, nibbling dry toast, repressed a shudder.

'What stuff?' she enquired, to take her mind off the mess on her husband's plate. 'I thought you were still building the store in Moonshine.'

Edward looked slightly guilty. 'Well, so I am. But I knew the break would come when they first struck oil, so I've been bringing stuff in from all over for a while.'

'Where's it been stored?'

I've got a lot in Rigsby's big barn, and some in our hayloft.'

'Ted! Not *food*? What about rats?'

'No, it's all right; I couldn't expect food to keep, could I? Well, there's tinned stuff, of course, and dried stuff, but . . .'

'You should have told me. And before you rush off, what about that letter from Dunedin?'

Edward reached for the bread, doubled a slice over, and took a huge bite. 'Darling, we talked that over yesterday. This Sue is obviously nearly illiterate. She says Mark's run away and left their son in her charge, but what about Wen? I think it's a confidence trick – to get us to send money to her. But I told you I'd write to father and find out what's going on. As you say, it's odd that we've not heard from him since we've been here.'

He swallowed the rest of his bread, gulped his coffee and stood up, patting her shoulder. 'Got to go now,' he said rather thickly. 'Will you be all right, you expectant mother, you? Ribbons will take care of you! I may not be home tonight, but I'll be back by tomorrow evening, I promise.'

'Yes, I'll be fine. Take care of yourself.'

She jumped up, hugging and kissing him, reminding herself, as she always did when he went away, that he was the most precious thing in her life and never again must she let misunderstanding grow between them, as it almost had in Liverpool.

But the New Zealand letter continued to worry her, and in the end she got it out, re-read it, and then wrote to Karl herself. To make sure the letter went she told Ribbons she was driving into town and got Rube to harness the pony to the neat little dog-cart she used for short journeys.

It was a fine, crisp day, chilly but nevertheless pleasant, one of the really nice days in their short winter, and she drove at a spanking pace along the quiet road. She reached the schoolhouse and dropped the boys off, since school was in session, then continued on to the Bender Commissary, where the post office was located. Commissaries were still a novelty to her, and watching the men buy their goods with tokens instead of cash was intriguing, like a game. But she was quite acute enough to realise that it was good business for the mill-owners to open these shops and to allow their employees to trade only with tokens. That way prices could fluctuate according to supply and demand, making it difficult for the lumber workers, in a good week, to drink themselves silly on Commissary whisky.

She posted her letter, then decided to call on her friend Sal de Valdos, who worked in the hotel. Sal was a beauty, with rich auburn hair, a creamy skin, and a magnificent, if voluptuous, figure. She greeted Tina warmly and called her round the counter, since she was on duty that morning behind the reception desk.

'Come on, honey,' she urged, giving her deep, delightful chuckle, 'tell liddle ole Sal your news!'

Tina sank into the chair which Sal dragged forward with one lazy foot, and remarked, 'You might just as well set up as a public news service, Sal! How on earth did you know?'

'In this here burgh? Tina, honey, everyone knows everything! 'Cep' you, you Britisher! 'Sides, you went to see doc, and anyone can see you're in good health.'

'I see. I might have saved myself the journey. Do you know when my baby's due, or can I tell you *some* news?'

Sal's slanting green eyes dwelt thoughtfully on Tina's waistline.

'January now. Let me see. Should I say July?'

'Well, not bad. End of June, anyway. I say, Sal, I would like that coffee! And did you know that Jenny Branch, that pale coloured girl who works for the Edells . . .'

The two heads were close; the coffee came, and the special coconut biscuits which Tina loved, and the gossip session was in full swing.

*

It had been sheer bad luck that Mark missed Edward in Beaumont; with nothing but a vague memory of sending letters to a post office, he had repaired there first, only to be told that incoming mail was usually picked up by anyone with time to spare to 'do mailman', or that those expecting letters would go through the incoming post themselves.

Baulked, Mark decided that the only thing to do would be to plug away at the stores on Spindletop until he found Edward's. Or someone who had been friendly with Edward. And in the fullness of time he would undoubtedly have discovered the store and his brother, had he not heard of the discovery of oil in Humble, and the winter gusher.

Some sixth sense woke in him at the mention of the place. He had looked round Beaumont, asked everyone he could, and no one knew where Edward was, though several were sure they had seen a yellow-haired Englishman around.

So Mark took the railroad train to Humble, got down in Main Street, and walked straight into the Thomas Payne Hotel. Coming in from the sunny, chilly day it was dark in the foyer and he had to stand still for a moment to accustom his eyes to the gloom. Then he saw, behind the reception desk, two very pretty young women. They were talking together in hushed yet excited tones, and he guessed (wrongly as it happened) that they were discussing Moonshine Hill and the difference the gusher would make to their lives.

He walked forward, then cleared his throat, his eyes on the darker girl. She was so pretty! A small, heart-shaped face, skin like milk, and a mischievous, kissable mouth!

She glanced up at him and he had just time to see that her eyes were dark blue and that, when she smiled, dimples sprang into being, when the terrible thing happened.

Her face seemed to quiver and dissolve, and then it was not the happy face of an unknown young woman, but the face of his dead wife.

It was the first time it had happened since he left New Zealand and the unexpectedness, the sheer horror of it, rooted him to the spot for a moment. He swayed, put his hand up to his head, made an ugly, choking noise in his throat, and then turned and fled, his one thought to get away before the dead eyes opened and the dead mouth trembled into agonised life.

He had meant to visit Moonshine Hill, but he was in no state for anything of that nature. He found a hotel – not the Thomas Payne – and went and drank beer until he could scarcely walk. Then he staggered to the railroad depot and bought a ticket back to Beaumont.

That very evening, he found Edward's store by the simple expedient of walking into it, going to the counter, and asking the skinny black man in charge whether he knew Edward Neyler.

'Sho' do, sah,' the man replied cheerfully. Mark's heart leapt joyfully.

'Can I speak to him?'

Sorrowfully, the black head shook from side to side, and the man hitched at the apron drooping around his inadequate hips.

'No, sah, sorry sah. Mr Neyler he done gone home. Sole do sto'e an' gone home.'

The disappointment was overwhelming. Mark plunged blindly out of the place, his mind full of pain, and made his way back to his lodging house. He was absolutely certain in his own mind that he had only just missed his brother, and now he had gone home, to England. For a moment, wild thoughts of killing himself, putting an end to his miserable existence, chased themselves through Mark's head. Then he gritted his teeth and pulled himself together. What did it matter, when all was said and done? He could follow Edward back to England. He had plenty of time, if nothing else.

He was in his room, and he crossed to the wash-stand and produced a bottle of whisky from its hiding place behind the fly-spotted mirror. He would have to get work for a while to earn enough money to buy his passage, but it would be good to work for a change. He had not brought a lot of money with him, because it had seemed wrong to take money when he was leaving Su and Toddy and the others in the lurch. But there would be plenty in the bank for them, plenty . . . His thoughts stopped short. Plenty indeed, but how were they to get it? He realised with remorse and guilt that they could not get at the money, might even have trouble in running the farm without his signature to allow them to draw on his account.

For the first time, he thought of Johnny, not as a nuisance without Wen, but as Wen's dearly beloved son, and his own. He loved Johnny! How Wen would ache if she knew her son had been abandoned, perhaps even to starve, by her husband!

Then, with immense relief, he remembered his father. Of course, Karl would take care of them until he could get home or send them money. Karl had adored Wen, worshipped his little grandson.

Comforted, he continued with his plans to travel to England.

23

The new baby was a girl, and they called her, after some argument, Stella Anne. She was a pretty, fair-haired creature and Edward adored her, dandling her on his knee, talking to her, singing to her, behaving like the infatuated father he was.

And as Stella grew, so did Moonshine Hill. It grew larger and nearer to their smallholding, and one night Rube disturbed a man stealing hens from the coop. He shouted, Edward came running, and the man pulled a knife before disappearing into the woods.

Next day, Edward came home with a handgun for Tina.

'But I don't know how to use it,' Tina said anxiously. 'It frightens me more than the chicken thief did!'

'Then you'll learn,' Edward said. He set up a pile of tins in the yard and made his wife fire at the tins until not only could she hit them with every bullet, but she could pull the trigger without closing her eyes or screaming.

'I don't say you'd rival Jesse James,' Edward admitted, rumpling his wife's curls. 'But you'd scare hell out of an intruder and that's what matters.'

'If I could pull the trigger at flesh and blood,' Tina rejoined. 'And I don't think I could!'

'You could. You must keep it under your pillow at night and in your skirt-band during the day. Do you understand?'

'I suppose so,' Tina said. But it soon became as clear to her as it was to Edward that things were changing. A huge tent-city had sprung up around the hill, and there were dozens of shops and saloons and brothels, and some of the boomers were dangerous men when drunk or penniless.

'It wouldn't be true to say that life is cheap,' Edward told her. 'But folk die every day on the hill. They are gassed, or burned to death, or get caught up in the machinery . . . well, that's what you might call the accidental death roll. But there are others. They fight to the death over a woman, or when they're drunk, they quarrel and pull guns. Little Grinning Jackass fell in the mud when he was liquored-up and couldn't get up again. He drowned in the stuff. So you see, if a woman says "no" when they want her to say "yes" . . .'

He left the sentence unfinished, but Tina knew what he meant. And kept her gun handy.

Despite the dangers, however, she began to work in the store as soon as Stella was weaned. She felt safe enough, with Ribbons beside her, and whatever casual help Edward had been able to bribe away from the actual drilling. And, of course, there was Daddy Zeke. For a tiny wage and a bunk set up in the store room at the back Daddy Zeke stayed with them day and night, and was the greatest comfort to them all.

'I'm a hunderd, but still quick on ma pins,' he would boast, and though Tina privately thought him no more than eighty he was both spry and trustworthy, and could be relied on to nip out for help if customers got difficult. Zeke had once been a slave, working on a nearby cotton plantation, and he told the Neylers many a hair-raising, and probably apocryphal, story of the days of plantation slavery. He was good with his hands, helping Edward to make shelves and drawers for the stock in the early days and, once they were established, whittling tops and hoops and small toys for the Neyler children.

Edward's worries over Mark and his father had been answered in part by a solicitor's letter in reply to the one he had written to Karl. It was quite a simple, brief communication, merely stating that after the loss of his wife, Mr Mark Neyler had left the country and Mr Karl Neyler had suffered a severe heart attack, death being almost instantaneous.

Terribly upset and worried, Edward wrote again, at much greater length, asking for details of the tragedy and begging to be told what had happened to his nephew, John Neyler.

The solicitor's reply was reassuring. He explained that a cousin of Wendy Neyler's, Sue Young, had been living in the house at the time and helping Mrs Neyler with her work and her child. She had taken over the running of the house and was looking after Johnny and would continue to do so until Mr Mark Neyler returned, as the solicitor was sure he would. In the meantime, since a letter had arrived from Mr Mark Neyler giving Miss Sue Young a power of attorney to draw sums of money from the farm's profits, he hoped that this would seem satisfactory to Mr Edward, who, he understood, was still a part owner in the Neyler property. He went on to explain, however, that Mr Karl Neyler had left his Waihola farm to Edward, on condition that Edward gave his half share in the Peninsula farm to Mark's son, Johnny.

Edward wrote back by return, assuring the solicitor that this would be perfectly in order, asking that a reliable farm manager might be put in charge of the Waihola property, and that all profits accruing from the property might be handed over to young John Neyler's guardians for him, until such time as Mark either returned to the Peninsula farm or got in touch with himself.

'I'm certain that if he left New Zealand, it would be to find me,' he said definitely. 'The trouble is, we were moving around so much at that time. I wonder if he'll go to England? Look, Tina, do drop Charlotte a line and tell her to point the poor fellow in the right direction if he turns up in Liverpool. Better still, you exchange letters with Billy Snelling, don't you? Well, ask him to do the same. The Spanner's Row address was the last one Mark had for us, I suppose.'

Once these letters had been despatched, Edward relaxed. He felt he had done his utmost for Mark and now must look to his own life. He was sure too, strangely enough, that Mark was reasonably content, wherever he was, and that one day he would be reunited with his brother. In the meantime, he had a business to build up, a wife – pregnant once more – to take care of, and two sons to tear his hair over.

For the Neyler boys must be quite the naughtiest children ever to live in Humble! Their exploits, especially when in the company of the Hessler twins, were rapidly becoming legendary.

There had been the affair of the fire in the Humble underground tanks, for instance. It had raged for days, while a pall of darkness hung over the neighbourhood and a fine film of oil covered everything so that the smell and taste of the stuff was everywhere, proving, if anyone needed proof, how easily such a fire might spread and devour everything flammable for miles.

And who rode on the cowcatcher of the first train to go through that mighty conflagration? Dessy and Boss, equipped with an old Kodak camera with which to take photographs which would make their fortunes. The other two boys would have gone as well, if there had been room.

Who released the foul-tempered cross-bred bull terrier

kept by the porter of the Tullos Hotel? It had killed a visitor's cream coloured pug dog and stolen a pile of T-bone steaks before the boys had bribed it home again with liquorice sticks, for which, most fortunately, it had developed a great liking. That had been Frank's fault; he thought the dog needed more exercise than the porter gave it. Edward, grimly paying for the steaks and promising to tan the hides of the guilty, found himself remembering the exercise the dog had attained whilst being chased by every muleskinner on the Hill, and could scarcely forbear to grin.

Then Dessy and Frank had driven a mule team without asking anyone's permission, and had narrowly escaped death when the mules had overturned their load – and their amateur drivers – in a fast-running bayou. Only prompt action on the part of Boner Harris, the muleskinner who owned the team, saved them. Though, as he proceeded to fish them out and paddle their backsides with a hand hard as a plank, they did not wait to thank him.

There had been other incidents, all of a similar nature, including an attempt to dig an underground tunnel for themselves which would end in a large cave where they might lead private and interesting lives with the twins their only visitors. It was first begun in the rainy season when they could not go far, and commonsense decreed that the work should be started beneath the house, in the shelter of the stacks, a place where they spent most of their time during the rains.

It was scarcely their fault, as both boys pointed out later, that the tunnel, passing beneath one of the stacks which held up the house, should not have been quite as deep as they would have wished. Consequently, after a particularly heavy fall of rain, the family was sitting at supper one night when, very slowly and with great dignity, the house appeared to collapse under them. Edward, rushing outside to see what had happened, was at a loss at first to understand why the house should be leaning sideways, with one of the stacks hidden beneath the mud and the corner of the dwelling, once four feet in the air, now firmly resting on the ground.

He had still been wildly conjecturing when Tina's head appeared in the open kitchen window.

'Dessy and Frank have gone,' she remarked mildly. 'It's jam doughnuts and cream for pudding, but they've disappeared.'

He knew at once then that they were in some way responsible, and presently Rube appeared and suggested that the tunnel he had seen them digging might be responsible.

'I know it's not entirely their fault,' he said later to Tina. 'I know they've got inventive minds, and a talent for engineering, and a dozen other things. But I really think they ought to go to boarding school. Your Uncle Paul keeps offering to put them up in New York, and see that they're well. Wouldn't it be for the best?'

At the very thought of the boys leaving for New York, Tina felt a lightening of the burden their naughtiness laid upon her. But she was firm in her resolve to keep Dessy and Frank with her, and with their younger sister and the baby soon to be born.

'It's bad enough being carted around by your parents without being sent away from them,' she told her husband. 'I can remember how I hated being moved from place to place when I was small. The least I can do for my own children is give them some sense of permanence by always being with them.'

In both their hearts they knew their time in Humble would soon be over. The oil boom was settling down, the pipelines marched steadily to the coast, tent-city was a thing of the past. There was still a good living to be made from the store, but Edward longed to get into the building and construction business once more and realised there would be little chance for him in Humble, where builders were established and thriving.

Another reason for remaining was Edward's ever-present feeling that Mark might suddenly appear in Humble, searching for him. But gradually, as time passed and no Mark came, this feeling began to die. Mark would find him wherever he was; he knew that in his heart.

Then a letter came from Arthur. The Timber Hill Building & Construction Company was for sale, since old Marius Tremblatt was dead and his son had no interest in the business. It had been a thriving business, but had fallen into the doldrums lately, Arthur wrote. It was going at a give-away price; was his son-in-law interested?

Edward hesitated – and then Rick Platter came into their lives. He was buying property around Humble, hoping to find oil away from the hill itself, and he offered them a small fortune (not so small, either, said Tina) for their store and the smallholding.

Now there was no choice. They remained in Humble long enough for Tina to give birth to her fourth child, a boy as dark as the others were fair whom they called David, and then they headed for England, and Norwich.

Mark sat at breakfast in the kitchen of the Pinner house on Calder Avenue, Beaumont. Outside the room he could hear Hannah singing as she carried down Miss Stacy's morning tray. He cut himself a wedge of Hannah's home-baked bread and spread it liberally with butter. He was working with a construction gang and working hard, for the new rich of Spindletop spared no expense to provide themselves with beautiful houses.

The sun came slanting down through the branches of a pear-tree which grew just outside the window. It was in blossom, beautiful as a bride, and he felt his eyes dazzle with tears at the brilliance of it even as he felt his spirit swoop down from its normal, cheerful, sunny morning height to the depths of a black depression.

It happened like this from time to time, and he dreaded it, calling it 'the missing' in his mind, never knowing when it was going to strike, how long it would last, how deeply it would affect him. Days would come and go in hard work and peace, sunny days, steaming hot days, rainy days; and then, out of a clear sky, the hunger for her would come. It was as sharp as a knife and as persistent as toothache, a pain so cruel that it blotted out all other feelings. Women meant nothing to him, nor heat, nor cold. The only thing that dulled the hunger was work, and when it was bad he worked like a man possessed, until his back shrieked for rest and his muscles cracked with the strain. But at least he could ignore the pain of knowing that he lived in a world which no longer contained Wen, that their love had been snapped like a too-tight thread so that Wen, who had been a part of him, had been torn from his living, suffering flesh and that the pain of that tearing still crippled him, body and soul.

Hannah's voice saying anxiously 'Mr Mark, sah?' brought him back to the sunny kitchen. She was an ancient black woman, wrinkled as a walnut, but her eyes were calm and content, her voice young and fresh because she was happy.

'Yes, Hannah?'

'Yo' am sufferin' agin, hey? Jus' yo' git off ter work, but don't forgit you'm tekkin' Miz Stacy to de opery tonight, Mr Mark.'

He got stiffly to his feet, trying to banish the blackness which robbed the day of its sunshine. 'As if I'd forget, Hannah! What are they singing tonight?'

Hannah was packing his lunch-box with rapid but careful movements. 'It's an Eye-talyan comp'ny, Miz Stacy says, singin' a noo opery. Ma'am Buttahfly, I t'ink.'

'Mm hmm.' He had never heard of it, but however he might feel he would not let his landlady down. Miss Eustacia Pinner had been so good to him. He had been in miserable lodgings in a dreadful house in Deep Crockett and had fallen ill with influenza aggravated by too little to eat and too much to drink. He had been staggering along the road, dreading the return to Mrs Donnell's sour-smelling house, when he had collapsed in the Pinner driveway. Hannah, returning from a shopping trip, had almost fallen over his inanimate form. She had fetched the hired man and the two of them had carried Mark into the kitchen, meaning to call the sherriff, Ras Landry, and ask him to remove the drunk.

But Miss Stacy, veteran of the childish ailments of a score of nephews and nieces, diagnosed a high temperature and infection of some kind and had him tucked up in the spare room with the doctor calling before Hannah had recovered her breath. Despite the frequently voiced doubts of her faithful retainer, the doctor, and half her acquaintance, Miss Stacy had remained firm in her resolve. She had no intention of allowing a sick young man to be removed to a house like the Donnells', where he would undoubtedly die in a few hours from the smell alone.

A thin, chilly-eyed spinster in her mid-fifties, she had seen something she liked in Mark, and as he gradually recovered they became good friends. When he announced that he was well enough to work once more, she tartly recommended him to remain in her spare room as a lodger. 'At least you'll eat well and lie clean at nights,' she said grimly.

So he had remained, saving his money, reading his way voraciously through every book Miss Stacy recommended, talking, arguing, making her take a good hard look at the new Beaumont and Spindletop, instead of remaining in the old colonial house where she had been born, criticising everything new and then condemning it out of hand.

Now he took the filled lunch-box from Hannah and said: 'I'd best leave now. But I'll be back in plenty of time to smarten up for this entertainment. Shall I book us dinner somewhere special?'

Hannah sniffed. 'Dere's nowhere special in dis town! Sides, Miz Stacy tole me to buy lobsters.'

'Oh, that's different! I wouldn't miss your lobsters for anything, Hannah. We'll come back when the opera finishes, then. I'll order a cab.'

'Yo' will not! Rufus bin tole off to fetch yo' in de carriage.'

Mark, at the back door, said over his shoulder: 'You don't let me do much, do you? I suppose it was in order for me to buy the tickets?'

Sarcasm, however, was wasted on Hannah. 'Bless yo', Mr Mark, 'course, when yo' knew well Miz Stacy wanted to go an' hear de singin'. You-all 'joy yo'selves.'

The day's work over, Mark, in all the glory of his only

dark suit, handed Miss Stacy out of the carriage outside the Kyle Opera House. Miss Stacy looked fine, he thought, in an imposing gown of coffee-coloured silk, with creamy lace and a lace-trimmed parasol.

Conscious of his debt of gratitude to this remarkable woman, he had booked the best seats in the house, and handed her into her red-plush armchair as if she were royalty. He sat down beside her, produced the large box of candies he had purchased from Fullerton's, and handed her the story of the opera, since it was to be sung in Italian.

He looked around at the audience, amused and a little touched at the grandeur. Old Peg-leg Fryer was here, decked out in tails of all things, with his daughter Sukie – a flighty piece if ever he saw one – on his arm in a purple dress which was cut low enough to show her navel if one was close by.

He glanced cursorily at the story, gathering that it concerned a beautiful Japanese girl called Butterfly and her American lover, Pinkerton, who first married her and then deserted her. He settled comfortably into his seat and took the chocolate which Miss Stacy was offering, then prepared himself to be impressed and touched by Puccini's music, and perhaps a little bored by Italian dialogue and a conventional opera story.

Instead, from the first moment that the curtain rose, he could not take his eyes from the stage. It was as though his own story was being re-enacted before his eyes, with Wen as Madam Butterfly and Pinkerton as himself. Oh, the story was different, he knew that, but some underlying sentiment, that of indescribable loss and unbearable sadness, was his own. When the interval came he moved from his place with the utmost reluctance, scarcely able to tolerate the friendly people who stopped to chat to Miss Stacy, feeling that even a moment spent outside the auditorium was time wasted. The girl who played Butterfly was so like Wen! The same heart-shaped face, the smooth, ivory skin, the long, liquid black eyes!

When, in the last act, Butterfly's world falls apart with her discovery that Pinkerton never considered his marriage to her legal or binding, and that his only reason for re-visiting her home is to adopt their son, her pain was his. He knew what the outcome must be, saw her fall on her father's sword, heard the last agonised chords of that beautiful music rend him before the curtain fell for the last time. Then he left the theatre in a daze, three-quarters of him still watching the girl on the stage, hearing her lament for lost love in his ears mirroring his own crying loss.

He settled himself into the dark carriage beside Miss Stacy and then a terrible thing happened. He began to cry for Madam Butterfly as he had never cried for Wen. Or was he crying for Wen? He did not know, he only knew that difficult, racking sobs were forced from him, seeming to tear his heart from his body, so that Miss Stacy put her arms round him as if he were one of her little nephews and rocked him, and told him, 'Have your cry out, Mark. It's time you did.'

It was a long journey home. He found out afterwards that Rufus had driven round and round the town until his sobs abated, and then he had returned to the Pinner house.

When they climbed out of the carriage at last, he had some control over himself and had schooled his features into normality. Hannah led them straight into the dining room and left them facing a table on which there was a tureen of hot chicken soup, fresh crusty rolls wrapped in napkins, the pink and white succulence of two large lobsters, a salad, and potatoes baked in their jackets oozing sour cream and chives. On the sideboard was a strawberry shortcake with whipped cream, and simmering on the spirit-stove a great jug of black coffee.

'Hannah has prepared everything so that she could go off to bed knowing we could manage for ourselves,' Miss Stacy said, sitting down and unfolding her napkin. 'I knew, as soon as I saw which opera was being performed, that we might need time to talk.'

'But . . . but how did . . . you kn-kn-know? I mean, I never . . . s-s-said . . .' Mark stammered.

'You said quite a lot while you were ill,' Miss Stacy answered crisply. She began to spoon out the soup, then gestured to him to start. 'And since, too. Nightmares tell stories, and many a time I've come into your room and woken you with some cock-and-bull story of hearing noises, so that you could come out of a nightmare. There was a girl, too; she came from Deep Crockett after you'd . . . ah . . . visited her there. She'd been very upset by something you'd said in your sleep, my dear boy. Those girls from Deep Crockett aren't easily moved.'

'Miss Stacy, you make me ashamed! It's . . . when I'm . . .'

'I know, Mark. You go to Deep Crockett when you're drunk. And apparently, you only talk when you're drunk or delirious. Since I could make you neither, I thought of the opera. Deep emotion can sometimes go to the head just like alcohol. Because I wanted you to talk, Mark. You've told me nothing, do you realise that? You've never said you were a married man with a child, nor that you had a father living, nor that you dearly love your brother. You said you were looking for a brother, but even then, you would volunteer no information. You never said if he was married or single, older or younger than yourself. It isn't good for anyone to keep everything that matters locked away so deep that his conscious mind never acknowledges them. I know that from my own experience. So I decided that perhaps Madam Butterfly would break down your defences and give me a chance to help you.'

'You . . . you knew Wen was . . . was Chinese, then? And that she's . . . dead?'

'I did. And now I want to know what happened, my dear boy. For your own good, not for the satisfying of my curiosity; though, being a woman, I am curious. I want to help you!'

'Do I need help? I thought I was putting it all behind me, building a new life for myself.'

Miss Stacy snorted. 'Huh! Building up a new nightmare, pushing yourself to the brink of madness with your reticence. Is that your idea of a new life? And what about your farm, your dependants? What about Wen's little boy?'

To think about Johnny hurt him so much that he had to take a deep breath and hold it until the gas lamps lighting the room began to waver and tilt. Then he released the breath in a long sigh. 'All right. I'll tell you everything.'

He talked that night as he had never talked to anybody, ever. He talked until the stars began to fade and a greeny line on the horizon heralded another dawn. He kept nothing back, not the guilt he felt because he would not listen to Wen's voice when she tried to communicate with him, nor the feeling he had that Johnny would be better off with Su than with himself.

'You wouldn't listen to Wen because you knew what she was trying to tell you,' Miss Stacy said at length. Her tone was not accusatory, merely factual.

'Yes. I think she wants to tell me that Su's the next best thing to her. Wen wants me to face up to Dunedin, and Johnny, and life. She wants me to marry Su and go on from where we left off. I can't do it.'

'Why not, Mark? Mistaken loyalty? Death cancels that, dear boy.'

Mark flinched, but answered her steadily: 'No. It's just that she looks a bit like Wen, but she's totally different. I couldn't marry her. It wouldn't be fair.'

'Does she love you?'

Mark felt his face grow hot. But this was the truth at last. He had lied to himself down the years until he scarcely knew how to face the Mark he had become.

'I believe she does. It frightens me more than anything, that. She loved me even when my wife lived, but we thought she'd grow out of it, meet someone her own age. And now I'm not even Wen's Mark, I'm just . . . Wen's leavings. Just half a man.'

'Would she mind? Wouldn't she rather have you as you are than nothing?'

'I don't know.' Mark frowned down at his plate. 'I've treated her so badly! Oh, I sent a letter to our solicitor telling him that she was to draw money to run the farm, pay her salary and so on. But . . . but . . . '

'There's something else, isn't there? Another reason

why you won't go back?'

'Yes. When I was with her after Wen's death, her face . . . sort of changes. It turns into . . . into . . . '

'Go on, say it. Then it won't ever seem so bad again.'

'It changes . . .. Miss Stacy, I *can't*!'

'It changes into the face of your drowned wife, doesn't it, Mark?'

He stared at her, mouth dropped open.

'Sweet Jesus! How in God's name did you know?'

'Because it kept happening while you were delirious. One moment you seemed rational, asking for a drink, something to cool you down. The next, I'd bend over the bed and you'd try to push me away, babbling about hair waving in the water, sand clogging my eyes, my mouth. I tell you, Mark, it was so frightening that I had to send Hannah out of the room as soon as you started. She's a good soul, but she has deep-rooted superstitions which would have made her uneasy in your company.'

'Then you do understand, Miss Stacy, why I can't go back.'

'My dear boy, I understand why you *must* go back! You loved Wen more than you love yourself, and that's a rare thing. Do you think she'll always come to you as a corpse, when you face up to your life again? Of course not. It's your own guilty conscience which makes you see such terrible things, not your good little wife! You've neglected her child, the person she loves most in the world next to yourself. It is *you*, reproaching yourself, that horrible experience. When you face up to your responsibilities and go back you'll see her as she really was. Beautiful, smiling, full of life and love.'

'Really? Do you really think so?'

'I really do, Mark. I think the time has come for you to go back to Dunedin. You've saved money here, and Johnny must be five or six. He needs you, and Su needs you as well.

'But what about Edward? I was saving the money to go to my brother.'

'You may need your brother, but he doesn't need you. You've got responsibilities to Wen's son, Mark.'

They had been sitting at the table, the food ignored on their plates. Now Miss Stacy pointed to the cold jacket potatoes, the congealed butter, the uneaten lobsters.

'And by the same token, young man, we'd best eat this meal up or Hannah's feelings will be lacerated! She planned this dinner for a special treat, and her pleasure will be spoiled if we don't eat every scrap. Come on, start eating!'

Mark laughed and dug his fork into the lobster. Suddenly, he was ravenously hungry and could scarcely wait to swallow one mouthful before tackling the next.

'Should I start tomorrow? I know you're right, you see.'

A spasm, quickly suppressed, crossed the thin, humorous face in front of him.

'I think you had better write fully to Su, and your father, and your lawyer tomorrow. The following day will be quite time enough to leave Beaumont.'

He nodded, eager to begin once the decision was made. 'All right, Miss Stacy, I'll do as you say. You're a brick, do you know it?'

She smiled primly at him, then began to eat. He would never know what it had cost her to drive him away, nor the dullness he would leave behind. He had been like a son to her; no, more like a beloved younger brother, and she would miss him sorely.

'Shortcake, Mark?'

She cut a helping, then spooned cream over it, telling herself firmly that her comfort would be the knowledge that she had done the right thing. It would be, she knew, her only comfort.

24

'Poppa, oh, Poppa!'

Tina flung herself out of the train and into Arthur's arms, tears running down her face. Clutching him convulsively, she said, her voice breaking: 'It's been so long, Poppa! More than five years! You've never even *seen* Stella, or baby David!'

Arthur, weeping copiously, the tears streaming down and disappearing into his abundant grey moustache, patted her shoulder and reached for Edward's hand.

'My best, Tina mine! So you've brought her back to me at last, Ted, and grandchildren, too. Boys so fine and big, and a girl so pretty! The baby, even, is handsome! Dessy, Dessy, come and kiss your old grandpoppa before he's drowned in your momma's tears!'

The platform seemed to be full of Mummy's relatives, Desmond thought dispassionately, as he was enveloped, first in Grandpapa's whiskery embrace, then by little, plump Aunt Cecy, then others to whom he could not put a name. But all were moist-eyed, all smiling, obviously delighted to see the Neyler family back in Norwich once more.

But I am not glad to be back, Desmond thought rebelliously. I am an American, and so is Frank. They cannot turn us into English children just because they bring us back to this cold place, away from our wonderful farm in Humble, away from Moonshine Hill and the glamour and excitement of the oil rigs.

'How old are you, Dessy? Nine? Ten?'

That was a girl-aunt – would it be Rachel, Mummy's

youngest sister? Her obvious admiration warmed Desmond a little.

'I'm eight, Auntie. Frank's seven.'

She smiled sweetly at him, her dark eyes warm and understanding. 'So young! You are much bigger than our eight-year-olds, Dessy. I expect you think England is very cold and strange, but you'll soon learn to love it, I'm sure. We've had a bad winter, you see, and spring's rather later than usual; but it will come.'

She turned to where Stella stood, thumb in mouth, solemnly regarding the milling adults. 'Hello, you pretty thing, I'm your Auntie Ray! If I bend down you could climb on to my back and I'd be your horsie and take you to the motor cars.'

A little bell of recollection rang in Desmond's head. 'I'll be your horsie'? Who had said that? It had a bitter-sweet ring, as of some much loved time, now past. Then the word 'motor' registered.

'Has Grandpapa got a motor? We've seen them, of course, we rode in one in New York.'

'No, Grandpapa doesn't own a motor, he thinks . . . well, anyway, he hired one from Mr Wigg to take the family home. And your Uncle Abe has brought his motor too.' She caught his hand. 'Those who reach the roadway last will have to ride in a hansom; will you run with me?'

A little of the pleasure which had been wiped away by the unabashed sentimentality on Thorpe Station began to creep back into the day. He and Rachel, with Stella bobbing in her arms, ran across the foyer and out into the cold spring air.

Frank watched them, feeling betrayed. He said defiantly: 'It will be an English motor, I suppose. They're no dam' good! American motors are the best. I wish I was in America right now!'

To his chagrin, no one took the slightest notice. On all sides aunts, uncles and cousins were watching Grandpapa, who was telling what appeared to be a funny story, waving his arms around, talking in his odd, cracked English, the tears still wet on his cheeks though his grin stretched from ear to ear. Frank was embarrassed and repulsed by his grandfather. Horrible old man, crying like a baby in front of all these people. He should know better at his age – he had to be a hundred at least!

He took Desmond's desertion philosophically. It was always thus; Desmond was easily swayed. But he would harbour his hate, he would not let them make him English! It was cold and he was wearing his best overcoat which had lovely grey and black diamonds all over it and a high black fur collar. Desmond wore an identical one, and looking round him he realised that no one else was wearing anything nearly as smart as his coat. Nor as bright. It was a good thing he knew that he and Dessy were well-dressed, or he might think these miserable little country cousins were laughing at him. They certainly had smirks on their faces. He guessed they must be Aunt Cecy's boys; Bertram was the elder at six; the other, small and dark as a monkey, was called Conrad. Frank grinned scornfully to himself.

By now they had reached the motor cars and he saw that Desmond was saving him a place beside the uniformed chauffeur. He wavered. It would be better, perhaps, to announce that he preferred a hansom, but . . . but . . . Well, they were rather good motors. The one with the chauffeur was a beautiful dark blue colour with a silvery lady-statue on the long bonnet. The other car, with Uncle Abe climbing behind the wheel, was also glorious. A dark and throbbing red, with a silver line painted round it.

Mentally shrugging, he climbed up beside Desmond and even smiled at his grandfather when Arthur heaved himself into the seat beside him and leaned over to take baby David from Tina, then grabbed the small Conrad so that he seemed to be drowned in a sea of grandchildren.

'By Jove, Ted,' Grandpapa called over his shoulder, 'you grow boys big in Texas! This pair are twice the size of my Cecy's lads.'

'We grow everything big in Texas,' Frank muttered. Conrad turned on his grandfather's knee and looked seriously at his cousin. Then, suddenly, the little monkey face broke into a broad and toothy grin.

'Yes, but we're very tiny for our ages, Bertie and I. Your sister's big as well, isn't she?'

His clear, precise little voice sounded funny to Frank and he found himself grinning back, quite without meaning to do so.

On Grandpapa's other knee, Stella's small voice piped up.

'Gonna git me a sody-pop when we're home, ma granpappy says.'

'I say, she speaks with a Yankee accent,' Bertram remarked in a superior voice. 'Odd to hear a young kid talk like that.'

Frank began to bristle, but his father's hand fell, light but warning, on his shoulder.

'I guess we all sound a bit odd to you, Bertram, but the children will soon lose their accents.'

'Lose them? I don't want to sound cissy, like . . .'

'That's enough, Frank. Soon be at Bishopsgate. See the Cathedral, children?'

Tina, sitting squashed between Ted and Cecy, with her body warm beneath the car-rug and her face freezing, knew just how her sons were feeling. Like two puppets, dragged out by the grownups and made to dance to the tune of their choosing. Dragged around from one place to another, never allowed to say defiantly: 'No, I won't go, I want to stay here.'

But it happens to all of us, she thought resignedly, as the car turned into the drive. However old, we are all at someone's mercy, to go or to stay.

She glanced up at Edward, staring at the house, his expression one of nostalgic interest, and squeezed his hand. For his love, she would have travelled twice as far.

'Daddy wants us to look at a plot of land he's interested in, so he's hired one of Mr Wigg's motors, and we are to leave directly after breakfast.'

Tina chivvied her brood to the table, and soon they were all piling into the motor behind Reg Gallows, a sturdy and reliable fellow who had driven Edward around Norfolk quite a bit already, examining various places where Edward thought he might build a house. His company, the Timber Hill Construction Co., had already got contracts for work all over the country, but the family house which Edward intended to build was still in the planning stage. Ahead of him he saw the turning looming up. He tapped Gallows, indicating the entrance, and the big car swung into a tunnel-like drive. On either side of them mossy banks reared, planted with beech trees which stretched silver-grey branches up and into a leafy canopy which almost hid the blue of the sky.

They reached the top of the drive and burst into brilliant sunshine and what looked like parkland. Wide stretches of lawn, immense trees, a wood, a hollow, a sloping hill.

'What a wonderful place! But why the drive? It seems to lead somewhere and then there's just this.' Tina indicated the stretch of parkland.

'This is part of the Conisford estate, and I suppose the beech drive led to Conisford Hall before it was burnt down. It's beautiful, isn't it?

'Yes! Why, I can see traces of a garden, I do believe! May we . . .'

But the boys and Stella had broken away and were whooping down into the wood hollow. They disappeared into the trees but even though they were no longer in sight their progress could be charted by the noise as they crashed through the undergrowth.

'You want to explore, too? So do I. Is David asleep or do you want to bring him?'

Gallows cleared his throat and touched his cap respectfully. 'I'll look after the nipper, ma'am, if you'd like to leave 'im with me.'

David went happily to the chauffeur and Tina and Edward began to walk around the land. The traces of where the hall had once stood were overgrown but visible still, and Tina pointed to them.

'I'd like the house there, where the other house stood. I'd like our bedroom facing the cedar tree, so that when I woke I could look out and see those lovely flat wedges of green, and smell that glorious cedar-scent.'

'I agree. Shall we follow the boys and work our way round?'

An hour later they climbed back into the car, all excited and exhilarated by what they had seen.

'There's a stream . . . a grove of nut trees . . . a *huge* yew, big enough for a real tree-house . . . trees with bendy branches by the water . . . pink blossom . . . buildings which used to be stables and coach houses . . .'

They bombarded each other with their finds, every face alight with discovery.

'Dad, did you see the little round cottage in the wood? It has windows like a church, only there's no glass any more, and it's all full of twigs and bird-droppings and dirt. But we could live there! We'd love to!'

That was Desmond, blue eyes afire with enthusiasm.

'I don't think that little house would hold all of us, Dessy, but I think we've found the right place to build our house. I think it's what we all want.' He turned and hugged Tina, but gently, because of the baby. 'Goodness knows, darling, you've waited long enough for it!'

Above them, a lark spiralled into the sky, its song growing fainter as it rose.

'Ten years,' Tina marvelled. We've been married a whole decade, Ted! But this house will be worth waiting for!'

EPILOGUE

They stand in front of the new house at last, but this time the baby in Tina's arms is another blond boy; Henry Arthur, called Henny by his siblings because of a certain chick-like down on his small head, and his cheerful, chirping voice.

David has lost his place as the baby of the family, but his hand is securely held in Stella's little soft paw and he rather likes being a 'big boy'.

Before them, the house is complete and looks settled, comfortable, as if it had always been there. It is built of warm red bricks – old bricks. Tina's fancy led her to demand old bricks, old tiles, an old oak front door, and Edward decided to humour her. Looking at it now, he's glad he did. It is the old bricks and tiles which give the house its air of happy permanence.

Already the garden is beginning to take shape under Tina's guidance. She has never made a garden before, but she seems inspired. Almost as though the ghost of the old garden which once was there whispers to her how things used to be.

The stables have been beautifully and imaginatively restored and a man and his wife already live in the old groom's quarters, with their own tiny garden and running water and many other amenities which the owners of the hall certainly never knew, let alone their dependants.

The lodge in the woods has been restored too, and a gardener, his wife, and daughter Mabel moved in three days ago. Mr William Walters is an expert and has two under-gardeners and a boy under him, but he takes orders from his diminutive mistress because he knows she is willing to learn and wants the garden to be a credit to them both.

The servants' quarters in the attics will be occupied soon. Already Tina has employed a cook, two housemaids, two kitchenmaids and an odd-job man. They are looking forward to furnishing the house, starting with the carpets, Tina says authoritatively. She remembers the house in Spanner's Row, and how hard they worked just to get a few sticks of furniture together. This house is so different!

'Well, shall we go inside?'

That is Edward, full of pride in his achievement.

'In a moment.' Tina grabs Stella, who has begun to move towards the front door, towing David behind her. 'First of all, Ted, what are we going to call it? A house like this needs a name. We can't just refer to it as the Newmarket Road house.'

'A name? Yes, you're right. How about Moonshine House, after the hill?'

Tina thinks, frowns, shakes her head.

'How about Yew Tree House, Mummy?'

Desmond's suggestion makes Tina smile, but again she shakes her head.

Excited, the children bombard her with suggestions: Humbleside, Pinewood, The Croft, The Beeches.

Every suggestion brings the consideration, the little frown, the shake of the head.

'You choose then,' Edward says, knowing she has every intention of doing just that.

She looks up at him, her eyes twinkling, the dimples coming and going beside her mouth.

'All right, I will. We'll call it Neyler's Pride, because you made it, and you're as proud of your handiwork as a dog with two tails!'

Immediately the children tear towards the front door, shouting and pushing to be first inside. But Tina and Edward wait a moment longer.

'Neyler's Pride. Hmm. Yes, I think it'll do,' Edward says. 'I've certainly got a lion's pride of cubs, and most of 'em with golden manes as well.'

He chuckles, hugs her. Then, hand in hand, they enter the house and stand for a moment in the cool, tiled hall, whilst the children's noisy footsteps recede up the stairs.

The door swings shut behind them.

Judith Saxton

THE GLORY

arrow books

Author's Acknowledgements

A great many people have helped me with research into the early twentieth century for this book, including Barbara Miller, who sorted through the early records of the Norwich High School for Girls and showed me some fascinating books and photographs, Adelaide and Alan Hunter, who found me magazines, postcards and cuttings dealing with the twenties in Norwich, and C. Wilkins-Jones of the Local Studies Library, who patiently photostated masses of material concerned with Norfolk during the Great War.

In the North-West, Adele and Reginald Mayorcas of Chester helped me with details of Jewish weddings, customs and even cookery; and in Wrexham, Maureen Jardine's knowledge of Judaism kept our mutual phones busy as I checked facts with her.

Librarians in Wrexham Library are always helpful particularly Lynne Butler and Marina Thomas, who make time to help me solve my many and various problems, no matter how busy they may be.

Lastly, I'm indebted to my father, Ivor Saxton, who told me many 'family' stories, and particularly school ones which helped me to understand the workings of a boys' boarding school; and to my grandfather, Alfred Saxton, whose sensible and delightful habit of photographing everything he could point a camera at, and saving newspaper cuttings, old menus, old bills and family documents, helped me to build up a picture of Norfolk and New Zealand at the beginning of the century.

THE NEYLER AND ROSE FAMILIES

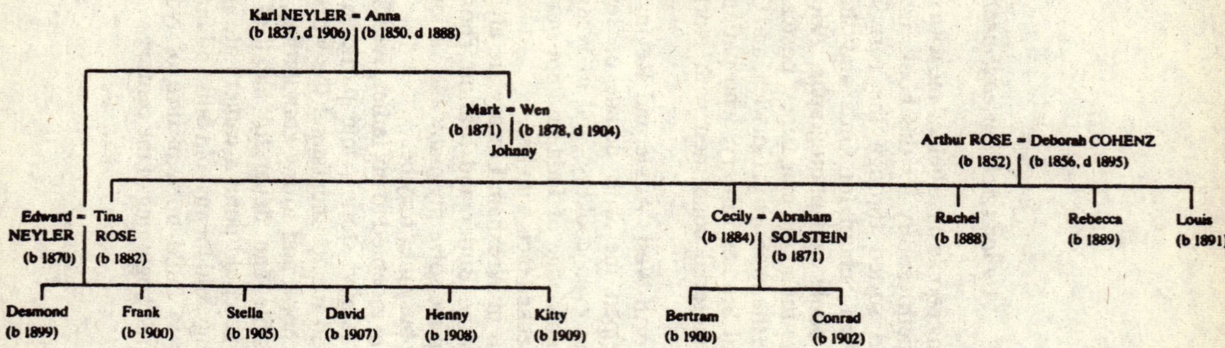

1: 1912

Tina was dreaming. She lay on her back in the big bed, one arm flung up above her head, her bedtime plait lying like a black rope across her shoulder and breast. A small sound, something between a squeak and a whimper, came from her half open mouth, and she moved her head restlessly on the pillow.

Ted, wide awake and far too hot even at six o'clock on this bright July day, touched his wife's shoulder. She kicked out, then whimpered again.

Ted rolled on to his stomach and leaned over her.

'Tina? Come on, love, you're having a nightmare. Wake up!'

Her eyelids flickered but did not open so he kissed her mouth gently, then with increasing firmness. It did the trick. Her lids trembled apart to show eyes still fogged with sleep. He smiled at her, their faces only inches apart, but she scowled, snuggling into the pillow again.

'Go away. 'Tisn't time to get up.'

'You were having a nightmare, sweet. Wake up, there's a good girl.'

She hunched up her shoulders and screwed her eyes tightly shut. 'No. I'm asleep.'

'How can you sleep in this heat? It's like an oven in here!'

It was no use; she was asleep again before he had finished speaking. Facing him now, she curled up and her breathing steadied into a regular rhythm once more.

Ted glanced towards the wide open windows. The trouble was, their room faced east and got all the early morning sun. In the nursery and the little slip of a room off it, the three youngest children and Stella, who was seven, would be quite cool, for their rooms faced the pinewoods at the back of the house. And the boys, Frank and Desmond, would be sleeping still because their room faced west, towards the beech drive. Only he and Tina got the benefit of the early morning sun, blessing it in winter and cursing it in summer.

Even in bed he could see the cedar tree and imagine the flat slabs of shade which it would be casting on the lawn. He heard furtive sounds and knew that the servants were creaking their way down the attic stairs. He glanced at his gold watch on the bedside table. It was barely six, so why were the maids getting up? They had no fires to lay or light in weather such as this, and . . .

Recollection flooded in and he nearly groaned aloud. Of course, today was his father-in-law Arthur Rose's sixtieth birthday. Today he and Tina were to host a large birthday party, with Arthur as the gratified guest of honour. Later, there would be a family dinner party, also held at The Pride. In theory, the work would be shared between Tina and her three younger sisters, but in fact most of it would fall on the servants and inhabitants of The Pride. Sometimes he wished he had not built such a very large house! It seemed to attract guests as honey attracts bees. In winter the billiard room was always full, the playroom bulging at the seams with children. In summer he practically had to put his name down to play tennis on his court, and the garden swing seat, the croquet lawn and the terrace always seemed to contain sundry friends and relatives. So of course when the party had first been suggested, the decision to hold it at The Pride had been unanimous.

He wondered, a little wistfully, why it was that he, Arthur's only non-Jewish relative, should end up entertaining all those good Jews. Today, in my kitchen, kosher things will be happening, he thought. He teased Tina sometimes that she crossed herself and asked forgiveness in Yiddish before eating bacon, because her beliefs must be so mixed up. She had eloped with him when she was only sixteen and before then she had been a good Jewish housekeeper, running her father's house, knowing everything there was to know about the Jewish dietary laws. They had married in the face of fierce parental opposition from Arthur, and against all the odds the marriage had prospered and strengthened until it was the best thing in both their lives.

Religion was one subject which never worried them. Sometimes Tina went to Shul with her father and sisters. Sometimes she accompanied Ted and her own children to morning service at one of the churches in the city, or at Christchurch, which was so conveniently at hand. Ted told Tina that he wanted his children to have the choice between one religion and another, but in Texas, where they had spent half a dozen very happy years, they had attended a local church, and the children took churchgoing for granted.

Tina, brought up with Judaism but completely accepting her husband's beliefs, was happy so long as the children knew right from wrong and had a stable background, and Ted knew, without conceit, that nothing mattered to her which did not involve them both.

Thinking of his children's upbringing made him remember his own. He had been born and brought up on the South Island in New Zealand, his brother Mark almost his only companion on their farm in the mountains behind Dunedin. Owning his own farm had been his dream, yet when he and Mark had run a successful dairy business, been people of standing in the community, he had not been content. He had gone off to England and fallen in love with Tina. He was ashamed to think that in fourteen years of married life he had never once seen Mark. They had been inseparable until his marriage, united against a harsh and violent father. And after? When he was in England with his adoring wife? Mark, too, had married. He and his wife, Wendy, had been happy too, but not lucky, like he and Tina. Wendy had been killed and Mark had simply left the farm, his little son, and his wife's cousin who kept house for them. He had gone to Texas, in search of the big brother who had once been everything to him. And by a cruel twist of fate, he had arrived in Humble, Texas, just as Ted and his family had left.

No one knew much of what Mark had gone through in the next few years. Unhappiness, misunderstandings . . . there must have been plenty of both, for Mark's rare letters were curt, raw with the pain of his loss.

Then a letter had arrived saying that Mark had come to his senses and was returning to Dunedin and his son. Later, they had heard that Mark had married again, to his first wife's cousin, whose name was Su. Ted supposed they were happy, but he knew that his own behaviour in the affair had not been good. During the four years that Mark had been in America he had written constantly to Su, suggesting that Johnny might be sent to England to be educated with his cousins; had even said that if Su agreed he would go to Dunedin and fetch the boy himself. But he had done nothing. Even when Mark was home and planning a wedding, when he could almost hear his brother's unspoken pleas for a brief reunion, he had let Tina argue him into putting off the trip. For Tina was jealous of his affection for Mark, and on this one point he had allowed her to persuade him against all his better judgement.

He knew that it was partly fear. Fear that he would be torn between life in South Island and life in Norwich, fear that he would want to stay with Mark. Whenever he acknowledged this, he saw himself too plainly and his conscience smote him bitterly.

To turn his thoughts from their painful, relentless track, Ted turned on his side and stared hard at Tina, trying to wake her. She *was* hot, he could see tiny sweat beadlets forming on her forehead. He stroked her silky skin and felt desire clutch at his stomach as he held the weight of her breast in his palm, rubbing his thumb over her nipple until it stood proud. Her lashes stirred and he saw the tip of her tongue moisten the fullness of her lower lip. He swallowed. In all the years he had shared her bed he had never known what it was not to want her. Even when she was huge with child, bad-tempered, weeping at nothing, she was the lodestar to which he turned, the magnet to his steel. He could not imagine life without her.

He put his arms round her and pulled her against him. His pyjamas had been abandoned long since and the touch of her excited him as it always had and always would.

'Go away! It's too hot!'

'I agree, sweetie. Take your nightie off.'

She giggled and then kissed his cheek, butterfly fashion, with her long, trembling eyelashes. He pulled the silly little silk straps down over her shoulders and her eyes opened into gleaming slits. As the nightie slid down to her hips he cupped his hand over her breast and felt her heartbeat quicken.

'Do stop it. Someone might come in!'

'They won't. It's very early. The servants are only just up.'

He pulled her nightie right off with only limited help from her and took her fully into his arms, then kissed her. She tensed, her mouth softening beneath his, and then she was clutching him, as eager, suddenly, as he.

The party, the heat, his own shortcomings, were forgotten as they made love.

In the nursery, luncheon was over and the little ones, David, Henny and Kitty, were washed, dressed and brushed to within an inch of their lives. Kitty was to give her grandfather a bouquet of roses and the little boys were presenting him with an immense box of cigars, and they had been rehearsed in their parts until they could have delivered the presents blindfold and in their sleep. Stella, who was seven and at the awkward age when she was neither nursery nor schoolroom, sat on the window-seat, watching the backyard.

'Mabel's gone into the kitchen. She's helping Ruthie with the tea.' Stella sighed and shot a meaning glance at Nanny Sutton, ironing hair ribbons at the nursery table. 'At least *she* isn't bored and shut up with the babies!'

Nanny Sutton finished ironing and stood the flat on its end.

'Nor need you be any more, miss! The boys are back

after their luncheon, so you can come along with me, see if they're ready for the tea party. But for goodness sake don't mess yourself up.'

Stella followed in Nanny's rustling wake, a smile already brightening her face. It was her life's ambition to be with her older brothers, but it was so rarely possible! They were at boarding school during term-time and though it was now the holidays they had their own ploys and their own friends, leaving little time for a child nearly half a dozen years younger than they. But today, because of the party, they might be with her until her bedtime!

At the door, she hurtled in ahead of Nanny, her voice high with excitement.

'Hello, Des, Frank! Nanny said I could . . .' She hesitated. 'You aren't in your suits! You'll catch it!'

Nanny's irate voice proved her point.

'Boys! What on earth are ye thinkin' of? Here's the little ones, bless them, sweet and clean as primroses and Miss Stella here a perfect picture, and you two sulky as bears just because of a stiff collar and a decent suit of clothes. Get *on*, will ye? Your mama wants you down in an hour, no more. Will ye get a move on, just?'

Nanny Sutton was twenty-five, extremely pretty, and Irish. When she was roused, her brogue deepened. Desmond looked across at Frank and winked.

'Sure and wouldn't we dress up as the Angel Gabriel himself for to please ye, Nanny?' he enquired innocently. 'For 'tis yourself we love dearly, me darlin' little bog-trottin' leprechaun!'

'Cheeky varmint!' Nanny Sutton took a half-hearted swipe at Desmond's golden curls. He was a great favourite with the servants and got away with a good deal more than Frank did. 'Now will ye get them suits on?'

'For you, Nan, anything!' Desmond bowed and smirked.

'Oh, get on with ye, Master Dessy! Just go to your room and get changed, the pair of ye!'

Desmond and Frank repaired to their room and began to don their best clothes. Frank, dabbing half-heartedly at his face and neck at the washstand, glanced out of the window at the heat-haze shimmering above the lawn.

'What a spiffing day for Grandpa's party! Though I don't see why we have to dress up like this. It's only family.'

Desmond was pulling a face, tying his tie in the mirror.

'Yes, but it'll be the same for everyone. You don't think Aunt Cecy will let the cousins off because it's hot, do you? No, they'll dress up for the honour of the Solsteins, same as we are for the honour of the Neylers.'

'I suppose you're right. Even Nanny Sutton was glistening a bit, wasn't she? I suppose she'll bring the kids down?'

Desmond, finishing his tie, shrugged himself into his jacket and gave his brother a knowing look through the mirror.

'Noticed she was a bit pink, did you? Know why?'

'No. Why?'

Desmond was about to answer when the door opened and Stella pranced in. She was charmingly dressed in pink and white, her pinafore so starched that it would have stood up by itself, her hair ribbon perched, like a gigantic butterfly, on the back of her head.

'Nanny says I can stay with you if you're respectable,' she announced, with the air of one giving them a high treat. 'I'm so bored with the little ones! Even David's only a child, really.'

She bestowed her sweetest smile on them both, then turned and took the towel away from Frank, arranging it strategically on the towel rail so that the dirt was not immediately obvious. Frank's washing had not so much removed the grime as repositioned it.

'We're not. Respectable, I mean,' Frank said crossly, giving Stella a glare. She ignored it, turning, with a whisk of her long, dark gold mane of hair, towards Desmond.

'Oh, Dessy, I *can* stay, can't I? I'm so bored! You do look lovely in that suit,' she added, with serpentine cunning beyond her years.

Desmond, laughing, nevertheless turned back to the mirror for a moment, smoothing his curls flat with his palms.

'Oh, I suppose you can. But shut up. Frank and I don't

want you prattling.' He turned away from Stella, to give Frank a meaning wink. 'Is Nanny taking the kids down? Will she wear her uniform?'

'Not uniform. She's got a lovely, summery dress with frills. It's sort of yellow.' Stella, sharp as a needle, glanced quickly from Desmond's grinning face to Frank's puzzled one. 'Why? Do you have to stay with Nanny?'

'Of course not, we're handing,' Desmond said. He straightened his lapels and it struck Frank abruptly that Desmond and Stella had a lot in common. They both used their looks to get what they wanted, Stella tossing her pretty little head at Nanny and making eyes at servants, uncles, anyone she wanted to get round. Desmond might not do precisely that, but he teased Nanny by imitating her brogue, or complimenting her on a new dress, and he made up to the servants to clean his room or make his bed for him, to give him little extras, to make him hot buttered crumpets when schoolroom tea was dull. Frank, watching the two of them charming their way through life, sometimes wondered what was lacking in him that he never tried to do the same. It did not occur to him that it was not a lack but a strength, that he neither needed nor wanted to captivate others for his own ends because he made his own way, was content to do his own work.

'We'll go down then,' Desmond said, making for the door. He held out a hand to Stella and it occurred to Frank that he was the odd man out in this trio for another reason as well. Despite their protestations, there was nothing Stella and Desmond liked more than getting dressed up and parading themselves before an admiring throng of relatives.

When they reached the hall they could hear the hum of voices coming from the living room. They went in and Grandpa was there with their parents, and Auntie Becky and Auntie Rachel. They stood back politely, waiting to be noticed, and Frank remembered that whatever he had been going to say about Nanny, Desmond had not finished. He sighed. It probably hadn't been very interesting, anyway!

'Ruthie, Mama sent me to tell you they're ready for the urn

now. And she said to say could I help?'

Mrs Ruthven, scarlet and sweating, dashed a hand across her brow and turned away from the oven.

'All right, Master Frank, run and tell Mrs Neyler I'll be up directly. And then you can give young Mabs an 'and with them strawberries.' Mrs Ruthven, reared from kitchenmaid to cook in a blackbeetly basement kitchen, had not got used to working in a house where the kitchen and scullery, living room and dining room, were all on the same floor. 'Alice, can you come?'

Alice, Arthur's housekeeper specially lent for the occasion, smiled at Frank and took the other end of the trolley with the urn on the top and big jugs of milk beneath.

'I've got it, Ruthie. Has someone taken all the sandwiches up? What about the savouries?'

'They're ready. Nellie, get them savouries out on to the salvers and bring 'em up directly.'

Nellie, in her blue print dress with her best apron over it, reached for the oven cloth even as the two women, pushing the trolley between them, disappeared into the corridor. Frank glanced round. He was to help finish off the strawberries, but where were they? The kitchen seemed to be cleared for action. But Nellie, turning from the oven, remembered Cook's instructions.

'In the scullery, lad. Young Mabel's at 'em,' she said briefly, loading her salver and hurrying out of the kitchen in the wake of the urn.

Frank went into the scullery and there were the strawberries, a great, gleaming pile of them in Mama's cherished cut crystal bowl, with a smaller pile at the side which Mabel was speedily reducing still further as she hulled the fruit. She said nothing, but glanced up at him and grinned – the fascinating, three-cornered smile which Frank liked so much. He grinned back, then nudged her along the wooden bench on which she sat.

'Budge up, Mabs, or I can't give a hand. How many've you eaten? I bet you're busting!'

'I'm not! Too busy.' Mabel pushed a large berry into her mouth and chewed ecstatically, but her fingers never stopped their brisk work. 'Go on, take one!'

They worked side by side in silence for a while, then Mabel said a little wistfully: 'What's it like, the party? Bet them dresses are pretty, eh? My mum helped to make the cucumber sandwiches this morning. She said there were forty people coming!'

Ada Walters, Mabel's mum, helped out in the house and was always much in evidence at parties. Mabel's dad, on the other hand, seldom came indoors. He was the gardener and gifted at his work, but being a man of few words seldom hung around the kitchen to flirt with the maids or gossip with the cook.

'Dunno. We just went in and kissed Grandpa and the aunts, and then Mama collared me to run this errand and Dessy to hand cups. Is that the last of the strawberries?'

'That's right.' Mabel dusted her hands, purple-pink with juice, briskly together and pushed the bowl to safety in the very centre of the table. 'The trolley and all the dishes and that are there, see? My mum'll be through in a mo., and she'll take them in when Ruthie says. That way, everyone gets a squint at the party, see?'

'What about you? Why don't you bring the cream jug or something?'

Mabel, heading for the back door, turned and smiled condescendingly.

'The best part of the party's on the terrace, and I'm going to skulk. I'll see everything I want to see!'

She whisked out of the door before he could say another word and was gone. Frank sighed and made his way back into the kitchen, then along the corridor, through the green baize door, and across into the conservatory where the party was in full swing. He *did* like cheeky young Mabel!

'Here's the cake, Poppa! Ted's lighting the candles and then you must blow them out – all at once, mind! With one blow!'

Arthur allowed himself to be led to where the enormous, three-tier birthday cake, iced in blue and white and crowned with sixty scarlet candles, stood waiting. Ted lit the last candle, then stood back, beckoning the guests nearer.

'Fine it is, Tina mine,' Arthur said. He felt tears come to his eyes, but he smiled through them at his family. 'Ach, it is good to be sixty and have my family around me. How I wish my dear Deb could have lived to see this day!' He blew his nose so vigorously that the nearest candles dipped and swayed alarmingly, and his son-in-law, about to put the matches down, held them ready for an emergency.

'Speech, speech!'

That was the Rabbi, his handsome, eagle-beaked face shiny with emotion and strawberries. Arthur had noted with awe the number consumed by his guest.

'A speech? You don't want to hear an old man talk! Don't I talk enough for you, hey?'

He looked proudly around him at his family. At Tina with her big, blond Ted; at Cecy, small and plump, standing close to her little, dark husband. Abraham was no beauty, but he was a good husband and father. Then there was Becky, watching the candles, and Rachel, his youngest girl, standing near her fiancé, Solomon Hurtz. His gaze rested longest and fondest on Louis, his only son. Louis was his pride and joy, so incredibly beautiful, with a height and assurance that made him the cynosure of all female eyes. At twenty, he stood at the threshold of life and Arthur knew he would grasp it with both hands. He had brought a young lady friend with him, and stood with one hand resting carelessly on her drooping shoulder. Arthur's heart swelled with pride. That Louis should have brought Sarah Kelpmann, rich, beautiful, and a good member of the Shul, to his old father's birthday party made his day. It showed that the boy had sowed his wild oats and was now settling down with a good Jewish girl of excellent family whose prospects it turned Arthur quite dizzy to contemplate. Landed Jewish gentry, that described the Kelpmanns! That his son, with his curly black hair, sparkling dark eyes and satyr's sensuous mouth, was the best looking man in the room Arthur never doubted. Nor that Sarah Kelpmann, given the opportunity, would leap at a chance to change her name to Rose!

'My dear, good children!' He held out his arms, then clasped them to his chest as if he were literally embracing his offspring. 'Such a party to make, and for the old man! Good food, that lovely cake, and after, just for family, a dinner party! What can I say but thank you all for making an old man very happy?'

There was laughter, then applause. The Rabbi, with a strawberry in one hand, cried: 'Old? Oh, Arthur!'

'Well, sixty feels old,' Arthur admitted. 'Fifty-nine, a boy, no less. Sixty, old.' He turned to grin engagingly at his assembled grandchildren. Tina's large brood; Cecy's two boys, Bertram and Conrad. 'If the old man's to blow out sixty candles, he needs a helper or two!' The little ones, dark-haired David, Henny with his plume of yellow fluff, Kitty with her dusky, clustering curls, ran to him, jostling and shouting with cries to be chosen. Stella hovered, not wanting to seem a baby. 'Three? Only three of my grandchildren to give me a hand? What about the men? Hey, boys?'

Little, dark Con, with his monkey's face and wiry body, caught Stella's hand and the two came forward. Desmond, smiling, self-consciously stroking his chin, was next, with Frank and Bertram close behind.

'That's better! Now we have a chance. But listen, chaps, we'll need strategy!' The eight young heads gathered close to his as his whisper made the little ones nod eagerly, the older ones choke on giggles.

'At the count of three! One . . . two . . . wait for it, wait for it . . . and *three!*'

The table rocked as the boys leaned on it, causing Tina to squeak with alarm and Cecy's little hands to fly apprehensively to her mouth, and the cake tilted perilously, but the candles went out to a man. Someone clapped, it was taken up by others, there were cheers, and then they were singing 'Happy Birthday' at the top of their voices and continuing, without a pause, into 'We all wish you *mazel tov*'.

Arthur, beaming, conducting with both hands, caught the Rabbi's eye and saw him cock a glance from the fair

Neyler grandchildren to their fair father, then look across at Bertram's dark, aquiline face and at Con's wrinkled monkey grin. The non-Jewish children were singing as loudly, and with as much enthusiasm, as any member of his Jewish family.

2

The tea party had been an enormous success, there could be no doubt of that, Tina told herself, and hoped fervently that the dinner party, and the subsequent bridge game, would also go off well. Bridge being Poppa's favourite way of spending an evening she had little choice but to propose it, and the family had agreed, with kindness if not enthusiasm.

At first, the gap between bidding the tea party guests farewell and sitting the family down to dinner had seemed an insurmountable problem. But then Ted had thought of the tennis court. So the women were advised to bring tennis skirts and the men flannels and straw hats, and though no one was particularly expert they enjoyed several sets, which were watched indulgently by Arthur and the older members of the party.

The only thing that had marred that part of the day for Tina had been her visit to the nursery. She had left the tennis party to check on the younger children and had found Millie, the nursery maid, supervising the eating of bread and milk by three nightgowned youngsters, all washed and brushed, whilst Stella, grimly determined to keep to her slightly later bedtime though her eyelids were drooping, ate bread and jam and an apple cut into quarters, and waited for her hour to strike.

'Well done, Millie. Everything went beautifully and the children looked lovely. I want to congratulate Nanny. Where is she?'

'She's changing out of her afternoon dress m'm,' Millie said. 'Back into her print, I daresay.'

Heaven alone knows what sent me along to Nanny's room, Tina told herself afterwards. Am I glad or sorry that I went? She could not answer the question since it raised an even harder one – having pried on Nanny, what was she going to do about it? In the end, as with all her problems, she took it to Ted, changing into his dinner jacket in his dressing room.

She opened the door, half fearing that Abe might have come up too, and be talking to Ted as he changed. But Ted was alone, already clad in black trousers and a white frilled shirt. She crossed the room, put her arms round his waist, and laid her hot cheek against his back. He turned round, still holding the ends of the black bow tie he had been in the act of tying, and kissed her.

'Poor darling, are you worn out? Never mind. In another three or four hours they'll be going home and it will all be over!'

'Oh, Ted, it's something much worse than tiredness!'

He always knew when she was genuinely distressed. His face became alert at once and he dropped the ends of his tie to put his arms round her.

'What's upset you?'

She had blurted out the whole story then: the trip to the nursery, Millie telling her that Nanny was changing out of her afternoon dress, her own visit to Nanny's small bedroom to thank her for bringing the children down looking so delightful.

Here Tina paused for a moment. Edward looked quizzical.

'Well? Tell me the worst! Had she gone off and left Millie in charge?'

Tina shook her head, her eyes on the floor.

'Oh no, she was there all right. *And* changing. In fact, she had h-hardly anything on at all!'

'And that upset you? Nanny's only human, you know. I expect she was feeling hot!'

'She was being human and feeling hot,' Tina said in a small voice. 'So was Louis. On Nanny's bed! In a c-compromising p-position.'

'My God!' Ted's face darkened. 'That little swine! I won't have him treating my servants like whores! I'll forbid him the house!'

'It's all right, Ted. I shall have to dismiss Nanny, so it won't happen again. But . . .'

'You will dismiss nobody! What good would that do? She's a damned fine nanny, you've said so a score of times. It's your unprincipled, immoral brother who's at fault, not the girl.'

His fury astonished her. She blinked nervously up at him as he shouted.

'But, Ted, I *must* dismiss her. I can't have a loose woman looking after my children!'

'She isn't a loose woman just because she succumbed to Louis's blandishments. Knowing him, he probably forced himself on her. I won't have the girl suffer for Louis's passions.'

'No, Ted, you don't understand! She was *enjoying* it! Truly! She was p-pressing Louis's head to her breast and he was mumbling on her skin and she was groaning, moving . . . it was horrible!'

He had been holding her close but now he put her away from him, looking down at her with gleaming eyes, slowly shaking his head.

'Tina, I'm ashamed of you! This very morning, when I . . .'

Her face flamed scarlet and she stood on tiptoe to put her hand over his mouth.

'Don't! There's nothing cheap or sordid about our love, Ted. We're married, it's different! What we do is . . . in the eyes of . . . well, with the approval of . . .'

He let her stutter herself into silence. They had been married in a register office, while she was still a minor, without her father's consent, and had kept well away from Norwich until Tina was pregnant and an annulment would merely have plunged her family into the sort of scandal they would most want to avoid. When she was quiet he took her shoulders and shook her gently.

'I'm not comparing our lovemaking with Louis's sordid

affairs, my darling. I'm merely saying that just because you saw Nanny at a very private moment you mustn't judge her by it. Physical ecstasy isn't something that can be turned on and off like a tap. She could have fought like a tiger to keep Louis at bay, but by the time you saw them . . . Damn it, she's probably as deeply in love with Louis as she can be by now! I'd like to wring his neck!'

Tina heaved a huge sigh and leaned her head against his chest.

'I see. But I'll never be able to look at her again without thinking about . . . that.'

'What about her? Hasn't it occurred to you that she'll feel just the same? She may even give her notice because of it!'

'She didn't see me,' Tina said bitterly. 'I daresay the Black Watch could have played the bagpipes marching round the bed and she wouldn't have let it disturb her.'

Ted's mouth twitched.

'You must forget what you saw, love. I'll have a word with Louis. I won't mention that you saw anything, don't worry.'

'Must you? Speak to Louis, I mean. If I'm not to dismiss Nanny, couldn't you just forget I told you? Then we can be comfortable again.'

Ted sighed. Sometimes his wife could be very difficult!

'Could you be comfortable if I didn't speak to Louis? Knowing that every time he came into the house he was just waiting for the chance to nip up to the nursery and get Nanny into bed?'

'No . . . yes . . . I don't know! Don't you *see*, Ted, that if I dismissed Nanny I wouldn't have to worry at all? Louis is my brother, I can't forbid him the house, but there are always other nannies wanting work.'

'That's the most stupid and immoral suggestion I've ever heard!' Ted was angry, and she hated him to be angry. She watched his face harden against her and could have killed Nanny, whose fault it was. 'Tina, don't you understand that with Louis, if it wasn't Nanny it would be the nursery maid? Or the cook? Can't you see that? Louis likes women!'

'You keep blaming Louis! It's never Nanny's fault! I wish I'd not said a word to you, then I could have . . .'

He caught hold of her and shook her till her teeth rattled.

'If you dare to dismiss Nanny Sutton, my girl, you'll answer to me for it! Is that clear? This house is run for your convenience and mine, not for Louis'. The truth is that you won't look facts in the face and see Louis for the rascal he is, but this time I'm going to make you. And now get into the bathroom and wash those tears away. Comb your hair and put on your best dress and come down to dinner with me. And for God's sake act as if nothing had happened. You may be sure Louis will!'

They sat round the table and Arthur beamed at them all and loved them, every one. He thought them happy and this pleased him, for he loved his family to be happy. Indeed, looking round the table at the façade each put on, they did seem to be a happy gathering. But beneath the surface the worries and miseries, the uncertainties and the disillusions, worked on each adult member of the party.

Tina was unhappy because she could not dismiss the children's nanny, and Ted was dreading having to tell Louis what he thought of his behaviour. Becky was eating her heart out because she was a year older than Rachel and still unmarried.

Rachel, sitting beside Solomon, was unhappy because she did not love him. He was suitable, Jewish, and he was fond of her. But he was so *dull,* so self-righteous! Last term she had been invited by Louis to the end of term ball at his college. She had gone and Louis, typically, had turned up with some dreadful, fast-looking female on his arm, introduced Rachel to a couple of his friends, and disappeared. But one of the friends, Frederick Sansom, had danced with her all evening, taken her into the summer-decked gardens for chicken salad and icecream, and rowed her down the river as dawn broke, to make discreet love in the shelter of some willow trees. It had been a night to remember, and Rachel could not forget it. Frederick had not been handsome or charming, but he had had a warmth and a liveliness of mind which Solomon patently lacked.

Four weeks had elapsed since that occasion, and Frederick Sansom had written to her five times. Day after day she nerved herself to write and tell him she was engaged to Solomon, or to write and beg him to rescue her from her loveless match. But as yet she had done neither. She had replied to the letters in the most colourless and guarded tones, and now she sat at the dinner table, crumbling her bread roll in thin, nervous fingers, and wishing she was brave, like Tina. Tina had thrown convention, parental affection and security in Poppa's face, and gone off with the man she loved. Would she, Rachel, have the courage to do likewise? She doubted it.

Louis was not experiencing any pangs of conscience because he had enjoyed the children's nanny; he considered such moments to be life's small compensations for the many dullnesses he suffered daily, such as this confounded dinner party. But he was unhappy because Sarah was furious with him. Most unfairly, for she knew nothing of the Nanny episode, she was angry because he had promised they would play bridge with the old man after dinner. So now she sat beside him, icicle cool, scarcely saying a word to him, though she laughed and flirted a little with her other neighbour, his confounded, cocky little nephew, Desmond.

'What's for pudding, Tina mine? That bird . . .' Arthur kissed the tips of his fingers extravagantly as the wreck of the roast goose was borne away. 'The recipe for that stuffing Alice would give her right hand to possess! You're still the queen of cooks, Tina mine!'

Cecy tried to strangle the jealousy which rose in her breast whenever Poppa praised Tina, and partially succeeded. She was not a jealous person by nature, but it was hard not to envy Tina Ted's astonishing good looks, and those tall, broad-shouldered sons of hers with their blue eyes and fair hair. She adored Abe, but he looked every one of his forty-five years and the beauty of his soul did not show in his dark-skinned, beaky face. Her own sons were clever and good looking enough, until they sat round the table beside the Neyler boys. Desmond and Frank made her darling Bertram and even little Con look foreign, small; insignificant almost. But Tina was answering Poppa and Cecy banished her envy.

'Well, Poppa, there's orange and lemon sorbet, because the children love iced puddings, and then there's raspberry meringue or apricot mousse. We thought we'd have cold sweets after the goose, and I know how you love meringues.'

Arthur was delighted with everything, and, when the table was cleared and Ted had announced that they would have coffee and mints on the terrace, he was the first to get to his feet, offer his arm to Becky, and lumber off, leaning on her and on one of his sticks, anxious to get the coffee over so that the game of cards might begin.

It was at this point that Louis approached Tina.

'Can I have a word with you, big sister?'

He was laughing because he was over a foot taller than she, but to his surprise she went very red before nodding curtly and preceding him out of the room. In the hall she glanced up at him, her eyes having difficulty in meeting his. He thought she must have been arguing with Ted. They had quite violent rows at times for all they loved each other so desperately. He put his arm round her shoulders.

'Poor little sis. Are you tired? Look, I just wanted to tell you that I'm in Sarah's black books. I wondered if you could possibly get me off the hook?'

Her eyes rounded and her mouth dropped open.

'Me? Get you off the hook?'

'Who else? Sarah's mad as fire with me because I've agreed to play bridge. Apparently she hates the game, though she's quite good. I wondered if you could arrange something – perhaps play with two tables instead of three? Or I'd willingly fetch the Rabbi and his wife to make up numbers.'

'No, I could not! I wonder you dare suggest such a thing, Louis!' She shot her brother a fulminating look. 'I won't have you hurting Poppa so, and at his own birthday party!'

She turned her shoulder on him and made for the conservatory. Louis, following, touched her arm.

'Don't get your rag out! I'll calm Sarah down. I just thought I'd ask, that's all!'

He kept his hand on her arm and despite herself Tina softened towards him. Louis was abominably spoilt, that was the trouble, and she had done her share of spoiling him when he was small. No use turning on him now because he still wanted his own way!

'Look, Louis, would it help if I told Sarah that Poppa is always in bed by ten thirty? You might take her on somewhere else. I'm sure you'd find plenty to do at that time.'

'No. Leave it to me. She's a good girl, really.'

He crossed the conservatory and slumped elegantly into the vacant chair next to Sarah, then leaned across and began to whisper in her ear. Presently, Tina saw the girl smile.

She was a handsome girl, the heiress to old man Kelpmann's millions, with a magnificent figure – she must have stood quite five foot ten inches in her stockinged feet. For the first time, it occurred to Tina to wonder why Sarah had consented to come here tonight. Would such a girl seriously consider allying herself to Louis, a twenty-year-old student without a penny to his name?

Tina looked at her brother, at the broad shoulders, the curly black hair, the slight, but undeniably attractive, air of dissipation which hung about him. She thought wryly that had he lived a hundred years earlier he would have done very well in the Regency, when young bucks fought and womanised and drank deep. But in 1912 he would not get much tolerance from people who mattered if he continued to seduce servants and barmaids, and to offer gratuitous insults to young ladies. For she knew, though she supposed that Louis did not, what an insult to Sarah his seduction of Nanny had been.

There was one spark of light in the midst of so much darkness, however. Surely, having so recently slaked his appetite, he would behave with decorum when he took Sarah home, and would not try to seduce her in the front seat of his father's Delaunay?

If Tina has underestimated Louis, she had also underestimated Sarah. When the brand-new, dark blue Delaunay drew up outside the Kelpmann mansion it carried one very furious but still virtuous young lady and one scratched and equally furious young man, nursing an incipient black eye.

'Damn it, Sarah, I was only trying to *kiss* you,' Louis said mendaciously, as the car stopped with a swish and scatter of the deep gravel. 'If that's what you're going to do every time you're kissed . . .'

'Louis, kissing I understand, kissing I enjoy. Mauling, however, is another thing entirely. You must learn to keep it for your kitchen maids and shop girls, because young ladies are not used to such treatment!'

'The young ladies I know don't punch,' Louis growled resentfully. He now knew how Sarah had learned the backhand which had been much admired that evening on the tennis court! By punching ardent suitors in the eye, just as this particular ardent suitor had succeeded in getting his hand down the provocatively low-cut front of her evening gown!

'I don't think you know any young ladies,' Sarah said reflectively. 'Your reputation has gone before you, Louis, and rumour has it that you prefer the easier manners and morals of the lower classes.'

'Damn it, what a thing to say! And what about my sisters? Do you think they punch and scratch their gentlemen friends?'

'I daresay they would, if their gentlemen friends tried to do what you tried to do!'

Louis sighed patiently and put his hand, with a certain amount of caution, over hers as it lay on her lap.

'You're very young for eighteen, Sarah. I assure you that *all* men want to touch nice things, and that doesn't mean . . .'

She interrupted him without apology, her fine eyes sparkling in the faint light from the gas lamps which flanked the front door. Her lips were curved into a half-smile, and a dimple appeared in one flushed cheek.

'Louis, I'm by no means as inexperienced as you would like to think! I've been to a great many dances and parties when staying with my mother's relatives in London, and I've been kissed by any number of young men, and none of them behaved as you did. Look, it's absolutely useless your trying to justify your actions, because it's impossible, so the discussion's getting us nowhere! Do you want to take me out again?'

Fifteen minutes earlier, being punched in the eye in a country lane, nearly breaking his wrist when extracting his fingers from their warm and comfortable resting place, he had vowed he never wanted to set eyes on her again. But she was laughing up at him, her lively, sensual face caught in the golden light, the outline of that magnificent body, those splendid breasts, tantalising him with their nearness. He knew that he must see her again. Such stern resistance was made, he told himself, to be conquered.

'I do, Sarah,' he said humbly. 'I really do.'

'Then there must be no more nonsense.'

He sighed, then crossed his fingers behind his back.

'I promise you. Not until . . .'

'What?'

'I was only going to say not until you were willing! That's all! If you were willing there could be no harm . . .' He looked at her and grinned. 'Damn it, Sarah, you're laughing at me!'

'Oh, Louis, you're incorrigible.' But she was smiling, and he knew she had relented. 'Will you come indoors for a drink before driving home?'

Louis pulled a face and touched his swollen eye, the long scratch down one cheek.

'Like this? No, I think your father might put two and two together and make five. I'll come and see you in a few days, if I may, when the wounds have healed.

She chuckled softly, then said a little impatiently: 'Well? Aren't you going to come round and open my door?'

He put a tentative hand on her smooth, bare shoulder.

'But I've not kissed you goodnight yet. Surely you'll let me kiss you goodnight?'

She laughed again and leaned across towards him. He touched her lightly on the shoulders, drawing her near, and felt her firm breasts push against his dinner jacket. Only the throbbing of his eye kept his hands where they belonged. She kissed him and he kissed her too – the most gentle and decorous of salutations. Then, before he could forget himself, he jumped from the car and went round to open the door. He saw her up the steps and watched until the front door closed behind her, then started the engine, and drove back down the drive.

It did not occur to him at once, but when he had reached home and was garaging his car the thought struck him. He had enjoyed that brief, inglorious struggle with Sarah more than the entire seduction of the Neyler nanny! Could this mean that virtue would bring its own reward, in time?

It was a new idea and one to which he intended to devote some thought. Until that evening he had considered women as man's natural prey and nothing more. He had cared nothing for the mind behind the pretty face; all he had demanded was good nature allied to complete compliance with his desires. But Sarah, he reflected, was different. Time alone would prove whether different would also mean better!

3

Parties, Mark reflected as he drove back along the coast road towards the Peninsula farm, seemed to be in the air today. He had driven into Dunedin to collect the mail and had just finished reading a letter from Ted in which he had described his father-in-law's sixtieth birthday party and the family get-together which had followed.

Mark, who had been to see the principal of the largest school for boys in the city, was planning a party of his own, too. There were several reasons for it, the most overt one being that he and Su had been married three years, which was a very good reason for celebrating.

When he thought of the doubts and fears which had preceded his actually asking Su if she would marry him, he could only marvel at his own stupidity. But of course it had not been so simple then. There was the twenty-year age gap for a start, and the fact that he had fled from the farm and spent four wasted years in America fighting to get over the raw, scarlet pain of Wen's death. Throughout those four years, the longing for his home and for Su had seemed to him not natural and good, but evil, a betrayal of his perfect relationship with Wen. Yet though he always thought of the years in America as the wasted years, it had not been so. It had taken those years to make him see that another woman could not supplant Wen, because their life together had been perfect, and was over. Another love-affair could take nothing from Wen – indeed, it would give, because he would be able to remember the good times without stirring up the aching sense of loss which made him wince at the mention of her name.

Now, driving back to the Peninsula farm, he beguiled the time by remembering that other homecoming, more than three years ago.

He had been a little hurt when the ship had docked and there had been no one to meet him. It seemed strange that, after a four-year absence, there should be no one at the quayside. He had cabled, but had kept it short and succinct. Had he been too short, too succinct? So far as he could recall he had simply said he was coming on the *Boston Star* and asked them to meet him. Surely that was plain enough? The exact time of the ship's arrival would have been given in the local paper, so there should have been no reason for their absence.

He did not have much luggage, just a large and shabby

trunk, a suitcase, and a Gladstone bag containing a stuffed crocodile for Johnny, a pair of china figures for Toddy and Freda to put on their mantelpiece, and a feather boa for Su. He was doubtful, now, about the boa, which had got crushed on its long journey and looked somehow tatty and disreputable, as though it had once graced the shoulders of a dance-hall girl but had been cast aside as too shabby. Still, perhaps Freda could wash it, make it look perky again.

He went over to where the cabs and their patient horses stood and hired one of them, then helped the cabby to lug his baggage over and stow it in the capacious boot. The cabby was taciturn, not in the least interested in Mark or his homecoming, merely climbing ponderously back on to the box and clicking to his horse.

Going through the city, Mark pressed his nose against the window. It had changed, perhaps, but not enough to hurt. Still beautiful, with its gracious houses, tree-lined streets and quiet, green parks, it warmed his heart as did the backdrop of blue hills in the distance. Over there was Waihola, where he had spent his childhood, and as the cab turned on to the coast road he heard the mew of the gulls and the muted surge of the surf and thought of the enchanted beaches and the sting of the wind and the freedom that to him was part of New Zealand. He could not forget that he had found Wen's body on a beach, lying in the surf, but knew that it would no longer have the power to numb his enjoyment of the shoreline. It did no good to dwell on the sad times. Wen herself would never have permitted it, he knew that now. He would remember only the good times, the loving, the laughter.

When he saw the farm his heart jumped, but not because it was different; it seemed to have stayed exactly the same. He and his luggage were set down outside the white-walled garden. He opened the gate, remembering how he and Wen had made it Johnny-proof, for their son had been a terrible one for wandering. The proofing had been simply chicken wire to block the foot-high gap beneath the gate. It had gone, and Johnny, he guessed, would find it somewhat difficult now to wriggle beneath the gate! There was a good deal of difference between a two-year-old and six-year-old!

He looked at the house as he walked up the path towards it. The front door, when he left, had been painted green; it was green still. The roses had bloomed around it, deep red and palest yellow; they bloomed there still. They were taller, further up the stones, but they were still as colourful, and their scent, hauntingly sweet, brought tears to his eyes which blurred their brightness.

His hand went to the door knob, then drew back. After four years, he had no rights here. He should knock. He was a visitor, someone scarcely considered now, who had deserted them when they needed him most. They had made their own lives, and no matter how little he might like it he was alien here, wanting acceptance but not daring to demand it. He knocked.

There was no answer from within the house but he was content, for the moment, to stand in the sunshine and dream a little. On such a brilliant day he guessed that the farmworkers would be in the fields, and probably Su and his son had driven into Dunedin to meet him. He must have missed them. He knocked again, then cautiously tried the door knob, but the door resisted him. Locked, of course. Well, the back door was never locked; he would go round the back.

The back door was locked as well and that really startled him. They *never* locked the back door; friends, family, the hands, knew they could wander in and out at will. Then he chided himself. Things changed, and people too. Su was a very pretty young girl, living alone but for the boy. He knew she had not married, for, though he wrote rarely and though his letters were stiff and uninformative, Su had not treated him to such a correspondence. Her letters were frequent and lively, full of chatter about the child, the farm, her daily life. And Toddy told her of milk yields, wool yields, haycrops and horses.

He waited by the back door for another moment, then went over and peered through the window. At once, fear clutched at his heart. The fire was out in the stove! What was happening? A faint premonition of disaster touched him with its icy bat-wings. Not . . . Oh, God, don't let anything have happened to Su! Not that innocent, charming child! Dear God, take the farm, take me, take the whole of the Otago peninsula if You must, but let Su be unharmed!

He took to his heels and ran across the yard to Toddy's cottage. Freda would surely be in. She was always either in or at the farm. She must be in!

His impetuous knock was followed by an even more impetuous entry; he stood in the middle of the small kitchen, his heart beating like a drum, smelling the good, comfortable smell of baking, floor polish, fresh logs on a fire.

'Freda!'

She came hurrying through, a duster in one hand. She looked exactly the same, her bushy grey hair sticking out untidily round her head, her good-natured, weathered face placid as ever. She entered the room smiling, with words on her lips. The words died, the smile faltered. The duster went to her mouth. Round eyes stared at him above the yellow stuff.

'Mark? Oh, Mark!'

Then she was in his arms, kissing him, crying, breaking free to rub her eyes with the duster.

'Wait till Toddy sees you! You've been to the farmhouse?'

He nodded. He felt calm now. He knew that they were all right, just by seeing Freda's expression.

'Ah, then you'll know they're away. Oh, poor Su, poor Johnny! They'll break their hearts to find they've missed your homecoming, honest, Mark. To think of them missing you! And Toddy was worried because they'd gone off quiet-like, only left a note, no address. But they won't be gone long if I know them, no fear!'

She patted his shoulder, her eyes tear-shiny.

'You could do with some feedin' up, I can see that! Sit down and I'll make coffee. There's some of them ring doughnuts you and Ted used to be so fond of in the jar in the pantry – cooked them barely an hour ago. Johnny likes 'em, too.' She glanced at the clock above the dresser. 'Toddy'll be up for his dinner presently. My word! To see his face!'

He enjoyed her voice like a good meal; the comfortable, New Zealand twang which he had sorely missed. He sat down at the table, sniffing the coffee pot as she added boiling water to the freshly ground grains.

'Away? Didn't Sue get my cablegram?'

She was in the pantry now, getting the cooky jar down from the shelf. She returned to put it down in front of him and bring the coffee pot over from the stove with two mugs and a bowl of brown sugar.

'There! I'll just fetch you some milk.' She bustled out and was quickly back. 'What cablegram?'

'Hell, didn't it arrive? I sent one from New York, asking them to send someone down to meet my ship.'

Freda poured the coffee and sat down, a frown creasing her brow. She helped herself to sugar, two heaped spoonfuls, then stirred it thoughtfully.

'A cablegram! So it was that . . .'

'They got it, then? And *left*? Ran away?'

His voice reflected his hurt.

'It can't have been yours which disturbed them.' Freda's sharp eyes had seen the change which came over his face at the suspected rejection. 'Look, Mark, it won't have been your cable. Toddy'll know. Johnny tells him everything, and . . .'

The door opened behind him and Freda's hand shot out, keeping Mark, who would have risen, in his seat, back to the door.

'Toddy, guess who's come visiting?'

There was the sort of silence that speaks. Then Mark turned and was on his feet in one movement and he and Toddy clutched each other, faces working with emotion.

'Mark!' Toddy's deep voice cracked with the depth of his feeling. 'After all these years! And the varmints away!'

'Where, Toddy?' Freda's voice was carefully disinterested. 'What sent them flying off, d'you suppose? I know you've been close with me and the others, but Mark's got a right to know. He's Johnny's father.'

Toddy went over to the dresser and took down a mug, then returned to the table. He poured himself coffee, added milk, and pulled up a chair as Mark sat down again.

'A cablegram; that's sure. But *where* they went . . .' He grinned across at Mark. 'Your brother Ted's caused the young 'uns a deal of worry, though Freda and I told them over and over Ted ain't the sort to throw his weight. Or poke his nose where it ain't wanted. Tell him straight and he'll back off, I told young Su. Not that they listened, I daresay.'

Freda tapped her husband's arm.

'Toddy, Mark sent a cable. He's thinkin' it might have been that sent 'em off. I told him no, but . . .'

Toddy's grizzled eyebrows rose and his mouth scoffed.

'You think young Su would have gone *anywhere* if she'd known you were comin' back? She'd have driven us all mad. that's for certain, gettin' the place ready, shampooin' all the sheep like as not. She'd . . . ' He stopped, to stare very hard at Mark. 'What did you say in that there cable, any road?'

Mark strained to remember. It had been such an innocuous cable!

'I think I said *Neyler returning on SS Boston Star stop Please meet.* Or something like that. No, I've got it! *Neyler arriving Dunedin on SS Boston Star stop Please meet.* That's clear enough, surely?'

Toddy was grinning, the relief written all over his broad, homely face.

'Oh, sure. Plain enough if you've been gettin' cables from Ted Neyler, askin' if he shouldn't send for young Johnny to come to England for schoolin' and upbringin' with his own kids. Clear enough when there hasn't been a mention of yourself comin' home!'

Mark felt light suddenly, as if he had woken from a nightmare.

'Then – it was just a misunderstanding? They thought I was Ted, coming to take Johnny?' He gave a crack of laughter and reached for a doughnut, cramming it into his mouth and speaking thickly through it. 'What a thing! How can we get in touch with them to bring them back? I can't wait to see them both.'

'That's goin' to be difficult.' Toddy's face was thoughtful. 'Johnny ain't secretive, but it was all done in such a rush, and not a murmur did he let out as to where they was goin'. Just goin' on a visit, that's all he said.'

'Oh, curse!' Mark absently reached for another doughnut. I've waited so long, he thought, that a few more weeks won't kill me. 'Well, what'll we do?'

Freda got up and went over to the stove.

'We'll let it be known that you're home, Mark. That's what'll bring 'em, feelin' foolish, you bet! It's a word-of-mouth country, this, and news travels fast. Give it time and one morning you'll wake up and they'll be squabbling up the garden path like kids, to see who'll be first in the door.'

'You're right. I'm really not in a hurry, though it will be marvellous to see . . . to see them. In the meantime, it's been a year or two since I worked the farm. Toddy'll keep me busy, giving me lessons.'

Toddy looked across at him, his faded blue eyes very bright.

'You're home for good, then? This ain't just a visit?'

Mark gripped the table top and bit his lip. Suddenly he wanted to put his head down on the table and weep like a baby, but it would only embarrass Toddy. Instead, he leaned across and grasped the other man's work-roughened hand.

'For good, Toddy. I'll not leave again.'

4

'A card! There's a card, Mark!'

Toddy burst into the farmhouse kitchen, his face shining,

evidence of his hasty journey from the stable to the back door. Mark, sitting at the table devouring stew and dumplings, dropped his spoon. Joe, one of the hands, stared. Even Freda, usually so calm, dropped her ladle back into the cauldron and exclaimed.

'I thought they'd never write,' Mark said, reaching out a hand. 'Can I see? Who's it addressed to?'

'Freda and myself.' Toddy sank down on to his chair and wiped his forehead with a large and rather grubby handkerchief. 'But you wouldn't expect them to send a card to anyone else, not when you consider they don't know you're here!'

Freda rescued her ladle and began to serve stew into another plate for Toddy. She carried it over to the table and plonked it down in front of him, then turned to Mark, her face eager.

'What's it say? Read it aloud, Mark!'

'It's quite short. It says *Having a good time, but missing you all very much. Home soon, I hope, love to everyone, Johnny and Su.*' Mark leaned back in his chair and cast a helpless glance at Toddy. 'I'm glad you've heard, of course, but what good is it? No address, and only a beach scene, which could be anywhere.'

Toddy spooned stew into his mouth, then spoke thickly through it.

'Use your eyes, lad. The postmark!'

Mark examined the postmark, then slapped his thigh jubilantly and waved the card under Freda's nose.

'Sydney! See, Freda? By God, they've gone all the way to Australia. No wonder none of the newspaper appeals reached them!'

'Sydney! Crikey, we ought to have thought of that,' Freda remarked. 'Johnny's grandparents are there. I remember Su telling me that she still wrote to them, regular as clockwork. Her uncle and aunt, of course. They've got a restaurant there, I believe. What'll you do, Mark? Write and tell 'em to come home?'

'I could do that, though it seems rather tame. What I'd rather do is . . .'

'Mark!' Freda was laughing, shaking her head. 'You wouldn't go all that way! She says they hope to be coming home soon. Suppose you missed them? Again!'

'You're right, of course.' Mark reached out and pulled his plate near him again, beginning to eat the cooling stew. 'I suppose I could send a cablegram, asking them to come back.'

'You do that. You'll find the Lengs' address somewhere in Su's desk. You'll look through it, surely, when you know that by doing so it'll bring them home quicker?'

Mark had steadfastly refused to interfere with Su's desk, not liking to examine the contents when the owner was far away. Su had done all the necessary paperwork on the farm in his absence and the desk, after so many years, was very much her property. But now, of course, he would feel differently. There was a reason to go through it; he would be searching for an address, not merely prying into what might be her private affairs. Mark finished his stew and took a slice of bread, using it to wipe up the last of the gravy.

'I'll do it! As soon as I've finished my meal I'll find that address. And when I cable, I'll be sure to make myself crystal clear!'

The waiting was hard. Being *almost* sure that she had fled because she thought his cablegram came from Ted, being *almost* sure that she had once loved him, made for disturbed nights, attacks of depression that were foreign to his old nature. Toddy and Freda were seen to exchange quick, worried looks when they thought themselves unobserved, but Mark knew that they were judging his behaviour solely on that of the old Mark. They scarcely know this me, he thought miserably once. They knew the old, easy-going Mark who had had Wen to bolster his confidence. They did not know the emotional cripple he had become without her, nor how easily the black moods had beaten him, once.

Fortunately, there was a great deal to do. He went over to his father's farm at Waihola, where he had been brought up, and was assailed by so many mixed emotions that he dared not go straight to the house. Karl had died during his time in America, Anna had been dead these past fifteen years or so, yet still they haunted the place: Anna with her fair, good-natured face, Karl with his striking looks and abrasive personality. And perhaps the young Ted, the young Mark, haunted the place too. His had not been a happy childhood in one sense, for his father's brutality had overshadowed it, but there had been compensations. His mother's overflowing love, the closeness which existed between Ted and himself. There was no substitute for that, because a woman's love was different. Better, perhaps, but still different.

I have not set eyes on Ted for fourteen years, but we are still close, he told himself, lurking in the big barn and staring towards the log cabin. It was a cabin still, with flowering creepers around the windows as there had been in his day. The new people had built on another room, but the main building was still logs, wattled with mud. Su had written to Ted, and Ted had authorised the employment of a farm manager, a youngish man with a wife and three small children. Despite their occupation, the place had changed remarkably little. Perhaps it might have been easier if he could have looked at the outside, traced the changes. The hurt was all in the mind, because you knew that if you walked up and opened the door the very air would be different, would repudiate the Neylers. It came home to him then that love and hate can run in harness, for he had hated Karl, yet loved him too. He wasn't so bad, the old man. He had mellowed with age, and his grimness had lessened. He had adored Wen, too, and his grandson.

As he walked away, down the hill towards the lake, it occurred to Mark that until he had returned to Otago Karl had, in a sense, not been dead to him at all; or no more dead than Toddy, Freda, Su. They had been away, that was all. It was only with his homecoming, and his visit to the Waihola homestead, that he was forced to acknowledge Karl was indeed dead. It would be a while, perhaps, before he was ready to meet the new manager and his wife.

Work on the Peninsula farm occupied him fully too, once

he and Toddy had got him into useful harness once more. Toddy had had ideas over the years which he had been unable to put into practice, lacking Mark to give him authority to do so. All he had done was to keep the place ticking over, the flocks in good heart, the crops bearing. He wanted to increase their beef herd. Beef was one of Scotland's most successful exports, he had heard, and he had also heard people say that the climate of the Peninsula was very similar to that of Scotland. Why not take advantage of the climate, then, and rear good beef stock?

Mark, grinning, said that it must rain a hell of a lot in Scotland and Toddy, also grinning, said he believed that to be true. As they spoke, the Peninsula was veiled in that light but persistent rain known to some as a Scotch mist.

Change must take place now that he was home, and Mark had a good deal of faith in Toddy's judgement. His own keen interest in farming reawoke as soon as he got back to his own place, and he and Toddy spent many comfortable evenings in the cottage, planning and dreaming.

He refused, however, to move back into the farmhouse. It did not seem like his home. He told Toddy and Freda that he felt like an intruder there, but this was not quite true. He felt like an intruder only in his old bedroom. Su had not used it, but had remained in the small room he had built on for her six years before, when she had first arrived at the farm to give Wen a helping hand when the baby was born. He remembered her so vividly, stick-thin and big-eyed, talking with the most appalling cockney accent and loving them, loving Johnny when he arrived, being just what they all wanted, only they had never known it until she was there. Su Yung, Wen's little Chinese cousin.

When he thought of her like that he knew a twinge of conscience over his present feelings for her, but he dismissed it briskly. She was no longer fifteen; she was a young woman and quite capable of either dismissing him or accepting him. Time alone would tell which she would do. And in the meantime, he did not wish to sleep in the big bedroom with the view of the harbour where all the most important things had happened to him and Wen. Their wedding night had been spent in that bed, Johnny had been born in it. One day, such memories would be sweet, but now because he was alone and uncertain still the sweetness was tinged with bitterness. It would take a lot of love to reconcile him to moving back into that room.

The day came when the ship carrying Su and Johnny was due to dock. He was restless and ill at ease all morning, shaving himself twice, cutting his chin quite severely so that he had to go out decorated with a sizable chunk of cotton wool, looking infuriatingly like a Santa Claus with a nasty attack of alopecia. He and Toddy left the farm, Toddy driving the trap. Sudden fear that they might not be on the ship after all, that he might not recognise them, that their attitude might be cold, impersonal, had assailed him, and he felt that with Toddy beside him he would be able to bear any or all of these things better. Of course, his thoughts, obediently saying 'they', really meant 'she'. Johnny was a child and as such his reactions worried Mark not at all. Su, on the other hand, was of an age to resent both his arbitrary leaving and his arbitrary reappearance. Even his cablegram might be resented! Who was he to demand their return, after all? He had listened to no one whilst he was in America, heeded nothing but his own wishes, his own fears. Was he to be paid out now?

They reached the harbour just as the ship was docking. There was a long line of tethered horses and carts, cabs and carriages, but Mark left that part to Toddy. Suddenly, he could not wait for the moment when he would see her, and he pushed his way to the quay, only to watch in agony as the gangplank was lowered. He saw her then, with her hand in the child's, standing as near the top of the gangway as she could get.

A whole new set of worries promptly reared their ugly heads. She was so young! His forty years lay on his shoulders like a ton weight. He could feel it dragging him down. How dared he aspire to her, who was so young and beautiful!

They joined him and he was seized with shyness, ruffling

the boy's hair perfunctorily, then staring at Su. She stood there, smiling, her dark eyes alight with amusement at his stupidity. But as their eyes met her gaze faltered, and she began to fuss the child, straightening his sailor collar, smoothing his thick hair.

He took her hand. It lay in his like a child's, the fine skin covering bones as fragile as a bird's. He felt clumsy, a great oaf, beside her. He saw that her long black hair had been tied into a knot on top of her small head, that she wore a dress with a skirt which was gathered on one side, reaching fullness at ankle level. There was a little cape round her shoulders, trimmed with fur.

'So you've come home at last!'

He had meant it to sound welcoming; with dismay, he heard his own gruff voice and knew it had sounded accusatory. Su knew it too. She stepped back, her colour rising, her hand sliding from his slackened grasp.

'I'm s-sorry. It was a misunderstanding, truly it was. If I'd known it was you, wild horses wouldn't have dragged me . . . Johnny away. He's longed to see his daddy, haven't you, Johnny?' Johnny continued to stare impassively towards Toddy and the pony cart. 'Did Toddy tell you how it happened? Your brother Ted kept writing, asking if he could have Johnny, to bring him up with his own children, and I was worried stiff – Johnny was my responsibility, yet what right had I to deny your brother? I shouldn't have gone, of course I shouldn't, but . . .'

'It doesn't matter.' Hang it, he had meant to sound understanding, not bored or impatient, yet he knew he must have sounded both. Desperately, he sought for something to say which could not be misunderstood, which might retrieve the magic he had dreamed about. He found it. 'Here comes Toddy!'

Toddy reached them and, without a word, bent down and picked Johnny up, holding him close to his weather-beaten face, beaming at the boy.

'Hi, Johnny, old sport! What did you think of the Aussies, eh? My, but you've grown! Did you see Ho John and Li? Were they well? Gee, you've sure done some livin', boy!'

Mark sensed the criticism in Toddy's action, and leaned over to take Johnny's hand as Toddy stood him down on the ground again.

'I'm sorry, Johnny. I'm afraid your dad isn't too used to children.' He squatted down so that he could look into the boy's face. He was a handsome lad, and big for six, and the smiles which Toddy's greeting had brought still lingered. But his eyes refused to meet Mark's. 'How are you, son?'

He thought Johnny's face flickered at the last word, and hoped he had at last said something right, albeit by accident. The word 'son' had been inadvertent.

'I'm all right.' Johnny still looked steadfastly down at his own stout boots and wrinkled stockings. He sounded sulky, but he might have been consumed with shyness. 'Where did you leave the trap, Toddy?'

Mark pointed it out and the small boy picked up his suitcase and staggered off, listing heavily to port. The three adults watched him go in silence for a moment before Toddy spoke.

'He's a grand lad. You're lucky, Mark. I wish he was mine. You'll be real proud of him once you get to know him.'

'I'm sure I shall, if he ever looks me in the eye,' Mark said a little resentfully. 'Damn it, the kid was two when I went, a charming, naughty baby. Now he's a proper boy, and if you ask me he's no keener to find himself saddled with a father than I . . .'

The words died on his lips, too truthful, too awful, to be contemplated. Toddy bent and picked up Su's suitcase and without another word the three of them made for the trap. Mark cast a haunted glance at the slim, upright figure walking beside him without so much as a word or a look in his direction. It had all gone wrong! It was plain that Su thought of him only as her cousin's husband and her own employer. She had had a crush on him once; Wen had teased him about it, said it was a fine thing when one's husband attracted fifteen-year-olds. Had she been right? Was it just a crush from which Su had recovered as one recovers from a head cold? Her letters had been so warm and friendly, so full of artless confidences, that he had allowed himself to believe otherwise. Of his own feelings there could be no doubt. He loved her and wanted to marry her. The thought of living at the farm and watching her marry someone else sent a shaft of pain through him.

In the trap, Johnny sat beside Toddy on the driver's seat and chattered ceaselessly. Behind them, Mark and Su exchanged only the most banal remarks and then fell silent. Miserably, Mark sought for subjects of conversation which would bring him back on his old friendly footing with Su, and could think of nothing. If he talked of America, she would think about the years he had left her to carry on alone, selfishly wrapped up in his own loss and sorrow. If he talked of their lives before he left for the States, she would think of him as Wen's husband, a father figure.

The result was, of course, that he sat beside her, stiff-faced, and endured the journey. She was wearing some sort of perfume, very faint, flowerlike; he remembered enough to know that it was different. Four years ago she had smelled of baby powder, soap, and peppermints, of which she had been inordinately fond. He cleared his throat.

'That perfume – what's it called?'

She turned to him, eagerly almost, probably as glad as he to end the too-long silence.

'I'm not sure. One of the boys bought it for my birthday last year.'

His discomfiture increased. Not once, in all the time he had been away, had he sent her so much as a birthday card. Nor had he remembered his son's anniversaries. Guilt swamped him. He turned his face to the sea and said nothing more. He hated himself.

For a month he remained in Freda's cottage, only visiting the farm at lunchtime, when as many of the hands as possible ate there. He avoided speaking to Su, because he was afraid that when he told her he could not spend the rest of his life in Freda's tiny spare bedroom she would announce that she was leaving. That, he thought, would be unbearable. As things stood, at least he saw her daily, watched her laugh with the hands, move about the kitchen serving the meal, bend over Johnny's books. And during that month, he took Freda's advice and tried to get to know Johnny.

'Mark, he's your son – Wen's son, if you like to look at it that way. Have you *no* feeling for him? No recollection of how you and Wen adored him?'

He could be truthful with Freda, whereas with anyone else he would have prevaricated.

'No, I haven't. My mind's muddled where the boy's concerned. He's changed, you see, so that I can't associate this big chap with the naughty, loving kid I left. He seems to belong to Su, and he doesn't like me one bit! I suppose I resent the time Su gives him, too. Teaching him lessons, taking him walks, riding out to see the Dodmans with him. He absorbs all her time and energy, you know. If I do happen to go over to the house, hoping for a word with Su, he appears. Just a pair of narrowed black eyes and a resentful mouth. No matter how politely I ask him to do something, what's more, he ignores me and turns to Su for her approval before he'll do it. I'll try, but I think I'm batting on a losing wicket.'

Freda chuckled.

'You wouldn't be the first to resent his own child, and I know Johnny doesn't help, but you must persevere! Take him for a walk one afternoon, just you and the boy. Don't let Su insist on accompanying you. Take him down to the beach, teach him how to fish, or row – something Su can't help with. You'll find he'll chatter away easily enough once you're by yourselves.'

'That's not a bad idea. I've had the feeling once or twice that it might be easier to get to know him without Su there. He feels a bit torn between us, perhaps.'

'Perhaps. And then why not take Su out somewhere one evening? You've got to get things sorted out between you. You'll have to move back into the farmhouse eventually, even if you have to get a maid of all work to move in as a sign of respectability. And why don't you ask her to marry you? All this talk of the age difference is bunkum, and you know it. She's a pretty girl and she's had plenty of offers, but she's turned them all down without a qualm. Toddy and I, we always had the feeling that she was waiting for someone, and why shouldn't it be you?'

'I'd love to ask her, but suppose it spoils even what we've got now?' Mark said miserably. 'Suppose she just goes?'

'And leaves Johnny? I don't think you need fear that! Now take my advice, there's a good fellow.'

He did. Despite some grumbling on Johnny's part, he took the boy into Dunedin and between them they selected and purchased a small sailing dinghy with a pair of oars. Johnny was not a successful actor, and it soon became obvious that he adored the boat and enjoyed his afternoon sailing lessons with Mark more than almost anything else he did. Mark, who had not sailed a boat himself for more years than he liked to admit, was pleased by his own skill as a teacher and soon extremely proud of Johnny. The boy was only six, after all, yet he handled the boat with confidence and competence; and, though his attitude to his father could be somewhat ambiguous, when they were sailing together they were the best of friends.

'And now,' Freda announced firmly, after she had seen Mark and Johnny returning from the beach, each talking as hard as the other, 'you must tackle Su. There's a play on in Dunedin tomorrow night. Ask her to go with you, and to have a meal afterwards. And even if you don't ask her to marry you, you might at least get on a friendly footing. I'm sure Su is as miserable as you are – she wants to be friends, if nothing more.'

'Suppose she won't come out with me?'

'Of course she will! Why shouldn't she? I tell you I'm sure she's as keen to get something sorted out as you are!'

It took the sort of courage that Mark was rather short on at the moment, but he forced himself to go through with it. He strolled over to the farmhouse that afternoon and walked into the kitchen, determined to ask her at least to go to the theatre with him.

She refused.

'I'm terribly sorry, Mark, but I can't leave Johnny alone all that time, especially in the evening. If it was an afternoon performance we could take him as well, but I don't think they do matinees.'

Johnny, sitting at the table devouring Bovril sandwiches, smirked, and Mark, sorely disappointed, lost his temper.

'If I'd wanted to take Johnny to the theatre I'd have invited him, not you! Very well, we'll forget it.'

He turned and slammed out of the house, and went straight across to the cottage, where Freda was peeling potatoes at the sink. He was so upset that he stuttered out his explanation.

'She w-won't come! She can't leave Johnny! That damned b-brat!'

Freda straightened, and dried her hands on a tea-towel.

'Less of that language, Mark, if you please. Here, finish them potatoes!'

With that she swept out of the house and returned ten minutes later, flushed with victory.

'You can call for her at six o'clock tomorrow evening. I'll take care of master Johnny!'

Mark, having finished the last potato, cast the knife down on the draining board and turned to hug Freda.

'You're marvellous! Of course I know she doesn't want to come and you bullied her into it, but I can't stand this uncertainty any longer.'

'Doesn't want to come? Nonsense! She's as mixed up as you, that's the trouble. She's convinced herself that you still think of her as Johnny's nanny and nothing more. I told her that even if you do think that (and it's up to you, Mark, to convince her that she's wrong about it!) you would still expect her to have some time to herself. You left Johnny for them other lads, I told her, pretty severely. If you won't leave him for Mark, then what's he to think? That took her aback, I can tell you. "Oh, I'll go then. Tell him I'd love it," she says, quick as a flash.' Freda tutted, regarding him with mock severity. 'You two! I'll be glad when this charade is over, I tell you straight!'

He called for Su the following evening, sharp on six

o'clock. Su was ready, and looking splendid in a dark blue silk skirt and jacket, the skirt fashionably gathered at one side, the jacket tight fitting, with a low V neck which ended in a large butterfly bow just below the breasts. A white blouse with a heavy lace jabot, and a blue silk hat with a plume of ostrich feathers which curled around her face, completed the ensemble.

'You look so pretty,' Mark said spontaneously, and was rewarded by her flush and the gratified little smile which curved her lips. 'I wish the trap was a bit smarter!'

Beneath the brim of the hat dark eyes sparkled at him with delicious coquetry.

'You look pretty good yourself. Once we're on the road, though, I'm going to take my hat off! The feather tickles. But I'll put it on as soon as we reach the outskirts of Dunedin.'

'Good enough. Then you won't mind if I do the same with my tie?'

For the first time since her return, they were at ease together, and when he drew the reins in a sheltered part of the road where it ran between trees, and suggested that they might talk since they would arrive at the theatre very early otherwise, she agreed peacefully. He looked into her calm face and knew that, in some mysterious, womanly way, she had made up her mind about him, about their relationship. He realised too that she might have decided to reject him, yet it no longer frightened him. If she had made such a decision then it would be up to him to change her mind, for her resolve could not be stronger than his!

He drew the trap right on to the verge, then loosed the pony's head so that she might crop the grass, keeping the reins over her back so that she did not get entangled in them. Then he turned to face Su, and smiled. He had prepared a beautiful speech about responsibility and the boy, the farm, the fact that Su had not yet met a man she liked well enough to marry, all working up to a peroration which was to be his own proposal. He spoke not one word of it. Instead, he took her face between his hands, seeing the lean palms and the long, tanned fingers curved round her heart-shaped countenance.

'I love you.'

He half whispered it, and knew that he was right, that the best way is always the straight way, in the end. Love was what it amounted to; all the other things, responsibility, convention, even his proposal of marriage, were only important because he loved her.

'I love you too.'

An hour before he would not have believed she could say such a thing. Now, he simply lowered his head and kissed her lips.

What followed was inevitable. Lovers' talk, sometimes happy, sometimes wistful, boring to everyone save the lovers themselves. They laughed at each other's diffidence, at the many ways they had planned to gain the other's love, then discussed their life to come.

It was nearly midnight before it occurred to either of them that they had missed the play, left it too late to get a meal, and were, in fact, ravenously hungry.

'Never mind!' Su snuggled close to him, tucked in against his dark suit jacket, blissfully happy. 'I'll make you something nice if you come back to the farmhouse with me.'

'I'll accept that kind invitation, ma'am, though it seems pretty shabby of me. I was supposed to be entertaining you, not vice versa.'

'There'll be other times. Oh, Mark!'

He squeezed her small waist.

'Oh, Su!'

Presently, they drove into the farmyard. The cottage was in darkness but a light burned in the farmhouse window. Mark got down, then held up his arms to Su.

'Down you come. You can go in and cook me a meal whilst I rub the pony down and put the trap away. How about a beer, too? I'm pretty thirsty.'

'All right, though I could rub the pony down; I'm a farmer too, you know.'

He smiled at her, then pointed to her suit.

'Not in those clothes! Where's your hat?'

The hat had been carefully placed on the seat between

them some six hours earlier. Now, one look at it was enough. It would never be the same again.

'Goodness, that hat cost me a week's wages,' Su exclaimed. 'How furious Freda will be! She thought it a great extravagance and scolded me soundly for buying it. And the suit, of course.'

'What did you buy it for?' Mark asked, leading the pony into the stable and pretending not to notice that Su was following him. 'It's almost as beautiful as you are!'

'For this evening.' She smiled naughtily at him. 'I thought if I looked very grown up and stylish you might treat me less as a little girl and more as a woman!'

He was incredulous.

'Never! When could you have bought it?'

'I cadged a lift from Joe the minute Freda said she'd sit with Johnny. Joe went into town for more cattle cake. I didn't tell Freda how much it cost. She guessed it was expensive, and she barely had time to denounce me for a spendthrift before you arrived to pick me up. And now she'll have to admit that it was money well spent, since it was Su in the suit you asked to marry you, and not the ordinary Su.'

He was rubbing down the little mare, but he turned at that, raising his eyebrows at her in the light of the lamp he had lit in the stall.

'Who's jumping to conclusions? I don't remember actually asking you to marry me at all! I just took it for granted that you would!'

She put a hand, cool and small, on the back of his neck.

'True. Ask me now.'

He finished the pony, stood back, then took her in his arms. He rested his chin on the smooth crown of her hair.

'Will you marry me, Su, and make me the happiest man on earth, etcetera, etcetera? I don't care now that you're just a baby, and that I'm far too . . .'

'So you're back at last.' Toddy's would-be accusatory tone could not mask a certain satisfaction in his voice, nor the scowl on his face hide the gleam in his eyes. 'I'll finish off here, Mark. You go on in. Did you have a good evening? Where did you go for a meal?'

'We didn't actually eat,' Mark said guiltily. 'But Su's going to cook me something now. I'm afraid I'll be a bit late in, but I'll come quietly and won't slam anything.' He still had his arms round Su, and now he turned her so that they both faced Toddy. 'Are you going to congratulate us?'

'What for? For taking leave of your senses? Keeping the poor lass out till this hour and not feeding her!'

'We're going to get married.'

Toddy walked around the pony, checking that Mark had finished with her, then doused the lantern and walked out of the stable.

'I knew that! It took you enough time, the pair of you, to come to your senses and realise what everyone else has known this past month! A fool could tell you were plumb crazy for each other. Tell Freda to bring some grub with her when she comes to the cottage. She's made you a late supper.'

They were left, standing in the stable doorway, staring open-mouthed at each other as Toddy stumped towards his cottage.

5

It was a fine Saturday morning, and the children were in the tree-house. Strictly speaking, it was several tree-houses in two trees, the first a yew and the second a great tall chestnut in whose lofty branches only the older children were allowed to perch. The yew had stout platforms on three of its boughs, and the boughs themselves were so close that climbing it was like climbing the stairs.

The top platform in the chestnut tree needed considerable agility and nerve to reach, and was reserved for Desmond, Frank and Bertram – not that they ever succeeded in keeping Mabel and Conrad from climbing up there whenever the fancy took them. Indeed Mabs, in her black stockings and black button boots, with her skirts tucked shamelessly into her bloomers, could climb like a monkey and was totally fearless. Neither Desmond nor Frank could forget the day they had been playing tennis when the ball, walloped by Desmond and sped on its way by a fair gale, had disappeared through the trees and into next door's orchard. Mabel, watching, had galloped to the chestnut tree and ascended it with almost shocking ease, not even bothering to discipline her skirts, so that the wind, billowing them out like a balloon, did its utmost to pluck her from her perch. The boys had watched, terrified, as the great trunk swayed and the branches whipped to and fro, but Mabel slid down to the ground and trotted over to them, remarking placidly that the ball was clearly visible from the upper platform, and telling them precisely where to find it.

The boy who will admit himself worsted at tree-climbing by a small girl has yet to be born, however, so Desmond and Frank thanked Mabel casually and went to fetch their tennis ball. They were careful, after that, never to enter into competition with such a superb tree-scaler!

But on this particular Saturday there was no wind and, though the colours of the leaves proved that summer was limping to its close and autumn would not be long arriving, it was still a glorious day. The four youngest children were playing at tea parties in the yew tree; from his loftier perch Frank could see the little pink china cups and saucers and the little woven baskets containing food, either real or make-believe, set out in the centre of the platform.

'When'll the Sollies be here, Frank?'

Desmond, his eyes half closed, was gazing out through the leaves in the direction of a distant boarding school's grounds. He had recently discovered that from this particular spot he could watch the boarders as they strolled in their garden, or played tennis, and it was a favourite pastime now to climb up here with a pair of binoculars and watch. Frank disapproved of this new craze and sincerely hoped that his own fourteenth birthday would not bring a sudden preoccupation with anything as soppy as girls!

'It's Saturday, you loon. They won't be here until after luncheon.'

'Of course. Damnation! Well, where's Mabel, then?'

Frank had a grubby piece of string round his hands and was trying to work out a new form of cat's cradle. He shot a quick, sly look at Desmond through his lashes. He only hoped his brother did not count Mabs as a girl. She was his, Frank's, friend and companion. He had no desire for Desmond, who thought her a silly kid, to suddenly decide she was worth his attention!

'Probably caught in the kitchen, peeling spuds or stringing beans or something. You know how Ruthie grabs her. It isn't fair, really. It isn't as if she's paid to help.'

'I daresay she's quite glad of the chance to nick buns and that. Anyway, she helps Mrs Walters, doesn't she?'

'I know. But it isn't as if Mrs Walters gets off early or something because Mabs helps her. She just gets through twice as much work!'

'Mm hmm.' Desmond flung himself back suddenly on the platform, abandoning his vigilance. 'I forgot, on a Saturday the girls go home, or most of 'em. It's a dratted weekly boarding school!'

'You weren't watching those daft hens?' Frank sighed disapprovingly. 'I wonder why they go back to school a week before we do?'

'Because we're term boarders, not weekly. We'd probably *starve* if our terms were as long as theirs. One of those girls is quite pretty, though. Lovely legs.'

'Don't be so bloody stupid,' Frank said sharply, resorting to term boarder's language. 'I'm going to fetch Mabel. She doesn't keep on!'

Desmond rolled on to his stomach.

'Don't bother. I'll go.'

Before Frank could gather his wits – or free his hands from the over-intricate cat's cradle – his brother was disappearing down through the leaves. Frank, left behind, sat down and felt resentful and uneasy. Why Mabel? She was three whole years younger than Desmond, and not a bit grown up for her age. A vague, formless worry began to nag at his mind. Mabel was *his* friend! Desmond had better leave her alone!

In the absence of a companion, Frank decided he might as well climb down. He supposed he could go along to the kitchen as well as Desmond, and then they could both escort Mabel to the tree.

He had barely reached ground level, however, before Mabel and Desmond came into the clearing, Desmond carrying an enamel jug and Mabel a string bag full of iced buns.

'It's our elevenses; Ruthie said we might as well have it out here as it's such a nice day. The littles must go to the conservatory, though.'

Elevenses were always served in the conservatory on sunny days. Drinks of milk, iced buns and apples or bananas were handed out indiscriminately to anyone who happened to be playing, so that Mabel got her share and even daft 'Arry, the gardener's boy, if Ruthie happened to be in a good mood. Luncheon, on a Saturday, meant that Desmond and Frank ate with their parents, a doubtful privilege, though the food was always much better than nursery fare. Best manners as well as best clothes must be donned, however, and usually conversation was confined to the older members of the company.

The littles, hearing that elevenses were being served, promptly deserted their 'house' and made off towards the conservatory, only Stella glancing back, rather wistfully, before diving into the wood.

'Ruthie forgot mugs for the milk, but Mabel says if we go back she'll change her mind about letting us stay here. We'll drink from the jug. You first, Mabel.'

Mabel tilted the jug and solemnly drank. Her dark eyes were lowered, looking into the jug, and her remarkably thick black lashes lay on her cheeks. Her pinafore was stained with one or two tiny pinkish marks and the hem of her blue gingham dress dusty and too short, so that her petticoat dipped into view. Her hair was done in a long, thick braid this morning, and seeing her in profile as he moved towards her to take the jug Frank was reminded of Red Indian maidens in books, with their remote, stern little faces and their high cheekbones.

'Hurry up, Frank!' Desmond jerked his brother's elbow and took the jug from him, hastily gulping down the remaining milk. 'Now let's go back up the tree for a bit. We can eat the buns and watch the world go by.'

'Watch the boarders, you mean,' grumbled Frank. 'Let's not climb right to the top for the buns. We'll only have to climb down again to take the jug back.'

Rather to his surprise, Desmond agreed without demur and the three of them stretched out on the lowest platform, a mere eight feet or so from the ground. They lay on their stomachs, eating the buns and arguing softly what they should do next. Frank wanted to give his rabbits a run on the side lawn before luncheon, Desmond wanted to play hide and seek, which made both Frank and Mabel stare, and Mabel herself wanted to dam the stream.

They were just growing heated when the sound of someone pushing through the undergrowth brought instant silence. They lay very still, hearts beating. No grown-up, except for Walters the gardener and daft 'Arry, knew about the platforms in the chestnut tree. They knew that somewhere in the wood the children had a tree-house in a yew – a lovely safe place for them to play. They had no idea that platforms had been built in the great chestnut tree and the children had no intention of letting anyone find out. They craned their necks to see through the screen of leaves into the clearing. It was far too soon for the little ones to be returning after their elevenses, and Walters or daft 'Arry would come along the path, not push through the woodland. They were astonished when Nanny Sutton emerged from the trees, then turned to someone behind her.

'It's all right, Louis, there's no one here. The kids have all gone in for elevenses, and if we stay here and someone calls I can say I was looking for them.'

The children exchanged startled glances as Louis followed Nanny into the clearing, put his arms about her, and began to kiss her with a fervour which shocked Mabel and Frank into an involuntary glance at each other. But presently Louis led Nanny over to the lowest platform in the yew and they sat down upon it. It was sturdy and well built, and scarcely creaked as Louis dragged Nanny Sutton across his knees and into a reclining position in his arms.

'How long'll the kids be gone? I don't fancy any interruption for the next few minutes.'

'Twenty minutes or so. Longer, if Millie gets in a flap with the iced buns. Which she will, because she's very partial to them herself and tries to keep a couple back.'

Louis laughed deep in his throat and began to kiss Nanny again whilst the three watchers exchanged glances. They loved Louis, but what on earth was he doing here, kissing Nanny? Everyone knew he was going out with Sarah Kelpmann and all the grown-ups were as pleased as if he had done something rather clever. When Louis kissed the side of Sarah's neck or turned her hand over to kiss the palm, their mother gave a little smile and Grandpa beamed so widely that one felt he would presently begin to applaud. The children had accepted that Louis was doing the right thing in kissing Sarah. But kissing Nanny Sutton?

As they watched, however, Frank realised that this was going further than mere kisses. To his horror, his charming, respectable uncle began to unbutton the front of Nanny's dress and, having opened it out, plunged his hand inside, convulsively squeezing some part of Nanny and causing her to give a moan of pain. Frank hissed in his breath, then saw that Nanny was not attempting to stop Uncle Louis; on the contrary, she was giving him every help and encouragement in a number of things, all of them unlikely and wicked, which Uncle Louis promptly began to do.

Frank looked at Mabel. She was watching without expression, her face once again reminding him of a Red Indian, so impassive was she. He glanced at Desmond and quickly away. Then he reached out and shook Mabs's arm and nudged his brother. This was the perfect moment to escape unseen, whilst the couple on the platform were so engrossed in what they were doing.

Frank sneaked, on his knees, to the back of the platform and then dropped to the ground. His feet thudded against the leaf mould, but he knew he would be safe enough. Mabel, following, landed more lightly still, and Frank stood for a moment, looking up at the platform edge, waiting for Desmond.

Mabel jerked at his sleeve, rolled her eyes upwards and then shook her head. He got the message that Desmond would not be following and took Mabel's hand, leading her the quickest way out of the wood.

They crossed the kitchen garden and walked quickly through another belt of trees and down to the stream. Some day, Mother threatened, she and Walters would turn the stream from its present bed so that it could run through the garden proper and not just through the wood where no one could see it. The children sincerely hoped that it would be as expensive and arduous an undertaking as Pa protested. They loved the stream, with the tall beech trees growing beside it and its deep, fern-fringed banks. Frank broke their companionable silence.

'That was Uncle Louis and Nanny!'

Mabel slanted an enigmatic look at him.

'Yes, I know.'

Without having to consult one another, they sat down on the bank to remove their shoes and stockings. Then, with the shoes laced together and dangling round their necks with the stockings stuffed into them, they began to paddle downstream to where the water would dive under the cart-track which bounded the property just there, and emerge in the meadow on the other side.

'But Mabs, he's going out with Sarah! Why was he kissing Nanny? And squeezing her?'

Mabel shrugged and kicked up a foot, sending a shower of sparkling drops ahead of her.

'My mum says your Uncle Louis's a devil for the women. Perhaps that's what it means – that they kiss more than one.'

'Well, if that's so . . .' He hesitated, then turned to another subject, or at least another facet of the same subject. 'Why wouldn't Des come away when we did? He's changed, you know, Mabs. It was just the sort of thing he would do now, stay and stare; I suppose he thinks Nanny's a girl!'

'I know what you mean, Frank. I been thinking of getting that girl who's in my school to come up here, before you go back to school, specially for Des. Do you 'member me telling you about Suzie Canning?'

'No . . . oh, yes! You don't mean . . . '

'I do, then.' Mabel nodded solemnly. 'She and Des would get along fine.'

Frank was silent, digesting this information. Mabel had told him about Suzie when he first came back from school – how Suzie was turning into a 'real nasty creature' because she sold 'looks' for a farthing, 'touches' for a halfpenny, and 'feels' for a penny. He had been mystified until Mabel had explained, and then both disgusted and fascinated. Familiar with the anatomy of small sisters, he felt, first, that money so spent was money wasted, and secondly, when Mabel had told him about the enthusiastic response evoked amongst the boys, that in some way Suzie was preying upon ignorance and that, when the payers had seen – or touched – or felt – what she had to offer, their fury at the deception would be very great.

Mabel had speedily disabused him.

'She sits in her grandma's outside privy, holidays Monday Wednesday and Friday, from nine until ten in the morning,' Mabel assured him. 'School times, it's four until five in the afternoons. And there's always a queue; some of the lads go back twice in the same day! I tell you, she's making a mint!'

Now, remembering this, he felt he must question Mabel further.

'You think *Des* would give her farthings? Honest?'

Mabel grinned. She had a delightful grin, a three-cornered smile which dispelled all the impassivity from her small face and made her look twinklingly alive.

'Farthings? He'd give her pennies! I daren't walk past him in the house if there's no one around.' She adopted a recognisable imitation of Desmond's voice. 'Mabs, why don't we go for a stroll in the wood one evening?' She returned to her own tones. 'And he's forever pinching my bottom and rubbing up against me.'

'Well, I knew he'd got a thing about girls, but you! You're only a kid! Younger than me, even. Now if it was . . .'

Mabel interrupted him.

'It will be. He'll start mucking about with girls like Suzie, and then it'll be kitchen maids, and then bigger girls – he won't ever be with us again. Not proper.'

'You're right. I didn't know how bad he was, but I do see that you're right.' He shot a suspicious glance at Mabel. 'Why are you laughing?'

'You make growing up sound like measles! And then I thought what your Uncle Louis'd say if he knew we'd seen. And Nanny Sutton, who tells us off and scolds, lying there with her chest all open and groaning and carrying on!'

Frank laughed too.

'I suppose it *is* funny, in a way. But . . . well, I'll be fourteen in nine months! Will I get like Des?'

Mabel's sharp gaze softened as she took in Frank from head to foot.

'You won't be horrible with it, like Des is. You'll be grand, Frank, when you grow up.' She patted his hand. 'Are the Sollies coming after luncheon? What'll we do?'

'Yes, they'll be here. We'll build the submarine, I expect.'

Some time ago the children's imaginations had been fired by undersea warfare, and they had begun, using as the main part the body of an ancient carriage found in the loft, to build themselves a play-submarine. Up in the dim and dusty loft they had played some memorable games in their sub, but it had recently been borne in upon them that they would soon need another. Warfare was best if there was an enemy, for one thing, and the rapid growth of Stella and David and the fact that they constantly besieged their elders for a place in the *Waterspout,* as the submarine had been christened, made it clear that if war was to be waged in peace a second craft must be built.

They had received with cries of joy a number of tea-chests from Uncle Louis and had borrowed tools and advice from Mr Walters. But the second submarine still needed a good deal of work to make it playable.

'I'll bring some food, if I can,' Mabel said magnanimously. It did not seem strange to her that she, very much the poor relation of the crew, should be the only one capable of nicking food. Nursery meals were not easy to purloin, and Ruthie did not encourage the children of the house to wander around her kitchen. Mabel, on the other hand, constantly working there, had many and various opportunities of slipping food into her pockets, to say nothing of the fact that Ruthie would often show her appreciation of Mabel's hard work by slipping her a bag of buttered scones or a basket of fruit 'for the crew'.

'That'd be spiffing. Here's Des at last!'

Desmond strolled through the trees, sat down on the bank and shed his shoes and socks. His cheeks were flushed and his eyes very bright.

'Paddling? I don't blame you. It's hot enough!'

He said nothing of the scene he had left and neither did Frank or Mabel. They talked of the submarines, and the Sollies. Safe, childhood topics.

'More pie, Louis?'

Tina presided over the luncheon table, slipping the wide silver pie-slice beneath the next wedge of plum pie and handing it across the table to Louis, then catching Ted's eye so that the small silver cream jug was also nudged in her brother's direction. She did not offer more pie to the boys, for she was sure that such rich food could not be good for young digestions. Ruthie should have provided a nice rice pudding, or caramel custards perhaps, but she had probably forgotten that the boys lunched with the grown-ups today.

Louis poured cream over his pie and dug his spoon into

the golden pastry.

'Ruthie makes a superb plum pie, as good as Alice's,' he remarked. 'Don't make me feel greedy, boys. Have some more!'

Frank and Desmond, who had been watching him with unusual intensity, blushed and disclaimed any interest in the plum pie. Tina put in a few words about the inadvisability of the young being encouraged to eat hot pastry and cold cream in the middle of the day.

'Oh, rubbish,' Louis said blandly, keeping his eyes on his plate so that he would not see the small figure stiffen with annoyance over her baby brother's words. 'Look at the stuff you used to guzzle when we were children! Pickled onions, and salami, and . . .'

'Really, Louis, if you're in a mood to reminisce . . . '

'Touché, little sister!' Louis's more recent past was not a subject upon which he wished to hear his sister's opinion. 'I'm sorry, boys, I cannot influence your mama into giving you any more pie!'

'Influence! Well, well, the less said the better, perhaps.' Tina smiled a trifle maliciously at Louis. 'And what have you been doing today? Dancing attendance upon Sarah?'

Louis found himself the object once more of two pairs of blue eyes, trained on his countenance like machine guns. Whatever was the matter with his nephews today? But his limpid gaze fixed itself on Tina's face, supremely innocent.

'That's why I didn't get here until one o'clock. I had to meet Sarah. I've arranged to take her for a run this afternoon in Poppa's motor. We'll go over to the Horning Ferry for tea. After that we'll hire a boat, I daresay, and I'll row her up the river. Very romantic, don't you think?'

Frank and Desmond exchanged glances. Louis had been at The Pride at eleven o'clock, not dancing attendance upon Sarah but kissing and cuddling Nanny!

'You met Sarah this morning? Oh, Louis, you should have invited her here to luncheon,' Tina said at once. 'She would have been very welcome – she's such a charming girl. I do believe she's having a good influence on you as well. You haven't been nearly so . . . well, so wild, dear, since you took up with Sarah.'

'I couldn't. She had a luncheon engagement,' Louis explained. 'But I'll take her home to dine with Poppa, I expect.'

He sounded a trifle resigned.

'I don't know where you get your energy from,' Ted remarked. 'Taking Sarah rowing, on a warm afternoon like this!' He smiled at his brother-in-law. 'I'll have the last piece of that pie, please, my love. That's about all I'm capable of on such a day!'

It was fortunate that, at the moment he had remarked on Louis's energy, he had not been watching his eldest son's face. It was a study.

'I wouldn't be so energetic if I'd not had a quiet morning,' Louis began, 'but . . .'

Desmond, catching Frank's eye, suddenly gave a most awful snort which he tried, without success, to turn into a cough. He choked and spluttered, turning scarlet, and Frank, banging his brother on the back, began to snigger beneath his breath. Louis looked at them, then quickly away. Tina, leaning across the table, smacked Desmond's hand sharply.

'Des, what on earth's the matter? You'd better both leave the table and apologise to Uncle Louis for this behaviour when you're calmer.' She turned to Louis. 'Thank goodness you *didn't* bring Sarah back to luncheon, if the boys are going to behave like hyenas!'

With Frank and Desmond gone, Louis was able to finish his plum pie in peace. Remembering his own youth, he could only sympathise with their abrupt fall from grace. How often had the giggles caught him at the most inappropriate moments! They were nice kids, though, Tina's boys!

'Did you hear Uncle Louis? What a whopper, a quiet morning! And he said he didn't get here until one o'clock!'

The two boys stood in their bedroom, still pink-faced from their recent attack of untimely mirth. Desmond began to remove his collar and best tie, shaking his head reprovingly at Frank.

'Our uncle is without doubt a terrible liar. But I don't blame him for not telling Mama what he had been doing. You should have waited, Frank, I can tell you!'

He proceeded to give Frank every detail of the passionate scene which had been enacted below his perch. Frank, striving to follow a story which sounded anatomically impossible as well as dreadfully sinful, comforted himself with the thought that Des must be exaggerating. Must he not? Yet he was uneasy. The recollection of his uncle's hand plunging into Nanny's bodice, the convulsive closing of that hand, the groan which had been wrenched from Nanny's lips, made him realise that he did not really understand grown-ups at all.

He was spared having to comment on Desmond's tale, however, by the thump of feet in the corridor outside, closely followed by the bursting open of the door. Con stood there, hair on end, monkey-face wreathed in grins.

'Are we late? Sorry. It was the porridge. Here comes Bertram.'

Bertram, smooth and unruffled as ever, stalked past Conrad and greeted his cousins.

'Hello, chaps. Sorry we're late. It was the porridge.'

Frank, wrenching off his suit in favour of play clothes, turned to stare.

'Still? Con, you're a rum 'un.'

Con grinned deprecatingly.

'If you could have seen it this luncheon, you would have thought me mad. It had whiskers growing on it, and no end of mould. But it's been awful at home. Mama cries at every meal and Papa storms and then goes all icy. And today our Nellie started bawling when she put the dish on the table. So I ate it.'

'You never! With the whiskers and the mould? *Why*, Con, when you've held out for ten days? You weren't starving, were you?'

Con shook his head, his grin never faltering.

'Of course I wasn't starving, you oaf! Bertie got me food, and Cook kept slipping me bits and pieces. Mama insisted that I had milk and biscuits to make up for no breakfast or luncheon, and I had a proper meal at night. No, I changed tactics when I realised that Papa didn't actually want me to eat it, he just wanted me to give in. And the women wailing . . . well, it got a bit much.'

'So you did give in, in the end! Oh, well, you did pretty well for a kid, Con.'

That was Desmond, patronising as ever. But he had reckoned without Bertram.

'You don't understand, Des! He ate it *all*, every scrap! Mama wept and tried to snatch it away from him, Papa kept saying, "That'll do, Conrad. Now I've proved my point you may leave the rest," and Nellie wailed, "It'll kill 'im, Mr Solstein, it'll kill the boy!" It was a triumph, I tell you. And when Con had eaten the last little smear, he pushed the empty plate away from him and said . . .' Bertram, the grave, the sensible, was suddenly convulsed with mirth. He could not go on with the story, so Conrad took it up.

'I said it was the only decent porridge I'd ever tasted, and if they wanted me to eat porridge in the mornings they must always serve it with whiskers and mould. And Nellie started to giggle, and Mama clapped her hand across her mouth and she was laughing and crying at the same time, and then Bertie and I went off. Only Papa didn't even smile.'

Frank could imagine his Uncle Abe's ugly, self-righteous face, set in disapproval, furious because he had suddenly realised he had lost the battle he thought won.

'I just hope they don't take you seriously, Con, and offer you porridge with whiskers every morning!'

Bertram wiped his streaming eyes on a clean pocket handkerchief and pulled himself together.

'Don't worry. They won't do that. Con was s-sick all over that turkey carpet in Papa's study! Oh, you should have seen . . .' and he was off again, his face turning scarlet.

Presently, when they were sober once more, they set off for the stables and the submarines, Frank eyeing his cousin Con with considerable respect. To have the nerve to stand out against his father, and then to have the nerve to eat cold ten-day-old porridge! Frank had always been a bit scared of Uncle Abe and thought him a stern and unsympathetic father to his two sons. So different from their own dear Pa, who adored and spoilt them all indiscriminately.

'Wait until Uncle Louis hears,' Frank said, as they climbed into the loft. 'He and Mama have talked over the porridge story, wondering how it would end. They won't dare say so to you, but I bet they're pleased, Con.'

Desmond, starting to take a tea-chest to pieces with Walters's big claw-hammer, looked up at the mention of their uncle.

'Have you told them about Uncle Lou and . . .'

'No! Des, you mustn't! Really, we shouldn't have been there. It was spying, and eavesdropping, and all sorts.'

'It doesn't matter, then,' small Con said placidly. He picked up a piece of tea-chest, fitted it into place, and began to push tacks through it. 'I like Uncle Louis. He lightens my life.'

Frank grinned at this, but he saw Bertram and Desmond exchange a glance, and then the two of them disappeared down into the stables, with a furtive air which made him turn apologetically to Conrad.

'Des is taking Bertie down to tell. But you won't say anything to the others?'

'Of course not.'

At the end of Frank's conscientious recital, however, Con squatted back on his heels and frowned at Frank.

'Well, I know Uncle Louis kisses people. I thought you and Des knew as well. We were at Grandpa's once and Uncle Lou caught Nellie in the downstairs cloakroom and pinched her bottom. She let out such a squeak that I ran in, thinking it was Stella messing about – we were playing hide and seek. And there was our Nellie, pushed right into the coats and things, with Uncle Lou sort of leaning on her, and Nellie's skirt up round her waist, most peculiar! So I said: "What are you doing to Nellie, Uncle Lou?" and he said a mouse had run up Nellie's skirt and he was trying to catch it.' Con snorted. 'It sounded silly, but Nellie's face was so red, and Uncle Lou wouldn't turn round and talk; he just sort of spoke over his shoulder. So I went away. But in the carriage going home I asked Nellie what Uncle Lou had really been doing – it was just Nell and me, because it was the time Bertie and I had measles, only I got better first – and she said Uncle Louis was a right varmint and he'd pinched her bottom, and that was why she'd squealed out. And not to tell, if I pleased, because she would get into trouble if my mama thought her flighty.'

Con ran out of breath and beamed triumphantly at Frank.

'Well I never!' Frank's astonishment was genuine, for he had always thought the Solsteins' Nellie the height of respectability. But now that he considered the matter, he realised that she was no older than Nanny Sutton and every bit as pretty. 'And there's something else I meant to ask you about, Con.'

He told Conrad, without going into too much detail, that Desmond had started some bottom-pinching on his own account, with Mabel as his victim.

'She doesn't like it at all,' he finished impressively. 'I ought to say something to Des, only he *is* the older, and he may just say something smart.'

'You tell him to leave our Mabs alone,' Con said fiercely. 'If he wants a stupid girl, let him find a stupid one, not our Mabs.'

But in the event it proved far less embarrassing to tackle Desmond than Frank had anticipated. He stumbled and muttered his way through a couple of short sentences before Desmond, far from denying it all or pretending to be offended, simply said: 'Oh, you needn't worry about that stupid kid. She's only a child! Now that I've seen what I saw this morning I shan't bother Mabel again. No fear!'

'Then who will you bother?' asked Frank, expecting to hear the name of the High School boarder with the lovely legs, or a sister of one of Desmond's friends. Instead, Desmond gave him the benefit of his most superior look.

'Nanny, of course!'

Frank stared at him, round-eyed, for a moment, then

laughed scornfully.

'Oh, yes, I can just see Nanny going for a walk with you in the woods, or letting you pinch her bottom in the laundry-room! She'd give you a clip that'd send you into Suffolk!'

But Desmond neither rushed at him nor grew hot and flushed as he so often did when he was laughed at or disagreed with.

'Don't forget what I saw, baby Frank! And what I could describe in every detail to Mama. Nanny likes working for us, I've heard her saying so. And no wonder, with Uncle Louis . . .'

'Des! You wouldn't! Tell, I mean.'

'I shan't have to,' Desmond said cryptically. 'I'll play you at chess, if you like.'

And when he lost, he only smiled, patted Frank's head in a manner which seemed more consoling than congratulatory, and left the room, humming a sprightly tune.

Frank put the chess pieces away thoughtfully. Desmond had taken a big step away from him today, but they were returning to school in a week; then he would just be old Des again. Neyler Major. Until Christmas.

6: 1912

'Of course I'd love a party! But you said a combined party, for us and for Johnny. What did you *mean*?' Su, enveloped in an outsize apron, was baking bread. Mark laughed, and crossed the kitchen to kiss the tip of her nose.

'That smells good. I hope it's one of those milk loaves! I went into Dunedin earlier in the week, and whilst I was there I had an interview with the headmaster of the boys' school. I've arranged for Johnny to start there as soon as the school holidays are over.'

'Mark!'

'He's running wild here, love. You do your best, but he's ten now and needs more work than we can give him, and he's dropping behind boys of his own age. Where is he now, by the way?'

Su turned back to her baking board, but her shoulders drooped.

'Rabbiting. With Sam, in the high pasture. Why?'

'Well, there's a good reason for sending him to school! There's no one his own age to play with, so he hangs about with Sam, who's thick as porridge and as cunning as a weasel. *And* nearly three years older than Johnny.'

'Boarding school.' Su tried to assimilate the idea. Not to see Johnny every day, not to read to him at bedtime every night. Not to set his schoolwork, not to cook his meals or darn his socks. Not to see him coming into the house after spending an afternoon rabbiting with his friend Sam, dirty, tired, happy as Larry! 'Oh, Mark, I'll miss him terribly! I don't think I can bear it!'

Mark had been watching her face, his eyes full of concern for her, and now he took her in his arms, swaying her gently from side to side.

'It's for his good, darling! I know what you were thinking, you were thinking about the good times. But think deeper, my love!'

She obeyed, wrinkling her forehead. Other things. Johnny's truancy, the times he ran off and just did not bother to return until he was ready, careless of the anxiety he caused. His obstinacy which meant that sometimes he hurt himself, either physically or mentally, refusing to listen to advice. His increasing dissatisfaction with her teaching, his grumbles that the work was either dull or 'babyish'. His eagerness to play with other boys, and the diffidence he was beginning to show in the company of his peers.

'I do see what you mean, I suppose. But have you told Johnny? What does he think?'

'When I first sounded him out he was furious, and said he'd run away,' Mark admitted cheerfully. 'But when I told him that behaving like that simply proved how badly he needed the discipline of a decent school he took me a bit more seriously. He tried bursting into tears and when that didn't work he tried to punch me on the nose. Unsuccessfully, I might add. He's getting quite interested in the idea. I think he'll stick to it and end up enjoying it, once he's made some friends.'

'Well, I suppose you're right, and he needs school. But I've been so careful these past years never to make him feel an outsider, or unwanted. I'd hate him to feel that.'

'I know. In a way, it's a bad time to send him away, when he's becoming difficult and a bit headstrong, but we didn't do it a couple of years ago because you couldn't bear it, and I won't see the boy ruined by either of us. Darling, you fret over him like a mother hen, you know you do!'

'What does Freda think?'

He sighed and kissed her, then pinched one of the hot scones standing on the table and bit into it.

'I haven't asked her. How could I, when you didn't know? But I did tell Toddy, and he's all for it. Especially when I explained that he'd only be a weekly boarder, and come home every Friday night until Monday morning.'

He watched Su's transparent face light with relief, and congratulated himself upon his acumen. He had deliberately let her believe that Johnny would be a termly boarder, knowing how much less terrible, by comparison, weekly boarding would seem.

'Home every weekend! Gracious, that's nothing! He'll enjoy it, and he'll have every weekend to play on the farm and boss us about. Oh, Mark, you're the most wonderful, clever, darling man!'

'Tell me something new! Let me go, you insatiable woman, and put the kettle on. Scones need tea with them, and I could do with some butter, too!'

Johnny accepted the idea of school in the end because he knew Su wanted him to go and thought it was for the best, and Su was the most important person in his life. His father was a good companion, but he had always known that, though Mark loved him, there was an ambiguity in his attitude to his son. Had Johnny realised that Mark was jealous of him he would have been astonished and more than a little gratified. And had Mark known that Johnny was equally jealous he would have been just plain astonished. But Freda knew. Knew, too, that boarding school would probably improve the relationship out of all recognition. It had not occurred to any of the Neylers that it was strange that Mark and Johnny got on best well away from Su, but Freda had noticed. Johnny's horizons were so narrow that he concentrated too much on Su.

Freda, a childless woman, had given all her maternal love to Johnny. She hated the thought of him going, for she realised, in a way that Su and Mark did not, that the Johnny who returned from boarding school would not be the Johnny who had left.

But she loved him truly, so gave her blessing to the scheme.

Johnny sat in the trap with his suitcase on the floor behind him and Toddy's thigh rubbing his own. His parents were in the back, strained and awkward in the face of the impending parting, but Johnny watched the barrel-sided bay mare jogging along the road and felt the cold wind plucking at his hair, and was reconciled to the thought of boarding school because he would play games, team games, for the first time in his life. Also, he knew his education had been neglected, and he was a competitive boy who liked to be at or near the top. But what had finally decided him was the knowledge that if he continued to fight he might win the battle, but lose the war. He would stay at the farm and find himself disciplined more and more firmly, whilst Su's affection and companionship, which he valued more than anything else, would stray from him because he was 'difficult'. Better, by far, to accept a degree of parting, knowing that when he returned at weekends he would have almost all her attention and affection to make up for their time apart!

So when he finally kissed his parents quite warmly, shook Toddy's hand, and humped his suitcase into the school hall, he was sure he was doing the right thing. It was also in the back of his mind that the intimacies between Mark and Su, which he hated and most bitterly resented, could take place whilst he was out of the way and would not even have to be thought about.

He had reckoned without Freddy Fawcett.

Freddy was his roomer; the younger boys shared two to a room and Freddy, a thick-set, fair-haired boy with twinkling blue eyes and a cherubic countenance which hid a mind like a sink, fell to Johnny's lot. A little lost at first in the echoing corridors and crowded classrooms, Johnny turned to his roomer as to an old friend, and on that first evening, as they got ready for bed, told Freddy about his father and Su.

'Your pater married a *Chink*? I call that disgusting!' Freddy drawled the words in a man of the world fashion, for he was a good deal more sophisticated than Johnny. 'Got her in the family way, I suppose? Doin' the decent thing, eh?'

'I don't know what you mean,' Johnny muttered, knowing only too well. 'Su's beautiful. She had heaps of boyfriends before my father came back to Otago and married her. I like her awfully.'

Freddy's twinkling eyes scanned Johnny's countenance and saw there was more here than he had realised. Freddy's father was a notorious womaniser, his mother a meek, much maligned woman who adored her son, so Freddy had rather naturally assumed that Johnny would be contemptuous of the woman in his father's life. Instead, it appeared to be the other way round. Despite his prodigality with his father's money Freddy was not popular with his classmates, and he had hoped to make a friend of the new boy; it would not do to antagonise him by making remarks of a derogatory nature about Chinese women, evidently.

'Nice, is she? Your pater's done well, then, because I've

heard Chink women are good lays – my father says so, and he should know. Now that you're out of the way, I daresay your father's got her in his room and . . .'

His conversation became obscene and Johnny, not understanding that this was Freddy's way of championing the woman in his roomer's life, weighed the pros and cons, decided that an ally was only worth so much, and hit Freddy on the point of the jaw.

Against all the laws of commonsense this instant and open sign of disapproval started a friendship which would last all the time they were together and do Johnny and Freddy a great deal of good. Freddy, nursing a bruised jaw, put the word about that 'young Neyler' was both aggressive and capable. Johnny, not a boy to bear a grudge, was impressed by his roomer's immediate apology and explanation that his words had been meant in a complimentary fashion.

In the days which followed, Johnny grew to understand why Freddy spoke as he did. In Freddy's eyes, it was natural and right that a man should both want and take the woman of his choice. When Johnny let it be known that he felt slighted by Su's preference for her husband, Freddy told him bluntly that he had his facts muddled; an adult male wanted at least one adult female of his own and women were the same. A boy of Johnny's age could in no way take the place of a mate.

It was a startlingly frank way of explaining sex and marriage but it was easily absorbed by Johnny, a farmer's son. Freddy, a farmer's son too, could not understand why this basic fact of nature had escaped Johnny, but as the boys grew to know one another he realised that Johnny's circumstances were very different from his own. Johnny had only seen the man-woman relationship working between Mark and Su and no one else, for Freda and Toddy, the only other married couple he knew at all well, were not in the habit of exchanging so much as a kiss in public. He could – and did – accept mating as natural in farm stock, for the procreation of the species, but he had thought Mark's preoccupation with Su disgusting. All in all, Johnny's education was lacking in certain areas.

Johnny, for his part, was puzzled by Freddy's attitude to his parents. Joe Fawcett treated his only son with sublime indifference, but Freddy adored him. Beryl Fawcett worshipped her constantly erring husband and her swaggering son, yet Freddy thought little of her. Johnny had always assumed that feeling begot feeling; this was certainly true in his own case, for he loved Su who loved him and suspected Mark, who suspected him. Now it seemed that you could love someone who did not love you at all. Or Freddy could. It was very strange.

After a week, Freddy found himself less puzzled by the fact that Johnny's pater and Johnny could both love a Chink. Freddy had absorbed, without ever thinking about it, his father's precept that women were made for man's pleasure, and that when their period of supremacy was done they could and should be cast aside. A Chink, he felt, should never actually be married! Yet he respected Johnny, and Johnny respected Su. He found himself eager to meet Johnny's people, and wanted Johnny to meet his.

Though neither knew it, the boys were educating each other, both broadening their minds in a way which would have been impossible under different circumstances.

Johnny found his first close friendship very satisfying, and actually accepted an invitation to visit the Fawcetts' sheep station on the first weekend of the term. He also invited Freddy to accompany him home on the following weekend.

He wrote and told his parents of this change in plan, and as he sealed the letter he felt independence push out the last echo of complaint with his lot. He was growing away from them, living a life of his own, and it was good!

7

Mabel was cleaning up the tree-house, because in a few days the boys would be back and it would be in use once more. It never occurred to Desmond and Frank, of course, that during its long winter loneliness the tree-house got messy; bird-droppings, piles of dead and rotting leaves, the scatterings of prickly nut husks, piled up on the platforms, transforming the tree-house into a sort of repository for anything that could be blown on the wind. But Mabel knew, and enjoyed this annual clean-up because it meant that the boys, and therefore the summer, were almost here.

Today she was armed with a bucket of hot soapy water and a cloth; yesterday she had done the main job of clearing the rubbish, using the hand-brush which hung all summer, unobserved and unremarked on, in the thick, tussocky growth of shoots around the roots of the elm next to the chestnut. It was not easy, for all her nimbleness, to scale the tree with the full bucket, but she had managed it and was rubbing away now, enjoying the smell of the wet wood as, board by board, she cleaned. Very soon she, the boys and the Sollies would be occupying their eyrie once more.

She had a lot to tell them, too, this year. She emptied her bucket airily through the green of the leaves, then hoped, too late of course, that there was no one prowling about below. But no one was. On the second platform she stopped, rubbed her hot face with her bare arm, and gazed across to where Stella was strolling round the lawn, her arm around the waist of her friend Heather. Stella was a pupil at the Norwich High School now, and Mabel often saw her setting out in her green tunic and cream blouse, with her black felt hat on the back of her head. Mabel, a pupil at the Bullock Street Board School, was in with a chance of going to the High School too if she got a scholarship and viewed the possibility with faint alarm, but it increased her interest in Stella. She had taken the examination several weeks previously and awaited the results with mixed feelings. She was in the same class as Suzie Canning and they were best friends, drawn together by the fact that they were easily the two most intelligent girls in the scholarship class, but even if Suzie got a scholarship Mabel knew full well that her friend would never be allowed to use it. So if she did get through she would be alone at whatever school she qualified for; no one else in Bullock Street stood a chance of passing.

Her parents were torn by two perfectly natural desires – that she might get a scholarship and continue with her education, and that she might take Mrs Neyler's offer of a job as kitchen maid at The Pride.

'That'd be nice, Mabs, to have you workin' with me,' Mrs Walters had said wistfully. Mabel pointed out that she worked with her mother quite a lot already, and was told that it was not the same. Mabel thought it was – boring work, and long hours; she had no desire to be a kitchen maid to anyone. But time would pass before she had to break it to her mother that nothing would induce her to work in the kitchen. It had given additional impetus to her studying, however, to know what fate might have in store!

Sitting in the chestnut tree and wondering about her chances of getting a scholarship made Mabel think about Suzie. The two girls might have been thrown together at first because of their brains, but now they were genuinely fond of one another. Suzie had strange morals, perhaps, but she was a good friend. She was a year older than Mabel and had the kind of beauty that rarely blossomed in Bullock Street Board School. Smooth, light-coloured hair fell gleaming to her waist, rippling like a fall of heavy satin. Her eyes were almond shaped and green, fringed with incredibly long, dark lashes. Her brows were two wings of black above those unusual eyes, and even at thirteen her figure was bidding fair to be exceptional. But it was not for these attributes that Mabel valued Suzie. It was her quick wit, her humour, and her courage in adversity which drew Mabel to the other girl. Suzie's mother was a Frenchwoman who had run away from her hulking bully of a husband when her baby was little more than a year old. By the time Suzie was four she was an orphan, her father having succumbed to a thirst for meths and a conviction that he was a skilled diver, proving himself incontrovertibly wrong one hot summer day when he had made his unsteady way to the topmost diving board at the local swimming pool and died as a result of his amazing leap.

'Couldn't he swim, then?' Mabel had asked Suzie, fascinated by this weird tale.

'Dunno. Didn't really matter, 'cos the pool had been emptied. Splat!'

Splat must have been an understatement, Mabel concluded, and viewed Suzie with even more respect, for her friend lived with her sour and disapproving grandparents, a reminder of a son they had feared and despised and a daughter-in-law they had scarcely known. Yet Suzie, who should have been meek and downtrodden, was lively and easy-going, never blaming her parents for their desertion or her grandparents for their mean, grudging attitude towards her.

'They can't help being old, and they didn't ask to be landed with me,' she said, when questioned about her grandparents. 'No good grumbling; but they wouldn't let me take the scholarship, they want me to earn.'

'What'll you do?'

'Depends.' Suzie pulled a face. 'I in't going to work in a factory, that's for sure! But a shop'd be different. Selling pretty clothes, or food, or shoes – I wouldn't mind that. I say, any chance of me visiting your place, come Saturday?'

Suzie adored visiting the Walters, loving their tiny, crowded cottage which looked so quaint from the outside though it was really dark, damp and inconvenient. But it was a home with love in it, and Suzie appreciated that and was frank enough to say so.

Mabel, dreaming up in the chestnut tree, suddenly

remembered that tomorrow was Saturday and Suzie would be having her dinner with them, and began to climb down as fast as she and the bucket could make it. A problem was going to arise fairly soon, and she would have to think how best to tackle it. Suzie, who had been such a good friend this past year, would not expect their friendship – and visits – to cease just because the Neyler boys were home, nor did Mabel intend this to happen. But she must make it plain to Suzie that there must be no 'carryings on' with the boys. It would lead to trouble, she was sure of that.

So when Mabel went to meet Suzie the following day she broached the subject as soon as they climbed off the tram and began the walk up the long, beech-lined drive. To her intense relief, Suzie admitted that she was thinking about giving up her money-making scheme completely.

'No one who's more than a month past their fourteenth birthday in't coming near nor by,' she said darkly. 'No fear, not any more! That's dangerous!'

Mabel, with no idea of what her friend was implying save that obviously someone had got difficult – perhaps demanding his money back? – nodded sagely and told Suzie that Des, Frank and Bertie were all above the legal limit and that Con, though younger, was exceptionally strong for his age. Suzie cocked a quizzical eye at Mabel, but forbore to say anything other than that she would not dream of suggesting any of the boys might like to visit her. Suzie respected her friend's innocence but did not envy her for it. Armoured against the world by her knowledge of its various sins and wickednesses, she thought herself far more of a match for what life might hurl at her than her little friend.

'Ted, do pay attention! I'm trying to talk to you! I asked you what you thought about the Walters' idea of sending Mabel to the High School?'

Ted and Tina were sitting in the drawing room whilst outside rain fell steadily. Ted was trying to read the paper. He grunted at Tina's impassioned words, then glanced up at her over the spectacles he had lately taken to wearing.

'What? Who's Mabel?'

'Oh, Ted! Mabel Walters!' Tina's voice came out in a wail of exasperation. She knew full well how Ted hated being dragged into discussions of affairs over which he had no control, but this was important and she was determined to get his opinion before she said anything further to Mrs Walters.

'Oh, that Mabel. Go on then, fire away. What's she done now?'

'Mabel's got a scholarship, and she passed well – so well that they've been given their choice of schools. She's a very clever little girl. Well, Ada was telling Ruthie that she thought she and William might send the girl to the High School and when I came into the kitchen she asked me what I thought. I said I'd talk to you, because it might be better for the child to go to one of the more practical schools. You know, with more emphasis on useful subjects and less on academic.'

It seemed she had caught Ted's attention at last. He put his paper down and frowned across at her.

'She should go to the High School, of course. The Public Day School Trusts provide about the best education available, I think, which is why Stella's there, and why Kitty will go when she's old enough. I don't believe in boarding school for girls but I do believe in giving them the best you can manage.' He picked up his paper again, hopefully. 'Is that all?'

'Ted! How can you prefer reading the paper to talking to me! You're very unkind, and as it happens that isn't all. Mabel brought the most extraordinary child to the house last week – if it *was* a child! Skirts almost to her ankles, hair looped up on top of her head! Just the sort of girl I don't want Des mixing with, and he and Frank were both with them. Of course I don't want to interfere with Mabel's friends, but . . .'

'Then don't.'

'What?' Tina blinked. 'Oh, but I wasn't interfering. It's just . . . Ted, you're horrid to me!'

Ted put down his paper and stood up. He walked over to

Tina's chair, then pulled her to her feet. His expression was rueful.

'Poor darling! Let's go for a ride in the motor, just the two of us. It's raining too hard for a stroll in the grounds, but we could go round to Bishopsgate, or up to the Sollies on Ipswich Road, or out into the country to the Mainwarings.' He paused, then smiled at her. 'As a matter of fact, I'd rather like to visit Abe; we're working hard over bringing the Motor Show to the city, but it occurred to me the other day that Abe does most of the dull work and I do most of the exciting things. Poor Abe sits in the car showroom and does the ledgers and sells, whilst I go off to meet the big manufacturers and try out the cars. So I thought he and I might go up to town for a few days next week and do some business, see some new models. I could sound him out on the idea tonight, if you like.'

'I don't know about Abe, but *I'd* love to come,' Tina said with alacrity. 'Nanny takes excellent care of the little ones and the boys amuse themselves very well. Why, if Cecy came too . . .'

'Heaven preserve us! All I said was . . .' Ted flung an arm round her shoulders and led her towards the door. 'All right, all right, I'm not being horrid to you again! It'll just teach me to make rash statements, that's all.'

The car was kept in the erstwhile stables, in what had once been a loose box at the end for sick animals. Ted, holding up a huge umbrella, ran out, fastened the doors back, then bent to the task of starting the engine, turning the handle with increasing vigour until at last the engine roared sweetly into life. Tina, standing in the shelter of the side door, muffled in a long raincoat and with her own umbrella rampant, darted out and flung herself breathlessly into the passenger seat. Ted slammed the door on her, then went round and climbed behind the wheel.

'Here we go,' he shouted, for the engine's roar in the confined space of the garage sounded painfully loud to unaccustomed ears. 'We'll go and visit the Sollies and suggest a trip to town.'

Tina furled her umbrella and snuggled up beside him,

patting his arm and almost purring with contentment. A trip to London! This evening was turning out better than she had hoped!

'Ted,' she said presently, when they were heading down the drive towards the road. 'What I *meant* to talk about . . .'

Without taking his eyes off the road he leaned over and patted her knee.

'I thought as much. You've not forgotten! Look, young lady, if you want to come with me to London, you'd best forget about little Mabel's friends, and her education. Leave both problems to her parents.'

Tina glanced sideways at him and did not fail to note the sternness of his profile.

'Edward Neyler, sometimes you're Teutonic, you are really!'

'Teutonic!' He pretended to lurch in his seat, pressing a hand to his heart. 'What a rare insult! My darling, all I do is save you from yourself. I just make sure that you remain as sweet as I know you are.'

'You try to rule me! You want to make me think like you do! You won't let me . . .'

The car slowed, then came to a halt beside the kerb. The rain continued to bounce off the windscreen, and even above the noise of the engine they could hear it striking the roof and sides of the vehicle.

'Tina.' Ted turned from the wheel and caught her hands in his. His palms were warm but his eyes were cold. 'Darling, just because we employ Mabel's parents, it doesn't give you the right to pick the child's friends. Nor, to be blunt, does it give you the right to "advise" Mrs Walters to send her daughter to some school other than the one your daughter attends. If you want to come to London with me, you must remember that everyone is a human being with rights and desires, not just you and your family!'

Tina coloured hotly and her gaze faltered.

'I didn't mean . . . but Ted, that girl was dreadful, not a bit like sweet little Mabel! And I truly thought that perhaps a more practical school would be best. The thought that

Mabel would be at Stella's school didn't worry me.' She glanced quickly up at him, then down again. 'Well, not much.'

He pulled her towards him and kissed her lightly on the mouth.

'That's my own girl; it's settled then. If Abe and Cecy want to join us they shall, but I'll book us a suite at Wilde's Hotel first thing tomorrow morning.'

The car drew out into the middle of the roadway once more and proceeded on its way. Tina snuggled up against Ted again and sighed happily. She wanted her own way, of course she did; she still thought that Ted was soft with the servants. But it was lovely to see herself being effortlessly managed into good behaviour so that she appeared in the best possible light in Ted's eyes. He outmanoeuvred her, persuaded her, even bribed her – but she loved every minute of it!

'We're having a tennis party at the weekend, Mabs. Pa said we should ask our friends, so how about asking Suzie?'

Mabel and the boys were in the stable loft. The craze for submarines had suffered a temporary setback with the fine weather, but it was wet today and though the *Waterspout* needed little doing to it the younger craft, *Tornado,* still lacked certain essential items of equipment such as guns and a conning tower.

Mabel reached for one of the few remaining apples and bit into its wrinkled sweetness, watching the boys as they hammered empty tins into gun barrels.

'Suzie plays a good game of tennis,' she acknowledged. 'But your mum wouldn't want us at one of her smart parties.'

'It's a party for us, not Mama, and you're always at our summer parties, so why not Suzie?' Des demanded. 'And you're a cracking good tennis player.'

'Mm hm.' Mabel finished the apple and hurled the core at Desmond, who ducked and grinned. 'But a tennis party's more . . . oh, more grown up than the usual sort of party. It sounds it, anyway.'

'Well, I'm fifteen,' Desmond said. 'We're having Una and Richie, and the Sollies of course, and that girl who stays with the Tatsons. You *must* come, Mabs, otherwise what shall we do?'

'Without,' Mabel said, smirking. 'What about numbers, though? Your mama's crazy about even numbers. Many's the time I've heard her beating your dad about the head because he's asked someone home and unevened her dinner table.'

'That's why we want you and Suzie,' Desmond said patiently. 'We've got to have ten, and Mama says we can count Stella as one, because she's beginning to play tennis, though very badly. But Mama says we must include her more. Of course, we shan't get many sets with so many and only the one court, but we can play croquet, and Pa's putting up the net for quoits – deck-tennis, I mean – and . . .'

Frank, patiently hammering away at the tins, turned and winked at Mabel.

'Say yes, Mabs, or he'll pester you to death. He says he thinks Suzie's got . . .'

Desmond shouted and launched himself across the loft, landing squarely in the middle of Frank's back. Frank tipped forward and the *Tornado* lurched beneath their combined weight.

'Get off, you swine!'

'Then shut your bloody gob!'

There followed a brisk exchange of blows and insults until Mabel, well used to such behaviour, picked up the hayfork and began jabbing both contestants indiscriminately.

'Stop it, you two, or someone'll hear and we'll be for it,' she said breathlessly. 'I'll ask Suzie if you're so set on it, Des.' Her fork landed on Desmond's behind and he reached back, thumping wildly in the general direction of Mabel. She, not one whit worried by this, merely increased the pressure on the fork until Desmond, swearing, removed himself from on top of Frank and cast himself down on the pile of hay Mabel had vacated.

'All right, all right, there's no need to be so damned vindictive, Mabs. I wasn't going to hurt precious boysie! I just didn't want him repeating . . .'

Frank, spitting dust and hay out of his mouth, rolled over and grinned at his brother.

'Forget it, Des. If I'd known every word you uttered had to be treated as a state secret . . .'

'Frank! Oh, for goodness sake, you two!' Mabel threw the hayfork down as Desmond began to growl, and headed for the ladder which led down into the stable below. 'I'm going. You can fight without me. Look, I'm meeting Suzie tomorrow. I'll ask her if she'd like to come to the party. But I can't promise anything.'

Desmond hastily abandoned his seat in the hay and followed her to the top of the ladder.

'Is she coming to see you tomorrow? If so we'll ask her ourselves; then we'll know straight away if she can come or not.'

Mabs was halfway down the ladder, but her head was still just in the loft. She stopped and flashed a glance pregnant with mischief at Frank.

'No, we're meeting in the city. We're going to have coffee and cakes at the Salonica.'

'Why on earth?' Desmond's fair brows rose.

Mabel shrugged and grinned across at Frank. Plainly the whole thing amused her very much.

'Dunno. Just for a lark. The thing is, Suzie got a scholarship too but her grandparents won't let her use it and she'll be starting work in a few weeks. She won't have trouble finding a job, she's so smart, and she dresses ever so nicely. But once she's working there won't be any time for larking. See?'

'We'll come too,' Desmond said eagerly. 'We'll treat you. Won't we, Frank?'

'I don't mind, though girls' larks are pretty slow,' Frank said. 'I suppose we could, though. We could tell the parents we were going to the museum and catch the tram into the city. Now that we're older we don't have to ask permish anywhere near so much.'

'No,' Mabel said firmly. 'It's a lark for the two of us, see? Me and Suzie. I don't want to get wrong with her by letting you come along. Whatever plan she's got, it'll be just us.'

No more was said and Mabel continued on her way down the ladder, leaving the brothers to continue their work. Desmond hammered away for a while, but presently he suggested that whatever Mabel had said they might go along to the Salonica next day to see the fun.

'We could. I've been there with Mama. Their cakes are prime,' Frank agreed. 'But it's a swanky place for kids – is that why Suzie chose it, do you suppose?'

'Probably. She's a little cracker, that girl. If you're game then, we'll go. There's no law against two fellows having coffee and cakes there on a Saturday morning.'

Frank continued to hammer, nodding his agreement. He had no particular desire to annoy Mabel and even less to cross the deeply carpeted confines of the Salonica. But a lark was a lark, and he rather agreed with Desmond, for once, that a ringside seat was not to be missed!

'A table for two, please, miss,' Desmond said to the waitress who came forward as they entered the low-ceilinged, sunny room. 'By the window, if that's possible.'

The waitress was in a black dress with a white frilled apron, and a white cap was perched on her glossy curls. She smiled at Desmond, then turned to smile at Frank.

'This way, sirs. A table for two.'

But halfway across the room Frank suddenly remembered their plan. In a voice which came out much higher than he intended he said: 'Four! A t-table for four, if you please!'

'A table for four. Two young gentlemen and two invisibles,' the waitress said cheekily, and led them to the most favoured table, where they could sit and survey through the windows the market place spread out beneath them – for the Salonica Refreshment Rooms were on the first floor – or watch the other customers as they sipped their coffee and ate their cakes.

Frank, taking a seat beside his brother, was glad he had

put on his best clothes. It was early and there were only half a dozen other customers in the place, all ladies and all immaculately clad in light summery gowns. Desmond was smiling up at the waitress as she stood, little pad and pencil poised, waiting to take their order.

She thought them a handsome couple, both so tall and fair, broad-shouldered in their dark blazers, their beautiful, deep young voices occasionally cracking into falsetto as they argued over what they should order.

'If you was to order coffee, then I could bring the trolley over and you could choose your own cakes from there,' she remarked at last, since the discussion over the respective merits of chocolate éclairs and cream doughnuts seemed to be getting dangerously heated. 'You can have whatever you like, see? There's lovely cream meringues an' all.'

Relieved of the responsibility of mutual choice, the boys did as she suggested and presently the coffee pot and cups and the silver cream jug arrived in front of them. Desmond insisted on telling the waitress that they were expecting a couple of young ladies, and would be obliged if she would bring fresh coffee and the trolley of cakes over as soon as their companions arrived.

Agreeing with a smile the waitress, who was in fact only Desmond's age though she felt centuries older, went back to the kitchens for another order. She wondered with a good deal of curiosity what sort of 'young ladies' would presently join the boys. They were a right couple! Lads of that age, she knew, often took up with proper little tarts – but they did not usually then take them to the most respectable coffee house in the city!

Twenty minutes later, when both boys had succumbed to temptation and eaten a cake each, Mabel and Suzie came in. They were scarcely recognisable as the children Frank and Desmond knew. Mabel wore boots with heels, a long dress and a hat. The very thought of Mabel in a hat would have convulsed Frank at any other time, but somehow today, in conjunction with the grown-up dress and the way she walked, it no longer looked funny. It made him wish he had never come; this was not a lark, it was an attempt to grow up, and he hated it! The two girls crossed the room in the waitress's wake, arm in arm, and Frank saw Suzie looking wonderful in a peach-coloured, gauzy dress, with her hat tipped forward so that it shadowed her small face. He could appreciate that Suzie looked very grown up without a qualm. It was just Mabel who must stay the same.

The waitress, catching Desmond's eye, steered the two girls over to their window table. Mabel, so self-conscious that she had not looked at anything except the distant windows, suddenly focused on the boys and became scarlet with embarrassment, then succumbed to a terrible urge to grin. She clapped a small hand hard over her mouth, but giggles bubbled out from between her fingers despite Suzie pinching her arm and frowning down at her with the utmost severity. Frank, also infected, began to snigger, but the two older ones were solemn, Desmond pulling out a chair for Suzie who, after one cold, infuriated stare, sank into it.

'Might we have the trolley . . . ? Here we are, ladies!' Desmond said affably. 'Which cakes do you prefer?'

Suzie turned gracefully towards Desmond, then cast her enormous, expressive eyes in the direction of the trolley.

'What a surprise to see you here, Mr Neyler! I say, look at those meringues!'

Both girls stared with unabashed greed at the creamy confections spread out before them.

Once coffee had been poured and cakes chosen, however, there came one of the small, awkward silences that can be so difficult to break. But Suzie, having accepted their presence, did not intend to let her 'lark' lose all its savour.

'Well? Didn't you two take us for young ladies out for a good time? We've been round the smart shops, and bought some hat trimmings and some ribbon, and made the shop-girls wrap it neatly for us. We even went into Garlands, and I was very gracious to the young lady on the haberdashery counter. Wasn't I, Mabs?'

Both girls dissolved into irritating giggles. At least, they irritated Frank and Desmond, who simply could not see the joke.

'Well? What's so funny about Garlands?'

Suzie pulled a face and took a large bite out of her meringue which promptly exploded softly, showering her with pieces. She said a short, sharp word and both boys blinked, then she turned to beam at them.

'What's funny? Why, by this time next month I'll be a young lady on the haberdashery counter in Garlands myself. I got a job there, that's why the lark! Though I bet they never recognise me in my shop blacks after seeing me in this!' She indicated her finery with an eloquent wave.

Desmond began teasing Suzie, telling her she would be the prettiest girl ever to serve on haberdashery and easily the prettiest girl at their tennis party, and Frank turned with relief to a second cake, offering the plate to Mabel as he did so. It struck him that there was something sad, almost wistful, in her expression as she looked at the older girl.

Frank frowned. Surely Mabs did not envy Suzie? And then, suddenly, he knew that it was not that. Mabel thought it a shame that her friend was being forced to cast aside her scholarship in favour of a job in Garlands. She must realise, as Frank did, that being forced to grow up before one was fourteen was not a lark at all, but a wretched business.

'Mabs! Have another cake! Go on. Des and I are rolling at the moment, because Uncle Louis tipped us yesterday.' Frank spoke impulsively, wanting to make Mabs smile, to take that haunted look out of her eyes.

He succeeded. Mabs eyed the plate with her head on one side, like a sparrow, then pounced on a cream meringue.

'All right then, money-bags! Take the éclair, Suzie. They're really good!'

The four of them laughed together, the boys beginning to boast and show off, the girls to nudge each other. A party of smart ladies at the next table smiled indulgently. Frank knew that Garlands was forgotten. But he was terribly glad that Mabs would be safe from the world for a while yet.

8

'Today Poppa's gone to Cecy's house, which is right and proper. She'll give him a *cholent* at lunchtime and so on. But tomorrow he must come to us. It's Alice's weekend off, and I'd feel guilty not to do my share.'

'Tomorrow? But Tina, love, you know Sunday's the only chance I have to get out into the countryside! Old Blake's got a boat for sale which sounds just what I've been looking for, and I told him we'd pop over tomorrow and take a look at it. I thought you might get Ruthie to make a picnic and I'd bring some wine – make a day of it.'

Tina and Ted were in the kitchen talking, whilst Ruthie scraped new potatoes at the sink and enjoyed the almost plaintive note in the master's voice. Ruthie was a feminist and it always amused her to watch tiny Mrs Neyler dealing with her tall, commanding husband. She could charm him with a glance, make him laugh with a few words, or reduce him to silent disappointment with a frown. Yet he was one of the foremost businessmen in the county, always thinking up something new and profitable. He sold cars, ran a kinema for the moving pictures, built office blocks and beautiful houses. She knew, of course, as all the servants knew, that Mr Neyler was the boss over the things that mattered. But Mrs Neyler knew how to get round him, nevertheless!

'Not tomorrow,' Tina said firmly now. She glanced meaningly at Mrs Ruthven's broad back. 'Ruthie, why are you scraping the potatoes? I thought Mabel helped out on a Saturday?'

'So she do. She've gone to pick a foo raspberries,' Ruthie said. 'I'll goo and give her a holler.'

She rolled out of the back door and presently could be heard 'hollering' in the kitchen garden.

'Now that you've got rid of Ruthie I suppose you think we can quarrel,' Ted said approvingly. Tina was mixing something in a big yellow bowl and he put his arms round her waist and rested his chin on her shoulder, peering down at the mixture. 'Why can't we go today, then? And what're you cooking?'

'Ted, you're impossible,' Tina said, dabbing his chin with a floury hand. 'Have you forgotten the children's tennis party? I'm up to my eyes as it is. And tomorrow is Poppa's day. I'm cooking in a kosherish fashion right now, so don't think you can persuade me to change my mind!'

'Well, how about taking Poppa with us?' Ted suggested, clinging to the faint hope of retaining his outing. 'Imagine it, my love! The whole family packed into the Rover, a picnic on the bank of the broad; champagne, if you like. Then coming home late in the moonlight, singing the old, sentimental songs, breathing the good fresh air . . .'

'Topping up with oil every ten miles, breaking down, you swearing fit to give Poppa a heart attack, the children cross and argumentative – oh, I can imagine it all too well,' Tina said. 'Goodness, Ted, it would be awful! Family motor trips are fine for us and the children, but it would be fatal to expect Poppa to enjoy our sort of outing. Besides, he hates fresh air. He thinks night air injurious. He . . .'

'As it happens the car's going like a bird at the moment. No, honestly, don't snort in that disbelieving way. And you could pack Poppa a special kosher picnic. You need a break. Be a sport, my love!'

'It's out of the question,' Tina said, but she softened the remark by turning in his arms and kissing his chin, keeping her hands well clear of his dark jacket. 'Poor darling, you *do* enjoy your outings, but . . . I know! Why not go today instead? Ruthie can get a picnic in no time at all, because there's heaps of food for the tea this afternoon. You could take the little ones. Actually, it would be . . .'

‘What do you mean, *“You* could take the little ones”? What about you? Why can’t you come?’

Tina shrugged helplessly, pointing to her mixing bowl and then waving vaguely round the kitchen.

‘How can I? Not only do I have to prepare the meal for tomorrow myself, but there’s the children’s tennis party this afternoon. What sort of mother would I be to abandon my children at party time? Besides, Cecy’s coming over, and the girls.’

‘And with my four favourite Roses present, you expect me to take a picnic out?’ But Tina saw the look he shot at the golden summer day through the kitchen window. ‘Don’t you need me here?’

Tina shook her head.

‘Not really. As I was saying, it’s Nanny’s afternoon off, so I’ve been wondering how on earth to keep the little ones amused. If you took them with you it would be wonderful – a real help. And then I’ll arrange an early dinner so that you and I can go out for a drive this evening. What do you think of that idea?’

‘Not so dusty. And it would mean I’d see Blake’s boat.’

Mrs Ruthven surged back into the kitchen at that point with Mabs, bearing a colander full of raspberries, in her wake. Tina, who had heard all about the exploit in the Salonica from a friend who had been having coffee there at the time, looked narrowly at Mabel, then dismissed her. Small, skinny, with straight black hair and black eyes, she seemed very ordinary to Tina. It seemed that the Walters had decided to send their daughter to the High School, but clever though she might be she would never compete with Stella for beauty. Tina caught the thought back guiltily. How absurd, when Stella was nine, quite four years younger than Mabel!

‘What delicious raspberries, Mabs! Can I take some of them for the picnic?’ Edward grinned down at the girl and she smiled back, and immediately her face was transformed into pixie-like prettiness. Tina, catching sight of the smile, reflected that the child had character and, with her boys in mind, would have to be watched.

'Well, Ted? Will you go today?'

Ted nodded, taking a handful of raspberries out of the colander and popping them into his mouth.

'All right, then, if it'll help. What's for dinner tonight, and what time's early?'

'We'll dine at seven.' Tina turned to the cook. 'What's for dinner tonight, Ruthie?'

'Iced cucumber and yoghurt soup, my special lobster mayonnaise with a crunchy salad, and pears in brandy with whipped cream,' Mrs Ruthven said. 'You said not to serve a savoury, ma'am, because of having a big tea for the tennis players.'

'There, Ted, a dinner worth hurrying home for! And you'll pack the master a lovely luncheon to eat by the broad, won't you, Ruthie? Enough for the three little ones too, of course.'

Mrs Ruthven agreed at once.

'Beer for you, sir, and milk for the children. Cold chicken's nice, I always think. But we've plenty of food, I'll put you up something a bit special. How about some of them strawberries?'

Edward groaned, patting his waistline.

'I've got a weakness for strawberries. And chicken. Don't worry that I'll be late home, not if it means missing your lobster mayonnaise. Seven, you said?'

'Not a moment later,' Tina said gaily, pushing him gently towards the kitchen door. 'Go and tell Nanny to get the little ones ready.' She prodded his back where a roll of flesh showed against his jacket. 'You're getting fat, my darling!'

'Rubbish!' Edward said, but even in his own ears his tone lacked conviction. 'I'll go and fetch the children, then.'

He disappeared round the kitchen door and Tina, closing it gently behind him, bustled back to her cooking bowl, smiling at Ruthie and Mabel.

'There, all settled! Thank goodness the little ones won't be underfoot when the guests are here. Are you looking forward to the party, Mabel? I hope so, since you're working so hard to make it a success! Have you a nice tennis dress?'

'I've the skirt and blouse the High School wear for games,' Mabel answered politely. 'They're very nice.'

'Of course. I expect you're getting the uniform together now. I'm coming to watch the tennis, of course, and from what my sons say you really should win!'

Since a trip in the car with their adored father was the height of bliss, and the thought of seeing a boat one degree better, it took David, Henny and Kitty only a few moments to get ready. Nanny co-operated eagerly. She had plans of her own for the afternoon which would be all the better for having most of the morning free as well. If her employers had known that she was being picked up by Louis and taken to Wymondham Gala and Fête, they might not have been so ready to allow her to leave early. But they did not know, and Ted was grateful for her cheerful co-operation as they got the boys into their sailor suits, thick stockings and sturdy boots, and Kitty into a pink and white smock dress and white stockings – though her shiny black boots were every bit as stout as the boys'.

As soon as the children were dressed they rushed out to the Rover, cramming themselves into the back seat with squeaks and giggles and dragging the lap robe over them, although this was speedily discarded since the day was warm.

As soon as the picnic basket was aboard they set off, talking and shouting cheerfully as they drove along. Ted, driving serenely with the wind ruffling his hair, felt totally happy. It was often thus. An easy-going and good-natured man, he needed only a fine day, a smooth-running car and the company of his children to have his good fortune brought home to him so forcibly that only in song could it be released.

He began to bellow; tunelessly, alas, but the children knew what he meant to sing and joined in. 'I'll be your sweetheart,' they carolled, and Kitty's little pipe, Henny's husky tones and David's choirboy soprano mingled with Ted's flat and tuneless bass to make a beautiful sound on a sunny day.

They reached the broadland village without incident and drove down the main street, then turned into the Blake boatyard. Mr Blake was nowhere to be seen; the sheds, the yard, and even the boats bobbing at anchor, were deserted. Everyone promptly abandoned the car, David holding Henny and Kitty firmly by their hands.

'Blake will be having his luncheon,' Ted said, consulting a large gold hunter. 'We should have stopped and eaten our picnic on the way down. We can't very well sit and eat it here, in someone else's yard.'

The children were hungry and three faces fell at the thought of having to wait, without so much as a bite, whilst the Blakes finished their meal.

'I know!' Ted said suddenly. 'I'll drive a bit further down the street and through the village, and turn down a lane I know. There's a bit of a staithe down there and we can eat our luncheon overlooking the broad. How will that suit you?'

The children, with squeaks of enthusiasm, promptly piled back into the car. Ted walked into the house, acquainted the Blakes with both his arrival and his intention of lunching before seeing their boat, and then returned to the driver's seat. He duly drove down the village street and turned into a dusty, tree-lined lane. They emerged, as he had predicted, on to an open space where the boarded bank proclaimed a safe mooring place for craft. Despite the brilliance of the day the staithe was deserted and the broad likewise. Spread before them like silk, not a ripple disturbed the surface of the water, and it seemed as though the whole world snoozed in the breathless noon heat.

As soon as the Neylers arrived, however, silence was at an end. Ted, a born organiser, had everyone working at a task within minutes. Kitty unpacked the basket and arranged the contents on the tablecloth which Ted had spread in the shade of some alders. Henny and David searched for dry sedge and twigs to build a fire and Ted himself filled the tin kettle, lit the twigs, and made himself a cup of tea. He had no particular desire for a cup of tea, since there was beer in the picnic basket, but knew how dear to the heart of a child is a fire, burning merrily in the open air.

As soon as the picnic was spread out everyone fell to upon cold chicken, salad and fresh bread rolls, then turned their attention to a large skep full of cherries which the thoughtful Ruthie had included instead of strawberries, which were inclined to travel badly.

Ted, reclining on his back with his straw hat tipped over his eyes, heard the shrill voices move away from him towards the edge of the water. He said drowsily: 'I'll just have a little rest to let my luncheon settle and then we'll go back to Mr Blake's place. Be good, won't you?'

He heard David say obediently, 'Yes, Daddy,' before he drifted off into delicious slumber.

Left to their own devices, the children were good, at first. They tidied up the picnic things and threw the crumbs into the water, then lay on their stomachs and watched the shoals of tiny fish which appeared as if by magic to browse upon their sudden largesse. When this amusement palled, David showed the younger two how to make boats out of leaves and twigs, and then how to drive the craft across the broad with the aid of leafy sallow branches, which were dipped into the water and sloshed vigorously around to cause waves which carried their tiny craft, bobbing and lurching, further from the shore.

Unfortunately, a slight disagreement over who had upset whose boat led to Henny, a stocky and determined child, swiping his elder brother with a soaking wet branch, whereupon David retaliated. Within seconds a fight was in progress, both boys dipping their branches in the water and lashing each other mercilessly. Kitty, despite her four years and her pink and white appearance, joined in lustily, and it was only after a particularly brilliant swipe by David had actually bowled her into the dust that she retreated, stumbling into Ted's recumbent form and inadvertently waking him.

Sitting up suddenly, still fogged with sleep, Ted received a wet and dusty branch right across the face. He gasped and swore, and Kitty swung round, catching him across the face for a second time, uttered a cry of 'Daddy, Kit's all wet!' and, running across to claim his protection, trod on his hand.

Ted's shout of pain and rage frightened his daughter and she promptly burst into tears, putting small, dirt-streaked hands to her face and knuckling her eyes vigorously as she wailed. David and Henny, grimly battling on, were first aware of their father's participation in their game when their weapons were grabbed, snapped across Ted's knee, and tossed into the water. One glance at their father's face, usually so mild but now red with temper, put both boys to flight. Kitty, tugging at Ted's jacket, was crying steadily, the tears channelling white lines down her face, and the boys, fleeing in opposite directions, were out of sight in seconds. Ted hesitated for a moment, then, with a sigh, relinquished thoughts of revenge on his sons and turned instead to his woebegone little daughter.

'Come on now, Kit, you aren't hurt,' he said. He knelt before her, holding out his handkerchief. 'Spit on this and I'll clean you up a bit.'

Kitty paused in her howling to say testily: 'You c-could dip it in the w-water, Daddy,' and then howled louder than ever as the significance of her remark made her remember the battle. Also, she felt a lot safer from Daddy's wrath whilst howling and hiccuping.

Ted silently stood up, went to the edge of the staithe, soaked his handkerchief and returned. Mopping Kitty's hot and dirty little face he said: 'That's enough, Kitty, or I'll give you something to cry about.'

Two blue eyes, framed with dusky lashes, opened and gazed at him searchingly, then Kitty stopped in mid-sob and said in a trembling voice: 'You won't hit the boys, will you, Daddy?'

Feeling the grittiness of the mud drying on his face and knowing his shirt was smeared, its stiff collar drooping, and his three children resembled nothing so much as three ragamuffins, Ted found it quite an effort to say truthfully: 'No, I won't hit them. If you can find them, Kitty, you'd best tell your brothers to come back here whilst I pack the car. Don't be long.'

The boys returned once Kitty had assured them that it was safe to do so, and Ted did his best to clean them up. Their hair was so muddy that he had to get them to kneel on the edge of the staithe whilst he poured water from a picnic mug over their heads, and then rubbed them dry on the lap-robe. Then he found he had no comb on him. But at least they looked clean. He tried not to notice their rumpled hair and crumpled, damp clothing. Boys will be boys, he thought, climbing back into the driving seat. They've got the mischief out of their systems now, and they'll settle down for the rest of the afternoon.

He knew his children a little less well than he imagined. David and Henny were both inventive and high-spirited and the battle had merely whetted their thirst for action. But their father, driving into Blake's boatyard, was unaware of that.

Old Fred Blake, telling Mr Neyler that the boat for sale was in fact his son's, and was moored on the opposite side of the broad, suggested that the children 'might prefer to goo to Platt's landin', together, and git some fishin' ', but Edward felt he wanted the boys under his eye.

'Besides, they'll enjoy the trip across,' he said, giving them a minatory glance which was lost on them completely, since they had every intention of enjoying such a voyage.

And enjoy it they did. They leaned from the boat and dabbled their hands in the water, spying for fish in the clear depths. They saw a swallowtail butterfly, huge and colourful, fluttering over the reed beds, and a flock of moorhen chicks paddling along like a flotilla of tiny ships.

Once ashore, they congregated by the boathouse until young Mr Blake, a mere stripling of fifty-five or so, joined them. He owned a trim bungalow with two boathouses built over the broad and a glorious garden, landscaped by himself, with groves of small trees, and miniature lakes, streams, islands and bridges. Kitty was enchanted by this child-sized world. It seemed built especially for her, and as soon as the Blakes and Ted had disappeared into the larger of the two boathouses she and the boys wandered off on a tour of inspection.

At first, it really was a tour of inspection. They crossed tiny bridges, explored wooden slopes, examined an artificial ruin and some wooden pagodas. Heavy booted but on tiptoe, at first they treated the garden reverently. Then David was struck by the possibilities of one particular island. With its thatched pagoda, its surrounding streams and its beds of irises, it would have been easy to defend had it not had two bridges, one to the east and one to the west.

It was the work of a moment to explain to Henny and Kitty that he would defend the island and they would attack it, and then he positioned himself in the centre of his property and announced that the attack must begin. The response was immediate and the fun fast and furious. David ran, skidding and shouting, from one bridge to the other to repel the enemy, pushing Henny into the stream, never noticing when his brother's desperately anchored boots scored the bank into twin furrows, nor when Kitty, following her leader, trampled almost flat a very fine clump of Japanese iris, the blue and lavender *kaempferi,* which had taken the Blakes months of anxious cosseting to rear.

David did not notice, but someone else did. Young Mrs Blake, a gimlet-eyed woman in her fifties with a passion for gardens and a deep dislike of children, had seen from afar and, on wings of fury, traversed the garden at astonishing speed, unnoticed at first by any of the three combatants.

'Come you outer that!' Mrs Blake shrieked, arriving on the scene like an avenging angel. She saw the furrows on the bank and moaned. 'See hare, you young varmints, what . . .' She spotted the bent and bleeding irises and her sudden scream of rage brought David off the island by the far bridge and sent all three children scuttling for their father and the boathouse.

Mrs Blake, still buoyed up by fury, followed them, announcing shrilly as they all arrived more or less simultaneously in the boathouse that 'Gardings in't no place for damned kids!'

Ted began to apologise but she shouted him down, her

mouth working, her cheeks bannered scarlet.

'There's a dam' big hoole in the stream-bank, and them iris what took Father and me such a power o' work to raise, they've tromped 'em flat. Thass too bad!'

Ted, seeing that action spoke louder than words, slapped both boys briskly across their tingling ears until they sought refuge behind their sister, gave Mrs Blake a handful of cash to 'make good the damage', and promised that the boys should suffer more fully for their sins when he got them home. The two male Blakes, eyeing their termagant female with a degree of embarrassment, mumbled that the iris would doubtless survive, and that it didn't do to expect old hids on young shoulders. Then, before Mrs Blake could voice further complaints, old Mr Blake steered the Neylers out of the boathouse and back to the dinghy.

'Don't you worry yourself, sir,' he said to Ted, clearing his throat and patting Ted's shoulder in an avuncular fashion. 'She hev got a bee in her bonnet regardin' that garden, and thass the truth. Silly old mawther! Now we'll go back to the yard an' talk business.'

Poor Ted, still simmering, cast his offspring a speaking glance and ignored them completely until Henny leaned too far out over the side of the boat and dropped his sailor hat overboard. Instead of helping his brother to regain his headgear, David smacked his head for carelessness and Henny, stung, seized David's hat and flung it from him. A fortunate breeze, springing up, carried the small object a good way off, twirling it merrily, and Henny crowed over David, who was about to begin a proper fracas when a glimpse of his father's face sent him sinking into his seat once more.

'Boys will be boys,' Mr Blake said tolerantly, rowing in pursuit of the floating sailor hats. 'I've 'ad four of me own, sir, so I should know!'

'Boys will have sore bums!' Ted roared, forgetting himself. 'Letting me down, behaving like hooligans . . . can't take them anywhere . . .' His words became lost in incoherent threats, his fury even greater because David and Henny were, by now, in the extreme stern of the boat and he was in the bows and therefore unable to inflict the swift punishment which would have given him so much satisfaction.

By the time the bank was reached and the boat moored safely, it would have seemed churlish to have whacked the boys, now the picture of innocence as they jumped ashore, helped their sister out of the boat, and then stood meekly waiting for their father, dripping sailor hats in hand.

'Get into the car and stay there,' Ted said, scowling at his offspring. 'I want to talk business with Mr Blake and I can't do so whilst I'm wondering what you three are up to. Stay in the car! Do you hear me? If you want to see one solitary strawberry when we get home this evening, don't move out of that car.'

With that he turned on his heel and marched into the house. Mr Blake, tipping them a wink, followed. The door closed behind them. Silence descended on the boatyard.

The Rover was parked at the top of a slight slope overlooking the broad, and directly in front of her, joined to the edge of the staithe to increase the mooring area, was a stout wooden platform which extended into the water for a distance of several yards, a sort of cat-walk, so that it and the staithe formed a letter L. The yard being deserted by visitors and workmen alike on Saturday afternoons, the boys and Kitty had no one to complain to, no one to watch, and no one to watch them. However, they were all a trifle subdued by their vigorous afternoon and climbed into the back of the Rover, where Kitty, cuddling down on top of the lap robe, almost immediately fell asleep.

'What did we do, Davie?' Henny enquired presently, his voice expressing injured astonishment. 'All we did was tread on her old lilies by accident, and – and anyone's hat could of fallen in the water! It isn't fair! I don't wanna sit in the car all afternoon!'

'We got a bit muddy after luncheon,' David pointed out, trying to be fair to their absent persecutor. 'But you're right, it isn't fair. I bet old Blake's giving Daddy beer right this minute! I'm thirsty too. Is there any milk left?'

At once the picnic basket was lugged out and rifled, and

though the milk was no more, there were two bottles of beer which, as David said, 'would have to do'. Presently, with a bottle of beer in one hand and a chicken leg in the other, David said brightly: 'Let's play we're driver and navigator, exploring Africa in our car!'

No sooner said than done. No orders had been given forbidding them the front seat so they climbed over, with their provender, and David settled behind the wheel to take first go as driver. Like most small boys, David had a very fair idea of how to drive a car from watching his father closely on outings, and though he knew they could not get down to start the engine he fiddled with various levers, twisted the wheel and finally, not without difficulty, released the handbrake.

By this time, David had swigged half the bottle of beer, and was delighted when the car began to trundle slowly down the slope. This was proving to be an excellent game and they had not disobeyed a single one of their father's commands!

'Spiffing, Davie,' Henny shouted, his voice a little slurred, his bottle emptier even than his brother's, for he had not got the car to drive, but merely had a road-map spread out on his lap. 'This must be Africa. I c-can see giraffes! Wake up, Kitty, Davie's taking us for a drive!'

But Kitty slumbered on and David, suddenly realising his responsibilities as a driver, began to tug fruitlessly at the handbrake, looking anxiously ahead to where the broad loomed. However, they were heading straight for the wooden cat-walk, which was not on a slope but ran flat and straight right out into the deeper water of the broad. He calculated that the car would stop of its own accord before it reached the end of the cat-walk.

The big car trundled down the last slope of the staithe and on to the wooden planks, which reverberated beneath the unaccustomed weight. All might have been well had David only continued to concentrate on his steering. Instead, he leaned over and began to heave again at the handbrake, allowing the car to head where it would for a split second.

It was their undoing. The right-hand wheels spun for an instant in space, then the car turned turtle.

The boys saw a confused kaleidoscopic view of sky, water and spinning landscape, and then they struck the water, the sudden shock of it making them gasp, even as the weight of the car above them pushed them under. Kitty, perhaps not even waking, did not cry out. David knew a second of guilt – what would his father say to this? Henny's frightened yelp was lost as the water surged into his mouth.

There was a tremendous splash as the car hit the surface, but soon enough the ripples which surged against the staithe settled back into calm. Quietness descended once more and the moorhens, which had fled when the leviathan suddenly crashed in amongst them, came back to paddle indifferently across the muddied water.

Ted, returning with Mr Blake, their business satisfactorily concluded, looked unbelievingly round the empty yard where the Rover had stood when he left it barely forty minutes earlier.

'What the . . .' Ted took off his straw hat and scratched his head. 'Oh, no!' He turned to Mr Blake. 'The young devils! I reckon they managed to get her going and they've gone joy-riding into the village! I'd best chase after them.'

But Mr Blake had him by the arm.

'Mr Neyler, sir! There's tyre marks on the cat-walk. Look!'

Ted ran across the yard, his heard suddenly thumping with fright, half expecting to see the car in the water on the far side of the cat-walk, with three repentant figures perched on the hood, for the water was not deep near the bank.

He saw only water. Calm, still.

He saw the tyre marks, but they ended halfway along the cat-walk – they *must* have gone into the village! He was turning away, almost faint with relief, when he noticed how muddy the water was further from the bank. Beside him, old Mr Blake began to run along the cat-walk. Ted stood still, and the world suddenly stilled too, so that an uncanny pause seemed to grip the moment. He saw, faintly through the muddied water, the dark shape of the car a foot or two below the surface.

Wheels uppermost.

9

Stella stood in the kitchen with her nose pressed against the window pane and watched the first cold flakes of snow drift down from a leaden sky. All the buildings which surrounded the kitchen yard had slate roofs, and Stella traced the slow spiralling of the flakes from the bare branches of the beech trees right down on to the roofs. It looked chilly and forbidding out there. Behind her, she knew, all was warmth and light. Ruthie was making a cake, Ethel and Edie were sitting on either side of the fire, praying that the bell would not ring, and Millie was making Stella's tea.

She did not have to turn round to verify the scene, for she had been home from school for thirty minutes and routine had taken over. Tea in the kitchen was her favourite time of day, now.

For Stella's life had changed so drastically since the death of the little ones that she felt she was no longer *that* Stella Neyler; that Stella, a pretty, heedless creature, had died as surely as the little ones on that day in July.

After the first shock of their loss, Tina and Ted had sent the children away. They had gone to Cromer, staying with Alice's cousin Maude, and had remained there for six weeks, until the school holidays were all but over. Twice a week they telephoned their parents, once a fortnight their parents spent Sunday with them. In between they went for long walks, played games on the sand, ate strange but delicious meals and tried not to think about the little ones.

Stella still remembered the awkwardness of those Sunday visits. Mama and Daddy, clad in black but with bright, artificial smiles, had taken them for car-rides and picnics. But the smiles were apt to slip if they thought themselves unobserved, and they held each other's hands tightly when they went walking. Too tightly. Eyes were shiny for no reason, one was suddenly kissed or hugged with undue fervour. The children breathed sighs of relief when the visits were over, and returned to their Cromer world, glad to be allowed a fortnight before the next descent.

On their return home, they found other changes. Nanny Sutton had left, and the nursery wing was locked up.

For the boys, going back to their boarding school, this was not so hard. For Stella it was a cruel deprivation. She knew no other life save the nursery one; her little bedroom, leading off Nanny's, had been her refuge in times of trouble and her favourite place in times of happiness. It was small, to be sure, with large boxes for toys all along one wall and a chipped little dressing-table with a mirror the right height for a nine-year-old and whitewashed walls on which her successful drawings were pinned. But it was cosy and familiar, unlike the guest suite, to which she had been promoted.

'It's just right for you, separated from the other bedrooms and with your own private bathroom, just like a grown-up guest,' Mama had said, pointing out the guest room's advantages. But Stella hated the new room with its pale carpet, fitted wardrobes and velvet curtains. There was nowhere for her toys, she was not allowed to pin anything to the walls, and though she had brought Gungy, an earless, eyeless toy monkey, and Alison, a doll with eyes that swivelled and real hair, they seemed no more at ease in this new magnificence than she did. In her old room she had formed the habit of curling up on the window-seat, feet on the cushions and fingers in ears, whilst she committed poetry, tables and spellings to memory.

Here, she had a real little desk and a table lamp, but the basket chair creaked frighteningly, and the table lamp sometimes cast funny shadows on the smart wallpaper. She had a gas fire, but was bidden to use it sparingly, and to treat the bathroom with respect.

Treating the bathroom with respect was not difficult. In the old days bathtime had been a communal affair, with Nanny supervising, the small room hot and steamy, the other children wanting their turn, leaving boats bobbing on the surface of the water, while Kitty sang, slapped the flat of her hand on the water, squealed, ducked . . .

The new bathroom had pink tiles, one mirrored wall, matching towels. Here Stella bathed herself, washed her own hair. She hated and feared bathtime and was, suddenly, afraid of drowning. Once she had driven Nanny mad by ducking her head beneath the surface and holding her breath for as long as possible, emerging, scarlet-faced and panting, to Nanny's scoldings and Kitty's admiring squeals. Now, she ran a tepid inch or two of water, soaped herself with thumping heart, took a flying leap back on to the bathmat and dashed back into her chilly bedroom. There she would crouch before her lonely gas fire, dripping and shivering, until boredom and a sick feeling from hanging her head down drove her to bed, still damp-haired, uneasily to sleep.

Above everything else, she was lonely. The maids were kind, especially Millie; and Ruthie, too, welcomed Stella to the kitchen, understanding how bereft the child was. But Mama did not approve of her spending so much time with the servants. When she came into the kitchen and found Stella there, a slight but definite frost seemed to form; Stella, recognising it without understanding the reason for it, soon learned to slip out of the back door as Tina entered the room. But now that Christmas was behind them and the hard cold of January had arrived, it would be too chilly to hang about in the yard or the coach-house. She would have to retreat to her room after tea, and she dreaded the thought of the long, lonely evenings.

The war, of course, had made changes in everyone's lives.

Uncle Louis had left Grandpa's house and was living in London somewhere and learning to fly an aeroplane at Hendon airfield. He wanted and intended to go to the war when he had got his 'ticket', whatever that might be, but Stella knew that Mama and Grandpa thought it was just a phase, that Uncle Louis would realise that his place was with Grandpa and the business and not in France. Anyone could fight in France, Mama had once said, but only Louis could cope with Grandpa and the factory. He and Sarah were to marry in the spring, their wedding having been postponed last summer after the death of the little ones. Stella never doubted for one moment that Uncle Louis would go away, once he had married Sarah. She understood that this must be so, even though Mama could not see it that way. Uncle Louis had explained it to her, kindly and rationally, but she worried about him because he was her favourite uncle. Indeed, her only real uncle, for though Daddy had a brother she had never met him.

Behind her, Stella heard Ruthie lift the now filled cake tin and carry it across to the oven. She listened and heard the bell go; Ethel – or was it Edie – got to her feet with a martyred sigh and the kitchen door opened, swished shut. Millie poured milk into Stella's blue mug. Outside, darkness was falling as well as the snow. In the reflection on the window glass Stella could see the quiet, domestic scene. Her tea was set out, her milk poured. She even saw Millie's mouth open, preparatory to calling her name. She turned back with pleasant anticipation to face into the warm and cosy kitchen. Faces were flushed from the warmth, and everyone smiled or looked good humoured. They had mourned the little ones quite as fervently as her parents, but they did not have time to let the loss continue to weigh on them. She basked in their smiles.

'Oh, Millie, that looks delicious!'

Stella's praise was genuine for Millie liked to 'keep her hand in', as she always said, and her teas were beautifully presented. Today there was a thick hedge of mustard and cress in a horseshoe-shaped container, egg sandwiches in white bread and potted meat in brown, two tiny fairy cakes with pink icing and silver balls on top, and a slice of fruit cake. A plate of thin bread and butter, a jar which looked like a pineapple filled with raspberry jam, and the blue china mug full of milk.

'It don't take long to make things look nice,' Millie observed. She smiled at her solitary charge. 'I see your calendar marked out again! Never you mind, my chick, the time'll soon pass. You're too much by your own, together.'

Stella, used to the anomaly which caused Norfolk people to address one person as a crowd, nodded, her mouth full of egg sandwich.

'I know. Daddy says he might let me go to boarding school soon, though. Then I wouldn't get so lonely because I'd only be here in holiday times, like the boys.'

Millie, tidying away the remnants of tea-making, turned and stared, dismay evident in her large, light blue eyes.

'Oh, miss! You'd 'ate that, surely?'

'I wouldn't, I'd like it. You don't know what it's like, Millie, being alone when you're used to . . .' She paused, aware that there were some things which should not be said, however true they might be. 'I miss living in the nursery,' she finished lamely.

'You in't the only one,' Millie said briefly. 'If you go, miss, I will an' all.'

Stella's hand stopped, sandwich-laden, halfway to her mouth. Her dismay was as complete as ever the nursery maid's had been. Millie was the last link with her old nursery life, and to part with her, unthinkable. Her protuberant blue eyes, her flyaway hair that would never stay under her cap, her knobbly legs and the big-knuckled, chilly hands – they were as familiar as and a good deal dearer to Stella than her own mother's.

'You wouldn't! Oh, Millie, you wouldn't go!'

Ruthie murmured something warningly, but Millie was not to be turned from her purpose.

'I would, miss! I'm right fond of littl'uns; I wouldn't know what to do with meself if there weren't no childern here. Who d'you think does your mending, and keeps your room tidy? To say nothing of polishing up in the nursery and keeping it all nice.'

'Millie, thass enough!' That was Ruthie, coming straight out with it now. Millie flushed and hung her head, then she tossed back a hay-coloured lock and faced Stella.

'Well, I do, Miss Stella.' Millie glanced defiantly at Ruthie, then back at Stella, sitting white-faced at the table. 'And let me tell you, it have struck me, times, there's more life up in that there nursery than in the rest of the house, lately!'

She turned and fled then, into the darkness of the scullery, and Stella scraped her chair back, ignoring it when it fell over with a clatter, and flew after her. In the small room, smelling of cabbage and earth and scouring powder, she flung her arms round Millie's stringy waist.

'Do you really go up there, Millie? Can I come? It *was* a good place, wasn't it? I miss it so terribly – and Nanny, and them.'

Millie's scrawny arms were round her, she was pressed close to Millie's bony chest. And for the first time since the tragedy, she knew a sense of comfort and protection as great as that engendered by Nanny's comfortable, well-padded embrace.

'Yes, my woman, you shall come up there with me! There's nothing frightening in a place where kids ha' been playing. Do you come with me tomorrer, when I goes up there!'

'Come you outa that, the two of you,' Ruthie called. 'The bell have rung for Miss Stella to go to the study. You'd best cut along there, love.'

Carefully, Stella detached herself from Millie's arms.

'Daddy probably wants to talk about boarding school. I'll tell him I've changed my mind, Millie, and don't want to go after all.'

But Millie really did love children; far too much to let Stella make what she now realised would be a great sacrifice.

'Look, my woman, I was talkin' daft just now. You go, if the master'll send you. I'll stick on here, and that's a promise!'

* * *

'Miss Kelpmann to see you, ma'am.'

Tina, knitting khaki mittens for the men in the trenches and warming her toes in front of a lovely fire, put her work down and rose as Ethel stood aside to let Sarah into the room.

'Sarah, my dear, this *is* an unexpected pleasure! I thought that, with Louis being home, we should see very little of you. Louis's with you, I presume?'

Sarah stood in the doorway for a moment, tall and striking in an earth-brown coat with a fox-fur collar turned up to frame her pale, patrician countenance. But it was the look in her large eyes which brought Tina hurrying across the room towards her.

'Sarah! My God, what's wrong? Is it Louis?'

Sarah shook her head and came into the room. She undid her coat and sank into the chair which Tina indicated, then put one hand to her brow. Worried as she was, Tina still noticed that the little fur hat she wore exactly matched the reddish-chestnut of the fur collar and that, in turn, her Russian boots were the same dark brown as her coat. Even in obvious distress, Sarah was elegance personified.

'Oh, Tina! He's postponed the wedding again!'

Tina sank into her own chair and picked up her knitting, but made no attempt to start work on it.

'He's a thoughtless scamp! Why, for goodness sake?'

Sarah pulled the little fur hat from her shining dark hair and leaned forward earnestly.

'Oh, if only I knew! He says he'll be getting this certificate or whatever shortly, and then he'll go to some wretched place outside Liverpool, and then he's going to ask to go to France! Yes, really, with the RFC, of course. And Tina, there's no earthly need. He could just as easily apply for a flying job in England! They *need* pilots, and though I dare say you'll think I'm prejudiced, I do think Louis is good at his job. As for postponing the wedding, whyever should it be necessary, whether he's in England or France?' She fished a tiny square of cambric out of the pocket of her coat and dabbed at her eyes with it. 'I'd rather have some happiness than none!'

'I can't understand it,' Tina muttered. She reflected that she would dearly have liked to smack Louis. How could he behave so to someone as eligible as Sarah? She bit the thought back, trying to substitute the word charming instead. 'Do you have any suspicion that . . . well, that there might be someone else?'

Sarah shook her head hopelessly and stuffed the handkerchief back into her pocket.

'He says there's no one else, but I suppose he would. He says it wouldn't be fair to me to marry me and then go off and perhaps get himself killed, but that really is for me to decide! He's put me in an unbearable position, Tina! I dare not go round to the Bishopsgate house, in case Mr Rose has a heart attack when I say that Louis is going to France. And that means I can't enlist your father's support for the marriage. As for my parents, if Papa knew that Louis wanted to postpone the wedding again goodness knows what he'd say. I don't mind telling you, Tina, that several times Papa's been very difficult about my marrying Louis! It has taken Mama and me all our time to bring him round. There were rumours . . .' She paused delicately. 'But I daresay you heard them, too. I promised Papa that Louis's philanderings were a thing of the past, but if I admitted that the wedding was to be put off again . . . well, I don't think I could persuade Papa that Louis was not keeping a dozen mistresses!'

Tina stood up.

'Where is he now? I brought him up, so perhaps I can talk some sense into him. The trouble is, dearest, that he believes you'll wait. I shall disillusion him on that score.'

Sarah got up too, her eyes beginning to sparkle once more.

'Would you? Oh, Tina, that would be such a help! He met me as we'd arranged, to talk over wedding plans, and just told me about the postponement and walked out, back to the Bishopsgate house! I didn't know which way to turn, truly!'

'I'll speak to him,' Tina promised. She crossed the hall to

the cloakroom and got down her blue wool coat with the silk lapels. 'Is your car outside? May I borrow it to save ringing for James and letting the whole house into the secret?'

'Of course! Dickson's outside still, I daresay. Unless he's gone into the kitchen to chat to the maids.'

Dickson was a handsome young man with dark hair and a rosy complexion; Tina had little doubt that he was at this very moment sitting on the kitchen table, swinging gaitered legs and flirting with Ethel, who was a pert and handsome girl much sought after by young men despite her occupation, for 'skivvies' were not generally thought to be much fun to 'walk out' with, due to their job being a living-in one, with very little spare time.

'I'll ring and ask the girl to send him round.'

Tina, as it happened, was in luck. She arrived at the Bishopsgate house to find her father was dining out with a friend, Becky had gone round to visit Cecy, and Louis was alone. In fact, he answered the door when she rang and seemed pleased to see her, waving a chicken leg hospitably at her and taking her straight into the kitchen where he sat her down in Alice's favourite chair by the range and seated himself opposite, his wicked face alight with curiosity.

'Excuse me continuing my meal, sis, but it's Alice's night out and she didn't trust that young flibbertigibbet Annie alone in the house with me, so she sent her off to visit her mother in Bull Close. And since Poppa's gone a-visiting and Becky's with the Sollies, here I am, alone and starving, forced to subsist on cold chicken and a few other trifles. Want a cup of coffee? It's good – Alice made it before departing. Becky makes lousy coffee and Rachel's staying with someone this week.'

'Yes, I'll have a coffee, but I'll make it myself, thank you.' Tina felt sorry for Dickson, stuck out in the car in the cold, but she could scarcely send a maid out to fetch him in when there wasn't a soul in the house save herself and her brother. 'Louis, what's this about putting the wedding off again?'

Louis took a large bite out of his chicken leg and spoke thickly.

'What sort of life would it be for Sarah, married to me when I was off with the RFC? Can you see her in a little flat in town whilst I finish my course? She would go mad! And then, when I leave to fight . . .'

'Louis, that's just making excuses! You know very well that her father's giving her – both of you, I mean – a very beautiful house on Ipswich Road as a wedding present. As for a little flat, why on earth should she? You can spend weekends with her here in Norwich.'

Louis looked sulky. He stretched out his well-polished shoes and scowled at his reflection in the gleaming toecaps.

'I don't want her old man's charity, I want a wife who can be with me. If we're married, we should be together. At least until I go to France.'

'Go to France! Louis, your place is here. Even more if you've a wife. You'll break Poppa's heart, and Sarah's.'

Louis's brows rose and his expression became knowing.

'Indeed? Like you did? But he survived, Tina mine!'

'Don't rake up old forgotten stories,' Tina said sharply. 'Tell me the truth, Louis. Is there someone else?'

'Only Sarah. Truly, old girl.'

It relieved Tina's mind more than she had believed possible. She had suspected for a long time that Louis was having an affair with someone, and when she had asked the question she had been watching his face. There had been mischief there, and a certain triumph, but no trace of deceit, none of the little tricks she had come to expect when Louis was lying to her. For the first time it crossed her mind that her brother might actually be sleeping with his fiancée, but she banished the thought as soon as it was born. Such a thing was impossible, Sarah being such a closely guarded, well brought up young woman. And yet the predatory air which Louis wore when he was not having an affair with some woman had been noticeable, of late, by its absence. Shocked by her base suspicions, Tina burst into rapid speech.

'Only Sarah? Well, that's wonderful, Louis! And when

you lose her, what then? Because you will lose her, if you try to put the wedding off again.'

It set him back on his heels, she could see that. The dark brows drew into a frown and there was an arrested expression on his face.

'Lose her? But she's crazy about me!' He grinned suddenly, his brow clearing. 'There are hundreds of pretty girls, Tina, but only one Louis Rose.'

'You've forgotten one thing, Louis.' Tina was keeping her temper with difficulty. The conceit of the man! 'Sarah isn't just a pretty girl. She's an heiress. And she's got style.'

Louis did not answer for a moment but transferred his gaze to the flames, flickering in the fire. It was almost, Tina thought, as if her brother were weighing the pros and cons! And when he spoke, it was wearily, as if he were tired of the discussion.

'All right then, if it means so much to everyone! I'll marry her at the end of April. Tell her, would you?'

Tina got briskly to her feet and buttoned up her coat.

'If you wish. Shall I tell her you're here, and alone in the house?'

He got to his feet, holding the kitchen door for her, and shook his head.

'No. I'm leaving in a few minutes.'

She crossed the hall, then turned in the doorway, her expression puzzled, the finely curved brows arched.

'Leaving? But you're here for another three days!'

He almost pushed her out of the door, into the chilly, snowy darkness.

'I was. But even though I may be forced to marry Sarah, none of the rules say I've got to spend the remainder of my leave here!'

Before she could say one of the words burning on her lips, the door slammed and she was alone, unable to vent her spleen on anyone with Dickson watching her, jumping down to start the car engine, and with something so final in that slammed door that she knew instinctively that had she returned to beat upon it there would have been no answer.

More than a little shaken by the vehemence in Louis's

last remark, Tina climbed into the car, settled herself into the deep leather upholstery, and planned what she would say to Sarah. She wondered at her own lack of satisfaction, for even if Louis had been ungracious in his defeat, defeat it undoubtedly had been. She had won, hands down, and Sarah would be married in the spring.

Sitting back as the car slid through the thin fall of snow, she tried to plan her wedding outfit and decide on presents. But all she could think of was the fact that Louis, who had courted Sarah with such ardour, no longer seemed to want to marry her, but seemed determined to join the rest of the army in France.

The roads were a little treacherous so Dickson drove with great care, which was as well, since by the time they reached The Pride again Tina had tidied away her tears and fixed a bright smile to her face. Sarah was a bride-to-be once more, and Louis's resolve to go to France might easily be weakened by a wife.

But in her heart she acknowledged that he would go.

Louis had a small, brightly painted two-seater Ford Tourer whose engine, lovingly tended, could do a good speed on a deserted road. He left a note for his father propped up on the kitchen table explaining that he had been called away, donned his thickest overcoat and a long striped scarf, and threw his few possessions into a Gladstone bag. Then he and Flossie, his car, set off on the road back to London.

Despite the fact that he was to be married, he knew a wild and exultant happiness as he drove. The snow had stopped and the sky was clear, the moon and stars bright in the deep blue-black above. The wind was cold but Flossie's engine purred, there was a bag of peppermints handy so that he could suck one as he drove and a flask of brandy in his pocket to keep out the cold. One way and another, he enjoyed the journey.

He threaded his way through London to Golders Green, parked the car in a mews garage and made his way softly across the courtyard to a cottage with a blue painted back door, robbed of colour by the moonlight but as familiar to

Louis as his own hands on the steering wheel. He unlocked the door, slipped through it into the small, red-tiled corridor, then locked the door behind him. He stood for a moment, head cocked, listening. Nothing. He had woken no one. Then, very quietly indeed, he mounted the stairs with their squeaky treads. At the head of the stairs was a tiny landing with two doors leading off; he opened one of them and let himself into the darkened bedroom.

'Darling?'

His whisper was barely audible, but it woke the sleeper in the old-fashioned double bed. She stirred and sat up, and in the dimness he saw her smile, saw her arms come out to him. He knelt on the bed and reached for her, kissing the sleep-blurred mouth and eyes, pressing her softness harshly against his still driving-coated chest.

'I've come home early. Are you all right, my love? How's the boy?'

She snuggled against him for a moment, then kissed the side of his face and settled back against the pillows as he began to undress.

'He's got a name, Lou! Call him James, not the boy! It's lovely to have you back so soon, but – why?'

He stripped naked and stood for a moment smiling down into the cradle at the foot of the bed without answering her. The child within, dark-haired, its small face scowling in sleep, stirred as though conscious of the scrutiny and Louis turned quickly back to the bed.

'He's grand.' He murmured the words as he slid between the sheets and turned to take her in his arms. 'My son! Sarah Sutton, you've done me proud!'

And Sarah Sutton, once the Neylers' nanny and now the mother of Louis's son, relaxed in her lover's arms and let her mouth soften beneath his lips. It was only when he began to tug impatiently at the neck of her nightgown that she spoke again.

'Lou, why've you come back so soon? Is it all arranged – the wedding, I mean?'

'Button your lip, Say. I've been away nearly a week and all you want to do is talk.' Persuasive fingers slid down the neck of her nightie and began to caress her swollen breasts. 'Can we make love? Is it all right now?'

She sighed and began to unbutton the gown, then, with his help, wriggled out of it. The curtains at the window were drawn back and in the moonlight the new fullness of her body pleased him immensely. Anticipation made his touch suddenly tender, almost hesitant. He stroked her waist, and then down the smooth curves of her buttocks, pulling her gently closer.

'Well? Is it all right?'

'Baby's nearly eight weeks old, so I suppose so. The doctor did say after six. But do you think we should?'

He raised his eyebrows at her, continuing to caress her back, their bodies just touching. He felt the shudder run through her and felt the push of hardening nipples against his chest.

'Do *you* think we should, Say? I don't want to do anything you wouldn't like!'

She giggled, a delicious bubble of amusement deep in her throat, knowing her own weakness as well as he did. She adored him, she adored making love, and tonight, after their long abstinence, she could not even pretend coyness or unwillingness.

'I think . . . perhaps . . . we should.'

In the past, Louis had been a sensual and demanding lover, greedy, sometimes rough, always taking rather than giving. But tonight he made love to her leisurely, wooing her in a way he had never bothered to do before, taking delight in the full ripeness of her body, teasing her with kisses and caresses until she was completely relaxed and eager for him, the baby in the cradle, who must not be woken, totally forgotten. Then he took her engorged nipple in his mouth, playing with it, drawing off some milk, until she was clutching him, pushing her hips forward, mutely appealing for consummation.

'Oh, Lou, you're driving me crazy! Oh, Lou, I want you so!'

It was a delicious loving, made more so because they felt like prisoners released from their recent abstinence. When they were quiet at last, Sarah with her head on his chest, Louis on his back, one arm behind his head, staring up at the ceiling, they had never felt more in accord. It was easier to ask the question which had to be asked, and to answer it truthfully.

'Louis, are you going to marry her?'

He stroked the rich, tumbled brown hair away from her brow, and sighed.

'Yes, dammit! If I'd put it off again she'd have smelt a rat. As it was, I nearly gave the game away to my sister Tina. Your one-time employer, sweet Say. She asked me whether there was anyone else.'

'And you told her . . .?'

'Only Sarah, I told her. Which couldn't be truer.' He grinned, his caressing hand still smoothing her hair. 'When I think of the times I've said "Sarah" and meant you! I never thought having two women with the same name could be so convenient!'

'I'm glad. That you're going through with it, I mean. When you go to France, you'll have a wife to write to.'

'And you. If you think that I'll marry and forget you and the boy you're wrong! This' – he slid his hand down to caress the curve of her stomach – 'this is for ever.'

'Or until I meet another man and marry him.'

'Why should you do any such thing? I've *got* to marry Sarah so that I can afford to keep my mistress in luxury. And my son.'

She laughed, and turned her head to kiss the hand near her face.

'Oh, Lou, you'll have other sons! Do you think Miss Kelpmann will be barren?'

He turned her on to her side, then put his arms round her waist, holding her close and covering them both with the bedding.

'Forget it now, Say. Sleep. God knows, the morning will come soon enough, and the boy will start his demands on you.'

She sighed and cuddled down and very soon she slept. But Louis lay awake and thought. Many things had touched him about young Sarah Sutton – young she was not, he reminded himself, since she was four years older than he, yet she seemed young. He had been at the house when Ted had returned after the children's fatal accident. He and Sarah Sutton had been out in the country, making love under a haystack, and he had brought her as far as the bottom of the drive and then driven the rest of the way up himself, to visit his sister.

He had barely assimilated the news before Sarah was back, and the full shock of her loss broken to her. Tina had been white-faced, shocked, silent. Sarah had screamed and then keened, and he had not comforted her, nor gone to her, nor tried to ease her pain. Later, he had been deeply disgusted by his behaviour. To stand by as she blamed herself – who was blameless – and agreed to leave at once, refusing money, swollen-faced with grief. It had been, he thought, the worst thing he had ever done.

Afterwards, anxious to make what amends he could, he had followed her in his car and picked her up, asked her where she would go, what she would do. By then he was bitterly angry with Tina for virtually turning the girl from the door and it helped to ease his own sense of shame. But Sarah was conscious of none of it. She sat beside him in the car, all her tears cried out of her, shaken now and then by a deep, dry sob, and waited for him to tell her what to do next. It was not until a fortnight later, when he had moved her and her belongings into the mews cottage in Golders Green, that she had told him she was pregnant. Even then, he had admired her. She had told him, neither accusingly nor reproachfully, of her condition, and waited for him to turn her out, or suggest an abortion, or send her back to her mother in Ireland.

He had not, at that stage, intended to live with the girl. He shared a flat in Hendon with a fellow flier, and had merely meant to visit Sarah. But something about her, the gallant way she had kept her condition a secret, or the way she immediately began to plan what work she might do to keep herself, changed his mind. He moved in with her, took over the finances of the small house, and, with considerable amusement, insisted that the neighbours should call him Louis Sutton. When his son was born, he knew that he could never leave her to struggle with the boy alone. He adored the child, was proud to tell the neighbours that they had a son, and wanted to give the boy the earth, to acknowledge him openly.

And yet, side by side with his love for Say was his love for Sarah Kelpmann. Sarah had character, determination, a lively and original intelligence. Poor Say had a placid disposition, a generous spirit, and a straightforward attitude to life. One day, he suspected, he would love Sarah deeply and possibly only tolerate Say.

In the moonlit bedroom he turned cautiously away from her to lie on his back. Immediately, she turned round too, snuggling up against him, underlining her own dependence and the depth of her love. Yet she had done everything in her power to get him to marry Sarah Kelpmann! Did she know that he was not by nature faithful? That if she had not borne him a son he would have moved back from her a little, gradually allowed her to drift away from his life and back into her own? Perhaps. She had said something of the sort, just before he left for Norwich earlier in the week. He screwed up his eyes and brought the scene clearly back into his mind. Say feeding the baby in the low armchair by the fire in their tiny sitting room. Himself sitting on the table, kicking at the dining chair nearest to him. Say smiling up at him, speaking.

'You're not a one-woman man, Lou, you've got time and energy for two. I'd rather you married Miss Kelpmann now and went on loving me than blamed me later.'

'And you the mother of my boy? As if I would.'

She had smiled almost indulgently, as if she knew him better than he knew himself.

'Oh, Lou! Marry her, to please me!'

He had muttered something and left the room but he knew now that she had been right. If he lost Sarah Kelpmann, in the very depths of his mind he would blame Say. Because, dammit, he loved them both, in his way!

He turned on his side at last to settle down to sleep, and

knew that he would go through with it now whatever might happen. By the end of April Sarah Kelpmann would be Sarah Rose, and he would have two homes: a large house on Ipswich Road and a mews cottage in Golders Green. But the thought did not worry him. Things had a way of working themselves out, if you trusted to providence to guide you!

10

It was a beautiful wedding. The synagogue was decorated with branches of early lilac, white, mauve, and purple, and the poles of the Chupah were wreathed in vineleaves, cunningly twisted, with the pink and lavender motif of the lilac echoed in the hothouse blooms peeping from between the foliage.

Ted was sitting with the boys but Tina was with the wedding party, an 'interferer' in place of her dead mother, for she had helped to bring Louis up. Watching his wife's small, determined face as she, in turn, watched the bridal couple, Ted thought wryly that the Jews knew what they were talking about when they referred to the parents or parental representatives at a wedding by that name. Tina, bless her, could no more stop herself interfering in the lives of those around her than she could have stopped loving him. It was, he knew, both her strength and her weakness. And because it was part of her he could be indulgent about it, stepping in when he saw that her strong-willed 'guidance' was going to cause unhappiness, applauding her when it caused joy.

This was Ted's first Jewish wedding, and he noticed that apart from the bride – who looked absolutely radiant in white wild silk, with a coronet of lilies of the valley shining in her dark hair – Stella, who was a bridesmaid in blush-rose muslin, and Tina and Mrs Kelpmann, there was not a woman in sight. They were all up in the women's gallery, behind him. Mrs Kelpmann was crying steadily, the tears making glistening tracks down her bunchy, olive-skinned face. Would Sarah look like that one day? It seemed impossible – certainly Sarah would never have chosen to wear plum-coloured velvet and sables!

Mr Kelpmann was not crying; he was standing, very straight and upright, with one hand lightly touching his wife's, and as the bridal couple moved slightly – the ring was about to be placed on Sarah's finger – Ted saw Mr Kelpmann's expression change as his eyes fell on Louis. Ted looked away quickly, and when he looked back Mr Kelpmann – 'You must call me Ernest' – had controlled his features once more. I hope Louis realises that this time there's got to be no messing about, Ted thought, or my irrepressible brother-in-law might live to regret it. Ernest Kelpmann was a powerful man and he adored his only child.

There had been a lot of Hebrew spoken, but suddenly English words caught Ted's ear.

'Blessed thou art, consecrated to me by this ring, according to the law of Moses and Israel.'

The ring slid on to Sarah's forefinger and she raised her eyes to Louis's face. Her smile was sunlight on dark mountains, day dawning. Yet it was a private smile, meant for Louis alone. Louis was still holding her hand; Ted saw his fingers tighten, saw his brother-in-law's glance soften yet burn, and then they turned back to the Rabbi and the Chazan to drink the toast, their private moment over for now as Louis grinned his reckless grin and put his foot on the wineglass, symbolically significant in some way no doubt but to Ted it looked remarkably like the end of freedom. No more wine, women and song, for the cup is broken and the free man fettered. He grinned to himself, but then the choir broke into a chant of heavenly beauty and the couple moved down from up by the Ark to walk through the congregation.

As Tina passed him she crooked a finger and he slipped out of his seat, crooking a finger in his turn to his two sons. Desmond and Frank, as tall as he now, fair hair water-flattened, dark suits drawing attention to their broad shoulders, followed him out.

Outside, the sun shone brightly and up the road a laburnum tree, leaning over a little cobbled courtyard, was already spilling its bright gold. A small crowd had assembled and Ted grinned at the servants who clustered near, anxious to see the bride and to offer their good wishes to the happy couple.

He saw Mabel, looking extremely nice and rather grown up in a gown which looked vaguely familiar. And next to her, looking straight at the boys, that friend of hers, what was her name? Sally? Susan? The one Tina disapproved of so strongly. Ted, watching her, blinked as she caught Desmond's eye and one of her own long-lashed orbs closed in a wicked, twinkling wink. He glanced round, but Tina was busy, talking to Ruthie and the maids, calling Sarah over to show her bouquet. It would never do if Tina knew that already Desmond was bidding fair to rival his Uncle Louis over his interest in women!

The cars were waiting to take the wedding party and all the guests back to the Kelpmann house, where the reception was to be held in a vast marquee erected on the lawn. Desmond, standing beside Tina, murmured something and slipped away. Ted knew where he had gone but pretended not to notice. The boy was only human, the girl both young and extremely pretty. It would do more harm than good in any case to try and stop Desmond talking to her. Frank had followed his brother and the four of them stood in a small group until Tina, ending her conversation, called the boys to join her in one of the cars. Ted watched them drive away. The wedding is over, he thought sentimentally, and today a new life will begin for them both. If it was even half as happy as his own married life had been, they would be fortunate indeed.

*   *   *

'Suzie!'

Suzie, watching the bride, had been aware of Desmond with the tingling excitement that always overcame her when she was attracted to a man and knew it was mutual. He was, of course, much too young for her; Suzie, at nearly fifteen, usually sought companions of at least seventeen. But he looked much older; you could have taken him, she considered, for nineteen or twenty quite easily. Besides, there was something about him, though she did not quite know what. Louis had it too – though he, of course, was out of her class, and would not spare a second glance for someone of her age. Suzie, who made a point of knowing most things, knew that he and Sarah Sutton had been lovers right up to the time the Neylers' nanny left the family. She suspected, though the suspicion was completely unfounded, that Louis still had another woman tucked away somewhere.

'Oh, hello, Des.'

Her voice was calm and friendly, her smile the same. It was as if she had a little voice inside her, advising her how to behave with men, and with Desmond the little voice advised that he should be allowed to do all the work, all the pursuing; that he would not value her if she showed the slightest sign that she would welcome his attentions.

'Suzie, you look grand! Meet me this evening? At the tree-house?'

He spoke so low that only she could have heard, she told herself. Frank was telling Mabel about the ceremony, his voice still at the stage when it sometimes ascended the scale for a word or two, coming out as a squeak instead of the deep, masculine voice which was almost identical with Desmond's.

'I was surprised, Mabs; it's very colourful. Odd, in places. Do you know, before Uncle Louis went under the sort of canopy thing, he lifted Sarah's veil and they smiled at each other. Uncle Abe says it's tradition that the groom lifts the veil so that he can tell he's getting the right woman – not being palmed off with some spotty sister that they couldn't marry off. Weird, isn't it?'

'He'll lift more than her veil tonight,' Desmond said salaciously, and noticed Mabel's blush with interest. Three months ago, she would not have known what he was talking about. On the other hand, Suzie merely smiled and made as if to turn away. But as she did so he heard her murmur, scarcely above a whisper:

'Nine o'clock?'

'It's a date.'

Then their mother called them and the boys turned away. The colour in Mabel's cheeks was fading and Suzie caught her friend's arm.

'Shall we go out for tea, now we're so fine? To the Corner House, if you like – my treat. I'm rich this week. Want to know why?'

'Yes. Why?'

'I've left Garlands.'

They were walking away now, leaving Ada and William, and all the other servants from The Pride who had come down to see their dear Mr Louis wed, to make their way back home. Mabel shot a glance at Suzie.

'No! But I thought it wasn't so bad, and the money was all right. Where are you going next?'

'Nursing. That way, maybe I'll get to France one of these days.' She shot a dancing look at Mabel out of the corners of her long, green eyes. 'I don't mean to be poor for ever, Mabs. I'm going to marry a rich feller and live in luxury, I am.'

'I don't blame you. I suppose you didn't fancy munitions or working on the land or anything like that because . . .'

' . . . because there's no men in jobs like that. That's the idea. Perhaps I'll nurse a rich, fat old major, and marry him. Or a dashing young captain, who's an earl really, and then I'll be an . . . there's no such thing as an earless, I suppose?'

Mabel giggled and elbowed Suzie briskly in the ribs.

'Fool! If you're aiming for an earl, why did you say you'd meet our Des in the tree-house tonight?'

Suzie groaned. Mabel must have excellent hearing to have caught that low-voiced conversation!

'Meeting Des? Oh, that's just a bit of fun. I don't mean anything by it. Why? D'you still think he's too young for me?'

'I don't know that I ever thought he was too young for you. I thought you might have trouble if you messed around with Des. And I still think it.' Mabel could be frank to the point of crudeness when she liked, and she faced her friend frankly now. 'You don't want to take your drawers off for Des, I'm telling you, Suzie, or you'll get more than you bargained for. You'll end up rocking a cradle and that won't get you an earl!'

'I don't see why. I've given lads a good time before, and I'm not nursing a big belly yet.' Suzie looked curiously at her friend. 'I didn't know you knew about . . . well, that!'

'I'm not any too sure,' Mabel admitted. 'I'm repeating what Ruthie said to Nanny Sutton, ages ago. Only it was Louis she meant, of course.' She pursed her lips, then began to speak in a very good imitation of Ruthie's motherly tones. ' "Thass oonly fair to warn you, gel, that them as takes their drawers off for Mr Louis gits more'n they bargain for. You'll be rockin' a cradle in nine months." That's what Ruthie said,' Mabel finished, returning to her own voice.

'And you deduced from that . . . ?'

Mabel frowned and scratched her head.

'Lumme, that something *happens*, of course! No one's ever said what, so I don't know.' She raised a brow. 'Do you know?'

'We-ell, I know you can have a lot of fun without rocking no cradle,' Suzie said a little defiantly. 'You've got to be careful, that's all.'

'Oh. Well then, be careful.' They were on the Walk now, heading for the Corner House. 'Aren't you going to tell me what people do? When they make babies?'

'I am not!' Suzie sounded disproportionately indignant, Mabel thought. 'You'll find out for yourself soon enough.'

Once in the Corner House at the window table they favoured, eating cream cakes and drinking tea and eyeing the dresses of the ladies around them, it crossed Mabel's mind that, for all her talk, her friend might well be as ignorant as herself. Comforted, she continued her tea.

Louis and Sarah honeymooned in London. At first, Poppa had been taken with the idea of the two of them going to Yarmouth where, so many years before, he and his beloved Deb had been so happy. But then, in January, the town had been heavily attacked by Zeppelins and since then the east coast had been sporadically bombed, so he had suggested London. The theatres were still doing business as usual, the restaurants too.

Louis, of course, was all in favour of a London honeymoon. There would be opportunities, he thought optimistically, of getting over to Golders Green when Sarah was otherwise engaged.

So they travelled up to their hotel by car and made their way to the suite of rooms which Poppa had reserved for them. He considered it his right to pay for the hotel, he explained, and had also given Louis a generous cheque to pay for other pleasures during their stay.

And now, even as Desmond tiptoed across the croquet lawn towards his rendezvous with Suzie, Louis, who had been banished to the bar for a drink whilst his bride prepared for bed, tapped on their bedroom door.

'Sarah? Can I come in now?'

She opened the door and he slipped into the room. The curtains were firmly drawn across the wide windows which overlooked the park and the subdued, pinkish glow from the bedside lamps was the only illumination.

Sarah's hair was loose. That was the first thought which occurred to him, for he had never seen it loose before, flowing in deep, rippling waves down to her waist. She was wearing a white satin nightgown, quite grand enough to be a ball-dress, and she had bathed and powdered herself – he could smell something flowery which almost combated another scent: Sarah was nervous, despite her apparent calm.

He took her in his arms. She had always seemed almost as tall as he but now, barefooted, she seemed much smaller and more vulnerable. He decided to be gentle with her. Releasing her from his embrace he pushed her gently towards the bed.

'Lie down whilst I undress.'

She sat on the edge of the bed, brushing her hair, scarcely glancing across to where he was hastily stripping. He glanced at his maroon silk pyjamas, then decided that it would be a waste of energy to put on garments which would so soon come off. He sat beside her on the bed, put his arms round her, then rolled her, quite gently, on to her back and began to kiss her.

At first, she responded well and eagerly, almost as he would have expected an experienced woman to respond. But with the first attempt at real intimacy, she tensed and drew back a little. Not before time, Louis thought prudishly. A decent virgin of just twenty should not part with her nightdress willingly. He was subconsciously judging her by Sarah Sutton's standards, for Say had never allowed the light to remain on whilst they made love; he had never seen her naked in anything but moonlight, and then only, so to speak, by accident.

Suddenly, as if she could read his thoughts, Sarah began to resist him. Strenuously. Louis had expected coyness, perhaps a few tears, and was prepared to deal with such maidenly faltering in his best and most seductive style. He was not prepared to be kicked, scratched, punched, and finally to find himself kneed in the groin.

'Look, Sarah, I'm not going to hurt you. I'm . . .'

An expletive he had never expected to hear on a woman's lips was hissed at him.

'You are hurting! For God's sake, what do you think you're doing? Ouch! Stop it! *Ouch*!'

All Louis's good resolutions deserted him. It had always been like this, right from the start! On their very first date she had blacked his eye and scratched his face, and for what? For daring to try to touch her breasts, when if she had not worn such a provocative dress he would never have dreamed of doing such a thing! Well, this time it would be different. And to think that he had allowed her to retain her nightdress, when the bloody thing was confoundedly in the way!

He hurled her on to her back and ripped the nightdress off her, hearing the material rend with a good deal of satisfaction. She screamed at him and hit out and he captured her wrists, then began to force her legs apart with his knee. With some difficulty, for she was wriggling like an eel, he got both wrists clamped in one hand and shut her mouth with his own, then he tangled the other hand in her loosened hair and pulled it savagely until, beneath his mouth, he felt her lips part. He dared not loose her, though she was responding to him now, moving her body into a more comfortable position, her breathing steadying. In the muted light he watched her thick, white eyelids droop and then widen with pain and shock as he took her. She jerked convulsively, and tears welled up in her eyes, but she neither screamed nor tried to tear herself loose. He admired her then, wanting to explain to her, to move less savagely, to give as well as receive pleasure, but unable to do so, transported by a lust to which she was a stranger. And presently, when he was sated, he knew that he was forgiven. She cuddled up to him, sighing, and took his hand and put it on her breast, and laughed at the great black bruise disfiguring one cheek and the scratches on his chest.

They slept for six hours, heavily, and he was woken by her, kissing him. She was lying on her stomach leaning up on her elbows, and her mouth was on his own, firmly, and then her tongue probed at his lips and her breathing quickened.

Desire was roused to white heat by the sheer unexpectedness of the caress. He reached for her and she came willingly into his arms, though having deliberately begun to seduce him she proceeded to make him work hard for her capitulation.

An hour later, she remarked, in a slow sleepy voice, that her nightdress was ruined, and that it had cost twenty guineas.

'You shouldn't have fought,' Louis reminded her. 'If you hadn't, it wouldn't have been necessary to tear it.'

'You raped me,' Sarah said in a wondering voice. 'Now I think back, you raped me! Shame on you, Louis Rose!'

'Did I? I suppose I did. And you enjoyed it. Shame on you, Sarah Rose!'

'Mm hmm. Oh, Louis, I love you so!'

'You must do. You've scratched half the skin off my shoulders and it still stings!'

He propped himself up on an elbow and looked down at her. She pouted at him, her skin shiny, her hair tangled, her poise quite gone. He let his eyes linger on her mouth, beestung into soft plumpness by kisses which had known little of tenderness. He had marked her beautiful body, he knew that. Bruises on her wrists and breasts, on her soft inner thighs. With tenderness now, he kissed her lips.

'I'm sorry, darling. I didn't mean to be rough, but . . .'

He stopped talking.

'Who blacked your eye for you then, Des?'

Frank's far from innocent remark earned him a baleful look from his elder brother.

'What black eye? You did it, Frank, when you shot your elbow out last night over the billiard table. And don't you forget it!'

Frank, undeceived, grinned.

'Was it Mary? She's getting a big girl, isn't she? Lovely tits, as the upper school would have it.'

'Think what you like.' Desmond's tone was airy. The two boys were in their room, getting ready for a shopping trip into the city with their mother. They were only home, officially, for the wedding, but it would be a couple of days before they were returned to school, possibly four or five if they played their cards right. 'I say, Frank, have you got my blue tie with the white polka dots on it?'

Frank was sitting on the window-seat, with a copy of *Chums* before him, open at a Frank Shaw adventure story. He had been reading, with only half his attention on his brother, but now he looked up, his face darkening.

'You've not been mucking about with Mabs? Des, if you . . .'

'Not with Mabs, old bean. What riles me about Mabs is that you've no desire to muck about with her yourself, yet you're dead against anyone else having a go at her. You want to grow up, young Frank.'

'That's just where you're wrong,' Frank said placidly, returning to his story. 'You being a year ahead of me is a great help, because if you're an example of what growing up's like, then I don't want to do it.'

'If I have any more of your lip you won't live to do it,' Des said. 'And answer your elders and betters, will you? Where's my blue tie?'

'Don't know. Look for it. Lazy bugger.'

'Hey, just you look as well! Lazy bugger yourself! You're the younger, and if I say move, you move.'

Usually the boys avoided direct conflict since they were of a height, of a build, and of boringly identical strength, so that a fight between them tended to last for hours rather than minutes. But on this occasion, though neither knew it, there was just sufficient needle in both remarks to make them throw caution to the winds. Frank was uncomfortably aware that there was more than a grain of truth in Desmond's accusation – he would have killed anyone who hurt Mabel, but he had no desire to start what he termed 'nonsense' with her himself. And Desmond, smarting under the recollection that Suzie was nothing but a little tease, who would let a fellow go so far and no further, was jumpy and quick to take offence at what he imagined to be a slur on his manhood. They met, head-on, like stags in the rutting season, and it was thus that Stella found them when she came in to tell them that their mother was waiting. Locked in what appeared to be mortal combat, they swayed and staggered around the room, butting, punching, wrestling, whilst Stella squeaked and circled them, her small, shrill voice almost unheard above the rich medley of threats and swear-words pouring from her brothers.

'Boys! What are you doing? Stop it at once! Remember you are supposed to be gentlemen!'

Their mother's outraged voice had the effect of bringing them both out of their fury. One last push, a muttered 'You swine!' and then they were shaking their heads sheepishly and muttering, being forgiven, departing to the bathroom to wipe away bloodstains – Desmond's nose had bled copiously over them both, a tribute to a lucky head butt from his brother – and to tidy themselves.

'I didn't mean to nettle you over your eye,' Frank said, as he cleaned up. 'It's ages since we fought.'

'True. I rose to the bait like a fish to a fly, I suppose,' Desmond admitted. 'I'll tell you who it was, anyway. Suzie.'

'No!' Surprise and a degree of envy fought for supremacy on Frank's face. Surprise won. 'What was she like? As hot as Mabs painted her?'

'Yes and no. But when I come home in the summer I'll make jolly sure it's yes and yes! C'mon, let's get back, or Mama will ring a peal around our ears.'

Frank, following his brother down the stairs to where their mother would, by now, be impatiently awaiting them, wondered whether it would be politic to tell Des that, by the summer, Suzie would be a nurse and probably far away. He decided, perhaps a little regretfully, that it would not. He must keep his own counsel – for the time, at any rate.

'Well, Say my dearest, I've got my ticket, I've done most of my training, and any day now I'll be off to France. We really ought to get the boy saying "Dada" before then, though.'

It was a lovely bright day towards the end of May, and Louis, Sarah, and the baby were out walking in the park – or rather Louis and Sarah were walking whilst baby James rode in style in his perambulator.

'Oh, Louis, we'll miss you, Baby and me! Do you get a leave before you go?'

Say was wearing a white muslin dress with little blue flowers scattered over it, and a blue ribbon tied up her hair. She looked young and innocent, and although he knew that strictly speaking she was neither of these things he still felt his heart move at the sight of her. She was a good girl, was his Say! Nevertheless, both duty and desire prompted his next utterance.

'I get leave, but I'll go back to Norwich and my wife. Of course.'

'Of course,' she echoed, ashamed of a natural wish to have his company, and Louis put his arm round her shoulders and squeezed her lightly. She was growing plump; not that he objected. It was nice to have a plump woman and a slender one, he considered, for then one made fewer mistakes in bed. Awful, to roll over, grab a tress of thick hair, clear the back of a pearly neck for his passionate kisses – and discover himself murmuring the wrong name! Fortunately, this had not yet happened. He was training himself to call them both either by their given name of Sarah or by a love-word – darling, sweetheart, my love – during moments of passion.

He acknowledged ruefully that each Sarah had cause to be grateful for the existence of the other. Living with Say was a little like living with a contented and affectionate cow; living with Sarah more like cohabiting with a tigress who could love you one minute and rake you down the next. Lovemaking with Sarah was strenuous, she made him work for her and fight for what he wanted, but when he got it, God, it was sweet! He never quite knew where he was with her. She was unpredictable, beautiful, capable of sweetness, fierceness, sulkiness, generosity.

He found her exciting but exhausting. He knew that, had it been she in the Golders Green mews, he would probably not have won his flying certificate. But Sarah Sutton was different altogether. With her he could relax and be himself. On his weekend leaves he walked slowly around the summer city, or sat in a pub drinking and talking, or slept in the square garden, stretched out on a deckchair, Say content to lie on a rug at his feet and make daisy chains or sing lullabies to their son.

But now he had come to say goodbye to her for a while. He would see her when he had leave since he intended to go back to Norwich via London on each occasion, and to spend either the greater or lesser part of each leave with his mistress and the boy, depending on whose companionship he felt most in need of.

No one knew about his double life. The chaps at Hendon had known there was a woman, the chaps at Filton, where he had completed his training, assumed that he had married her. Walking with Say's hand tucked into the crook of his elbow, with the precious burden before them in the high perambulator, he mused idly on the undoubted fact that he felt a lot more married to Say than he did to Sarah. Sarah was excitement and escape, Say and his life with her the very stuff of marriage – bills, lines of washing, plain cooking.

'I'll leave after luncheon,' Louis said now, squeezing Sarah's shoulders again. 'Poor old darling; but you'll manage very nicely. You always do.'

Her smile was a little sad, a little abstracted. She told herself continually that one day he would go and that, when he went, she must make a good life for herself and her son without him. She knew Sarah well enough to guess what an exciting and challenging wife she would make. And yet each parting hurt a little more, made the possibility that there might be no return a little less easy to bear.

'Yes, we'll manage, Baby and me. We'll write, as well, as soon as you send us an address.'

She kept a brave face until she waved the little car off that afternoon, then she went indoors and wept over the washing.

'London's been bombed! Father always said a Zeppelin would get there one day!' Sarah scanned the newspaper eagerly, heedless of the sudden, icy stillness of her husband on the opposite side of the breakfast table. 'Oh, Louis, Golders Green's been badly hit. You had a flat there, didn't you? I do hope all your friends are all right.' She glanced up. 'A motor omnibus was hit and a score of people killed. And a great many injured. Do you . . .'

Louis plucked the paper out of her hand, scanned it quickly, then stood up, throwing his napkin down on the table where it knocked over the marmalade pot. His coffee cup was untouched; his toast, buttered but not yet spread with the marmalade, lay on his plate. Sarah stared up at him, her mouth dropping open.

'Louis? What . . .?'

'I'll have to go.' He walked round the table and patted her shoulder. 'I've scores of friends living in that area. Some of the fellows are in France already, but they left wives and children. I'll not be above a day, but I must go at once.'

'Of course you must.' She was immediately practical, immediately understanding. 'And I'll come with you. There might be something I could do.'

He was in the doorway, but turned at that.

'No, darling. It may be . . . a bit gruesome.'

She was on her feet, following him.

'War's gruesome, Louis. I'm coming. I'll just get my dark coat.'

But when she went round to the garage ten minutes later, the little car had gone.

Louis drove into the mews close and parked his car outside the cottage. Passing down the main street, he had been appalled by the damage. Houses with the frontages sheared clean away so that one saw the cracked washstand, the warm rug by the bed; the tiny, intimate details of the life that had once filled the house bared to the world at last. Louis turned away his head. He felt, obscurely, that the little back-to-back houses were like plain, fat little women who had found themselves stripped by the blast and were trying, in vain, to hide themselves. He would have liked to catch hold of the walls and close them around such pathetic, embarrassed nakedness, and failing that he would not stare at them.

But in the mews all seemed quiet and placid enough. There were geraniums in the windows of No. 4, salmon and scarlet, and the books which had lain on the sill of No. 7 lay there still. He walked briskly to his own front door, and rang the tinkling little bell. No answer. It was then that he remembered the motor omnibus and the people killed. He fished for his key and opened the door. It was quiet and cool, the low-ceilinged living room deserted. He went through to the kitchen. There was a fire burning, and the smell of cooking. He glanced out of the window, and saw Sarah. She was pinning washing on the line, nappies over one arm, the other reaching up. Her hair was untidy, wind-tugged, and in the loose grey gingham dress her bulges looked less appealing, but his heart, nevertheless, lurched with pleasure because she was all right. He opened the back door and whistled. She turned towards him, and he saw the pink fly to her cheeks, her eyes brighten.

'Louis! Oh, darling, is anything wrong?'

She ran into his arms and he patted her shoulder, trying to stifle an impatient desire to be sarcastic and biting at her very ingenuousness. Anything wrong indeed, with half the main street torn asunder by bombs!

'I thought there might be. I thought you might have been caught in the raid.'

She smiled up at him, then gently detached herself from his arms to pick up the washing, which she had cast down on seeing him.

'No, I'm all right. And Baby too. The noise was dreadful, but no one we know was hurt. Except Mr Tollworthy, the butcher. He's in hospital.' She returned to the line and began pinning the rest of the nappies out, speaking loudly above the rollicking wind. 'I would have let you know, but I didn't think.'

'No. Anyway, a letter wouldn't have reached me before tomorrow. We've got to arrange something, because I'll go mad with worry now, knowing that no one would contact me.' He gazed at her back view. When she stretched up like that her skirt lifted unbecomingly, revealing thick, wrinkled stockings and over-chubby calves.

She finished with the washing and turned to him, taking his hand and leading him back into the house.

'Worrying's silly, Louis. We'll be all right.'

'It won't do! London's going to be the most dangerous place in England for the rest of the war.' Inspiration struck him and he caught her shoulders. 'Of course! You must come home, to Norwich!'

Her eyes widened, then narrowed with laughter.

'Norwich? To Ipswich Road, I suppose? Oh, Louis, if only I could! But I'll be all right here.'

'I'll get you a little flat. This place is rented, and I daresay a flat in Norwich would cost no more. We'll choose one in a part of the city where the family don't go much. Why on earth didn't I think of it before? You'll be Mrs Lewis – you can remember that – and I'll be Robert Lewis, your soldier husband. Then I can divide my leaves up between you. God, it's the best idea I've ever had!'

She gazed up at him, adoration shining from her eyes.

'Could we? I'd love it, of course, because I've friends in the city. But we'd be found out, Lou, that's the rub. Someone would recognise you, or me, or both of us. We wouldn't be able to stroll in the streets or anything without being afraid.'

But his quick mind had already grasped both the advantages and the disadvantages and he had an answer ready.

'Yes we would! I'd keep special clothes at the flat, ready for Robert Lewis, and if anyone saw me by chance they'd think how like Louis Rose was, not that I *was* Louis. It'll work out whilst the war's on, at any rate, and when it's over we'll think again. It might be better for you to live in London then, because in peacetime I come up to town quite a bit for Poppa. But for now you'll live in Norwich, somewhere where you won't keep running into the family. And everything'll be prime, you see.'

'Louis, it wouldn't work. We'll find some means of keeping in touch so that you know I'm all right. But going back to Norwich – it would be far too risky. I'll stay, and it'll all be for the best.'

The flat was more of a bed-sitting room really, on Pottergate. It was next door to a pub, the landlady was fat and good-natured and made a great fuss of James, and Louis left mother and son there with no qualms.

'Your furniture will go into store until I get you somewhere better,' he told Say as he prepared to leave her. 'I'll send you an allowance, of course, and I'll see you every time I'm home. And I'll write. Now take care of yourself, and if you need anything either write to me or speak to Mrs Tuddenham.'

He had three more days of his leave left and she knew that he would not see her again. He had brought her straight back, after giving notice to the landlord of the mews cottage, and found her a room in a boarding house for one night. Then he had found the flat and moved her into it, barely remaining with her for an hour before rushing off back to his wife.

Now, in the stuffy, over-furnished living room with the gas-ring in the corner, he was saying goodbye to her. He kissed her, his mouth clinging for a moment, then he put her from him and instructed her again on how she was to behave.

'And take care of James,' he ended as he turned from her to go back to his other life.

She stood at the top of the stairs and waved, not liking to go rushing into the road because he had hidden his car further along so that no one would see him with the vehicle and later put two and two together. She knew that with the change of venue their relationship would change, but she did not know how. Time alone would tell that.

11: 1916

Dawn was breaking as Louis's aeroplane gained height, and the first rays of sunshine glinted on the edges of the retreating night-clouds in the lightening sky. It was 4.15 and this was the dawn patrol, a routine flight which could be boring or exciting, depending on whether the German aircraft were also dawn patrolling, trying to spy on or bomb the trenches below them.

Louis yawned jaw-crackingly and turned to glance at Nick, flying on his right and a little behind him in the formation. Nick raised a hand, and then, with a grin, mimed someone drinking, then clasped his head. They had had a hard night of it at the local *estaminet* the night before, and Louis's mouth felt like the bottom of a birdcage. He swallowed, and licked his dry lips. A cup of hot coffee would be nectar now, but he wouldn't get anything to drink until they landed in about an hour's time. Roll on breakfast, he thought longingly.

They were over the Allied trenches now. It was always grim down there, in winter a sea of mud and bodies, in summer a sea of dust and bodies. Now, in the March chill, it was gleaming clay, puddles reflecting the steely, cloudy sky. The shell holes were pools of thick, treacherous mud; horses could and did fall into them and were entirely swallowed up. Men, too. Louis shuddered and looked ahead to where Flight Commander Tillett led them. He saw the captain waggle his wings, then the nose of his aeroplane lifted as he began to climb again, straight up into the cloud cover. This probably meant that, having seen the sky clear above the trenches, he was checking that there were no enemy aircraft coming from the east, whence they always came. If everywhere was clear he might signal them to break formation and go off separately, keeping their eyes peeled for enemy formations of course, and then they would make their own way back to Petitpasteur, and breakfast.

The cloud, cold and clammy, closed round Louis and immediately he was alone. He could not see the wing tips of his own aeroplane, let alone anyone else's, but he held his course with the supreme confidence of one who flies in formation with men as experienced and skilful as he, and presently burst out into brilliant sunshine, the sky deep blue, the clouds a snow-scape just beneath his wheels. And company; the rest of the flight, all in exactly the same positions as they had held upon entering the cloud.

But there was nothing else of interest, save for some fast

vanishing specks in the east; German bombers, probably, making their way home after shedding their deadly loads over the trenches. They were a good way off, but it was possible that the captain would decide to chase them, or send a pilot or two in pursuit. Louis watched the leading aircraft eagerly, but instead the captain made signs that they were to split up, some going one way, some another. He tapped his wristwatch, then held up one finger, then gestured back towards the aerodrome. Louis, breaking away to the north, waggled his wings in acknowledgement; he would be landing in an hour, old Tilly might rely upon that! With a thirst like his he was not likely to be tempted into strafing balloons or chasing off to terrorise the German trenches. No, today he would be a good boy and patrol along his territory until it was time for breakfast.

It was as he broke away from the others, doing a rather showy roll, that a thought occurred to him. There was a farmhouse out in this direction where only the previous day he had gone with Nick. They had bought an excellent meal there – scones, new-baked and thick with cream, the real clotted sort. Afterwards, they had been pressed to accept delicious sandwiches made out of smoked ham. Louis swallowed. And though the coffee was only ersatz it had been good!

If he continued to fly in this direction, he could be over that farmhouse in five minutes. And landing in the big pasture at the back in five minutes and thirty seconds. And drinking hot coffee and eating ham and eggs in . . . say ten minutes? The prospect was irresistible. He continued to fly towards the farmhouse, noting absently that the area had been heavily shelled since he last passed over it. Last night there had been shelling, and he had heard the whine and crump of bombs, too.

He knew his plan was going to come to nought two minutes later, but for a moment he could not bring himself to believe it. The place must have taken a direct hit. The grey stone walls still stood but where the roof had been there was only a smoking ruin, and plainly nothing could have escaped from the fire that had raged in the farmhouse.

He circled, remembering the old couple, the woman's beaming, toothless smile and the old man's friendliness, the way they had pressed the ham sandwiches on the two young men who were in their country, fighting their war. The talk, almost philosophical, of their son and daughter, both dead in the war, and of a nephew, fighting in Egypt. It was impossible that the old people had lived, and yet . . . the ruins were still smoking, and the place was a good way from the village. It was all too probable that no one had yet been near the farm, and if not . . .

He knew he would land. Impossible to fly back to Petitpasteur not knowing whether those good people were alive or dead! He knew, of course, that they were probably, almost certainly, buried in the ruins and as probably dead. But if they were down there, suffering . . .

He landed neatly, climbed down from the cockpit, and walked over to the farmhouse.

He found them almost at once. They were both very dead, without dignity or individuality. They must have been sitting or standing close together when the bomb hit them, and now they were just fragmented. Louis walked away from the jumble which had once been the farmer and his old wife towards the stabling, which was, paradoxically, standing as untouched as though there had been no bomb, no blast, no sudden deaths. He had best take a look, make sure that there were no beasts waiting to be milked or fed or something.

Afterwards, he wondered what had taken him along to the darkest end of the apparently empty stable, to peer right inside the last stall. Could it have been providence? But for whatever reason, he went along to the end stall and saw its occupant.

'Hello! You gave me a fright! You aren't hurt, are you?'

The small, skinny child curled up beneath the manger neither moved nor spoke. Only the eyes glinted, to show that it lived. Louis moved closer. He tried in French.

'Bonjour, mon enfant. Que faites vous?'

Not a movement nor a sound. Louis moved nearer. He put out a hand. Still nothing. Making a quick decision, he lifted the child up beneath her armpits, for she was definitely a girl, with a skimpy, thin little cotton dress and shoulder-length hair. She hung in his hands like a rag doll; her head even lolled a little to one side. But beneath his right hand he could feel the thunder of her heartbeat. She was deathly afraid.

Louis loved children and had always been at ease with them. Now he simply sat down on the floor, cross-legged, and cuddled the little girl as unselfconsciously as though she were his own little niece. He sang to her, he played games with her, going 'round and round the garden' on the palm of one small, grubby hand, burying his head in her neck and blowing raspberries against her soft skin, teasing her in a mixture of English and French over her silence, her dirty face, her lack of movement.

He was hours overdue, and never even thought of it. His thirst no longer mattered. Nothing mattered but bringing this filthy, tattered girl-child back from whatever far country she had been driven to by the bombardment.

It was when he began to play 'This little piggy went to market' that he knew he was winning. She withdrew her foot from his fingers with a little jump. And then she laughed – a small enough sound, certainly, and although he knew it was a laugh he also realised how nearly it might have been a cry. But it was a beginning.

Thirty minutes later, he took her to the pump in the yard and solemnly washed a small part of her face, 'so that I can see if you can smile at me'. She could, and, presently, did. When he climbed back into his cockpit and wedged her on to his knee she showed not a trace of fear, though when they landed and his mechanic came running towards the aircraft she shrank back, her eyes widening and darkening like a cat's.

He picked her up, for she was featherlight, and walked with her to the squadron office. Captain Tillett was there, worried in case he had managed to crash his aeroplane and kill himself. The story, briefly told, was explanation enough of the child's presence.

'What's her name? And what was she doing there? I've

been there myself, but there was never any mention of a child.'

Louis shrugged.

'I don't know, and I doubt whether she can tell you. Her shoes are almost worn through; I'd say she's walked for weeks. And the dirt on her isn't just ordinary muck, it's engrained filth. If you ask me, she just turned up at the farmhouse last night, and hid in the stables to avoid the strafing. What with the noise and the shock of the farmhouse coming down, I daresay she's not yet able to think straight.'

'I see. Well, you'd better take her to the base hospital. The girls down there are wonderful. They'll see her right.'

So Louis put the child into the squadron's ancient lorry and drove her to the hospital, and tried to leave her with the prettiest nurse he had seen for some while. But the child would not be left. She clung to him, and when the nurse took her and Louis turned away she spoke for the first time.

'Non! Non! Avec vous, monsieur!'

He returned to her side at once, explaining that the nurse was good and kind, and was merely taking care of her because she was a little girl and needed food and a nice hot bath.

'If you tell me your name, I'll come and see you tomorrow,' he assured her, in his best French. 'And then, if you would like it, I could take you to my home and you could meet my family.'

'Josette,' she murmured, clinging to his hand. 'I am Josette. You swear you will come back, monsieur?'

He put a hand to his heart, squatting down so that their heads were level.

'I swear it. You'll be good with this lady?'

She glanced indifferently up at the nurse, then back at him. She nodded vigorously.

'Yes. If you will truly come back.'

It took them a month to make all the arrangements and to get Josette respectable once more.

'There was nothing physically wrong with her,' Louis

told Nick. 'But she had worms, and fleas, and lice, she still doesn't know her surname and she had no idea where her relatives might be. She and Maman were walking when the aeroplanes came over and Maman fell. Then, later, Maman died. And she went on walking, because she didn't know what else to do.'

'And she's been cleared to go to England?'

'That's right. She's a Belgian, and England's full of 'em at the moment, so there's a slight hope that someone might recognise her, I suppose. But more to the point, my sister's got a little girl, Stella, about Josette's age, and she's said she'll give Josette a home and bring her up like her own. She will, too. She's a sharp little lady, my sister Tina, but she needs this kid as much as Josette needs her.'

'Why's that?' Nick suddenly did a double-take. 'Hey, you say she's a *Belgian*? and she *walked*? Good God, man, it could be a couple of hundred miles!'

'That's right. Kids are odd little creatures, but they can cover the ground when they decide to keep moving. Tina lost her own younger children in an accident in the summer of 'fourteen. That's why she'll welcome Josette.'

'I hope you've explained to her that England's an island, or she'll probably set right out to walk back to you,' Nick remarked. He had not been able to help noticing how very attached to Louis the small girl had become. 'Does she understand that she's to live with your sister and her daughter?'

'She does. She's sharp as a needle, you know,' Louis said with almost paternal pride. 'Only until the war's over, mind you. Then she's going to live with me!'

'Hmm! What will your wife say to that?'

'Oh, by then Josette will have settled with the Neylers and probably wild horses wouldn't drag her away,' Louis said with airy optimism. 'It'll all work out for the best. Things always do!'

Desmond thundered down the stairs, skidded across the parquet flooring in the hall, and then, just outside the dining room door, adopted a careless pose and sauntered into the room. Because it was Saturday morning no staff members presided over breakfast, only two prefects, and the boys were talking freely, opening their letters and eating vast quantities of toast and jam. The butter, which was rationed, had gone long since and the jam itself, being rhubarb and ginger, was detested by every pupil of Pursell's School from old boys to the very youngest midget in the juniors, but food was food. On weekday mornings two rounds of toast only were allowed, so at weekends one ate one's fill.

Desmond grabbed a chair and flung himself into it. He was immediately hailed by Frank, sitting opposite him in deep conversation with his friend Puggy.

'Des, there's a letter from Mama and Daddy. I bags first read.'

'Be my guest. Where's my egg?' A boiled egg apiece was a Saturday morning ritual and Desmond did not intend to miss out just because he was late. 'Come on, did someone bone my egg?'

'No, young man, no one's ate it,' the cook said placidly, entering the room. 'It'll be like a bullet now, and cold, too, but I daresay you won't mind that. If you 'adn't been late, acourse, you could have 'ad it 'ot. I heard you thunderin' down the stairs, so I brought it through.'

'Ta, Cooky, you're a princess,' Desmond said, decapitating his egg. It was hard. 'Any bread and butter for your favourite customer, Cooky?'

'It's all gone long since. You'll 'ave to make do with plain bread,' Cook said tartly, but she snatched a slice of bread from the plate and presently returned it, smeared with either butter or margarine; it was such a scraping that Desmond could not tell which. Nevertheless, he thought, devouring it and giving Cook a grateful beam, it was better than nothing. And it was Saturday. If Frank was in the right sort of mood they could take themselves off to the Copper Kettle and get themselves coffee and cakes.

'It's from Mama, with a bit on the end from Daddy,' Frank remarked, reading the letter. 'Mama's going on about the Belgian child. She's dark-haired, and has dark eyes. Mama says she's teaching Stella French faster than Stella's teaching her English.' He broke off to chuckle and help himself to a pale and tepid cup of tea. 'Auntie Ray's nursing somewhere in France, and Aunt Cecy made a cake with grated carrots instead of dried fruit – ugh, horrible!'

'Shut up! Let me read it!' Desmond grabbed the pages and skimmed them with only faint interest. Josette – soppy name – interested him not at all. Girls were fine, but ten-year-old girls did not count as such in his book. On the other hand, it seemed as though Stella and the new brat got on pretty well. That would mean he and Frank would have peace during the summer vac, to say nothing of Easter, which was almost upon them. So good would come out of evil, in fact. He grinned at the thought. One could scarcely describe the taking in of a ten-year-old brat as an evil action, but it really would be jammy if it got Stella off their backs!

Daddy's few lines were typical of his father. He had gone up to London to see if the army was interested in putting him in khaki but it appeared it was not, or not yet, at any rate. He had a contract to make special boots for officers and was putting men and women on to the work at more than he had ever paid anyone before. He was giving free cinema shows to the wounded soldiers twice a week. He was their loving father.

Desmond finished the letter and shoved it back into its envelope and then into his jacket pocket.

'We go down to Austin's for our fruit today, Puggy. You coming, or shall little brother and I go off on our tod? If so, we can bus.'

Puggy, thus appealed to, shook his head and stood up.

'Not today, Neyler. I'm playing in a match after grub, so I'll go and punt a ball about. I know you two. You'll be up to something, and I want to be in tip-top condition. We're playing King's, and they're good.'

'Tip-top condition?' Frank got up too and punched his friend lightly in the shoulder. 'With all that soggy school toast inside you? And about ten gallons of Cook's worst tea, laced with snail's milk? You'll be lucky if you can trot, let alone gallop!'

Puggy grinned and punched Frank back. He was a thick-set boy with greenish eyes, ten million freckles and ginger hair. He was also a very fine rugger player.

'Do me less harm than cream cakes and black coffee,' he observed. 'Why aren't you playing, Neyler?'

'Because I went to Ely last time, and young Horton-Smythe needs a game,' Frank said. 'I might watch, though, so do your best, laddie!'

Desmond snorted. He had got his cricket colours at the end of the previous summer and was longing to sport his white blazer with the purple raven on the pocket, but he had little time for rugby, which he considered a crude and dirty game, easily leading to black eyes, broken noses, and the consequent loss of the good looks of which he was so fond. Frank and Puggy had acquired their first fifteen colours this year despite their youth, and at match times wore purple blazers with silver ravens on the pocket and velvet caps with tiny peaks and silver tassels on the crown. If his brother watched the match in all the glory of his blazer and cap, then Desmond would not do so for the world.

'I'll do better than you would,' Puggy jeered. 'Going to give us the benefit of your support, Des?'

'No, it's a game for ruffians,' Desmond said. He had remained seated, finishing off the last of the toast, but now stood up. 'Well, if you're not coming, Pug, we might as well go. Ready, Frank? Shall we catch the bus?'

During the autumn and winter terms the pupils of Pursell's had to walk or bicycle everywhere to keep them fit for rugger and football, but in the summer term they were allowed to travel by bus since the headmaster did not believe that cricket was as exacting a sport as 'footer'. However, an exception had been made for the Neyler boys, when they visited the greengrocer for their Saturday order.

The whole business had come about after their father had visited the school and had been impressed by everything except the quality of the food.

'It's like food on board ship in the sixteenth century,' he grumbled to their mother. 'I'm not having my sons going down with scurvy, or losing all their teeth by the time they're twenty. Boys need decent fruit and vegetables as well as meat stewed to rags and great suet puddings.'

Accordingly, he arranged with a greengrocer in the town that each Saturday during termtime his sons might go into the shop and spend up to five shillings between them on fruit, the bill to be settled by him at the end of each term. The town itself being out of bounds to the boys except on special occasions, he had made his arrangements with Mr Austin, a greengrocer who was right on the outskirts of Cambridge.

And then one day Desmond was forced to go for the fruit by himself, since Frank was in sick-bay. Seeing a chance to gain additional privilege, Desmond had pointed out to his house tutor that with the weight of oranges and grapefruit in his bicycle bag making him unsteady he had been forced to unload half the fruit and to make two trips. His house tutor, a sensible and easy-going man, agreed that in future the boys might catch a bus 'when necessary' to fetch their weekly order. It immediately became necessary on almost every occasion for a while, since one must not allow privileges to lapse. And now they frequently caught the bus, not just as far as Mr Austin's, but right into the centre of Cambridge, for there were a hundred good reasons why it might take them most of the morning to fetch their fruit and, unless they were seen, very little fear of being apprehended.

Today, however, was sunny and relatively mild.

'No, let's walk,' Frank said now, as they clattered across the hall to the front door. 'We can always get a bus back.'

They were dressed in sports jackets and flannels, their caps in the regulation position on the extreme back of their heads, but when they were well clear of the school both boys stuffed their caps into their pockets, removed their school ties, and tried to look as though they came from anywhere but Pursell's. It would not do to be seen in Cambridge sporting the school colours. The dons and other college officials were quite capable of informing on them to their teaching colleagues at the school.

'Here, I brought our civvy ties. Is yours the red or the blue?'

'Doesn't matter.' Frank slung the red tie round his neck and tied it, then scrutinised the road ahead. 'There's old Ma Hogman! D'you think she'll notice our ties?'

Desmond whipped his cap out of his pocket and was about to jam it on his head when, by some trick of fate, a bus drew noisily up at a stop some half a dozen yards ahead of them.

'Quick, run for it!'

Before Mrs Hogman was anywhere near they were on the bus, making their way to the top deck, triumphantly bound for the town centre.

As they climbed down from the bus Frank remembered something.

'Des, I meant to ask you. Did you see the notice board this morning? Anyone mention Tufton?'

Tufton had been head boy last year, and had beaten Desmond for taking a shop girl to the cinema when he should have been attending a demonstration of small boat sailing organised by the prefects. There had been no love lost between them after that, for Desmond considered himself too old for beatings. He frowned now.

'Tufton? No one said anything. Why, what's happened to him? Nothing pleasant, I hope.'

'Killed. At Verdun. There were four of ours.'

'Oh.' Desmond looked blank for a moment, then pushed his hands into his pockets and began to saunter nonchalantly up the street, gazing into the shop windows as he went. 'Well, he was a swine so I can't feel any great loss, though I wouldn't say that to anyone else, of course. Four of ours, you say? D'you know the other names?'

'I wrote them down so I can tell Uncle Lou when I write. He won't have known them. They would have been midgets when he was here if they were here at all. And over there I shouldn't think subalterns have much to do with the elite of the Flying Corps. Tuffy had only been out three weeks.'

'Three weeks!' His voice subdued, Desmond added:

'Who were the other three?'

Frank fished a crumpled piece of paper out of his pocket.

'Paget, Carruthers, Coe; that's William Coe's elder brother. He was called out at suppertime a couple of days ago and didn't come back. We guessed then what it must be. I can't remember Carruthers at all but Paget played in the old boys' match last year. Big fellow with a yellow moustache. Remember?'

Uneasily conscious that in just over a year he himself would be taken for military service unless he had managed to get into a classified job by then, Desmond tried to change the subject.

'That reminds me, I've not heard from Suzie lately. I wonder if she's in France? She wrote to me a couple of times when she first went into nursing, but I've not heard for ages.'

'Don't show your ignorance, Des. Girls can't nurse in France until they're eighteen. Anyway, she writes to Mabs, so I think she must be all right.'

'And Mabs writes to you. I see. Well, next time you write to Mabs you might ask her to remind Suzie I exist. Come on, here's the Kettle. Going to risk it?'

It was not, in fact, as much of a risk as it might have appeared. The Copper Kettle was an attractive little tea-room with a wide window looped with net, giving an excellent view down the street in both directions. At the back the tables were partitioned off, and there was also a very convenient rear exit so that if one were careful one could slip out if a house tutor's wife, or a couple of prefects, looked like entering. And now that the younger masters had been caught up in the war effort, so that even the older ones were involved with sporting and other extra-curricular activities, it was less likely than ever that they would be caught.

Accordingly the boys went in and sat down at their favourite table, a sheltered nook near the back, and beckoned the elderly waitress. All the staff, except the older women who could not stand the pace of war-work, had been employed elsewhere by now.

'Coffee and cream cakes, please,' Desmond said, giving the waitress the benefit of his most charming smile. 'Have you any meringues?'

Presently, with a plate of mock-cream cakes between them and a jug of coffee steaming in the middle of the table, Desmond leaned towards his brother.

'See those girls over there? What d'you think?'

Frank followed his brother's meaningful glance. Two girls, both personable, wearing fashionable light wool suits and with their hair short and curled, were sitting at a window table. They were glancing now and then towards the two boys in their alcove in what could only be termed an interested fashion.

'Des, will you never learn? It'd be bad enough just being caught in town, but to be caught talking to girls . . .'

'We shan't be caught! We could take 'em to the cinema this afternoon, since you aren't playing in the match. Or we could meet them down by the Cam arter dark this evening. Be a sport, Frank. Let's go and see if we can click with 'em!'

Frank hesitated. They were very pretty girls; the smaller of the two had a roguish look in her dark eyes and he admired the way her suit clung to her small, high bosom. He nodded, only half reluctant.

'Righto. I don't suppose they're interested in us, but it wouldn't hurt to have a word with them.'

They finished their coffee and cakes, paid the bill, and got up. Crossing the room and heading for the door, Frank saw Desmond preparing himself for the usual opening gambit just as the two girls got up as well and came towards them. This threw Desmond slightly, Frank realised, but his brother gathered his wits and held out his hand to the taller of the two girls.

'Good morning! Miss Ferris, isn't it? I was just saying to my friend that . . .'

'Why aren't you at the Front?'

That was the taller of the two, the one Desmond had addressed. She was blushing deeply, colour spreading patchily across her face, but she held her ground, repeating the words loudly.

'Pardon?' Desmond was completely bewildered.

'At the Front! Why aren't you fighting in France? The army needs you, but my friend and I don't! We've got no time for a couple of windy shirkers.'

Briskly, she pressed something into Desmond's nerveless fingers. Her small friend, eyes downcast, came forward and fumbled something soft into Frank's hand. Then the two girls marched out, heads held high.

Frank opened his fingers and stared down at a pigeon's feather. For a moment it meant nothing to him. Whatever had that girl been prosing on about? And then he realised he had been given a white feather. He felt warmth rise in his cheeks. Desmond stood there, crimson-faced. Someone sitting at one of the tables muttered that they should be ashamed of themselves. Frank turned round, clenching his fists. Bland female faces beneath feathered hats, linen cloches, avoided his gaze. Every face seemed suddenly condemnatory. He wanted to explain, or to hit someone, but instead he shoved Desmond in the back, then walked past him, opened the door, and pulled his brother outside. Cool, crisp air! After the malignant stuffiness of the Copper Kettle it was like wine out here! The girls had disappeared.

The boys walked blindly, away from the Copper Kettle, around corners, until they reached Regent Street, with Parker's Piece on their left. Frank jerked his head at the green grass, and the two of them walked out to where some philanthropic soul had propped an ancient wooden seat against a gnarled tree-trunk. They sat, wordless for a moment. Frank opened his hand again to let the feather flutter free, but the wretched, crushed thing clung to his sweaty palm and he had to wipe it off against the slats of the bench. It was not even white, he noticed, with wry humour. Stupid little sluts. They had not even had the commonsense to pick up white feathers to round the insult off nicely. They had just grabbed for the first thing they saw – and for the first two boys they saw as well. One each. Neat.

It occurred to Frank then, sitting quietly on the bench whilst the fresh March morning erased the stupid, spiteful words from his mind, that if he looked eighteen to a couple of girls he probably looked eighteen to a lot of people. And it followed that in that case he would be accepted into the army without any fuss. In a way, then, the girls had been justified in telling him that the army needed him, because it was true. Conscription had come in at the beginning of the month and any young male who was not in an essential job ought to be fighting in France! His blood raced for a moment, then doubt cooled it. He was a good shot, he enjoyed the OTC manoeuvres carried out two or three times a week on this very piece of ground, he was head of his platoon whilst Desmond was a mere squaddy still. It had not occurred to him to try and join the army because he knew himself to be too young and believed the war would be over before he was old enough to take part in the conflict. Yet that morning, when he had read the list of the old boys who had died at Verdun, he had had a cold feeling, an intimation of mortality, perhaps. What could happen to a big, tough ex-head boy like Tufton could also happen to him. Yet thousands of soldiers did not die; look at the generals. They seemed to be all right. And more than four of last year's sixth form had gone to France. Uncle Louis had been in France for ages, and to be a flier, like him, would be prime!

When he thought that Desmond was calm enough, Frank suggested that they make their way back to Mr Austin's shop and thence to school. But all the way back along Regent Street and Hills Road Desmond brooded and muttered about the stupidity of the two girls and the cruel unfairness of what they had said and done.

Frank, on the other hand, bore them no ill-will; he was too excited by the thought that they had put into his head. Why should he not take up the challenge and join the army?

12

'My arms are stiff! When we come in on Monday, Esther, let's have a change round. I'll rinse the sheets, and you can jolly well mangle them.'

Mabel and her friend Esther Smallwood were changing from overalls and caps back into their outdoor clothes after a session in the laundry of the Norfolk & Norwich hospital.

'I wouldn't mind that. Just look at my hands!' Esther exhibited small, pink hands, the fingers wrinkled and ancient-looking from constant submersion in water. 'It isn't so bad in the summer, but this evening the water was icy!'

'I know. But if you don't get a move on the Figg mutters about "young ladies what in't never done a hand's tarn, together", and that's maddening. Are you ready?'

The two girls called goodnight to the regular laundry workers and made their way out of the hospital to the main road. They usually walked home together since their homes were not far apart, though Esther's father was a timber merchant living in a mansion and owning two motorcars, and Mabel's father was a gardener living in a cottage and owning two bicycles. But the war, and Mabel's scholarship, had made them as nearly equal as it was possible for two girls to be.

'You're doing post next week, aren't you?' Esther said presently as they trudged along the sandy pavement. 'I'm doing clerical work for my father.'

'Yes, I'm postlady. And I'm on at the hospital from four till six as usual, and I'm due to help with the allotment as well. We'll be busy, holiday or no holiday. Still, I daresay we'll have time for a bit of fun!'

'I daresay. And it's all to help the war effort. My brother says the home front is just as important as the fighting.'

Esther's brother was a subaltern in France. Mabel had been watching her friend's face once when Esther had been skimming down a recent casualty list. It had made her glad she was an only child.

'I suppose that's true. Everyone works hard now, don't they? Mrs Louis Rose drives an ambulance and helps in the wards, and my mother's full time at Bolton & Paul's. Even Mrs Neyler works hard. She does nearly all her own housework!'

They reached the end of Esther's drive but paused for a moment, Esther swinging on the wrought-iron gate as she spoke.

'Will you call for me on Monday if I don't see you before?'

'You'll see me before then, delivering your post,' Mabel reminded her. 'And I might take your fare on the buses if I'm doing that on Monday, or . . .'

'I know. If I died tomorrow I'd half expect to meet a High School girl on the gate with a temporary worker band on her arm, explaining that she was standing in for St Peter! But do call for me!'

'Righto. Cheerio for now!'

Walking the few hundred yards along the Newmarket Road which separated the Smallwood home from The Pride's driveway, Mabel thought about the changes the war had made in everyone's lives. Women who had never so much as dusted their own bedrooms now scrubbed floors in hospitals, drove motor buses, manufactured parts of aeroplanes, or worked on the land. Her own horizons had widened remarkably, but she loved the opportunities to see how other people lived, and hoped sincerely that after the war was over people would not return to their old dull and narrow paths.

Reaching the dark driveway, Mabel struck up it without a qualm, well used to returning in the late evening after her work was over. She wanted to visit the house tonight, though, so did not strike across the top of the drive and into the pathway through the trees which led to her parents' cottage. She knew that Mrs Neyler would be in the kitchen, preparing the evening meal, so she made straight for the back door, tapped, and slipped in.

Her guess had been right. Mrs Neyler was taking a meat pie out of the oven. On the bottom shelf Mabel glimpsed jacket potatoes and a rice pudding. The war was a great leveller when it came to food, too. Mr Neyler refused to take advantage of his position, and there was little difference in the way the Neylers and the Walters ate now.

'Hello, Mrs Neyler. Is my mum here?'

Tina, who had heard the door open, straightened and smiled.

'No, dear. She came in for a few minutes, but she left half an hour ago. You're on holiday now, aren't you?'

'Yes, we broke up for Easter today. Only of course our war-work goes on. I'm doing the post on Monday, and I was wondering . . .' Mabel hesitated, then glanced down at her boots and up again, to meet Mrs Neyler's dark blue eyes. They were very like Frank's eyes, she thought. 'Well, Frank will be home by then, won't he?'

'Yes, that's right. And Desmond, of course.'

'I was wondering whether Frank might come with me to do the deliveries. I do rather hate the post job.'

Tina smiled, half teasing.

'Not worse than mangling sheets, surely? Your mother was telling me about it. It sounds horrid.'

'Not as horrid as the post. Last winter I took an official letter to an old lady in Suffolk Street. I had to read it for her, since her sight was failing. It – it wasn't a nice letter, and though I stayed for a bit, and made a cup of tea, I've never forgotten how awful it was.'

'That's too bad. I suppose it was a sad sort of letter? Frank will enjoy coming round with you on Monday, I'm sure.' Tina turned to the oven and began to take the potatoes out. Curiosity and delicacy were fighting a battle, and curiosity won. 'What did the letter say, dear?'

'Her boy had been killed.'

'Dreadfully sad. Frank will be home tomorrow morning,

so if you pop in at luncheon time you may make arrangements with him.'

Making her way home, Mabel remembered the letter. I was too young to know I should have lied, she thought with anguish. Reading the letter aloud to the old lady had been almost as wicked a deed as writing it had been.

It had been brutally brief. Your son has been court-martialled and shot for desertion, it had said.

'Well, love, they've found a use for me at last, even though it's only as an organiser! They won't send me to the Front, but I'll free some other fellow to fight for his country, and that's what matters.'

Tina stared across the kitchen at Ted, the angry words held back, with the tears. He had longed to be part of the war and now he was. Weeping or reproaches would not change the army's mind about accepting his services. It would merely make him less happy.

'Ted, darling, I'm very glad for you! It's what you wanted, and knowing you're in a safe job makes it easier for me to bear you being away from me.'

His delight was transparent and he kissed her, beaming.

'You're a woman in a million! You'll manage without me, I know. You did it once before, my clever girl!'

'Of course I will. Look, this meat pie's cooked to perfection. Could you fetch Ruthie and the girls? They trooped out to the garage with William to watch him doing an oil change, of all things!'

'I know. I asked them to bring me down some apples from the loft, so that I could have a few words with you before they came in. I'll give them a shout.'

He went to the back door and shouted, while Tina began putting meat pie out on the plates. They all ate in the kitchen now, the girls, Ruthie, herself and Ted. It was rather cosy, sitting round the scrubbed wooden table in the warmth of the fire, though a far cry from pre-war dinners!

In response to Ted's call the children came hurriedly into

the kitchen, closely followed by Ruthie. Tina, watching the children settle, mutter grace, and begin to eat, realised what secret lives Stella and Josette led. Like two little mice, or two sisters, they whispered and giggled together over private jokes, shared a bath at bedtime, pooled their pocket money. With Ted gone, it would fall to her to live more closely with her daughters. It might be fun to get to know them better!

'Actually, I don't mind delivering round here.' Mabel stood on tiptoe and pushed a bundle of letters through a letter-box, then descended the steps to join Frank on the gravel sweep once more. 'It's impersonal, you see. No one wants to chat to you, or asks you to read the letters for them. The other girls hate doing round here because there's so much walking up and down drives, but I rather enjoy it. They have lovely gardens, some of them.'

'I like it today,' Frank agreed, smiling at the bright sunshine. 'But yesterday – by gum, didn't we get wet? I was half drowned by the time we got home. Even my rubber boots were squelching.'

'I don't mind a bit of wet,' Mabel said with airy inaccuracy. 'It would be much quicker if we just pushed through the hedge into next door's garden, but I daresay they'd complain and we'd only catch it.'

'We couldn't, it's holly,' Frank said briefly. 'Go on. You were telling me about the concert you gave at school for wounded soldiers.'

'So I was. Where had I got to? Oh, I know, the little ones. They did a black and white minstrel show. Stella and Josette took girls' parts so they didn't have to black up, and they looked so pretty! They had frilly muslin dresses, and little ballet shoes, and they did a topping dance! The men cheered and clapped! And then there was a toy symphony. That was awful!'

'I believe you!' Frank laughed. 'I suppose they had combs and triangles and all those fearful noise-makers?'

'Well, yes, but that wasn't the reason. There was this man at the back, you see. He was pretty bad. I think he only came because he was related to one of the mistresses. She did a lot to help and wanted this chap to come. He had awful scars on his head and neck, Frank; purply, raw-looking places. Then, when a girl began to whack a big tin tray to start the symphony off – oh, it was awful!'

'Why? Do go on, Mabs! What happened?'

'He went a bit mad, I think. He howled like a dog, and he was crying real tears and banging his head against the wall, and not even the biggest girls knew what to do. The other soldiers got up and stood round him so we couldn't see, and someone called for a car and they took him away. Then the soldiers came back and sat down and said carry on, only they were . . . . twitchy. I don't know how else to describe it. We knew they were longing for the whole thing to be over, only we didn't know how to end it. And then Miss Leman – she's a wonderful woman – stepped forward and said would the men like to put the chairs back against the walls and come through to the kitchens for a buffet tea. We'd meant to serve it to them in the hall, but this way they all milled around and helped to get the cakes out of the tins and made their own tea, and cracked jokes about how handy they were. And before we knew it everyone was comfortable again. We'd got them boxes of home-made sweets and a string bag of fruit each, because everyone else gives cigarettes, and they really liked them, you could tell. Then they went home.'

'I wonder what happened to the man who went a bit mad?' Frank said. 'Poor devil!'

'Yes, I know. I wonder, too. Now tell me about your school. What do you do towards the war effort?'

'Not as much as you, I don't think. Des and me are in the OTC and we've learned how to shoot and drill and read maps. Bayoneting, attacking, using cover, throwing grenades – that sort of thing. I'm pretty good. I command my platoon already. Daddy's leaving in a day or two, you know, and I reckon I'll be next.'

'No, Desmond will. He's a year older than you.'

'Doesn't matter. I want to go and Des hates the thought. You know what he's like about getting his hands dirty, and in the trenches you get more than dirty hands! People get in by lying about their age and that's what I'll do. I look a lot older than I am, you know.'

'Oh, really? Where's your beard, then?'

He grinned down at her from his considerable height, not annoyed by the slur on his apparent age as Desmond would have been, but amused by it. He is older, Mabel thought, and was dismayed.

'I can't help being blond. Fair-haired fellers always seem to have pretty feeble beards. Daddy can still go two days without shaving and no one would notice. It isn't that which counts, you know. It's height, shoulders – general strength, I suppose. You could take me for eighteen.'

They reached the roadway again and Mabel stopped, pulling Frank to a halt too. His very coolness and self-confidence was convincing.

'But you wouldn't, Frank! You wouldn't join up and go out there. Your mum and dad would mind terribly, and I daresay Des would as well. And what about school – your future?'

'Daddy can't say much considering he's off himself in a few days, and Mama cares for Des more than she does for me. As for school, I've had enough of it. And if everyone says "I must think of my future" and doesn't go and fight, there won't *be* a future. Or not a future worth living, at any rate.'

They walked the rest of the distance between the driveways in silence but as they turned up into the next property Mabel tried another tack.

'Why, Frank? What brought this on? You're happy at school, for all you may pretend you hate it, and you aren't the aggressive type. You don't want to kill people, do you?'

'Not ordinary people, no. But the Huns aren't ordinary people, Mabs. They do things that make your blood run cold! The stories I've heard . . . there's a chap who writes in *Chums* who's pretty straight, and from his reports it just doesn't bear thinking about that the Huns might win and come over here.'

'Are all those stories *true*?' Mabel shuddered. 'But even

so, you're under age! I know you'll go when you're eighteen, but before then why *should* you? Desmond won't.'

'He won't, not till he has to. But Mark Neyler's gone.'

'Who's he? What does he matter?'

'He's Daddy's brother.'

Mabel scowled.

'Just because your uncle's a fool you don't have to follow his example and be a fool as well.'

Frank did not take exception to this remark but reached over and rumpled Mabel's hair.

'Oh, Mabs, Mabs! There are other reasons. My grandfather, Karl Neyler, was a German, you know.'

'Was he? I didn't know, and it doesn't matter. No one could accuse your family of being German sympathisers! They're all as English as anything.'

'Then two girls in Cambridge gave Des and me white feathers. It made me think. You see, I *look* eighteen and I'm as strong as any eighteen-year-old, so in a way if I don't fight it could be because I'm afraid. If I was a weedy type it would be different, but I'm not. I'm more capable of defending myself than a good many lads who'll be sent out now that there's conscription, and anyway I'm itching to go! I want to prove that I'm capable of kicking the Hun in the guts. And I'm going.'

'Frank, don't.' The day seemed grey now, though the sun still shone. She could sense his determination, but she had to try to stop him. 'Please, Frank! I've got a friend at school whose brother's a subaltern, and she told me once that young officers only last two or three weeks in the trenches. Her brother's been there six months and he's experienced, but the new ones . . . oh, do listen! Think of the casualty lists! Hundreds and thousands are dead already. Don't go, Frank!'

'I know all that, old girl, but I'm not going to be an officer. No fear! I'll enlist as a squaddy and get all the fun and none of the responsibilities. I'm a crack shot, and I reckon it's cushy out there if you keep your head down! Look, I wouldn't go if winter was coming on because I've read the letters in *Chums* about mud and blood, but it'll be *summer*, damn it! I'm not keen on cricket and it's end of year exams, and I reckon the war'll be over by September, so I can get back to school for the rugby season. I'd never forgive myself if I missed out on this!'

'All right then, I'll tell!'

He laughed at her, running his hand through his thick fair hair which the summer sun would bleach to an even lighter shade.

'You wouldn't, my flower! I'll write to you and tell you what's going on. News from the Front! You'll be quite a heroine at school with a fellow of your own in the trenches.'

'A fellow of . . . Frank, don't be silly!'

'I'm not being silly, you are. You must know very well that I like you more than I like anyone else.'

They were halfway up the drive of yet another house, with the trees overhead shutting out the sunshine and the curve of the carriageway in both directions ensuring privacy. He moved close to her so that their bodies touched and put his arms round her as naturally as if he was always hugging girls. They stood thus for a moment, hearts pounding, then he bent his head and Mabel felt his lips, cool and firm, touch hers.

Her body knew what to do better than she. Her arms went round his neck, her mouth softened beneath his, and when he moved his tongue with gentle intimacy against her full lower lip she shuddered with pleasure and made no attempt to stop him. But neither did Frank attempt to go further; instead he released her.

'There! Now does that prove you're going to have your own fellow in the trenches?'

Mabel sighed and they moved up the drive towards the house once more, but this time with Frank's arm around her shoulders.

'If I'm your girl then surely you see that I don't want you to go? I don't care if other girls think you're a coward or if you've got a German grandfather, I just want you here, whole and safe!'

'That's very nice of you. But I'm not here, I'll be stuck away in Cambridge as soon as term starts, and then I'll be at university. And all the time you'll be growing up, getting prettier, probably marrying some damned chap whose only claim to you is that he's on the spot.' He swung her round to face him, holding both her shoulders now. 'Mabel, I want to *deserve* you! How can I deserve you if I won't fight to keep things as they should be for you!'

'That's not the reason, though. You want to go despite wanting me,' Mabel said shrewdly. 'Don't you see? I want you without any old nonsense about deserving! I want you because I . . . like you best.'

'What's wrong with saying "love"?'

'It's soppy, that's what,' Mabel said austerely. 'I don't *know* about love, but I know about like. I like you best.'

He laughed and squeezed her, then set off towards the house once more.

'I wish I had a ring to give you . . . something special. To show you that you're mine. A token, something to remind you . . .'

'Half a sixpence? Like in *Kipps*?'

They laughed and continued with their delivery of the mail, but that evening, just before Mabel went to bed, a note was pushed under the cottage door. William brought it through to the kitchen where his daughter was dutifully making cocoa as a bedtime drink for them all.

'Note. For you, Mabs.'

Mabel took the envelope and knew she was blushing as she spread out the single sheet of paper it contained.

'*I'll pick you up at seven,*' the note said briefly. And then, in smaller letters, '*Look in the envelope.*'

She put her fingers into the envelope and fished out the small object which she knew, instinctively, would be there. A sixpence, mangled in half. She crumpled the note into a ball and threw it into the fire in the kitchen range.

'It's from Frank. He's calling for me at seven to deliver the post.'

She took her drink up to bed and put the half-sixpence under her pillow, and next morning slipped it into her pocket before leaving to meet Frank.

'I had the devil's own job to get that coin in two,' Frank

greeted her, displaying his own half-sixpence. 'I hope you appreciate that I cut myself quite badly with the chisel? Don't laugh, you Jezebel, give me a good-morning kiss.'

'I don't think we ought to kiss any more until we're courting properly. Not until we're engaged. Or is it married?'

'Good Lord, if Des could hear you now he'd know I'd taken leave of my senses,' Frank exclaimed. 'You're a silly little kid with a moral code fifty years out of date and no brain, and now that it's too late and I've plighted my troth I find you think kissing's the seventh deadly sin. What have I done?'

'Don't be a fool. I didn't say that! It isn't sinful so much as more-ish,' Mabel explained. 'I don't think we ought to start a habit like that – not if you're going so far away.'

'You cunning little serpent!' Frank said. 'Are you trying to bribe me to give up the idea of joining the army, with your lily-white body as first prize, so to speak?'

Mabel, who had indeed allowed a vague plan on those lines to form in her mind, blushed fierily and hit him as hard as she could.

'I hate you and you're very insulting! As if . . . I just said . . .'

He grabbed hold of her and tried to kiss her, but she fought stoutly, furious at his embarrassingly accurate guess, and finally broke away and tore into the trees. There he caught her, as she must have known he would, and they kissed, wildly and innocently, before going down to the sorting office, arms entwined, to deliver that day's mail.

Both knew that the subject of the army would lie fallow for a while, though it would be uppermost in their minds.

13

It had been a gargantuan row with Mark that made Johnny run away. It was one of those very violent rows which blow up from time to time between people who are secretly jealous of each other. Since neither knew they were jealous, however, each put the row down to a weakness in the other's character, Johnny deciding that Mark was narrow-minded, Mark that Johnny was a libertine.

For once, the row had not involved Su in any way, though a woman was definitely responsible. Johnny was tall and strong, looking a good deal older than his years. His thick black hair and eyes were the only signs that his mother had been Chinese; his height and build came straight from his German grandfather and his personality was his own. What Mark thought of as a libertine streak was, in fact, no more than a certain precocity, brought about partly because he looked older than he was and partly because he was mixing with boys of sixteen and seventeen.

Freddy Fawcett's father had at last left his long-suffering wife and moved away to Canterbury, taking with him his latest mistress and his son. This would have left Johnny high and dry, had he not already begun to form a tentative friendship with Phil Rawson, who was two years older than he. And Phil, in his turn, introduced Johnny to Shirley.

Shirley worked in the coffee shop nearest the school. She was a buxom, rather simple-minded girl of about sixteen, whose generosity might have been termed promiscuity by some. The boys who benefited, of course, merely said that Shirley was 'good fun'. Johnny, going for a walk with

Shirley down by the sea one evening, thought her very good fun indeed, for he was a perfectly normal healthy young animal. Offered cream cakes, he ate them every one. Offered Shirley's temptingly rounded body, he enjoyed it with very much the same appetite.

Since more than half Phil's class were members of the Shirley-club, Johnny was very pleased with himself when it became obvious that she liked him best. His enthusiastic and puppy-like approach may have had more to do with it than his performance, but this, fortunately, did not cross Johnny's mind. He thoroughly enjoyed the spring term, despite missing Freddy badly at first.

But then came the long Christmas holidays, and Johnny began to make excuses to visit Dunedin, until it occurred to him that Shirley's chief attraction had to do with being a girl. And if one girl was willing to accommodate him, surely other girls might be equally willing – and girls, furthermore, who lived nearer home!

He soon found a suitable candidate in Chloe, the young woman who helped with the farm work now that several of the men had gone off to fight in the war. She was older than Shirley, quite nineteen, but even more attractive, being the possessor of the finest bosom Johnny had ever seen and a physique much improved by all her hard work on the farm. She had a boyfriend fighting in foreign parts; she often spoke longingly of 'Billy', and as soon as Johnny began eyeing her up he could not help noticing that she was doing the same to him. She missed Billy, she told him, and her eyes continued the story. One evening spent together in the hayloft was sufficient to prove their mutual interest; henceforth she literally as well as figuratively took Johnny to her bosom.

Su, blissfully unaware of Johnny's chief preoccupation, thought that life had never been so smooth. He and Mark did not quarrel so much, the boy worked hard on the farm during the day and at his books in the evenings. He slept like a log, admittedly, but always rose betimes. If, after the second week of the holidays had passed, she noticed that he was sometimes worn out after the evening milking, she put it down to his youth and let him slumber on the couch with his mouth and book both open and both unregarded.

Johnny and Chloe restricted their sessions in the hayloft to Tuesday and Thursday evenings, after milking. This was because Su and Mark visited friends on those particular evenings; on Tuesdays the Dodmans, on Thursdays the Campbells. And twice a week was enough to satisfy Johnny, if not Chloe.

Then, one warm Saturday afternoon, Mark announced that he was going to take Su over to Dunedin to visit a sale of work in the Presbyterian church hall, and then go and have a word with the manager who ran the Waihola homestead for Ted.

'Come with us, Johnny,' Su urged, but Johnny, very conscious that he had a holiday task of gargantuan proportions untouched, declined the trip.

'I'd better get my maths done,' he told her. 'I've got to do it, and the place will be quiet, being a Saturday afternoon.'

So when his father and Su left, Johnny settled down at the kitchen table with his work spread out round him, contentedly figuring. The contentment was genuine, for maths was his favourite subject. It never crossed his mind that Chloe, like a love-hungry mare, might come seeking her stud.

Yet that was exactly what happened. Within five minutes of Mark and Su departing, Chloe slipped into the kitchen.

'Johnny, your ma and pa went! Toddy's give me the afternoon off. What d'you say?'

'Well, why don't you go down to the beach?' It was a hot, sunny day, the sort of day when Johnny would have enjoyed a swim had it not been for the maths. 'I might come down later, if I finish this before teatime.' He frowned down at the sum in front of him.

'Oh, Johnny!' Chloe pouted. She was clad in a cotton blouse and a short, practical skirt. She bent forward, examining his book upside down, and Johnny noticed she was not wearing anything beneath the blouse. Two buttons were undone and he could see bare skin through the gap. 'Ain't there some other time you could do them sums? It seems such a waste!'

Johnny sighed and bent over his work again. He really must get on. He wanted to be finished by the time Mark and Su returned. A swim would be nice, of course, but he could swim in the evening when the maths was off his conscience.

'It's got to be done, Chloe. If you go down to the beach I might join you there after tea. Su and my father will be back for tea and they might come down as . . . oh!'

Chloe, losing patience with subtlety, had undone all the buttons on her blouse. Two large, melon-shaped breasts faced Johnny across the scattered papers. Chloe leaned forward and her breasts swung amongst the papers, nosing into them like a couple of impatient, pink-tipped balloons. Johnny swallowed.

'Aw, come on, Johnny! We ain't never done it on a real bed!'

Enlightenment dawned. So it was not a swim she was after! Slowly, Johnny closed his maths book.

'That's true. But . . . I don't know . . .'

Chloe moved round behind him and leaned on his back. Johnny felt the soft fullness of her pushing against his spine through the thin cotton shirt and her fingers beginning to slide across his shoulders, and swallowed again. He stared unseeingly at the answer paper in front of him. He could not, at that moment, have added two and two with much hope of getting a correct result.

'Aw, come on, Johnny!'

He turned and clutched her, burying his face in her ample plumpness. In less time than it takes to tell they had got themselves through the kitchen and across the hall, and were disporting themselves on the Neylers' big, soft bed. Chloe undressed him; Johnny, quick to learn, undressed her. They had never made love naked before, never seen each other's bodies in full daylight, and their lovemaking, for obvious reasons, had been mutually silent.

But not now! Chloe crowed and groaned, uttered small shrieks and mutterings. She also bucked and reared beneath him, bit him, and scratched him.

Johnny, not to be outdone, was equally uninhibited.

Their lovemaking became mobile, first here, now there. They rolled off the bed on to the floor, progressed to the washstand, returned to the bed. And all the while Chloe cackled like a hen laying an egg.

It was the noise of Chloe enjoying herself, in fact, that brought Mark, returning to the house for some papers, round to his bedroom window.

At first, he could scarcely believe his eyes. He saw a naked man coupling with a naked woman, first on the floor, facing away from the window, then moving on to the bed where, with cold shock, he recognised his son and Chloe. He knocked on the window, his temper such that afterwards he realised he had actually cracked the glass; neither Johnny nor Chloe heard a thing.

Fury, which was possibly partly envy, brought Mark round and bursting into the bedroom before he had thought what he was going to say to the evildoers. Fortunately, perhaps, words were not needed. The pair of them had left the bed again and were on the floor, on Su's beloved white fur rug. Mark's roar made Chloe jump quite perceptibly, and brought Johnny's head round, his eyes widening with dismay.

'Dad! Oh! Oh crumbs!'

For the rest of their lives, the people involved would remember the next ten minutes with the most acute embarrassment. Chloe, naked as the day she was born, trying to scramble into her skirt and blouse, clumsily fumbling with buttons and fastenings, copiously weeping. Johnny, trying to get a word in edgeways as Mark roared and Su came in, round-eyed, begging for an explanation. Then Chloe gave up the unequal struggle with her buttons and rushed from the room, her big breasts bouncing as she ran, her sobs becoming wails of terror and despair.

Johnny was in his trousers; that was about the extent of his attempt at regaining his respectability and, since the fly-buttons were unfastened, Su was not taken in.

However, Su's presence at least calmed Mark down a little. He had been attempting to roar at Johnny and lay him out cold at the same time, but now that his wife had arrived Mark sobered a little.

'Come into the kitchen,' he said gruffly, and they followed him meekly through, Johnny not daring to look at Su nor she at him. Once there, the row really got into its stride. Mark, cuddling Su, told Johnny that he was an animal and would in future be treated like one. Su, sobbing, moaned, 'Suppose she has a baby? Oh, Johnny, what will we do if she has a baby?'

Su's tears hurt Johnny far more than Mark's ill-aimed blows or abuse.

'She won't, don't worry, Su,' he said earnestly. 'Girls don't have babies with me.'

This ingenuous remark led to the story of the girl in the coffee shop and the preoccupation with 'Shirleying' which had gripped the upper school last term. This, not unnaturally, led to another eruption from Mark, together with the grim warning that the headmaster should be told, the guilty boys expelled for corrupting his son's youthful innocence, and the practice of after-school fornication stopped once and for all.

Having made that decree in his most impressive voice, Mark grabbed Johnny – very unfairly, since his son was sitting meekly down on a kitchen chair at the time – and leathered him with his belt. It was the first time in his life that Johnny had ever been beaten, certainly the first time that he felt his beloved Su was actually in agreement with his punishment, and it left him trembling, sick and furious. What would the school say when they found out who had put an end to Shirleying? And how would he face Chloe, knowing that he would never again dare to do the exciting and altogether delightful things she had taught him that very afternoon? Glowering at his parents, he slunk out of the kitchen and locked himself in his own room, where he twisted and turned, gloomily counting the pink, raised welts on his back and buttocks. Life in future would scarcely be worth living, here or at school. He would go! He would run away to somewhere he could be sure of appreciation and a place in the adult world.

It never occurred to him to try to join the army. Instead,

he thought of that other running away, when he and Su had fled together. He had loved his grandfather and grandmother, still wrote to them, and had long promised them a return visit when he grew up. Well, he would go to them, and nothing would make him return to New Zealand, where they treated him as a child when he was as adult in most ways as his father!

By the time Mark and Su were in bed, Su having fastidiously changed the bed-linen, they were already realising that they must not make a mountain out of a molehill.

'I'll tell him that such behaviour is irresponsible, and must stop,' Mark promised. 'But I shan't say anything at school. It was probably nine days' wonder there, and Johnny'll warn the boys that they've been twigged.'

Even as he spoke, Johnny was tramping the coast road. By the time his parents woke next morning, Johnny was stowed away on a ship bound for Australia.

For the first two days, the Neylers searched the district. Then they informed the authorities that a boy of fourteen who could be mistaken for seventeen or eighteen had run away from home, and the authorities suspected the army.

Johnny, landing at Sydney, had little difficulty in persuading his grandparents to keep him. He was young and strong, a good worker, and quite willing to be employed in any capacity, provided that he was not despatched home. They wrote to Su, but two days before she got the letter Johnny took off once more on a cattle-lorry bound for the outback. He had seen his grandfather addressing a letter to Dunedin, and he had no intention of being so speedily collared.

He might have felt differently had he known that Mark, worried by reports of the state of affairs in Europe and fired with patriotism by the sight of all the uniforms in Dunedin, had lied about his age and joined up.

'You can cope, love, because you coped before,' he said tenderly to Su as he prepared to embark for the battlefields of France. 'Toddy's here, and Freda of course, and this time I'll write every day and let you know what's happening. I'd hate myself if I didn't fight for my country and my wife!'

'I'll cope. They say the war won't last much longer anyway,' Su said, her voice carefully bright though her eyes were wet. 'Take care of yourself, darling.'

Bereft of Mark and Johnny, she prepared to be very lonely.

Frank had laid his plans carefully and thought them foolproof as, indeed, they proved to be. On the last day of the holidays he got on the train with his brother and a pile of luggage, to get off again at the first stop, leaving Des with a note, forged, purporting to be from Ted Neyler to the headmaster of Pursell's School.

The note explained that Desmond and Frank had fallen victim to mumps during the holidays and that Desmond, stricken first, had recovered first also. Frank, the note continued, was still very poorly and would not be returning to school until half-term.

Desmond also had a number of letters, written in advance by his ingenious brother, to be posted weekly along with his own parental bulletins.

'I'm going to join up in London,' Frank said, drilling Desmond in the part he was to perform. 'It's easier not to be noticed in a big city. You'll have to stand buff for a few weeks, old fellow, and then it'll be too late. Once I'm trained and at the Front, the army won't give me up just because the parents make a fuss. Don't forget to post the letters each week, though. I don't want Mama and Daddy finding out too soon.'

'I'm not putting them in the same envelope as mine,' Desmond muttered. 'Then, if there are questions asked, I'll say you must have left them with some bit of fluff in Cambridge to post for you. And I'll say I knew you were off on some lark, but I didn't know what. I don't see why they should expect me to stop you just because I'm the oldest. It isn't fair! Why should I get stick because you run away?'

'You do that – post the letters and deny all knowledge,' Frank advised. 'Look, why not say that we both wanted to go, and tossed for it, and I won? Say you gave your word, then they won't blame you.'

'Yes, that might work.' Desmond hated the thought that his parents might secretly believe him to be windy, even if it was true! 'If I say I gave my word not to split, Daddy wouldn't expect me to go back on it. Though Mama's a different kettle of fish! Anyway, Daddy's in the army himself, so he can't blame you all that much.'

'Suppose I meet him in France?' Frank's grin faltered, then returned. 'But I won't. I reckon he's in London for the duration. Anyway, it'll be over by Christmas, everyone says, so all I'm doing is having my share a bit earlier, or I'll miss out! I bet hundreds of fellows are doing the same.'

'Maybe. If it wasn't the summer term, and I wasn't in the eleven . . .'

'Don't you go changing your mind, Des!' Frank said. 'You've got to be in school to keep my cover!' The train began to get up steam and he raised his voice above the racket. 'Cheerio. I'll write. Care of Tilly Catcher.'

The train steamed out and Frank's adventure began. He got to London and sold his luggage, or most of it, having spent the journey cutting out all the name tapes and burning them with a box of matches he had bought. Clothing sold would disappear utterly; clothing found would start an immediate hue and cry.

He reached Liverpool Street Station and made his way to the nearest recruiting office. Though he did not know it, the staff there was recruiting for a big offensive planned for the early summer. Questions were not likely to be asked of a tall, upstanding youth who gave his age as eighteen and looked every month of it. By the time he went to bed that night he was in the army, and next day, in company with a number of other youngsters, would be sent to a training camp on the Downs for a few weeks before being despatched to France.

That first night, wrapped in blankets and lying on a rickety camp bed, Frank felt the first faint stirrings of doubt. This was to be an adventure – but it was so like school! Boys everywhere, and adults stamping and shouting and ordering one about. But soon he would not be classed as a boy any longer, and would be able to prove his manhood by shooting at something other than a wooden target!

Without the slightest conception of how he would really feel when he first saw bullets tearing into living flesh, Frank turned on his side and slept soundly till morning.

Flanders. A city of canvas tents pitched on marshy ground, criss-crossed by duck-boards. Mark was a lieutenant by March, training other men for the big battle which was said to be imminent. They were stationed a few miles outside Steenbecque and for the most part the men were New Zealand infantrymen who had already fought their way through the fronts in Egypt and Gallipoli. They were experienced fighters, certainly, but new to the war as it was being fought in Europe. Mark had been trained for this type of warfare, and now he was passing his knowledge on.

Sometimes, as he lectured, he thought how odd it was that he should be expected to teach something he only knew from his own teachers. But he did his job well and was liked by the men. Off duty, he and a few fellow officers would go into the town, which was packed with refugees, and have coffee and the plainish cakes which was all that was available, and buy postcards to send home. It intrigued him to see the women doing work the men had once done, and doing it well. And their traditional tasks, lace-making, sewing, and cooking, still went on as before.

He wrote to Su about the good things, never about the bad; never mentioning the fever which sprang up amongst the men billeted in this low and marshy area, nor the violence he taught. And her letters speaking of the farm and her life there were a great joy, as were Toddy's brief notes, Freda's scribbles. It gave him immense pleasure to know that they were cutting corn or clamping potatoes; he could see the scene so clearly in his mind's eye when he read the words. The seasons were upside down here; even the stars overhead no longer danced in their familiar places. He had given a lecture only last week on the stars – one day, if you were lost in no man's land with the stars your only guide, knowing them might make the difference between a safe landfall and a bayonet in the belly.

Then, one miserable, rainy day when he and Jamie Jamieson were squatting on boxes in their tent, gloomily contemplating the unceasing downpour, a hand threw a bundle of mail into Mark's lap. He sorted the letters out, and the first one he opened was from Su. Jamie, reading his own post, jumped as Mark suddenly leapt to his feet, knocking the box backwards into the mud.

'Christ! Su's pregnant!'

Jamie righted the box and grinned up at the older man.

'Good on you, mate! When's it due?'

'At the beginning of July, but it's her first child, so she says it will probably be late.' He glanced down at his friend and read the startled look aright. 'She's my second wife. Johnny – my son – he's not Su's child, though she treats him as if he was.'

'And she's pleased, is she? The wife?'

'Pleased? She's in seventh heaven! We've been married a while and not a sign until now.'

'That's great. You'd better write back at once, tell her we're on the move again. Our letters travel even further than we do, and that's saying something.'

'I will. But we'll be in France before she gets it.'

Mark refolded the letter and returned it to its envelope. It would be read and reread many times in the weeks to come, and always with increasing pleasure. He knew how unhappy it had made Su when she thought herself unable to bear him a child. It had not made him unhappy – Johnny was sufficient proof that having children was not all honey – but now that he knew she was pregnant he found his joy and pride so great that he wanted to tell everyone he met. He longed to see his child safe in Su's arms, longed to be back on the Peninsula once more. Yet it gave him, he told himself, an even better reason for fighting this war. To make the world a better place for Su and his child. For his son or daughter. He had not much minded which at first, but as the brigade marched across into France his desire for a daughter crystallised into a positive longing. A little girl, just like Su! That would be the best thing that could happen.

Weighed down with all the impediment of a continental war on their backs – the rifle and ammunition, the bedroll and greatcoat, the gas mask, steel helmet, water bottle and entrenching tool, to say nothing of the emergency rations – the men could not hurry. Mark had a horse on the march now, and as he rode beside the column of men he often thought of Ted. Ted wrote too, long, newsy letters, and nothing could hide his longing to be in France with Mark, where the action was! Mark, lean and tanned and fit after his years on the farm, his hair untouched by grey, had given his age as thirty-eight and been believed. Poor Ted had not been so lucky, and he chafed against the restrictions of the Ministry and longed for a horse between his knees and the comradeship of soldiers.

When, after days of marching, being billeted in barns to recover their strength and then marching on again, they neared Armentieres, Mark saw an aeroplane with the British colours clear on its wings and remembered that Ted's young brother-in-law, Louis Rose, was in the Royal Flying Corps and stationed somewhere near here. How strange it would be, after all these years, if he and Ted and this Louis should meet up, in the middle of the biggest war the world had ever known, in a country which was foreign to them all! His heart contracted at the thought of seeing Ted. The years could not change his feeling for his brother; Ted was dearer to him than any other person on earth except for Su.

As the column clattered into the church square he glanced up at the clock, long stopped at half past eleven – giving the square its name of Half Past Eleven Square – and vowed that when this lot was over he would find Ted. Go to England and find him, if necessary. They were too near to miss seeing each other again as they had missed each other in America, a decade ago!

He had seen no action yet, or he might have qualified the thought.

14

It was raining again, a fine, drizzling rain that did not look much, but soaked you through in a moment. Frank and Hoss, crouched in their trench with the rest of their platoon strung out along its length, regarded the rain with true British phlegm; not only had they grown used to it, but they were about to be rescued from it. Any minute now another group of men would come marching up to take over this particular position and they would be sent back to the rear for a rest period.

'A good 'ot barf,' Hoss said, narrowing his eyes dreamily. He hitched his puttees up and stood, head cautiously bent, looking out to the west, whence their relief would come. Frank looked up at his friend and grinned. After the war Hoss would have a permanent stoop. It came from being six foot four, which was taller than the man who had dug this trench, obviously. Hoss spent a good deal of time trying to get his height down to a decent five foot ten, with a noticeable, if understandable, lack of success.

'Tomorrow, that'll be, if we're lucky. Yes, *and* clean clothes.' Frank, crouching in the mud at the bottom of the trench patiently checking his equipment, thought of a newly ironed shirt, underpants smelling of soap and – best of all – soft, clean, sweet-smelling socks. He sighed, and picked up his war trophy. It was a German helmet of black patent leather, the brass badges missing, alas, but the spike on top still intact. An admirable trophy, and one which would be much envied by the rank and file – but what would his officers make of it? Was such looting allowed? There had been no one *in* the helmet – it had been abandoned when the Huns had left the trench – but he supposed it was still loot. He tapped the helmet, and dug Hoss in the back of the knees. 'Is it all right to take this back with us, or will some officer swipe it off me?' He grimaced at his friend. 'Think what we suffered because of it!'

Hoss grinned. It was useless to think of the real suffering which had gone into the helmet's gain – the men killed, the heavy, red-faced sergeant who had been such a brick to them lying in the mud, his face drained of colour and his right foot blown to a scarlet pulp. All he and Frank had suffered had been a nasty attack of crumbs. They had 'won' a couple of German greatcoats, thinking, in their innocence, that, propped up on a couple of rifles, the coats would make a decent tent against the weather. The greatcoats, however, had been alive with lice, known as crumbs since they looked just like fawny-white breadcrumbs, and by morning so had Frank and Hoss.

They did their best to get rid of the pests, but the older and more experienced soldiers told them it was impossible to clear them without civilised conditions, just as it was impossible to heal bleeding and blistered feet whilst out here in the soggy trenches.

'We'll be in the rear again in a day or so,' a cheerful corporal assured them. 'Then it's bathhouse drill and clean clothes. You'll not be chatty after that, or not till the next spell in the trenches, at any rate.'

'Chatty? Why not crumby?'

The corporal laughed at Frank's question.

'I'm Indian army, lad, and a chatt is 'industani for our friend the crumb. Or louse.'

Now, however, with the greatcoats hurled well clear of the trench and a bath imminent, Frank was more interested in the fate of his helmet than in his louse-bites.

'Well? Can I take my loot back?'

'Yes, if you hide it from the officers and NCOs; otherwise they'll take it off you,' Hoss advised from his own experience, for, in the backstreets of London from whence he sprang, hiding possessions from those in authority was a way of life. 'Put it in your bedroll. That'll do until we're in billets.'

Frank began to wrap the helmet with his waterproof sheet, then noticed movement at the far end of the trench.

'Hey, look there!'

Further up the trench a dixie was standing and the men were in a line by it. Steam rose and they could see hot liquid being ladled into mugs.

'Is it char? I could do with a cuppa!'

The two of them, packs on back, rifles slung, joined the queue hopefully, tin mugs in hand.

'There won't be no rum in it; we 'ad that yesterday.' Hoss held out his mug to the corporal dishing out the strong, sweet tea and grinned at him. 'Rum issue for swaddies, eh, corp? Per man, per day per haps!'

The corporal, not a man renowned for his sense of humour, grinned back. He had been a coal heaver in civilian life and was wont to compare coal heaving favourably with heaving dixies, and to accuse officers various of seeing off the rum ration rightfully belonging to other ranks. Nevertheless, this embittered man grinned at Hoss.

But the memory of yesterday's rum issue brought yesterday back too vividly into Frank's mind. It was given out before the raid. Get into a German trench, grab some equipment and a prisoner if possible; spread alarm and despondency. That was what their officer said, and Sergeant Fellowes echoed it. Frank thought that the taste of rum would always bring that moment back to life, when he and Hoss stood side by side in the rainy darkness, their faces and hands blacked out with burnt cork, the spirit coursing fierily through their veins. It was the first time he had tasted rum; having no liking for spirits but a great enthusiasm for sweets and chocolate, he and Hoss usually bartered their rum ration and their cigarettes for whatever was going in the way of sweet things.

When the rum was finished they scrambled out of the trench and crouched beside the parapet, waiting for the last man up before putting into practice all the things their sergeant had impressed upon them – spread out, crouch, move silently.

Even divested of their packs and the paraphernalia of the soldier on active duty, they sounded awfully loud to Frank as they clinked and clattered over the parapet and into no man's land. The mud itself was noisy, sucking at their boots, squelching whenever they moved. Darkness, of course, was a friend – but it was an enemy too, unless you kept your head, remained cool, and forced the little picture of the terrain you were crossing into your mind and kept it there. He knew that at a certain point they would probably need to crawl; the long grass would almost hide them, if it wasn't rain-flattened by now.

Hoss was close to him and the rain eased momentarily and he smelt summer on the breath of the wind and was transported for seconds back to England, a wet night in a summer lane. Then he pushed through the grass and saw Hoss rise to the crouch and suddenly this was exciting, there was a wicked thrill in it greater than climbing someone else's flagpole in someone else's college grounds, a chamber pot clamped beneath your arm, ready to hang it insultingly above their flag.

He got his night-eyes then, and could see the treacherous terrain with the mine craters yawning at him – hungry mouths waiting to devour if you put a foot wrong. Their objective – an advance enemy trench, probably lightly held, the Staff said with the callous optimism of those who will never have to find out – was close now, on their right. They could hear soft voices, and a burst of laughter. Frank's hair prickled on his scalp and he held his rifle more firmly, his hand already fumbling for the small bomb in his pocket.

He could not have said when they were spotted, only that they were. Machine-gun fire rattled and flares suddenly illuminated the hellish night. Something went past his cheek and he flinched back before realising it was only a bird, disturbed and terrified by the sudden light and noise. He and Hoss dropped on to their bellies and suddenly the night was full of other members of the raiding party, word was passed to get back, the enemy was too strong, their wire impregnable, get *back,* damn you! Crawling now, the dark friendly, the mud an enemy, making you slip and slither. Hoss muttering, reminding Frank to keep his head down, to keep on crawling. Bullets, the wind of them over your frightened head, sweat in your eyes so that every instruction, every piece of good advice, was forgotten. Only Hoss, cool, by your side, cracking a joke of all things, about the mud. Keeping you moving, taking away the terror. Then the parapet, the slither down into the trench. Their officer, counting heads. Two dead, three wounded. Frank's thoughts taking over, full of confusion, excitement returning now that the danger was less. Could this be war? Where was the glamour, the charge, the wounded heroes, the sullen prisoners? He had imagined it all so clearly! And the other thought, which would not go away though it seemed so petty and trivial. Damn it, this is *summer,* the cricket season's in full swing, flaming June and all that. And I'm in *France,* everyone knows about France – yet it's done nothing but rain for days on end!

'Wake up, Frankie. No time for dreamin', lad! Get that char down you and I'll hump your pack on to your shoulders. We're off to the rear in ten minutes!' Hoss grinned again at the surly corporal. 'There ain't gonna be no push yet, then, or they wouldn't spare lads like us! Eh, corp?'

It took them the best part of two hours, in fact, to change places with the relieving mob and a further two hours to reach their billet. It was a good seven miles behind the lines, a farm with the men sleeping in the big barn amongst clean straw and the officers taking over the farm itself. You could still hear the shelling and see the distant smoke, but you were not woken by it. It constituted a nuisance, in fact, rather than a threat. In the trenches it was impossible to discount.

They settled in, and routine took over. Hoss's longed-for hot bath came the following day when the platoon was marched to the divisional bathhouse and thoroughly cleansed, and Frank's body knew the delights of a freshly laundered shirt and he pampered his sore and bleeding feet with whale oil and soft clean socks. The German helmet was too desirable an object to leave lying about – he hid it at the very bottom of his kit-bag. Then the kit-bag was deposited safely in a corner of the 'room' he had made for himself, walled in with straw bales.

Two days after their arrival the rain stopped. The sky was a clear, rain-washed blue and the countryside decked with its summer foliage. There was a real wood, where the trees still knew the seasons, where birds built nests in the branches and bluebells grew in shady spots. And corn-fields, green still, where larks rose straight up, singing as they headed for heaven. There was a river, with willows along its banks and a deep, quiet pool where trout lurked. Discipline was eased and the soldiers became young men again, hurling themselves into the water to bathe, eyeing the young woman who strode, sturdy and barefoot along the river path with her milking buckets on a yoke across her shoulders.

The guns still grumbled and muttered to the east but they were able to push the war out of their conscious minds, though at night the thoughts that one could rigidly control by day had it all their own way and men twitched and whimpered in sleep as they would have scorned to do when awake. June neared its end. Frank and Hoss, two tiny cogs in the great wheel of the war, waited, and knew they might die, and could not believe death could touch them.

'If this is air supremacy, let there be an end to't,' Louis misquoted, helping himself to smoked salmon. It was breakfast time in the mess and he had only been back from leave a couple of days so the smoked salmon – or what was left of it – was his contribution to civilised living. It had been a present from Ted, gloomily working for the Ministry of Defence in London and itching to be off to France, and had been much appreciated at dinner the previous night. Louis was finishing it off as a sign of ownership whilst opposite him at the table sat Nick, far more conventionally eating bacon and eggs. At Louis's words, he nodded vigorously.

'I know what you mean. We keep air supremacy, but at

the most horrific cost. We're losing about a hundred and fifty men a month, I believe, and the same number of aeroplanes. Seasoned men are replaced by kids, and *that* means we're hardly ever on terra firma. When this big push starts we'll all be worn out and useless.'

'That's about it.' Louis got up. 'Well, I mustn't grumble! I had my leave and spent a good deal of it in bed, one way and another. Now I've got to buckle down to knocking a few Boches out of the sky. We're on standby, you said?'

Nick nodded.

'Yes, for the next six hours. After that we can go off somewhere, if you like. We're on dawn patrol tomorrow, though, so we mustn't be late back to kip.'

'I've got a friend in the trenches, a chap I was at school with. I thought I might go and look him up later. Don't much want to go up to the line, not with so much going on, but when he goes to the rear, which ought to be around now, I'd like to see him and have a jaw.'

'I'll come with you. Better than going on the batter when we've an early start. I always feel horribly sorry for the lads in the Camel Corps, and the odd thing is, they feel horribly sorry for us! It's a good thing we don't all think alike, I suppose.'

'Yes. Ours is a solitary calling, as the poets say. I think that's what they've got against it. But those trenches!' There was a ruminative pause whilst both men thought about the trenches which they flew over so frequently and visited so seldom. 'Mind you, it was pretty grim for Cotterill yesterday and the blokes downstairs risked all sorts to get him out. We ought to nip down to the dressing station and find out how he is.'

'Christ, Louis, he couldn't have survived those burns!' Nick had a snub-nosed, cheerful face but now he looked savage. 'I hope for his sake he's gone west.'

Walking over to the squadron office, Louis reflected that Nick was right; Cotterill had been a living torch when his aeroplane had crash-landed in no man's land. In such circumstances survival would be far worse than death.

'I wonder why Cotterill didn't use his pistol,' Louis said

thoughtfully as they strolled along. 'He had one, I know.'

It was accepted amongst them that those who carried pistols did so in order that they might spare themselves the agony of death by burning. Louis, blessed with an optimistic nature, could never have carried a revolver with such intent; something would save him, something always did. But he understood that others did not have his disposition.

'I've always suspected that whatever happens, it happens too quickly for you,' Nick said. He did not carry a pistol either. 'Well, at least it's fine and dry, so we can sit on the grass.'

He drew a copy of that much coveted publication, the *Wipers Times,* out of his pocket and was soon chuckling.

Louis lay on his back on the grass and remembered his leave. It had been a wonderful ten days, mostly spent with Sarah though he had managed to arrange a brief, two-day holiday with Say and the boy. He had sent them ahead of him to a cottage on the coast and, since he had hired it for a week, had left them there too. Say was quite content in the tiny thatched house with the seashore just outside her door and a farm nearby to deliver her milk and a few groceries.

Say, sweet and fat, wanting only to make her menfolk happy, was easy company. Not so Sarah. Slim and practical in dark, well-cut skirts and jackets, she drove ambulances and practised first-aid and was proud of her achievements. She had delivered a baby all by herself, she boasted. And Louis, having just made vigorous love to her, had said that when he next came home he hoped she would be *having* a baby and not merely delivering someone else's, like a postman!

'I can't understand why you aren't pregnant already, darling,' he said rather fretfully. 'God knows, the way we spend my leaves you ought to be!'

Sarah did not care to be reproached. She allowed her voice to cool considerably.

'There's plenty of time for babies. Any woman can produce a baby. But I'm being really useful for the first time in my life, and I like it. It means a lot to me.'

'I don't like useful women,' Louis said sulkily. 'I like decorative ones.' Then, relenting, because she was so very decorative, he rolled over – they were in bed – and kissed the side of her neck, just below the ear. 'Never mind, sweetheart, you'll have a baby. I'll see to it!'

Say, on the other hand, was 'taking precautions', as she phrased it. This involved a certain loss of spontaneity whilst Say pored over the calendar, counted on her fingers, frowned and re-counted – or, almost worse, jerked away from him at the very moment when he most wanted her to lie quiet and submissive beneath him.

'Sure and I can't bear to think of it, Lou, but suppose you were killed?' she said mournfully, when he complained. 'I could support the boy, but if I had two or three more I wouldn't know which way to turn.'

Louis had to acknowledge the truth of her remark. Whilst he lived he could support her and his son, but if he were to die she would be totally alone. She would get no widow's pension because she was not married to him, his relatives would not help her because they did not know about her; her own mother, knowing nothing of her daughter's circumstances and in any event pitifully poor herself, would be unlikely to assist her.

'Very well then, Say, take your precautions. But don't, I beg of you, ever shove me back and pull away like that again at such a . . . delicate moment. Something very precious to us both might have suffered irreparable damage.'

They had laughed together, but he knew that lovemaking with Say had lost a good deal of its charm. Once fear of consequences entered a relationship, he thought selfishly, natural pleasure tended to fly out of the window.

In the mess office, the phone rang. Nick flung his paper down and got stiffly to his feet just as the door of the office burst open.

'Enemy aircraft sighted and heading this way. A number of bombers with a fighter escort. Presumably to bomb the trenches.'

Minutes later, Nick and Louis and the rest of their flight were in the air and climbing to gain height. They were over the trenches quickly, glancing below at the desolation; the trees that knew nothing of June, the craters filled with sticky mud, the thin, poisoned weeds.

Climbing still, they saw another squadron of Allied aircraft and signalled to them that enemy aircraft were approaching in force. And then, coming from the east, they saw the Huns and flew to meet them.

The action was brief but bloody. Louis was jinking, stalling, keeping his aeroplane moving briskly and, he hoped, unpredictably, firing bursts from his Lewis gun whenever an enemy appeared in his sights. He saw British aeroplanes spin out of control, spiralling down into no man's land, and a German bomber burst into flames directly beneath him. He saw the thick black smoke and pulled away from it, his heart going out to the crew of the doomed aeroplane.

Within moments, he saw Nick, gesturing, and following his friend's eyes knew that his own wing was on fire. He gauged the fire's strength and the speed at which it would travel as best he might, then turned the nose of his bus downwards. A forced landing in no man's land did not appeal, but it would be better than roasting. He began to coax his aeroplane into a long glide, taking it as slowly as he dared. The flames crept back, devouring more and more of the wing, and he knew that if he slowed too much the flames might go up the struts into the upper wing and if he went too fast he might find the flames in the cockpit with him. Why did they make the material which covered the wings so inflammable? he thought inconsequentially. Did the women who stretched the fine linen so carefully over the frame know that it burnt like a torch?

The ground, pitted and scarred, was close now, the aircraft tipping crazily. She touched down, bounced, touched down again. A crater yawned. He could not avoid it. She was travelling too fast, one wing all but consumed, the flames licking at the cockpit. He felt her tip and slide, then somersault forward. He was hurled out, felt his face smash into something yielding – and knew no more.

He awoke in bed. Hearing returned first, before he had strength enough to open his eyelids or move his lead-heavy limbs. He listened. There were voices, talking English. He felt faint amusement because he found this reassuring. Why on earth should he have expected to hear foreign words? It occurred to him next that the voices were all male. Then he heard something clicking and wanted to open his eyes, but his lids felt so heavy, like two great pillows on his cheeks. He listened for a moment longer, then drifted into sleep.

When he woke again he felt stronger. He listened for a moment, then blinked his eyes open. He was in a sort of hospital, he could tell that by the lines of iron cots and the identical regulation bed-coverings. Oddly, though, the floor was just earth, the walls greenish canvas through which he could see sunshine. He could hear gunfire too, and shellbursts. He moved his head a fraction and blinding, red-hot pain shot through it like needles being driven into his brain. It surprised an involuntary shriek from him, only the sound emerged as a moan, no more. He heard a soft voice near him and his eyes, which had clamped defensively shut as the pain struck him, opened cautiously.

A girl leaned over the bed. A fair face, red lips. He closed his eyes, then opened them again. She was still there. She had large blue eyes with thickly curling fair lashes. Her hair was almost entirely obscured by a white cap. A nurse, of course.

She spoke to him but he could not be bothered to listen, not yet, and then she stroked his cheek, her fingers cool and comforting. He wanted to laugh because she was only a child and yet she seemed to accept her role as his comforter. It was ridiculous because she was a child and he was . . . he was . . . confound it, how old *was* he?

Presently, despite himself, he slept again.

The third time he woke he did so because someone was speaking to him. He opened his eyes and there was a young man, fair-haired and freckled, with a cheerful, open countenance, grinning down at him.

'Woken up at last, eh, Louis? How're you feeling? The nurse says you're one of the lucky ones – you gave yourself a terrific bonk on the bonce and they had to shave your hair off and stitch up your scalp, but otherwise you got off practically unscathed. Some broken ribs, wasn't it? But I thought I'd pop over and cheer you up. Here, I've brought your mail and some strawberries.'

Louis smiled and murmured his thanks, taking the letters. Who was this fellow, and how had he come by his, Louis's, post? Odd, that the name Louis struck no particular bell. And who were the letters from? He recognised neither handwriting, only registering that they were quite different. One, written in black ink with flourishing capitals, looked forceful and distinctive, the other was small and sprawling, not easy to read. Women?

He turned his head cautiously to look up at his visitor. He was filled, suddenly, with panic so fearful that he could have screamed. He felt the colour drain from his face.

'What's the matter, old man?' The visitor looked concerned. 'Feeling off, are you? You've gone very white.'

'I don't know who the hell you are!' The visitor's eyes widened uneasily. 'And I don't know me! For God's sake, *who am I*?'

It did not worry the doctor nor the nursing staff that he could not remember who he was. They assured him that it often happened after a blow on the head, and when his ribs and scalp wounds had healed they discharged him and sent him back to the squadron. He knew by now that he was Louis Rose, and a good few other things about himself. He was intrigued to find that he had a wife and gazed at her photograph with lustful thoughts whizzing round in his otherwise empty head. Nick, the young man who had come hospital visiting, was his closest friend, it appeared.

'She's stunning! And you mean to tell me I've just got back from leave?' He scowled. 'I bet I had a good time with her, and I can't remember a thing! Pretty name though, Sarah Rose.'

He wrote home of course, explaining what had happened, and the family responded at once and very thoroughly. Almost too thoroughly, Louis thought, as the letters came flooding in. Sisters, brothers-in-law, nephews and nieces deluged him with photographs. His father was a grand old boy; he liked the look of him, though he was sorry that his mother had died so long ago. It would have been rather nice to get to know a mother!

The doctor said his memory would return bit by bit, and that very probably, once he got home again, everything would come flooding back. He certainly knew without any bother how to drive a car and fly his beloved aeroplane, though he could not remember one solitary detail about his crash. Friends in the squadron, who had watched, horrified, as he tipped into a mine crater, had told him all they knew, but, perhaps fortunately, the crash itself remaind a blank in his mind.

When he returned to the squadron he had been offered Blighty leave so that he could give his memory a chance, but he had refused it. The big push, the moment they had all been waiting for, was to take place in less than forty-eight hours. He wanted to be here, with his friends, guarding the trenches against German attack. It was bad enough to be down there with all the shelling going on without knowing you might be bombed as well!

In fact, he no longer worried over his memory loss. It was coming back already, as the doctor had predicted. His father's photograph could not tell him that his father walked with a stick, talked with an accent, was warm and outgoing, yet Louis knew all these things. He remembered some incidents at his own wedding, though his bride was still a mystery to him. He knew she was dark, so why did he often think of her as light-haired? She was slim, yet he remembered a delicious plumpness. It crossed his mind that he might have been a one for the girls – that would account for it. He was rather ashamed that with such a beautiful wife he still received affectionate letters from another woman, a girl called Fay, or at least that was how she signed herself. She did not seem to know he was married; he ought to write and tell her, but that was not so easy. There was no address on her envelope, nor a surname. He sighed. He got tired rather easily and the doctor had warned him that straining to remember would do more harm than good. Memory would return when it wanted to and not because he tried to make it.

He read Fay's letter again, then put the whole business out of his mind. It was an odd sort of letter anyway, very domestic, talking about 'the boy' and the little, everyday things that go to make up a woman's life. It did not occur to him that it was, perhaps, a wifely letter.

'Desmond, darling!' Tina hugged her son delightedly, then stepped back, tilting her head to look up at him. 'I declare you're taller than ever, if that's possible! And you'll be home in another week or so, won't you?'

Desmond returned her hug, for they were in the seclusion of his study, and was glad that he had such a pretty little mother, one who might easily be taken for a chap's elder sister. He adored her! It made a difference, perhaps, that he was her favourite child and knew it, but he told himself he would have adored her anyway.

'Mama, what a lovely surprise! Yes, I'll be home soon, which makes it even more surprising. If I'd known you were coming over I'd have asked my study mate to buy us some cakes – he's gone into town on an exeat. But since you kept your visit a secret you'll have to ring for a taxi and take me out in style and buy *me* cakes instead.'

Tina hugged him once more, then stepped back briskly, beaming up at him.

'Des, darling, what a bounder you are! I've every intention of taking you out to tea and, what's more, out to dinner as well. I want to talk to you seriously, for once.'

Desmond, holding open the door for her, groaned.

'Not about Frank? We had that all out at half-term, surely? Daddy gave me such a dressing down, and you know I couldn't stop Frank. I gave him my word! Confound it, Mama, you wouldn't have been able to stop him, so how could I?'

'No, it isn't about Frank. We've forgiven him for running away, we write regularly, and everything's all right between us. He's young, I know, but he's a trained soldier now. I couldn't insist on the army sending him back even if I wanted to. Of course I worry terribly – and nearly losing dear old Louis made me doubly nervous – but I doubt if there's a woman in England now who isn't worried about some man over in France.'

They descended the stairs, crossed the tiled hall, and emerged into brilliant sunshine. It was the first of July, and it seemed as though summer had decided to arrive at last. Tina had ordered a cab and the driver dived out of his vehicle at the sight of them and opened the back door. Desmond ushered his mother inside, then ducked his handsome head and followed her. He shot back the partition between the passengers and the driver, then hesitated, turning to Tina.

'Where shall we go? Would you like me to take you on the river for a bit? It's a lovely day and I adore sculling a boat with a pretty woman in it. Who's to guess that you're my mama?'

She agreed enthusiastically, patting her curls. She wore a small straw hat perched on her head and a cream coloured suit with a sailor collar and dark brown piping.

'Won't it be fun? And afterwards we can have tea at that place you and Frank liked so much – the Copper Kettle, was it?'

'Yes, but I've gone off it. There's another one, awfully good, on King's Parade.' He leaned forward and addressed the driver. 'To Snidger's Yard, please.' Leaning back again, he eyed his mother quizzically. 'Now, what is it you want to talk about?'

But she would say nothing until she was comfortably ensconced in the bows of a boat and he was gently sculling upriver. Then she took her hat off, ran a hand through her black curls, and dangled the other hand in the water.

'This is blissful, Des! I wonder what Frank's doing now?' She laughed gently. 'Probably sculling up some meandering little French river, with a nice little French girl reclining in the back of the boat. *Not* his mama, you dull dog!'

'Mama, he's a soldier. What on earth makes you think he might be on the river? Soldiers don't get weekends off, you know!'

'Don't they? I don't see why not. They've got to rest sometimes; they can't fight without rest, I suppose? Anyway, I've had several lovely letters from him. He's got nice billets, and a really charming friend, and it all sounds frightfully exciting.' She paused, shading her eyes with one hand to look across the glinting water. 'Oh dear, I didn't know there was a hospital near here.'

Dcs followed her eyes to where a blue-clad soldier strolled along the bank and nodded indifferently. He wondered why Frank was writing a lot of lies to Mama, for from the letters that he received he had gathered that life in the trenches was appalling.

'Yes, there's quite a large hospital, I believe. So you've had letters from Frank saying he's enjoying the army? I'm glad, because if he's happy who can blame me for letting him leave? But that isn't why you've come all the way over to Cambridge just for an afternoon, and right at the end of term, as well.'

'I know I shouldn't hate seeing wounded soldiers, but I do.' Tina moved carefully so that she was no longer facing the bank. 'There are such a lot in Norwich – London is worse, and I suppose they're a reproach to us civilians, living such pleasant lives really. Though of course the shortages are horrid, and then there are the raids, and conscription. Anyway, I'm *not* here just for the afternoon. Didn't you hear me say that I'd give you dinner tonight as well as tea? Your father is meeting me here tomorrow and we're having a little holiday together. He hasn't been too well, so he's got some time off from the Ministry and we thought we'd get right away from everything for a few days.'

'I see. Come on, Mama, cough it up!'

'Des, what a horrid expression!' Tina stared severely at her son, an expression of distaste crossing her face. 'All I want is your word that you won't join up. Not until you're eighteen, and then I can't stop you. Unless we've managed to get you into a reserved occupation by then, of course.'

The boat was floating gently beneath the overhanging willows which grew in the gardens of one of the colleges. Faintly, they could hear young voices in the distance, mingling with the chimes of a church clock striking the hour.

'*Stands the church clock at ten to three?*' Desmond quoted, '*And is there honey still . . .*'

'Stop it!' Tina fairly shouted the words. 'Des, don't! I don't want to think about dying!'

'Mama, Rupert Brooke wasn't writing about dying; that wasn't a war poem.' Desmond stopped rowing and leaned forward, taking his mother's small hands in his own strong clasp. 'That's a poem about Cambridge; or Grantchester, at any rate!'

'I know that, but he was killed in the war anyway, and all those lovely words . . . thoughts that no one else could have . . . he loved all this . . .' Her voice faded away. In his grasp, Desmond felt her hands trembling and knew that his mother was hiding behind a cheerful mask, the same mask she had worn when the little ones had died. She did not fool herself that Frank was safe, but she made his vulnerability easier to bear by pretending. And not only for herself; it was easier for others not to have her love and fear constantly before them. Desmond, loving her, could do only one thing.

'I won't join the army, Mama. I swear it. Not until they make me.'

It was not a great sacrifice; he had no desire to join the army, but at that moment he felt noble. He could almost feel the tension draining out of her. She leaned back, averting her face. He had never seen her cry and was glad that she was too proud to do so in front of him. And presently, when she turned to face him once more, her eyes were dry and a slight smile curved her lips. She was in command.

'Thank you, Des,' she said quietly. 'I know it's a lot to ask, but we've lost so much, your father and I.'

'It was a lovely weekend; thank you, darling!' Tina leaned across the table in the sunny window embrasure of their riverside hotel and squeezed Ted's hand. 'Do you feel better for the break?'

Ted, crunching toast and honey, smiled and nodded.

'Much better. The truth is, I get tired far too easily. And there's not a lot of time to be tired in wartime. The flat's very pleasant and I always eat well but it isn't like home.' A waitress entered the room with an armful of newspapers and he beckoned her over. '*The Times*, please, and the *Mail*, I think.'

Ted paid for the papers and Tina took the *Mail* and began to turn over the pages.

'Oh dear, Ted, doesn't life come rushing back when you see newsprint? I dread looking at the casualty lists, but I always turn to them first.' She rustled through the pages, then lowered the paper to stare incredulously at her husband over the top.

'Ted? There isn't a list in here. Is there one in your paper?' And then, as he frowned and shook his head, she added tentatively: 'Do you suppose that the war's come to an end at last?'

'I'm afraid not, love.' He put his paper down and took both her hands in his, holding her gaze with his own.

'Oh, but Ted, why should there be no lists?'

'Because there was to be a big battle at the weekend, the biggest yet. The troops have been massing along the river Somme for weeks now. I'm very much afraid that probably it's impossible to print casualty lists.'

'Impossible to . . . you mean *too many?* Oh, my God!'

The weekend crumbled to ruins as they sat there.

15

On the night following the beginning of the great push, Mark lay in a forward dressing station whilst a harassed orderly dressed a bullet wound in his stomach – the bullet had merely entered the flesh and come out again – and tried to assess the battle so far. A fiasco was the best description he could think of for his own particular part of it. Charging into smoke and a hail of bullets, he had only had time to realise that the trenches which should have been empty were not before he fell, his rifle jerked from his hand.

He must have blacked out for some moments – it could have been an hour or more – because when he came round he was amongst a sea of bodies. He had crawled, with infinite labour, back to the trench he had so lately left and when the body-snatchers came up someone had helped him on to a stretcher and seen him back to the dressing station.

'Well, lad, you've got yourself a Blighty one, by the looks!' The orderly patted Mark's neatly bandaged torso. 'Though you're a Fernleaf, aren't you? Don't suppose a Blighty one 'as much significance, eh?'

Mark sat up, gingerly, and swung his legs over the side of the makeshift bed. When he did so, the room tipped and swayed alarmingly.

'Not a lot. I've a wife and child in New Zealand, though, and they'd like to think of me in England. I've a brother in the Ministry in London, you see. I've not seen him for years.'

'Well, now's your chance, feller! Someone'll walk wiv you – if you can walk – dahn to the ambulances.'

Is this the end of my war? Mark wondered, as he limped with painful slowness further from the lines. He wondered if he would be allowed to send a field postcard to Su, then forgot everything except that he must walk forward and must not faint. And that soon, he would be able to lie down. And sleep.

Louis fell into his bed; he had never thought to fly so constantly, with so little rest, yet the days passed – they were in mid-July now – and the battle still raged. The skies were crowded with shells, screaming through the air and bursting with a sound like an express train hitting the buffers at full belt.

To be alive was a miracle. In the trenches and in no man's land the bodies piled up; a constant stream of wounded limped or were carried to the rear. Louis tried never to look down on to that carnage, but sometimes he could not help it. He flinched back, his stomach turning, when he caught a nightmare glimpse, then fired his Lewis gun into the enemy with more determination than ever. If killing Huns would bring the war to a stop, then he must kill, for what was happening on the ground was not war but slaughter.

He often thought about Frank. He knew now he had a nephew in France, and Tina had sent photographs of a fair, fresh-faced boy with an engaging grin. It seemed impossible that the lad was still alive but he could not find out. When he asked he was told that when the Staff finally decided to call off the push it might be possible to trace his nephew. But until then . . .

Once, after a particularly determined assault on a brigade which had just pulled out of the battle for a short rest, he was told by a weary, filthy, fair-haired soldier who looked no older than Frank that he knew a chap called Neyler; Nails, that was what they were calling him. He'd been wounded in the stomach right at the beginning of the push. He had no idea what had become of him.

'No, I didn't notice what he looked like,' he said wearily, rubbing his eyes with his knuckles. 'Thin and dirty, like the rest of us.'

After that, Louis saw Frank's face in his nightmares, and there was blood on the smooth, girlish skin, or wounds so terrible that they brought him out of sleep on a yell. It was not uncommon, however; few men could sleep peacefully after the first of July.

Nick of the cheerful face and freckles was dead; it ought to have been a comfort that he had taken a German fighter and a German bomber aircraft with him, but Louis only missed him. Others, too. And his memories were slow to return now, as though pleasant recollections had no place in a mind so crammed with horrors. It pleased him that he had his family more or less sorted out in his mind and he felt worried and guilty because Sarah was oddly blurred. But as soon as the heat eased off here he meant to take some leave and go back to her. Find her again. He knew he loved her, but the complexity of his feelings baffled and confused him. He would go home just as soon as he could be spared for a few days, and see her for himself. Until then he would fly, and fight, and do his damnedest to get this terrible war over with.

Frank and Hoss, alone in a crumbly, part-dug trench, lay on their backs, using their packs as pillows and their great-coats as covers. Too tired and hungry for sleep, they could scarcely even relax, for the tension which had started with the unbelievably heavy barrage on the first of July was with them still. They had not left the front lines in all that time and their weariness had reached a stage where to shut their eyes was impossible. All that mattered was resting and perhaps getting some food, the will o' the wisp of their billet seeming to have retreated past remembrance.

From the moment the bombardment had begun, Frank recalled, they had blindly obeyed orders and they had gone on doing so ever since, even when the orders seemed as if they must have been issued by madmen, or murderers, or both. They had been told, on that first morning, that there would be a tremendous artillery barrage and when it ceased they would go over the top, the officers and men equipped with wire-cutters first, and then the mass of the infantry.

They were to press forward at a run up the slope in front of their own trenches and fling themselves into the German trenches which, according to the confident predictions of their masters, would be empty, save for mangled bodies or men driven to the extremities of terror and shell-shock by the aforementioned bombardment.

It had not happened in the least like that. The effect of the barrage, which had induced a state of nervous terror in several members of their own platoon, had been minimal, for when the men scrambled over the parapets and slogged forward – Frank, a tall, strong lad, had found it as impossible as the rest to run up that hill with upwards of sixty-six pounds on his back – they were met by withering blasts of machine-gun fire which mowed down the foremost, crippling and killing, shattering the impetus which had carried them onward.

At the time, they had no idea why the wire was not cut, nor indeed that it had not been until they found themselves facing it. Beating in vain against the barbed wire, with the German gunners still very much alive, they had continued to throw themselves into the attack, wave after wave of them, until darkness had seen the pitiful remnant of that once huge army dragging itself back to its own trenches.

Men died in their thousands but still they attacked, days and nights passing like a nightmare until there was no counting them. Frank and Hoss, always together, had seen their officers and their companions killed; they had seen sick and bewildered reinforcements, green boys out from home, come up and shake and go in to attack – and be killed. Now, death-hardened before they were seventeen, they found themselves increasingly astonished as day succeeded day and they were still alive. Filthy, red-eyed, exhausted, they did as they were told without more than a grumble or two because, so far, their number had not been on any of the bullets, whizz-bangs or bombs the enemy had hurled at them, and because life, any life, was preferable to being shot. They had seen, with unbelieving horror, a young officer turn and shoot one of his own platoon who had half turned back towards the shelter of the trenches on facing the deadly hail of German bullets. On their way back, when their own officer had ordered them to retreat, they had passed the murderous officer and his victim – both dead. Such a waste, Frank had thought bitterly.

'What'll you do when the war's over, Frankie?'

Frank shifted his head on his pack and squinted across at his friend.

'Do? Dunno. Go into business with my old man, I suppose.' He sighed, rubbing his dirty face with his dirty hands. 'God, I could do with a bath!'

'An' a good scoff. Blimey, I wish me lugs'd stop ringin'! Does your guv'nor want you to work wiv 'im?'

'I don't know. But I think he takes it for granted that me and Des will work with him, one day. He's got what you might call wide interests, so it wouldn't be dull. What about you?'

'My old man thinks I'll go into the shop; there ain't no other kids, see? But I can't see me standin' behind a counter all day, slappin' jellied eels or sausage an' mash on to dinner plates. Though it's better'n this!'

His gesture included the trench, the waste of mud and cadavers that was no man's land, the enemy on the ridge above them.

'Anything's better than this. I'd rather sell jellied eels for the rest of my life than charge up that bloody slope tomorrow morning.'

Hoss grinned. Frank could see his teeth flash in the summer darkness.

'Too true, old pal. Tell you what, I'm glad I lorry-hopped into Amiens before this caper started.'

'I bet you are, you jammy blighter!'

Frank's words held no grudging note, though the two days Hoss had spent in Amiens, just before the barrage, had been the only two days they had been parted since, as raw recruits, they had stood together on the Downs, painfully learning to slope arms, to charge, to march. Hoss was more than a friend to him, dearer far than a brother, for if war did nothing else it showed people in their true light. Hoss was a tall, skinny cockney with a long face creased with laughter lines and mousy hair clipped so close to his skull that his steel helmet seemed in perpetual danger of engulfing the knobbly features beneath it. But it was not his comical face, his scarecrow figure, which made Hoss so special for Frank. It was his ability to laugh at discomfort, to joke his way through rules and regulations as prickly, and often as unnecessary, as the barbed wire which ringed the trenches, which had enabled Frank to survive the war and remain sane.

'It was jammier than you know, my son!' This, said in an effete and languid voice, was meant to amuse. What followed was not. 'It was the first time I'd ever bin off, wivout you, and I missed you suffink rotten at first, old pal. Then, later . . .'

'You were glad to be alone?' Frank stiffened like a terrier who sees a rat. 'Aye aye, here's a thing! Good little break, was it? The barrage started within thirty minutes of you getting back or I'd have asked before.'

'It was *bloody* good.'

'Enna pleace but hare's blooda good, bor!' It always amused Hoss when Frank dropped into the broad Norfolk dialect which was the *langage de guerre* of all the Neyler children. 'What did you do? Flirt with one of the nurses? Get blotto on cheap champagne?'

'Nah! Got meself . . . well, guess.'

There could be only one answer to that. For months Hoss and Frank had experienced only war and loss. They knew, none better, that a shell could come whistling out of the night sky and blow them to oblivion between one breath and the next. Tomorrow they might scramble over the parapet and die before they had even set foot in no man's land. They might make the barbed wire and be savaged by machine-gun bullets, they might actually reach the enemy trenches and be spitted on a bayonet. They might even get back safely to their own lines. But the experience which they knew, sharply, they might never taste beckoned irresistibly.

Frank dropped his voice, though they were alone.

'A woman?'

'Yeah.'

'Jee-*sus*! In Amiens? Tell!'

Slowly, choosing his words, Hoss recounted his story.

He had gone into an *estaminet* to buy a card for his mother and to have a few beers. Nothing unusual about that, save that he was alone. And then, coming out into the street again with a lacy, embroidered card in one hand, he had been accosted by a girl of no more than fifteen or sixteen. She had asked him for chocolate and, when he admitted he had none, had walked along beside him, chattering. She told him she lived on a farm just outside the town where he could buy bread and farm butter, and bacon and eggs too if he was rich enough.

Alerted at the thought of food, for he had the healthy appetite of most youngsters of his age, he had gone willingly with her to the farm whilst she continued to talk to him in a mixture of broken English and too-rapid French. She told him about her father, who had been killed in the army the previous year, and her mother, who had been killed when Amiens was bombed.

'I want to train as a nurse, one day,' she had confided. 'Or, perhaps, as a dancer.'

The farm, she explained, was merely a place where she worked in order to keep herself and her small brother, Albert.

Hoss, with money in his pocket, bought crusty bread, fresh butter, and half a dozen eggs which the farmer's wife willingly hard-boiled for him, since there was no bacon available. With this feast the two of them climbed up into a dusty, sun-speckled hay-loft where the girl and her brother slept at nights. The farm itself billeted half a dozen officers, she explained. She was very willing to accept a share of the food, and as they ate Hoss told her something about himself.

'About me dad's shop, and me mum charrin' at the big houses up west when she was a gel, and she told me about cleanin' pigsties and muckin' out the 'orses.'

'And you understood each other?' Frank said incredulously. Despite his years at boarding school his own

French was still slow and laboured.

'Well, it was a bit of a bovver,' Hoss admitted. 'We got along all right, though.'

'And then . . . ' urged Frank, longing to get to the point of the story. 'When did it happen?'

'Then. And there.'

'You were bloody lucky, Hoss. What's it like?'

'It's all right. Not like I thought, some'ow, but good. She's a nice kid, too; not like some.'

'Going to see her again?'

'I should say! But . . . Frank?'

'Mm hmm?'

'Just *see,* like. She's a good kid. If it 'appens again, good. If not, good. D'you see?'

Frank, who did not, was about to question his friend further when he heard a shell-whistle and ducked apprehensively, his head curling protectively into the shelter of his arm. There was a dull crump as the object struck the ground, but no explosion followed so he stood up and looked over the top of the trench, which was easy because it had no parapet or places to fire from but was just a digging, about five feet deep.

Bouncing leisurely downhill towards him was a smallish object, no more than a dark shape in the night. It rolled to a halt and Frank said cheerfully: 'It's a dud,' but turned and snatched up his rifle. It seemed unlikely that an offensive would start now, but you never knew.

He stood there, his senses prickling alert, for a moment. It was a warm night and faintly, on the breeze, he could smell flowers. Geraniums? It made him think nostalgically of his mother's garden. There was a bed beneath the small sitting room window which was particularly her own and he pictured her kneeling there, setting geranium cuttings in the sunshine, her hair stirred by the breeze, fingers deft and gentle on root and stem. For a moment he was off guard, relaxed; soothed out of his customary vigilance by the memories stirred by that innocent flower scent.

Then the breath caught in his throat and he coughed and with the cough shouted: 'Gas! Hoss, it's gas!'

Dropping his rifle, he dived for the bottom of the trench where his mask rested. Hoss was on his feet, peering towards the gas cylinder which Frank could hear hissing faintly now, but he too turned and with the movement came another shell-whine.

The gas, heavier than air, would roll down into the trench. Frank fumbled with the mask, knowing that he must get it on or run; there could be no safety without it in the trench. And even as he rose to his knees, all hell was let loose upon them. There was the shattering roar which presaged the shell-burst and he saw, in slow motion, the ground ascend as the shell struck and felt the precursor of the impact patter, like rain, upon his steel helmet. He had the mask to his face when something struck it from his hand and the earth rose up before him like a black curtain.

He tried to shout to Hoss to get down, but he could only wheeze as pain stabbed his lungs and throat. And then the earth descended, the weight bearing him down as he took one more desperate gulp of what should have been air but was not. He felt his face smash into the soil, felt it pressing, cold and cruel, upon every pore of him. Stifling, inexorable.

His last thought was for Hoss, who had been standing when the gas came pouring over the ground, when the shell burst.

Then, nothing.

Tina came slowly down the steps of the small hotel where she and Ted had spent the night, drawing in deep breaths of the fresh summer air. It had rained most of yesterday and most of the night as well, but half an hour earlier the sky had cleared as if by magic and the sun had come out, sparkling on a million raindrops, making the world look new-painted. And Tina, bursting with *joie de vivre,* had decided that she simply must go out and see what London looked like, after her long absence.

Her step was light, because today was a red-letter day. After all the worry of the last few weeks, Frank was to be discharged from hospital and allowed to come home to The

Pride to recover from being gassed and buried. He had been in hospital in France for weeks, but at last they were releasing him. He would come, by ambulance and hospital train, by ship and by another hospital train, as far as London, where they were to meet him with the big Daimler, the back seat covered in blankets and pillows for the journey down to Norwich.

As if that was not reason enough for rejoicing, they had heard a couple of days ago that Ted's brother Mark had made a good recovery from his wound and would be back on active service shortly. And Louis, the beloved baby brother, was being given a home posting and would be in Norwich almost as soon as they.

It was the combination of all these things that had driven her out on her solitary walk. Indeed, she could not have sat in the dining room a moment longer, sipping coffee and nibbling toast, watching the sun dazzle on the raindrops whilst Ted, reading glasses perched on his nose, worked his way through the morning papers.

Ted, best of husbands, had been quite willing to let her go off by herself. He suspected her, she was sure, of a desire to visit once again the really good dress shops in the West End, but she had no desire to shop. She wanted to walk, and think, and enjoy being in London again after so long away.

She was dressed, with wartime simplicity, in a plain, dark blue coat and skirt with a matching broad-brimmed hat trimmed with a large pink rose. Because of her small stature she had taken enthusiastically to the prevailing mode for Russian boots and today she wore elegant blue ones, with red side buttons and red heels, and she felt very fashionable and was sure that Frank would appreciate her appearance.

She tapped her way briskly along the pavements, her mind busy with her day. She longed to see Frank again, yet part of her dreaded the meeting. It was that padre, she though vindictively. He had written to her, telling her of Frank's bravery, his cheerfulness and his determination to recover completely. But he had also warned her that his experiences had changed her son; that she must do her best not to be distressed by it.

She told herself now that such experiences must change any man; surely no one who had fought in the trenches would ever be quite the same, let alone someone who had been buried and gassed and whose life, for a while, had been despaired of? Yet she was very sure that all parents did not receive letters warning that their sons had altered. Why should she, in particular, be warned? Then she shrugged the niggling little worry away. She would be seeing Frank for herself soon enough; the time to worry was then!

She came to a wide window with a display of austerity fashions and stopped, ostensibly to admire the array of gowns and hats, but really to use the glass as a mirror to check her own appearance. She saw a small, slender woman with a hat perched on a mass of glossy black hair, her skin clear as a girl's, with no hint in her figure that she had borne six children. She seldom allowed herself to think of her babies, lost to her for ever, but she thought now, examining her reflection critically, that sorrow had marked her little. Or not outwardly. To herself she hugged the scars of her loss, allowing no one to guess at the pain and guilt which had threatened to drive her out of her mind until she had come to terms with it.

She wished she had chosen something a little more dressy than her blue coat and skirt, though. It seemed severe for so joyous an occasion. And then she was visited by an inspiration. If she could buy a corsage it would make her look almost bridal. Pink rosebuds would be best, to match the rose in her hat, and it would smell sweet too.

No sooner thought than done. She was walking along a smart, tree-lined road and could see no flower-sellers, but she would probably find one easily enough if she sought in the side streets and squares. Unhesitatingly she turned a corner and hastened along a side road, for she had not the smallest fear of being lost. Like most pretty women she had implicit faith in her ability to charm any man around into assisting her. And besides, she only had to hail a cab and within minutes she could be back in the hotel with Ted, or even at the station where they were to meet Frank.

She turned another corner and, ahead of her, saw the flowers. A mass of them, spilling out from the small, rather shabby corner shop to stretch almost to the gutter, so that passers-by had to walk right round them to avoid treading on the blooms.

I'll get a rose corsage there, Tina thought.

She hurried forward, the scent of the flowers borne to her by the breeze so that her pleasurable anticipation was heightened. Lovely, lovely day, when Frank was restored to her from the jaws of death, when Louis got a home posting, and she was looking younger and prettier than any thirty-five-year-old mother had a right to look! Before her, the blooms spilled out across the flagstones, a living Raleigh's cloak of colour.

She reached the flowers and paused, arrested by their beauty and by the sheer quantity of them. Roses in full bloom, their scent heightened by the sunshine on their pink, crimson, white and yellow petals. Some were in huge bunches with ribbons of satin, gauze, velvet, others were more formally placed in bouquets. She looked further and saw lilies, white as snow with powdery gold hearts, and tall, proud gladioli, crimson, flame, tangerine. Dahlias and asters too, and all the flowers of summer, woven into hearts and crosses.

Wreaths.

Flower shops sold wreaths, of course, as well as ordinary flowers. Yet now that she thought about it, she had never seen such abundance outside a florist's, so that the flowers had invaded the pavement, the wreaths lying amongst the rest.

Her eyes went uncertainly to the legend above the shop window. 'Albert Findlay', it said in curly black letters on a white ground. And below that, 'Purveyor of Jellied Eels, Hot Pies, Sausage and Mash'.

Still she did not understand. Could it be that it was now a flower shop and the new owner had not yet painted out the previous owner's sign? She moved towards the open doorway and noticed for the first time that though the door was open the blinds were down. Through the doorway she could see small tables laid with chequered tablecloths, and a long, marble-topped counter.

There was a notice in the window, stuck to the inside of the glass. It was written in a shaky, wandering hand, the writing of someone who did not feel at ease with a pen. Peering, she read it.

Due to the death in France of our son, Cedric, this shop will be closed all day Thursday. We are sorry for any inconvenience to our customers.

Tina stood there staring at the cheap, lined paper with the stiff little sentences written on it, and then she was not seeing it, nor the flowers. They had blurred together into a hot dazzle as tears formed in her eyes and spilled, burning, down her cheeks.

16

Louis was heading homewards at last. He had been in England, to be sure, for the best part of a week, but he had been busy, seeing people, taking part in discussions. And now, when he could no longer put it off, he was going home to Norwich.

The home posting, which would mean six months at least away from the Front, was by no means unwelcome, and once he had got to London and talked, with all the persuasion at his command, to the Powers that Be he had managed to arrange a secondment to the aerodrome at Great Yarmouth, where he would be principally occupied in instructing. But his actual arrival home was something to which he was not looking forward. It would be such a strange experience, to face a woman he could not recognise across the room, to take her to bed, and not to be able to recall what pleased or did not please her, yet to know she was remembering many previous nights with him.

He knew what she looked like, of course, and had managed to give the impression in his letters that his memory had returned. But when they met face to face, would she not guess?

The train was nearing Thorpe Station and Louis reached up to the rack and got down his haversack. This next bit was bound to be awkward! He had not told anyone the exact time of his arrival, but suppose someone recognised him at the station, someone he could not remember? He would just have to pretend, he supposed resignedly. He had been in London when Frank had arrived back from France and had been tempted to arrange a meeting there, because the Neylers were pretty clear in his mind now. But at the last moment he had decided it would not be fair to his wife, so had continued with his plan to arrive in Norwich unheralded, and surprise them all.

The train slowed and he slung his haversack over one shoulder and lowered the window. The haversack was not all his luggage; there was also a canvas bag full of presents. A dusky pink muslin dress with cream lace inserts for Sarah, a big box of *marrons glacés* for Frank because he had been gassed, some pieces of embroidery for his sisters. Collars and cuffs, made of the exquisite Brussels lace and embroidered with silk so fine that the designs could have been painted on. Then there were toys for his nieces – he counted Josette as a niece – and French perfume for Tina and for his wife. And the lace stole. And the white woolly dog with the floppy red tongue. He frowned. He had bought the lace stole for . . . whom? And that toy dog must have been for someone, perhaps an employee's child. Sometimes, if he picked up the toy, a child's face seemed to blur before his eyes, becoming tantalisingly clear before it faded away. A very young child, little more than a baby, with dark hair and eyes, rosy cheeks . . . the train jerked to a stop and Louis put a hand to his head, which was aching abominably. Forget it, he told himself, getting down on to the platform and lugging his belongings down too. He glanced round, but a station was a station, it seemed. It might have been anywhere. He handed in his pass though, crossed the echoing hall and went out into the station forecourt. The cabs were lined up just where he expected them, but that might have been commonsense rather than memory. He climbed into one, gave the cabby his direction, and settled back in his seat, half excited, half reluctant, now that the moment was so near.

The cab drew up outside an imposing house with turrets on each corner and he got out on to the gravelled drive, paid the fare, and then climbed the steps slowly. It was evening, but the sky was still light. He put his finger on the bell-push, but did not press for a second, struck suddenly by the ghastly thought that any pretty, dark-haired woman who answered the door would look like his wife. Nervousness had, for the first time, made him forget the photograph at which he had stared for so long.

He was sweating. He, who had been flying aircraft over enemy territory for a longer tour of duty than most, was afraid of a slip of a girl. It was ridiculous! He pressed the bell, keeping his finger on it, then snatched it away as another thought occurred to him. Suppose a maid or his wife's sister answered the door! He was so tense he might make an unforgivable mistake, and then . . .

The door opened. She stood there. Tall, slender, in a clinging dark dress, her hand flying to her heart as she saw him, the big, dark eyes widening, the soft, full lower lip trembling.

'Louis! Oh, Lou!'

She was in his arms, slim and strong, deeply satisfying. His body knew hers; he knew everything about her, it seemed, as her perfume caressed his nostrils and the way she clung brought the memories rushing back. So many things, so many times! The touch of her mouth, the way her lips parted for him as her body fitted neatly against him was reminder enough of his kissing, fighting wife with her sweetness that was spiced, always, with astringency. He groaned and buried his face in her neck, opening his mouth on her skin, tasting it and feeling her gasp and shudder as he lifted her off her feet.

He carried her across the hall and halfway up the stairs before she made him stand her down. She leaned against him then, laughing up into his face, her eyes blatantly adoring.

'Lou, you can't take me straight up to bed, no matter how much I . . . well, you've left the front door open and your luggage is still down there, and . . . well, you can't!'

'I can,' Louis said. He glanced ahead of them, to where three white painted doors were ranged round the landing. 'It's the one on the right, isn't it?'

She took his hand, stroking between his fingers in a manner which had him pulling her up the stairs two at a time. She laughed, breathlessly, but followed close.

'Louis, you haven't changed one bit. But you know I've got a companion living with me now – the house is so big, and it seemed foolish to stay here alone – and you've not met her yet.' They reached the bedroom and he closed the door and tugged her into a sitting position beside him on the bed, then began to kiss the side of her neck. 'Now just stop it. I won't be seduced before we've exchanged more than a few words. And I've some news for you.'

'Really?' He was unbuttoning the dark dress in a determined sort of way. She tried to prevent him and he captured her hands and held them out of the way whilst, one-handed, he continued to undress her. As he did so, it occurred to him that he was no stranger to the buttons and laces and hooks and eyes which fastened women's clothing. But why should he not know such things? He was a married man, after all!

'Louis, do *listen* when I'm talking! I've got some . . . oh!'

He tossed her last garment airily over his shoulder and began stripping as well. She watched, smiling. It was so typical of him and she had missed him every bit as much as he had missed her. He came over to her and took her in his arms, gentle now.

'Louis, I'm pregnant!'

He shouted with joy, laughing, proud as a dog with two tails, holding her away for a moment so that he could stroke the slight bulge of her stomach before he began to make love. And in the excitement and wonder of their love-making he knew complete satisfaction, a joy and fulfilment greater than any, he was sure, he had ever known before. It was a terrible thing, he thought, that such bliss could have been forgotten for so long, or that he could ever have felt confused about her. She was a marvellous woman. He would never grow tired of her, never so much as glance at another female. Marriage to such a one as Sarah was a rare privilege.

Presently, dressed again and holding hands, they went downstairs to bring his luggage into the house, to shut the front door and adjust the black-out curtains, and to make themselves a meal.

'I eat in the kitchen, as most people do,' Sarah explained. 'There's no maid, of course, but we manage very well.'

'Good, because I'm ravenous,' Louis said fervently. The kitchen door opened and he added: 'I only had a sandwich on the train . . .'

The words died on his lips. The kitchen was occupied. In a high chair by the table sat a chubby child, bibbed and busy, a spoon in one hand, a dish before him. Sitting at the table, drinking tea, was a young woman. She had very pretty golden-brown hair and blue eyes, and she was wearing a blue and white print dress with an apron over it. The dress bulged pleasingly.

'So you and Jamie have started tea, Sally! This, my dear, is my husband Louis. Lou, Sally Lewis.' Sarah seemed quite unaware of the stillness which gripped Louis in an iron hand, or of the faint colour which had surged into her companion's cheeks. 'As soon as I knew I was pregnant, I began to look in the *Eastern Evening News* to see if anyone wanted to share a house. And I found Sally's advertisement. We knew right from the start that we'd get on, didn't we, Sally? We like the same kind of things. And of course Sally can't go out to work, because of Jamie. So when my baby's born, she's going to take care of them both whilst I work. Good idea, isn't it?' She leaned over the baby. 'Jamie's got lovely dindins, hasn't he? Can Auntie Sarah have some?' Jamie chuckled and pushed the spoon inaccurately towards her mouth. 'Oh, my, what a kind boy he is!' Sarah turned back to Louis. 'Isn't he a pet? I just hope I'm lucky enough to have such a beautiful baby.'

Louis, muttering something, felt that he was caught up in a nightmare. The woman with the baby wasn't Sally Lewis, she was . . . he could *not* remember! But he knew one thing; it was the memory of this woman which had got so inextricably mixed up with his memory of Sarah that he had scarcely dared to come home. And now, to find them living under the same roof . . . he sank on to a chair and put a hand up to his head. His face felt drained of colour and he was very sure his legs would not support him any longer.

'I'm sorry, I don't feel too good.'

The women were immediately all concern. The Lewis female jumped up and made him a cup of tea, then whipped the baby out of the high chair, her face pink and flustered.

'I'll take the boy to his bath, shall I, now? Sure, and it's not easy for your husband to find a scrap of a wee boy in his kitchen when he wants nothing more than a quiet meal with his wife.' She took off the child's soiled bib and pushed it into a linen basket standing just inside the door. 'I'll say goodnight to ye both, for I'll not be down again. There's a good casserole of lamb simmering in the oven, Mrs Rose.'

'You're worn out, dearest,' Sarah said anxiously, when her companion had disappeared. 'Sit quietly there, and I'll dish up and cut some more bread.'

'I need a wash and brush up,' Louis said, suddenly seeing a way to find out a bit more. 'You dish us up a good helping of that lamb, love, whilst I tidy.'

He found his way upstairs, then followed the sounds of splashing bathwater up another flight. He hesitated outside a door, then opened it and slipped inside. It was a pleasant bedroom and Mrs Lewis was sitting on a chair with the child, towel-girt, on her lap and the enamel bath on another chair in front of her. She turned at his entry and smiled without selfconsciousness. It was the smile, he saw with dismay, which one gives an old friend.

'Well, Lou? I'm sorry if you're annoyed with me, now, but I thought you were dead, see? You didn't answer my letters and I'd no rent-money, nothing. I advertised, then, and Mrs Rose offered me the job. A soldier's widow, she thought. I was desperate, Lou.'

'Well, that's all right, I suppose.' The words sounded feeble, even to himself. Deciding suddenly that truth was his only course, he added? 'Look, who *are* you?'

She still held the child and over the top of its head he saw tears fill her eyes. She said forlornly: 'I'm Sarah Sutton. I knew you'd lost your memory when I moved in, but sure I never thought you'd forget me entirely!'

She rubbed the baby dry, then began to dress him in a vest, a bodice and various other garments to which Louis could not give a name. Then she laid the child in its cot and turned once more to Louis.

'I'm sorry. D'you want me to go?'

He shook his head, frowning. He was not really listening to her.

'The baby. Is he mine?'

'That's right. James. You chose the name.'

'Does my wife *know*? Forgive me, but were you my mistress?'

She gave a watery laugh.

'Oh, Louis, what a question! I was, I suppose. You took care of me, first in a wee place in Golders Green, and then you moved us to a dear little flat right by the Coach and Horses. But when you stopped writing you stopped sending money too, and I had to do something! I thought you were dead, or never would I have come here.' She looked up at him, helplessly. 'What'll I do?'

'My wife doesn't know, then. You do realise that there can be nothing more between us? I behaved – badly – in the past, but that *is* the past. If you wish to continue to live under this roof, you must forget the boy is mine. I'll arrange that you're paid a fair sum for his upbringing, of course. My wife pays you as a companion?'

She was speechless, tears running freely down her cheeks, but she nodded, then sniffed dolorously and rubbed her eyes with her apron.

'Good. Then I hope we may be friends.'

He left the room, shutting the door firmly on her grief. I have nothing to reproach myself with, he told himself virtuously, as he seated himself opposite Sarah at the kitchen table and began to eat the casseroled lamb, for what happened between me and that girl upstairs happened to another man, in another life. He also reflected how fortunate it was that whatever had caused him to make the girl his mistress in the first place, whatever attraction she had had for him, had obviously gone. He had felt no flicker of desire for her in that bedroom upstairs, only embarrassment and a faint distaste. Eating his good meal, watching Sarah's glowing and vivacious face across the table, he was very sure that he would remain faithful to his wife.

Ten days later, Louis was sitting in the kitchen alone on the last afternoon of his leave. It was a miserable, rainy afternoon, what was more, and he felt resentful because Sarah had insisted on going out and leaving him behind.

'Darling, it's wonderful to have you home,' she assured him earnestly. 'But you're stationed so near now, you'll probably be home each weekend. And I really am needed. Trained drivers who can also do first-aid are always needed.'

'I need you as well,' Louis said fretfully. 'Tell them it's my last day and they can get someone else to drive the wretched bus.'

'No. Just amuse yourself. It's only for a couple of hours.'

She had gone, looking very pretty in her dark skirt and coat with her high boots, and Louis had mooched around the house for a bit, feeling neglected and badly-done-by. Deserted by hard-hearted Sarah and condemned to a lonely, boring afternoon at home. It was raining far too hard for visiting. Or for visitors, come to that.

He played dice for a bit, then tried to read a book, then tiptoed into the conservatory at the back where Jamie, in his perambulator, snoozed amongst the plants, with the doors wide open so that he got the air without risking a wetting. Jamie was fun to play with when he was awake but today he was most soundly asleep. He was on his side, his legs curled up, his arms clutching his faded blue wool teddy-bear, and not even when his father tentatively rocked the pram did he stir.

The thought that he was the boy's father was one which Louis did not wish to have intruding; it reminded him that, once, he had been unfaithful to Sarah. Now, having made quite sure that Jamie would not oblige him by waking up for a game, Louis decided that he might just as well pack. Then there would be less to do this evening. The other woman (he did not appreciate how apt this title was) must be upstairs in her room, either knitting for her son or for some soldier in the trenches or perhaps even resting on her bed. At any rate, she would be unlikely to appear downstairs until teatime.

Louis went to his room and got out his haversack and the canvas bag. The bag would do very nicely to hold the brand-new flying boots which Poppa had made for him; they were magnificent objects lined with thick sheepskin, and would ensure that his feet kept warm no matter how cold it might be down on the east coast.

He opened the bag and saw the lace stole and the woolly dog. Immediately, he knew they had been bought for Say and her son, though he had not known it before. Say! The very use of the pet-name brought it all back as her own stumbling words had not been able to do. The mews cottage, the sweet, plump, easy-going woman who had given him her love, her body, and a son.

How could he possibly have forgotten her? Without a second thought he took the lace stole and the woolly dog and made for her room. Up the flight of stairs and into the wide attic which had been so charmingly converted into a bed-sitting room. He did not knock – why should he do so, when this woman had been closer to him than almost anyone in the world except his wife? He knew that he must apologise to her for his former coldness, explain that memory had just returned – and give her the presents he had brought so far for her.

She knew, at once. She had been lying on her bed, propped up by pillows and reading a magazine, but she threw it aside, sat up, and held out her arms.

Seconds later he was squeezing the roll of fat round her waist, teasing her, cuddling her; intending to do no more, he told himself, than to establish good relations. Unfortunately, she was only wearing a flounced white cotton petticoat – no drawers, no bodice, no corsets. And it was a double bed, with plenty of room for manoeuvre. She seemed to *expect* to be seduced, he thought plaintively, as he obliged.

When he left her they both knew that their relationship, in the fullest sense of the word, had been resumed. She was his mistress. Any feeling that it was wrong or unusual to make love to two women had completely disappeared. How could it be wrong to make three people happy instead of two? After all, he was not giving Say something which he was not also giving Sarah!

He decided to make Sarah a meal so that when she came back from driving her ambulance she would find something delicious all ready for her. It also crossed his mind that if she was not forced to cook she would have more time to give him later.

Humming to himself, he began to assemble the ingredients for a macaroni cheese, which he happened to be able to cook. As he worked his mind dwelt pleasurably on such problems as how to make sure, when he was next home on leave, that Say got her fair share of his attentions. On a weekend leave, for instance, Sarah would be very unlikely to go ambulance driving. He wondered, idly, if the attic stairs creaked; whether Sarah would notice a somewhat prolonged absence in the middle of the night. He rather thought she would; a pity. He liked the idea of stealing from the slender and energetic arms of his wife to the plump, pillow-like embrace of his mistress.

By the time Sarah arrived home, Louis was glowing with virtue and affection. Had he not used his afternoon to good effect, cooked her a delicious supper, and thought about her constantly?

When she asked, remorsefully, if he had been bored, he told her – truthfully – that he had not; packing his clothes and effects had taken longer than he anticipated, as had a little rest on the bed – he did not say whose bed – and then he had done some cooking so that they might have an undisturbed evening.

Louis, with his arms full of Sarah, was himself again.

Frank lay in the creaking wicker garden lounger with striped cushions beneath him, looking up through the branches of the cedar tree at the cloudless sky. But he was seeing the base hospital. The ward had been full of gas victims, and it reeked. He knew it and so did most of the others. The nurses were wonderful, putting up with the stench, never letting the patients see their distaste, clearing up the foul green vomit which, days later, was still being voided. But Frank had felt like a leper. He still did.

The cedar tree smelt very good; a clean, fresh smell which mingled with the scent of the crushed weed which proliferated in the grass just here. The grass was thin because of the cedar's roots and because of the carpet of needles it laid down in the autumn, yet the weed flourished; small, nameless, with a tiny white flower and little, round leaves. Frank breathed the good clean smell in, yet, stronger than the flower scent, he could smell and taste in his mouth the evil stink of the gas.

Firmly he forced his mind away from the past and into the present. To his right there were wide herbaceous borders, blurred with colour now; the scarlet of poppies, the blue of delphiniums, the vari-coloured dahlias. And behind them, like sentries sloping arms, were the cordoned apple trees. They were all eating apples – Cox's, Pearmains, James Greave – and the trees leaned decorously, linking arms, marching in splendour on either side of the long gravel path which bisected the garden, bordered with box, separating the flowers from the vegetables.

He could not, from here, see further than the apple-walk, but he knew what everything would look like. On the further side of the path there were other apple trees, mostly cookers, and beyond them the two asparagus beds. At this time of year the green fern would be fully out, the delights of the asparagus stalks themselves long over. He remembered lying in the trough between the asparagus beds once, hiding, whilst Desmond and the Sollies searched for him. The earth had been warm and crumbly beneath him, the sky brilliant above, but dimmed by the green of the fern, already turning gold in places, with the occasional hot scarlet of a bunch of berries to make the colour scheme complete. He had been the last person discovered, though who had found him, and how, had long since faded from memory.

By concentrating on the garden he hoped that it might be possible to stop seeing Hoss, outlined against the night sky, and the inside of that canvas dressing station, greenish, smelling of blood and vomit, the pain thick in the air – thicker even than the fear. He had not known, until then, that pain and fear could be seen and felt if you were weak enough – not your own pain, but the pain of others. There had been men in there much worse off than he – men with wounds so terrible that he could not now contemplate them without beginning to shake. A nurse, too, had been hit. Her face – what was left of it – would haunt him for ever, he thought.

After the dressing station came the base hospital, where they had kept telling him he would soon be going home, and then not letting him go. There had been a padre to whose hand he had clung when . . . he pushed the black thoughts back, out of his mind. No! They would give way if he thought about the garden.

Behind his closed lids the garden came to life. Wrongly. Instead of asparagus spears in the beds there were crosses – grey, crooked, mud-blackened. They moved! They limped nearer him! And there were tangles of wire around the apple trees – the trees were leafless, crucified, their branches crippled and bent.

He wrenched his lids open and sat up, sweat running down his face. Why could he not forget? Why could there be no peace for him, no clean, sane sweetness? If he relaxed his iron hold on himself the bitter memories spilled into his quiet mind, galvanising it into sick horror.

'Frank?'

The voice made him jump. He turned his head jerkily, making the wicker seat creak, and there was Mabel, standing quite close to him. She looked cool and pretty in a green and white striped cotton dress with a white straw hat on the back of her head, her hair plaited into two long tails, but the expression on her face was anxious.

'Sorry, Mabs, I didn't hear you come up. How pretty that dress is!'

'It's only school uniform.' Mabel indicated the end of the seat with a jerk of her head. 'If you were a gentleman, Frank Neyler, you'd offer me a seat. Or do you still need to lie down?'

He swung his legs round and sat, then patted the striped cushion invitingly.

'Sit down. If you can bear . . .'

She sat, then turned so that she faced him. Her eyebrows, he noticed, were beautifully shaped and now she raised them with delicate enquiry.

'Bear what? To be near you?' She giggled and took his hand in hers. 'Darling Frank!'

It was the first time he had seen her, he realised, since the Easter holidays before he had run away to join the army. Not so long really, only about five months. Yet it might have been forty years, he had changed so radically. He had left her behind. She was a carefree child still. He . . . he did not care to think what he had become.

'If you can bear the smell of gas.'

Looking into her guileless eyes, he could see no revulsion, only love and a desire to help.

'Gas? Oh, that! It's ever so faint, honestly. Is it just that?'

He loved her honesty and understood her at once. She knew it was not only the smell of the gas that haunted him. But to put into words what he felt was more than he could manage. How could one say that before, he had watched life from the point of view of an actor in the centre of the stage, but that now he watched from the back of the stalls? Once, he had been so busy *being* that questioning had never occurred to him. Now, he watched the antics that men call living and marvelled that it still seemed important to others. Even death no longer seemed so terrible; now it was merely inevitable. Did he see it simply as a sleep? He could not sleep. His eyelids would open of their own accord, forcing his starting eyes to stare into the darkness and see the past. The recent past. School might never have happened, the good times gone along with the bad. Only the war had reality.

'I can't sleep.'

He mumbled the words, incapable of explaining to this child who loved the old Frank what was happening to this new, older Frank.

'It'll come, Frank, honest. Your friend died, didn't he?'

He stared at her, surprised, for a moment, out of his indifference. How on earth had she known that? He had mentioned Hoss to no one because there was no point, now that Hoss was dead. For the first time he found himself hurting for Hoss, wanting to cry for him as he had never done before. He nodded, keeping his gaze lowered so that she would not see that his eyes were wet.

'It must be a huge thing, to see someone like Hoss die,' Mabel said.

He was surprised anew. Everyone else would say how sad, and then point out that thousands had died at the Battle of the Somme. No one else could realise that he and Hoss were almost one, that they had shared the certainty of immortality, knowing that they could not die. So Hoss's death had been a foreshadowing of his own. It had been terrible to be gassed and then buried alive, to feel the earth snapping your ribs, cracking a shin-bone, thrusting fragments of rock into soft, flinching flesh. But to lose in a blow not only one's dearest friend but one's own immortality – it was that which had finished him.

'It was a huge thing, Mabs,' he said humbly. 'I can't

explain, but . . .'

'Don't try.' Mabel was brisk now. 'Was that why you were snoozing out here – because you can't sleep at night?'

'That's right. I've never not been able to sleep before. The nights are so long, and yet I can't read or look at pictures or anything because I'm too tired. Isn't it mad, Mabs?'

He tried to grin, to make light of it, but the small face turned to his was serious.

'It's awful. Can you get out of the house without waking anyone?'

The abrupt change of subject made him smile. Good old single-minded Mabs!

'I suppose I could, if I wanted.'

'Then meet me outside your kitchen door tonight at eleven o'clock. I've got a cure for not sleeping.'

'All right then.'

He guessed that she meant to walk him around to tire him out. He had tried it himself, tried a dozen other things, but none of them had worked. Sometimes he wondered how he went on, without rest; surely, one day, he would have to sleep, like a clock that must falter as it runs down. He had nightmare-haunted naps, of course, but they left him tenser and less refreshed than ever. How long could he go on?

'Don't forget, Frank. Eleven o'clock.'

She gave his hand a last squeeze and then jumped down off the wicker chair and headed for the wood which screened her home from the big house. She was running, and her hat fell off; he could see the impatience in the way she snatched it up and let it trail and bounce behind her as she held it casually by the long, dangling ribbons. He smiled again. A nice little schoolgirl, that was his Mabel!

He was there on the dot, and so was she. It was a fine night, the warmth of the day still lingering faintly in the air. She took his hand, smiled up at him, then led him at a brisk pace across the garden and into the wood. Through the trees, never hesitating, seeing each obstacle long before he did, she led him to the tree-house. At the foot of the chestnut tree she paused, then pulled his head down to hers so that she might whisper.

'Can you climb, Frank? In the dark? It isn't too windy.'

'If you can I can, you cheeky brat! My gammy leg's quite strong now. You go first though.'

She climbed fairly slowly, and he watched and copied her holds exactly. She stopped on the second platform and to his surprise he saw that it was spread with blankets and pillows. She sat down, pulling him down beside her.

'Good thing it isn't raining, Frank! I've often slept up here. It's nice. I'm sure you'll soon drop off.'

'Literally, you mean? You're quite mad, girl, but I suppose I may as well humour you!' They both lay down and rolled themselves in the blankets. The pillows were thin but comfortable and Frank followed her lead and lay on his side. 'Of course the planks are a *little* harder than a bed, and the wind a trifle more forceful out here, but just for half an hour I'll stay up here with you.'

'Shut up and go to sleep.' She sat up on her elbow and firmly tucked in a stray end of his blanket, very much as she had tucked in her dolls when she was small. Then she leaned over and kissed him softly on his cheek. 'Goodnight, young Frank!'

'Goodnight, Mummy,' he whined in shrill mimicry of a small child. He heard her give a smothered giggle, then there was silence. She had closed her bright eyes and was obviously determined to go to sleep herself.

In his turn, Frank pushed his head into the pillow and closed his eyes. He knew it would not work, he just knew it! The wind moved the branches and there were two above him which creaked abominably. He could not possibly sleep with that noise going on, not even when Mabel moved a little closer and slipped her small hand into his. It was nice, being so close to her. He was in a room of his own at the house, because it was not fair to expect Desmond to share a room with him, what with the nightmares and the smell of gas. But this was different; he was not being selfish, because the wind would take the smell of gas right away, and he was scarcely likely to have nightmares when he knew perfectly well he wouldn't sleep. How could he, high up in the branches of the chestnut tree, for all the world like rock-a-bye baby!

Five minutes later he was snoring, his head flung back, his mouth open, little grunts competing with the creaking branches. Mabel scarcely dared to move in case she woke him. She was determined not to sleep in case he wanted her, or had a nightmare, or in case someone noticed he was missing from his bed and started a hue and cry. Of course, when morning came, she would pretend that she had fallen asleep before him and slept soundly all night; that way he would not feel guilty. And then, when the sun came up, they could both go . . . both go . . .

Two children slept on the high platform, rocked by the wind, soothed by the rustling branches of the chestnut tree. Neither dreamed.

17: 1919

Tina dipped her cloth into the bowl of warm water and applied it to the window, sponging it slowly across the four-inch strip of black paper down each side of the pane. It had been there, that black-out paper, for more than four years, and was reluctant to move; but go it must, for Ted had gone to London to fetch his sons home and they must not be welcomed by relics of the war. The years of darkness were over; light could now show around the edges of the curtains, through chinks in the shutters, could even spill out in great golden slabs through open doors! Peace might still feel new after less than five months of it, but at least one need no longer fear being seen by an enemy overhead.

Behind her, one of the twins stirred and muttered. Tina glanced round. As she had thought, the mutterer was Valentina. Nicholas slept soundly, his dark head burrowed into the pillow. It was usually thus; Valentina had been small, wizened and red-haired at birth, and was small, wizened and red-haired still and a poor thriver into the bargain. Constantly vomiting, grizzling, given to attacks of evening colic just when one thought one had a moment to relax, Valentina kept her parents busy walking her up and down, draped over one shoulder, whilst she drew up her tiny knees, screwed up her little face, and bellowed with pain.

My Armistice babies, Tina thought proudly, glancing at the two small sleepers once more before turning back to her self-imposed task. She adored them both, though giving birth to twins at the age of thirty-six had been no light matter, and presenting two sons, both in the army – for Desmond had not escaped conscription – with a tiny brother and sister had given her moments of embarrassment.

Tina caught the top of the now well-soaked strip of paper and began, with infinite care, to peel it from the pane. It came smoothly now, curling round her wrist like a cat, leaving no trace of its presence on the glass. When the window was clear she stepped down from the chair which she had used to reach the topmost pane and turned towards the children. They were peacetime babies, born on the eleventh day of the eleventh month, if not at the eleventh hour, and now that her sons were coming home peacetime could be enjoyed to the full.

The children slept and Tina turned to leave the room. She was a lucky woman. Two sons and a husband had gone to the war and two sons and a husband would return. A nagging fear that Frank had been so deeply marked by his experiences that his mind was, in a sense, injured still, she pushed to the back of her mind. Ridiculous to have such fears; Frank had gone back voluntarily after his gassing and no one had noticed anything unusual in his attitude. No official recognition of 'strangeness', at any rate. Compared with poor Cecy, she was fortunate indeed.

Cecy had lost her elder son. Brilliant, arrogant Bertie, totally unsuited to a soldier's life, had been killed just before the cease-fire. The news of their loss had reached Cecy and Abe four days after the cessation of hostilities and had been all the more stunning, harder to bear, because the rest of the world was rejoicing. Tina had had a heartbreaking glimpse of Con at that time; she had taken the girls to a bonfire which had been lit on the cattle market and had found it too rowdy for her liking, with the brewery giving away free beer and every man seeming to think it his right to kiss every woman. She had the girls clutched close and was pushing her way towards the nearest tram stop when she had seen Con. The grief on his face, the way a small circle of quiet seemed to have formed round him, was unforgettable.

There had been other deaths, scores of them, but none had touched Tina so deeply. Ted's brother Mark had been wounded twice but had gone back to his wife and daughter in New Zealand with a chestful of medals and a limp.

Tina, trotting down the front stairs, thought guiltily that other people's time always went a good deal more slowly than one's own. Mark's daughter Emily must be around two now, a little bit older than Louis's son, Simon. Yet it seemed only yesterday that Mark had written so jubilantly to announce her arrival.

Tina entered the kitchen and went straight to the oven. Since she was not sure what time Ted and the boys would be back, she had decided on a beef bourguignonne – or plain old beef in red wine, as her sons would tell her. It was looking good, she decided judiciously, and popped the casserole back into the oven, then turned to check everything else. Potatoes, peeled and in a pan of water, cabbage shredded, some dried peas soaking in a bowl.

Next she would prepare the twins' bottles and the rest of the paraphernalia which was necessary at bedtime. She had every intention of getting a nanny again just as soon as possible, and had put the word around that if Millie, her one-time nursery maid, cared to apply for the post she would be very welcome to do so. In the meantime, she managed as best she could, though Thursdays, being Ruthie's half day, were worst.

Mabel loved the twins, fortunately, and often came in to give a hand after school on a Thursday. Tina, assembling Woodward's Gripewater, vaseline for bottoms and shampoo for tops, cottonwool and bibs, tried to concentrate on her work, but it was difficult. Her mind would keep on going off at a tangent, into wild and unnecessary speculation.

One thing she kept thinking about was Ted's expanding business interests. The construction company had suffered – though he had been busy enough, in all conscience, with repairs – and the motor salerooms had closed quite soon after the start of hostilities, but Ted's cinemas, which she had gloomily thought of as a wildcat buy, were booming. People needed entertainment when things were as black as they had been for the past few years, and they had flocked to the cinemas.

She had suggested the other day that when the boys came back he could hand over some of his enterprises to them; he had grunted noncommittally but later, with seeming casualness, had said it was a good idea, particularly as he had another idea which needed working on.

Tina, with a sigh, had resigned herself to once again scarcely seeing her husband whilst he flung himself heart and soul into some new scheme. She had realised long ago that he got little pleasure out of his successes once each peak had been conquered. What he really enjoyed was the struggle to reach the summit; he was far too energetic to relax once he got there!

There was a big tray with tulips and daffodils painted on it down beside the stove. Tina fished it out and began to assemble everything necessary for the feeding, changing and putting to bed of the twins upon its multi-coloured surface. Last of all, she stood a pan of hot water, with the filled bottles in it, upon her tray. She was about to pick it up when she heard giggles and scuffling outside the door, which presently burst open so that Stella and Josette might erupt into the room.

'Hello, Mama! Have they arrived?'

Stella, very pretty in her school uniform, threw her new black felt hat on to a chair and ran a hand through her fair curls.

'Not yet. I'm going to feed the babies and put them to bed now so we can have some time to ourselves this evening. It's Ruthie's day off and she won't be back until six, and of course Mrs Walters only works until three. Would one of you . . .'

'Golly, we've got a heap of homework,' Stella said at once. 'And we've not had any tea, and . . .'

'If I helped with the twins, Mama, Stella could get tea,' Josette remarked in her clipped, precise little voice. 'You don't mind, do you, Stell?'

'Well, I'd rather . . . wait a mo., here's Mabel,' Stella said thankfully. She was turning into a lazy little madam, Tina thought, but she said nothing, only smiling with special warmth at her adopted daughter. She turned the smile hopefully on Mabel as the girl entered the kitchen. She was in her dark school coat and hat but she began to take them off at once, putting them neatly on the hooks behind the door before crossing the kitchen to Tina's side.

'Here I am, Mrs Neyler. Just in time to help to feed the lions!'

'And how glad I am to see you, my dear. As a special treat you may feed Nicky, instead of having to tease Val to drink.'

Mabel took the tray firmly from her and backed into the kitchen door as many a maid with a laden tray had done before her.

'No, don't spoil my pleasure! I'm getting quite a dab hand at persuading Val she likes her bottle, and anyway, Mum says you've advertised for a nanny. When you get one I don't suppose I'll have nearly as many chances of cuddling the twinnies.'

Tina snorted. 'I can't see one woman coping with Val, let alone Nicky as well, so I daresay you'll get plenty of opportunities to cuddle them. I've asked your mother to see if she can find Millie – do you remember Millie? She was so good with children, and I'd love to have her to take care of the twins. Nanny Sutton's with Mrs Rose now, of course, so I can't have her back.'

'No, that's true.' They mounted the stairs and turned into Ted's dressing room, where the twins slept. 'Don't they look charming when they're asleep?'

Tina's face softened as she looked down at the cots. They were her darlings, even if they were naughty sometimes!

'Yes, charming,' she agreed softly, and picked Nicholas out of his nest of blankets, then cradled him in her arm, sitting in the comfortable old nursing chair whilst Mabel handed her the bottle and made her own preparations for feeding the younger twin.

'Well, darling? What did you think?'

Sarah and Louis faced each other across the spacious living room of the house in Ipswich Road. The war had been over eight months and the house was fully lived in again, and fully staffed, so that the moss-green carpet, the delicately coloured rugs, the well-polished furniture and ornaments, had an expensively cared-for look. As did Sarah. She no longer drove ambulances or dug the garden but lived the life of a lady of leisure. She had more freedom, Louis sometimes thought, to poke her nose into the concerns of others; as she was doing now, for instance. He had gone up to The Pride to see his nephews because she had urged him to do so. Now he pulled a face, prevaricating because he did not want to have to face the truth. There was something odd about Frank.

'Think? Darling, don't insist there's something wrong with the boy because he won't pretend an interest in construction, or cars, or cinemas, when he finds them boring. Isn't it enough for Ted that Des throws himself so wholeheartedly into the family business? Look, I've told you before that shoes and boots – the whole set-up – bore me and sicken me, but you don't think I'm odd. The very *smell* of leather – ugh! But do you worry about me, say I must be ill in my mind? Of course not! I've been leading a life where intense danger was part of every day, and my skills were all that saved my life. I can't expect to settle down at once, you've said it a hundred times. So why do you and Tina make such a fuss about Frank?'

'Because Frank's such a decent boy – not like Des – and he had a rotten time. Tina's blind to Des's faults, but even she's worried about Frank.'

'Why do you say Des isn't nice?' Louis said, visibly bristling. He had frequently noticed a resemblance between his own attitude to life and that of his eldest nephew. 'Just because he's attractive to women, and charming with it . . .'

'Oh, charming! That's so important, isn't it?' Sarah threw herself down in one of the deep, cream-upholstered armchairs and looked up at him ruefully. 'You think charm's important because you're so well endowed with it yourself, but you've other qualities, my dear love! And how you can deny Des's faults when already poor Ted's having to make excuses for finding him with his fingers in the till . . .'

Sarah was pregnant again and the July heat was very trying to her. He bent over her and kissed her brow, pushing the heavy hair off her face, seeing tiny seed-pearls of sweat forming on her upper lip.

'Don't talk like that, darling. Des only took a bit of money because Ted wasn't paying him enough to . . . to manage on. And you must know that he does love the business while Frank hates it so, yet Ted pays them both. I really do think he was justified in feeling a little sore with his father.'

'Oh, do you! Frank hates it, but he works hard, and Des loves it but spends an awful lot of time drinking in various bars and carrying on . . .'

Louis had been stroking his wife's shoulder but now he snatched his hand away as if she was red hot. His thick brows met in a furious scowl. He knew what was coming next: a reminder that Desmond had not just taken money, but had put a car on his father's account and expected Ted to pay all his bills, including those he ran up because of various girlfriends. If the boy has a handsome face and figure and likes women, what's wrong with showing his appreciation by taking them out? Louis thought crossly. Why did it have to be stigmatised as womanising? His own reputation in that direction had been bad once, and sometimes, when Sarah made remarks like those he realised she was about to embark on, he suspected that she knew more than she possibly could about his present peccadilloes. After all, she could not have the slightest suspicion about his continuing affair with Nanny Lewis; but there had been others. Small indiscretions, but ones he would prefer to keep to himself. There was a barmaid called Patty with a glorious fall of golden blonde hair who had been more than generous to him on several occasions. She worked in an ancient inn out at Horning and at first, he told himself defensively, it had been the hair which had attracted him, only the hair! He had longed to see her with it loose, flowing around her plump shoulders, and from there it had been a small step . . .

And then there was Rita. And Beryl. And Wilma. All employed at his father's shoe factory, all falling willing victim to his charms. In the large, quiet stockroom in the basement, between the aisles of shelving crowded with shoes and boots, he had spent many interesting and productive hours with Rita, Beryl and Wilma. Of course he had been careful to choose quiet times and had tried very hard never to enter or leave the stockroom with any of the girls, but it stood to reason that some of the bored, nasty-minded clerks must have hazarded a guess or two as to why he spent so much time checking stock. And it stood to reason that one or two of those guesses would be correct, since not only the law of averages but also his confounded reputation was against his appearing entirely innocent. He felt no guilt, of course, because nothing whatsoever would have happened if he had not been so terribly bored. He reflected now that during the four years of the war he had been faithful as faithful could be to the Sarahs. It was just that now, with no excitement or danger, and with shoes being thrust, metaphorically, down his throat all day, something had snapped. The urge to add a little danger, a little spice, to his existence had tempted him into a few acts which might, by the critical, be construed as adulterous.

' . . . with a score of unsuitable women, not even paying for his pleasure, and . . .'

'I'm going out!'

He had slammed out of the house before he reflected that her condition was probably making her critical. He was sorry then, though he felt no inclination to go back for another lecture. He had too much on his mind. Although Sarah did not know it, Say was also pregnant, as though his welcoming in of the peace had been unusually prolific. Say, of course, had been tearful and terrified at first, saying she would do away with herself or run off, sure that Sarah would guess who had fathered the child and sack her after a hair-tearing session.

'I'll have to go,' she said tearfully. 'But I'm that used to you, me darlin', and having Simon as well as Jamie to mind, that the dear knows how I'll get on without ye, and burdened by a new babe.'

It was to Louis's credit that the thought of procuring an abortion for his mistress never even crossed his mind, and when Say suggested it he was firm in his rejection of the idea. She was not to blame for getting pregnant. She must be patient for a little longer, and then he would set her up in a nice little cottage somewhere and visit her as often as he could.

'You'll have to tell folk you were widowed in the spring,' he said, after giving the matter some deliberation. 'And you'll have to change your name again and keep clear of the city for a bit. But later, when the child's a year or two old, you must bring him to visit us and pretend you've married again. See? It's quite simple, really.'

Say, poor soul, had looked doubtful, but Louis was sure it would work out. It was a nuisance that his delicious existence with two eager women would have to change, but he was sure there would be compensations.

So now he crossed over to the garage and started the car. He would go for a spin and put silly women right out of his head. He drove out into the road, hesitated, then turned down towards St Stephen's Street, heading for the Wroxham Road. He would go down to Horning and forget his troubles and Sarah's fault-finding. It was a beautiful evening and he enjoyed a drink twice as much when he could drink it sitting by the river. If it had been suggested that he was going down to Horning to see Patty he would have repudiated the suggestion righteously. He was going down to Horning right enough, and if he should happen to bump into Patty . . . but it was in the lap of the gods, after all!

Frank lay in bed staring at the ceiling and wondering why he could not pretend better. His father was being so good, dragging him around every building site, every cinema, every car showroom in the city, trying to interest him in one of them. His mother arranged for him to attend parties, brought young people to the house, made him a member of every club in sight. All he wanted – and it showed – was to be left alone.

For his thoughts, after so much anguish, were no longer a torment to him. In his own quiet way, if left alone, he simply savoured the peace. No one ordered him about, no one slung bombs at him or assailed his ears with deafening noises, no one tried to kill him. But though he preferred this life to that of wartime, he still wanted no part in it. He was perfectly content just to watch.

Others, unfortunately, thought he should participate. Mabel, for instance. She seemed to expect something from him and he was not at all sure that he wanted to give it. She snuggled up to him when they were alone, touched his hand, his cheek, yet there was no thrill of excitement, no response, in him. It was as though he had spent all his emotions in the first months of the war and now had none left to give. No enthusiasm, either, and only the mildest interest in one or two things. He was interested in the babies his mother was so proud of, for instance, but had no desire to hold them or play with them. He could not love them.

Sometimes he tried to arouse such feelings but mostly he did not bother because he was sure it was no use. Desmond and his friends who had survived the war wanted something he did not; Stella and Josette seemed almost afraid of him, giggling in corners, squeaking, enjoying a fund of private jokes. Con came closest to him, with an understanding which was strange when you considered that he had never even been in the army. But he had lost Bertie, and whatever Frank may have felt about his own brother he did understand Con's grief. However, Con was almost as detached these days as Frank was, filled with a determination to get into Cambridge University and working extremely hard, so that the two rarely met.

He worried most over Mabel, though. His feelings towards her now were so negative, yet had once been so positive. He knew he had loved Mabel and had intended to marry her one day. What was almost worse, she had known, and knew still. He could read it in her eyes, see it in the sudden way she would turn to him, feel it through her fingers when they touched him. She loved him in an uncomplicated and almost childlike way, and was waiting confidently for his feelings towards her to return to normal.

He was nineteen, yet felt ninety. No rage flowed in him, no hate. No passions, in fact. Nothing but calm acceptance of life as it was, with no desire at all to interfere. He watched Desmond's increasing greed with indifference, his frenetic affairs without even faint disgust. Sometimes he supposed, vaguely, that he too should be pursuing girls, or settling down with Mabel, but he had no desire to do any such thing. He watched.

Earlier in the evening Mabel had obviously decided to try and change things. In a few days, she explained, she would be breaking up from school for the summer holidays. She thought it might be fun to take their old bicycles and have a cycling holiday, perhaps touring down on the coast.

'Just us, Frank,' she had urged. 'I've got some money saved, and it would be so peaceful and pleasant. I know you'd like it.'

For a moment he had actually felt fear, as sharp and

acute as in the early days of the war when he had heard the approaching whistle of a shell and wondered if his number was on it. He would *not* like such a holiday, because Mabel expected something from him. A response that he did not know how to give.

Would she understand, though, that it was not a deliberate snub? He was too fond of the girl to want to hurt her, but she had to know some time. He groaned, bored by the look of the familiar ceiling, and turned on to his side. Immediately the faint, hated smell of the gas wafted up into his nostrils. He felt sick. As if any woman could want him, stinking as he did!

Presently, he slept.

'I *do* understand, Frank, honest I do.' Mabel's dark eyes were fixed earnestly on Frank's face. 'It can't be easy to fit into life at home again. I mean, there's a big gap because when you left you were a schoolboy, and now you've come back you're a man and you've been sort of catapulted into a job without any of the middle bit. Sort of.'

Frank grinned. 'You've "sort of" hit the nail on the head, young Mabs. Des had nearly a year of being in Daddy's business before he was conscripted so it hasn't been so difficult for him to pick up the reins again, but I've got no reins to pick up. All my friends were army or school and most of 'em are dead anyway. That's made things worse.'

They were sitting on the wicker garden lounger, in the shade of the cedar tree, a foot of striped cushion between them. Mabel could have closed the gap but Frank's whole attitude warned her that it would not be a wise move.

'I know. That's why I suggested you and I might go off on our own. You wouldn't have to please anyone but yourself, Frank, and it would be so restful in the evenings, just strolling by the sea or along a country lane. We needn't cycle very far or very fast. You're fit, I know, but we'd take it easy.'

'It isn't that. I feel I'm cheating you. Things have changed in a way you *don't* understand, though you come nearer to understanding than anyone else has done.' He took a deep breath and turned to face her. 'I don't think I'm ever going to marry, and once I wanted to marry you very much. *Now* do you see why I don't think we ought to go on holiday together?'

She stared, and he saw her cheeks flush beneath her summer tan. 'Do you mean . . . were you wounded *that* badly? Oh, Frank, if . . . '

He stared, then laughed aloud. 'Lord, no, I don't mean I'm incapable of . . . anything! Just that I'm not terribly interested any more. I feel so cold and detached, as if I was a different species from a different planet. How could anyone marry me when I'm the way I am?'

Mabel was nonplussed and showed it.

'What way? For goodness sake, Frank, don't you *see*? If you don't come on holiday with me I'll never understand what you're talking about! I'm not trying to tease you into marrying me or – or loving me. I just want us to have a nice holiday!'

In the end, for the sake of peace, he agreed to the cycling holiday. He knew his parents would be very relieved if he went, and he also knew that it would be pleasant to be with Mabel and away from the worried eyes of the family. In the end, he grew enthusiastic. He took over the planning and booked single rooms for them at small country pubs for the first three nights of their journey. He overhauled both their cycles, drew out his savings, accepted gracefully when his father insisted on giving him a generous sum for a holiday bonus, and at last waved a cheerful goodbye as they set off one warm, breezy morning with a drizzling rain blowing in their faces.

'We've got beds tonight at Cromer, so we shan't have to hurry.'

'Lovely. Whereabouts in Cromer?'

'The Lion. Does that suit your Majesty? And I thought we'd stop at Aylsham for some lunch, since it's about halfway. Think you can make it that far?'

Mabel beamed at him, her dark eyes sparkling. It occurred to Frank for the first time that this really was a holiday for them both, and that Mabel had never had a holiday in all the time he had known her. How selfish he had been, never considering her very real and natural wish to see a bit of the countryside and sleep under a different roof each night! For her sake, they would have a good time and enjoy themselves!

'Can I make it? I'm not soft, you know! High School girls play a vicious game of hockey, and us Walters have to walk or cycle everywhere, unlike you pampered Neylers!'

'Really? What about buses? And trams? And trains? And . . .'

She giggled and they rode on, the drizzle gradually giving way to watery sunshine which turned the wet road into a ribbon of pale, reflecting blue and the trees into faery palaces with diamond drops on every leaf. Mabel talked, sang, or was silent. Frank felt dreamy contentment steal over his senses, a feeling that soon he would know what had been wrong with him and would be able to conquer it. He would be the old Frank again, or the young Frank, rather, able to join in life wholeheartedly. For the first time, he acknowledged that it was possible to step out of his niche as audience and become an actor once more. He began, cautiously, to be happy.

'Sarah, darling, you've found a treasure in that cook. This kedgeree is first rate!' Louis beamed at his wife across the snowy surface of the dining table, then reached for the coffee pot. 'All well in the nursery?'

'As far as I know.' Sarah pushed her cup towards her husband. 'Pour me another as well, darling! I do think Mrs Bristow's a good cook, and she's longing to have a go at a dinner party, she says.'

'It would be nice to entertain again,' Louis agreed thoughtfully. 'Nothing too big, of course, because people aren't giving big parties yet, but we could invite . . .'

'All the people we owe, now we've got Mrs Bristow,' Sarah said. The servant problem at least was now fading from memory, though food was still sometimes difficult. The young Roses had a cook, a parlourmaid, a woman to do the scrubbing and a girl to help Nanny Lewis with the children. 'Your sisters might like to come around and meet some young men. It's about time! Since Ray broke off her engagement I don't think she and Becky have had any fun at all.'

Louis was about to reply when the door opened and Nanny Lewis entered the room. She smiled rather apologetically at them but shut the door behind her and came across to the table.

'Good morning, ma'am, sir. Could I have a word with ye?'

It was not so long ago that they had all breakfasted together around the kitchen table. Sarah smiled and pulled out a chair, gesturing the other woman towards it.

'Of course, Sally, and sit down whilst you say it. Now then, fire ahead!'

'I'm gettin' married, ma'am.'

Louis could not prevent his involuntary start, but Sarah was looking somewhat taken aback herself and would merely have thought his surprise natural.

'Indeed? This is rather sudden! Have you known the lucky fellow for long?'

There was just sufficient censure in her tone to bring a flush to Nanny Lewis's cheeks, but she continued with her explanation though her voice wobbled a little.

'Not too long, in one way, Mrs Rose. The truth is, I'm afraid, that . . .'

'That you're pregnant? My dear girl, I've known it for several weeks! I must say I did wonder whether you were ever going to confide in me.'

It was Nanny Lewis's turn to look startled.

'You knew? Well, ma'am, I was that ashamed I should hope I couldn't say a word to ye! I'd not seen me laddo for a while, you see, so no chance of tellin' him the way I was in. Then a week ago he came back for good – he was on leave when we . . . well, anyway, he come home. And when I told him how it was he said we'd marry as soon as we could. It'll mean movin' out of the city because he wants to be near his mother, but I'm a country girl at heart. If only there's someone who can love Simon as I've loved him, ma'am!'

Louis was listening, at his ease now. This was obviously Say's way of getting out of the house without rousing his wife's suspicions, and a very clever way it was too. He hoped she had invented a good name for this mythical would-be husband, though, or they might yet be in trouble. Sarah was asking the question now – he determined to drop a cup or stage some similar diversion if Say hesitated or was at a loss.

'His name, ma'am? Well, it's Winkie Butcher. He helped out at The Pride once or twice before the war.' She turned to Louis. 'I daresay you remember him, sir? He was in business for himself, what you might call garden contracting I suppose. We've been on good terms for years, even after I met my first, but this time, when he came home on leave and found me actually in Norwich and at a loose end – well, we clicked at once, you might say.'

Louis could think of a much more basic word for it, but he was too confused to do more than grunt. Winkie Butcher? He just hoped Say was not making an almighty fool of herself, because he remembered Winkie well. A tall, well-set-up young fellow with a high colour, dark twinkling eyes, and a way with the girls. Louis knew he had survived the war and had met him in Norwich only days before, and he knew Winkie would not take kindly to Say telling people he was going to marry her. Unless . . .

But Sarah was being gracious, telling Nanny how much they would miss her, promising her a month's extra salary and some useful presents for the new baby.

'For I daresay we shall reach our time within days of each other, and last time I was given more presents than I could possibly use.'

As soon as Say had gone, Sarah began to tell Louis how hurt she had been when Nanny had not confided in her. Louis sympathised, nodded, shook his head, but underneath he was thinking furiously. Could Say have been telling the *truth*? Was she really going to marry that bombastic young Butcher? If so, he would be bitterly hurt! How could she do such a thing to him? He would have arranged something, seen her right! The more he thought about it, the more he knew he should have been consulted; he did not want Jamie brought up by some horny-handed agricultural labourer. Damn it, he would have made arrangements, given time! But he was worrying unduly; it could not be true!

It was, of course. He had believed it in his heart from the first mention of the man's name. And Say, when reproached, defended herself tearfully.

'Sure, Lou, and I know you meant well for us but you'd done nothin', and the dear knows your wife had noticed. 'Twouldn't have been long before she was puttin' two and two together and then what could we have done? And then Winkie came along with talk of gettin' a place of his own, marryin', settlin' down. So I said I'd got a bit put by. I knew Winkie liked me, you see, and I was desperate, and when he pricked up his ears and said he'd take me and the children too if I'd provide the home, it seemed just the t'ing. Oh, Lou, love, what else could I do?'

Her brogue always got thicker when she was distressed and Louis hated to see her distressed. They were in her room, not a safe place to be even though Sarah was out at a coffee morning. But he put his arm round her plump shoulders and squeezed her gently.

'All right, all right, you probably did the best thing. And fancy you having a bit of money put by! I thought you were as improvident as me!'

'Oh, I am! But you did say you'd set me and the babies up somewhere, and I thought if you'd buy a cottage as a kind of farewell present then you wouldn't need to do anything else. Well, a few shillings to buy the boy presents, perhaps, though Winkie says he'll treat him like his own. And I know he thinks the new one his, for . . .'

Louis's outraged yelp frightened him almost as much as it did Say, for in the nursery next door they could hear the two little boys murmuring as they played, and Janet, the nursery maid, would not be out of earshot. Hastily Say put a muffling hand across his lips and dropped her own voice to a whisper.

'Oh, Lou, do hush! Suppose Janet comes in?'

He tore her fingers away from his mouth but dropped his voice to a whisper nevertheless.

'His? How can it be? You're nearly five months gone! The man isn't an idiot! He couldn't . . . or are you telling me you were carrying on with him . . .' a hasty calculation ' . . . last January?'

'Sure and weren't you and the missus off to London like two lovebirds last January?' Say said sulkily. 'If it hadn't been for Winkie I'd have died with the boredom and the jealousy!' And then she, who had never reproached him, added almost sharply: 'And there was that wench in Horning, to say nothing of the girls at the factory! It's unfair of you, Lou, to be angry with me!'

'Unfair? You dare to accuse me of unfairness when it's you who're leaving me?' Louis was totally sincere in his feeling of rejection. 'Taking my child to another man – and now you tell me you were actually carrying on with Winkie back in January . . .' Another thought darkened his brow. '*Is* that child mine?' An accusatory finger pointed at Say's middle. 'Were you trying to make me responsible for another man's brat?'

Say began to cry in good earnest. She put her hands to her face but Louis pulled them down, then he tilted her chin until her tear-drowned eyes could not avoid his stern gaze.

'Well, Say? Is the child mine or his?'

'Y-yours, Lou, I th-think. B-but it's useless to say it c-couldn't be his, because it c-could!'

Louis could no longer ignore such real distress. His arms went round her and he cuddled her tightly. He kissed her brow, then her tear-wet cheeks, then her lips. Then he gently held her back from him.

'Then you want me to buy you a cottage? Well, it may take me a week or two, but I'll raise the cash somehow!'

He left her then, and went to his own room to ponder on how to get hold of some money quickly. He was fortunate in that Sarah's father paid her a handsome allowance which entirely covered the cost of running the house and paying the servants. His own salary was generous, he supposed, but somehow he had never managed to save anything. On

Monday he would have to look round the factory and see if there was any way he could raise the money. A loan from his father seemed the obvious thing, and Arthur had never been mean with his only son. It would, Louis told himself philosophically, work out in the end.

Louis leaned on the bar of the Fye Bridge Tavern and felt that the iron had really entered his soul. Despite it being a Monday he had entered the factory cheerfully enough, with a whistle, if not a song, on his lips. He had put on his best tie, a cheerful floral one, and his dark suit to please Poppa. A quiet talk with Say had informed him that what she and Winkie would most like was a small shop in the main street out at Blofield. The asking price was reasonable, the accommodation adequate. Jamie would not lack a decent garden to play in and the village school was barely five minutes' walk along the wide street, so Louis felt confident that he would be able to explain matters to Arthur's satisfaction. Sally Lewis was a faithful employee, the shop would be an investment. He would pay Poppa back in a few months and all would be well once more.

Arthur had been indulgent enough, had even praised his son's generosity in wanting to set the young woman up in business, but nevertheless he had advised his son that if he wished to purchase the place he should apply to Sarah's papa and make sure that the gift came from his wife rather than himself.

'For talk there must not be,' he pointed out jovially. 'Ah, I know you say the young couple will pay you back, my boy . . . ' for Louis had protested as much, 'but such talk we must not have, for the sake of your good little wife.' His eyes were full of affection for Louis, but there was shrewdness there, too. 'She's a good, generous girl, your Sarah. Speak to her, eh, before doing such a thing?'

Louis guessed that Poppa thought the gift of the shop was a preliminary to a relationship with Say, and was tempted to tell him the truth and get the money anyway. But there was worse to come. He had gone down to the stockroom for a legitimate purpose and was in between the shelves ticking off the required sizes of boots on an order when Wilma appeared around the corner, a gleam in her rather watery blue eyes.

'Thank God I've found you, bor! Hare's a pickle! I think I'm in the family way!'

For a moment horror froze him to the spot. It could not be true! But it was soon clear that Wilma believed it. She began to talk wildly of putting an end to it all, of how her father would kill her when he found out, of how the shame of it would probably kill her anyway.

Louis fought with and subdued an unreasonable urge to encourage her death-wish, and instead asked her what she wanted from him. It was money, of course. Money to leave the factory, to go away and have the baby somewhere where she was not known; money to set her up when she returned, having given her child for adoption.

He made enough promises to calm her, and then hurried out, not to Backs, where he would meet half the clerical staff and very probably Poppa, but to the Fye Bridge Tavern, which was a goodish walk away. There was a charming barmaid too, but for once Louis was impervious to her blue eyes and softly curling fair hair. He simply did not know which way to turn. Ghastly visions of all his chickens (so to speak) coming home to roost, of Rita, Beryl, and Patty from Horning all claiming to be in the family way, floated nightmarishly through his head. What could he do? It was going to be next to impossible to find the money for Say's shop, let alone Wilma, and to Louis's inflamed imagination the others were already lying in wait for him, ready to bombard him with paternity summonses for twins at least. What on earth was he to do?

'That'll be one and eightpence, sir, and would you kindly move away from the bar if you've finished?'

The pretty barmaid, tired of being ignored by one of her most fulsome admirers, grabbed his empty tankard and his equally empty sandwich plate and held out her hand. Louis put the money in it without one single joke, nor did he tickle her palm as he took his change.

Must be ill, thought the barmaid remorsefully as she saw

him moving – almost slinking – out of the crowded bar-room.

Later that afternoon, Louis was back in the stockroom checking off the boots once more. He was preparing a vast and extremely unexpected order for more army boots, and knew he ought to be pleased, for Poppa had been convinced that he would have the boots on his hands for the duration now that the peace had broken out. Instead, this mammoth order had been telephoned through that very morning. But he had been so sick and worried that he had not thought to tell Poppa. In fact, he might as well wait now and hand him the cheque, which would be arriving in a few days.

He blinked. Just suppose the money never appeared on Arthur's desk? It would not be in the books, of course, because he, Louis, had not thought to put the order down. He frowned. There must be some snag. It simply couldn't be that easy! Surely his father would miss the boots!

Only a little thought convinced him that this problem could easily be overcome. He would suggest to Arthur that the boots be moved into the warehousing at the back until such time as they had some use for them. In fact, there would be no need to make any such suggestion; he would get the job done now and tell Arthur that it was a *fait accompli.* And then no one would remark on the absence of army boots which Arthur had been resigned to making a loss on anyhow. The money would pay for Say's shop, perhaps even with enough left to tide Wilma over her 'trouble'.

I'll put money aside each month, as I'd planned, and pay the business back, ran Louis's thoughts. It's only borrowing, after all; if Poppa hadn't been so difficult I'd just have borrowed the money direct from him instead of having to use my wits to get hold of it.

By thc time he left for home that evening, the plan had been perfected and all but concluded. The boots had been moved to the warehousing, save for those which he had sold to the army; he had even arranged for the money to be paid direct to him since he was managing the sale.

Louis, without really thinking about it, had embarked on a life of crime.

18

The cycling holiday was a great success, Mabel thought as she went up to her room in the grey stone fisherman's cottage, just outside Happisburgh village, where she and Frank were staying for a few nights. Frank was laughing again, teasing her. To be sure he was not very amorous yet, but even that was improving. Better still, he was telling her more, no longer holding back his thoughts and feelings.

It was beginning to show in his face, she thought now, taking off her short, practical cycling skirt and the dark blouse which was stained with sweat and dust. He was smiling more at other people and she had heard, that very morning as they cycled through the village, two women talking.

'He's a handsome lad,' one of them had remarked. 'And she in't so dusty. Nice couple.'

Mabel was used to hearing the Neyler boys admired for their fair curls, regular features and good figures, but now for the first time she saw that Frank was really very handsome, and knew that one day other girls would envy her her tall, blond husband.

Because it was going to come out all right. The knowledge that he did love her, whatever he might say at the moment, warmed her, and she was bold enough to tell him that he must begin to battle with his self-doubt.

'It isn't just that,' he had protested. 'I'm shy, though I can't imagine why, and it's horrible to me to see Desmond acting like a randy tomcat. And then I know I smell of gas . . .'

'That smell's almost entirely your imagination,' Mabel assured him. 'I hardly notice it, truly, and if we were married and together most of the time I bet I'd *never* notice.'

He had smiled at her and it was very nearly his old smile, and then, so casually, he had put his arm around her shoulders. They were sitting on a shingle bank above the sea, which pounded the pebbles below with a surge and drag, and above them the seagulls gave their melancholy catcalls. Mabel could taste salt on her lips and, though the wind was cold, she was hot with happiness. For Frank had flung an arm round her shoulders and she could sense how near his restraint was to disappearing altogether.

'Never notice? I'll hold you to that, Mabs, one of these nights!'

'I wish you would.'

The words, almost whispered, had been going too far and too fast for Frank; she realised it as soon as they were out of her mouth. His arm had moved, absently, as though he were merely a little stiff in that position, but she felt his withdrawal keenly and would have given a good deal to have the remark unsaid. It was both fast and forward, she told herself crossly.

But it had given her a Plan, and she intended to put it into execution this very night. Frank used the smell of gas as the main reason for not making love to her; she would prove that it was no reason at all. She intended to wait until the fisherman and his wife had gone to bed in the converted shed they slept in when they had overnight guests, and then join Frank in his room. After that, she would play it by ear. If he wanted her to, she would go to bed with him. If, as was far likelier, he did not even wake, she would sleep in his room and assure him, in the morning, that the gas was nothing, a mere figment of his imagination; certainly it would not prevent a woman from sharing his bed!

She knew, of course, that it was not just the smell of gas which had made Frank so withdrawn. It was that night, the night that Hoss had died. Something had happened on that night, four years ago, which had made him believe that being close to a person would result in death. Vaguely, she believed that something had happened which had connected death and girls in Frank's mind, but what it was she had not the faintest idea. Nor did she think that it mattered. Frank was getting better so quickly that the whole worry would probably slip from his mind soon and cease plaguing them both.

Darkness was thick as she crossed her bedroom on bare feet and opened the shutters. She had donned her thin cotton nightie and now she opened the window, and then simply stared, her purpose forgotten for a moment. Her room overlooked the beach and the moon was full, painting a path across the sea, silvering the pebbles and turning the breakwaters and their long-fingered shadows into pitch. Out at sea there were lights – ships, sailing up and down the channel. And a thin cloud slipped, scarf-like, across the moon's bright disc. Beauty, and magic, were almost tangible out there.

The sleepy chirp of a bird in the lilac bush by the front gate brought her back to earth. She pushed the window wider and leaned out. She could just see the shed. The curtains were drawn, the windows tight shut. She sighed with relief and turned back into her room. Now for it! She wanted to help Frank and this was one way to do it. They had had a full and exhausting day; only excitement had kept her awake so long as this and already she could feel her eyelids drooping. Frank, she was very sure, would be fast asleep. There was no need for the fluttering in her breast nor for the sudden dampness of the palms of her hands. She rubbed them briskly against her nightgown, then opened Frank's door. It creaked. He lay facing the window, his breathing deep and even. She crossed the room and lay gingerly down on the extreme edge of his bed. There was the faintest smell of gas, but it was so faint that it could disturb no one. She made herself comfortable, and began her vigil.

* * *

It was most unfortunate that she overslept and that Mrs Mitton had walked in on them. Shaming to have her stumbled explanation of noises in the night being patently disbelieved not only by Mrs Mitton but by Frank too. He had shot up in bed, his fair curls on end, his face creased with pink lines down one side where he had slept on it, looking disproportionately astonished. Mabel had slunk from his room back into her own feeling like a Magdalen and cursing her ability to sleep through a hurricane.

Breakfast, served by a tight-lipped Mrs Mitton, was an uncomfortable meal; they agreed to move on without exchanging more than one swift, beady-eyed look. Indeed, they did not speak a word during breakfast and left almost as silently, Mabel not even wanting to thank Mrs Mitton, though she did stumble through a couple of ingratiating sentences which their hostess listened to with cynical detachment.

It had been raining, too. They rode off along the coast road towards Sea Palling. Mabel wanted to explain but she felt thoroughly misunderstood and furious with herself. Why on earth had she not told Frank what she intended to do? What did he believe, anyway? Surely not that she was trying to compromise him?

The thought made her smile and she shot a glance at Frank through her eyelashes. He was looking at her.

It was just at that moment that she noticed the rain had stopped and the sun had broken through the cloud. She raised her brows at Frank and he grinned.

'Mabs, you're a silly fool! What on earth did you do that for?'

'I wanted to prove to you that the smell of gas didn't bother me.'

'Was *that* it!' For a moment they cycled in silence. Then he spoke again, with a certain wry humour. 'Do you always sleep so soundly in a strange man's bed, then? Or were you actually overcome by the gas fumes?'

She giggled and leaned over to push his shoulder and their front wheels grazed. There was a moment of wild wobbling and then two cycles were down on the wet road and two riders, inextricably entangled, were gasping and laughing on the rain-soaked grass.

'I wasn't in your bed, Frank, I was on top of it! I don't want you to do anything you think is wrong. I just wanted you to know that if you *do* want to . . . well . . .'

Their faces were inches apart and they were laughing still, completely without guile. Frank took her shoulders in his hands and for a second they were quite still, their very breathing suspended. Then his lips grazed hers, returned with less diffidence, and then he grabbed her, holding her crushed close, the kiss burning her, devouring her so that she threw her arms round his neck and seemed to fuse against him, oblivious of the wet grass, the mud, the public highway.

He broke the kiss at last and moved back, his face reddening.

'Mabs? Oh, God, Mabs, I want . . . Mabs, could you . . . would you . . .'

A car, skidding to a halt, brought them apart and on to their feet like a pair of marionettes jerked by invisible strings. Someone jumped down and came round to the nearside of the car, leaving the engine still running.

'Whatever were you doing, sitting there on that wet grass? Honestly, Frank, if you want to ravish Mabel at least do it on dry ground!' It was Desmond, a loud chequered cap on the back of his sun-bleached hair, his shirt sleeves rolled up. He put his hands on his hips and grinned mockingly down at Mabel, dusty and dirty, vainly trying to clean the mud off her skirt. 'Hello, Mabs, old girl! Are you wounded?'

Mabel bent and retrieved her cycle with as much dignity as she could muster. She scuffed with her sandalled feet and saw that Desmond was looking at her long, bare legs. She blushed and moved round to straighten her handlebars, which were at odds with the rest of the machine.

'Shut up, Des. We had a horrible crash. What do you want?'

'Yes, and what are you doing in this neck of the woods? Not hunting for us, I hope?'

Frank sounded slightly annoyed, to Mabel's glee. So he had enjoyed the interruption as little as she!

'Of course we're hunting for you; what other reason would I have for being on the Palling Road at this unearthly hour?' Desmond sounded testy. 'I've got an old friend in the car, and she absolutely refused to come out with me unless I could find her old chum Mabs, so here we are.' He turned to the car. 'Come out, come out, you charming surprise!'

The door shot open and a vision appeared on the running board, putting back the short veil which hung over her long green eyes.

'Suzie! Oh, Suzie!'

The two girls were in each other's arms, laughing and exclaiming, neither caring that Mabel looked a regular ragamuffin and Suzie, in a green silk suit and biscuit-coloured shirtwaister, her pillbox hat trimmed with pale green ostrich feathers, looked like a model.

Presently, when their first transports were over, the girls stood back from each other, smiling.

'I've a million questions to ask you, Suzie Canning,' Mabel said severely, picking up her much-maligned cycle, which had been cast down the moment she set eyes on her friend. 'But Frank and I are having this holiday the hard way. We pedal! So why don't you meet us in Sea Palling? You'll get there a bit before us, I daresay, so you can find somewhere nice for us to have lunch. A pub, perhaps, or a small café. And you'd better think up a good excuse for not writing to me for such ages.'

The two cyclists mounted, the car shot past them, hands waved, and they were alone once more, with the road rapidly drying in the sun and Mabel thoughtful.

This had changed everything, she was very sure of that; whether it was for worse or better she could not yet say. But the ice had been broken, and Frank had kissed her. She did not think he would go back into his shell, therefore it stood to reason that though the presence of the other two might delay the cure, it would scarcely let the old illness take grip again. She had made up her mind to help Frank, and she was perfectly willing to lose her virtue to him if that would bring her old love back. No doubt Suzie and Des would spend the day with them and then go back to Norwich, which would suit Mabel very well. She and Frank had already prolonged their holiday, with everyone's approval, from one week to two, and their fortnight still had three days to run. And nights. Three days – and nights – would be time to break the spell that had so cruelly bound her love.

They made their way to Great Yarmouth in the end, having lunched at Sea Palling, and booked two double rooms at the Royal Hotel. It was all perfectly respectable, of course, for the two girls would share one room and the brothers the other. Frank did mention the smell of gas but Desmond waved this aside – with a wink and a knowing smile which puzzled Frank somewhat.

'Nonsense, old boy. The rooms are big enough, God knows, for a regiment to sleep without disturbing each other. Shall we go to the show on the pier tonight?'

But at this point Suzie looked at her friend and remarked that in no circumstances would she appear at a theatre with Mabs unless Mabs changed.

'I've brought a couple of thin dresses,' she said casually. 'You can borrow one of them, Mabs.'

And up in their room it became apparent that Suzie had planned an overnight stay, for she had a bag full of exciting things. A silk nightdress, fine as gossamer. Directoire knickers; two pairs, one in salmon-coloured silk and the other in black lace. Silk stockings. A flame-coloured voile dress with a low neckline and long, full sleeves. Another, cream-coloured, with flared sleeves and brown piping.

'Suzie, how elegant it all is,' Mabel sighed enviously. 'Your nightie's pretty enough for a ball-dress.'

She spread the garment out on the bed the better to admire. It was of palest rose, trimmed with deeper rose at the ribbon-tie waist and around the neck.

'Yes, it is pretty.' Suzie threw it a casual glance. 'It's the new Magyar style that's all the rage in town. It cost a bit, I can tell you.'

Mabel, in her darned drawers and camisole, was washing at the washstand. She rinsed the soapsuds off her face, dried it, and then turned to her own bag, pulling out a rather crumpled cotton dress.

'D'you think someone would iron this for me? We didn't mean to stay in hotels, Frank and me, and so we didn't bring anything smart.' She tossed the dress down on the bed and smiled ruefully at her friend. 'Not that I possess anything as smart as your nightdress, even!'

'No. You aren't working yet. I said I'd lend you something to wear and so I shall. The cream one is more you, I think.'

'I ought to refuse, but I'm not going to! Thanks, Suzie. I'll enjoy wearing it.' Mabel slipped the dress on over her head and surveyed herself in the mirror. For a moment she was too startled to do more than stare. Could it really be she, this elegant woman with the subtly outlined figure and the golden skin? What a lot a dress can do, she thought, honestly astounded.

'Suzie, it's so lovely it's almost wicked!'

Suzie was putting on the flame voile dress. It was too low-cut, Mabel thought, but she smiled at Suzie anyway. If her friend wanted to ask for trouble, she was quite capable of handling it. She was very glad that the cream-coloured dress was not like that, though.

'It does suit you.' Suzie patted her own slim hips, then scrutinised Mabel carefully. 'Let me do your hair, and that'll complete the transformation. I've got an ivory comb somewhere which will just make that outfit.'

Presently, looking so fine she hardly knew herself, Mabel sat down on the bed to wait whilst Suzie brushed and pinned up her own tawny locks.

'Suzie, are you still nursing? Or have you got some other job now?'

Suzie was putting lip-rouge on. She had already used some black stuff on her eyelashes, to Mabel's astonishment.

'I'm still nursing. It's a good way to meet men.' Suzie

finished outlining her mouth and stood up. 'Look, sweetie, we'll talk later, all right? Now I want my dinner!'

They had an excellent dinner and saw an amusing show on the pier, then returned to the hotel. Mabel noticed that Desmond kept sidling up to her friend but thought that Suzie was quite capable of dealing with the elder Neyler. She and Frank said goodnight, their eyes saying much more, and then they separated, the boys to go to their room, the girls to theirs.

As soon as they were in the big double bed, washed and nightgowned like two little girls again, Mabel turned to her friend, eager to talk.

'Now, Suzie, tell me everything! How did you meet up with Des, for a start, and where do you get all those wonderful clothes? You aren't married or anything, are you?'

'No. Not married or anything. Men give me clothes, or money, or even both. Dear Des said if I'd spend a few days with him he'd give me a good time and see I went back to London richer than I came down. But I'm on *holiday*, dammit! I just wanted to find you again. I daresay he's furious now, because you must have guessed he thought it would be you sharing with Frank and me with him.' She snorted. 'He doesn't know you very well, that's clear enough – or his brother. And as for me, a holiday's a holiday.'

'He doesn't know either of us at all,' Mabel admitted. 'Suzie, if you're nursing, why do you keep saying you're on holiday, as if . . .'

'As if I didn't enjoy being paid for and having presents from men? You great noodle, of course I enjoy that part. It's the going to bed part that can be boring.'

'Boring?' Mabel's voice squeaked. 'But I thought . . . you always said . . . '

Suzie laughed. It was a cynical sound. Mabel winced.

'I'm telling you now, Mabs, that if you start sleeping with someone for what you can get out of them instead of because you like them, there's no fun in it. I should know. Some of them are old, nearly all of them are married, and nine out of ten I find boring. Now you know.'

'Then why . . . ?'

'D'you want my life story? It started when I met this young officer who seemed ideal. He swore he loved me and would marry me. We slept together. Though why they call it sleeping when it's the last thing you do I can't imagine. A man thought of that one, I'll bet. Where was I?'

'You slept with the young officer.'

'That's right. And after three months or so, he told me he'd changed his mind. I was upset, but then I thought it out and it was fair enough. All I wanted from him was a nice home and plenty of money. The old how-d'you-do was fun, but it wasn't that I was marrying him for. I decided then that I'd please men for a return, not for bogus love. So I do.'

'Oh.' Mabel tried to sound sophisticated and nonchalant. 'Then you aren't really a nurse at all?'

'Bless you, I told you I was and I *am*! I meet well-to-do people when I'm nursing. And my . . . friends . . . need to be well-to-do.'

'Oh. And you said they're often married?'

'Sure. Married men need someone like me worse than single ones.'

'Oh.'

'Do stop saying "oh" like a silly goldfish,' Suzie said wrathfully. 'If you think I'm a tart why not say so?'

'You're a tart,' Mabel said promptly. They both giggled.

'Oh, Mabs, I suppose I am, but at least I'm honest. And I won't just jump into bed with Des because he wants me to. He's young and very good-looking, and I daresay he'd be good enough in bed to be a change from my present elderly admirer, but I've got a feeling about Des. I've always had it, ever since I was fourteen or so. I don't want to get involved with him. Odd, isn't it?'

'Not at all, really. Do you remember Con once, when we were kids and Des had suddenly gone berserk because he couldn't have his own way, and then he'd rushed off into the house? Frank was making excuses for him and Con suddenly looked up from whatever it was he was doing, with those bright, round eyes of his fixed on the doorway Des had just disappeared through, and he said, "Des is bad." Just like that. Everyone went quite quiet, for a moment.'

'I wasn't there,' Suzie said. 'But I know what he meant. I think Des would want his money's worth, if you understand me.'

Mabel nodded in the dark, though she had not the faintest idea of what Des's money's worth would consist.

'What about marriage, Suzie? Don't you want to get married one day?'

''Course I do. It may have escaped your notice, old Mabs, but there aren't a lot of spare men around since the war. If one wants to marry me, that's fine. Until then, I'll work hard and save up and buy pretty things.'

'I see. Look, Suzie, I don't want to seem mean, but when are you and Des going back to Norwich? Frank and I need some time on our own, and . . .'

'Mabs, you aren't sleeping with him, are you? That'd be a laugh, and me manoeuvring to keep Des from forcing you into it!'

'We aren't. Not yet. But I would, if he wanted me to. I love him.'

Mabel turned over in bed and looked into Suzie's face. She had her night-eyes now and could see quite well in the dim light. She saw the startled look on her friend's face, and then the genuine smile which followed.

'That's wonderful, Mabs! It sounds odd coming from me, I know, but why don't you marry him first? It could save a lot of heartache.'

'He hasn't asked me. Not for either, if you know what I mean. But I do think he will, if you and Des will just go!'

'That's my girl, you say it straight out! The trouble is, I think Des had planned to stay for the weekend. I can't pretend I'm keen; I want to get back to Norwich and look up some of my old friends and see how Auntie Vera's treating Gran – you know the sort of thing. How would it be if I got Des to take me home after breakfast tomorrow?'

'It would be marvellous for us, but if Des really means to

make love to you he might easily do something on the way home,' Mabel said shrewdly.

'Rape, you mean?' Suzie sniffed. 'I don't fancy that! Tell you what, Mabs, I'll steal away at dawn – very romantic – and catch the milk train up to the city. And you tell Des I've gone straight back to London, otherwise he'll probably try to catch me, and he might do it at that.'

'All right. Have you got an alarm clock or something?'

Suzie had a neat little travelling clock in her case and now she leaned out of bed and set the alarm.

'That's done. Goodnight, Mabs, and don't think you've seen the last of me, because you haven't! I'll be staying with my Auntie Vera in Bull Close Road, so you can visit me.'

''Night, Suzie. Wake me when you leave.'

When Desmond discovered Suzie's defection next morning it immediately became clear that her decision to cut and run had been the right one. He was furious and his temper grew ugly, even including Mabel in his wild threats because she had connived at her friend's escape.

'What rubbish! I didn't even wake; she left me a note pinned to the pillow,' Mabel said truthfully. She refused to hand the note over, however, since it was pinned, not only to the pillow, but to the rose-coloured nightdress.

'*When you decide to make Frank a happy man, wear this*,' the note said. '*Enjoy yourself. Love, Suzie.*'

'She's an ungrateful little trollop, that's all I can say. I paid for her meals, her hotel room, everything, and then she sneaks off without so much as a thank you . . .'

'Without paying you back in kind if not cash, you mean,' Frank said, gently mocking. 'Desmond Neyler, what would Mama think of such behaviour? And Daddy paid for the rooms and well you know it. Suzie's too nice a girl to let you have your evil way with her, so perhaps it's a good thing she's gone.'

'Well, I think she's a nasty piece of work,' Desmond said sullenly. 'Now I suppose I've got to drive home by myself tomorrow. I only meant I wanted company for the journey, you know, and perhaps a goodbye.'

'Tomorrow?' Two faces turned towards him, both falling, but Desmond, not a sensitive soul, failed to notice anything unusual.

'Yes, I've got to go back tomorrow, worse luck. Oh, curse you, Mabs, if only you'd woken you could have warned me and I could have talked her round! You are too bad!'

'Don't speak to her like that.' Frank took Mabel's hand in his, caressing the inside of her wrist secretly with his forefinger until he felt her pulse speed up. Then he winked at her. 'We're going swimming, aren't we, Mabs? Coming, Des?'

Desmond had not brought a bathing dress but went and bought one whilst Frank hired a bathing hut. As a matter of fact, Mabel was extremely pleased with her bathing dress. She had outgrown her school costume so she had been forced to buy a new one before they left Norwich, and it was easily her most fashionable garment. It was navy blue with white trimming and had quite short sleeves and a daringly short skirt, a little way above the knee, though the dark blue bloomers came to just below the knee until she began to swim, when they rode up alarmingly to mid-thigh. Because it was for seaside wear, the costume had a wide sailor collar and an even wider sash tie with anchors embroidered on it, and Mabel felt herself to be truly elegant in it, especially as she had always been a strong swimmer.

They spent most of the morning in the water, and Desmond's temper seemed to improve, though Mabel was annoyed by his persistent and oft-voiced grudge against her friend. When dinnertime came, and Desmond suggested going to a dance at one of the other hotels, she was adamant that she wanted no such thing. She was annoyed with Desmond and saw no reason why she should have to dance with him as well! Frank, she was sure, would not wish to dance. His new-found ease with her had not yet reached the heights of being in each other's arms in public.

Instead, the three of them strolled down by the harbour. There was a French ship anchored there and one of the men came over to the side and Mabel practised her French on him with some success. He blew her a kiss as she left, and both boys thought this extremely amusing, Frank teasing her with being a *femme fatale,* Desmond almost forgetting about Suzie for a moment.

Back at the hotel, Mabel pleaded tiredness and the brothers admitted that they too were tired, but would stay downstairs for one drink at the bar before seeking their beds. Mabel left them to ask at the desk that she might be woken with a cup of tea at eight o'clock next morning. As she stood there, waiting for someone to answer the bell, she noticed that Frank was standing at the bar alone. She glanced around. Desmond was making for the back of the hall, where the telephone stood. Perhaps he was going to telephone his parents, to tell them he would be back next day?

Then, in a flash, Mabel remembered that she was sleeping, tonight, in a double bed. Alone in a double bed. And Desmond had said their room was so huge that a regiment could sleep in it and not disturb each other. Or words to that effect. Which simply *must* mean that they had single beds, and were probably at opposite ends of the huge room.

To think was to act. She seized a sheet of paper and reached for the pencil which lay near at hand on the counter so that hotel guests could leave messages for the staff. She scribbled her message, folded it, wrote *Mr Frank Neyler* across it and walked a little uncertainly towards the bar. Could she go in and slip the note into Frank's hand? But there were no other women there!

'Can I help you, miss?'

A uniformed pageboy was at her elbow.

'Oh, please! Would you give this note to Mr Neyler? He's in the bar.'

'Certainly, miss.'

The boy took the note, saluted, and turned towards the bar. Mabel ran quickly up the stairs, her hands shaking a little. The die was cast! She had invited Frank to spend the night with her in Suzie's half of the bed. She opened the door, closed it behind her, then laughed at herself. She had said no such thing! All she had said was that she would miss Suzie's companionship tonight. But if he chose to construe the message as meaning the other, she would not complain!

The Magyar nightdress lay on the bed. Mabel washed, brushed out her hair and slipped the flimsy garment over her head. A quick glance in the mirror astonished her once more with her own beauty and glamour when clad in the right sort of clothes, and then she was in bed, the curtains pulled back and the window just wide enough to let in the cool sea-breeze.

She lay there, content to wait, feeling no shame, no curiosity. If she felt anything it was peaceful pleasure at the thought of a closer intimacy with Frank than she had ever known. She did not doubt that he would come, but she hoped, in her heart, that he would insist on marriage before the final intimacy. It is not that I'm a prude, she told herself firmly as she cuddled down beneath the sheets, but I do think he loves me as much as I love him, and if that's so it seems a shame to have to hide what you've done and how you feel.

She thought she was wide awake but she must have dozed a little for she came to herself when she heard the door shut gently. She glanced round and saw the light glinting on his fair hair and then he was sitting on the bed, pulling back the covers, whispering that she was beautiful, so beautiful! She lay still, her face hot as he feasted his eyes on her in the gossamer gown and then quickly, because she felt horribly shy and unsure of herself, she sat up, half turned her back on him, and pulled the Magyar gown over her head. He put his hands on her waist, then slid them round to grasp her breasts, and even as her body began to tingle into a response, everything in her died, and fear brought her heart thumping into her throat. She turned in his hold, beginning to struggle fiercely.

'Desmond! Oh, my God, I thought you were Frank! You pig! I hate you! Get out of my room or I'll scream the place down!'

He laughed beneath his breath and threw her back on the pillows, holding her still with his weight. His eyes gleamed savagely, palely burning.

'If you scream, who do you think will believe you? The pageboy gave me your note – he doesn't know one Mr Neyler from another – and it's destroyed, so no one can prove what it contained. I'll tell Frank it was an invitation and he'll believe me because he thinks he's a poor bargain. D'you want to hurt him? Because if you scream . . .'

She hesitated for long enough for his hand to gag her, then, though she squirmed and tried to bite, she could not free herself.

'You told Suzie to run away,' he said through clenched teeth. 'If you hadn't, she'd have been with me now instead of you. It's a punishment for interfering. And the more you fight the more you'll get hurt.'

She continued to fight until she could fight no more.

In the early hours of the morning, a small, battered figure left the Royal Hotel, stealing across the dark promenade, heading for the harbour. It was Mabel and she looked as if she had been fighting a heavyweight boxer all night. Her face and neck were blue with bruises, except where they were pink with abrasions. Just past the hotel she stopped to vomit, her hair hanging down unregarded, matted and lank. She knelt there for a little, and once she glanced wistfully over her shoulder, as if hoping for pursuit, but the hotel was in darkness. Frank slept, unknowing. Desmond slept too, sated.

Presently she dragged herself to her feet and moved on. She was limping and so stiff that each step felt as if it must be her last. But she must get away! It took her what felt like a lifetime to reach the harbour but she got there at last. She looked over the side, into the dark and oily water. She moved on, slowly, making for the big ship which she remembered seeing a lifetime ago. The gangplank was down. She was nearly at the foot of it when the giddy, spinning darkness which had been surging at the edges of her consciousness began to engulf her. She took two wavering steps, then knew she was beaten. She slumped across the gangplank and fainted.

19

'I don't know when a year's brought more trouble than 1919 did,' Tina remarked, from her perch on top of the stepladder in the hallway of The Pride. 'Can you take this star, Ted?'

It was Twelfth Night and they were dismantling the Christmas tree and, since Tina had no trust in servants when perched on high, she had insisted on stripping the top of the tree herself. Ted, reaching up and taking the once-a-year treasures, nodded in gloomy agreement.

'Yes, it was a bad year; let's hope 1920 turns into something really good. Though, when I think about it, I don't know that it can undo many of 1919's dirty tricks.'

'Well, Louis could come back, I suppose. And so could Mabel. And Frank could change his mind about that wretched old boatyard. And that's only the start. We could . . .'

'That really wouldn't solve many problems, darling!' Ted put a clutch of glass birds carefully into their cottonwool nest and held out his hand to his tottering wife. 'Come down now. You've got everything from the upper branches. Stella and Josette can do the rest; goodness knows they're longing to!'

'It *would* solve problems. Well, some of them,' Tina said defensively, coming cautiously down the ladder backwards, one hand holding her skirt clear of her heels. 'Oh, I know it wouldn't put back the money Louis took, or get those poor, wicked girls out of trouble, but it would be so nice for Sarah, trying to cope with the new baby and with Simon by herself.'

Ted grunted noncommittally. He was fond of his brother-in-law, and Louis's sudden flight had been as complete a surprise to him as it had been to everyone else. He thought he would never forget that dark night when the front door bell had suddenly pealed and pealed again, so that he, halfway up the stairs on his way to bed, had hurried down and fairly wrenched the door open.

Cold air had rushed into the warm hall and his breath had turned to fog, almost obscuring the figure on the doorstep. Then she had pushed blindly past him into the house and he had recognised his sister-in-law. Wild-eyed and white-faced, she had clutched his hands, her own trembling violently.

'Ted, it's Louis,' she had said. 'He isn't in London on business at all. He's on his way to Australia. He's left me!'

Even then he had been unable to stop the thought flashing through his mind: ' . . . and Sally Lewis, and Wilma, and Patty, and . . .' because it was so obvious that poor Louis had fled not so much from Sarah as from his suddenly onerous love-life. Paternity orders had been fluttering around his ears like leaves in autumn; his shocked and horrified father had thought to unveil a villain who was systematically stealing from the firm and had found the thief to be his own son. One way and another, Ted found it difficult to blame Louis, in his heart, for his abrupt departure.

But Frank's loss of Mabel had been a real tragedy, with no subsequent explanation to make it in the least amusing. She had simply gone, it seemed, disappearing into the Yarmouth night, leaving her possessions, her bicycle, and a nightgown which her mother had tearfully declared was never one of Mabel's. That mystery had not been solved, though the immediate fear – that she might be dead – had been cleared up within twenty-four hours by a letter, posted from a town further up the coast, in which Mabel declared briefly that no one was to worry and that she would be 'all right'.

After that, it just seemed that Frank had sunk back into the old apathy from which Mabel had aroused him so successfully. He was a spectator, remote from them all. Until the incident of the boatyard; and whilst Ted praised God for the chance that had flung Frank and the boatyard together, Tina, with less understanding, kept insisting that she wanted her boy home again and that he would waste his life away stuck down at Oulton Broad with never a game of bridge or a tea-dance to brighten his days.

Ted had gone to look at the boatyard partly from curiosity and partly because the man who was selling it had a Sunbeam for sale which might be just the thing to get Frank interested in driving a car. They reached the yard, and Ted was intrigued, despite himself, by the beauty of the site and by the remains of what must once have been excellent buildings.

The cottage interested him not at all, and he saw Frank poking around in it without a second thought. But his son's expression, when he began to discuss the possibility of bringing the yard back to commercial viability once more, was another thing altogether. Frank's face wore a lively, listening look.

Driving home he had ventured a question or two, and had known at once that if Frank wanted to do anything with his life it was to rescue the old yard and build beautiful boats there once more. Ted was a loving father and a man endowed with great generosity of spirit. He had wanted to invest in the yard himself, build up the business, see it prosper, but now he watched such plans whistle, unregretted, down the wind. It was far more important to him to see Frank regain his interest in life.

'Well, Frank, what do you think? A bit too much of a challenge, eh? It would take every bit of a fellow's hard work and concentration to bring that place back into shape and I've just not got that much time. I suppose someone might come in with me, but . . .'

'Could I do it, Daddy? I'd love to try, if you'd let me. I'd live down there, and I could tackle a good bit of the work. I've always loved working with wood, and if there was someone locally who could teach me . . .'

It had been as good as bought from that moment on. Of

course Ted had not bargained for a good deal of it. Frank's savings, for instance. He had put every penny into the yard and had been adamant that his father's money was only a loan, which he would pay back at the earliest opportunity. And then he had proceeded, despite Tina's tearful protests, to move into the terrible, derelict cottage. Just him and a mongrel dog he had picked up somewhere. They had been there, the two of them, for ten weeks now, and whenever Ted got the car out and drove over to Oulton Broad to visit his son he felt like an interloper. Frank had employed an old fellow who knew everything there was to know about building boats and the two of them were always busy, seldom talkative. It is hard, sometimes, to let someone else do what is best for them, Ted told himself as he pulled the ladder away from the tree and called through into the kitchen for the girls to come and finish the work. But it still has to be done.

Stella and Josette, bursting into the hall, put an end to their parents' musings upon the unsatisfactoriness of 1919.

'Here we are, girls. Mama's done the top of the tree and will leave the rest to you. And if you do a good job you may join us presently in the study and I'll give you some roasted chestnuts. I'm going to cook some for Mama and myself.'

'Oh, Daddy, what stories you tell!' Stella cried boisterously. 'You'll give us some nuts even if we make the most awful bosh of the tree and break all the decorations, so don't pretend.' She began to untangle a bell from the tree whilst Josette, dark-haired and remarkably pretty at fourteen, unwound a great mass of tinsel. 'Leave it to the experts, darlings!'

'Perfect foils for each other, those two,' Ted remarked to Tina as they settled down in front of the study fire. 'Stella's fair as a Viking maiden and Josie's got that lovely, richly brown colouring that makes her look intense and gives her skin a glow.' He cut half a dozen nuts open with his pocket-knife and spread them out on the brass shovel. 'They look very grown up this evening, for some reason.'

'I know, I noticed as well.' Tina sighed and lay back in her chair. 'They're awfully naughty – they've let their skirts down at least four inches lower than I said they might. Isn't it absurd to want to grow up so badly?'

'It's human nature, darling. My, they're going to break some . . .' He stopped, an uncomfortable pain stabbing at his own chest. How could he make such a cruel remark, when Mabel had almost broken Frank's heart?

He had liked Mabel very much and had a great respect for her father. When the letter had arrived assuring her parents of their daughter's safety, he had spoken to Frank with as much tact and consideration as he could find.

'Could it have been anything you said or did, old boy? Mabel was such a good girl. I can't imagine her leaving for no reason and frightening everyone so.'

'I think she suddenly realised she couldn't marry me, and felt ashamed to come right out with it after she'd got me round to wanting to marry her again,' Frank muttered. 'She came to my room, Daddy, and spent the night with me without my knowing until next morning. She wanted to prove that the smell of gas didn't bother her. But then, the next night, she ran away. I suppose she couldn't face telling me that she'd changed her mind. She always was a kind little creature.'

'Yes. And not stupid, either, Frank. I'm certain there was a reason for her leaving and probably it had no connection with you. We'll find out some day, I daresay, and in the meantime don't let it hurt you. I'm sure her feelings for you are the sort that will bring her back, one day.'

'I'd like to think so.'

Ted did not believe that Mabel would return. Whatever the reason for her flight it must have been serious. He could not imagine what had happened, he just knew that something had. And in the meantime, there was the boatyard. If Frank could make a go of it he might come back to them again. Ted prayed nightly that the miracle would happen.

Louis stood at the ship's rail as she steamed into Sydney Harbour. The water winked in the sunlight and the city on the shore looked wonderfully inviting, the very place to start a new life.

It was hot, though it was early January. Louis thought wonderingly of the land he had left, of the people muffled in coats and scarves and boots. Yet here there were bathers in the surf and even at this distance he could see the light cotton clothing of people walking along the front.

Looking back, he could only wonder what miracle had made him suddenly cut and run. He knew, really, that it had been misery and desperation as his troubles increased, backed by the boredom, the soul-destroying hours spent in the factory, with its smell of hides and leather, of feet and sweaty humanity. He had left for all the wrong reasons and had found much more than he deserved even before he put a foot on shore. Peace of mind and clarity of self-vision had come to him; he had seen himself, idle, pleasure-loving, lazy, and had not liked what he saw. Of course he had loved Sarah, she was beautiful, witty, and an ideal wife and mother. His children were grand kids. But he had been content to let Poppa pay him a wage for being bored. He had not worked for his money! Here, in this new country, there would be no one willing to pay him for doing nothing, no one to wait on him hand and foot, pay his bills, see to the preparation of his favourite meals.

Oddly enough, too, stories of Poppa's came back to him. Stories of the American west, the great stretches of prairie, the mountains, the sense of being part of the country. Before, he had not really understood the wistful note in Arthur's voice as he told of these things, but now he thought he did. To go out into the burning blue distances of Australia and to survive by his own wits and muscle; that really would be something!

He wanted to work manually, to make roads or dig for coal or round up cattle. He knew now that he had been playing at life, playing at being a man even, and that even the war years had been cushioned for him. Out here, for the first time, he would be given the opportunity to come to grips with reality. He must seize it with both hands or regret for ever.

He leaned on the rail, symbolically gripping it hard. The challenge would be accepted! He would not regret!

*   *   *

I am a deserted wife, Sarah said to herself as she held Cara to her breast and watched her suckle. I am a deserted wife, she told her reflection as she applied skinfood to her face before going to bed. I am a deserted wife, she reminded herself as she got behind the wheel of her car. But she did not really believe it. Louis had been away so much during their marriage that she never quite got over the feeling that one morning she would turn over in bed and he would be there, that look of loving affection dawning on his face and his mouth quivering into a teasing smile at her surprise.

She missed him horribly, but she was an independent young woman with a good deal of courage and was determined not to show anyone how she felt. Her father, equally determined that she should divorce Louis, could not persuade her to make any move yet.

'I'll make arrangements when I'm ready and not before,' she told him coolly. 'I'm not unhappy, living alone with the children – I'm too busy to be unhappy.'

It was not quite true, of course. She would have had to be a good deal harder than she was to have taken his defection as anything but a near-mortal blow. At first, it had seemed that her world had come to an end; her cosy coffee mornings, her bridge parties, her good works, all needed a husband somewhere in the background, though she had never realised it. And then there was the letter. Louis had left her a letter, and if confession was indeed good for the soul then Louis's soul, she thought, must be in mint condition! The letter had Told All: the story of his long affair with the other Sarah, including the admission that he, Louis, had fathered both the nanny's children; the begetting of children on two females at his father's factory and a barmaid out at Horning; the seduction of a landgirl, a chorus girl at a London theatre, another factory worker. And his embezzlement. The deceit and the lies necessary to get the extra money for his women. All written down in his six-page letter, almost proudly.

At first she had reacted as any woman would. The letter had been like a knife in her side; the pain had felt physically real so that for days she walked carefully, moved slowly, as if a sudden jerk or an incautious step might open the wound and bring the blood pouring out.

She had been saved from despair by something which still caused her family a good deal of distress. She had seen an advertisement in the *Eastern Evening News* for a lady to help in a small coffee shop, 'hours by arrangement'. She had applied, agreed that she would work three mornings a week, and got the job. What was more, she loved the work. Her three mornings might be a source of embarrassment to her relatives, a time when they felt they could not go into Dorothy's for fear of being served by Sarah in a frilly apron, but to her they were escape from household routine and a feeling that she could, if she wished, be completely independent of everyone.

At first, she had tried to blame Louis's weakness on the war, but she was far too honest a person to lie to herself and she soon saw that it *was* a lie; the war had scarcely affected her husband. The war had hurt Frank terribly, but he was neither dishonest nor immoral. In fact, of all her relatives-in-law, Frank was the one with whom she was most in sympathy. She knew how Mabel's sudden disappearance had shattered him; even Desmond had been affected. He had got his car out on the fateful morning and had searched the countryside for hours, not even pausing for food. Of course, it had only been a temporary worry with Desmond; he had forgotten the girl in a couple of days. But Frank, she knew, would not forget. He had moved into a derelict cottage in the middle of the derelict boatyard and was said, by his fond father at any rate, to be working miracles there.

I do the same, in my small way, when I'm serving coffee and cakes at Dorothy's, Sarah told herself. Frank builds boats to forget and I serve impatient ladies with delicious food. And both of us, whether we know it or not, are building up a life for ourselves which the deserter knows nothing about, and that is good for our self-respect. Across the gap in their ages and the miles that separated them, she mentally saluted Frank. His was much the harder lot. She only hoped he would reap a rich reward of forgetfulness.

* * *

Frank was in the boathouse, waxing the first craft to go out of the Neyler yard. She was a little beauty, commissioned by a man called Claud Grundy so that he could teach his son to sail, and everyone who saw her was impressed.

'We won't hurry over her, Mr Frank,' Benjamin Coates said when Frank first read him the customer's requirements. 'He in't going to want to sail her in mid-winter, so we've plenty time. When we're established, then we'll ha' to work fast, but now it'll pay us to be leisurely.'

So they had taken great care and worked with pride, and the result pleased them both. Gleaming with careful polishing, every plank – for she was clinker built – smooth as satin, with the name *Dancing Lady* picked out on her bows in gold and black, she was a first-rate advertisement for the yard.

Frank hunkered back on his heels and glanced around him. The waxing was finished and it must be nearly time to repair to the cottage for a cup of tea and a chat over the next day's work, but since there was no sign of Benjamin yet he could afford to stay where he was and dream a little. Staring out of the boatshed door he saw the sight he loved most – the Broad, steel-grey and calm as evening galloped over the flat country, the sky as pale as the water, birdsong lulled, only the occasional *plop* as a fish rose disturbing the silence.

To this place he had come last year, and in the time he and Benjamin had worked on it improvements had been made almost daily. Their first task had been to make the big boatshed, the one he was in now, watertight and fit to work in. They had done so, and it was now a good deal more weatherproof than his cottage. But he spent hours working in the boatshed, and he only slept in the cottage and spent the long, dark evenings there. Then he built up a roaring fire, lit the lamp, and read or figured or just stared, dreaming, into the flames. Rain came through the tiles and drove in at the gaps beside the windows but it bothered him not at all. He slept downstairs, so what did a bit of rain upstairs matter? And after living in the trenches the cottage was luxurious in the extreme. He had a roof over his head, a fire, and a couch to sleep on. And, best of all, he was happy.

For he had never expected to be happy again, after Mabel's defection. He had moved here to get away from the family, puzzling over his inability to enjoy the same things as his brother, his quietness, his lack of friends. And he had found happiness. And Patch. Patch was a skinny mongrel with guilty eyes and the air of abject apology common to most dogs who have been unwanted and unfed since puppyhood. He was a sly, furtive little animal but he adored Frank and Frank adored him. He slept on the foot of the couch at night and could be found with his nose an inch from Frank's heels during the day. Despite the fact that he was now well fed he stole whenever the opportunity presented itself and slunk away from raised voices as if perpetually conscious of wrong-doing. He remained aggravatingly skeletal too, apparently quite capable of wolfing down two enormous meals a day and never gaining an ounce. But he was all the company Frank wanted.

Apart from the invaluable Benjamin, of course. Benjamin had worked for one of the big boatyards, a foreman, invaluable to the firm. But they had not wanted Donnie. Frank, desperate for someone who really knew about the business, would have taken on a dozen Donnies provided that Benjamin came with them, and anyway Donnie was a hard worker. It was just that he had to be carefully watched and carefully instructed. His father knew that Donnie was simple so he was prepared to take the trouble, and Frank was prepared to follow suit not only because he was genuinely fond of Benjamin but because he liked Donnie, and saw no reason for making the lad's life difficult by giving him orders which he could not carry out.

Without saying much, Benjamin watched Frank with Donnie, and then threw himself, heart and soul, into the new yard. It would succeed because Benjamin wanted it to, and with this in mind he taught Frank everything he knew, everything he would have taught Donnie if his son had been normal.

''Tweren't the bosses,' Benjamin explained to Frank once, when Frank had shown curiosity over the other yard's rejection of Donnie. ''Twas th'other men. They couldn't leave orf teasin' the lad. When he done something wrong everyone lost time horsing around with him, and they teased him into doin' wrong.'

It was not difficult, as Frank well knew, to fluster Donnie into doing peculiar things. Once, his father, visiting the yard on a muddy, rainy day, had asked Donnie casually to 'pass a cloth over my windscreen, lad, to clear off the mud splashes'. Two hours later, when Frank accompanied Ted out to the car, Donnie was still there, standing drenched in the downpour, the cloth going automatically over and over the shining clean windscreen. One had to be a lot more definite than Ted had been when giving Donnie orders!

There had been other occasions. Asking Donnie to chop some logs and finding him patiently trying to cut them up with a kitchen knife because he did not know where the axe was kept, finding the lad weeping dolorously because a frog had glanced at his sandwiches and he thought they were now unfit for eating – these were samples of Donnie's behaviour when rattled.

But they had no trouble with Donnie if they phrased their commands with care and kept an eye on him. Indeed, some of the finest polishing on the *Dancing Lady* had been done by Donnie, because he was endlessly patient, never fretting to get on with the next job, always content with what he was actually doing.

'Mr Frank? The boy Donnie and me, we're finished. See you tomorrow, shall us?'

'What about our cuppa?' Frank, guiltily aware that he had quite forgotten to put the kettle on – or to light the fire for that matter – scrambled to his feet and clicked his fingers – needlessly – at Patch. 'I'll go and light up and put the kettle on.'

'Not tonight, Mr Frank. You've a visitor,' Benjamin said gruffly. 'She've been here a moment or two, I reckon. We're orf.'

Recognising a note of finality in the other man's voice,

Frank knew better than to press the invitation. 'See you in the morning, then. Goodnight!'

He hurried across to the cottage as soon as the Coates had gone, conscious of faint curiosity mixed with annoyance at an unsolicited visit. He much preferred being alone, but no doubt it was his mother, or one of his aunts. He knew it would never be the only woman he would have welcomed.

He stepped into the kitchen and blinked. The lamp was lit, the fire roared up, lighting the whitewashed walls and the low ceiling criss-crossed with blackened beams. Good old Benjamin. He must have done the necessary before leaving.

'Hello, Frank!'

A slim, smart young woman sat on the easy chair by the fire, with a slice of bread impaled on a fork held out to the flames. She was smiling at him though her eyes were watering and her cheeks flushed from the heat.

'Suzie! What on earth . . .?'

'I've come to see you. Mabel asked me to.'

'Why?' The smile left Frank's mouth and he felt his heart begin to bump unevenly in his chest. 'Why couldn't she have come herself?'

'I'll tell you in a moment, if you'll just fetch me some butter for this toast. I suppose you *do* have butter? And a knife would be useful, too.'

Frank went into the walk-in pantry and picked up the butter. It was a big pantry because the family who had lived here last had half a dozen children, or so he had been told. For himself, it was useful because he could buy in large stocks of food and this made trips to town rare events. With the butter in one hand he went over to the dresser and got down two plates with pink roses all over them – his mother's gift – and then fished a couple of knives out of the drawer in the table.

'Here you are.' Frank put the butter down and held out his hand for the first round of toast. 'You can eat it, since you suffered for it, and I'll make the next bit.'

Suzie smiled but shook her head. 'No fear. This bit got

scorched. You can have it. Besides, I'm getting used to being part toasted myself. Just sit down and eat the meal I've cooked for you and don't be ungrateful, and if you'll pass us another slice of bread I'll have the next one.'

Without another word Frank picked up the loaf which Suzie must have brought with her and cut a thick wedge. He handed it to her, watched her impale it on the fork, and then began to butter his own slice.

Presently, the task done, he sat down in the easy chair opposite hers and began to eat, staring at her as he did so. She was thinner than she had been in the summer, and he sensed a brittleness about her which he had never noticed before. As though she was made of fine glass and might easily be broken. Her glorious hair was not bobbed, he was relieved to see, but left unfashionably loose and just tied back with a piece of narrow velvet ribbon. She had always been very pretty but now she was something more. Her intelligence was showing, Frank thought confusedly, and smiled at the thought. Absurd! But she was lovely to look at. He could sit here and enjoy watching her as he enjoyed watching the Broad when sunshine and wind bedevilled the water into a multiplicity of dancing, sparkling ripples.

'Well? Aren't you going to ask me why I'm here?'

He shook his head, and smiled when she pouted.

'Oh, Frank, where's your curiosity? You're unnatural!'

'I'm not.' He took an enormous bite of his scorched toast and tasted the salty butter and the charred bread with a gourmet's pleasure. 'This is delicious, Suzie! I don't ask because I already know what you've come to tell me. Mabel's alive and well and isn't coming back.'

She stared, delicate tawny eyebrows climbing.

'How did you know? *Did* she write to you, after all? At The Pride, I mean? She wouldn't know this address. Do you know where she is? If so, why . . .'

'She hasn't written, not as far as I know. She writes to you, then?'

He could not prevent the hurt from sounding in his voice and Suzie spoke quickly, eager to soothe.

'No! She's only written once and that's why I'm here. She

said to tell you there was a good reason for leaving and a better one for not coming back. She said she's sorry.'

He continued to munch. Silence drew out until the kettle, on Suzie's side of the fire, began to sing and spit droplets of water out on to the fiery logs. As Suzie reached to take it off the flames he seemed to recover from his abstraction.

'Sorry? What for? She's done nothing to me. It's her parents she should apologise to, going off like that. I believe her mother nearly went insane with worry. It was unforgivable.'

'She's been in touch with them now, and they've forgiven her.' Suzie turned away from him, looking into the heart of the fire, her green eyes reflecting the gold as it danced so that they seemed to have a life of their own. 'She's married, Frank.'

The silence stretched out. Frank just sat. Suzie waited a moment and then panic filled her. His eyes looked so empty! She jumped to her feet, dropping her toast and the toasting fork in her haste, and came to stand close to Frank, her hands on his shoulders.

'Frank? Are you all right? Did you . . .'

'I heard.' He sounded composed, a little amused, even. 'It came as a bit of a shock, that's all.' He pushed her gently away, then gestured to the floor. 'You've dropped your toast. Don't waste good food.' He waited until she had picked up the toast and was pouring the tea, then added: 'Bit quick, wasn't it?'

Reassured by his calmness, Suzie nodded and passed him a cup of tea.

'Yes, it was. He's a Frenchman, apparently. I expect she'll come home one day, but not yet. Not so soon. He's a bit older than her, I gather, and . . . well, that's why she said to tell you she was sorry. Because of getting married on the quiet, I suppose.'

'Very understandable. Did she give you an address to write to? Because if so, do write and tell her I'm not furious, or anything like that. But I would like to know . . .'

'No. No address.' She sipped at her tea, then glanced at her watch and jumped. 'Gracious, look at the time! I've a car picking me up here in five minutes. I must drink up and go.'

'You've got to leave now? That was a very short visit!'

'That's your fault, old Frank, for living in such an inconvenient neck of the woods! But I'll come and see you next time I'm home. If you want me to, of course.'

'I'd like to see you, but warn me next time. If I'd known you were here I'd have come in sooner, for a start.' He put his empty cup down. 'Are you still nursing, Suzie?'

'Yes. I don't know whether I'll go on doing it for very much longer, though. I get terribly tired.' She grinned at him, a naughty grin. 'I lead a very full social life, you see, and nursing is becoming little more than a time-consuming and exhausting hobby.'

'I can imagine.' He spoke drily. 'You're terribly thin, girl, but I suppose it's fashionable.'

'It is. But actually I'm not being fashionable, it's the result of burning the candle at both ends; one tends to lose weight. It suits me, however, so I don't repine.' She pulled a face. 'Better than being fat!'

The car, tooting outside, brought her to her feet. She was wearing a brown wool dress with a belt of plaited gold silk, and now she flung her coat across her shoulders and picked up her hat and gloves. The coat was a pale, rich fur. It looked very expensive and Frank said as much as he helped her into it.

'Yes, it's mink. And before you ask me what I did for it, I'll tell you. I was very kind indeed to a very boring old man – the husband of one of my patients. There, now you know that I'm a scarlet woman!'

He could not tell from her tone whether she was serious or not but he bent and kissed her cheek, then pushed her out through the door, back into the cold and the winter dark.

'Yes, you always were ever so wicked. Goodbye, Suzie, and thank you very much for making the effort to come and see me. Don't forget to come next time you're in Norfolk!'

He stood and waved until the cab had disappeared down the long drive and then turned back into the kitchen. It was not until the sound of the engine had faded into silence that he began to cry.

20: 1924

The twins were in the sandpit, which was tucked out of sight between the vegetable garden and the wood which hid the Walters' cottage. It was a delectable spot, made especially for them by their father and William Walters, and whenever the weather permitted Nicky and Val could be found there, digging, lugging slopping buckets to and from the standpipe, building towering edifices, or just sitting and dreaming.

Today was hot, so they were clad in bathers, and June, so they were eating cherries. The cherry tree overhung the sandpit and dropped an abundance of fruit on the white Yarmouth sand, and though this brought the hazard of flies and wasps the twins were quite ready to put up with the trifling inconvenience for the sake of unlimited cherries.

Their nanny, who had not thought much of the sandpit at first, now frequently blessed it. To be sure, it meant sand in everything, but the sand was clean and regularly changed and it kept the twins happy and relatively mischief-free for hours on end. As witness today; a bright and beautiful Sunday when the rest of the family were attending a cocktail party at Frank's yard, to launch his latest boat. Val had bargained briskly for today.

Their mother had been dressing for dinner when they had tackled her about it. Sitting on the little round stool in front of her dressing-table in a slim-fitting black georgette dress with fringes that swished gently when she moved, she was fastening around her neck a beautiful string of topaz stones, yellow as cat's eyes. She raised her eyebrows when they appeared round the door and smiled at them.

'Hello, bandits. Has someone broken it to you that we're not taking you to Frank's party tomorrow after all? You'll be much happier at home with Nanny, though. A quiet lunch, nothing which will give you tummy upsets, and then a walk to the park perhaps. Far better for you than a grown-up party.'

'We want to come with you!' Val's voice was calculatingly close to a wail. 'We don' wanna be left on a Sunday! Nanny won't let us do *anything* except the park and picture books!'

'Oh, but you'd hate it at Frank's party, pets,' Tina replied, her eyes widening with horror at the thought of being saddled with two five-year-olds. 'You'd be so bored!'

'We want to come!' Nicky said in a high whine.

Val was opening her mouth for a fresh onslaught when their father, coming through from his dressing room, called their bluff.

'Nonsense! You'd hate it. What do you really want?'

Nicholas glanced at Val. She always knew what they wanted. That was the advantage of being a twin!

'We want to play in the sandpit all day in our old things. We want strawbs for tea, please, and late bed, because the rest's at Frank's party, having fun.'

'It's a deal.' Their father was already dressed for his dinner party, in white tie and tails, but he bent down and shook hands on the bargain in the approved manner. 'I'll see to the details. All you have to do is be good.'

And now, the day having been won, so to speak, they were enjoying the fruits, both of their endeavour and of the cherry tree. Their mother disapproved of greed and would have forbidden cherries had she thought of them, but the twins, bitterly used to seeing delicious, indigestible food being borne into the dining room and steamed fish and macaroni pudding making its way nurserywards, believed in striking whilst the iron was hot. Last year Val, stricken by sickness after an excess of cherries, had thoughtfully rushed out and vomited behind the coach-house sooner than draw adult attention to the whereabouts of the cherry tree. This year she was too sensible to over-eat. Besides, it was a leaner year for stoned fruit.

Everything had gone well, with cold chicken at luncheon followed – treat of treats – by icecream and by Stella, returning early from the party, with a present for them from Frank. A beautiful little sailboat, carved and rigged just like his own boat, *Sayonara*.

Since the stream was forbidden territory to them, their mother showing signs of going into strong hysterics if they mentioned playing there, they had a galvanised bath full of water in the sandpit. On this hot afternoon, having first buried the bath up to its rim in sand, they filled it to overflowing with buckets of water, threw in some shells to add verisimilitude, and floated their new acquisition on its gleaming surface. One at each side of the bath they crouched, each with a hand in the water gently stirring to keep the model boat on the move.

They were sitting thus, dreamily playing, when the boy found them.

He was a very little boy, with bleached fair hair and tanned skin. He must have been about three, Val thought. He came through the trees and there was something in the way he looked over his shoulder which led them to suspect that he had escaped from a parent or a nanny who would presently hotly pursue him.

Val's maternal instincts were not pronounced, but he was a charming little boy. She lifted him over the stout little brick wall and sat him down on the soft sand.

'Hello! What's your name? I'm Val and that's Nicky.'

The boy stared thoughtfully from one to another but vouchsafed no answer.

'He's too little to talk,' Nicholas said condescendingly. 'Much too little, aren't you, old chap?'

'No he isn't. Babies know their own names ever so young. Come on, tell Val your name.' The little boy's mouth curved and a small, plump hand shot out and tugged at her limp red hair.

'*Tu es fillette,*' the small boy said solemnly.

'What?'

'*Je m'appèle André,*' the little boy said in a squeak. 'Ooh!'

The last exclamation was caused by a slim young woman in one of the very short skirts which caused their father to roll his eyes and their mother to purse her lips. She came quickly out of the trees and addressed the erring André in a torrent of quick and angry-sounding French. Then she turned to the twins and spoke to them in perfect English.

'Hello! I thought at first that you must be Mrs Neyler's twins, but I believe I'm wrong because you aren't a bit alike.'

'We're the twins.' Nicholas spoke rather gruffly. He and Val were very different because of Val's flaming red hair and his own light brown thatch, but it always annoyed him when someone showed obvious scepticism over their relationship. Twins did not have to be identical, after all!

'I'm sorry.' The lady sank on to the sand as though she were well used to sitting on the floor and pulled the little boy on to her lap. She was very thin, Val saw, and her eyes were huge, black and sparkling with long straight lashes. 'I ought to know better than to make remarks like that, because people annoy me by saying that André and I don't look like mother and son.'

'He is your little boy, then! But he's French!'

The lady had a small velvet purse dangling from her wrist. Now she rummaged in it and brought out a packet of cigarettes and a gold lighter. She turned courteously to the twins. 'Yes, he's French. Do you mind if I smoke?'

'Please do,' Val stammered. She was intrigued by this lovely lady who actually asked children if she might smoke in their sandpit! 'How can he be French if you aren't? You aren't, are you?'

'No, only by marriage. My husband's French, you see, so I'm called Madame de Recourte.'

She put the cigarette between her lips and snapped the

lighter. The cigarette was pale blue and the paper between her lips was gold. A faint flame appeared, then she inhaled and the tip of the cigarette glowed red. She sighed luxuriously and blew a thin stream of smoke towards the upper boughs of the cherry tree. Val had already noticed that the lady's fingers were tense, gripping the lighter, and now she took in the rest of her appearance. The sleek, black hair was short and held close to her head by a band of amber-coloured velvet which matched the long beads round her neck. Her dress was a fine black voile, sleeveless, tubular, ending just above her knees as she sat. Her shoes were very elegant, with high heels. They were made of shiny leather and had huge velvet bows on the toes. She wore a tiny gold wristwatch on one wrist and on the other three or four thin gold bangles. Around one ankle was a fine gold chain with a heart hanging from it. Her stockings were the sheerest silk that Val had ever seen.

'Well, will you know me again?'

The lady's voice was teasing, but Val knew herself understood; her staring was a compliment and had been taken as such.

'You're very pretty, and you have lovely clothes. But I don't know you, and you don't know me. Do you?'

'I did tell you my name was Madame de Recourte.'

'Oh, yes, and I told you we were the Neyler twins. But I don't know who Madame de Recourte *is*!'

The lady laughed and let the little boy down on to the ground, where he sat down with a thump and proceeded to scoop sand into a pile with great energy.

'Nor you do! Well, would it help if I said I was . . .'

'Children, Nanny says tea's ready. She doesn't want to wait too long, because . . .'

Tall and slender, as blonde as Madame de Recourte was dark, Stella stood there, one hand fluttering towards her mouth. She stammered something more about the tea, then, with her eyes fixed on the twins' new friend, added: 'Is it . . . can it be you, after all this time?'

Madame de Recourte got to her feet and held out one hand, dropping the cigarette on to the path and letting it smoulder there unregarded. She was smiling, but Val could tell that the easy air which she had begun to wear had gone, and she was, for some reason, on her guard. Against Stella?

'Yes, the prodigal daughter's returned for a few days. I wondered whether you'd recognise me, Stella. Four years produce many changes. I didn't intend to visit but my son ran away and when I followed him I came across the twins and we got talking. I'd better be getting back, or Mother will worry.'

'Oh, Mabs, hang on for a minute! It's so good to see you. You look terribly chic and elegant. We were all awfully worried when you went away, and curious too, I suppose. Is the little boy really yours? He's – he's very nice.'

The Fench lady bent down and picked André up, ignoring his shout of annoyance and his pleas to be let alone. She held him close to her chest, almost defensively, and continued to speak to Stella over the top of the lint-white curls.

'Yes, he's mine. My husband, Matthieu, wanted André to meet his grandparents and he was coming to England on business so he brought us. I truly didn't mean to come near The Pride. I knew we could stay quite safely in the cottage. Your parents have always respected our privacy, and I should have let Mum run after this chap . . . .' She squeezed her son, kissing his neck and making him squeal and giggle. 'Please forget you've seen me, Stell.'

'Mabs, I can't! Please come up to the house! Not today, because everyone's away at a party, but tomorrow. Mama would be terribly hurt if she knew you were here and had gone without seeing her, to say nothing of Daddy and the boys. Desmond's married now, you know, but Frank . . .'

'No!' The word was said so sharply that it sounded like an expletive. 'I'm leaving almost at once and I know better than to open old wounds. It's only by chance you've seen me, so please don't tell your parents or brothers that I've been home. If you *knew*, Stell, you'd understand! Please?'

There was a noticeable pause before Stella said sulkily: 'All right, if you feel so strongly. Though how you intend to keep the twins quiet I can't imagine!'

Madame de Recourte turned to the twins, sitting in the

sand and staring from her face to their sister's. She smiled at them and dimples peeped for a moment.

'It's rather important, Val and Nicky, that no one knows I've been here. You won't tell?'

Nicholas glanced at his sister, waiting for her lead, and Val shook her head decisively. She had taken a liking to this French lady, whose profile reminded her of an Indian maiden in the nursery picture at home.

'We won't tell.'

'Thank you.' She bowed her head at them, then turned back to Stella. 'One day, Stell, when the wound's not so raw, I'll come home properly and we'll meet and talk about old times. But it's too soon. I couldn't face the explanations and exclamations. Try to understand, there's a darling!'

'I can't,' Stella wailed irritably. 'When you ran away I was only a kid and the hushed voices defeated me. Frank went round like a ghost and Des was too bright and cheerful, and we were told not to mention your name. It never occurred to me that there might be a rather . . .' She hesitated, glancing uneasily at her small brother and sister. 'Well, more in your sudden flight than met the eye. Oh, well.'

'Don't jump to conclusions, Stell, and don't worry. I really am very happy. *André, chéri, dis adieu.*'

Then she was gone, the child in her arms chattering away in French nineteen to the dozen as he was borne off. Stella stood for a moment, gazing after them, then rounded on the twins.

'Gracious, you two always seem to be in a mess! Nanny wants you for your tea and what she'll say when she sees your faces I don't know. Where did you get jam from out here?'

'It's not jam, it's cherries,' Nicky corrected placidly. 'We'll wash in this water if you'll go and tell Nanny we won't be long.'

As soon as Stella, grumbling, had disappeared behind the apple trees, he and Val leapt from the sandpit and grabbed the still smouldering cigarette.

'Turn and turn about,' Val said crisply, sucking frantically at the gold-coloured filter. 'Ugh, it's strong. Worse than those leaves you and Simon smoked.' She removed the cigarette from her mouth and regarded it thoughtfully. 'Lots of the papery stuff's got left on my lips,' she concluded balefully.

'You can have it *all*,' Nicky said. 'You've chewed it! You aren't supposed to chew it. I heard Uncle Frank showing Stella how to smoke a cigarette and he kept saying "Don't chew it, girl!" which is how I know it's wrong. Go on, hurry up and finish it and then we can have some tea. It'll be strawbs, because Daddy promised.'

Ten minutes later, tottering back to the house, Val remarked that she really was not hungry and thought she would miss out on tea; twenty minutes later Nanny, holding Val's head over a basin in the nursery bathroom, remarked sourly that sooner or later young ladies who made pigs of themselves with cherries would get their come-uppance.

And Val, sheet-white and still pathetically heaving, could only snivel and curse the demon tobacco whilst endeavouring to assure a frankly unbelieving Nanny that it was nothing to do with cherries!

'I shouldn't have come back.' Mabel faced Suzie across a small table in the window of the Corner House. 'It was just that you said you'd be in the city this week and Matthieu really did think we should have "*des petites vacances*" with my parents. It seemed meant. If only I'd sent Mother chasing after André into the Neylers' den! All I can think of is that Stella will blab and great unhappiness will result. She wasn't very reliable as a child. And at the back of it all, I suppose I hoped that if I came home a miracle would happen and everything would come right again.'

'Mabel, that's for babies, dreams like that. How can it "all come right", as you put it, when you're married to Matthieu and happy too? For all I know, Frank may be pursuing some girl, and no one can just roll back the years like a cheap carpet that's worn badly! Beds have to be lain on, dear.'

'I didn't mean anything like that,' Mabel said, colouring.

'I'm not that stupid! No, I meant that Frank and I might meet and be friends again and understand each other without having to mention Des. But as you say, it was just dreams.'

Suzie nodded rather abstractedly. She was examining the large plate of cream cakes on the table between them and now her hand hovered, unwilling to select too quickly.

'Cream cakes are my biggest failing! I love those éclairs but they're gone in no time, and the cream puffs with coffee icing don't last much longer. Cream horns, on the other hand, are quite substantial *and* they have jam at the bottom.' She took a cream horn and bit into it, continuing with a full mouth, 'I've never really understood why you left! Oh, I know about Des, but you couldn't have known you were pregnant then! I really thought Frank was nerving himself to pop the question, you know, and it was plain as the nose on your face that you loved him. So why, Mabs? Why let Des spoil it all? And then why on earth did you slam the door on Frank by marrying Matthieu? It really mystifies me.'

'I ran away because I didn't want to hurt Frank by admitting what Des had done; at least, that's what I told myself. But I think it was instinctive, really – you're badly hurt, so you crawl away and hide. And having left, I didn't know how to go back without entering into explanations which would probably be disbelieved and would certainly bring great distress. Then there was Matthieu. He really is the kindest man, Suzie, and he really did love me. And I him, though in a different way from the way I loved Frank. When I told him I was pregnant he was so good, so generous! It made no difference that the boy wasn't his. He insisted that we marry and he's treated me so well. He adores André; nothing is too good for his son. Well, one day you must come and visit us and you'll see for yourself how lucky I am!'

'Mm hmm. How did you meet this paragon, anyway?'

'I worked for him.' Mabel smiled. 'The classic case, my dear! He has an import-export business and a flat in Paris and a beautiful country home, rather like a farm. I worked at his Paris office for a few weeks, translating English into French and French into English; languages were always my strong point. Then I found I was pregnant and Matthieu came in to pick up a batch of translating and found me weeping over the sheets. He was wonderful. It was Friday evening and I expected him to give me a week's notice – I hadn't even started the translations, you see – but he told me the work was rather important so I must go back to my room, pack a bag, and he would take me down to his country house where we could work on the translations together.

'Once there, I saw that I'd have to explain, so I did, and he asked me if I'd be prepared to stay at the château, do some translating for him there at weekends, and keep the place nice during the week. He said it would be less arduous than the job in Paris, and that I could have my baby quietly, with the village doctor and midwife in attendance, and then put the child out for adoption, or at least write to my parents after the event. But no more than three weekends later he proposed. And I accepted. And we've lived happily ever after, I might add!'

'A château's a castle, isn't it?' Suzie said, seizing on the most important detail. 'Is he immensely rich, your Matthieu?'

'Yes. But that isn't why I'm happy with him!'

'I'm sure it isn't. But doesn't it coat the pill?' Suzie murmured mischievously. 'I'd bet a considerable sum of money on the fact that he's older than you.'

'He's forty-four, actually, though he doesn't look it. If you're imagining a bloated sugar-daddy, forget it.' She opened her purse and produced a small photograph. 'See?'

Suzie took the photograph and pursed her lips in a soundless whistle of admiration.

'Cripes and blimey! All that and money too. *Now* I know why you don't dream of Frank any more!'

'I do.' Mabel snatched the photograph back, her cheeks flaming. 'Oh, God, I dream of him! Just to see him in the distance, in a crowd, anything . . . that's why I came home!'

'You want to have your cake and eat it, my girl,' Suzie said severely. She shook the coffee pot and then beckoned to the waitress. 'Could we have more coffee, please?' And then, her attention reverting to her friend once more, 'Frank's doing his best to forget you, my dear, and the kindest thing you can do is to forget him as well. I don't think Frank could share friendship with you, not when he'd hoped to become your lover. Perhaps in a few years' time, when he's married himself, it might be different.'

'Marry? Frank? He wouldn't!'

'I think he will. You wouldn't want to deny him the happiness you've found, would you, Mabs?'

'Oh, no, but now that I'm married I shouldn't think it would even cross his mind.' She put her hands to her hot cheeks, aware of Suzie's censorious look. 'Look, I had to marry for André's sake, otherwise I should probably have bided my time and then come back to Frank. But I couldn't, not with his brother's child, and with Desmond stamped all over his face, poor little devil. So you see, it was different for me.'

'It always is. You leave Frank alone, Mabs. Now let's change the subject. I've got a brand new flat in London in a brand new block; why don't you bring Matthieu to visit me there? When my man-friend's not around, if you prefer.'

Mabel glanced pointedly at her friend's outfit. The honey-coloured fur cape, the pale gold voile blouse, the dark brown accordian pleated skirt, exactly matching the high-heeled leather shoes with their big brass buckles.

'Your man-friend's obviously not short of a copper or two, dear! What do you use your salary as a nurse for? To buy nail lacquer?'

'Miaow!' Suzie grinned appreciatively at her friend. 'I never thought you'd turn out so elegant though, love – you've got chic since we last met. I won't ask where you got your suit, or that divine little hat, because they shriek Paris, but I *have* to suggest that Matthieu and my friend Ronald must have one thing in common!'

'If you mean they both spend their money on bad women, I suppose I can scarcely deny it, now,' Mabel said quietly. 'You've always been proud of being a naughty girl, but I've been brought up to see what I did as . . . oh, Suzie, as ever such a sin! And it was all pain and humiliation, every moment!'

'I didn't mean that! Honestly, Mabs, how you take one up! I meant they both enjoyed spending money on pretty women!' Suzie cried, leaning across the table and catching Mabel's hands in hers. 'I just wish Ronald would decide he wanted to marry me and then I could be comfortable, instead of having to be careful never to offend him! It must be lovely to be cherished by a man whether he's rich or poor.' She glanced at Mabel through her long, tawny eyelashes. 'I'm going down to Oulton in a day or so, to see Frank.'

'Oh, are you?' Mabel stared at her friend, her eyes hardening. 'If you're thinking of trying to wheedle Frank to cherish you, you'd better stick to your sugar-daddy, because you'll just be wasting effort on Frank!'

'You really think Frank's yours, don't you,' Suzie said slowly. 'And it was true, once. But you've forfeited any rights, Mabs; you forfeited them the day you agreed to marry Matthieu. However, if you'll go down to Oulton and live with Frank as his mistress I certainly shan't go and visit him. That's fairly said, isn't it?'

Mabel caught the waitress's eye and asked for the bill, then turned back to Suzie.

'Frank deserves better than you can offer. Why should he take such *very* shop-soiled goods when he could have the best? I wouldn't go to him because of one man, so why should you go to him after a dozen? You leave him alone, Suzie Canning!'

Both girls were on their feet now, hissing at each other across the remains of their morning coffee.

'Shop-soiled goods? What did Matthieu get, then? It's marriage that's in question, remember. And at least I'm not trying to palm another man's child off on Frank.'

'You, have a child? When you've been sleeping with men since you were thirteen without producing one? I very much doubt if you're capable of giving birth!' Mabel's face, which had been pink with temper, suddenly drained of colour and she caught at Suzie's arm as the other turned to leave. 'Suzie, I'm sorry, that was a wicked thing to say! I didn't mean a word of it, I swear I didn't. It's just that I can't bear the thought of anyone else having Frank.'

'I know.' Suzie linked arms with Mabel and the two of them walked over to the cash-desk together. 'You might be right at that, and I'll forgive you anyway, because of the compliment you just paid me.'

'Compliment?' Mabel pushed the money across the desk and raised her brows at her friend. 'What was that?'

'You said if you wouldn't go to him after one man, why should I do so after a dozen? My dear Mabs, it must be nearer fifty!' She laughed as Mabel protested, but continued seriously: 'I know what you mean; Frank's an extremely eligible bachelor and could have his pick of bright young things – bright young virgins, if we're being honest. But he *likes* me, Mabs. I've been going over to the yard about once a month for ages now and I'm breaking down the barriers and giving him back his self-confidence and I do think that one day he may want to marry me. I'd hate to think that you grudged him a normal life.'

'I'm being a bitch in the manger, you mean,' Mabel said ruefully as, arm in arm, they turned right along Gentleman's Walk. 'I wish you good luck, Suzie, and happiness too. If those things go with Frank, then I still mean them. There, wasn't that big of me? Now I'd like to pop down to Garlands for some voile to make my mother a rather special dressy sort of blouse, and to Fullers for one of those oozy, gooey fudge cakes. Are you coming in that direction?'

'Yes, I'm coming; at least I'm not going anywhere else,' Suzie said. 'Can I tell Frank I've seen you and that you're happy? Or is that asking too much?'

'Tell him,' Mabel said, and, arms linked, they set off towards Garlands. They were a striking sight. Desmond, strolling along with his hat tilted jauntily on his blond locks and a rose in the buttonhole of his pale grey suit, stared and halted, one hand at his tie, the other held out, his most ingratiating smile directed at Suzie.

'My dear Miss Canning, it's been years! You must introduce me to your friend . . .'

His voice died away as Mabel, her cheeks flaming, brushed past him and hailed a taxi-cab. She was in it and being whisked off down the road before he had collected himself. Desmond blinked and rubbed his nose ruefully.

'What've I said to offend the little lady? I only meant to have a few words with such a pretty couple!'

'I daresay she's got a thing against being accosted in the street by an Englishman,' Suzie said consolingly. 'Madame de Recourte – that's her name – has been pretty strictly brought up, by all accounts.'

'Oh, French, was she? Well, she looked topping. Those very dark, silky sort of suits can only be worn by the French. I know you girls don't like to show your figures any more, you all want to look like sixteen-year-old youths, but the way that silk clung . . .' He whistled expressively. 'Oh well, there's no accounting for tastes, I suppose. But I'd like to meet her properly – be introduced, and all that.'

'Well, perhaps you'll meet her one day, though I believe she's going back to France tomorrow. And I'd better go too. I've got some shopping to do; some voile and a cake. So if you'll excuse me, Desmond . . .'

'Oh, Suzie, don't rush off!' Desmond's smile was engaging but the look in his eyes was predatory; Suzie remembered what Mabel had told her and shivered, despite the warmth of the sun. 'Let me buy you luncheon, for old time's sake. It's years since we met and we've not had a chance to talk yet, and . . .'

'And you're a married man with two children,' Suzie said briskly. 'Goodbye, Desmond. Give my regards to your family.'

The smile had left Desmond's face and there was a sharp glint in his eyes which Suzie recognised. She continued to stare unflinchingly up at him, however, reminding herself that he could scarcely do anything, not out here on the Walk with people everywhere!

'You've a sharp, nasty tongue, Suzie. I remember how

you let me down all those years ago, and I've not forgiven that yet. Now there's another set-down to add to the score I'm reckoning up against you. It'll be paid off though, one day.'

She turned away, unable to hide the distaste she felt, and hurried towards Garlands. Behind her, she heard him strike his cane viciously against something, probably the nearest lamp-post, but she did not turn her head. Was Desmond really dangerous, or just a foolish, greedy young man? Not so young, either; he must be twenty-three or four. He had slipped up in his amorous dealings about three years ago, Frank had told her, and got a girl of good family pregnant. Forced to marry her, he seemed to be acting in the belief that a pregnant woman was a happy woman – or at any rate, a quiet woman, for his wife had had three babies in three years, and was expecting a fourth, though Suzie knew that she had miscarried of her second child.

And Beryl was not his only responsibility. He had a mistress, a sharp-faced, avaricious, henna-headed woman called Zelda who owned a gown shop on Davy Place and lived in a small flat above it. Desmond had bought her the shop and set her up in business but she was shrewd and hard-headed and had soon gained her financial independence, though even Frank had no idea whether she was still in his brother's debt or had paid him back.

'I don't say anything to Des,' Frank had told her when they discussed the uneasy alliance between Desmond and Beryl and the torrid affair between Desmond and Zelda, 'because in a way it's to Beryl's advantage that he keeps the other one. You see, he's so busy with the pair of them and all the kids that he doesn't get up to other mischief.'

'Like what?' They were at the Swan, in Horning, eating strawberries and cream by the river and watching the passing boats – a busman's holiday, Suzie had teased him.

'Like cheating Daddy,' Frank said ruefully. 'He used to enjoy the devious methods he employed, I'm certain of it. Now he doesn't have time – he just demands.'

'And gets?'

'Usually.' Frank sighed and pointed to a passing yacht.

'That's one of ours. Beautiful, isn't she? The third . . . or was it the fourth? . . . that we built. Where was I?'

'That Des gets what he wants.'

'Oh, yes. Well, the only time I *did* say something to him about Beryl and Zelda he said it didn't matter, because neither minded about the other and, in fact, each was happier to receive only half his attentions.'

Despite herself, Suzie giggled. 'Your brother is an unmitigated cad, and terribly conceited; but he's probably got a point!'

And now, entering Garlands and realising that she could scarcely buy voile for Mabel's mother when she had not the slightest idea of the quantity or the colour required, she also realised that it might not merely be Desmond's amorous attentions which were best divided between his wife and his mistress. It was quite possible that Desmond was a bully.

On this disagreeable thought she turned out of the shop again, and headed for Fullers.

21

Louis sat on the third park bench in the gardens nearest the medical school, reading a letter. Balanced on the bench beside him were three more, as yet unopened. It was a hot day and sweat kept running down his forehead and into his eyes, making them sting. From his chin the drops descended on to the letter, making the ink run as though someone had wept over it. And, thought Louis, that might yet happen.

For the letter was from Sarah, and it asked for a divorce. She had waited for five years and still he said not a word about returning. For the first couple of years she had understood; he was working on a sheep station, living in a bunkhouse, messing with men like himself; there could be no place for her or the children there. But then he had written that he was moving to Sydney.

'You never really said why,' the letter said a trifle plaintively. 'Only something about a little boy called Sam falling into a turnip chopper. And still no word that you would either come home or send for us. Finally, Lou, dear though you will always be to me, good sense has prevailed. Simon is terrible naughty. He needs a father's firmness, and Cara needs a father's love. To save more time and heartache, would you please provide me with evidence? It need not even be real – just you and Another, booking into a hotel as Mr and Mrs Rose.'

Sitting on the bench in the shade of the acacia trees, Louis remembered his life on the sheep station, so abruptly shattered by Sam's accident. He had been the only man on the homestead that afternoon and he had driven the station wagon, with Sam's body tightly clasped in one arm, all the way to the nearest village where he might find a doctor.

The doctor had been there – drunk. So drunk that he had sat in a chair, boozed and bleary, and told Louis, step by step, what to do for Sam and how to do it. And at the end of what had been both the worst and the best three hours of his life, Luis had known one thing. He wanted to be a doctor.He had gone with Sam into Sydney when the boy was well enough to be moved, and had entered his name at the medical school there. Doubts had been expressed at his ability to do the course at his age, until they had examined Sam. Then he had been allowed to enroll, and since then he had never looked back with any sort of regret to what his life might have been.

Until this moment? But could he even say that? He knew now the deep satisfaction of somebody making something of his life, for he was well on the way to becoming a doctor, and a good one. His social life was almost nil, for in every free moment he worked to keep himself, to buy books, and instruments, and respectable, though not smart, clothing.

For a moment he thought about home, and his family. There was pleasure and pain in such recollections, yet both were faint, faded by time and by a life so much more interesting and important than the life he had left. He still knew that Sarah was a beautiful woman and that his children would be handsome and intelligent. But bringing them out here would never work – Sarah was used to a different sort of life altogether and would not appreciate having to live in cramped lodgings and work for her living when she could be at home in the Ipswich Road house, a gracious, relaxed hostess, a fond though never over-anxious mother, a generous and loving wife. Here, she would have to be breadwinner for herself and the children because he could not support them all and continue with his degree and nothing, not the love of his wife, not the cries of his children, would deflect him from his course now.

He looked at the letter again, half believing that he had misread it, but he had not. She wanted a divorce, and he knew she was entitled to ask for one. He grinned ruefully as he thought how far from easy he would find it to provide her with the 'evidence' she spoke of – she would not believe it, but he scarcely knew any women save for a few fellow-students. And the money to buy a 'companion' for a night would have to be earned.

But he would do it. It would cut the last link with England, and he suspected that it would hurt badly, but for Sarah's sake he would do it. He had never faced his own complete determination until this moment, but now, confronting it, he knew that his work had been made easier by the fact that, subconsciously, he had felt he could always drop his life here and return to Norwich; take up again his job in the factory, slip into the once-familiar role of Sarah's lover, the children's father.

He put Sarah's letter down on the park bench and picked up the next one; Tina. He would know that neat, decisive handwriting anywhere. She would know about the request for a divorce since she and Sarah had always been close. He opened the letter, half hoping that Tina would refer to the divorce, half hoping she would ignore it. He skimmed across the first page; his younger sister Rachel had married a middle-aged widower called Adolphus Siegal and much to everyone's surprise, since 'middle-aged' was a euphemism for a man in his late fifties, she had recently produced a son named Caspar. Tina enthused over the baby, over the motherly way his own daughter Cara behaved with the tiny cousin. She told of a party at Cecy's house, The Towers, on Unthank Road and for a moment Louis was back in the garden on a summer's day long ago, when, as quite a young child, he had hidden himself in a patch of pampas grass during a game of hide and seek. He had been unharmed but one of the little girls, searching for him when he had giggled, had cut herself quite severely on the razor-sharp pampas blades.

The house had not been Cecy's then, nor the garden; it had belonged to the Solstein parents. But they had moved out several years ago and the 'young people', as Abe and Cecy had been called by them, had moved in. Louis, dreaming, saw again the broad, daisy-speckled lawn drowsing in the sun, the wide herbaceous borders with their clumps of blue cultivated thistles and the huge Himalayan poppies, the air soft with the scent of flowers, sleepy with bee-hum. He blinked and shook himself back to awareness of the gardens where he was sitting, the acacia and eucalyptus trees, the parched grass, the brassy heat of the midday sun. Different – but every bit as beloved, he realised with surprise. Oh, England called him, of course she did! But so did Australia. England had been his dearly beloved home, but now so was Australia. And he knew which country would win, because Australia had won already. He might go back for holidays but he would never live in England again. In his heart, he did not even want to, save as a sentimental journey to a time when he was younger, seeing things with the clear, uncomplicated vision of a child. Here, life was harsher perhaps, but it was more real, more earnest. A quicker pace, a fiercer struggle for richer rewards.

He laid Tina's letter down and picked up the pad of paper and the pencil. He wrote firmly, not really thinking of anything but the need to get the deed done.

Dear Sarah, thanks for your letter. I'll do as you want, of course, and as soon as I can arrange it. Kiss the children for me.

He hesitated over the signature; he always signed himself 'Your loving husband, Lou' when he wrote to Sarah, but would it be appropriate in view of the impending change in their relationship? He thought about it, then shrugged and signed off as usual. He folded the letter, put it into his pocket and then picked up the last envelope. Without opening it, he knew it was from Say. He could see her penning it so clearly, sitting behind the post office counter in the village shop he had only ever visited once, but which was still engraved on his memory. The post office was just a bit of the counter, of course, but Say had a tall wooden stool and a pink blotter, and it was there that she sat and wrote her long, rambling, surprisingly shrewd letters to him. He loved receiving them. Say never asked for anything, not for vows of love, not for interest in her brood, not even for replies to her letters. She wrote because she wanted to, and it showed. Bits of village gossip, a fragment of talk she had heard which might interest him, the marks Jamie had got in his latest arithmetic test, all jostled with the weather, the state of her garden, the hen who laid astray, the flimsiness of the new sugar bags and how was a body to sell sugar when it come out at the seams of the bag the way it did?

He could see her so clearly, a little plumper, probably, with her pretty hair carefully tied back yet always coming loose, a curl bobbing against her broad, calm brow. She would be writing with one arm curled protectively round the letter, so that no one else could read it, and the tip of her tongue just peeping out from between her white teeth. Behind her, the sacks of flour and sugar, the tub of margarine with its scoop, and on the shelf, the big jars of boiled sweets, the colours inviting even in the gloom. Slightly to one side, there was a door, propped half open. Behind it was the wide, low-ceilinged kitchen where Say cooked their meals, did their washing, coped with her brood. She had a girl to help her now, Maureen Jarvis, and across the kitchen was the back door, also quite often open, affording Say a glimpse of her garden.

'Country children don't want nor need much garden,' she had written proudly once, 'because they've all the meadows and woods to play in. But we've got a sandpit and a swing and one day Winkie's going to build a slide.'

He settled down, after a quick glance at his watch to make sure that he still had plenty of time before his next lecture, for an enjoyable read, and as he read his contentment grew. For Sarah might cut him off, slam the door, take another man to her bed and her heart, but Say never would. She would always be there, cushiony, welcoming, his friend if he needed one, his lover if he wanted one. She was Winkie's wife, and a good wife too, he had no doubt of that, as he was sure that she was an excellent mother. But she could not give Winkie her love, because that had been handed to Louis, lock, stock and barrel, a dozen years ago.

Is it possible that I've ceased to love Sarah yet still love Say? Louis wondered, as he stood up at last and folded the letter back into its envelope, to be enjoyed over and over in the days to come. Surely that was not possible! No, the truth was that he loved both women in different ways, and probably would until the day he died. And he did not believe that Sarah no longer loved him; she wanted her freedom, but that was because she could scarcely do as Say had done, and marry again, without first obtaining a divorce.

Sarah's the same, really, he comforted himself as he entered the cool hall of the medical school. She loves me as much as ever, but she needs a father for the children, just as Say did.

The thought comforted his vanity, if not his intellect.

Suzie closed the door of Mr Abbott's room behind her and

then looked around the hall. Gleaming tiles, cream-washed walls, the hospital smell she had known for so long all about her, even here; antiseptic, carbolic, illness. She gave a little sigh and made for the front door. The last time! For Mr Abbott had told her, pretty bluntly, that if she wanted to get rid of the cough that had haunted her for the last six months, and put on some weight again, she must give up nursing for a reasonable length of time, if not for ever.

'Take a job in the country, if you can't take a long holiday,' he had advised. 'And don't do anything more than you have to; you've been burning the candle at both ends for far too long, nurse. How old are you?'

'I'm twenty-two, sir.'

'Hmm. D'you want to be twenty-five? Hey?'

'I do indeed, sir. But not for three years or so!'

She had smiled perkily but he did not smile back, frowning down at his blotter as though he had not heard her reply. His heavy, pink and white face looked solemn in a way she had seldom seen it and suddenly she was afraid. Was she really ill?

'That's right, keep cheerful, but I'm serious, y'know. If you don't give yourself a chance you won't see twenty-five. Nor twenty-four, either.' He had thick, bushy eyebrows and he glared at her through them in a manner she had often found comic when she was being lectured by him on some small point of hospital procedure. Now it was not funny. 'Take a year off from nursing, perhaps two. If you could get a job in the country, where the air's clean and the pace of life is slower, it would give your lungs a chance. Nurses are practical people, in my experience; daresay you could make a go of light housekeeping, eh? Giving orders, that sort of thing?' He leaned forward across his desk and smiled, the ends of his waxed moustache tilting upwards. 'What d'you think, eh?'

'Are my lungs diseased, sir?'

She got the words out through a horrid thickening in her throat, a fluttering of panic in her breast. Her palms were pressed to the side of her uniform skirt and she could feel them moist and hot, as she could feel the now familiar tightness beginning in her chest.

'Diseased?' He shot her another glance. 'We've all got Londoners' lungs; yours aren't any worse than mine, I daresay. But you're a nurse; you should've guessed that all the wheezing meant things aren't right.' He got to his feet and moved around the desk, putting a huge, well-manicured hand on her shoulder in a fatherly fashion. 'Hey now, missie, don't look so frightened! I'm not condemning you to anything but a change of scene for a while, and then you'll probably be fit as a fiddle again. Fit as a fiddle.' He paused, as though searching for the right words. 'If the cough doesn't clear up after you've been in the country for a few months you'd best come back, have a few tests done. All right?'

'Yes, sir. If you think that's all I need. Country air and rest.'

'Nothing better for the lungs than clean air and plenty of rest.' He cleared his throat. 'You're a pretty girl; got a beau? Any chance he'd marry you, hey?'

'I've got a – a friend, but he's an elderly . . .'

He interrupted her, his face reddening. 'I don't want to know any details, nurse! Does he have a place in the country? Any chance of you staying down there?'

Suzie laughed and shot the doctor a mischievous look. 'I wouldn't get much rest, sir! But I come from a country city, if there is such a thing – Norwich, down in Norfolk. I've a friend there who might need a housekeeper.' Her eyes dreamed. 'It's a lovely spot, quite near the coast, and the air couldn't be purer. I think I'll be able to go there.'

'Good, excellent, couldn't be better. I've a great fondness for Norfolk. Punting on the Broad, bagging a couple of wild duck – ah, yes, that's for me when I retire.' His relief showed in the way he pumped her hand and called his good wishes after her as she left his room, and Suzie wondered how far the doctor's kindness would have carried him had she not made it clear she knew a refuge. His gruff manner hid the most generous heart – indeed, it had been at his suggestion that she had consulted him over the wretched, niggling cough, the weight loss and the attacks of lethargy which no one else seemed to have noticed.

And now, she reflected, walking along the pavement in the general direction of the tube station, she had been condemned to idleness. Not that she would be idle, she would rather anything than that! She qualified this foolhardy thought by dodging across the pavement and touching wood on the façade of a small grocery shop. An elderly woman, booted and fur-coated, came out of the shop with a frown which melted into a smile as Suzie beamed at her; it was a cold winter's day but Suzie's stunned initial reaction to the doctor's advice was rapidly dissipating in delight and anticipation. She was going home! After all the years she was going home to Norfolk, and, what was more, she was going to stay there.

With Frank. Strangely enough, she had no doubts or fears about her destination. She would go back to the flat now and tell Ronald that she was leaving him – and London – for medical reasons. He was fanatical about his health and the slightest hint that she was ill would be enough to persuade him that she must, indeed, go away. Then she would go down to the station and get herself a single ticket to Norwich Thorpe. She would stay with her aunt for one night and then the next day she would go down to Oulton Broad and tell Frank he needed a housekeeper.

At the entrance to the tube station she bought a large bunch of freesias for an exorbitant price from the flower-seller sitting nearby, then dived down the steps. The freesias smelled of spring and despite her precarious position – no job, very soon no lover, no home – her heart was light. She had loved Frank quietly for so long, and now, at long last, she was going to be near him so that he, too, might fall in love with her!

The boatyard had turned into a roaring success; one had only to glance around it to see that. All the sheds were either repaired or rebuilt and there was a double garage housing a large truck and a shiny new Hudson-Essex, whose gleaming black bonnet paid a silent tribute to the hours the boy Donnie had spent waxing it.

Frank walked across the immaculate yard in the increasing dusk of the rainy afternoon, and pushed open the door of the cottage. It had changed very little in the past five years, though the roof no longer leaked and the window frames had been renewed and reglazed. But a glance round it would show that it was a bachelor abode, for it completely lacked the woman's touch despite all Tina's motherly efforts to see that her son lived in some style. Frank merely suffered the turkey rugs, the satin sofa, the modern pictures, until Tina had gone home and then sent them back to Norwich on the next conveyance city-bound. Once this had been a brewer's dray and Tina had suffered the shock of having the vehicle arrive outside The Pride, complete with the beautiful modern gold and white divan bed she had sent her son, just as six members of the Bridge Club arrived for dinner. It had been her last gift. Now, when she came to visit Frank, she might glance at his shabby rugs and worn sofa and cast her eyes towards the ceiling whilst tutting her disapproval, but further than that she did not go.

He stood on the doorstep, just inside the shelter of the small porch roof which he and Benjamin had added, removing his rubber boots and thinking rather mundanely about his supper. It would have been nice to settle down in front of the fire with a hot cup of tea, knowing that a meal would presently be brought in, but he would have to either stir himself into action with a frying pan or go into the village and order dinner at the Wherry. He took off his waterproof and hung it on a nail just inside the door, then turned for his last look at the Broad. He did this every night, and the sight never failed to soothe him and to give him a deep sense of satisfaction. Tonight was no exception. There was something fascinating in the sight of the Broad under rain, that mirror-smooth surface dimpled and pitted so that it resembled frosted glass, making the steel-dark sky above it seem lighter in contrast. And tonight, despite the lateness of the hour, there was a boat making its way across. Like a waterboatman, one of those Christ-like insects that skim the surface of the Broad, their bodies the boat, their elongated legs the oars, it came nearer and nearer to his mooring, partly obscured by the grey mist of the rain falling straight and mild into the water.

Frank paused. It could not be coming to the yard, not at this hour! He went through in his mind the number of people who might come to him across the water, rather than down the lane, but they were few and none of them would have ventured out in such a downpour without a good reason. He was on the telephone – it was essential in a business such as his – and even the most casual caller usually rang him since he was so often out, or too busy to attend to unexpected visitors.

Then a hand was raised in greeting. So he had best abandon thoughts of settling down for the evening just yet!

Only an idiot would have gone out again, into that relentless wet, yet Frank felt vaguely guilty, standing in the shelter of the porch, watching his visitor get rather clumsily out of the boat, shake masses of water off a huge, ankle-length water-proof cape and hand it to the boatman. No money changed hands and Frank guessed that only a substantial advance payment had lured old Pat Paterson out on such a night.

The boatman turned his craft and began to row out into the Broad once more, and the visitor turned and crossed the yard with quick steps.

'Hello, Frank. Can I come in?'

'Suzie! Come in, girl, you'll catch your death!'

He pulled her into the kitchen, closed the door, then surveyed her. Her dark tweed coat was soaked across the shoulders and hem despite the cape and her hair clung to her head, beads of moisture pendant on each lock, but she smiled up at him gallantly, though she was shivering and her lips showed blue beneath their paint.

'I've c-come to visit you, and you're s-so difficult to reach unless one has a car, which I've not! May I go to the fire for a minute?'

Her fingers were at the buttons of her coat and, seeing that her efforts to remove it were making no headway because her hands were numb with cold, Frank unbuttoned her like a child, threw the coat carelessly on the floor, and snatched the roller towel down from behind the door. He rubbed her hands until the fingertips began to glow pink, then turned his attention to the soaked gold of her hair, wielding the towel to such good effect that presently her hair, short as a boy's, stood up, soft and fluffy, like chick's down.

'There! Better? Now you can sit down!'

She sat down, smiling up at him. She was wearing a lemon jumper suit with a green chiffon scarf in the low V neck, caught in at the waist with a green and gold leather belt. The skirt was straight and very short and her legs were clad in such fine silk stockings that for one horrified moment Frank thought they were bare.

'For a moment I thought you'd come out bare-legged, in this weather,' he remarked, sitting down opposite her in the sagging but comfortable chintz-covered armchair. 'Anyone who's mad enough to cross the Broad in this sort of rain is mad enough for anything.'

'Bare legs are unfashionable, and you couldn't accuse me of *that,*' she protested. She held out her hands to the fire and Frank could not help noticing that her fingers were so thin he could almost see the flames through them. 'I didn't mean to come over until tomorrow, but then I decided the sooner the better. I would have hired a car, but someone was ahead of me. It would have meant waiting for ages, and then I remembered Pat.' She cocked a bright eye at him. 'Why? Aren't you pleased to see me?'

'Of course I am. But did you arrange for the car to pick you up later?' Belatedly remembering his manners, he added: 'I could run you to the station in the Essex, of course.'

'Never mind later!' She sounded impatient. 'Is there anything to eat in this place or have I got to face that rain again? Because I'm starving, I warn you!'

'There's some cold chicken, I think,' Frank said, guiltily remembering the inroads he had made on the bird during his lunch-break. 'Probably some potatoes – cold boiled ones, I mean – and half – nearly half – a marmalade pudding. And I've tinned stuff, of course.'

Suzie pulled a face. 'Marmalade pudding? But even in your beloved Essex, I'd have to get out and stumble into the Wherry. No, don't try to persuade me to let you buy me an expensive dinner; I'm too tired. A little cold chicken and some boiled potatoes will have to suffice for tonight.'

'There's no need for that; we'll go to the Wherry,' Frank said, grinning at her. 'And then I'll take you to the station and you can sit in the car until the train arrives; how does that suit you? We can talk over dinner.'

'No. I'm determined not to go out again tonight,' Suzie said firmly. 'I'll fry the potatoes and do the chicken in a sauce. I'll even heat up the marmalade pudding, if that'll please you.'

'It sounds delicious,' Frank said slowly. 'But Suzie, you said you didn't want to go out again tonight!' A tide of colour engulfed his face and he stared at her. 'Good God, you can't very well stay *here*!'

'Why not? I call it very inhospitable of you, Frank, not to insist that I stay. I even brought a nightie, to keep me snug.' She reached for her dull green leather handbag and produced from its depths a wisp of what looked, to Frank, like cobweb. 'See! Wasn't I sensible?'

'Is that a nightgown? My dear girl, you might as well be . . .' He thought better of it and cleared his throat. 'Look, of course you can stay! But I've no spare bed and I can't offer you mine because I don't know where the clean sheets are! Mrs Coates changes it for me, and takes most of the heavy washing home with her. But you're very welcome to the couch and a pile of blankets.'

She smiled and nodded. She looked very pretty now, flushed from the fire, and as he smiled back at her he noticed that her makeup had all been rubbed away when he vigorously towelled her dry and was touched that she had made no effort to re-apply powder and lipstick, as most girls would have done. She trusted him, even without the defence of her paint. It did not occur to Frank that girls were generally thought more attractive with makeup than without; he knew that, for his own part, Suzie was far more appealing with her skin clear and clean, her tawny lashes untouched by mascara, the line of her lips her own pale, soft pink.

'Then I'll go and check our supplies.' Frank got up and went over to the pantry. Suddenly he felt like a kid, flushed with the excitement of this new venture. It would be fun to have a visitor, fun to know that Suzie was going to share his breakfast next morning. 'I say, how about making a chicken curry? There's a jar of curry paste!'

'Yes, I think I could manage that, if you've got some vegetables.' Suzie got up and came across to the pantry. 'And you've got cheese, so I'll have cheese and biscuits whilst you guzzle marmalade pudding.'

'Except that I don't think I've got any biscuits. And what have you got against marmalade pudding, anyway? I think it's delicious; Mrs Coates nearly always makes me one when she comes in.'

'Well, I could learn to tolerate it, I suppose.' Suzie began to collect ingredients for a curry, ignoring Frank's startled glance. 'Here, you go and peel some onions. We'll talk over our meal.'

But once at the table with their soup in front of them, Suzie seemed to have lost her tongue. She began to speak, took a spoonful of soup, blushed, and then turned accusingly on Frank.

'Now that it's come to the point I'm nervous as a kitten! And why I can't imagine, considering some of the things I've said and done in my time!'

'Then nervousness becomes you, because you look very pretty, stuttering and stammering there,' Frank said. 'Go on, girl, cough it up!'

'I've given up nursing.'

'Really? Now that does surprise me. I thought you'd only give up nursing for marriage, and if you'd got married you'd have blurted that out first, not last.'

'No, I'm not married. And I've left the chap I was living with. I don't want to go back to him.'

'Why should you? Nurses are always wanted; get a job nursing in Norwich, then we could meet more often.'

Suzie sighed and put down her soup spoon.

'Frank, are you deliberately being dense? I don't *want* another job in nursing. I want to be a – a housekeeper for a change.'

'Lord, I didn't know you were so domesticated,' Frank said mildly. 'Have you any particular part of the country in mind for this new venture? Or any would-be employer, for that matter? Do you want me to speak to someone? Is that why you've come visiting in such foul weather?'

Suzie tried another tack. 'It's got to be fairly light work, that's the trouble. To tell the truth I didn't so much leave nursing as get told I must leave.'

'Sacked, you mean? Why, for God's sake?'

The long green eyes met his. Their sparkle was a little too bright.

'A doctor at the hospital said I must have rest and country air. Otherwise, I might . . . might . . .'

'Suzie! Are you ill, love?'

'Only a little ill. But I don't want it to get worse, which is why I'm here.' Suzie took a deep breath and squared her shoulders. 'Frank, wouldn't you like a housekeeper? A living-in housekeeper who just wants board and lodging? I'll sleep on the couch until I can get into Lowestoft to buy a bed, and I wouldn't be any trouble, honestly.'

'You're ill! Why didn't you tell me straight away? What did the doctor say? What is it? If you need treatment I'll pay for you to go into a nursing home, I'll do something!'

'I'm not terribly ill. It's just that I've been overdoing it, what with heavy nursing and – and everything. If you'd let me come here and take it easy for a few months, then maybe I could go back to nursing after all. The doctor seemed to think . . .'

Frank got up and lifted her carefully to her feet, then pulled her round to face him. He shook her gently and, when she tried to speak, put a finger across her lips.

'Shut up and listen for once, you bossy young ex-nurse! You'll come here as my guest and I'll see you get rest and fresh air and everything else the doctor says you need. What do you think Mabs would say if I let you get ill?'

Suzie flinched, then laughed, though tears stood in her eyes. 'What do you think she'd say if she knew I was living in the cottage with you?'

'Yes, that's true. And my mother! It'll be best if I pay you a fair wage and let you prepare the odd meal now and again. We'll go into Lowestoft and buy a bed tomorrow – there's a second bedroom, though it's full of lumber at the moment. I'll have Donnie clear it out. We'll be very snug, I'll be bound.'

He was grinning, his cheeks flushed, his eyes blazing with excitement at the plan. He had not known he was lonely until Suzie had made her proposal, but now he acknowledged that he would enjoy her company, that it would enrich his life. Patch, who had been snoozing in front of the fire, was woken by the excitement in his master's voice and gave a blurred half-yelp-half-yawn, and then, when they laughed, got staggeringly to his feet, tail wagging, and butted Frank with his head. What goes on? his eyes said.

'I'm going to live here with you and your old man, Patch,' Suzie said, kneeling down to pet the dog. He suffered it gracefully but his eyes never left Frank. 'How will you like not being the only pebble on the beach, old lad?'

'Two people to beg from, two people to take him walks – he'll be in clover,' Frank said at once. But it was a mistake. At the sound of the word 'walk' Patch rushed to the door and fixed the handle with a beseeching gaze. 'Hey, don't take me so literally, Patch. We're in the middle of a meal. Later!'

But Suzie walked to the door and opened it. Outside, the rain had stopped and a frosty moon rode high over the Broad.

'To hell with later, Frank. Nothing's going to spoil and the soup's gone cold already. Let's celebrate in all that wonderful romantic moonlight!'

'Well, just down to the staithe and back,' Frank conceded. He took her arm as they walked and was a little shocked by its fragility. In the darkness she clung close and her happiness was so strong that even the dog was affected by it, capering ahead, diving into clumps of bush, rousing the sleepers therein to a sleepy chirp.

'We'll buy that bed tomorrow.' Frank was planning busily as they returned to the lamplit kitchen. 'And a piece of carpet, some curtains – all the things you'll need.'

'Do you have a double bed, Frank?'

He had been eating curry in between sentences but when she spoke she saw him stop for a moment, perfectly still. Then he glanced up at her. There was a warning in his glance that she did not fully understand.

'Yes, I do. Why?'

The warning had been too open to ignore; she said feebly: 'Then may I have one too? In case of – of one of your sisters or – someone wanting to stay?'

'Certainly. And now you've got to try my marmalade pudding. I think you'll find it's quite delicious. You've been put off by the thought rather than the taste.'

As she ate the pudding and commented favourably, Suzie told herself not to be so brassy and brash. Frank was only human. It would not be long before he was as eager to share her bed as she was to share his. It was just that he was a decent, law-abiding man with a sense of responsibility and with a deep respect for the right way of doing things. He had seen what happened to promiscuous men – his Uncle Louis, far away in Australia, and his brother, with a whining and discontented wife and a demanding mistress. Frank would think very carefully before taking a step as profound as sleeping with her – but that he would do so in the end was a certainty.

So Suzie ate her marmalade pudding and then helped Frank to make up the couch in front of the fire, and when he had left her, she snuggled down quite contentedly on its narrow cushions. It would all turn out the way she wanted it to, now that she had been accepted as a member of the small household.

22

Frank telephoned Con's chambers in Cathedral Street from the alcove on Guildhall Hill, just beside the Public Benefit Tailor's shop. As luck would have it, however, Con's secretary informed Frank crisply that her employer was at the Guildhall today, prosecuting in a motoring offence.

'I'm not far from the Guildhall,' Frank told her, squinting sideways to where the façade of that building could be seen. 'Do they break for luncheon, or do they carry on, munching sandwiches or something when no one's looking?'

'If the case seems likely to be a long one, they usually adjourn at about one o'clock, Mr Frank. But if the magistrates see that the case may be brought to a speedy conclusion then they may well continue on past that hour. In my judgement, the court will probably adjourn at one o'clock today, since it is a somewhat complicated case. But I could be wrong, of course.'

'I see.' Frank consulted his wristwatch and saw that it wanted but ten minutes to one o'clock. 'I suppose I can pop in, can I, and take a look to see how things are proceeding? I very much want to speak to Mr Solstein.'

'I'm sure that would be acceptable, Mr Frank; it's not as if it were a matrimonial or were being heard in camera. Goodbye, sir.'

Frank replaced his receiver and emerged from his alcove, wondering how Miss Barker spoke when she was not being the perfect young solicitor's secretary. Probably very much as she had just spoken to him, for she was a middle-aged spinster who adored Con and seemed to live for her work.

He glanced up towards the Guildhall just as Con, beautiful in a dark suit and a dazzlingly white shirt, came round the corner of the building. He headed for the line of cabs opposite the market but heard Frank's shrill whistle and grinned, crossing the road to greet his cousin.

'What's all this? You up on the spree, old boy? I thought you'd have been ankle deep in sawdust at this hour, or munching your way through one of Suzie's ploughman's lunches!' He shot a penetrating look at Frank and his manner changed. 'What's up?'

'If you've got a moment, I thought we could lunch together and have a talk. I rang your chambers and Miss Barker told me where you were. Look, Backs is pretty close. We could have a beer and some sandwiches. Or if you want a proper luncheon there's White's.'

Con took his cousin's arm. 'Backs and sandwiches will suit me fine; I've got to be back here in an hour. Unless it's something very confidential, in which case you may find Backs full of friends.'

'I'll chance it,' Frank said briefly. 'And I don't have any friends who'd come up and interfere between us – they'd get pretty short shrift if they tried!'

They reached the Haymarket and turned into the Elizabethan room, with its panelled walls and ceiling, all dark and smelling of food and beer, crowded with men perched on every available surface, munching and drinking.

'There's my partner – he's just finishing. We'll grab that corner table,' Con muttered, steering Frank through the crowd. 'Hello, Symons, Felton; may we bag your places?'

Mr Symons was whitehaired and wore *pince-nez,* and Andy Felton, an extremely able barrister, was a tanned young man whose favourite recreation was sailing; and though so different the two of them were close friends. They greeted the cousins, then slid out of their settle behind the small round table.

'You're more than welcome, Solstein; I recommend the beef and pickle sandwiches,' Mr Symons said primly.

'Good day to you both.'

Behind his senior's back, Andy winked, then they were lost in the crowd.

'Nice chaps,' Frank ventured as he and Con squeezed on to the high backed settle and gestured to the waitress. 'I wouldn't change the boatyard for anything, but sometimes – just sometimes – I feel I need someone to talk to, and Ben isn't much of a one for conversation, though his grunts sometimes speak volumes.'

Con's eyebrows climbed. 'I thought you had someone? If I lived with Suzie I'm sure I shouldn't complain that I'd no one to talk to – does she ever stop for breath?'

'I can't talk to her about this.' The waitress came up and took their order, then left them again. 'I need to be told what to do!'

'I see; I hope you aren't after free professional advice, because if so you'd best not tell Symons, nor Felton neither; they'd both of them charge the Archangel Gabriel if he asked the way to heaven – and they don't belong to the Chosen People, either, so they've no excuse.' Con grinned his crooked, monkey grin. 'Now I wouldn't charge you – or not above a tenner, at any rate!'

The waitress, obviously harassed, dumped two foaming pints of beer and a plate of chunky sandwiches in front of them. Frank fished out the money and tossed it on to her tray and she gave him a distracted smile before disappearing into the crowd once more.

'It's about Suzie. You know she came to housekeep for me because they wouldn't let her go on nursing? Said she wasn't fit enough?'

'I know that was the story. True, was it? Your sister assured me that Suzie had been after you for years, and that it was just an excuse to get into your house. Well?'

'She's ill; in fact quite a lot worse than she knows. I took her up to London a couple of weeks ago, to see that doctor chap she's got such faith in – Mr Abbott. He did a lot of tests, told her to rest and get plenty of fresh air and good food, and told me to take her home. But when he rang through on Monday he got put on to me, out in the shed, and it was a different story. He told me she's going downhill, and of course he recommended me to see that she took his advice. But he said there were traces of blood in the sputum samples. The summer's a bad time for consumption, it seems, but he said if she made it through to the autumn she might regain a measure of health during the winter months.'

There was a short, shocked silence. Then Con spoke, his voice hushed.

'Consumption! And Suzie, of all people! Frank, I'm sorrier than I can say, but surely he doesn't mean she's going to *die*? Not if she takes care, heeds his advice? Damn it, she's only our age!'

'Have you seen her lately, Con? I swear I'd not noticed how thin she's got, how slowly she moves, until he pointed it out. And then I knew that the improvement she talks about is just an illusion.'

'Yes, but . . . did he hold out no hope? What about a sanatorium? I've heard there are places in Switzerland which do miracles. We'd all help with the cost, you know that.'

Frank shook his head. 'Mr Abbott seems to know and he says it's a disease that moves either slowly or very fast, and she's deteriorating fast. He doesn't think she'll last much longer than next spring.'

'Does she know?'

'She knows she isn't a lot better, but she definitely doesn't know she's worse. I think it's because nursing was such a strain that she finds the quieter pace of life easier and thinks she's getting stronger. But I'm afraid she'll notice, unless I can do something to take her mind right off it.'

Con took a huge bite out of a sandwich. 'Such as? You could send her to Switzerland under some pretext.'

'It wouldn't work. I've already suggested it and she just laughed at me. I thought . . . marriage.'

'Marriage?' Con's eyebrows shot up almost into his hair. 'But she's living with you – isn't that enough?'

Frank's voice sank to a mumble. 'I'm not sleeping with her, Con. I've never even tried to make love to her. I've found a thousand excuses for myself but the truth is I didn't believe I could make love to anyone. Ever since the war I've kept clear of women because I've thought that the gassing and the other business had combined to make me impotent – or different, at least. The way I see it now is that if I married her, showed her she was the one person I really cared about, then she wouldn't mind so much – that I've never seduced her, I mean.'

'I'm sorry as hell about Suzie, Frank, you know that.' Con regarded his cousin with open curiosity. 'But are you trying to tell me that you've never done it? Not even once, when you were sixteen or so?'

'That's right.'

'And you think that marrying Suzie will convince her she's the one you love? If so, she's remarkably obtuse. I've known for ever how you felt about Mabs, even when we were kids.'

'Yes. But Mabs is married. Gone. It's taken me a while to come to terms with it, but I think I've done it. She isn't going to come walking across my yard one day, like in a romantic novel, to tell me she can't live without me. She's happily married to her Frenchman and probably never spares me a thought.'

'Then Desmond's oft-voiced suspicions that you'd had a crack at Mabs in Yarmouth and it was that which made her bolt were false?'

'False as hell. If Des and Suzie hadn't turned up I don't say things would have continued so – so platonic, but as it was I didn't have a chance to blot my copybook. I meant to marry her; you know that.'

For a moment the two young men sat in silence, contemplating what might have been. Then Con sighed and spoke.

'Right, Franko, then I take it you want advice of a purely emotional nature. You want to know if it's right to marry a woman just because she's dying.' He paused, but Frank said nothing so he continued. 'Morally or ethically it might be wrong, I don't know, but in your shoes I'd marry her.'

'You would? I'm glad, Con, because I'm going to. Will you stand by me, old fellow? We'll have a quiet wedding, but I'd like you to be there.'

'Wild horses wouldn't keep me away.' Con took the last sandwich, then wagged a finger at Frank. 'One thing, though; have you thought that she might not . . . oh, hang it, that she might . . .'

'Might not die? I'd give my right hand to have her live, but if there was no danger to her life I wouldn't have considered marrying her. I'm selfish, I suppose. But having considered it, it's what I want. I'm fonder of Suzie than anyone bar Mabel. And I told myself last night when I was lying in bed and wishing I could sleep that Mabs is probably completely different now. Fat, with a family of spoilt little French kids and down-at-heel shoes. I might not even recognise her, let alone want her. No, I'm not afraid of regretting the marriage, even if it lasts a normal lifespan. I – I dread losing Suzie. It's going to be hard anyway, but I've a shrewd feeling it will be harder after we're married.'

'That's something you'll find the strength to face when it happens,' Con said sombrely. He pushed the table back and stood up. 'Walk back to the Guildhall with me? On second thoughts, I've got another thirty minutes before I'm in court again, so I'll walk back to the Essex with you – where did you park her?'

The two cousins walked companionably back along the Haymarket to where Frank had left his car.

Suzie crossed the yard, nodding to the men at work in the big boatshed, and dived into the woods which surrounded the yard. She had a special place down by the water which even Frank did not know about, where she went sometimes to be alone.

She reached the glade and settled herself comfortably on the fallen tree-trunk with the clear view across the water, deserted in the October sunshine, reached into her pocket for a packet of cigarettes and drew one out, then hesitated.

Frank hated her smoking and she had all but given it up, to please him. Only when she was very unhappy had she come here to smoke and weep, and now she was happier than she had ever been. She put the cigarette back, then knelt down and scraped at the soft, peaty earth until she had a fairly deep hole. She put the packet of cigarettes into the grave, laid her lighter on top, then snatched the lighter back before burying the packet and patting the topsoil into firmness once more. No point in destroying a perfectly good lighter along with the demon tobacco!

The gesture having been made, she leaned back on her tree stump and let her thoughts wander. Marriage! She had dreamed of so many things; of the moment when Frank would realise that he wanted her, would steal across the landing into her room, slip into her bed, make love to her! Or sometimes she would imagine herself at a party, the belle of the ball, with men vying for her attention and Frank at last realising what he was missing, so that he came to her, cast himself at her feet . . . yet strangely enough, marriage itself had never entered into her imaginings because it had seemed too unlikely!

For a long time, she had been unable to believe that he could resist her. She had worn her most provocative dresses, had planned 'accidental' meetings on the landing when she was in her négligé. She had tried dressing up and not dressing at all. And whatever she did he behaved with perfect friendliness and courtesy. She could not even reproach him for his apparent indifference to her, because he had made it crystal clear that she might live in his house as a guest or a housekeeper, but never as his mistress.

And now she knew that he was not indifferent! He had taken her to London to see Mr Abbott and insisted that they book into an hotel for a couple of nights so that they could take in a show. To be sure, they had had single rooms, but he had been sweet, putting his arm round her in the theatre, taking her to tiny, candlelit restaurants and buying the most exotic food on the menu, going with her to the smart clothes shops and splashing out his money on an absurd but gorgeous Chinese garment with a high collar and long, full sleeves, vividly embroidered, the soft silk of the skirt whispering right down to the floor so that when winter came she could be warm in the draughty cottage.

He was different himself, more relaxed, with a softening

of his attitude towards her. It was because she was better, of course. Mr Abbott was determined to get her right so had insisted on another year's rest, but he knew she was better too. In a year, she thought hopefully, when Mr Abbott told them, Frank will be used to me around his house and won't want me to leave. In the meantime, she would be very careful. Her cough had improved a little and she scarcely ever got breathless now, or wheezed when she hurried. Smiling to herself, she thought that she hurried so little – and would hurry less, for yesterday, when Frank had returned from a business trip to Norwich, he had stopped off in the village on his way home.

'There's a girl, Madge, coming in for a few hours each day in future to do the rough work. And I've brought you something pretty.'

'A girl to help with the rough work – goodness, Frank, I do little enough now; just a bit of cooking and cleaning!'

'You'll do less, then, because I want you fit again. Aren't you going to ask to see what I've bought you?'

She nodded, and he drew a small box out of his pocket.

'Close your eyes then, and hold out your hand.'

She obeyed, holding out her left hand palm uppermost. She felt it gently turned over, and then a ring was slipped on to the third finger. She opened her eyes and saw that it was a cluster of emeralds on a narrow gold band, and that his fingers still held her own.

'Oh, Frank, it's beautiful!'

She was still admiring it when she suddenly saw that it was on her engagement finger. She looked up at him, not daring to ask the question which hovered on her lips. Was it an accident, or . . . ?

'Darling Suzie, will you marry me?'

With true feminine logic she had promptly burst into tears and it was during his efforts to stem the flood that Frank had kissed her for the very first time. And then his arms were round her, he was cradling her against his chest, telling her that he had been *afraid* to ask her to marry him!

'Because of the gassing I've never been with a woman, my darling, and you've never pretended to be an innocent.

I'd begun to doubt whether I could be anyone's lover, and you – you were so beautiful, self-confident, that you frightened me!'

She remembered the evening with dazed pleasure. He was going to marry her. They would continue to live in the cottage unless there was a good reason for moving out – his face looked so shy and proud when he said that – but he would have the whole place redecorated and refurnished, and she should choose how it was to be done.

'I like the cottage the way it is,' she had insisted stoutly, and was rewarded by his relieved grin.

'So do I, but it isn't very smart or modern, I know. We'll do the bedroom up, though, with some pale sort of carpet and matching curtains, like my mother's room at home. And I'll buy a new bed, one of those divan things Mother wanted me to have. You deserve the best!'

'I've got the best, or will have once the knot's tied.' She reached up and kissed his chin. 'When can we get married? You said a quiet ceremony, just for family; but I don't have any family now except my aunt!'

'Share mine; goodness knows there are enough of them! Stella's got the most frightful bounder in tow now, Paul something or other, and then there's Josette – you always liked her, and she'll leave her social work in London for our wedding, I'm sure. Des and Beryl can't very well be left out, nor their batch of runny-nosed kids, and there's Auntie Sarah and Simon and Cara. What about your friends? Wouldn't you like to invite some of 'em from London? We'll have a cosy supper party at the Wherry after the ceremony, and we'll hire every available bedroom for the night so that no one has to drive home. How about it?'

'Not the London crowd, but a few schoolfriends.' She hesitated, glancing up at him, her eyes exactly matching the emeralds on her finger as he had known they would. 'You know Mabs was almost my only friend at one time, certainly my dearest friend; but she won't be able to come, so might I ask her parents?'

'You don't think she'd leave France just for a wedding? Probably you're right. As for the Walters, you don't imagine any Neyler could get married and not ask them, do you? I don't want any hurt feelings either, so Ruthie and Edie must come, and Alice – she's part of the family – and then there's Nanny Sutton, only she's Mrs Butcher now, and the Sollies, and Auntie Becky, and the Siegals . . . did I say a quiet wedding?'

And now, sitting on her tree-trunk with the cigarettes symbolically buried beneath her feet and a new life opening up before her, Suzie vowed that she would make Frank forget Mabel. She had seen the way his fingers had clenched when she had mentioned her friend, how the air had seemed, for an instant, to be charged with an emotion she did not understand. Love of a sort for Mabel still lingered, but she would dispel it! She would show him that real love was a two-way emotion with physical as well as mental harmony essential to its blossoming, and it was real love that they would share!

Through the belt of trees which hid her from the yard she heard a dog yap once, sharply, and knew that Patch had spotted Frank. She got to her feet. In a couple of weeks they would be man and wife and there was a lot to plan still, including the honeymoon. Frank was insistent that they honeymooned in style and had offered her the choice between a cruise, a month in France or a month in Switzerland. At the mention of a honeymoon she had cried again. She wanted so much to be a virgin for him, nervous of the thought of being alone with her lover in some strange hotel room. He knew the reason for her tears without being told and had hugged her and laughed at her, telling her that the Suzie he wanted to marry was the same Suzie who had delighted him with her naughtiness when they were children, and that her many love affairs were only the result of her sweetness and generosity.

She emerged from the shelter of the trees and saw Frank carrying a tin of paint from the boat which he had just rowed across the Broad to the shed. He called out: 'Hello, gorgeous; miss me?' and her heart thumped so hard that it made her cough, for he had said it in front of the men working in the shed, had proclaimed his partiality aloud for all to hear.

When he had delivered the paint they went indoors and Suzie made scones and then they sat down by the fire and discussed honeymoons, bedroom wallpaper, and where they should hold the reception. And Suzie tried to forget the niggling fact that never, for all his own sweetness and generosity, had he said he loved her.

'Didn't Suzie look charming? I'm sure she was delighted to have a proper wedding, even though Frank kept insisting they wanted to be married quietly. All that white satin, and the veil so fine it seemed to float after her down the aisle. Didn't Stella and Josette make charming bridesmaids, too, one so fair and the other so dark! Ted? Are you listening?'

Tina was sitting in front of her dressing-table, brushing her hair. The room had just been redecorated in pale green with a mossy carpet and curtains and bedding the colour of young beech leaves. Tina, her glossy black locks outlined against the reflection of an alcove of soft, dull sage colour, looked at Ted in the glass and frowned. Despite Frank's early objections it had been a very big wedding indeed, with a marquee on the lawn and two hundred guests thronging the garden and reception rooms of The Pride. It had been a great deal of work, Tina reflected now, quite a society wedding, but she was not one bit repentant, for naturally Frank and Suzie had preferred it, in the end, to a dull family affair.

Ted put his hands on her shoulders and grinned at her reflection. He touched her hair with his chin, thinking that it was still dark and thick, though there might be a white hair here and there if one looked closely. He never looked closely. He did not need to; he knew her as he knew himself and he knew, too, that her remark had been caused by guilt, that she had spoken because she wanted his reassurance that they had done the right thing by giving their son a big wedding.

'Yes, Suzie looked charming, and what's more she'll remember her lovely wedding all her life, and that's the object of the exercise, isn't it? But that dreadful Cunningham youth was drunk as a newt, and it grieves me to see Stella ignoring decent young men and taking up with bounders.' He smoothed down his hair with one hand and sighed. 'She'll marry in haste and repent in leisure!'

'Marry in haste? At twenty-two?' protested Tina. 'It's high time she was married. I just wish she'd never met young Cunningham. But I don't want to think about them. I want to think about Frank and Suzie. They're spending tonight in London, aren't they, and catching the boat-train to France first thing in the morning?'

'That's right. Remember our honeymoon? And that awful journey up to Inverness, and you falling asleep with all your clothes on and waking up in a bate because you'd had no grub? And blaming me for everything?'

'I remember.' Tina turned and rubbed her head against his striped pyjama jacket. 'I was so nervous, you know. That was why I smacked you, and shouted. They're much more sophisticated these days, though. I expect Suzie's quite experienced already. But I daresay Frank doesn't mind.'

'I daresay you're right. Come to bed, darling. We can lie in tomorrow, and let someone else bring us breakfast for once.'

They climbed into bed and presently Tina heard a small snore, then a deeper one. Sighing, she drove an elbow briskly into Ted's well-covered ribs and then, when he merely grunted, heaved him from his back on to his side. The snoring stopped. So much for romance, Tina thought ruefully, and curled round her husband, snug against him. How long ago was it? Getting on for thirty years ago he wouldn't have gone to sleep so promptly! She thought of Frank, in bed with Suzie in some large, impersonal London hotel. She hoped they would be as happy as she and Ted, but secretly she thought that theirs was a state of bliss which could only be achieved in rare cases. A housekeeper, however much Frank might pretend that she was a fully trained nurse, was still a housekeeper. Any girl who managed to woo Frank into matrimony had Tina's approval, but she was still a very ordinary girl. Unlikely to be one of those rare women who achieve complete matrimonial bliss.

Content with her lot, Tina joined Ted in slumber.

'Well, Suzie, home in three more days. Enjoyed it? What do you think of the sunny south?'

Frank and Suzie were strolling along the harbour at La Coquel, a tiny but increasingly popular fishing port on the Côte d'Azur whose shingle and sand beaches and tiny cafés had conquered the young Neylers' hearts. It was a day of peaceful, golden sunlight, the blue sky flecked with white overhead, the breeze no more than a whisper. Suzie smiled up at her husband and squeezed his hand.

'It's wonderful, and the holiday's been wonderful, and *you're* wonderful! But home's pretty good too, so I shan't be unhappy to leave. And to tell you the truth, I keep wondering how Patch is getting on and whether he's eating properly. Suppose he's a skeleton when we get back? Would you ever forgive me?'

He put his arm round her waist and hugged her to him. 'Naturally I'd blame you for insisting on a French honeymoon! Fool! Now look, are you sure you don't want to come with me to see this fellow? It's mean to transact business on our honeymoon, but this Bernard's got a new way of putting his cruisers together which interests me, and he's perfectly willing for me to glance at his plans and talk things over. It might mean business for the yard too, because there are one or two things we do which he's intrigued about. You know you can come if you like, but I don't want to bore you with technical discussions.'

'I shan't be bored because I'm not coming to the offices with you. See that café? The one with the green and white striped awning and the orange trees in tubs? I'm going to sit down at one of those little tables, order coffee and cognac and be peaceful. I'll write some letters and when you come out we can stay there and have a spot of luncheon. Does that sound nice?'

'Lovely, if you're sure.' He walked her to the café, then pointed to the other side of the harbour. 'See that tall building with the blue door? If you want me, just go through it into the reception place and ask for Monsieur Bernard. I shan't be long, if you're sure you don't mind?'

She laughed and that made him laugh too, then he raised a hand and set off along the cobbled quay and she watched him disappear behind the blue door where, if she was any judge, he and Monsieur Bernard would be engaged in dull discussions for a good deal longer than the hour or so he had promised. However, it did not worry her, for first she would drink the lovely dark coffee and follow it up with a tiny glass of sparkling cognac, and then she would nibble some of those delicious little biscuits, salty on the outside, sweetish on the inside. Then she would write some letters, whilst the pigeons who lived in the old warehouse buildings opposite came down and squabbled with the gulls for any scraps she might throw them, and finally she would walk further along the quay, to where the taciturn, bearded, bereted French artist usually sat, and buy a picture of the harbour to hang in Frank's office when they got home.

Her morning planned, she sat back in the surprisingly comfortable wicker chair in the dreamy sunshine and contemplated the harbour. Because of the increasing popularity of the place there were several yachts moored incongruously amongst the fishing boats bobbing on the dirty harbour water. One of them had only lately docked, she realised – a sleek navy blue and white hull, the sails already folded, and aboard the bustle which obviously preceded a party coming to land. She could see a man, a boy, some sort of golden retriever which barked once and was sharply reprimanded in French. Idly, she watched as the man and the boy crossed the deck and came ashore. They were strolling towards her now, the man tall and distinguished-looking, with dark hair winged with silver, deeply tanned skin and dark eyes which regarded the little boy affectionately as the child hurried beside him, chattering in shrill accents. Something about the man caught her attention. He was extraordinarily handsome and his clothes were good – a dark blue silk shirt and a pair of cream slacks. Of whom did he remind her?

She gave up the puzzle and looked instead at his companion, a little boy as blond as the man was dark. Blue-eyed, too, unless she was much mistaken, and with a look of . . . she nearly gasped with shock. Frank! How odd to see a little boy who could have been Frank's double at the same age in France, of all places! She was just thinking how funny it would be if the boy were a by-blow of Frank's, how she would tease him, when without any conscious effort she knew who they both were. A glimpse of a photograph years ago, a fragment of talk, and she knew without a shadow of doubt that this was Mabel's husband and her son by Desmond Neyler.

Suzie jumped to her feet. She must stop them, speak to them! If Mabel was here too, now was the time to lay the ghost, for surely Frank would accept her loss if he saw her with her handsome husband and beautiful little son? But in jumping to her feet she overturned her cognac, which splashed all across the peach-coloured linen of her skirt, and then the glass rolled off the table and shattered on the paving. Two waiters appeared, one with a cloth to sponge madame's skirt, the other with a brush and pan to clear up the glass. It only took a moment or so, but that was enough. When she looked up again, the couple had disappeared.

Slowly sitting down again, Suzie realised that she was bathed in perspiration and that her heart was beating uncomfortably fast. She felt as if a band enclosed her chest, squeezing her ribs, constricting her heart, and she could feel heat flooding her cheeks. She sat very still for ten minutes, feeling her heartbeats gradually slow to normal, the perspiration cool on her skin. Consciously she forced herself to relax, not to think, and only when the tension had ebbed completely did she allow herself to consider the situation.

What on earth would she have said, for a start, had she reached Monsieur de Recourte? It was a blessing that she had spilled the cognac. But the Recourtes had come off that yacht; she glanced towards it. If they had done so there was a good chance that Mabel was still aboard. She considered the question of what to do calmly. The town was a small one, and the yacht would probably remain moored in the harbour for the rest of the day at least. Should she suggest to Mabel that they behave in a sensible, civilised way and meet for luncheon, all five of them? Or should she cut her losses and try to persuade Frank to leave?

She turned to glance at the yacht and went cold, then hot. Standing on the deck, leaning on the rail, was a slender figure in a navy blue and white suit. She was staring across at the building into which Frank had disappeared not twenty minutes earlier as if she could sense that somewhere inside it was the man she had once loved. Or loved still? Suzie could not say, but neither could she sit here and wait for Frank to emerge and see Mabel.

She got up and went into the café, paying the waiter who was leaning against the bar and having a quick swig from a bottle of red wine. Then she sallied forth into the sunshine, heading with determination towards the yacht. When she neared it, she moved across so that she could see Mabel's face. It was calm enough, but her gaze never moved from the blue door, and the look in her eyes made Suzie ache for her. But she could not allow Frank to see that expression!

'Hello, Mabs. I thought it was you! I spotted you from the café over there, where I've been drinking cognac. Would you care to join me?'

Mabel started violently and one hand flew to her throat. Suzie's eyes flickered over her friend's glossy hair, the deep golden tan of her skin, the slim fingers loaded with rings, the nails, polished ovals of perfection. She looked very beautiful, and not old enough to be that little boy's mother.

'I'm sorry if I surprised you, Mabs, but I was sure you'd seen Frank, and would guess I was somewhere in La Coquel.'

Mabel shook her head, then came over to the gangway, gesturing to Suzie to join her.

'No. That is, I thought I saw Frank, but I often think I see . . . people. It didn't occur to me that it really was him, nor that you'd be with him. But just in case, I stayed aboard when Matthieu and André went ashore. I wouldn't want to bump into him accidentally, not with André in tow. Look, come aboard and have coffee with me. We can't stand out here all morning.'

She ushered Suzie on board and down into a large, airy

cabin where the remains of a continental breakfast still littered the table. A manservant was clearing away at lightning speed but in response to a volley of French from Mabel he picked up his tray and vanished in the direction of the galley.

'He'll bring us fresh coffee presently, and croissants. Do sit down and tell me why you and Frank – I take it you're with Frank? – are in France?'

Suzie lay back in her chair and looked coolly across at Mabel.

'Certainly. We're on our honeymoon. Didn't you know?'

'I believe my mother did write something about a wedding, but it seemed such ages ago, and I thought . . . well, let me wish you both happiness.' Mabel's smile was brief and barely changed the look of stunned disbelief on her face. She turned towards the door. '*François, le café vite, s'il vous plaît.*'

'Thank you. We are happy. Look, Mabs, I thought it might be better if we all met for luncheon, André as well, of course. But . . . I wonder now if it would be wise? It would be difficult for me to persuade Frank to leave here, but perhaps you might tell Matthieu that you'd prefer somewhere brighter, with more nightlife? I find I'm – I'm afraid.'

The manservant brought a tray with a silver coffee pot, a tall silver jug of hot water and another of milk which he placed before Mabel, then returned with another tray laden with a variety of bread and cakes. Mabel thanked him dismissively and when he had gone turned to Suzie once more.

'I don't want to meet. It seems incredible that you've forgotten who fathered André, but I'm trusting that you've never told Frank?' And then, as Suzie dumbly shook her head: 'Well, you goose, what do you think Frank would feel? To know, for certain, that I'd run away because his hateful brother had raped me? And even if you can bear to contemplate that, just think about Matthieu for a moment. He's never met Des, so he'll naturally assume that Frank is the man who treated me so badly, because André's very like both boys. As for leaving, Matthieu's come all this way to see a man who builds yachts and cruisers and I can't think of a single convincing reason for just abandoning the place without seeing Monsieur Bernard.'

'Oh, God!' Suzie felt the band begin to tighten round her chest. 'Monsieur Bernard is Frank's contact too. He's there now, in his offices.'

'No!' Mabel abandoned her pretence of calm and began to wring her hands. 'Suzie, what are we to do? I dare not let Matthieu see Frank. He might kill him! I beg you to go!'

Suzie put a shaking hand to her head. Her skin felt cold and clammy. She reached for the coffee which Mabel had just poured and raised the cup to her lips. The china chattered against her teeth for moments before she could summon the strength to sip it, but it helped. After half the cup had been laboriously drunk, she felt the band begin to loosen its grip.

'I c-could pretend to be ill. If I did, and said I wanted to go home now instead of in three days, I think Frank would take me.' She shot a look at Mabel, half defiant, half pleading. 'He's very fond of me – loves me – and he wouldn't make me stay here against my will.'

Mabel was staring at her friend. A shade of anxiety crossed her face, then she leaned over and put a hand on Suzie's forehead.

'You don't have to pretend; you *are* ill! Suzie, what's the matter?'

'Oh, I'm all right now, but I've had food poisoning. I adore lobster, but I do believe it was that.' She watched the concern leave Mabel's face. 'Very well, I'll persuade Frank to leave.'

She got up, and had to cling to the table for a moment before turning towards the door which led on to the deck.

'Suzie. I wish you didn't have to rush off, but I do understand.' Mabel had risen too and now she crossed the room and touched the other's arm. 'I know it's silly, but I would love to see Frank, just for a minute, close. To see how he's changed, and so on. Could you bring him past the yacht? I promise I won't come on deck or let him see me, I'd just like to see him again.'

'I can't tell which way he'll go when we leave Monsieur Bernard's office,' Suzie said guardedly. 'But I'll do my best.'

She left the yatch with a brief wave to Mabel, then made her way over to the blue door. As luck would have it, Frank had finished his business and greeted her warmly.

'Darling, how kind of you to come and meet me! Monsieur Bernard has recommended an excellent place for lunch, right round by the mole. We can stroll along the harbour and look at the boats and then try the seafood at Pierre's.'

Suzie's heart skipped a beat. 'Oh, not that harbour again! Why can't we strike into the centre of the town and then drop down that road with the vines growing on the hill and reach the mole from there? A change of scene.'

He agreed without demur and she led him away, past the artist, who scowled at them because they walked across his little length of cobbles, away from the yacht and Mabel. She thought of Mabel, pressed close to the cabin window, hungry for just a glimpse of Frank, and knew a pang of pity, but her steps did not even falter. Frank was hers now, and she dared not risk him so close to Mabel. Suppose he sensed her presence, as she had thought at first that Mabel had sensed his? Resolutely, she walked on.

23: 1926

Suzie had a bed downstairs in the main living room of the cottage, and Frank had a lean-to kitchen and a downstairs lavatory built on so that she should not have to climb the stairs. Today she was sitting up, writing a letter, with the pale spring sunshine flooding in through the small windows which looked out on to the yard. When it was really warm, Frank usually propped the door open so that he could keep an eye on her, call across, but it had been chilly when he left so the door had remained closed.

When the door opened, she put down her letter and at once smiled joyously, for she thought that Frank must have returned earlier than expected from Lowestoft, but instead Con came into the room.

'Good morning, my love! Frank rang yesterday and said he'd be in Lowestoft this morning so I thought I'd steal a march on him and come and visit you.' He crossed the room, put his hands on her shoulders, and surveyed her solemnly. 'You make an incredibly pretty invalid!'

'Oh, Con, not an invalid! Frank says that quite soon . . .' Her voice faltered, then picked up strength again. 'Quite soon I'll be up and about again, now that spring's come. However, I'm beautifully spoiled at the moment, what with Frank fussing, and Mrs Fennell coming in to cook when Madge is off for a few hours, and visitors bringing me pretty things.'

Con laughed and took off his coat, then produced from his pocket a small, square box with a cellophane lid. Inside it, a miniature rose tree with perfect tiny roses, each one no bigger than a fingernail, grew in a tiny pot.

'Oh, Con!' She took the rose from him, devouring it with her eyes. 'Isn't it perfect? Put it near me, so I can enjoy it. June roses in April! I told you people spoiled me!'

'Next time, it'll be a bird in a gilded cage,' Con said teasingly. 'You may be tied to your bed, but the cage gets prettier each time I visit you.' He sat down on the chair by the bed and examined her. Her hands were transparently thin, her face was shadowed by the illness, but indomitable courage shone from her green eyes and her smile showed only her genuine pleasure in his company.

'I'm not caged, not when kind gentlemen leave the door ajar!' She shook her head as he went to move. 'No, I was teasing. I want to know all the gossip, and you can't talk freely with half the yard listening! Go on, amuse me!'

'Why else have I come over? But what about your letter? If you've nearly finished it shall I leave you and go and make a cup of coffee whilst you sign off? Then I could post it for you on my way home.'

'My letter?' Suzie's voice was vague. 'Oh, it's nearly finished, but it's not urgent. I'll finish it tomorrow. To tell you the truth, Con, I find writing terribly tiring. I read a lot though, especially now that I've stopped trying to knit or crochet.' She picked up her letter and leaned across to put it on her bedside table and caught her breath on a cough. As Con watched, she froze into a dreadful stillness, deathly afraid to move, even to breathe, until she had mastered the urge to cough, when she sagged against the pillows, then pulled out a large handkerchief and pressed it against her mouth. Speaking through it, she announced cheerfully: 'Mustn't cough! Now, Con, tell!'

Con became aware that he was tensed on the edge of his chair and leaned back too, pretending to consider. 'What should I tell you this time, I wonder? You know that Sarah's changed her mind about the divorce? Women are fickle in some ways and towers of strength in others. I admire Sarah immensely, and when you think what she's put up with . . .'

He continued in this vein for a while, then switched to an account of Stella's wedding to Paul Cunningham, which had been held two weeks previously despite great uneasiness in the family. He described Grandpa's new lady friend, for Arthur was turning out to be a regular lady-killer in his old age and favoured spats, violet hair oil and gold-topped canes, accompanied by flappers who hung on his every word and voiced the opinion that he was a 'darling old gentleman'. There was nothing even faintly unpleasant in all this elderly gallantry, but it caused his grandsons a good deal of amusement.

He told her about Ted's latest brilliant idea, which had been to stage a mannequin parade at the car saleroom and to serve champagne and pâté de fois gras to his customers. One of the mannequins, perched on the bonnet of a brand-new 11.9 Bean (ridiculous name for a car, Suzie remarked), had got oil on a gown valued at over a hundred guineas, and Ted had calmly taken it from her and lent her a pair of mechanic's overalls in its stead, gone down to the kitchen, and scrubbed it clean with a mixture of petrol and carbolic soap.

'It worked, too, which was what infuriated the designer,' Con told her. 'Whilst she was raving about the fine fabric and the delicate material and the cost of every stitch, Ted was treating it like a bit of old sacking and getting away with it!'

Suzie gave her tiny, breathless chuckle and Con remembered with a pang her old, carefree laugh and knew that he would never hear it again, for Suzie dared not laugh too freely. Or move too suddenly. Or cough.

'Hasn't your hair grown?' he said idly, in a pause. It was shoulder length, as thick and glossy as ever, waving luxuriantly across the pale skin of her shoulders, for her nightgown was sleeveless and low-cut.

'Yes, hasn't it? They say hair goes on growing . . .' She paused. 'Well, it goes on growing whatever your health is like,' she concluded breathlessly. 'Tell me more, Con!'

Con began to rattle on inanely, about his mother's spring cleaning, about Grandpa's Alice, who had turned the house upside down to find her birth certificate because she could not remember whether she was fifty now or next birthday, and, when she did find it, insisted on giving a party because she was only forty-nine. And all the time he was speaking his heart was aching for Suzie, because he knew all too well what she had been going to say. Hair goes on growing even after you're dead, that was what she had choked back. Yet she did not know on how slender a thread her life hung, Frank had assured him of that.

Presently, he saw she was almost sleeping. There was a lovely smile on her face, but her eyes were closed and presently the smile faded and she turned her head into the pillow. He leaned over to pull the covers up across her bare shoulder, and sent her letter fluttering on to the floor. He tucked the blankets round her, then picked up the sheet of paper. She must tire easily, he thought, for there were only a few short sentences, written in Suzie's round, childlike handwriting. He read them at a glance, without any intention of prying on her.

For a long moment afterwards he just sat, the page in his hand. So simple the words, and so practical.

> *Dear Mabel, Frank married me*
> *because I was dying. It will be*
> *soon. Could we meet before I go*?

Presently, his composure regained, he put the letter softly down on the bedside table and leaned back in the chair. Of course she knew. She had been a nurse, she was a sensible girl still. And how much harder it must be to pretend ignorance, to join joyfully in the game of 'getting well' which Frank played so determinedly! After about ten minutes she stirred and gasped and he heard the wheeze and gurgle of her chest as she struggled against a cough. It was unbearably painful to sit there helpless whilst she fought her lonely, hopeless fight and Con's courage suddenly drained away. He got up and stole over to the door. His hand was actually on the doorhandle when she spoke.

'Con? Have you got to go now?'

He turned back. The game needed two people, and it must be played to the finish.

'No, I'm not leaving, I was just slipping out for a word with the men whilst you slept. I'm not used to people dropping off in the middle of my best stories, I might tell you! I hear noises from the kitchen, so I'll ask Mrs Thing to make us some tea, and then I'll tell you about Val's unanimous letter . . .'

Mabel came. She received the letter and read it, then cried all over Matthieu, who patted her and petted her and insisted that she should go back to England to see her friend for the last time. It was painful, perhaps, but it was his wife's duty and he knew she would not shrink from it.

Nor did she. Ten days after Suzie had despatched the letter Mabel walked into the living room.

'Suzie? Oh, my dear!'

The two girls embraced and Mabel felt the skeletal thinness of the body inside the frilled pink nightgown and tried to hide the shock that Suzie's appearance had given her. That lovely hair had been cropped short again and was dull and lifeless, the once-glowing skin pale and waxy, and her eyes and teeth seemed far too large for her small face, fined down to bone by the disease.

'It was good of you – to come so far, Mabs. It's taken some – arranging!'

Suzie's voice was a thread, but the mischief was there, the life-force. It seemed impossible that she could be dying, yet Mabel had been aware of the nearness of death as soon as she touched her friend.

'Yes, I'm sure it did. I do hope, darling Suzie, that you managed to send him off with Con for the day? Con said it was all arranged when he spoke to me on the phone.'

Suzie winked conspiratorially. Death parodying life. Mabel clutched her handbag tightly and tried to listen and not to think.

'Yes. We had to think of – something really good. I pretended I wanted – one of the new mattresses.' She paused. It was clear that she could not talk for long without rest. 'He won't be back till late.'

'I see. Is there anyone else in the house?'

'Yes. I'm never – left. Madge is in the kitchen. She'll bring in – the trolley – presently.'

'That's fine, then.' Mabel was wearing a suit in what was described as crushed strawberry wild silk, and a dull pink cloche hat. She saw Suzie's eyes taking in every detail of her appearance and was glad she had not worn dark clothes. Taking off the hat she shook her hair free and then shed the suit jacket, for it was a warm day. The blouse beneath was a paler shade of pink and admirably tailored. She caught Suzie's eye and grinned.

'Paris, and fiendishly expensive! But Matthieu takes a pride in my appearance.'

Suzie touched her frilly nightgown.

'London. Frank likes me to look – nice, too.'

Mabel sat down on the edge of the bed and took her friend's hand. It lay in her own warm palm like a little claw, so cold and dry it felt.

'Darling Suzie, I know you asked me to come here so that we could talk about more important matters than Paris suits and London nighties! Is there anything I can do to help you, make things easier? I'll do anything within my power, or within Matthieu's.'

The head on the pillow nodded.

'Yes. I want to know – about your – marriage.'

'Very well.' It was more or less as she had expected, though she had not realised that Suzie would come straight out with the question. But time was short and they both knew it. 'Matthieu wanted a wife and, even more, a child. He's a fine person, Suzie, but he doesn't make love to women. Not to any woman. He *isn't* a sissy, really, but ours has always been a – a marriage of convenience, and the agreement is that he'll treat André as his own son and me as his wife in every sense but one, if I'm faithful to him and treat him as I would a more – more ordinary husband.'

'I see. I'm not terribly – surprised. Men that – handsome usually – marry young.'

'I suppose so. Matthieu hurts me sometimes by his jealousy and suspicion, though it's obvious why he's jealous and suspicious, even though I've not given him the slightest cause. He knows I once had intercourse with a man and gave birth to a son. He's afraid that one day I'll want what I'm obviously missing.' She sighed. 'He can't believe that my one and only experience of sex was horrible and frightening beyond belief. So he's safe, my poor Matthieu. I've got no desire to let anyone . . . well, anyway, that's our secret. You won't tell.'

'I won't. But you're still – in love with – Frank.'

It was a statement, but Mabel nodded.

'I suppose so. When we met last autumn I envied you so much! I feel terribly guilty now, but then all I could see was a normal marriage to a loving husband, the very things I had once wanted and needed, and which fate has denied me. I saw you touch, kiss, walk away with your arms round each other, and I knew you were in love. Then, for a moment, I wanted it *all* – the pain, the closeness, everything I can't have.'

Suzie's eyes closed. 'And me. And me.'

'I know, love. I know. But at least you've *experienced* these things, even though you've got to lose them! Frank loves you wholly, not . . .'

'No.' It was just a faint, husky whisper. 'It's the same – with us. All goodness, kindness, but no – physical marriage.' A tear slid down the pale cheek and one frail finger wiped it away. 'Dear Christ, Mabs, do love him! For me.'

'I do.' Mabel could not see Suzie's face through the shimmer of tears in her eyes. 'You know I do. I always have, and I can't change now.'

'Yes. But love's no – good from five – hundred – miles away.'

There was a clatter, then the kitchen door opened and Madge wheeled the tea trolley into the room, beaming at them both.

'In't that nice to have a friend come calling all the way from France? Afternoon, ma'am, I've made a foo of my own scones, what no one else don't know the recipe for, and thass as nice a cuppa tea in the pot as ever I made.' She swung the trolley dexterously around the rug and brought it alongside Mabel. 'Shall I pour, ma'am, or will you do th'honours?'

'I'll pour, Madge. Thanks very much. Everything looks delicious.'

Mabel poured tea into delicate china cups, arranged a slice of thin bread and butter, a dab of jam and a scone on a plate for her friend, and all the while she knew that Suzie would be fair; she would not make any deathbed wish to demand that she, Mabel, should desert her husband and come rushing back to look after Frank when she died. But she had left her friend in no doubt whatsoever that that was what she wanted. One day. When the time was ripe, she hoped and expected that Mabel would return to Frank, and she wanted Mabel to know that it was not only all right with her, it was her dearest wish.

'Here's your tea, love. You know I'll do my best. Is there anything else?'

Suzie sipped her tea. Her eyes had a dreamy, contented look, as if now the plea had been made she could stop worrying and rest. At her friend's question, she shook her head.

'No. There's only one other thing, and – Frank will see to – that.'

There must have been two hundred people at the funeral. All the Neylers were there, of course, and the Roses, the children subdued and miserable with black bands round their arms, for children had loved Suzie and she them. All the villagers came, showing their sympathy in the only way they knew, by wearing their best and subduing their voices; for East Anglians don't wear their hearts on their sleeves. And then there were friends. From London, from Norwich, from hospitals all over the country they came. And schoolfriends. Men, women and children who had loved Suzie in their different ways came to pay their last respects.

Con, standing at the graveside as the body was committed to the earth, thought bitterly that it should have been raining, then chided himself. A pale blue sky, new leaves clustering on the trees which surrounded the country churchyard, clouds scudding overhead gilded by the May sunshine and driven by the sort of breeze every yachtsman loves, that was the sort of day Suzie would have chosen to say goodbye on. She had been so full of life and laughter that it was fitting her last party should take place on a beautiful day.

The funeral tea was to be held, not at the cottage, but at the largest house in the village. The Matthews family had been good friends to Frank and Suzie,. and when they offered the use of their house Frank was glad to accept, knowing he could not have faced making the necessary arrangements himself.

Supporting his mother who had wept steadily throughout the very moving service, Con caught Frank's eye and they both grinned, the same thought occurring to each – how Suzie would have giggled to see Cecy, who had never approved of her, behaving like a human sprinkler!

Once they were all at the house protocol took over. Frank moved about being a good host, Con settled his mother in a chair between Auntie Tina and Auntie Rachel, and went off to fetch them some of the excellent buffet set out in the dining room. People were losing their diffidence now, and were beginning to talk, even to smile, and once again Con thought that this party was the poorer for Suzie's absence and blinked at his apparent inability to accept the fact of her death. Even in the churchyard, when Frank had stepped forward with a handful of the peaty black soil and dropped it on the coffin, he had been unable to convince himself that it was really Suzie down there, cold and silent in the dark.

A group of villagers were talking to Arthur and his Uncle Ted and he went towards them. Grandpa looked partriarchal and splendid in an old-fashioned black suit with his spade-shaped beard white as driven snow. He greeted Con cheerfully enough, but there was sadness and bewilderment in his eyes.

'A child so young, and the boy so new married,' he muttered to Con. 'A sad and terrible thing. Will you with your cousin stay, tonight? Eh? Would you do that for the old man? Alone he should not be, not tonight.'

'If he'll let me, Grandpa.' Con squeezed the old man's hand. 'I don't want to sound trite, but Suzie wouldn't want any weeping at the bar, you know. She'd have told you to have a drink and enjoy her last party.'

Ted, standing back, nodded and moved to stand between them. 'She was a good girl, and a gay one. It seems wrong that . . .'

'That the old man, who more than his share has seen, should drink at her funeral,' Arthur said. 'I would have gone to let the lass stay. Unfair, that I should live to see this day.'

'I know.' Con patted Arthur's arm. 'But consumption isn't fair; it doesn't attack only the elderly. Let me get you both a drink.'

After a couple of hours the rooms were thinning of people. Mrs Matthews pressed Frank to stay the night, but he refused, saying he had work to do and would be the better for doing it. By the time he and Con left, however, it was dark, and he was obviously glad of his cousin's company.

'You can keep mum or you can talk, old chap,' Con told him as he slid into the passenger seat of the Essex. 'But you've been on your best behaviour for hours; it'll do you good to relax and talk. I know more about the business than most, which might make it easier.'

Frank nodded and started the engine. 'Thanks, Con.'

They drove to the yard in silence, but as they walked into the cottage Frank spoke in a startled tone.

'There, Madge came back and I told her not to! I told her I'd probably get you to stay and that we . . .' His voice choked up and he stopped in the doorway for a moment. The kitchen door was ajar and through it they could hear Madge moving about and humming beneath her breath. A good smell of cooking reached them. The cottage did not have electricity but there were oil lamps which the girl had kindled and the fire crackled merrily in the grate.

'Madge? That you? I've brought my cousin home and the smell of cooking's very welcoming, but you shouldn't have come back. You've worked like a beaver for weeks and more than deserve your evenings free.'

The singing stopped and Madge put her flushed face round the door. 'You din't think I'd leave you hare alone tonight, without so much as a hot cuppa tea?' she said indignantly. 'Nor no fire nor lights? Fine thing that'd be!'

'We ate quite a lot at the Matthews',' Con began, but Madge brushed this aside.

'I saw what you ate, a foo sandwiches! Thass no food for a working man! I done you a casserole of beef with dumplings, plenty for both. And the fire's lit and Benjamin and Donnie and me set to and – and cleared the place.'

For the first time Con realised that the bed which had dominated the living room for so long had gone. He saw

Frank's glance go round the room and for a second his cousin's eyes closed as though he could not bear to contemplate the change. Madge saw too, but she spoke with determined briskness.

'That don't do to hang on to memories, even when they're happy, so we cleared through. Just you sit down to your teas, now.'

They ate, then helped Madge to wash up despite her insistence that she could manage alone, and just as they finished a knock on the door revealed Madge's 'steady feller', come to walk her home.

When she had gone, with promises to arrive in good time next morning to get them 'a bit of breakfast', the men sat down, one on either side of the fire, and leaned back in their chairs. Patch, close against Frank's leg, whined and pushed his nose into his master's hand. Frank's fingers began the automatic caress that Patch loved – fingers along the jawline, up round the ear, across the dome of his head, round the other ear, down the jawline again. Patch sagged, eyes half-closed, an expression of sloppy bliss on his furry face.

'Frank, do you want to talk about it?' Con said presently, when he had got his pipe going.

'Frank nodded. 'It's odd, but I do. Right at – at the end there was something so strange that I'd like to tell you. Couldn't tell anyone else, of course.'

'Fire ahead then.'

Frank sighed and nodded at Patch, comatose against his knee. 'He missed her fussing, that last week. She'd put her hand over the edge of the bed, and he'd push his head under it, but she didn't have the strength left for pulling his ears and tickling him. Poor chap, poor old Patch.'

Silence stretched. Con, looking at Frank, saw that his cousin was remembering, had forgotten his presence, the new emptiness of the room. His lips wore a half smile, his lids drooped, his hand caressed Patch automatically. But presently he sighed and came back to the present.

'Last Saturday, that was when I think she began to know. You remember, she decided she wanted a special sort of mattress and despatched us to Norwich to order one. When I got home she was quiet and peaceful, but next day I took one look at her and knew she'd never lie on the new mattress. Dear God, she went downhill fast once she loosed her hold.'

'Loosed her hold? That's a weird way of putting it!'

'Is it? It's what she did, you know. As if she'd hung on and told herself she'd make it if she kept up her spirits. And then, that day we were in the city, it seemed as if the strain of holding on was too great, and she'd decided – well, to let go. She wasn't miserable or depressed or anything like that. It was as though she'd stopped fighting and was saying, "I've done my best but now I'm tired; let me sleep." '

His voice broke on the last three words, but Con said nothing. He sensed that Frank would tell what had to be told in his own way and his own time.

'She slept a lot on Sunday,' Frank went on. 'But on Monday she woke up really early. It was one of those rare, absolutely still mornings, when a mist hovers above the Broad and sounds travel like billyo. I could hear the Franklyn boys squabbling over a bicycle pump as clear as if they were in our yard instead of right across in the village.

'She looked up at me when I took her a cup of hot milk – there was blood on her chin, Con, and on her pillow, and you know how fastidious she was – and she said, "Frank? Will you do something for me?" '

There was a painful silence. Con knew that Frank wanted to tell his story unemotionally and kept his eyes on the flames of the fire. Let the words come, he prayed silently. Let him find the words. To tell can often ease the pain.

'Of course I said I'd do anything,' Frank continued. 'And then she asked me to pick her up, wrap her in a blanket, and take her outside. Said there was a place down by the Broad where she'd been very happy, happier than she deserved, and she wanted to die there. I can tell you, it came as one hell of a shock, because I didn't know she . . . damn it, she'd let me believe she was as ignorant as – as I wanted her to be. Of course I thought how frail she was, and how chilly it can be before the sun comes up, and I kept telling her it wasn't wise, but she just fixed those great, tired eyes on mine, and when I'd finished waffling she said, "Please, Frank." '

This time the silence stretched on too long. Con spoke gently.

'Did you do as she asked?'

'Of course. I wrapped her in a blanket and carried her out. Hardly daring to put one foot in front of the other, she felt so light and brittle. She loved the air on her face, and when she felt the breeze she gave a tiny smile, just a tiny one. Then she pointed to the trees and whispered – she was past talking by then – where I was to go. Said you could see the whole Broad from there and that it looked so – so heavenly when the sun rose.

'I had an awful job to get through the undergrowth. It had grown a good deal thicker because no one went there once Suzie was bedridden, but I got through at last. It – it was a good place, Con, as good as she'd said. The sun came up red as blood, and the mist stirred and began to lift, and then she . . . she . . .'

Con spoke quickly, seeing Frank's haunted eyes, the way his hands shook.

'You did right, old chap, don't let it get you down! She died as and where she wanted to die, and that's a lot more important than being comfortable or getting another hour of life!'

'Yes, I suppose . . .' Frank stopped and shook his head violently. 'No! You see, I took too long, I was doubled up over her, shoving my way through blasted willow saplings and undergrowth, and just as I reached her clearing I looked down into her face. She'd closed her eyes and her face had sort of smoothed out. She looked young and blank and . . . and terrible. Oh, God, Con, she never saw that sunrise! She died before . . . before . . .'

And he was crying, painful, tearing sobs, whilst Con hugged his shoulders and knew himself powerless to comfort him.

24: 1927

Louis woke early, with a pleasurable sense of anticipation bringing his eyes open even before he had remembered what morning this was, in what way it was special to him. He rolled over in the big divan bed, and viewed his bedroom, newly decorated, with complacency. Pale wallpaper scattered with blue morning glory blossoms, a carpet whose colour had been described in the shop as 'midnight velvet', curtains of dark cobalt with silver embroidery, with a matching counterpane for the bed which reposed, at the moment, on the floor, the night having been a warm one.

Until ten days ago, it had been the bachelor apartment of any fairly successful man living along the North Shore. But then the telegram had arrived and, in a blaze of excitement, he had examined his bedroom. Fawn walls, brownish carpeting, mud-coloured drapes. He had acted at once, getting in touch with the most expensive interior decorator in the whole of Sydney and putting himself unreservedly in the fellow's hands. The result had been a bedroom of undoubted blueness, the bill a nine days' wonder at the hospital where he worked.

Fortunately, the other rooms had not been nearly so bad. There was a wide-windowed living room overlooking the harbour, and because he entertained there and, presumably, the man who owned the flat before him had done the same it was pleasantly decorated in creamy gold colours, with the carpet a square of brilliant orange and the curtains some sort of bronze silky stuff.

A white tiled bathroom and a yellow tiled kitchen completed the apartment and now Louis jumped out of bed and went through to run himself a bath. Naked, he admired his physique in the mirror, then began to wash. Humming, he soaped his thick, curly black hair, then rinsed it clean with handfuls of water. No doubt about it, he was a pretty good bargain for a man in his mid-thirties. When Sarah had written to him telling him that she had changed her mind about the divorce he had been rather pleased, expectant almost, but then the telegram had arrived and he had decided that he would not lose her twice! For she was coming to visit him in Sydney, and he knew that this was his opportunity. If he could not make her fall in love with him all over again – and with his new city – he would be extremely surprised!

Moving out of the bathroom and back to his bedroom, he picked up the telegram and studied it, though he knew it by heart. *Arriving Thursday 10th Tasmanian Queen stop Book hotel three week stop Sarah.*

He smiled scornfully at the very idea of booking a hotel room for Sarah whilst he had his apartment and his double bed! It would be absurd, for she was no longer suing for a divorce and she was still his wife! Oh, he had little doubt that she would try to get him to return to Norwich with her, but when she saw his work, his life, when she understood that there could be no question of his leaving his career and his home, he was sure he could persuade her to stay with him, send for their children.

He dressed quickly in white trousers and a white shirt, with a silk handkerchief knotted in the neck, for the day would be a scorcher or he was no judge, and then made his way into the kitchen. He poured himself orange juice, adding ice and a sprig of mint, then cut a thick slice off the loaf and put it under the toaster. When it was light brown, he added butter and a generous spoonful of honey and carried his meal through into the living room, sitting down in a comfortable chair in front of the sweep of the view.

My last breakfast alone, he was thinking sentimentally, when his cleaner, Klara, rattled on the door and then came through it, puffing, to announce that it was a good drag up the stairs.

'Too true,' Louis agreed. 'Morning, Klara! When I've done here you can tidy up my brekker things and then do the bedroom and bathroom. I'll be off presently to meet Mrs Rose.'

'Ain't that great, Mr Rose? She'll love dis apartment, she'd be a foolish voman else!'

He smiled at the Germanic turn of her words and got up to take his dirty plate and glass back into the kitchen. Klara was no younger an Australian than himself, but they shared both a tremendous love for their new country and an inability to lose their accents. Louis still spoke English as if he had never moved out of Great Britain in his life.

'You're right, Klara, so get it nice for her. Here . . .' He fished in his pocket and drew out a handful of coins. 'Before you leave, would you go down to that place on the corner where the flower-sellers sit and get me some roses? Red ones. Put half in the green glass vase in the living room and the rest in the blue and white china bowl in the bedroom. All right?'

'I'll do that, Mr Rose. There ain't none of your younk people coming, then?'

He shook his head, remembering that Poppa, too, said 'younk' like that, as did several members of the Jewish Congregation. He had scarcely thought about religion over here, though he did attend Shul if he had the time and felt in the mood. A man without a woman, he reminded himself now, could not afford the luxury of kosher eating, let alone slavish regard for the sabbath, not when he was a working surgeon at the biggest and best hospital in Sydney, at any rate!

'Not yet, but I'm hoping to persuade her to send for them. Don't forget the roses!'

He left the flat and ran down the two flights of stairs to street level, then regretted his haste as sweat broke out on his skin. It would never do to arrive at the quay sweaty and over-eager. He wanted Sarah to be impressed by the new Louis, the one who held lives in his hands and was trusted and respected in the community; he wanted nothing to remind her of that impetuous, idle young man she had married. Or nothing but his lovemaking, he amended. He was very sure that his performance in bed had been near-perfect when he left England, and it had probably improved as much as his general character had in his new country!

On the way to the hospital he popped into a florist and bought a bunch of white lilies with powdery gold hearts. The girl behind the counter smiled at him and added a pink satin bow *gratis,* and Louis pinched her cheek. Nice girl, nice flowers, nice morning.

He met a ward orderly just outside Casualty, a chap called Fred Biggins. Louis thought Fred a scrounger and a lazy blighter but this morning everyone shared a halo. He greeted him cheerfully, and was rewarded by his immediate response:

'Mornin', boss! Today's the day, then?'

Going through reception Mr Cargill came out of matron's office with a pile of papers and also stopped in his tracks.

'Morning, Rose. It's little woman day, I see!'

Louis flourished the lilies and admitted that Mr Cargill had guessed it, then went on his way to his secretary's office. Miss Shelley Porter sat at her desk, typing with incredible speed, working her way through the letters and reports which he had dictated to her yesterday. She looked up at his entrance and smiled beatifically.

'Today's the day, then?'

'That's right. Some flowers for you, my lovely!'

He had meant the flowers for Sarah, but he could soon buy some more, and it brought Shelley out of her seat, skipping round the desk to take the flowers, squeaking and burying her nose in their scented petals, then bending down to select a vase from the multitude tucked away in the bottom cupboard. She liked flowers. And she liked Mr Rose. Louis, who had not, if the truth be known, lived the life of a celibate since qualifying, admired her bottom as she bent down to get the vase. It was a charming bottom, satisfyingly plump, and he knew from experience that it would be encased in french knickers made of softest silk. It was a good bottom to stroke, to pinch. Miss Porter was a bright young thing and thought it a great feather in her cap to be having an affair with the best looking surgeon in the hospital. But now, of course, he would be a model husband. He knew he could be such a thing – indeed, it would be difficult to fall from grace once Sarah was installed because there was no opportunity for dalliance in the busy wards and he would be too tired after work to satisfy any woman other than his wife.

Shelley chose her vase and came out backwards. Louis put his hands behind his back, out of harm's way. He watched as she straightened and began to put the lilies lovingly into the container.

'Everything all right, Miss Porter?'

Shelley replied that everything was fine, thank you, sir, then glanced out of the window and towards the door. Having taken these elementary precautions she promptly threw herself into his arms. She was a satisfying armful too, for a man who had once spent five years without a woman. Louis tried to forget how successfully he had made up for those five years since! She had firm, high breasts which she could not subdue as fashion demanded, and lovely legs with well muscled thighs and calves. As he held her now, he thought irrelevantly that it was nice that she had decent calves. I could never make love to a woman with skinny calves, he told himself piously, nor with those awful bulging ones like Sister Watson's!

'Louis? Do you think you should, darling?'

His hands, quite without conscious thought, had moved round and were pushing themselves past the barrier of her waistband to grasp the tempting, melonlike curves of her bottom. He pulled himself together and stepped away from her. Today of all days!

'Sorry, sorry, I don't know what came over me. Because this is goodbye to all that, my dear. You do know that?'

'If you say so, Louis.' She smiled up at him, the tip of her tongue just peeping between her small teeth. He swallowed, and she moved closer again. 'Shall I get the photo of your wife out of your desk and put it on top? Or aren't you going to bring her back here?'

She was so close that he automatically put out his hand and patted her bottom. Oh. Hell. Think of *Sarah,* damn it!

'You're a thoughtful girl, my dear. Yes, put it on my desk. In fact, you can be the ideal secretary and nip into town for me and buy some roses to put near the photograph. Red ones. All right?'

'Will do, Mr Rose.' She took the money he offered her and went round to sit behind her desk once more, every inch the efficient secretary in her white blouse and dark skirt. 'Good luck with your meeting, sir, and give my regards to your wife.'

'Thanks.' He nodded to her and let himself out into the corridor again. It might be as well to agree to matron's suggestion, now that Sarah would soon be here. Matron, a lady with a weight problem and a rather fine moustache, disapproved of Mr Rose and said – loudly – that Mr Rose's secretary ought to work in the typing pool, with the other medical secretaries. Yes, he rather thought he would agree to the change; there was nothing like removing temptation – far more efficient than merely promising oneself to fight it.

As he walked through the streets towards the docks he found himself trying to conjure up a picture of Sarah's bottom, and was a little shocked, then comforted himself with the thought that it was probably a sign that he was settling down at last. At least if he took to staring at feminine bottoms the owners would almost certainly be unconscious of his admiration – he remembered a teenage obsession with breasts which had proved almost equally embarrassing to himself and to the owners of the breasts!

He lingered once he got near the docks, having a cup of coffee and a wedge of heavy fruit cake at a scruffy little corner shop, then set out, having first purchased a large bunch of red roses. It would please her to find her way strewn with red roses – they *were* the flower of love, and two hearts beating as one, and so on, weren't they? Then he saw the ship and his doubts and fears vanished, to be replaced by almost unbearable excitement. She was coming, the *Tasmanian Queen,* bearing down upon her mooring, heading for the shore! It did not matter that she was old and salt-stained, with rust showing around her Plimsoll line and barnacles encrusting her plates, she was carrying Sarah! Thoughts, lascivious and loving together, filled his mind. Sarah on their honeymoon night, pure and pale, first frightened, then generous. Fighting, kissing Sarah. With their first child in her arms. Walking across the bathroom naked turning to laugh at him. Weeping when he left her. Sarah. Sarah.

The ship docked, passengers thronged the rail. He stared until his eyes ached, but could not pick her out from the crowds. It occurred to him that she might have aged in six years, her hair might be grey, her figure fuller, less lissom. He grew anxious that she might find the heat too much, and pushed forward to the foot of the gangplank. Fat or thin, dark or grey, she was his own darling Sarah, and he would welcome and protect her as such!

'Louis? Lou, my darling! Over here!'

He looked. She had come down the gangway and was hurrying towards him, her hair coming down from its bun, her face shiny with perspiration and love. Plump, pretty, carelessly dressed in blue gingham which was stretched over her wonderful, expansive bosom, her hands held out to him, a tender smile curving her generous mouth.

Louis's heart faltered. Shock stopped his forward progress, mouth at half-cock, the roses tumbling from his nerveless arms to lie on the paving. Then she was close and he was grinning, grabbing her warmly to his chest, kissing luxuriously, then hungrily, the soft, eagerly parting lips she offered so ingenuously.

'Say! My darling girl, to come all this way alone! Say, you're more beautiful than ever and I adore you!'

They walked away towards the city, Say hanging on to his arm, chattering, looking up into his face as he, indulgently smiling, looked down into hers.

The wrong woman.

Or the right one?

The whole family were gathered in the Green Room at The

Pride, with most of their friends and all the Congregation. Ted, looking fondly round him, wondered why it was always The Pride. It was his father-in-law's seventy-fifth birthday, and 'Where else should we hold the party?' Tina had demanded. 'I'm the eldest child, darling, and this is the family home when it comes to a real get-together. We couldn't expect Cecy to help, with her tiny garden and cramped reception rooms. I know Rachel's home is quite spacious, but it's so tidy and dull, and besides, Adolphus is an elderly man, the planning and excitement wouldn't be good for him. And Bishopsgate wouldn't be fair because all the planning would fall on Poppa himself, and there isn't room in the drive for more than three cars, they would have to be left out on the road, and . . .'

The arguments were needless, of course. Ted liked to entertain and would have been hurt had the party venue been moved to anyone else's home. He just liked to ask, that was all! He got a considerable thrill, if the truth were known, out of looking round the motley crowd of Jews and Gentiles, family and business associates, knowing that each one of them saw him as one of themselves. They never thought of him as that young man from the Colonies who had done well for himself, he was just Ted Neyler, one of the best.

Ruthie had outdone herself with the cake. It was gigantic, and on the topmost tier seventy-five blue candles would presently blaze. Arthur was getting emotional of course, trumpeting down his nose, making extravagant promises of how he would mark his three-quarter-century by blowing out every single candle at the first attempt – if his grandchildren and great-grandchildren would help him!

'Simon mine, you're the eldest so you bring the little ones to the old man.' He beamed round at the assembly. 'Come on, don't be shy! Beryl, bring the cottontops over here. Come along, I shan't eat 'em!' Desmond's tired-looking wife pushed her three eldest children towards their great-grandfather but clutched the two youngest to her, as if to blow out a candle might cause them to disappear as well.

'Here we are – I'll hold baby Cas, eh, Rachel?' The

two-year-old Caspar had a strong-featured face and a tetchy expression, but he clutched Grandpa's beard and grinned to himself, a dark imp. Arthur counted heads. 'Simon, Cara, Val and Nicky, and little Dessy, little Art, Maudie.' Seeing the children clustered around him suddenly reminded him of that other party when other children had come running to blow out his birthday candles. David, Henny, and Kitty, who would come running no more. He felt tears come to his eyes, but smiled through them at his beloved family. 'Ach, how I wish my dear Deb could have lived to see this day!'

The Rabbi was a new one, a small, square man with glasses, a salt and pepper beard and a great sense of fun. He put one hand on Arthur's shoulder and indicated the children and their parents with a jerk of the head. 'What a femily, Arthur! What a grend femily you got!'

Arthur, blowing his nose vigorously, agreed, but there was a shade of enthusiasm missing, for Louis was not here. The others were lovely boys, but Louis was his only son and he missed him sorely, thinking wistfully of him every day, writing to him, talking about him. However, it would not do to think about Louis or he might make a fool of himself. He turned Caspar so that the imp faced the candles which Ted was lighting even now.

'A grand family; you're right, Rabbi. And now, children, you've got to give an old man a hand with all these candles!' They were ablaze now, and someone had drawn the curtains so that the only light came from the cake and its brilliant burden. He drew the children close.

'Now then, some strategy we must have! Our attack we must plan, eh?'

The young heads drew close to the venerable one and Frank, watching indulgently, remembered himself, fifteen years before. How Grandpa had planned the great blast of breath which would send each group of candle flames into oblivion, how even he and Des, though telling themselves they were too old for such nonsense, had nonetheless done their part with gusto.

'Now, *bubelehs!* At the count of three! One . . . two

. . . wait for it, Simon . . . and *three!*'

The candles went out to a man and the singing started, the whole assembly starting with 'Happy Birthday', and then, to wild applause, breaking into 'We all wish you *mazel tov*' whilst the children capered and clapped and the adults reached for their glasses, so that they could toast Arthur when there was a pause in the singing.

Frank noticed that the servants had joined them and were standing, singing and clapping, but obviously waiting for the moment when they could get at the cake. He moved towards them, meaning to congratulate Ruthie on her magnificent catering, when he heard, faintly, the chimes of the front door bell.

No one else heard, and after only a moment's hesitation, Frank slipped from the room, closed the door softly behind him, and went across to the front door. He opened it, and a tall man stood there, with a small woman holding his arm. Both were smiling, albeit somewhat nervously.

'Hello, Desmond! I've seen photographs of you, but I don't suppose you can guess who I am?'

The twang was somehow familiar, yet Frank knew he had never seen the man in his life before. He frowned, then laughed, standing aside and gesturing the couple into the hall.

'I'm sorry, but I'm not Desmond, I'm his brother, Frank. Do you want to see Des, or is it my father? You see, there's a family party going on, and . . .' At that point, it came to him. 'Good God, I thought your voice sounded familiar! It's Uncle Mark, isn't it? And you must be my Auntie Su!'

'Too right, and I suppose Ted's miles away, and we'll miss each other, like we did in America,' the man said ruefully. 'We're here for a bit this time, mind, so we could always come back . . .'

'No, no, he's right here, behind that door!' Frank was almost gabbling with excitement. 'You don't know how marvellous this will be for Daddy, Uncle Mark, because he's never had any family of his own at one of these great unwieldy gatherings, and . . . oh, he'll be so excited! Do you mind if I take you in right now and introduce you?'

Su, clinging to Mark's arm, spoke for the first time. 'Yes, but it's a family party, and we aren't family, not strictly speaking.' She cocked her head as a mass rendering of 'Seventy-five today', more generally sung as 'Twenty-one today', assailed their ears. 'It sounds like a birthday party.'

'Yes, it's my grandfather's seventh-fifth birthday,' Frank said. He had just realised that his Auntie Su was Chinese and was still trying to assimilate this extraordinary fact and to wonder why his father had never mentioned it. 'Look, they've quieted down now, so I suppose they're cutting the cake. Come on!'

He crossed the hall without more ado and flung the Green Room door open wide. The Green Room was separated from the conservatory by wide glass doors but this afternoon these were open to give the guests more space. As Frank entered, Ted was just about to propose the toast. He turned to gaze enquiringly at his son.

'Yes, Frank?'

'Two visitors to see you, Daddy,' Frank announced. 'They've come one hell of a way to be at this party – half a world away. Can you guess?'

For a moment they faced each other, the two brothers who had not met for nearly thirty years. Greying red hair, a thin, intelligent face, quiet grey eyes faced greying blond hair, a broad, jovial face, bright understanding blue eyes. Then the two men moved as one and were in each other's arms, thumping each other's backs, talking both at once, whilst tears streamed down Ted's face and Mark kept gulping.

'I never thought . . . it was mad to come all this way . . .'

'Mark! Nothing matters but that you're here!' Over his shoulder Ted roared: 'Edie! Get the bed aired and made ready in the yellow room – we've two guests who'll stay for ever!'

For the first time it occurred to Frank that his father was growing old, hair thinning, waistline thickening. He was barely twelve months older than Mark, but it could have been twelve years. Then Ted turned and beamed at him, and no critical thought could survive against the depth of affection he always stirred in his second son.

'Well, Frankie? What do you think of that? After all these years!'

'I think that you and Uncle Mark, and probably Mama and Auntie Su as well, ought to take your cake and your champagne and sit quietly in the study for a bit and catch up on things.' They went eagerly, the two women eyeing one another with open interest. They were really rather alike, Frank thought, two small, slender ladies with night-black hair and backs like ramrods. Su was a good deal younger than Uncle Mark, obviously, and a good deal younger than Tina, but his mother had kept her youthful figure and much of her youthful exuberance as well.

When they had bustled from the room, Frank turned to Desmond. Des was leaning back in a chair, gazing cynically at the now closed door. He had not, Frank realised, uttered one word of greeting to his uncle and aunt.

'Well, Des, what do you make of that? After all those years!'

Des pulled a face. 'Oh, they're after something, you may be sure of that. It's a long way to come to scrounge, but I daresay they know him too well back home. And Daddy'll shell out, that's for sure.'

Frank gave him a look of complete disgust and walked out of the room. It was so typical of Des, who always had his hand in someone else's pocket, to assume that everyone else was the same. Frank had only seen Mark for a few moments but he felt he knew him already. A strong, independent man, who would ask for help from nobody but would be quick to offer it.

He found himself outside the study door and hesitated, then made up his mind. He tapped and walked in. The men were standing by the window, deep in conversation, the women were sitting by the fireplace, equally engrossed.

'Thought I'd just tell you I'm off home now,' he said cheerfully. 'I've got some work I'd like to finish before the light goes. But I'll be round here first thing, to get to know my newly acquired relations!'

'Must you go?' Ted knew that Frank had intended to stay for the family dinner party, but he also understood his son. 'Well then, drive carefully. Come to luncheon tomorrow!'

'I will.' He turned and was immediately aware that they were engrossed once more before he had closed the front door behind him. It was right and proper that it should be so. As he gunned the car down the drive he found that he was thinking about Mabel. He had not thought of her properly since Suzie's death. She must miss family parties, too. He had looked for her at the funeral, half ashamed of looking yet unable to stop himself hoping that she would come. She and Suzie had been such close friends, after all. She had not come, though one of the most beautiful wreaths bore her name. And since then he had stopped thinking of her, had concentrated on his work, on a newer, faster boat that he was designing, and on living alone in moderate comfort.

He drove along the summer lanes and into the yard, parking the Essex in the end shed which served him as a garage. He went into the house and realised that there was no food in for an evening meal since Madge had assumed he would be dining at The Pride. Never mind, he could make do with cold stuff; or he could always nip across to the Wherry and get himself something hot.

He made himself a cup of tea and took it outside. The yard was quiet although the Broad itself was not – holidaymakers, yachtsmen and little boys in scruffy skiffs plied their way across its glinting surface beneath the hot sun. He felt content, sitting still for once, whilst a bee buzzed drowsily and gathered honey from the climbing rose near his head and the tea in his cup cooled. Patch pushed a cold nose into his hand, then sighed deeply and curled up at his master's feet. Frank slept.

When he woke, evening had come and the weather had changed. It was cold, and above his head dark clouds gathered ominously. He took his chair indoors and lit the fire, for the cottage could be chilly in the evenings even in the height of summer so the sticks and coal were always ready in the grate. Outside, it began, quite gently, to rain. Frank went into the pantry and began to assemble the makings of supper, for he would not bother to go across to the Wherry on such a chilly night. There was half a ham, some cold potatoes, a jar of home-made chutney and a wedge of marmalade pudding. He piled everything on to a big dish, stood it in the middle of the table, then went over to the window. The rain was really coming down now, fairly bombarding the water, turning the surface of the Broad to frosted glass. It was rather nice when it rained as if the heavens had opened, and one was snug indoors, with a fire burning, and food ready to eat.

And then he saw the boat. Who on earth would be coming here on such a night? It could scarcely be family or friends, for most of them would believe him to be still at The Pride, enjoying Grandpa's seventy-fifth birthday dinner. It could be Con – Con did not like him to be alone on family occasions – but why should Con come across the water, in Pat Paterson's row-boat, with Pat straining at the oars?

The boat had swung towards his landing stage now; there could be no doubt that he was about to receive a visitor. Someone small, swathed in oilskins, sat in the stern of the boat. Frank's heart began to beat a steady tattoo against his ribs. There had been another occasion once when a boat had come across the water in appalling weather, bringing someone very special to him. He had thought, then . . .

He walked out, straight into the storm, with the thunder rumbling overhead now and, far distant, lightning stabbing at the unseen hills. He was soaked to the skin in seconds but he walked steadily on as the boat drew in to the landing stage and someone clambered out, shed the borrowed oilskins and turned, a little uncertainly, towards him.

Frank quickened his pace. He grinned foolishly, even though she could not possibly see his expression through the driving rain. And in his heart, the sun came out.